The Griffin
Twin Books

PRESENTS

978-0-9725548-1-7

Published by Twin Griffin Books
Cover art by Ray Cosico
www.TwinGriffinBooks.com
www.AuthorJustinThomas.com

THE GHOST OF GABRIEL'S HORN

Book I of The Fable & Avenue Saga

BY JUSTIN THOMAS

To magic.

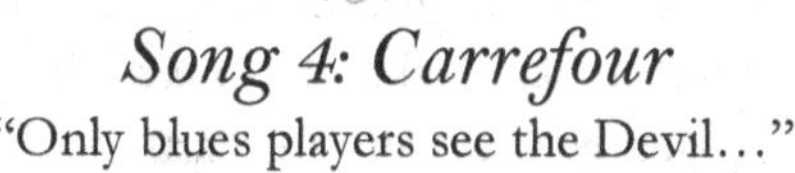

Song 4: Carrefour
"Only blues players see the Devil…"

The sky's age was calculated precisely at infinity, and it had seen so many things since it was born. This morning, close to noon, pale-blue and calm, and accompanied by a few puffy clouds, the sky was quiet with anticipation. The only movement was the sun, but that was expected. The sun's reason for rising today was different. The bright body inched its way up onto the sky to get a better perspective of the goings on below. The clouds remained still, holding back the urge to gather and hug one another tightly until they perspired rain. After all, the deluge ritual would disturb the story, which already suffered a long pause in its even longer narrative. Nothing happened for twenty years. Between 1937 and today, August 25th, 1957, nothing happened that interested the sky and the other celestial onlookers' ubiquitous gaze. Not the passing of another World War. Not a conflict in Korea. Not even the incrementally freezing cold, pretentious climate of world politics. Nothing below animated the sky's interests.

Cuba would change regimes in two years. The world would hold its breath as fear of atomic war continued to loom, encroaching early in the next decade. America was going to violently lose a beloved president. War would break out in Asia. A King would announce a grand dream of equality for all. Brave teens preaching peace and Flower Power would stage protests in an effort to cease ongoing conflicts around the world.

Mundane affairs.

And the sky couldn't care less should a gossiping soothsayer reveal the future movements of what would happen abroad. A bolt of lightning would be the price paid for any clairvoyant librettist that disclosed a line of prologue before this particular story's music unfolded of its own accord. Today, at the outset of this new act on an age-old story, gods reborn as jazz players moved into position to reclaim their rightful place.

There was a wide-open country field below. The field was split in two by a dusty road, a signature of Clarksdale, Mississippi. A lone car on Gaston Avenue disturbed the day's calm. The car's zoom staggered blades of tall, wild grass, bending them off balance as they struggled like drunkards to stand up straight. The dirt road, ground by the car's tires, sprayed up into a dusty, glittering, ethereal cloud that followed the vehicle for a brief moment before settling gently back onto the earth.

Inside the car Horatio Peters watched the world speed by. His mind was elsewhere as he sat back in the rumbling 1955 Chrysler Imperial automobile. The radio blared jazz but could not compete with the young man's thoughts. The music in Horatio's head had been haunting him since he was nineteen years old. First, just on paper, taunting him as musical notation, some of which were scripted in foreign characters—musical notation Horatio had never seen before. Then, after a few years, the music haunted him in his head. Finished pieces composed by his father played for him, but not through his horn, despite his ten-year dedicated practice to the trumpet. Growing up, his mother praised him, calling him a prodigy. Virginia Peters declared Horatio's trumpet-work proof that he was his father's child. But Horatio believed he was chasing his father's genius rather than following in his father's footsteps. He was good, but his father's book of original compositions proved there was more to learn. Some declared Pete Peters as the greatest trumpet player Harlem had ever known, and Horatio now understood why. Pete Peters was original.

Horatio turned his head and spotted his father in the driver's seat. Pete Peters' hands were on the wheel, his eyes focused forward on the journey ahead. He took time from his concentration, turned to his son, and beamed proudly. The smile only lasted seconds before Pete Peters returned his attention to the road. He didn't look too much older than his son. Pete Peters didn't look a day over thirty-three. Both son and father shared the same earth-brown skin and handsome face mounted on an oval-shaped head. Both possessed a tight curl to their hair that many thought was awkward and ugly. Pete Peters dismissed the claims whenever such nonsense was expressed. People's words regarding the music he played were mostly complimentary. But should the moment arise, a comment made about the way he kept his hair, Pete Peters would articulate, *"Man, let me tell you somthin'. The curls in my hair are the secret musical clefs that make my horn blowin' so powerful."* His line would make people jump and applaud no different than when he'd play one of those otherworldly notes from his horn. But his retort would not stop there. As Pete Peters was known to do with his trumpet playing, he made his audience holler louder as he'd conclude, *"Hell, these kinks are what keep a woman uninhibited from the dance floor to the bedroom. You ain't ever gon' find my hair conked. Shit, and that's no lye."*

Horatio liked that.

Nothing could slow his father down or bend his father's smile into a frown.

Why should it? Pete Peters was a celebrated child from birth. Born in Harlem in 1900, four years before the great real estate crash that led the way for a large, migration of blacks to the area, Pete Peters and his family greeted the colored drift when it happened in 1904. His father was a mortician and his mother was a nurse. Papa Peters was born in 1865, a child of the Thirteenth Amendment. Mamma Peters came three years later in 1868, a child of the Fourteenth Amendment. Their births marked milestones. They were of the first black children born to an America that included 'Negroes' as free and proper citizens, former slaves and newborn alike. Pete Peters' birth too marked a milestone. He was a child of the new millennium. Black people believed the clock started over for them. This was a new century with new possibilities for a new generation. It was fitting for Pete Peters to take up the trumpet and celebrate. He learned piano to appease his mother. He learned all the church hymns and old-time spirituals to satisfy his father. His dedication, where he immersed his musical talent, was in the newborn style dubbed jazz. Every note played was nothing less than a declaration of life and freedom, happiness and praise. Jazz was a budding and honest community organizer threatening change and progression. His rival was a stingy politician named Jim Crow who was violently keeping good on his promise of segregation and ignorance.

Horatio imagined his father's music echoing through the streets of Harlem and slapping against the walls of every building as if they were drums. Horatio envisioned Harlem's city blocks coming to life as the alchemical rhythm transmuted the dense buildings malleable, animating the city skyline into tall, dancing shadows. The lights in the windows flickering to the tempo of blaring jazz that screamed wildly. Every nightclub waving like water with people inside stomping to music and forgetting their troubles with outlawed gin, number slips, and the magic of reefer's aroma. The sweet breath of Pete Peters' horn tickling the people into gyration, making them swing, swish, and sway *"Like pay day was every day,"* so sang Horatio's mother in one of her many songs co-written by her husband.

Pete Peters' music throbbed inside Horatio's head. His whole boom band performed privately for his son. Horatio wanted to jump up and play along to the sound, blowing his horn in synch with his father. He wanted to use the roof of the car as a stage even now as it soared down the dirt road. Horatio's wild imagination frustrated him, the music continuing to play. He'd read and feverishly studied his father's music composed inside a songbook he received when he was nineteen. There were notes he just couldn't catch no matter how hard he studied the compositions. His father composed rhythms beyond existing musical notations. Horatio could hear them, but he couldn't play them.

He kept his gaze on his father. Horatio dared not blink, holding his eyes still until they burned. Then the muscles holding his expression trembled and lost their grip. He concentrated hard to keep his composure, but Horatio's smile faded. His eyes wavered and shut. *Blink.* The image of his father dissolved into his friend, Johnny Concheroot. Horatio's sight blurred watery at the edges. He reached for the radio and turned the music down. Johnny didn't mind. Horatio returned his gaze to the outside. The music in his head increased in volume. Horatio took a deep breath and let out a sigh.

Pete Peters was murdered in 1933 on the night Horatio was born. Horatio was minutes old, and he mourned his father's passing with his first cries into the world.

Horatio blinked again. The music scratched. He heard static the moment his eyes closed. There was an image, a flash. Pete Peters' music faded. Horatio strained to listen. He heard nothing but the lowered volume of jazz coming from the radio mixed with the car's humming engine. Horatio closed his eyes. He saw everything all over again. The scene was a nightclub. Midnight. His father. Three ruffians. A scorpion pointed a pincer toward Pete Peters. A lion circled the silent scene, its roar muted. The scene came with lyrics and music. A bass played slowly and prominently while a trumpet hummed softly behind it. Fingers snapped eerily. Horatio heard his voice narrate: *'My father was murdered minutes before I was born. He was murdered at midnight on a night as cloudy and unclear as the motives of his attackers. The stars' colors sang in dull notes while gravity pulled on hopes to get down to the sound of deceit. My father's friends shared new ideas for musical beats. Gunshots. Boom bass addressed to shoulder, head, and heart. Dead on the spot. Dead on arrival of my mother's screams that reached out to hold him, arms around to cloak him. My mother sure knows how to sing, even when she's screaming. Weeping. Crying my father's name to invoke him. Her eyes bathed in the image of the blood that soaked him. Shock produced me, and I cried too. In a doctor's arms – passed to my mother in the delivery room. I already knew before they delivered the news. The breath in my tiny lungs longed for a horn to breathe through. By the standards of conception I was physically minutes olds, but spiritually—like the sky above me—I was going on infinity. Sadly, I would only know my father through my mother's memories. Somehow I still see the flicker-flash ambience of ambulance sirens singing sanguinary symphonies. A new womb. My father's murdered body the delivery. Heaven is a mortuary where his father serves as custodian to the dead. Grandpapa Mortician."*

Horatio opened his eyes. The world sped by. His father's music resumed in his head. He took a breath, trying to remain nonchalant. Johnny Concheroot noticed but said nothing. He continued driving. Horatio calmed after several more breaths. He took a look in the back. There was his father's music book on the seat. An oak case rested next to the book. Inside the case was Horatio's trumpet. Both items were still, unmoved by the car's turbulence over the dusty road. Horatio relaxed and looked out beyond the road. The path seemed to stretch into infinity, challenging the sky for distance.

"How much farther you suppose?" Horatio asked Johnny.

Johnny checked the rearview mirror as if the answer lay behind them. "We're on Gaston now," he answered. "We should intersect with Jackson soon enough." He grinned. "You suppose we'll see the Devil himself?" Johnny adjusted his tall physique in the driver's seat.

"Long as he got answers, I don't care," said Horatio reaching for his fedora on the dashboard. He slumped in the passenger's seat and put his fedora atop his head, angling it over his eyes. "I got somethin' for him if he got anything other than answers, or should his ass be reluctant to give any." Horatio's hand went to his hip and felt the handle of the .45 caliber pistol holstered there. Both men chuckled. Horatio lifted his hat. He looked at Johnny and with a sincere smile that hinted at a sly grin, he said, "Thanks again, John-John."

Johnny replied in a matter-of-fact manner, "Ain't nothin' but mornin' glory and sweet potatoes, Horatio. I owe you this." He cleared his throat, stalling. His eyes moved away from the road ahead, looking as if he was searching for the right words. Johnny's demeanor turned serious. "Look. I'm at peace. I'll stay at peace even if the answers are what we already believe them to be." Again, Johnny adjusted himself in the driver's seat. His adjustment could not, however, shake the uncomfortable feeling that the subject of his words addressed. He concluded to Horatio, "I hope you can be at peace too." Johnny waited for an answer to his sentiment, but Horatio said nothing. He merely nodded his head to acknowledge Johnny's words. Johnny's grin returned. "Hope we can still be friends, despite the circumstances." He chuckled and caught a glimpse of Horatio's smile from the corner of his eye.

Horatio's smile broke into a low laugh. He slumped further down in the seat, his eyes covered by the fedora. He shut his eyes and relaxed. Johnny was referring to old politics. The same politics he'd been speaking about since he showed up on Horatio's doorstep five years ago, seven weeks after Horatio's mother passed from illness. Horatio remembered. His mother's death brought out many people from her and her husband's past. The church was as packed as the Harlem clubs she sang in. Followers of Virginia Peters' craft, family, and fellow musicians, attended her funeral to pay their respects. Characters from stories told to Horatio appeared before his eyes, legends turned reality.

Johnny knocked on Horatio's door seven weeks later, catching Horatio in a moment of struggle with his father's songs. Horatio had been making another attempt with the compositions, trying to honor his mother with a musical eulogy expressed through his father's music.

Horatio had always entertained his mother with his trumpet playing. She would join in with song, playing on the piano. When Horatio caught a wave of improvisation, Virginia would do the same with her playing and singing. Horatio's trumpet style reminded Virginia of her husband. Horatio's music made her happy, covering a sadness that was too often present. On Horatio's nineteenth birthday, Virginia presented him with his father's music book. She removed it from the old, dusty suitcase used for her travel from Harlem to New Orleans, days after her husband was murdered and Horatio was born.

That damn music book filled with songs Horatio wanted to play, but couldn't. These were the songs he believed his mother deserved to hear. It hurt more when Virginia's illness became worse. Horatio tried playing them again after she died. Nothing. In his frustration, he admitted his trumpet skills had a limit. Then, Johnny's introduction into his life put Horatio's frustrations on pause with a knock on the door that same afternoon. And so, Horatio answered the door, thankful for the distraction. On the other side was Jonathan Richard Concheroot, a tall black man sporting an elegant suit, and looking no older than him. He was polite, addressing Horatio as if he wasn't four years Horatio's senior. The tall, dark skinned man from New York could give any Southerner a run for their money when it came to hospitality. There was something beyond the hospitable demeanor, however, and that was a swagger only Brooklyn could produce.

Johnny introduced himself. He'd come all the way from Brooklyn to pay respects to Horatio's mother. After that, Horatio invited him in for a drink. Johnny assured Horatio that he was not just a Virginia Peters zealot. *"There's more to my visit,"* Horatio recalled Johnny saying as he inspected the house in awe and wonder. It wasn't the house Virginia Peters grew up in, but it was a place she called home for nineteen years. They sat at the table and drank. *"I play piano, like my father. His name was Joseph Concheroot. Of course, they called him 'Joe' for short."* Johnny clarified, *"He played in your father's band. They made music together."* Then came the news. *"He killed your father, my father did. He shot him. At least, that's what he's servin' time for."*

Politics.

It was an unusual way for a friendship to form, based on such a revelation. But from that conversation came a bond. Johnny was trying to make amends for his father's sin, and Horatio accepted. Then came their music, travel, women, and a few dollars in their pocket. Small clubs in the Southern region lit up with revitalized jazz from a piano player and a trumpet player, the sons of legends composing their own musical mythos. Horatio engaged musical elders in pretentious, yet hip, conversations on the subject of music theory and composition. His elders would ask him, *"You Pete Peters' boy, right?"* And then they'd tell him, *"That man had some band. Lord, yes he did. Made some heavy music up there in Harlem. Your mamma could sing too. She could saaaaang. Your father had more than theory. He had the law of music."*

Horatio all the while was an intelligencer. He gathered the old-time wisdom of musicians that witnessed sound evolve from spirituals to gospel to blues to jazz (and those lost styles in between) just so that he might crack the musical code penned inside his father's music book.

Those notes. Taunting. Irritating. Unplayable.

Horatio resumed the challenge to express his father's music. It was after a raucous show with his horn and Johnny's piano skills running across keys. There were wild patrons, and it seemed as if Rock 'n' Roll had a rival. Horatio was inspired. He mingled with his audience, indulging in a few drinks, enough to lower his timidity. He flirted with the female spectators long enough to impress upon them a faint signature should he return to the scene. Then he stowed away to partake in his private battle alone in a motel room with the curtains closed. His father's book lay open on the bed. He stared at the book for a few minutes. He sipped on a bottle of something strong. Bottle in one hand, horn in the other. Horatio eventually put the bottle down on the floor. He took a breath, gripped his horn, and played notes from one of his father's songs.

It sounded terrible.

Disappointment coupled with alcohol compelled Horatio to irrational behavior that involved the strong contents in the bottle being poured over his father's music book. A match. Lit. Dropped onto the open book now resting on the floor.

The fire hovered above the pages. Music played. Horatio could hear it, all the music he failed to translate with his horn. The notes were less irritating when heard. Horatio remained still. His eyes were not fixed on the fire, but on the unscathed book over which the flames hovered. The book's pages flipped, running through the hovering fire without being autographed with a burn or blemish from the flames. It might have been the alcohol that assisted Horatio's vision to perceive the written musical notes floating from the page, but there was something real about the experience. The notes, as melodic as they represented, snaked through the fire, intertwined and formed a double whorl that swirled around Horatio's body. The animated script crawled into Horatio's ears and nostrils.

The fire burned out. The book closed. The music remained. It played in his head. Horatio sobered, to say the least. He believed that if he could now hear the notes, he could also now play them. But there came nothing except terrible sounds mixed with the beauty of the music in his head. Horatio found another bottle of something strong and drank, not to get drunk, but to go to sleep. It didn't help. The haunting followed him into his dream, transforming into macabre images. Horatio witnessed the scene of his father's murder. It was a brutal scene adorned with beautiful music composed by the victim himself. This was the closest Horatio had ever been to his father. He woke excited, not because of the loud sounds of the gunshots, or his mother's shrills before going into labor. The gruesome scene produced two oddities, one of them a comforting thought.

Oddity one: Horatio saw a lion circling the scene, and a scorpion pointing a pincer toward his father. Oddity two: Three men were involved with the murder. Three men of different size and shape. Masked. No lone gunmen. Horatio told Johnny about his dream the next morning. Concheroot jokingly asked for a grain of salt. *"I need somethin' to spice the news with,"* he laughed. *"I'm a spiritual man, but c'mon, Horatio. Until reality shows otherwise, I'm gon' let a dream be a dream. My father killed your father. Simple. I'm sorry for that."* Johnny assured Horatio, *"I ain't tryin' to take your wind away, kid, so don't be afraid to sail on."* This didn't slow Horatio down, even as he and Johnny continued to play small, bawdy jazz clubs, the kind that boasted signs expressing in painted words *Liquor upfront, poker in the rear.*

Horatio held private after shows. The set list was always the same, but very pleasing. Five of his father's songs would play in his head. He'd sit and listen with nothing stronger than water to sip on. No lights. He'd pace, only daring to join in on the sound with finger snaps and foot taps. He never touched his trumpet. And when he slept, the music narrated the same dream: Pete Peters' murder by three ruffians, a reoccurring feature. The songs only found pause when Horatio would play on stage, never disturbing his performances to break his concentration. The music even serenaded his escapades with female admirers should he take a night off from his studies.

The music remained in his head. The same five songs, though there were more composed in his father's book. Jazz might be a cosmic word for *improvisation*, but Horatio believed his father had a plan. He wished he knew specifically which songs the five were. That was when he stumbled upon a song he could play. *Carrefour: The Intersection of Jackson and Gaston.* He gave no thought as to whether he'd seen the song before, or to what spirit possessed him to attempt to play it. There were no impossible notes of foreign script, just jazz. Horatio felt partially relieved as he brought the song to a sweet crescendo that equated to him sighing.

Handwritten liner notes appeared in the songbook, and Horatio knew he'd never seen them before. Then he considered the possibility that the writing had been overlooked because he didn't care for anything other than the musical compositions.

Carrefour. First song written. Took a long time to write, find a note I could play. Nothing incorporeal. I compose it late in this book. Song four. Just seems appropriate. Jackson and Gaston Fable opened their doors to me when I played it for them. October 10, 1925 – P. Peters

Horatio read more that night, turning to the book's opening and inspecting his father's prose. He found a list of musical notes, but they were notes that could be played on his own instrument. There was nothing ethereal. But the music book was again new to Horatio. At the opening of the book, on a page Horatio knew was once blank before his eyes, Pete Peters' handwriting appeared. He wrote:

The songs composed in this book are collectively known as The Son Dial Tone.

The rising sun's light drenched the motel room, pouring in like waves of water. The curtains burst into flames. Horatio stood up as the walls caught on fire. The light reached out for Horatio and devoured him.

He exhaled and opened his eyes. The world was speeding by but beginning to slow down. Horatio properly adjusted his fedora. He sat up in the passenger's seat. Johnny steered the car to the left, parking partially off the dirt road. They had come to an intersection. Johnny opened the door and jumped from the car to stretch his long legs. Horatio followed. Johnny shut his door as Horatio left his open. After shutting the door, he took time to check the revolver holstered on his left hip while Horatio bent down into the backseat to remove his trumpet and his father's music book. "I thought this was only for blues players," said Johnny as he put his hands in his pockets and inspected the area. The wind picked up. Johnny's suit flapped wildly. "I don't see any street signs, but this the intersection. Got to be. We on Gaston; that's got to be Jackson," he said tracing the intersecting streets with a finger.

Horatio didn't reply, his excitement garbling Johnny's words. He placed the oaken case on the passenger's seat and opened it. His trumpet gleamed as the sun caressed the instrument. Horatio removed his trumpet from the case. He stood up and put his father's book on the hood of the car, *4:21 The Book of Life* its label. Horatio flipped open to the music titled *Carrefour: The Intersection of Jackson and Gaston*. He examined the song. His eyes looked up at Johnny who was now standing in front of the car.

Horatio backed away from the book, which closed without the support of Horatio's fingers holding it open. He lifted the trumpet, puckered his lips, closed his eyes, and kissed the song into existence.

A high note bubbled and dipped to start the recital. It wasn't a blaring declaration, as often heard by trumpeters. It was a smooth ease into a song that turned ritual and tribute into music. The wind ceased. The dirt settled back on the dusty road, bending like a wild cat tamed into submission. The scenery rippled, bubbling as Horatio continued to play. Johnny turned around, aiming his gaze at the far right side of the intersection, hands still in his pockets. Waves of heat murmured from the grass, distorting the already rippled environment. Johnny leaned against the hood of his car and watched, his charming grin making an appearance. He let out a quick breath of air and shook his head. "Mornin' glory and sweet potatoes…" he declared in a low voice. "Ain't this about somethin'."

Horatio concluded his melodic paean. The concentric waves that rippled reality, bending and bubbling the corporeal countryside, flickered and flapped from existence, leaving only the stillness of the day. The waving breaths of heat, writhing upwards from the grass on the far right side of the intersection, were the only peculiarity that remained. The heat grew like stalks, becoming more opaque, intertwining and forming a solid image. A two-story house was sculpted from the waves of heat, a quaint country cottage that boasted a Moorish design to its façade.

Horatio lowered his trumpet and stared at the house. Johnny stood up straight, resting his hand on his holstered revolver as the arched doorway opened and out onto the porch stepped an old man. He was short and stocky, clean-shaven with an olive-shaped head. The old man was dressed in a mustard-brown collar shirt, a color tone several shades lighter than his skin. He wore crisp blue jeans and brown work boots that were caked with dust.

"Jackson or Gaston Fable," Horatio called as he adjusted his fedora.

"Jackson," the old man hollered back. "Gaston's my brother. He lives across the street." Horatio and Johnny turned their heads to look at the empty lot across from Jackson Fable's house. Both men returned their attention to Jackson. "He's not home," the old man explained. He squinted his eyes, concentrating on Horatio. "You Pete Peters' boy?" he asked. Horatio responded, *"Yes I am, sir."* To which Jackson replied, "You sure 'nuff look like him." He moved his eyes, still squinting to keep focus, and studied Johnny. "I take it you're Joseph Concheroot's child, yes?" And Johnny affirmed, *"Yes, sir, I am."* Jackson nodded his head and hummed in contemplation. He waved the young men forward and turned around, walking into the house. "Come on in from the outside, then, get yourself some lemon water with ice." He assured from over his shoulder, "You can leave your car there. Ain't nobody gon' disturb it."

Horatio and Johnny both took a breath. Horatio put his trumpet back into its case, closed, and locked the oak box. He lifted the case by a strap and slung it over his shoulder. He took his father's music book and walked toward Jackson Fable's house with Johnny Concheroot next to him. They entered into a circular front room that featured white walls and charming, rustic furniture.

A round coffee table lay in the center of the room. A trumpet case, much the same as the case carried by Horatio, rested on the table. Behind the table was a short set of stairs leading up into the kitchen and dining area where Jackson Fable was preparing tall glasses of lemon water with ice, digging into his refrigerator for a pitcher and a lemon to cut. A fireplace, absent of a flame, was positioned to the right. Above the fireplace was an Ayizan veve symbol, intricately designed from brass. Ornate, Moroccan amphorae was placed around the room, along with potted, exotic flora. Two antique pots hung to the right of the fireplace with two empty vases below them. Left of the door was a wicker chair, cushioned with a cumulus-like pillow. A mirror hung on the wall behind the wicker chair. A bench, carved from the wall, lay at the far end of the room, to the left of the stairs. It was decorated with a long cushion and pillows. A dark brown quilt hung as tapestry from the wall behind it. A wooden sofa, carved and branded with detailed, anomalous symbols, occupied the left side of the room. A crowded bookcase lay behind the sofa. Sconces were on either side of an arched pathway from the front room to the dining area.

"Come on in here," Jackson directed. "Have a seat."

Horatio and Johnny proceeded into the kitchen and dining area where the rustic and charming décor continued. Horatio and Johnny took seat at the table, removed their fedoras, and watched patiently as Jackson prepared their drinks. They noticed a doorway behind the old man, its window covered with a curtain. To their right were windows adorned with opened curtains that let the day's sunlight peek in on their meeting, brightening the area. To their left was a narrow, arched opening leading to ascending stairs.

Jackson filled three cups of water and removed a knife and cutting board for the lemon. He placed the contents on the counter, cut the lemon in half, and spoke, "We've lived here for forty years now, my brother and I, and our wives until they passed away through one circumstance or another." Jackson squeezed lemon juice into each glass. He stirred the added nectar with a teaspoon. "Gaston and I are from over-up-there north, a small town just outside Saint Louis. We wanted to stay even after the Klan killed our father—those cowardly men." He stepped back and wiped his hands on a towel hanging off a drawer's handle. "But on that same night we became outlaws, so our mother moved us south. New Orleans. We stayed with our grandmother, a woman with a terrible disposition. But, she was sweet enough to teach us most the tricks we know." He bent down, and examined the rims of each glass. He lifted one after the other and hummed a gentle spiritual over the contents. Cubes of ice clinked and clanked into existence. Their substance was not fabricated from the watery contents inside, but molded preternaturally out of nothing. The cubes then settled atop one another, floating in the glasses.

Horatio and Johnny said nothing. Their excitement was contained on their faces. Only small twitches and tics curled their lips into admiring smiles, the only hint of being impressed.

Jackson walked two glasses filled with lemon water with ice over to the table and placed them down on coasters. Horatio and Johnny simultaneously said 'thank you'. Jackson gave a quick nod accepting their gratitude. He turned around and made a walk back to the counter, a walk made sluggish by age and experience. Jackson retrieved his glass, turned, and made the same style walk back to the table, taking a seat across from his guests. He exhaled, giving a contemplative stare out the window. He cleared his throat and again looked at Horatio and Johnny, this time inspecting their guns. He smiled and billowed a low chuckle. "Were you boys expectin' the Devil?" Jackson's laughter became harder, but not offensive to the young men. "Only blues players see the Devil 'round here." He waved his laughter off and said, "I'm funnin' you boys. Them blues boys get the word out. Keep white folks and superstitious Negroes scared." He swallowed his laughter and exhaled another sigh. "I guess it ain't always enough."

Horatio put his father's music book on the table. "You taught my father how to compose and play these songs? You and your brother?" He slid the music book across to Jackson.

The old man took the book and smiled as he ran his fingers across the cover. He shook his head as he opened the book and corrected Horatio, "We gave him this book when he arrived, and we gave him a new horn. He wrote the songs. Couldn't tell you how he found us. Drove all the way from Harlem to get here. Must've come across rumors. He wrote this song with that earthly trumpet of his." He smiled and pointed to song four, *Carrefour: The Intersection of Jackson and Gaston.* "Sure did get us to open the door for him." Jackson smiled as he reminisced. He sat up in his chair. "Heard about your mother, Horatio. Sorry to hear of her passing. She had a beautiful voice. Her voice and the piano is where she had an edge on your father. They made some good music." Jackson took a sip of his lemon water. "Was expectin' you to be here sooner or later. Musicians from far and wide still flock to the area. We welcome their ambitions, though we don't always open the door."

"You and your brother play?" Johnny asked.

Jackson nodded his head. "Sure do," he said, memories expressed in his voice. "We play it all, music style or instrument. Well, there was one instrument we couldn't play." He looked at Horatio and said, "The trumpet we gave your father. Peculiar item. Found it one day, my wife and I. It was layin' in a field, in its case. It was just outside Red Leaf, a town twenty miles south from here. Use to be a town run by black folk. Then, white folks got involved. It's theirs now." Jackson waved his hand. "Anyway, we could move the case; we couldn't take the horn out. We brought it here. Your father showed up 'round six or seven years later, playin' his trumpet. We opened the door. We took him in as a student. He asked if he could hold the horn. My brother, Gaston, he said to your father, '*Go on 'head, boy. If you can lift it, you can keep it, cuz we can't do nothin' with it.*'" Jackson's grandfatherly smile appeared. "He sure 'nuff could hold it, and he could play it even better. The horn was his ever after. He wrote them songs, fillin' that blank music book with notation."

Horatio's eyes looked down at the book. He asked Jackson, "Could you teach me to play the horn?"

Jackson chuckled, considering Horatio naïve. "We didn't teach your father to play the horn," he said, his voice like a roll of thunder rumbling in the distance. "Not musically, anyway. He had the blessing to play music. He already put his time in. Practice. No different than you. All we taught him was how to express, through the horn, the tricks we learned from our grandmother. He hit notes no earthly instrument could. He took them lessons back to Harlem three years later. Your father got himself a band. He called them The After Mid-Knights. Hot damn! They could play." He said to Johnny, "Your father on the piano? Other boys was only playin' catch-up. That whole band. Spiritual sermons wrapped up in jazz." Jackson made a fist and swung excitedly. "Go 'head on, Pete Peters. This house, and my brother's across the way, always had the radio tuned to your father's music."

"My father never cut a record, sir," Horatio exclaimed.

Jackson again chuckled at Horatio's naivety. This time the old man expressed it. "You just saw a house appear from out of nowhere, you gon' question how we tuned a radio to hear unrecorded music playin' hundreds of miles up north?"

Horatio grinned sheepishly. "Sorry, sir," he apologized in the same manner. His grin remained.

"Ain't no need to be sorry," Jackson assured. "This type of thing don't happen to folk every day. Gaston and I goin' on more than forty years into all this and we still surprised. I can only imagine what your father showed people up there in Harlem. Your mamma knew what he was doin'. He brought her down here a year into his studies. She wanted to stay. She didn't want to go back to Harlem, but your father convinced her otherwise. I thought that was a good thing. We started havin' trouble not too long after your father left. Red Leaf. White folks in suits started comin' in. Movin' us like they did Indians to a reservation. They must've found gold." Anger molded onto Jackson's visage. "Didn't know Gaston and I was the gold." He grit his teeth, shaking his head. Then his calm, venerable demeanor returned. "Came in all nice-like. Promised change, inclusion into larger state politics. It was nineteen twenty-eight. Black folk just wanted a say, stop gettin' hung. But them suits left behind a honey badger of a man to oversee things. Cornelius "Curly" Burneside. Now, I don't recall myself or any other Negro gettin' a vote, but that cracker was de-clared new mayor and sheriff of Red Leaf." Jackson rolled his eyes. "And judge, and jury, and executioner. He wear his badge when he suited up in his white hood. That's how bold he be. He want you to know." Jackson took another sip of his lemon water, wishing it were something stronger. "Things escalated in Red Leaf. Them white folks started hangin' us. Then, one night, there was a lot of shootin'. A lot of black people died. Most of the town was burned, but the government helped them white folks re-build it. The whole thing took my brother and I and our wives off guard.

"From then on, we had us a war with him, Curly Burneside and his deputies. He knew tricks. Yes, he did. It was his tricks against our tricks, and he keep a hexed syringe on his hip in case you got any tricks. His soldiers carry them too. They been pricking us with them things since the ol' slave days. Stop African folk from usin' sorcery. Through all this war, listenin' to your father's music every night on our radios put us at ease. Glad them radios worked the way they do. Curly's tricks messed with some of these trinkets we got 'round here. The mirror couldn't tell us nothin'.'" Jackson gestured with his finger, pointing to the front room where the mirror hung behind the wicker chair. "That mirror there, show you things. Show you more than just your re-flection. But a re-flection was all we could see. Your mamma showed up five years later. She sang, and we opened our doors for her. It was a blues song, had a lot of heartache in her voice. She had with her another man. Leon Daniels, the bass player in your father's band. They told us your father had been murdered. She was holdin' you in her arms. Leon was takin' her to New Orleans." Horatio and Johnny didn't move, but the subject of Pete Peters' murder made them anxious. Answers. If nothing else, that was what they had come for.

The murder scene appeared in front of Horatio. It was a flash no different than any other time the dream sequence appeared while he was awake. Then, the vision overtook the environment surrounding Horatio. Everything around him dissolved, and the intangible image of the scene solidified in the evaporated absence of where he sat. All the players were in attendance, motionless as if in a photograph. There were the ruffians, the pointing scorpion, and Pete Peters with his back turned. The lion faded, replaced by a man hiding in a corner.

Leon Daniels.

"Leon witnessed the whole thing," Jackson voiced, taking Horatio from the vision. "Three men walked in on your father while he was settin' up at the club. Each man fired one bullet. That was enough." The vision returned to Horatio. The three ruffians pulled the triggers on their guns. The bullets broke through Pete Peters' shoulder, head, and heart. Pete

Peters' body hit the floor with a loud crash that ended the scene. Jackson said to Johnny in a sorrowful manner, "Your father told these men where Pete Peters could be found. Leon said your father and Pete had been arguin'. Someone took advantage of that. Pete Peters' good music made good enemies. Fifteen in total. Leon included, at one point." Jackson sat back. The old man looked uneasy, moving in his seat as he trembled with emotions.

Pete Peter's gruesome murder sprang back to life in Horatio's head, opening again with the three masked and armed ruffians. Leon Daniels hid in a corner. The scene had no motion. The image of the pointing scorpion washed away and was replaced with Johnny's father. He pointed a finger at Pete Peters. *There. He. Is.* Fade to ruffians pointing guns. And, scene…

Jackson's voice swallowed the image, and Horatio was back in the old man's kitchen. "Leon told me," he continued, "that all fifteen fellow-crafts of that peculiar class of musician were seduced into believing they were to preside over the secrets and lessons of your father's music. They didn't understand that Pete gave them the secrets every time they played. They music elevated too, even with them earthly instruments." Jackson's voice resonated with contempt and frustration. The emotions, once buried deep, were now more prominent, exposed and at the surface. "I mean, if you in Pete Peters' band, you playin' at his level." He sighed. "Three hoods dressed in tailor-made suits thought Pete was takin' money from them. Club owners. Everybody was goin' to the On The Hour club. People wanted to see and feel The After Mid-Knights. These ruffians had a club called the Mud Hare." Jackson stopped as he caught the excited flinch expressed on Johnny's face "You know the Mud Hare, boy?"

"Know of it," Johnny emphasized. "It was closed down, but it re-opened 'bout twelve years ago." Johnny continued to talk, and talk excitedly. "White people own it. It's called Harlem Dixie now. The woman who runs it with her son is from the South. Sarinda Fallows. It's a jumpin' spot. I played there a couple times. I love the crowd. Her son works on gettin' all the new Rock and Roll acts. Stanley Fallows. He's about my age. Miss Fallows keeps the flame of jazz goin', though." Johnny admitted, "That white woman can sing. She know how to bellow jazz. She writes her own tunes too; she puts on a helluva show. And I got to say, she a fine lady. Dark, red hair. Pretty, curvy frame. Like I said, she got a son my age, but she don't look a day over thirty herself. She must've had Stanley young." He slapped his knee and added, "And the way she like to be courted by a colored man behind closed doors, I'm surprised ain't no tint to Stanley's skin. Of course, he could be passin'. As the story goes, her husband, Stanley's father, he been done passed. Dead."

Jackson considered Johnny's words. "Well," he said, "The Mud Hare wasn't much a main attraction at that time, 'cept for gamblin'. On The Hour had that too."

"On The Hour been closed down for a long time," Johnny interjected. "It's all boarded up, burned. Black people been tryin' to open its doors back up. All their efforts get put down, though."

"That's a shame," Jackson commented. "Two black clubs in Harlem at war. White folks own one, the other been closed down." The old man huffed. "The way Leon tell it, them boys that owned the Mud Hare got other musicians, and everybody in Pete Peters' band to go along with the plot—'cept your mother, Horatio. Them boys conspired together to obtain your father's music book and horn, even if that meant having recourse to violence." Jackson asked as he lifted his glass, "You boys want somethin' a little stronger than the lemon water?"

Horatio and Johnny politely declined the old man's offer. Jackson finished his glass, letting the remaining lemon water not go to waste. He stood up, glass in hand, and with an old and sluggish walk, exhaled his age as he made his way to the cupboard to retrieve a bottle of gin. He said over his shoulder, "Leon confessed that on the eve of carrying out their conspiracy of execution, twelve of the fifteen recanted. He called the other eleven and stopped them from goin' along with the murder. Then he took it upon himself to interfere with the plot." Jackson removed one of his bottles of gin and returned to the counter. He opened the bottle, took a small sip, and spat a haze of liquor in four directions. He then poured a precise amount into his glass. He took a good large gulp and said after letting out a burning exhalation, "Yeah, twelve may have recanted in the deed, but three were more determined in their atrocious character than the rest. They persisted in them impious desires." He grinned as he inspected the bottle and said to his young guests, "I know thems a whole lotta words. Old folk tend to channel an education when we need it, even if old folk ain't ever had a proper one, which my brother and I have, just to let you know."

The tension blanketing Horatio and Johnny lifted. The old man knew how to turn the mood. It was appropriate. Both gentlemen laughed lowly. But they waited for the aged storyteller to continue.

Unfortunately, the tales continuance came with tension's reintroduction. Jackson's grin melted into a somber glower. The tension transformed the charming kitchen back into the scene of the crime, Horatio now experiencing the moment of his father's death through his father's eyes. Jackson's voice narrated. "Persistence, for which purpose these boys placed themselves respectively at the south, west, and east entrances to the club." Horatio, as his father, lifted the horn and spotted one of the masked ruffians in the reflection of the bell of the horn. To his left and right crept the other murderers, crawling from the dark. Jackson's voice penetrated the affair. "Because of Joe's tellin', they knew they would find your father there. It was the hour where he retired to pay his reverence to his lessons, as was his custom on a night off, at the hour of his band. Midnight."

Horatio turned. The three ruffians were upon him. They fired their guns. There was no noise. Not even his father's music accompanied the scene. He dropped to the floor, pushed by a force other than the gunfire. A flash of light covered his eyes, and then the gleaming shroud lifted and revealed he was still sitting inside Jackson Fable's kitchen.

Horatio and Johnny finished the rest of their lemon water in one large gulp. Johnny cleared his throat. "Mister Fable," he interrupted the silence in a voice as soft as his Brooklyn upbringing would allow. "I, uh, I'll…I believe I can speak for my friend here Horatio, when I take you up on that offer for somethin' stronger than lemon water."

Jackson looked at Horatio to see if the young man concurred. Horatio nodded in agreement. Jackson dropped his head, grinned, and chuckled in a boyish manner. He walked back to the table with gin bottle in hand, and he poured a sizeable amount into their glasses. Jackson left the bottle on the table, close to the young men should they need more than what was provided. He sat down. "We knew there was trouble before Leon and your mother showed up. Your father's trumpet case appeared. The horn wasn't in it. That was about a week before your mother and Leon came. Your mamma told us to keep the case. Keep it safe. It's been sittin' on the coffee table in the front room ever since." Jackson pointed his finger at the front room.

Horatio and Johnny turned around in unison, looking over their shoulders and gazing at the oak case resting on the coffee table. Horatio focused on the trumpet case, another piece to his father's puzzling and uncanny musicianship. He stood up and approached the case. Horatio circled around the coffee table to find the locks on the case. He bent down. His father's music, in his head, magnified. Horatio unlocked and opened the trumpet case. It was empty. Horatio kept a straight face as if not seeing his father's horn didn't matter.

Then, the music in Horatio's head seeped from his nostrils and lips as if he exhaled glittering cigarette smoke. It also precipitated from his ears. The animated notes twisted in a swarm of double whorls. Horatio hummed the songs pouring out of him, and he harmonized the notes perfectly, even the otherworldly ones. The swarm of musical notes filled the oak case, darkening and thickening. The black cloud congealed into a white light that faded into the colors of the rainbow, and then swirled again into a midnight colorant. Small glitters of light, acting like stars against the midnight wash, danced brightly. They reached out for one another and molded into a bright, golden light that culminated into the brilliance of an intricately designed brass trumpet that filled the blank space inside the case.

A watery haze clouded Horatio's eyes. His mouth hung open, shaped into a relieved smiled. Horatio looked up at Johnny and Jackson. Johnny stood up and walked to the open archway, leaning against the wall. Johnny smiled wide, proud like an older brother. Jackson got up from his seat. He went to speak, but a clicking sound interrupted him. The radio turned on, playing a live session of music from Pete Peters' band. An image appeared in the mirror, dissolving the reflection of the front room. The scene was a jumping nightclub in Harlem. The dance floor was a jumble of electrified bodies, kicking, arms waving, twirling to the unearthly sounds of a vibrant jazz band. The opulent opus coming from the band blared through the radio.

Jackson alerted Horatio and Johnny to the mirror's cast. He slapped Johnny on the shoulder and pointed, "Go on and have a look at your father's piano playin'." Excited, Johnny rushed to the mirror, standing close to the enchanted looking glass that cast history instead of a reflection. Horatio stood next to Johnny marveling at the sight all the same. Jackson grinned. He snapped his fingers and bobbed his head to the music. Then he turned around, made his way back into the kitchen, and opened the cupboard to retrieve another wooden case.

Horatio watched his father. Pete Peters' horn blazed like fire and roared like a furious wind. His fearsome trumpet-work pushed the troublesome world away, and the all-black patrons showed their appreciation through ritualistic dance steps. Pete Peters ceased his horn, but the band continued. Harmonious, incorporeal rhythms jumped loud from their instruments. Johnny pointed at his father, Joe Concheroot slapping the keys of his piano like rapid bullet fire. "Look at my pops go!" Johnny yelled. "Better days," he added with a warm smile as he nudged Horatio.

Horatio agreed. A tear slipped from his eye, unable to hold it. He sniffed back the potential threat of other tears and bent down and wiped his cheek, blurting out a joyous sound. He straightened and Johnny grabbed his shoulders, shaking him and laughing. Johnny let go, and then he spun coolly to the music and returned to the kitchen with a sly kick in his step. Johnny wanted to drink while the music played. He stepped into the room to witness Jackson Fable open the wooden case he'd recovered from the cupboard. Johnny stopped all progressive movement when he spotted a uniquely designed gun laying in the case.

Jackson looked up at him, his face completely remiss of a jovial spirit. Johnny stared at him. He fought against an instinct to go for the gun holstered at his side. Jackson watched the young man's hand as it trembled closer to the holstered weapon.

The music continued playing. Horatio observed his father turn and conduct his small orchestra. Piano. Bass. Drums. Trombone. Pete Peters jerked his hands wildly, trumpet in his grip. He conducted his band like a reverend exorcising the spirits of the instruments from their somatic selves. Horatio mimicked his father's wild, rhythmic arm flailing. Behind him, the old man and his friend stared one another down, Johnny's eyes going from the gun in the case to Jackson Fable's somber expression.

Horatio grooved with his father. Pete Peters played small notes from his horn, poking into the existing number every-so-often with his trumpet's voice. He snapped his fingers three times, smoothly twisted around to once again face the audience, and threw down a balled fist. The After Mid-Knights' cacophonous harmony ended. The audience threw up their arms and offered up a hollering sound of applause. The music hadn't stopped; it only slowed down. It segued seamlessly into a slow tune. Jazz and blues intertwined and fused to conceive and give birth to a new, mellifluous reality. The audience did the same. Suits black as night hugged up against the stars' light of sparkling gowns shimmering on the dance floor. Bodies swayed close to one another. Pete Peters' horn bellowed a pregnant mother's cry that announced Virginia Peters to the stage.

She was beautiful, a Harlem sweetie bragged about by Langston Hughes. Silver gown worn like a gray day wears the fog and haze. A glimmering, rhinestone headdress adorned her head, dangling bead strings, and covering a short, wavy hairstyle. Virginia resonated with the mix of her plum-tinted black father and walnut-hued mother. She didn't step, she glided to the microphone and sang: *"Do you remember when we came upon these shores? No, not in slavery, I'm talkin' way, way, way back when before Before's before. Only lost languages have penned our story in old tomes of lore. Will you come with me, all y'all slow dancin' on the floor?"*

The nightclub's scenery changed, but the imagery began to fade. The suits and glittering gowns were exchanged for other apparel that Horatio couldn't make out. His reflection, and the dangerous stand off behind him, folded back into the mirror's glass. The nightclub scene was gone, leaving Horatio staring only at his perplexed image. The radio's dial clicked off. Horatio turned around and walked to Johnny, interrupting the tough, yet nervous inspection his friend was giving to Jackson Fable.

"What the hell y'all two doin'?" Horatio questioned.

"Old man's got a gun," Johnny summarized in an uneasy voice.

Horatio looked at Jackson. The old man broke his somber gaze and grinned. He dropped his head and shifted his attention to the gun resting in the case in front of him. He said to Johnny without looking at him, "Calm your inner Brooklyn, boy. I got somethin' on my mind, and you boys gon' help me with that somethin'." He then called, "Horatio!" The young man stood up straight, at attention. "Go on and see if you can take up that trumpet."

Horatio walked backwards a few paces, and then he turned to the coffee table, went around, and reached for the horn inside the case. Jackson kindly asked Johnny to bring him the bottle of gin resting on the table. Johnny did so, apologizing to Jackson shortly thereafter. Jackson kindly dismissed the young man's sentiments. "No worry, boy. I'd likely react the same," he admitted pouring another drink for himself. He looked up and

Horatio was standing in the archway, trumpet in hand. A proud smile decorated the young man's face.

"All right, now," said Jackson. "If you can hold it, you can play it." Jackson took a breath and then asked, "You boys ever hear of Thunder John?" He took a sip of gin, his eyes on the gun. "He was a cowboy. Fearsome man. Black man. He rode in a gang. People called them the Wild Zulu-Indians on account them boys was Negroes mixed with Indian blood. But, you got them righteous scholars sayin' that some of us black folk been here before slave boats. Supposedly the Brother Dogs, as John's gang members liked to call their posse, they was what you call black folk indigenous to this land. Mean they was born here before white folks showed up. Their people wasn't brought here forcefully." Jackson considered aloud, "Black folk, we the first folk on Earth, we been all over this world at one time or another, under all conditions. Well, anyway, enough of a story. I just wanted to say this gun belonged to him. It came with the house." Jackson picked up the gun and added, "I like Thunder John, but growing up, my father always talked about Thunder John's mentor, Top Hat. Man was a runaway slave 'round the age of fifty. After the Civil War, he led a crew of ex-slaves called the Black Scarves. He and his boys helped newly freed Negroes find missing family members, or take down their cruel ex-slave masters for a price. Oh, he was old, tough, bad and brutal," said Jackson peering deeper at the heavy iron pistol in his grip. "But, he only killed bad, bad men, some say for sport. The pay was extra to him." Jackson contemplated and said, "I was always more partial to his stories. Of course, the women folk I knew, they all liked the tales of Thunder John's wife. She was a strong conjure woman, Ori Washta was. Tales of her say she governed a town out west. There she was referred to as *Queen* Ori Washta. Thunder John and his boys were loyal soldiers at her command."

The gun was an 1869 LeMat revolver, a well-built and mighty-sounding weapon with a nine-round cylinder and a short twelve-gauge barrel in the center. It looked like a small cannon fit for the hand.

Jackson placed the gun back in its case. "I was expectin' someone today," Jackson said looking at Horatio and Johnny. "The house made room for you boys. Two bedrooms. Upstairs. You can get your stuff from your car if you got spare clothes in some luggage. If not, I'm sure the closet and dresser drawers upstairs will provide clean clothes your sizes, each in your respective rooms. Move your car onto the grass, and then come back in. Get some rest. I'll make somethin' to eat. We gon' head to Red Leaf and pay a visit to ol' Curly Burneside. He holdin' my brother in a cell. We gon' rectify that. We gon' settle a lot of old business." He looked down at the gun. He aimed a grin at Horatio. "I got some new tricks for him." He walked over to Horatio and placed a hand on his shoulder. "Don't worry about the gun, yours or mine. I just need you to play your horn." He spoke to Johnny, "I want you to keep your gun close, however." He patted Horatio's shoulder and ordered, "Now go get y'all's car. Bring it on front."

Horatio and Johnny nodded together. They turned around and made their way outside, stepping back into the day. A lot was on their minds. Horatio spoke before Johnny could hold any protest. "He gave us answers, Johnny. We owe it to him to go."

Johnny wasn't as reluctant as Horatio perceived. He acknowledged, "Yes, he did. And, yes, we do. But them answers created a whole lot of questions."

Horatio stopped in the middle of the road. "You at peace? Completely? Your father ain't the murderer you thought he was."

Johnny looked around uncomfortably. His hands went to his pockets. He squinted and then focused his eyes on Horatio. "Still ain't good, but I'll see him when we get back to New York. Ain't visited him since I was…well, it's been some time. Been about nine years, or so." He pressed on toward the car, waving Horatio to follow. They slipped inside the vehicle, Johnny in the driver's seat, Horatio riding shotgun. Johnny started the car and pulled it up to the front of the house, driving onto the grass. They jumped from the car and went around to the rear. Johnny opened the trunk with his keys. The traveling jazz musicians removed their luggage and made their way back inside the house.

The front door closed and the music that brought the house into existence played backwards from out of thin air. The motions of the house's appearance did the same. The house's solid state faded into the waving lines of heat and sank back into the ground. Johnny's car, parked out front, dissolved along with it. The environment rippled and bubbled until the music washed away, leaving only the pristine countryside at the intersection of Jackson and Gaston.

The sky, and all the celestial onlookers, continued paying close attention to the story, resumed as it was.

Red Leaf In The Wind
"I'm about to be the envy of every Negro in the world."

Gaston Fable occupied a small room. He was tied to a chair and unconscious. An old desk and chair lay to his left. A faucet and sink were behind him. A light hung above him, the bulb of which was exposed without a shade. There were no windows. Shadows elongated and shrank as the light swayed to and fro. The door in front of Gaston opened, and four men stepped inside. Curly Burneside led the troupe. He stood at six feet two inches but looked taller because of his ominously confident demeanor. Curly was dressed in a button-collar shirt with a blue flannel pattern, tucked in and covered by a brown jacket that matched the color of his slacks. A wide-brimmed, felt hat rested atop his round, wizened head. His hat covered thin, silver strands that invaded the gold. A gun was holstered at his hip. One of his deputies carried a bucket of water, and with a signal from Curly, tossed the contents into Gaston's face.

Gaston's body jumped to life. His mouth opened, and water was sucked in hard as he inhaled deep. He choked, coughed, and spit the water from his throat. He opened his eyes. When the water cleared from his vision he'd returned to his youth, no longer tied in the chair. The scene was different, but the same. He was fourteen years old and scared. Water still drenched him, dripping as the white-robed and hooded man lifted him from the muddy puddle. It was night. A gentle rain ornamented the cold scene. The heat from the tall, wooden, burning cross shared its warmth, but was far from comforting. Gaston's brother Jackson was next to him being roughed up by another robed and hooded man.

Gaston shivered, he himself handled rough by the cold, Missouri night. His lip was split and bleeding. Bruises lined his face, billowing like dark clouds on his skin. Gaston's face throbbed. He wished for his right eye to continue swelling and hopefully shut. He wished his left eye would do the same. But, his eyes remained opened and fixed on what was in front of him. Calvin Fable, their father, tall and mighty, the strongest man he and his brother had ever known, was now subdued. Six hooded men, acting as if they were the offspring of the fabled boy Jack that climbed the beanstalk, snared this once great giant. Two, hooded men put guns to Gaston and Jackson's heads. This was all an ambush perpetrated by white grafted from the night. The other hooded men beat the boys' father who did nothing to fight back. He was warned that his boys would be killed should he do so. It was a warning without promise. The hooded men planned for all three to die. Father and sons were going to hang.

"If I don't cry, you don't cry," their father ordered before the beating commenced. Gaston and Jackson did just that, hard as it was to keep to their father's promise.

The ritual was taken further, and now, three robed and hooded men dragged Calvin's mighty, limp body to a tree. He was lifeless and beaten. But even unconscious, the might of Calvin Fable continued to challenge the men that struggled to drag him. A rope was already around his neck, tied into an elegant noose. One of the men tossed the long end of the rope around the branch of a tall tree. The second of the three tied Calvin's legs together at the ankle. The last tied Calvin's hands behind his back. The first man pulled on the rope, trying to elevate Gaston and Jackson's father. The other two men joined their comrade to help. Again, the might of Calvin Fable's body was stubborn, resisting even while insentient.

But up Calvin's body eventually went. His head falling to the left, as if trying to get a better look at his boys. But, his eyes were closed. The three men circled the tree, wrapping the rope tight. Calvin's body was displayed high above the ground, neck and head just below the branch. The robed and hooded men tied the rope into a stable knot and watched as Calvin's body trembled. Gaston and Jackson's father never resumed consciousness, or at least, never opened his eyes.

The man holding Gaston asked a hooded associate to retrieve a mason jar from their Sanford business-model truck. He hollered for the same associate to get his knife, and he commanded another to remove the pants from Calvin's hanging body. The hooded men set to their orders, one working Calvin's belt buckle as the body continued jerking.

And then, magic happened. The burning cross broke at the base. Its heavy weight crumbled and dropped straight down, landing on the truck occupied by the hooded man reaching for a mason jar. His body burst into flames. The other men jumped to attention, scrambling to their friend.

Gaston and Jackson remained still, watching their father dance a hanged-man's jig. Then Gaston saw his brother stand and run. He jumped to do the same, but he tripped and a man grabbed his shoulder. The hooded man shouted obscenities and slurs, but nothing hurt more than the punch he delivered to the fourteen-year-old's face, save the second and third hits from the man's fist.

A scream preceded a thunderous sound. The rain paused, too scared to drip. The hooded man beating Gaston soared away from him. He landed, sliding on the ground violently. His robe was covered in blood, torn and ripped just like the lower right of his torso where the buckshot tore through him. Gaston got to his feet. Jackson tossed the shotgun away and ran, grabbing his brother's arm. They ran and ran and ran and ran. They ran through the maze of trees, into the night. Voices were behind the boys.

Something popped, sounding like a firecracker. A bullet buzzed by Gaston's ear, its sound like an angry bee. Gaston's right earlobe split and bled. More pops sounded. More buzzing followed he and his brother. Thwacking sounds cracked against trees. Young Gaston became scared as to where his brother was leading him. His fears increased when they came upon a road. The borrowed car their father was taking them home in lay broken down on the other side of the road. Jackson dragged Gaston to the car and searched a compartment on the inside of the roofless automobile. Gaston watched his brother pull two firearms from the compartment. Their father had showed them the guns before they left the house, weapons kept by Mr. Franklin who owned the car. Two guns. One was for Mr. Franklin, the other for his wife.

Jackson jammed one of the guns into Gaston's hands. He hissed, *"Here. We gon' use these."* Gaston trembled with gun in hand. Rustling accompanied by cursing and slurs filtered from the edge of the woods. Ghosts appeared. Gaston turned, trembling ceased. He fired the gun. The force of the gunfire shook the young boy's body. He flinched. A bullet hit the chest of the first robed and hooded man that appeared from the darkness. The man grabbed his wound, coughed up blood on the inside of his hood, and dropped to the road to die. Young Gaston recalled a sad tune, hearing the piece of music as a gunshot from Jackson's firearm rattled him. The noise screamed in his ear, swallowing all sound around him. The music remained, a song recalling the ritual of clouds learning to fly.

Gaston and Jackson killed the robed and hooded men. The ghosts emerged from the woods, and the young brothers gunned them down.

Deed done, the boys slumped down against the car and panted to catch a breath. Ghosts as these white men were dressed. Ghosts they became. Jackson ran down the road, calling for his brother to follow and keep the gun in his hands. Gaston obeyed his brother. They ran and ran and ran, getting nowhere. Gaston followed his brother as Jackson ducked back into the woods. They found their father's body and dropped to their knees. The brothers held one another until the sun came up, all the time breaking their father's promise and crying. In the morning, Jackson wiped away the tears in Gaston's eyes. When Jackson's hand swept across Gaston's vision, he saw Curly Burneside's clean-shaven face staring at him.

Gaston Fable was tied to a chair, and he was dripping wet with water. Curly Burneside held Gaston's chin tightly, shaking his head and telling him to wake up. Curly backed away when Gaston came to. He slapped Gaston hard in the face as he took a step back. "Wake up," he said through a baleful, grumbling laugh. "Wake up, Gaston." Gaston looked up at Curly. Curly sighed, "There, you go, boy." He put his hands on his hips. He stood for a brief moment, contemplating. He got his thoughts together, made a noise, and lifted his eyebrows, exhaling. He removed his coat, folded it neatly, and passed it to his deputies. Gaston said nothing. His face was blank. He watched Curly as the sheriff unbuttoned the cuffs of his sleeves and rolled them up. Gaston focused on the silver ring worn on Curly's left hand. The ring was beset with a peculiar gray stone that was speckled with red markings.

Curly walked around in back of Gaston and turned on the water at the faucet. Gaston dropped his head, and one of the deputies screamed for him to keep his head up. Curly quickly interrupted and chastised his deputy. "Hey," he hollered at the deputized man. "You shut up," he told him. The deputy stood at attention. "Can't you see he's tired?" He looked at Gaston and asked, "You tired, ain'tcha, boy?" Gaston remained silent, which was enough of an answer for Curly. "Let him be," he said to his deputy, his voice a warning. Curly shook his head and said under his breath, "Goddamn ingrates don't know a fuckin' damn thing about respect."

Gaston breathed heavy. He chanted, "I do not apologize for having two eyes and a heart. I resonate green and indigo. Be afraid when I become violet, because then my black will be gold."

Curly washed his hands. "Whatchu sayin' there, Gaston? Is that there some of that nigger chantin'?" Curly's raspy, baleful laugh crept from between a smile. He turned off the water and dried his hands with a towel.

He returned to Gaston, pulled the chair from the desk, turned it around, and sat with his stomach against the chair's back. Gaston didn't look at him. "No prayer gon' do you any good," he said tapping on his ring. He went silent. Curly inspected Gaston for some time before standing up and sliding the chair back under the desk. "I hope you got some strength, Gaston. This is gonna be slow. It's the only way I can be merciful and show you that I really do have a heart." He knelt down and lifted Gaston's chin. "You see, now, I want you to know how your wife felt." Curly's smile widened. "Ain't that tender? You and her can still feel something together, share moments separated by time and place—you here and your wife where she is, on the other side of life. You'll know what she went through in her last moments—what we put her through. The beating, that is. No need to get into the other stuff. This ain't prison. But we do plan on stickin' you, boy. We got needles for you. Take them tricks away for a while so you can really feel this hurt."

Gaston didn't want to move, but his body trembled lightly, anger coursing through him. Curly looked at his hands and then balled them into a fist. He took a swing and hit Gaston hard. The sixty-one-year-old man rolled with the punch, but it hurt. The chair tilted to the left, and then it set back down. Curly hit Gaston with his left fist; Curly's ring added more of an effect. Then he threw his right fist straight into Gaston's face. Blood spurt from Gaston's nose. He took in a heavy breath to steady the pain, and he grit his teeth. Curly could see Gaston was hurt.

"Miss Fallows just wanted us to kidnap her—your wife—hold her until we got the attention of you and your brother." Curly wiped his knuckles. He removed his ring and set it on the desk. "Havin' that ring on is kind of like cheatin'. I want you to know my strength, boy." He grinned. "Anyway, I didn't think just holdin' your wife would be a good idea. I wanted to leave a mark." He turned suddenly and hit Gaston with his fist, the impact landing between Gaston's cheekbone and his left eye. "As much as you and your brother have been hidin' from me, with all them back—" he struck Gaston twice more "—and forth actions we've had against one another. You know how many deputies I've been through because of you two boys?" The deputies flinched. Curly stopped and took a breath. "I knew I'd catch you one day," he panted. "You at your wife's grave." He smiled proudly, reminiscing. "Here we are, even if it is years after we dealt with your wife. I knew you'd be there. I ain't got clue one as to why you didn't bury her where you and your brother hide. Ain't his wife buried on that invisible real estate of yours, that fucking translucent property, wherever it is?" Curly then rolled his eyes and huffed. "Miss Fallows is only halfway to happy, but she gettin' old. Sarinda don't look it or act it, but she gettin' on in years. She's impatient. But she knows me. I've always liked the chase, even to the point where I purposefully drag it out. Ironically, she taught me that. I use to be the impatient one, and she liked the chase." Curly took another gulp of air. "That's where I believe you should start to worry, cuz there ain't a reason to kill you just yet. No, boy. No reason at all." He again knelt in front of Gaston. "You see, I'm gonna beat you, boy. I'm gonna beat you cuz I've been beatin' you for so long. Why stop now? It's my job. Y'see, I'm different than most folk out there. I'm different cuz I like my job, and I'm honest about it. I like beating you, boy." He stood and continued to hit Gaston. Curly hit Gaston long after the old man's face was blistering with large purple mounds and scratched with blood.

Curly was impressed at how long Gaston was holding firm. The old man never lost consciousness. He never winced in pain, though Curly knew good-and-well that Gaston was hurting. Curly even appeared more exhausted than Gaston. The sheriff found himself taking a breath every-so-often following a salvo of heavy jabs. His deputies didn't move. They watched the scene with wide, curious eyes.

Then a melody played on a trumpet. The music's effect was felt before the first note was heard. Gaston noticed first. He lifted his head and moved his eyes to the desk. Curly's silver ring with the peculiar gray stone was where his gaze happened to land. Gaston's blurry vision focused. The stone beset inside the ring cracked and crumbled into ash. The trumpet's soft and slow bellow manifested audibly into existence. Gaston managed to smile through his throbbing bruises. Curly blinked wildly and pivoted toward the door. His deputies were unresponsive to the music, their eyes locked in Gaston Fable's direction. Curly blinked again, and within that infinitesimally small moment of time, he found himself sitting in Gaston's place, tied to the chair. A young black man stood in front of him playing a trumpet. There was another young black man standing there as well. He was taller and darker than the trumpet player. The young men flanked a familiar face. It was Jackson Fable. Gaston leaned against the desk, panting and rubbing his arms where the ropes that now bound Curly to the chair had dug into him. Curly's men remained unresponsive to the situation, their eyes not quite aimed at him, but staring down where Gaston's eyes would've met theirs had he still been bound to the chair.

The young trumpet player finished his song. He put one hand in his pocket, and the other dangled the trumpet still in his grip, held like a gun. Curly looked at the horn. Tension substituted for the absence of music. Curly's attention turned to his desk, examining his ring that was now crushed. The stone was like dust, its ash scattered on the desk. A smile fought to appear on his face, but the expression only managed to make his open mouth tremble. His wide gaze panned the brass instrument, admiring it. Curly's eyes, pulsing and blinking in rapid succession, moved back to Jackson. Moisture appeared on Curly's brow. He trembled. His breaths were quick. Curly noticed Jackson, much like the tall, young black man, was armed with holstered artillery.

Gaston moved away as Jackson grabbed the chair from under the desk and moved it in front of Curly. Jackson took a seat. He adjusted his fedora as he stared at Curly Burneside. "Go ahead and scream if it'll make you feel better," Jackson recommended. "I'm sure someone in the next town over will hear you, loud as I know you'll make yourself." Curly stayed silent, trembling as sweat poked through and dropped from his forehead. "You might as well piss and shit yourself now, Curly. Your body will do so anyway, even when you gone." Jackson removed the heavy LeMat revolver holstered at his hip. "You should feel honored losin' your life to this gun, old as it is." His eyes traced the gun's design. He looked at Curly and added, "Considerin' its previous owner too. You 'bout to make history like so many folk that done stared down the barrel of this gun." Jackson's eyes went to Curly's shuddering legs, and then returned to Curly's. "I don't know why I'm so surprised. Big as you carry yourself, Curly, and this is all you are? Scared?" Jackson's emotions fluxed between hurt and disgust. He turned to his brother and asked, "You want this?" He lifted the antique revolver.

Gaston shook his head, no. "Too tired," he assured his brother. He looked at Curly and said, "In my younger days I'd still have the strength. You best understand that, Curly. That's all that's keepin' my hand from that gun."

Curly slumped down in the chair like an apologetic animal backing away from an angry owner. Jackson nodded approvingly at Gaston's statement. He commanded, "Horatio, Johnny, help my brother to the car." The young men did as told, leading Gaston Fable from the backroom of the jail station out into the streets of Red Leaf, its citizens' movements paused in mid-stride and mid-conversation. Gossip was half spoken, proposals half given, and destinations were half reached. Nothing moved. Horatio and Johnny waded through the still citizens, leading Gaston to the car and helping the old man into the back seat.

Jackson stood. "Well, it's about that time, Curly." He cocked the revolver. "Now, you might hear the gunshot, but this gon' be quick. What I'm gon' hear is the collective applause of many Negroes you done sent to the other side." Then he declared, "I'm about to be the envy of every Negro in the world." Jackson aimed the revolver at Curly and fired at the sheriff's head, putting an end to a longtime rival. He holstered the gun, turned around, and left the jail station. He labored through Red Leaf's eerily immobile citizens and met Horatio and Johnny at the car. He ordered Johnny to get in and start the automobile. "Horatio," he said. "Play one last song before we leave. The second song I taught you." Jackson went around to the car's left side, opened the door, and slid into the back, next to his brother.

Horatio played. The trumpet blared loud and rhythmic. The music was like a succession of breaths, inhaling and exhaling. The sky applauded with thunder, and the clouds danced close together. The horn cried out, reaching out over the horizon. The harmony teamed with the sudden whipping wind and herded the clouds into a furious funnel that extended from heaven down to earth. The windstorm was magnificent, and would've made Prospero blush with envy. The beautifully menacing storm didn't move forward. It twisted and gathered strength in one area until one last note from Horatio's horn beckoned it to move closer, and move fast. Horatio stopped playing and entered the passenger's seat and Johnny sped the car away from Red Leaf.

Johnny didn't look back. Neither did Jackson. Gaston slept off his ordeal, dreaming of his wife and feeling better. Horatio peeked at the side mirror. The storm twisted closer to the small town. Horatio watched the violent, revolving storm cover Red Leaf. There it remained, gobbling up the town. Horatio looked away, putting his hand on the trumpet that rested on his lap. A red light appeared at the base of the monstrous storm and started ascending the maelstrom, changing colors, passing through the rainbow's spectrum. The light resonated a dark purple once it reached the peak of the twisting storm. A flash of lightning and a loud roll of thunder hailed the storm's dispersion.

Time commenced, and Red Leaf was gone. The sun set to close the day. Johnny continued driving. No one said a word inside the car. Horatio looked in the rearview mirror to see if Gaston was stable. He slept all the way to the intersection. Both houses appeared for their masters. It was dusk. The lights came on. Johnny parked in front of Gaston's Moorish-style cottage, the house a mirror image of his brother's. Jackson nudged Gaston awake, hating to disturb his brother's deep rest. Horatio and Johnny exited the car. Both came to Gaston's aid. Johnny opened the backdoor and helped the old man from the vehicle, Horatio kept back until Gaston was fully outside the car. Jackson joined in, dismissing Horatio. "Move aside, boy. Take up your trumpet and follow us into the house."

Horatio lifted his trumpet and walked behind Jackson and Johnny as they helped Gaston into the house, through the front room that was identical to Jackson's, into the identical kitchen, and up the stairs. Gaston was led to his bedroom and helped into bed. He closed his eyes and Jackson called Horatio to play a tune over Gaston as he rested. Horatio improvised a slow tune on the trumpet. Gaston was instantly lulled to sleep by the song. The bubbling blisters on Gaston's face deflated, flattening back into pristine flesh. Gaston's bruises lost their color, his brown skin shining through. The scars disappeared, the flesh mending back together. The rivers of blood evaporated.

Jackson ordered Horatio and Johnny to return to his house and allow Gaston rest. Jackson stayed behind, sitting in a chair situated next to the bed. He watched his brother sleep. Scars physical and emotional, once deep, were now filled in on Gaston's face. Much of the heavy weight of years was lifted from the younger Fable brother. Gaston dreamed of his wife, and he smiled wide. When Jackson witnessed the beaming expression, he knew his brother needed privacy for his dream, and so he left room and returned to his house across the street.

Horatio was upstairs in his bedroom. He'd put away his horn on return to the room. The case was still open, and Horatio admired the instrument. His father's horn was now rightfully his. He commanded its ethereal notes and profound music. There was so much to create with the horn's magic. Horatio had yet to attempt any of his father's songs, only learning the peculiar notes taught to him by Jackson. The magic he commanded today came with practice from songs composed by the Fable brothers and their wives. Horatio wondered how a man that never played the horn understood the otherworldly notes it could produce. Jackson knew its harmonies so well. No doubt Gaston knew as well, and their wives too.

But that was magic, considered Horatio. Convenient.

While Johnny enjoyed the mirror downstairs in the front room, peeking into yesteryears to observe his father in private sessions playing the piano or serenading his mother, Horatio perused his father's music book upstairs in his bedroom. The music from the book no longer haunted him since he'd lifted the horn. Tomorrow, he would make his first attempt at playing one of the songs with his newfound trumpet. He studied the songs long into the night, only taking pause when Jackson called he and Johnny to dinner. Horatio enjoyed the meal, simple as it was. Seasoned chicken, mashed potatoes, and vegetables. Cornbread and biscuits were also served. There was sweet tea to drink. Jackson went to check on his brother during dinner. Gaston was still asleep. Horatio and Johnny returned to their rituals, skipping dessert.

Later, Johnny interrupted Horatio asking him, "You excited?"

Horatio looked up from his father's book. "Sure am. Tomorrow, I go to work."

Johnny nodded his head. "Me too. I'm 'bout to turn in. Gaston's house looked similar to this house, but I saw one li'l difference there. He had a piano in his front room. If he's feelin' up to it, I'm gonna see what he knows, see if these tricks translate to eighty-eight keys." He beamed his charming grin. "We've seen some stuff, Horatio. I'm sure you got questions like me. Don't mean we can't jam in the meantime."

"Hell no it don't," replied Horatio. "We'll put together what we learn and take it to Harlem."

Johnny nodded. "Well, I don't mean to take up all your sweet time. This whole thing feel like a dream. Let me get some sleep." Then Johnny joked, "Dreamin' got me exhausted." He bid Horatio goodnight as he closed the bedroom door and left Horatio to himself.

Horatio changed into his bedclothes and crawled into bed. He was too excited for sleep, but he couldn't resist the overwhelming comfort offered by the bed, the pillow, and the covers. He yielded to their power and fell fast asleep.

Way, Way Back When
"Everything you've needed to know has made an appearance."

Horatio took a hot shower and then suited up in black slacks held up by black suspenders that folded over a white, cotton short-sleeve shirt. Black shoes covered black dress socks. There wasn't a need to be too sharp, just dressed. He snatched his fedora and flipped it along his arm, let it reach his hand, and then popped it on his head. He looked outside his bedroom. The sun's spidery physique was just crawling over the horizon. The sky blushed away its night visage, brightening from purple to red-orange. Horatio smiled and winked at the celestial body. He waved goodbye to the stars and slapped his hands together as he let out a holler.

"We 'bout to get to work," he expressed. He spun around and jived, "Hot damn." He looked at the trumpet case that lay on the dresser. "Today is the day I play with all the musical notes in sound's spiritual spectrum." He looked at the mirror and put his hands in his pockets. He said to his reflection, "Ain't that right, Pop?" A vision of Pete Peters did not appear in the mirror. Horatio waited a moment, trying to look beyond his image to see if he could find his father or mother. Nothing appeared. Horatio stared at Horatio. The mirror was just a mirror, but this didn't slow Horatio down. He slammed a foot against the floor and cocked his head to the side. "I'm gon' learn your songs first, Pop. Then I'm gon' compose a few of my own." He inhaled and moved his eyes to the trumpet case in front of him. He reached out and opened it. The brass brilliance was blinding, blaring from the horn that was once commanded by his father. He turned to the nightstand. There was his father's music book. Inside the book was music that could only be translated by his father's horn.

Horatio turned back to the trumpet case, closed it and tucked it under his arm. Continuing to gather his things, he took his father's book of music from the nightstand, opened the door, walked into the hall and made his way downstairs. Jackson was in the kitchen preparing a breakfast.

"Practice out back," he said without looking up. "Go through this door here." He pointed to the door behind him, the one with the curtained window. "Too early in the mornin' to be playin' in the front room. I could halt the sound of an earthly instrument, but not that one. Tried once with your father playin', only increased the sound. Wife had a fit," he smiled. Jackson opened the door as he maneuvered through the kitchen with utensils, produce, and other ingredients for the breakfast he was preparing.

Horatio nodded his head. He moved past Jackson and made his way to the door. He stepped through and found himself in a wooded area. Jackson's backyard looked nothing like the intersection. It was an entirely different environment from what lay on the other side of the old man's front door. There was no golden, sun burnt grass. The grass here was vibrant green, bloomed in color beyond viridescence. There was no dusty, dirty road. An earth-toned path parted the grass. The trees were tall, strong, and grew into one another creating a leafy dome that was purposefully imperfect. Cracks in the canopy provided entrance for the sun's light, which curved and twirled, supplying plenty of itself to show off the open space.

Horatio inspected the scene, hesitant at first to move further outside. This was not what lay behind the house when he and Johnny first pulled up to the intersection. This was somewhere else. He glanced at his father's music book and soaked in the inspiration to move forward, trumpet case still tucked under his arm. Horatio found a well-lit spot and set his belongings down. He opened his father's music book to the first song. *Pre-Conceived Notion*. Horatio trembled with excitement. He sat down in the wooded area, legs folded. He opened the trumpet case and lifted the horn. He twirled the instrument on his finger like a cowboy does a gun, as if the trumpet weighed nothing. Then he stayed the trumpet's twirl and snapped his fingers with the opposite hand. Horatio jumped to his feet and improvised a tune. He turned and blew short and distinct, bewitched trumpet chords in the four directions, like Jackson had done the liquor when he and Johnny first arrived.

Horatio's improvisation progressed from there.

His eyes were closed and witnessed a scene of his father playing a fierce, otherworldly tune on the horn. It was night, in the same wooded area. Pete Peters was attired almost identically, save a long-sleeved shirt and black vest covering his suspenders. Virginia Tara, Pete Peters' wife-to-be, danced merrily around a fire that seemed to twirl to Pete Peters' rhythms.

The flames reached up and formed clapping hands. Horatio's music quieted. Pete Peters' trumpet accented the scene. Horatio kept his eyes closed, lips puckered on his trumpet, continuing to play. The sound from his horn stitched the scene into existence. His music, like thread, wove together what he watched behind his closed eyes.

Pete Peters slowed his music. Horatio's improvisation simmered too. He stayed with his father's flow, but he didn't imitate the song. Horatio's playing complimented his father's groove. The fire retracted, flames flapping with a tender movement. Virginia danced in place, swaying her hips slow and gentle from right to left and back again. Her eyes remained closed, taking in Pete Peters' music. Her arms were out, bent, moving as if she was wading in water. Then Virginia Tara twirled around, her dress expanding like a trumpet's bell. She faced Pete Peters and beamed at him. His rhythm was majestic, poetic, magic perpetrating as music. Virginia stepped closer, stopped, and closed her eyes again for some time. Her eyes remained closed even when Pete suddenly ended his tune. Horatio continued playing, but his music was inaudible. The invisible notes formed the scene he observed.

Pete Peters lowered his horn. He dropped the instrument and walked over to Virginia. He palmed her shoulders, and she opened her eyes. She inhaled the air; her smile widening as her breath deepened. *"You heard that, Virginia?"* Pete Peters asked her in an excited voice.

"I did more than that, Pete," Virginia responded putting her arms around his neck. *"I was there. I saw you. I saw everything. I heard that music, and I did more than just feel it. Honey, I saw it. It was you and I. Our child narrated."* She teased Pete Peters with her wide smile and rubbed her nose against his. Pete Peters opened Virginia's embrace. She wasn't offended. Virginia gave a soft chuckle as Pete Peters rushed to his music book. He opened it and found a pen, scribbling wild. Virginia told him, *"I don't understand why you so mystified. Flummoxed, as I heard Gaston say. After all you've seen here? I know I ain't surprised at nothin' no more."*

Horatio's sight peered over his father's shoulder. Pete Peters penned the title for the first song in the book. *Pre-conceived Notion.* The scene flooded with fog and vanished as the dense, gray and cloud-like curtain lifted. Horatio's improvisation was complete. His eyes went straight to his father's music book. He played a note. The book flipped open to the first song and held its place. Horatio laughed at the cause and effect. He raised his eyebrows and took a breath. "Okay," he said still trying to get used to the tricks he could perform with the horn. He was like his father, Horatio guessed. He'd seen so much, and still he was surprised. Horatio tried another trick. Light splashed on the pages, which allowed an easy read for Horatio. He looked close and studied the notes for a moment as he stood over the music book. He was hesitant again. He inhaled and relaxed, and then he put his horn to his lips and played his father's song.

Playing the song with the horn was like putting a puzzle together. The notes that were skewered on what Jackson Fable called 'earthly' instruments, connected seamlessly with the telluric musical notations. Horatio's feet left the earth. His body curled, knees tucked to his chest. He played his horn over the hill that was his knees. His eyes shut. The music's notes scrolled behind his eyelids as if on an electric marquee. The sun's light disappeared. The woods disappeared, tree by tree by tree, enclosing Horatio in darkness. The atmosphere moistened. Strange symbols glowed in the blackness. The symbols hummed in and out of their glow. Horatio heard his own voice speaking lyrically over his father's music.

If Adam existed literally
In the flesh physically
Instead of meta-euphoric
    Allegoric-scientifically
I would be his flesh flickering
    Candle sunlight quivering
    Perfect molecular molded rendering
    Second manifestation
For on the Eve of my birth
I fed on information
And this is how I knew I was a male child
Not through the illusionary flesh fallacy
    Of the phallic waving serpent
    Of condensed masculine energy
    Swinging between me
But by the piece of the apple
    That would forever reside within me
The compiled music – the lump in my throat
So I ink penned, cried signature-signed and scribed a song
Scribbling rhythm on the inside of my mind

I began to take notes of the harmony vibrating
          Down my umbilical 'chord'
And there it roared – soared up from drowning
In the watery waves of the musical key C
Up and down into my mother's deep, dark Oshun
Where I lay surrounded 9 months, watery moist
There came the thunder of my Father's Voice
His music rolled on paper and lit this new joint
          with the spark of a pen's point
Poetry piled up in ashes
As he smoked shades of himself
Exhaling shadows of a former existence
Spooling and spinning into spinal energy
Standing on the corner of the galaxy
And suddenly, there came the breath that was me
Leaving ether winds as a trail, I wore 12 songs as my tail
To tell a tale made of 26 notes – 13 days and 13 nights
That my mother would take to compose and write – trials and crucibles
Time spawned metronome into psi-click [tick] intervals
My shadow casting its light onto me
Then my father's fingers snapped, and his hands clapped
And he sang me to life
There to throw back words working backwards
Into the past
So that we may move forward
Past the horrors – mirror spinal-dimensional spiral
Reflected through the dark corridors
Filled with the final note melodies
          Of my father's memories
Tickling me in my mother's belly. Mother Harmony.
My parents' story was a melody played on guitar strings
Floating and singing
All the way to their beginning
Of first kiss and serenity
To the conception of me, swirling inside
          Watching these memories
Vibrating past realities from my Father's Voice
          And Mother's Harmony

Etched in glowing hieroglyphs on the inside
        Of my mother's belly
My father left graffiti to speak to me
"We met in a square
Your mother's admiring stare
Watching the words forming, the poetry I shared
Recite, syntax flip, verbal gymnast
Poetry swirling between Arabic and African language
Add Italian, French, and Greek
Dazzled crowds seek every language shift
        Inciting puns, irony – tongue and cheek
My arrogance praised and encouraged
My poetry flourished
Piqued passion plucking a crowd's 'hurrahs'
I, the Sun, audience my solar system orbiting
        Caught in the warmth – the heat of my stanzas
Your mother a distant moon
My words' gravity pulled her higher to my noon
My words my tendrils of light offering a syllabic boon
A bold balladry birthing a lyrical atmosphere
        Spread and domed,
We admire one another long after crowd and applause
        Disappeared. Dispersed into the al-Andalusian night
Initiate, neophyte – neo-poetic Mason
Standing on this Moorish square
I, your Father Voice – she, your Mother Harmony
Calculating Maat-hermetic, mathematic future possibilities
We kissed destiny into existence – love into continuance
Life into remembrance, the present into future reminiscence
Circling love embraced there
We slow danced to intimacy's song
        In an al-Andalusian square."

The song ended. Horatio's feet touched the earth. The scene developed out of the darkness like a photograph. *"A Kingdom of Negroes,"* Horatio heard his mother say. *"We was there, Pete."* Horatio stared down at the music book. Its pages had already flipped to the second song called *Pre-Conceived Notion (Slight Return)*. Horatio started playing the tune, and again he lifted into the tucked position and the scenery faded from existence. The atmosphere became moist. The glyphs glowed in front of him. Horatio's eyes shut. The musical notes scrolled behind his eyelids. He played and listened as Pete Peters' lyrical chronicle unfolded.

"Hours fade
Churn time and make years from days
I, your Father Voice
She, your Mother Harmony
Continuing a black love story
> *In new bodies*
Wobbling waves of African dunes
Blazing beige and burnt by the sun
Or turned snow white by the blaze of the moon
There nature, man, and woman croon
Rising from a musically measured desert
Sings a kingdom's sandy song
> *Of sun-baked mud bricks*
Mixed with mud-based mortar and plaster
Sculpted smooth designed holy edifices
Towers placed at every corner of the city's wall
Coral stoned tiles bathing building interiors
Africa's Rome
Grand palace constructed from imported limestone
Wondrous worlds, family defined
> *Residential homes*
I, alone, walked the streets in the morn'
Coupled with thoughts of poems
Your Mother Harmony, I met her while she read an ancient ledger:
> *Metu Neter*
Mathematics spoken as sacred letters
Musical words conceived out of ancient breaths
She, your Mother Harmony, composed these lessons
Enunciating numerical syllables with the power
> *Of the third card in the tarot set*
Possessing the look of all four queens
> *In a fifty-two deck*
Her voice was as sweet as the scent of flowers

Though
She issued warning
Trickery trickling off the tongues of scholars
Scriptures infected, spoken inverted
Spiritual retrograde, regressive
Seventy-two holy names turned negative
On these incantations we prayed too long
> *Off key songs*
Prayers answered by sins turned flesh
> *Foul and hateful*
Created creatures, conjured ghosts
Smothering dreams and hope
Nations bleeding – bound
The sounds of muffled music jammed into boats
Notes sing melodies of slavery
Booming bondage verse-us freedom
Marching from kingdom to kingdom
> *Until it burned into our kingdom"*

Horatio tried to pull away from the trumpet, lost in the song. The melody was playing him. The rhythm moved him like a marionette. His fingers played the valves as he fed wind into the instrument. The sounds created by the horn produced the scene that Horatio's father narrated. There resonated an otherworldly groove that serenaded the scene. Also created were a set of strings that plucked at Horatio's fingers and formed a hand that pressed against his chest to push air into the trumpet, and a second palm that kept him pressed against the mouthpiece, forcing him to play. It was all a scary, symbiotic cycle. Horatio struggled to extend his legs and push his head away from the trumpet. He pushed, fighting against the uncontrollable desire to continue the song. The images were terrible. Opening his eyes did nothing but assure him the images were still there, the nightmare following him out of the dream.

He saw fires gnawing at an African city that was carved from the earth. Its towers crumbled into ash. African bodies lay scattered separate or piled high. All the black bodies were mangled. Every body had a story recounting its journey to death. Bullet riddled. Stabbed. Defiled. Broken. Beaten. Burned. A mix of each situation patterned the mortal remains of men, women, and children. Horatio tried to force the trumpet from his lips.

The music kept him in place. The floating glyphs burned brighter. The music screamed.

"We fled the violent deluge
And moved east
Behind us
I saw the rockets' red glare
The debris of earth's torn body
Turned foul and filth
> *Deviant*
To contaminate the air
The discharge of discord
Off beat pop that rocked the airwaves
Exhaust raged, flared, and fumed
Misguided alchemy consumed the sky
The smoke biting and devouring the golden eye
These gray and misty ghosts twirled and swiveled
Throwing obscene gestures to the sky as smoke signals
Choking the blue so the day could speak no more
Air smothered
The face of the sky suffocated into purple
The sun's warm intent extinguished
> *Its tendrils limp*
The off rhythm bombs birthed minstrels
> *Strolling streaks of erratic beats*
Some of us plead, plead, plead
Marched into slavery
Some bodies melt into the earth
Notes once singing life, decomposed of their melody
Your Mother Harmony leading us to safety
> *Or so we believed*
Her brother's kingdom a poisoned leaf
> *On the family tree."*

Horatio broke away from his horn. He collapsed to the ground, the wooded landscape appearing the instant the music stopped. Horatio lifted himself from the ground and wiped off his clothes. He lifted his horn and returned it to the case, shutting the wooden box. He turned around as he heard a raspy, aged voice comment, "I know you must be thinkin', *Where the hell did everything I know disappear to?*'"

There stood old man Gaston Fable dressed in an off-white buttoned collar shirt, covered by suspenders holding up gray pants. Gaston handed Horatio a glass of water that the young man knocked back. Horatio examined Gaston. He shared the same stocky frame as his brother Jackson but was more squared in physique than round. His skin was lighter, and his head was just as squared as the rest of his physique. His face was not as dour as his brother's, or perhaps just as dour in a different way. His face was bright and healed from his scars, though his eyes still looked tired with age. He wore glasses, which he removed and wiped with a handkerchief.

"When I was young," Gaston said putting his glasses back on, "I used my tricks to keep my eyes good, but I'm too tired with age now to do that." He chuckled lowly. "As for where-in-the-hell everything you know disappeared to, well, it's easier to think of it as everything you've needed to know has made an appearance." Gaston took the empty glass from Horatio, which Horatio thanked him for. "You ain't goin' crazy, Horatio. There's still magic in this world, sure as I stand and be. You can only go crazy denyin' it." Gaston looked down at the glass and continued to speak. "Now, magic's record might be a little scratched, the sound might be dull, but its music ain't ever died. That's the best explanation me or my brother can give you. You 'bout to play its song—all its notes and lyrics." Gaston chuckled again. "But, you don't need for me to tell you that. Shit. You just sent a whole town to Oz." Then Gaston considered, "Of course, I don't believe a lot of them people gon' land in Oz. They might meet the wrath of Gomar *Oz* Dubar, but there ain't gon' be no yellow brick road, and some singin', short white folk to greet them. They might meet a wicked witch or two. I know my wife, that wise woman, she got somethin' for them, the way they left her hangin' from that tree, body all beat, and worse." He waved Horatio toward him. "Come on in the house. Breakfast is ready. Grab your things."

Horatio went back to his trumpet case. He picked it up along with his father's music book and followed Gaston back into Jackson's kitchen. Gaston told Horatio, "Some of them people ain't stayin' in Oz. They comin' back. They gon' be all proper and nice with no hate in they heart. Town of Red Leaf gon' be re-structured." He slapped Horatio on the back and spoke before Horatio could reply, "Last time I saw you Horatio, ya mamma was holdin' you in her arms."

"Yes," he said to Gaston. "I heard."

"Go and wash up," instructed Jackson, preparing the breakfast as a buffet. Two plates had eggs. The first plate had scrambled eggs. The second plate was filled with eggs sunny side up. There was a bowl of buttered grits, a plate with bacon, another with buttered toast, and another with buttered biscuits.

Horatio ascended the stairs to the second floor. He saw Johnny in the hallway coming from the bathroom, all washed and prepped. "How you doin'?" Johnny asked Horatio as he neared him.

"Seein' things," Horatio replied. "Been practicing. There's a forest in the backyard."

Johnny shook his head. "Yeah, I know. I saw it last night. I took a peek out the backdoor. It was dark, but I could tell that I wasn't lookin' at what I thought would be the backyard. Did you play your father's songs?"

Horatio nodded and said, "Sure did. Took me places. I saw my mother and father." Horatio made a peculiar face, though smiling. "They weren't in Harlem, I can tell you that. Africa. Negro pride, and all that. Them righteous scholars would love it. My father composed a story in those songs, or unlocked another life. I can't say."

Johnny asked anxious but smiling, "Whatchu think we takin' up to Harlem?" He said before Horatio could answer, "How 'bout you see the rest of your father's story, and then we make one of our own? Find a Harlem sweetie for a muse." Horatio snapped his fingers in agreement. Johnny shook his finger and said, "Ain't nuthin' like a New York girl. Trust me." Johnny's laugh exhausted, and then he told Horatio. "I'm definitely gonna visit my father when he get out," he said as if trying to convince himself. "I want to ask him a few questions." He shook anxiously. "I was lookin' at that mirror. Your pops and mine, they composed songs together. Some of them wild ones, you know, with the horn. It was just them in the sessions." He stopped and gave Horatio a look. Both of them tried to hide their smirks. "Okay, man, I ain't at peace." He raised a finger as Horatio's smile came through. "But, I was before this trip." Johnny moved past Horatio. "You sure do got Harlem in your blood, readin' people like a numbers runner lookin' for his bets." Johnny moved down the hall and descended the stairs into the kitchen.

Horatio walked into his bedroom and lay down the trumpet case and music book. He proceeded to the bathroom, freshened up, and returned to the kitchen, jumping into the chow line behind his friend Johnny Concheroot. The breakfast buffet's hot aroma filled the kitchen and any nose in sight. Jackson and Gaston Fable were behind Horatio, allowing their young guests to prepare plates first. Horatio and Johnny took a seat after putting together full plates of breakfast and pouring themselves a glass of orange juice. Jackson and Gaston joined them at the table, plates just as full. They dug into their meals without saying a prayer. Their thanks and praise to a higher power very much assumed among the four of them. Gaston was the first to speak after the eating commenced.

"Found Lightning," he said to Jackson. "She was runnin' wild out back with Thunder."

Jackson rolled his eyes and huffed, jabbing his eggs hard. "Lot of damn good them dogs did." He looked up at his brother and asked in the same vexed manner, "Did you have both of them with you when Curly found you?"

Gaston replied 'yes' by simply nodding his head while sipping his orange juice. He put his glass down and spoke, "Both them dogs dropped dead. Made me look over my shoulder. I saw Curly comin' up the hill with his deputies. First they growled; backs all hunched up, hair standin' up. They turned in the direction Curly was comin' in, and then they dropped dead. Them hounds did they job, Jackson, as much as they could. I think Curly's ring was the root of his tricks. Saw the horn turn that trinket to ash." He took another bite of his food. "I also saw Louise. We danced. She look good. Her grave moved behind the house. Now I understand why she insisted on bein' buried outside of our protection, our spiritual jurisdiction," as Gaston referred to it. "I'm sure she saw somethin', a day or two before Curly found her." Jackson huffed again. Gaston reacted, dropping his utensils. "Stubborn old shit," he called his brother. "We got Curly. It's over. Smile."

Jackson's moodiness broke, and a smile came through.

"That's better," said Gaston. He went back to his food. "I get to dance with my wife now. Once a year. Like you and Zella Mae. Louise got her youth back too, just like your Zella Mae. Louise don't care what happened to her physically, what Curly and his boys did to her. She at peace." He turned to Horatio and said with a smile, "But, like I told you, that wise woman of mine had somethin' for some of them people you done sent to Oz."

Horatio smiled back.

"Sir," Johnny politely interrupted, getting Gaston's attention. The old man looked over at Johnny, attentive eyes appearing large through his glasses' thick lenses. Johnny inquired, "I noticed a piano in your house. I was wonderin' if I could play, learn anything from you, whether it be tricks or a new style."

Gaston went back to his meal. "Joe Concheroot's boy," he said lifting grits to his lips and taking a buttery bite. "I was very partial to your father's playin'. I want you to learn a song he composed. I got it stuck on one of them channels on a radio. I let that play while I sleep." He scooped up eggs and shoved them in his mouth. He swallowed and told Johnny, "Only trick you'll learn you'll learn yourself. That'll be stayin' in synch with Horatio when he playin' the horn."

Johnny looked excited.

Gaston called his brother to attention and notified, "Curly said a name." His old mind struggled to remember, and then it came to him. "Miss Fallows. Sarinda Fallows. He talked about her as if he worked for her. Said she wanted them to kidnap Louise. Gave the order."

Jackson and Horatio looked up, their eyes on Johnny. The young, Brooklyn man turned his head toward Jackson. He turned his head toward Horatio. Gaston did the same, and then the old man peered at Johnny.

Jackson put his fork down, food in his mouth. He chewed and leaned back in his chair. He asked Johnny, "Didn't you say a Miss Sarinda Fallows owns the Mud Hare? Call it what now?"

Johnny hesitated to answer, but his voice slowly crept up his throat and out of his mouth to say, "Harlem Dixie."

Jackson's chewing slowed as he thought. His eyes went to his brother, and his brother's eyes moved to him. Eyes locked on his brother, Gaston addressed Johnny with a question, "She a old woman?"

"No, sir," Johnny responded quickly. "At least…"

"She don't look it," Gaston finished, eyes still facing Jackson.

"Absolutely," Johnny said excitedly. Horatio watched Jackson and Gaston Fable hold a conversation with nothing more than stares. An unperceptive Johnny continued speaking. "I've said before, she must've had her son Stanley when she was mighty young. She couldn't be more than her early forties. And, again, she a fine white woman." Johnny said nothing more. The silence was tense. Johnny realized Jackson and Gaston were staring at one another. He turned to Horatio who looked at him with a concerned expression.

"If Curly had tricks she got tricks," Gaston said breaking the pause.

Jackson sighed. "Better tricks too." He stood up. "Considerin' she had Curly on a leash."

"Where you goin'?" Gaston hollered at his brother.

"This calls for somethin' stronger than orange juice," Jackson told him.

Gaston rolled his eyes and shook his head. "Negro, it could be Tuesday and that would be reason enough to call for somethin' stronger than orange juice or lemon water with ice."

Regardless, Jackson found a bottle of gin in the cupboard and poured himself a small glass. "You notice the way Curly looked at that horn, Gaston?" Jackson asked.

"I mostly noticed him lookin' scared," said Gaston continuing to eat his breakfast.

"I noticed, sir," Horatio affirmed as he sat up straight. "I was lookin' right at him."

Jackson knocked back a heavy wave of gin. Gaston dropped his fork and hissed in his raspy voice, "Negro, don't be stingy with the drink. Bring some of that on over to us here."

Horatio and Johnny's voices made a low rise with a concurrent, *"No, thank-you."*

Jackson slammed his glass on the counter and said forcefully, "Dammit, now! My old lady been gone for a good sum of years now, may her spirit rest, 'cept for one day of the year when we dance. But, I'll be damned if my house gon' have henpeckin' in it." He looked at his brother.

Gaston chuckled instantly at his brother's antics. He resumed eating, saying between chewing, "Negro, bring me a glass of gin. Shit."

Jackson laughed and went to the cupboard to retrieve a glass for his brother. He set the glass on the counter and tipped the gin inside, all the way to the top. He brought the glass to his brother, setting it down next to his plate. "House been quiet withoutcha. I should've left you with Burneside," Jackson joked.

Horatio and Johnny laughed. Gaston shook his head with a smile. "You know quiet bother you." He looked at Horatio and Johnny. "Both you boys get to my house after eatin'. It's music time. We gon' play for the rest of the day. We ain't gon' think about nothin' but the next chord in the song."

Jackson joined everyone at the table, bringing the bottle of gin with him. Everyone continued to eat. Horatio commented after a time, "I saw my mother and father when I played. My father was in the woods, practicin'. My mother was dancin' to the music. It was night."

"Yeah, Pete'd always do that," Gaston remarked. "Practiced out back. Your mamma'd be there. When it was just him, he'd only practice notes we taught him. Commandin' nature and so. Then, he brought your mamma down, impressin' her with what he learned. She'd keep his notes harmonized with her voice. Your mamma's voice would go from sweet and soft, to jazzy and rough. Hard. Helped your father's..."

"Voice," said Horatio.

"No. He never tried to sing," Gaston corrected.

Jackson smiled as he rummaged through the food on his plate with his fork. "Oh, no. That boy *tried* once. It was somethin' awful. Had the hounds howlin'."

Gaston nodded. "Oh, yeah," he remembered. "I think I forgot that on purpose. Glad he stuck to the horn, leave the singin' to your mamma."

"No, my father called himself Father Voice in the narration of his songs." Horatio kept his eyes on Jackson and Gaston Fable. He hoped to see a glimmer of something deciphered from what he revealed. Horatio disclosed more. "My father's songs took me to another time and place. It wasn't just my father's lifetime, twenty or so years ago. I saw my mother and father meeting in Africa. Well, they met again in Africa in a second lifetime. The first was somewhere I don't know. I think it was Europe. The buildings and background looked all exotic. I heard a description." Horatio paused. Then, he spoke with a slight stutter in his pronunciation of the word, "Al-Andalusian. My father narrated they were under an al-Andalusian night."

Jackson and Gaston both nodded their heads with their mouths full. Jackson swallowed first and answered Horatio as he shook his finger. "The Moors. Them was black folk that ruled a long time in Europe, mostly in Spain. They had tricks too. People say the Portuguese got a hold of an old book written by a mulatto. The Book of Cyprian."

Gaston swallowed and entered the conversation taking up the story from Jackson who sipped on gin. "Cyprian was supposed to be somethin' fierce with his tricks, creatin' all types of sorcery. Somehow he turned Christian. I'm sure a blade at his throat had somethin' to do with that. Must've done some good for white folk. They made that nigger a saint. But, his book remained." Gaston ingested the last of his food. "Mmm-hmm. Yeah, them Portuguese found his book. Christian as they called themselves, they used it to undo all the protection them Moors used to keep they kingdoms safe. Yes, they did. Them Moors were pushed out of Europe after that. They'd been there for over seven hundred years. Yes, they was. Brought all types of sophistication and culture to white folk."

"Cyprian's book supposed to have found its way to South America. Brazil," Jackson said. "They call it a book of the Devil." The old man shook his head, and along with his brother, bubbled with guffaws. "I tell you them white folks sure know how to scare us Negroes away from ourselves." Jackson and Gaston's laughter simmered down. Jackson looked up from his empty plate. He inspected Horatio and Johnny's plates that were speckled with crumbs and nothing else. "You boys finished?"

"Yes, sir," they complied.

Jackson stood up. "Okay. You know the routine, but I'm gon' say it anyway cuz young folk like to forget. Clear your space," he ordered in a grandfatherly tone. "Wash your dishes and utensils." Horatio and Johnny stood up and grabbed their empty plates and glasses. They made their way to the sink as Jackson concluded, "Gaston and I will put up the food. Go on across the street and wait for us."

Horatio and Johnny washed their plates under the faucet's running water. Gaston told them to leave their clean plates and utensils, now dripping with water, next to the sink. The young men followed the orders and then Horatio charged up the stairs to get his trumpet case. Johnny went into the front room, stood next to the door and waited patiently for Horatio who appeared shortly thereafter with the trumpet case under his arm. Johnny opened the door wide and moved aside for Horatio to walk through first. Horatio stepped outside, and Johnny followed. The two of them crossed the street to Gaston's house. At the front porch, Horatio tried the door. It was unlocked. He allowed Johnny entrance, and Concheroot was greeted by the fervor of two huskies. One of the dogs was a dark gray color, and the other dog was silver. The dogs' excitement was only playful. Horatio entered the house and joined in, standing still as the dogs frolicked between he and Johnny's legs.

Horatio moved slowly, walking forward. He put his trumpet down on the coffee table. The silver, female dog, Lightning, followed him. Johnny and Horatio allowed the dogs to smell them and again run through their legs before bending down and petting the animals.

"There's Thunder and Lightning!" Gaston exclaimed from the opened door. Jackson stood next to him filling a pipe with tobacco. The old men stepped inside. Johnny stood from petting Thunder. Out of courtesy he asked Gaston for permission to give the piano a play. "Go 'head on there, boy," Gaston permitted. "That's what we here for."

Johnny walked over and made seat at the center of the cushioned bench. His fingers immediately scampered across the keys and produced a clean, soft melody. Horatio took a seat on the couch. He observed that Gaston's front room was slightly larger compared to Jackson's front room to accommodate the piano. He sat back in the comfortable sofa listening to Johnny's elegant, improvised melody. Johnny was getting comfortable with the piano, feeling his way. Jackson sat in the wicker chair next to the door and lit his pipe, taking a puff and enjoying the music. Gaston flipped the radio switch on, and he tuned the radio to a channel that played his favorite song composed by Johnny's father. Joe Concheroot's cool piano playing trickled through the speakers. The sound scratched and popped as if played on an old phonograph. Johnny stopped to listen to his father. The song started slow, and then it progressed into a whirl of romantic chords. The song slowed again, a shimmering sadness to the music. Joe Concheroot played as if he was conducting a story. The song flowed into different tempos, stirring emotions. When it finished, Johnny attempted to play the chords he could remember.

Gaston flipped the radio on and off, stopping and starting the music for Johnny to mimic and learn. Johnny played carefully, keeping his ears tuned to nothing else but the song his father played. The song became more and more familiar, Johnny memorizing the keys and delivering longer playbacks. He learned his father's song in no time, adding his own accents to the music. Horatio joined in, removing his trumpet from its case and elevating the music past earthly notes and sounds. Johnny kept the piano's rhythm in synch with Horatio's trumpet-work. He didn't know how, but he was producing chords unheard of on a piano. Johnny commented that the Book of Revelation was nothing more than a holy concert held by angels and their horns, a whole heavenly boom band playing jazz. Gaston snapped his fingers and bobbed his head. Jackson tapped his feet as he puffed on his pipe. Thunder and Lightning lay on their stomachs and watched Horatio and Johnny jam.

The music played past midnight; only finding pause for a nice hot dinner. The jam session had its moments of improvisations and eases into well-known songs. Neither Horatio nor Johnny felt tired, but the two old men were. Jackson and Gaston broke up the music with Horatio and Johnny humorously rebelling against it. Johnny stayed at Gaston's house and Horatio and Jackson returned across the street, Thunder accompanied them. Horatio slipped into bed after changing into his nightclothes, and he realized how tired he really was. Or, it could have been the power of the bed. Horatio quickly fell asleep. He awoke to routine. It was early, the sun just making light for the new day. Horatio changed into fresh clothes after a hot shower. He put on a new pair of black slacks, the same dress shoes, and suspenders folded over a dark-blue, button-up collar shirt. Horatio unbuttoned the cuffs and rolled up the sleeves. He grabbed his trumpet case, his father's music book, and made his way downstairs. The house was dimly lit. Jackson was still asleep. Horatio figured he and Johnny exhausted the old men with their jam session that lasted several hours after midnight.

Horatio opened the back door and heard Thunder's whimper. He turned to the dog lying down in the front room, its head up and looking at him. Horatio slapped his leg and ordered the dog to him. Thunder jumped up excitedly and ran to Horatio who petted the animal with wild strokes. Horatio stood up and opened the back door wide for Thunder to run through. Horatio followed the dog outside. Thunder didn't run far, continuously circling back and waiting for Horatio while running around and around.

The sun's light crept through the foliage like an illuminated snake as it wound through the wooded area. Horatio came to the same spot he'd settled the day before and put his father's music book down along with the trumpet case, which he opened to remove the instrument. Thunder settled on the earth floor, spreading out comfortably.

Horatio decided to start with a warm up. He looked around for inspiration and his eyes rested on Thunder. He winked at the dog and exclaimed aloud that Thunder would be his muse. Thunder barked an approval. Horatio put the trumpet to his lips and aimed the horn at the dog. He played Thunder's bellow with chords that imitated the dog's howling sound. Then Horatio closed his eyes and everything disappeared as he improvised a tune that he wasn't quite sure if he was playing on his terms or by the will of some other influence.

Pete Peters hit the brakes suddenly!

The car stopped outside the On The Hour club. Virginia Tara was in the passenger's seat. Both she and Pete jerked forward from the car's immediate halt. It was just before dawn. Harlem looked abandoned. Pete Peters, eyes wide, stared up through the windshield and watched ghostly specters of smoke rising from the charred and blackened nightclub building. He exited the car in a hurry, and Virginia did the same. They both looked up and down the street, twirling around for a panoramic view. The sky brightened, but Harlem lay dull and abandoned. It was a gray day even with no clouds in the sky.

Horatio's jazzy groove coated the incident. His fingers worked the horn's valves in a wild rush. His lips breathed quick, sharp notes that expressed the sound of his mother and father's heartbeats.

Pete Peters ran inside the nightclub. Virginia followed despite Pete's decree to remain outside. The scene was as black and scorched as the exterior, but far more macabre with all the bodies spread across the dance floor and stage. Some of the bodies were burnt. Others were clean of sear. Many had been shot to death. Johnny's father was among them. Pete and Virginia walked backwards out of the club, their eyes locked on the horrible scene. They returned to the car and got in. Pete drove to his family's funeral parlor.

Horatio's trumpet wept a threnody as Pete Peters traveled through a quiet, empty Harlem to find his father's workplace. Then Horatio changed the momentum of the lament. He added quick and heavy pounding notes as Pete and Virginia exited the car. Then tension crept into Horatio's notes, and Pete Peters and Virginia Tara made a cautious walk to the Peters' Funeral Parlor. Eyes other than Horatio's, but just as curious, watched the couple enter the mortuary.

Pete Peters' family was propped up stiff against the wall, neatly lined together with their dead bodies tucked all tidy inside separate caskets. His father wore a black top hat to go along with his suit and white gloves, and his mother was dressed in a pearl-white skirt and a matching double-breasted suit jacket. His sister was dressed similar to his mother, with a veil covering her face. Her husband, Pete Peters' brother-in-law, was right next to her.

Virginia's eyes widened. Pete Peters put his hands in his pockets, dropped his head, and bit his lower lip out of anger. Horatio poured out an eerie plainsong from his trumpet. Pete backed away and exited the parlor. Virginia stayed fixed. She was so gripped by the sight that she didn't even tremble from the cold and grim display. It was like the moments in a dream that seemed brief, only to have hours passing in reality. Virginia didn't move for hours, or maybe it was only minutes. Pete Peters was gone. Virginia was here unmoved, but she jumped when she heard the horn play. It was loud, declarative. It was Pete Peters screaming to the heavens and cursing circumstance. The massive sound leapt from Pete Peters' horn like a djinn from a bottle. Life stirred in Pete Peters' family. Their color returned. Pete played louder, harder, funkier. The Peters' danced from their caskets to the sounds of supernatural jazz. Pete walked backwards, leading his family from the parlor. Virginia followed.

The left side of Mr. Peters' dark face became completely covered in white makeup. A black circle formed around his eye over the white, painted half of his face. Black dashes appeared vertically across the half of his lips covered in white. He clapped his hands and sang loudly, *"Call me Papa, Papa. I am Baron, Baron."* He sang the words over and over as if it was a holy chant. All-the-while his son Pete Peters continued playing a captivating, deep, full, and reverberating music from his horn.

Pete Peters led the procession through the streets. His entranced family and Virginia marched to the On The Hour club. The sound jumping from Pete's horn whipped left and right as his head jerked like an untamed stallion refusing to be broken in. Pete Peters blew a gust of rhythmic wind at the charred building, and the façade reconstructed anew. The horn's wild jubilance hopped into an open window and spread through the scorched interior. It cleaned the walls and renovated the flame-ravaged rooms. The music swirled around the charred bodies, wiped off their seared scars, breathed life onto their flesh, and mended the bullet wounds of the deceased. Pete's harmonized notes traveled through the noses and slipped between the lips of the fallen patrons and kissed their hearts to start, and tickled their lungs to breathe. The men and women opened their eyes, got to their feet, and joined Pete Peters' procession outside.

A truck appeared behind Pete Peters, separating him from his family. Virginia danced instep at his side. The truck behind them was equipped with a flatbed that was wide and long enough to accommodate a band. Instruments came into existence. Five men jumped onto the truck's back and took up their positions. Joseph Concheroot played piano. Percy Lewis hammered the drums. Leon Daniels picked the strings of his bass. Colin Heath respired sliding cadence through his trombone.

Harlem was alive again. Harlem became New Orleans with the thunderous boom from Pete Peters wondrous trumpet, complimented by his new band. This was their first gig, a resurrection. It was more than a concert. It was theater, operatic. But the musical production of resurrection and dance inspired a pair of devious eyes to bend, believing Pete Peters' ruckus dreary and mundane. And so did watch these contemptuous, dubious eyes that scowled at Pete Peters.

Horatio spun around and ended his practice. He stomped the ground and hollered. Thunder barked cheerfully. Horatio smiled at the dog. He took a moment to catch his breath, his eyes moving to his father's music book as he relaxed. He breathed deep and played a single, mystical note. His father's music book opened to the third song. *Pre-Conceived Notion (Reprise)*. Horatio turned, panning the wooded area. His eyes went to Thunder. The dog stared back at him assuring. No one but the two of them occupied the woods. But Horatio felt someone watching his mother and father. He looked around the wooded area again, eyes ending on Thunder. The dog turned away from Horatio.

"Okay, Thunder. I believe you. It's just us here." Horatio spied the open music book. "For now, anyway. Let's see what we can see."

Horatio played the tune. The story composed by his father resumed. He lifted from the ground, knees tucked to his stomach. His body curled in mid-air, and he closed his eyes to concentrate on the notes scrolling behind them. The scenery dropped away. Thunder disappeared too as Horatio's horn blossomed the story's continuance.

"A kinsman. A scoundrel wears royal robes
With a silk tongue salivating
          Odes to lies
Backward speech seeped
          A secret oath
Family bonds, in his heart
Bankrupt and broke
Family ties now a loop knotted rope
Mother Harmony and I
Took asylum in this madhouse of mirrors
Reflections, reversed heart, bad-blooded interior
The Governor, brother-in-law that was broken
Brother to your Mother Harmony
He opened his kingdom's gates with a perfect perfidy
          A lie hidden in his smile
While we came baring warning,

          "Violence across our African land ensues
          Nights of unrest have turned to mourning
The fetid aroma of war has left sacred land acridly perfumed
But, the dead lay fortunate
          While the living, chained together, by boats have been consumed
Wooden monsters make meals of us
Fed to them by the world's youngest children
          They tempered in tantrums
Are taking us across once charted waters
Our sun, rising since the first millennium, has set
The dark hour of alchemy
          Will transmute us to be
          As slaves in the hidden land to the west."

Brother-in-law gave us refuge and rest. Kindness. Comfort.
He hummed the song of deceit. Your mother and I
          Could not sense its rhythm or beat
But hidden behind curtain, pallid, profiteer Polonius
Plucking chords, playing him as a puppet
The foreign tongue, Captain Iago
          Speaking to this Othello

African sands freeze when he speaks coldly
Every limb of brother-in-law at his command
        A hold in his grip
Brother-in-law, on unkind command, turns kin into profit
First, molds deception, kissed on the lips of kith
We were seduced with wine and meal. Sanctuary.
This safe haven laden with traps and tricks
The deception revealed after the second day of reception
Citizens gathered, I among them, in exchange
        For the currency of gold and weapons
Brother-in-law a tool,
He preps us for slavery and rule

We the people would not go without fight
And the kingdom becomes a familiar sight,
        Worse. Civil strife.
War among one another. Family blood spilled.
I take advantage of the confusion with quick movements
I compose myself a song
        And sing myself into the wind
With nature I blend, wind, and bend
Looking for Mother Harmony to put my notes at peace
I team with three to breach a wall of enemies.
        African with sword, a woman.
        African with spear, a man.
        African with bow and arrow, a woman too.
Band together. Short blades caressed in my grip
        I play a song with the rhythm of my body
I move in a warrior's grace and manner
Carving a path through adversaries
        Like the heroes in the Legend of the Alchemist's Hammer
Throne room. Mother Harmony bound and sitting
Brother-in-law is left to die by my hands
Slave-capturing captain cowardly leaves his side
He hides away, but this act all a play.
Survivors of this civil fray will be made slaves
There stands an army, African and foreign
I twist my body to dodge the arrows and bullets coming my way

Loop, turn, cut and sway in a single breath
Arrows seem to pass through me, as I twist
*   Body shifts into air as I run my blade*
*   Along the necks of my opposition*
The warrior's song plays through me
*   Moves me forward*
I cover Mother Harmony's eyes from a gruesome sight
I stab her brother's chest with all my might

Horatio stopped playing. The forest returned, and his feet the same to the ground. Horatio was angry at what he'd seen. He paced. Thunder watched him, the dog's head following his movement back and forth. Horatio contemplated, trying to decipher the vision the music accorded him. The images again appeared in his head. His father killed his mother's brother. African people killed one another. African people sold one another. The three warriors at his father's side were killed; their deaths played like background music as the scene faded.

Horatio huffed, both to catch his breath and from his excited ire. Horatio's mind was everywhere. He believed what he saw as the truth. Then he tried convincing himself it was just a story. He stood still and looked over at Thunder. The dog stared up at him with wide, worried eyes. Thunder's cute expression caused Horatio to drop his head and let out a laugh.

"Past lives of my mother and father or not, Thunder," Horatio expressed ceasing his laughter and rolling back into a somber emotion. "I know things like this happened back in them days, Negroes sellin' Negroes into slavery. White folks created a violent market of human trade, and some of us tried to profit. Shit. Same thing still go on now in other ways." He took a deep breath. "Okay. Let's go way on, way back when." Horatio looked down at the music book. He saw the next set of notes, and he quickly shouted them into the air through his trumpet.

Up and curled Horatio went, and the story came to life as everything disappeared.

Mother Harmony explodes in pitch. She cries!
The palace cracks and crumbles from inside
I cut her from her ropes
She continues to scream

Force greater than thunder
    Erupting from her throat
She screams the palace and city into ash
    I hold her
She weeps a rainstorm over my shoulder
Her torrent tears collide and form a tidal wave
Everything is washed away
    Away. Away. Away.
We continue moving east
    Trying to recapture the day
A betrayal and war behind us
Laying in a pile of mud, ash, fire, and haze

Horatio dropped the trumpet, and he fell to the ground from his curled position in the air. He rolled onto his side just as his father's music book opened to the fourth song. *Carrefour: The Intersection of Jackson and Gaston.* "And this is where I came in," he said rolling his eyes. He took the book and flipped to the fifth song.

"Breakfast!" Horatio heard Jackson call from up the path.

Thunder jumped to his feet and bolted back to the house. Horatio smirked, and then he returned his attention to the music book, examining the first three songs for liner notes. His father only wrote two lines. *We were there, Virginia. Even war is romantic by your side.* If anything, Horatio could see that his father believed this was all real, in the sense that these three songs' melodies spoke of past lives. Horatio closed the book and packed his trumpet inside its case. He lifted the wooden box and returned to Jackson's house, stepping through the back door and into the kitchen. Breakfast food was again laid out like a buffet. Gaston sat at the table while Jackson set out the utensils and plates.

"Go and wash up," Jackson ordered. "Johnny's upstairs. He'll be down. He ain't feelin' well."

Horatio looked surprised.

"He saw somethin' in my mirror," Gaston explained as he got up from his seat. "Don't know what, but somethin' got him shook. Been playin' the piano all sad."

Horatio ran up the stairs. He tossed his belongings into his room as he passed by. The items landed neatly on the bed. Horatio hurried to

Johnny's room. The door was open. Johnny sat on the bed. He wore brown slacks with a white t-shirt tucked into his belted pants.

Johnny's face was buried in his hands. He heard Horatio near the door, and he looked up at his friend. Horatio asked him, "What'd you see, Johnny?"

Johnny didn't answer. He waved Horatio inside, and Horatio followed his friend's order. He sat against the dresser drawer, all the time he kept his eyes on Johnny. "I saw your father bring everyone back from the dead," Concheroot said looking away and remembering the magnificent scene. "I saw your father and mother pull up. They must've been returnin' from their time here. Harlem looked empty. New York looked empty. Dead. Gave me a chill seein' the city lookin' like it'd gone through the rapture."

Horatio folded his arms. "I saw it," he told his friend. "I saw it while I was practicin'. Played the music. I was there. Did you hear the horn playing?"

Johnny shook his head. "No, man. It was silent. I was lookin' in the mirror, but it felt like I was there. Only thing I heard, kid, was when your father started playing in his funeral parlor." Johnny's smile broke through, but he was still clearly shaken. "I liked that. Everyone got up." His smile faded. "My father was among the dead. That's what kind of got me shook, you know? I mean, if what we saw was real—if that really happened, then my pops had no business helpin' to kill your father." Horatio was about to speak when Johnny continued. He shook his finger and said to Horatio, "And, I felt somethin'. Someone was watchin' the whole thing."

"You got that feelin', too?" Horatio blurted as he stood up straight and took a step toward Johnny.

Johnny nodded. "I think someone was tryin' to test your pops. Someone wanted to see what he'd do with that horn." Johnny reached for his gun, still sheathed in its holster, the gun belt straps spread across the bed. He pushed out the revolving chambers and inspected the bullets inside. "We get back to Harlem, there's gon' be hell up in it."

"Hey," Horatio drawled. "Jonathan Richard Concheroot, don't do nothin' foolish, now. Don't do anything stupid, cousin. And, I'ma call you by all three of y' names like ya mamma when she mean business."

Johnny laughed as he slapped the gun's chambers back into place. He twirled the firearm like a gunslinger and then slid it back into its holster.

Horatio commented that the move was 'slick'. Johnny lost his smile and he confessed, "Them ain't my names, Horatio. Jonathan Richard Concheroot." Horatio's expression molded to show perplexity, and Johnny saw that. "That's my birth name, but not the name my mother calls me. To her I'm Jonathan Gregory. Gregory is her maiden name. She didn't want anybody knowin' I was Joseph Concheroot's child. I guess she was ashamed at where he went, prison, and all. Also, probably ashamed at what got him there. Helpin' to kill his friend. An accessory to murder." Johnny's grin pushed his dour mood aside. He stood up. "First time I ever thought of myself as a true Concheroot was when I showed up on your front porch. Not even when I visited my pops in prison those few times." He jabbed his finger hard on Horatio's chest. "But I'm goin' back to New York as a true Concheroot. People gonna see things. They gonna see the truth. We gonna draw out the real villains. Even if they got tricks, even if it's white folk out to hang us—Miss Fallows and her son. We gon' compose their eulogy with gunshots and magical jazz. Believe that shit. You got too much power in your hands with that horn to let it go to waste. We got some good to do with it; matters and thangs to set straight."

Jonathan Richard Concheroot walked out of the room. Horatio watched his friend leave. His eyes then went to the bed. There lay a gun the same make as the ones the ruffians used to murder his father. Horatio heard three gunshots. He flinched, and then the firearm faded away. He heard Johnny make his way down the stairs, and then he too left the bedroom, stopping at the bathroom to freshen up for breakfast.

Song 5: Sing You To Life
"That's what got you here, every lifetime."

Horatio and Johnny stood together in the wooded area outside Jackson's house. It was early the next day and the two of them were following Horatio's routine. Thunder was absent, staying inside. Horatio played a familiar, mystical note. His father's music book opened to the fifth song. *Sing You To Life.* Johnny smiled. He said to Horatio, "You do this everyday, man?" He pointed to the book as it raised and flipped open by way of the horn's hoodoo.

Horatio grinned. "Some groove, huh?" he inquired, raising an eyebrow. "It's impressive until you see what the songs bring." He asked candidly, "You ready, Johnny?"

No, Johnny wasn't, even if he desired to see more. That particular 'more' had the potential to be just as emotional as the scene he witnessed in the mirror the previous morning. "No," Johnny answered honestly. "But whatcha gonna do, right?" He put his hands in his pockets. "Play your songs, man." He stepped back, looking as if he was giving Horatio space. Johnny was trying to brace himself.

Horatio played the horn, a single note. The music book flipped backwards, arriving at the first song. "I'll start the story from the beginning," Horatio said. He'd already summarized the songs' stories, but Johnny requested seeing everything and experiencing the phantom visions up close. Horatio played the song's preternatural melody. He lifted and curled in mid-air while working the trumpet. Johnny watched, anxious and cautious. The woods faded black. The al-Andalusian scene of Pete Peters dazzling the crowd with poetry brightened into existence like a stage play. Johnny blended in with the people despite his contemporary attire. He was invisible to the black, Moorish onlookers, however. He didn't hear any narration the way Horatio could, but he understood the scene's narrative without lyrical commentary. The music was enchanting, jazz played with a bewitching twist.

Pete Peters was a lyricist. Father Voice. He spoke to a gathered crowd that was impressed with his passionate poetry. Of all those gathered around him, he only cared about one. Virginia Tara. Mother Harmony. She watched from an apartment window, but the scene played curious as the crowd moved away and Mother Harmony and Father Voice moved closer to one another. He spoke to her; she sang back to him.

The scene faded into a grand city in Africa as Horatio played his father's second number. Johnny watched the courtship happen all over again in another lifetime. War interrupted the affair. Europeans invaded and decimated the city while looking for slaves. Corpses and blood pools stained the streets. Johnny didn't move. He watched Pete Peters and Virginia Tara escape the city. Horatio glided into the third song. Johnny saw the betrayal, the civil discord. Europeans struck, taking slaves and the lives of those that refused bondage. Johnny cheered Virginia Tara's rescue and marveled at Virginia's aria that wiped away strife and disorder from the city before she and Pete Peters continued running into Africa's interior.

The music stopped. The woods appeared. Horatio's feet touched the ground. He asked Johnny, "Did you see it?"

Johnny walked toward Horatio and answered, "Sure did, man." He put a hand on his chest. "I thought I'd feel that same disturbance as the images in the mirror. What I saw was horrible—don't get me wrong, now. I know the Negro has been through a helluva lot. Go back one hundred years ago from this very day, and the Negro man and the Negro woman was still a slave. I know there were free communities, but that was rare. America was the land of the bleedin' slave, not the free and the brave. Not for colored folk." Concheroot waved his hand around at the trees, but he referred to the scenes created by the songs Horatio played from his father's music book. "I was relieved to see that the man who betrayed them didn't look like my father. I was nervous comin' to that part of the story."

"Man, I told you he didn't look like your old man," Horatio hollered. He grinned even though he was still frustrated with Johnny.

"I know. I know," Johnny assured. "But you know that's on my mind right now."

"I can respect that," Horatio replied. "We'll find your answers. I don't know if they're in these songs, but we'll find 'em."

"Your father thought all this was real, huh?" Johnny asked after Horatio played a note returning the pages of the music book to the fifth song titled *Sing You To Life*.

Horatio replied as he studied the opening music notes to the fifth song, "He did." He put the trumpet near his lips. "Ready?" he asked Johnny.

Concheroot nodded with a charming smile. "This time, yes."

Horatio played. He lifted and curled. The woods dropped away, fading into an African exterior. Father Voice and Mother Harmony camped under the moon as fugitives in their own land. Father Voice shuffled through parchment paper, his handwriting scribbled on them. Mother Harmony whispered in his ear. Johnny heard the music. Horatio heard his father's voice.

Mother Harmony sings
    Like a candied dream
Original melodies
Her supreme mathematics
Team with my supreme alphabet
    And there
Syllables and numbers turn
    A pirouette in the air
Coiled to build the anatomy of the
    Original prayers
Your Mother Harmony made me orgasm birthdays
    So that I would come of age
This lovely, mathematical sage
Her + time x 9 + coincidence = fate
She kissed my chest as I kissed her neck
Love leaks from her breast, her treasured chest
The milk of her honey, consecrated – blessed
I form a circle for our ritual

Johnny's loud protest broke through the scene. *"Whoa!"* Horatio stopped playing. His legs stretched and he touched the earth floor. The woods reappeared. He looked at Johnny who was shaking his head and hands. "I don't think we need to see your folks gettin' sweet with one another. Let that song be private."

Horatio laughed at Johnny's words with his whole body a flutter. "You hear my father talkin'?" he asked Johnny through a pause in guffaws. Johnny shook his head 'no' and said that all he could hear was the music as the scene played. "Okay, well, he's narratin'. My pops is talkin'. He talkin' to me, I think. But what I don't think is that he had any intentions of showin' me, as his son, anything he didn't want me to see." Horatio's reasoning didn't convince Johnny. He backed away, hands in his pockets and shaking his head. A small smile broke through his expression. Horatio pleaded, "We grown, man. Ain't nothin' we ain't seen or done ourselves."

Johnny waved his hand. "Ain't nobody was watchin' me while I was groovin' with my honeys, 'cept maybe another honey. But, okay, Ham," said Johnny to Horatio. "Go ahead and walk in on your father all naked if you want to." Then Johnny suggested as Horatio continued laughing, "You think you could skip a couple lines of music? Jump over this moment in time?"

Horatio paused in his laughter to address Johnny's sentiment. "Man, we need to see the whole story just in case we miss somethin' important."

Johnny arched his shoulders and said, "If you okay with watchin' your parents fuck."

"Whoa!" Horatio blurted, lowering his trumpet and stepping toward Johnny. "Ain't a reason to get vulgar, now."

Johnny put up his hands and waved them as he backed away from Horatio's approach. "I'm just sayin'."

"Ain't a need to say it like that," Horatio snapped back.

Johnny stood himself straight, taking a stance. "Wait, Negro. You can watch it, do it, but you can't say it?"

Horatio tried to clarify, "Hey, we're talkin' 'bout my folks here, the way you talkin' and all."

Johnny considered Horatio's words and then concluded, "Man, you got me more confused. You done flipped this whole conversation like a verse." Johnny raised his shoulders and said while moving his hands expressively, "I thought it was okay. Fuckin'. Ain't nuthin' wrong with it. That's what got you here, every lifetime. Right?"

Horatio signaled his yield with a sigh. He put the trumpet back to his lips, looked at Johnny out of the corner of his eye, and asked in a stern tone, "Can I play the song?"

"Go right on, man," permitted Johnny.

"You gon' be okay?"

"Yeah. I know how to close my eyes."

Laughter again spilled from Horatio. "Man, I tell you." He recovered from his guffaw and informed Johnny, "You'll still see it. Trust me. I got my eyes closed and I still see everything."

Johnny nodded his head. "That's cool. Go on and play your horn, man. Let's see your parents get it on."

Horatio made a face at Johnny. He inhaled and resumed the melodic and lyrical story. Woods gone. Horatio floated. Father Voice kissed Mother Harmony with all the passion of the spellbinding music that surrounded them. The stars and moon brightened. Africa's golden sands bleached into a wavy sea that resembled arctic tundra.

I compose your mother's beauty on my lips
Kiss her with closed eyes
 So that she may experience
 On the inside of her mind
What she means to me
Always locked in her memory
My words and breath
So that she will never forget
 My love to her, your mother
Forever be, etched on the inside
 Of her belly
If we give birth to a son rise
This feminine imprint I leave
 To study with your developing eyes
And later recognize
To choose the perfect woman to be at your side
 As a lovely bride
And if we give birth to a daughter
This feminine imprint I leave
 To study with your developing eyes
The way of which you carry yourself
Understand all the treasures of the world
 Do not add up to your wealth

I compose in the key of the watery C
      My legacy
Your mother's harmony adds rhythm
      Mathematics and precision
Split the light of music through our prism
We score ancient symphonies
Commit to memory a language that would
      Forever rest
      In Her and Hymns. Our Story.
All as we. Passed through our seeds.

Day rise.
      And we wait for this new day
      To break back into night
We align with twelve tones residing in the sky
This specific time of day
We chant to signs, harmonics in disguise
And the four elements must obey
      On command
The stars dance
My breath carried by seagulls
Three dots. I hum the dark sound
      Played in the background of Heaven
I breathe for my body to create a perfect seed
Our child. Cipher, circled perfect. 360 degrees.

I breathe in. A beat drops.
Heart. Half the song composed by Mother Harmony
The other by me
Beat. Beat. Heart. Breathe.
Invisible swarm. Electric fusion.
The gods strum life on a newborn's heart's movement
Guitarra moresca
Life amps. Lightning necklace, precious joule. Light watts.
Night watch
Your mother's earth forms the natural elements
      Of precious heavy metals and rock
I sample. Ample. Two lovers, music adorned.

Then came Horatio's voice. The notes whirling from the trumpet were an improvisation affixed to his father's song, complimenting the piece. Johnny could hear Horatio's voice overlaying the music, but it was barely audible. He concentrated more on the scene than the voice narrating it. Nothing between Father Voice and Mother Harmony became risqué. Johnny kept his eyes open. Father Voice and Mother Harmony sat back-to-back on the sandy surface and prayed.

"I am void of physical form
Soul cosmos-black
Inhaled through my father's breath
While my mother prepared in prayer
A place of rest
The might of my rhythm sung
>*When my father kissed*
>*My mother's lips*
Lifetimes ago on this spiritual trip
To the present of this reality where we exist
Sang to her when he described her beauty so precious
>*Sang my future lessons*
>*Future sermons*
Keeping determined the brave turned slaves
Pulled from the Heavens, temporarily leaving perfection
>*That above world*
>*When I was inhaled*
Caught by my father's voice like a whirlwind
I swirled like a mist-I-call a haze
Condensing into physical form in twenty-nine
>*And one-half days*

I am the Jesus Seed of antiquity
In my father breathes, believes, and prays
I possess the rhythm of a cannon to translate
>*What the thunders say*
I am the muse-I-call a breeze that makes a people
>*Dance and sway*
I as breath can breathe as I travel through my father's body

Sit at the right side of his creativity
This is the beginning of my journey
My rhythm. My flow. My name is Mojuba Kimoyo.

The heavens vanished and were substituted by the contemporary, wooded scenery. Horatio placed his feet on the ground. He had a wide-eyed expression on his face as he turned to Johnny. An open-mouth smile appeared. "That's my name, man!" he exclaimed. "That's my name. I mean, I'm a Peters. I'm the son of Pete Peters and Virginia Tara-Peters. But, that's my name!"

"Can't no one take that from you," Johnny commented, voice strong with pride. "You need to play for them Nation of Islam people. Brother Malcolm wouldn't have to have 'X' in his name. Shit, none of them brothers or sisters would. Hell, we seein' things only shouted about at Harlem rallies. Our history. All its glory. Good and bad. Ugly too."

"This ain't the whole story," Horatio remarked. "Jackson and Gaston always remindin' us that we the first people on Earth."

Johnny took a seat on the ground. "You know somethin', man. I think your father did see another life with that horn. The music of his past life probably gave him direction for this one." Johnny huffed. "That's what makes me so angry at *my* pops."

Horatio comforted his friend by saying, "Say, man, if this a story, then we all play a part. This where I came in." He chuckled. "And wasn't nothin' obscene in what we saw. Mamma and Papa just prayin' to the sky."

Johnny smirked and said, "They seem like they preparin' for a good night under them stars. Might as well get loose. Play your horn, man."

Horatio played a few notes of his father's fifth song before going back into an improvisation. The stars returned and formed the constellation of a man. Horatio floated, narrated, and played. Johnny listened closely to the groove, trying to memorize the freestyle notes performed in Horatio's off-the-cuff jam.

"My black body shaped as soul
Wearing a white robe
I speak musical odes that break down God's name
    To seventy-eight codes
My father's body a humble abode
Reproduced in his masculine image

Conceived through the love of Gemini
Fused as my father and my mother – plus "I"
Wearing their combined image in the flesh
As my soul's physical clothes, my code of dress
Future events
For now
My black glows the color of gold
Floating above green grass while seeking my spiritual task
The wind as my shoes
No need to use my feet to move
I glide on the wind, playing the breeze like an organ
My destination is the River Jordan
Travel halfway – meditate into space
Seated under the sun, I float in time and stay
   My father abstinent for three days
I absorb all darkness to wear every shade
Where all righteousness fades
Peace in God's final hour

Meditating in my father's world
Seeking my mother's womb-a-verse
Meta-terrain. Mother Earth.
My physical form given birth
Do I sit at the right side of my father's creativity?
   Or do I drown in my mother's musical key?
Her Meta-terrain-ion C
It's my father's choice on which gives birth to me
Eternity already knows of which way
   My fate sways

I continue my journey
Three days of adrenaline rush
Traveling up the River Jordan
   To receive God's touch
I sing in the key of inner-G
Condensed by my own gravity
I am the nexus
Ordained as my father's sun in the solar plexus

Under the heart's beating drum
I don't beat freedom. I caress freedom from the drum.
Musically eating this feast of bread in Bethla-hummmm

I travel up the tree of life
I receive judgment's light
Where Jacob matched the angel's might
Penuel. Where all is penned.
       O-penned at the Face of God
Mounted on skulls
I cross two thieves ready to judge me
On humble knee I bend
And I sing graciously, in my voice, and the proper key

"I am
In no sense—"

There came a sound louder than thunder. Horatio was pushed away from his horn. The instrument fell to the forest floor as the heavy force tossed Horatio backward. His back crashed against a tree, and he slumped to the ground. Johnny jumped to his feet, ran over to his friend, and helped him up. Horatio grabbed Johnny's hand and balanced himself against the tree he'd slammed into. He stood up, moaning. Letting go of Johnny's helping hand, Horatio stretched his limbs, rotated his arms, and bent backward to shuffle the pain around and from his body. He thanked Johnny as he wiped off the dirt from his pants and shirt.

"What the hell happened?" Johnny asked.

"That was my voice," Horatio said, mostly as a guess. "My Mo, uh, Mo-Mojuba K-K-Kimoyo voice—*Whoo!*" He said as an aside, "That name sho' is a mouthful." And then he continued, "And that's some powerful thunder." Horatio returned to his horn and picked it up. He dusted dirt off the mouthpiece and wiped the rest of the instrument's body. He waited for Johnny to take a seat back on the ground. Johnny asked if Horatio was confident he could handle the sounds of the voice. "I am," Horatio answered back. "It just took me by surprise. I can do this. I'm ready," he said. Horatio stretched his neck to either side and then started playing. He once again started with his father's melody and then flowed into an improvisation. Horatio lifted. The scenery changed back to the shimmering stars and the constellation of a man.

Mojuba Kimoyo's voice resonated, speaking to the thieves ready to judge him. Johnny could only hear Horatio's Mojuba Kimoyo voice as rumbling thunder. It was soothing, even with its heavy volume. Horatio controlled the notes of narration. They were heavy and powerful, but he never faltered from controlling them.

"I am
In no sense
Aware of guilty actions
     You call sins
Because my childhood has yet to begin

My mother, the virgin
She still bleeds the backwash
     Of future life
I as her son will give her light
Menstrual tunes from the womb
My father, he has yet to stop her waters
     And make her flower bloom."

And here am "I"
The Jesus Seed
Ready to see in which direction
     I breathe
Judgment received
Do I sit on the right of my father's creativity?
Or mature through birth in my mother's soil
     And earth
Watery rhythms of her Meta-terrain-ion C

The thieves give judgment
I am judged
1000 petals unable to open up
My lotus flower closed and shut
Time locked vault
My knowledge held at fault

My spirit churning into a body of salt
Blazing like a comet – all the fire of heart and hearth

Mother Harmony and Father Voice danced close to one another around a fire and under a beautiful, starry, African night. They flirted and laughed. Horatio's song narrated a new scene into reality. The setting lifted from the African sands as the two lovers undressed. They were left to their privacy. A comet flared, its brilliance radiating magnificently as it traveled toward a prodigious, blazing sun.

Tunneled from my father's body into my mother
To be as life, on Earth, as it was not yet to be
In Heaven

Horatio's music made the stars twinkle. The melody was low and soft, but continuous like a rabbit's sprint. The comet undulated to the horn's rhythm.

From my father's body
I was gala-x-haled
A comet of thunder
With lightning for my tail
The winds of ritual and prayer
          Guiding my sails
Led into a trail of mother's womb-a-verse
To sing spiritually inside her seed
Until I am born physically
As rhythmically I sing in the Anu-Na-Key
I am the Anakim here to descend through black hole
Message on black radio – into black womb
Played on space's black winds
My body, now a comet is the essence of Seraphim
Here to negotiate in space with the Elohim
Creator of the sun's race
Their bodies split into stars to constellate

Horatio's tune shifted into his father's song, losing its improvisation. It was morning. Mother Harmony and Father Voice were found and captured by European slavers. The music boomed. The thunderous notes pounded on Johnny and Horatio's chest. The music broke through their corporeal exteriors and boxed with their hearts. Father Voice was knocked unconscious and chained. The white slavers overwhelmed Mother Harmony, pushing her to the ground and crawling over her like a mass of giant spiders. The scene again panned up into the heavens. Mother Harmony's screams could still be heard. Her voice was operatic and matched the music played by Horatio. There came a flash of light and suddenly the lone comet was pursued by many more. The new comets were dull, barely emitting light.

I watch as foreign seeds conspire and contemplate
> *The burgle of my mother's egg*
It blazes bright in the center of her space
The warmth of my birthplace
Disturbed by a paler race

How could my father have let these foreign seeds penetrate?

No matter
This Jesus Seed must protect destiny and fate
I define my namesake
I am Mojuba Kimoyo
I flow with stealth
Discover language in star formations
Speak to the constellations, pleading for help
I am imbued with the power of Taurus
> *And the passion of Aries fills my heart*
I, comet, a spiritual dart
I blaze quickly as paler seeds fire Cancer toward me
I weave through space's field using dark harmonics
> *And large lodestones as my shield*
Sagittarius fires air-rows from rain-bows, dissolving foreign seeds
Virgo sings righteousness into space
Leaving my mother's womb-a-verse to heal

Paler seeds come close
But I hold the proper keys

To break my mother's egg's seal
So I may rest, expand into a physical form
From a single breath
Deep in this egg's core

As a comet, I soar
Lead paler seeds to be ensnared
By Leo's roar
Paler seeds continue to attack in hordes

But I got it
Keep my rhythm on topic
Duck, dive and weave
Straight through space
To make these paler seeds understand
And truly believe
When it comes to me, they can't stop it
I'm sailing with the physics and tidbits
Of Afro-nautics

My rhythm truly natural
All original
Black magical
Giving my speed a boost
Soaring through my mother's space
Paler seeds giving chase
Their rhythm a limping bootleg
Taurus imbued
Rhythm of my hue
I sing to penetrate my mother's egg

The reverberation
Of comet-sun
Penetration
Creates a dazzling light show
Bass flow, guitar rave
Sound and shock waves
Burning throughout the womb-a-verse and space

Paler seeds crumble to dust
And by the waters of Aquarius, they are washed away

The scene panned down from space to the wooded property that lay beyond Jackson Fable's backdoor. Horatio landed on the ground gentle and slow from his floating and curled position. He lowered his trumpet and turned his head toward Johnny. Horatio looked frustrated. Johnny said to calm him, "That's how life was, and still is for the Negro. That's part of our story." He patted Horatio on the shoulder. "Come on. Let's go get breakfast before we continue. This all a little intense, man."

Horatio agreed, nodding. He packed up the trumpet, closed the case, and lifted it and his father's music book into his grip. Horatio and Johnny walked back to Jackson Fable's door and stepped through. Jackson sat at his kitchen table working a crossword puzzle. Gaston was in the front room sitting in the wicker chair near the door and reading a newspaper. The counter, to Horatio and Johnny's surprise, was lined with deli meats, bread, and condiments instead of breakfast food.

"There's lunch on the counter," Jackson directed. "We called y'all for breakfast, but I guess y'all was deep into your study. Didn't bother to disturb you after the fourth or fifth time callin' you."

"Sorry, sir," said Johnny. "We got lost in some music and images. Didn't know that much time passed."

"That's alright," Jackson assured. "Go wash yourselves up. Come get somethin' to eat. I know you boys is hungry."

Horatio and Johnny scurried upstairs. Horatio asked his friend as they made their way into the upstairs hallway, "Another song for later?"

"Yeah, man," said Johnny. They split into their respective rooms. Horatio put down his trumpet case and his father's music book. He joined Johnny in the bathroom where they both washed their hands. Horatio excused himself and went downstairs to start on his sandwich. Johnny followed a few minutes later and joined Horatio for lunch.

"There's chips in the cupboard," Jackson notified, his eyes still concentrating on his crossword puzzle. "I forgot to lay them out. And you ain't got to be light on the meat. We already ate, breakfast and lunch."

Horatio pulled the chips from the cupboard. He opened the bag and poured some onto his plate next to his sandwich. He asked Johnny, "You want some, man?" Johnny said 'yes', and held out his plate for

Horatio to dump a mound of chips onto. They each poured a tall glass of lemonade and then sat down at the table to eat their sandwiches.

"You boys goin' back out?" Jackson asked.

"Yes, sir," Horatio replied. He raised his sandwich and paused before biting. He put his sandwich down. "I learned I had a name in the past." Jackson looked up at Horatio. Their eyes met. "Mojuba Kimoyo. You know what it could mean?"

Jackson returned his attention to his crossword puzzle. "Mojuba where we get the word 'mojo' from. Never heard of Kimoyo. Ain't nuthin' I need for this crossword puzzle," Jackson joked.

Horatio laughed. Johnny nudged him and rhymed, "You got that mojo, Kimoyo."

Horatio took a bite from his sandwich. He swallowed and yelled to Gaston, "You know what Kimoyo means, Gaston?"

The old man replied, "You finally askin' me? I been sittin' here all this time. Your voice so lazy it talks to the closest person."

Horatio knew Gaston was joking. He responded to Gaston, "Your ears so lazy you can't hear the conversation?"

Gaston snickered, "Boy, I will put tricks to you. Let your mouth get fresh again."

Horatio put his hands up and said to Johnny, "I'd say trick his tricks, but I don't know what he can do." He looked over at Gaston. "So what does Kimoyo mean, Gaston?"

"I don't know," Gaston confessed. Horatio slumped in his chair and huffed at the old man's response. Gaston added, "But we got books here and at my house 'cross the street. You might stumble on somethin'."

"Well," Horatio began speaking as he lifted his half eaten sandwich. "It's my name." He again paused from taking a bite. He inquired to both old men, "Did my father mention that name to you two?"

Jackson shook his head. Gaston stood up from his seat and trudged into the kitchen. "No," Jackson replied as his brother stepped into the room. "Your father said he was composing a story out them melodies. That much he told us. We just let him be. He'd come to us if he needed to learn a note or two."

Gaston sat down at the table.

Johnny asked, "How'd you two know how to play the notes if you couldn't lift the horn?"

"Our wives," answered Gaston. "They knew. They could reach them notes with they voice, one note at a time, not long enough to sing a song. We guessed the horn could play them notes. We knew the horn was special after Jackson and Zella Mae found it."

"You have a music sheet with the notes?" Horatio queried.

"Check your father's book," Jackson told Horatio. "I know he wrote down musical notation."

Horatio remembered the notation written at the beginning of the book. There was nothing special about the symbols. He considered that now that he had the horn, other notes might appear to his eyes.

Horatio declared, "After my father's story, I'm gon' write my own."

"Am I gonna have to call you Mojuba Kimoyo when we get to Harlem?" asked Johnny.

Horatio shook his head. "Oh, no. Negroes might have a little more wiggle room up north, but there still white folk up there. I got to keep my American name for cover. Ain't a need to get hung."

Johnny slapped Horatio's shoulder. "Your slave name? Like them boys hustlin' Islam say."

"Yeah," Horatio chuckled as he dived back into the remnants of his sandwich. He was finished after a few more bites and washed his heavy swallows down with the last of his lemonade. A few chips were left on Horatio's plate. Johnny asked if he could have them, and when permitted, moved them to his plate. Horatio wiped his hands on a napkin, crumpled it and said, "We could do some good for them scholars. We could show them our tricks, just like you suggested, Johnny. We got too much power to let go to waste. There's some good we need doin'."

This got Jackson's full attention. He put his pen down on his crossword puzzle and leaned back in his chair. "Whole Negro towns been burned and ravaged because color folk showed the power we can command with commerce among our own. You want to scare these white folks with tricks? That's what the war of Red Leaf was about."

Horatio already had an answer ready should Jackson or Gaston protest. "We do our work behind the scenes," he said with conviction.

"You are," said Gaston as he flipped the pages of his newspaper, eyes glued to the periodical. "You help takin' out people like Curly Burneside. There's more." Gaston's eyes scoped the new page of the newspaper up and down until he found his place to continue reading. "You got that Sarinda Fallows lady. Mmm-hmm, them stories connect."

Jackson moved his stern expression between Horatio and Johnny, mostly eyeing Johnny. Concheroot answered the old man's severe gaze with words. "There's no need to worry, Mister Jackson, Mister Gaston. We gonna raise Hell to bring Heaven on Earth when we get back to New York," he told the two old men. "Best you believe. I want answers as to who tricked my father into going against something righteous. If Miss Fallows, and any of her associates, including her son, has anything to do with it, they gonna be the first to burn."

Jackson bobbed his head as he considered Johnny's words. "We can't stop you from seeking the truth, but I can warn you to be careful in your actions after you locate it." He turned to Horatio. "You may be surprised to find that in your cru-sade to show the world what is and what is not, that some folk in this world—powerful folk—done already know. And, that is the real motive behind their hatred of you."

"Yeah," Gaston agreed flipping his paper to another page. "Color folk been modified to have so much subjugation, we don't think straight or quick. Sometime, we the last to know," he noted. "Don't know nothin' 'bout ourselves 'til white folk say its okay to know." He bent back the newspaper and finally addressed Horatio and Johnny while looking at them. "Stick to your story. Mmm-hmm. Don't wander into another picture show and get your roles all confused." Horatio and Johnny looked at one another with an expression of perplexity for what Gaston meant. They returned their attention back to the old man, their faces fixed respectfully. "Keep learnin' your father's song. See where that story take you. There's other conjure folk to deal with them bad people."

"Others?" Johnny probed.

"Others," Jackson repeated. "Look, we all tryna stay hidden like our property. We studyin' every myth and superstition we can get our hands on. We tryin' to manifest that great conjure known as the right moment."

"Well, shit, sir," Johnny cursed. "Ain't a need for magic to create a moment. The right moment can be now. As is."

Jackson addressed the young Brooklyn man in a grim voice, "It just might be." The old man began contemplating more than the present moment. He told Johnny and Horatio, "Gaston and I ain't been overseas in a war, but we done seen war. We've lost friends, wives. Good conjure folk killed with the help of laws that don't care if a hex takes conjure away, and that a nigger conjure man or woman is found hangin' on a tree."

Horatio dropped his head. "I do believe my father wrote this story for me," he said. He stood and excused himself from the room. Everyone watched as Horatio ascended the stairs, and in a short time, returned to the kitchen with his trumpet and father's music book.

Horatio walked outside, leaving through the front door. Johnny followed him. Jackson and Gaston rose from the table and walked to the front porch where they observed Horatio, standing in the middle of the intersection, put down his father's book and play an enchanted note from the horn.

The book opened to the sixth song. The first melodic notes breathed a succession of music and then stopped mid-tempo to repeat. This occurred nine times. Reality rippled as the horn hollered the music. Horatio then eased into a smooth, otherworldly stream of jazz that pushed out with such force it blew the surrounding scenery into dust that swirled up like a tornado and burst into a new environment.

Johnny, Jackson, and Gaston watched large slave ships move across the Atlantic.

Horatio lifted, but his body didn't curl into position. It continued to rise as he played. The ships passed under him. Only Horatio could hear Pete Peters narrate the scene as Father Voice.

Waves of aqueous reverberations
    Rise and dip below us
Boats dance saturate rhythms
While Yemaya sings somber
    Our chorus
Swelling cadence, crying chained
Caustic acoustics
Foul odors wail like banshees
My eyes become blind
Caused by effect
Harmony becoming off key
    I drown in C
Diving to search for me
Splitting my trinity
Self, sitting lonely on shelf

Purchasing me alone – I buy myself
We are currently currency

Buried under me is me, buried atop I
Black sea of bodies cry sweat
Wept, wicked carried away – captivity
Divided, but chained in unity
I swallow the collective, humming moans
            And breathe out mutiny
My voice rolls through the mass of packed
            Flesh sea of black
Captured hymns and hers, off rhythm words
            We curse instead of sing
My voice caresses the bruised cheek of she,
Mother Harmony
She sings, and our breaths connect
            To life past death
The effect, black turns rainbow
            And King Alpha's song resurrects
A cosmic kiss falls from the Heavens
            Down to our world
Twist, twirls, and swirls into the East winds
            Settling gently on the green of our heart
Beat. We hum a collective cosmic stream
The dead speak hauntingly as they cast ghost spells
            Rumored spirituals
We sing in the key of the deceased, gospel songs
Quietus psalms

Humming resonates, and a light the color of dawn
            Burns in our palms
We clap sunshine and cry sunbeams free
            To drain the color in our eyes
Clap and cry until the sun rises back into the sky
And the stars' little cousins drink our tears
            To become fireflies
The vessels shift and lift, floating over the sea
We sing, we sing, we sing!

Slavers bring winter when they enter below
Our warm glow cannot be cooled by the cold
But somehow they know
         All the breaths flow from me
I am the epicenter from where the music breathes
And so these slavers scream!
They cut, whip, and grab me
I cry one last note to put Mother Harmony at peace
         No protest. She drifts to sleep.
Color fades to darkness. The nightmare resumes.
Slavery over the watery horizon looms

Fettered. Plucked like feather.
I, Father Voice, am made to fly
Shoved until above
Beaten until I feel nothing
Thrown overboard to sing
         In the sea as I sink
Wine and wafer for sharks
Poseidon's communion
I am now the voice of the sea untamed
One day, I will be a hurricane
My scream moves the waves
Settling in the belly of Mother Harmony
Whispering
My voice as my son's heartbeat

The last notes put reality back together again. Horatio lowered from the sky. His feet touched the top of the ocean, and he didn't sink. The dusty intersection rose from below the waving water. 1957 Clarksdale, Mississippi reappeared. Johnny Concheroot stood just off to Horatio's side, hands in his pockets. Jackson's front porch and house formed around he and his brother Gaston. The old men stood still, continuing to observe the scene folding back into the present day.

Horatio dropped his horn. He bent down and scooped up his father's music book, franticly flipping through the pages. He saw the titles of other songs. There were fifteen more songs, but he'd just seen his father die, tossed overboard while making the journey from Africa to America as a slave. He wondered if these songs continued the story from his mother's point of view. He returned to the seventh song. *Merkaba Jazz.* It was co-written by *The Fable Brothers.* Horatio turned around and walked with a quickened pace toward Jackson's front porch. He looked at the other songs again. Some were co-written by his mother or Joseph Concheroot. Horatio held out the open music book toward Jackson and Gaston Fable as he asked them, "Did you see a past life scene when you composed this song with my father?"

Johnny came up behind Horatio.

Jackson took the book and inspected the seventh song. He smiled as he remembered. "*Merkaba Jazz,*" he said. "We just gave your father some ideas, he did the rest." Then the old man explained, "A merkaba look like the Star of David. It's a symbol 'bout how we all connected. Your father liked that concept. He was a beatnik before the beatniks." Jackson chuckled. "He just gave us credit 'cause of the idea, but we didn't craft any notes." He kept his smile to mask his concern. Gaston could see beyond his brother's façade. Horatio was too involved with his excitement to notice. He turned to Johnny and told him there were songs co-written by his father. Johnny reminded him that he already knew. "More information 'bout these songs appear after you play and learn them," Jackson said returning the music book to Horatio.

Horatio flipped to the beginning. Familiar and unfamiliar mystical, music notations were scribbled on the page. The writing hadn't been there before. Horatio closed the book and went to retrieve his trumpet. He lifted it off the dusty road and walked back inside Jackson's house. Johnny followed him.

Jackson exhaled, his expression melting into concern as the air left his body. He put both hands on the rail of his front porch and looked at his brother. Gaston said nothing, waiting for his brother to give the word. Jackson asked, "My eyes seein' things, Gaston? Now, I know I saw one of them slavers lookin' like our friend Curly Burneside."

"Your eyes more focused than mine," Gaston told his brother. "I caught it too. Horatio just excited about seein' his daddy in them flicker-show-like scenes. He missed it." Gaston recalled peculiar words spoken by Curly Burneside back when he was in his custody. *I'm gonna beat you cuz I've been beatin' you for so long.* Gaston relayed the words to his brother and asked him what he made of it. Jackson didn't know. Gaston stepped up next to him and asked, "You gon' tell them boys?"

Jackson nodded, yes. "When they leave for New York," he clarified.

The Fable brothers walked inside the house.

Horatio studied the music book in his room. He sat on his bed as Johnny leaned back against the dresser, removing the bullets from his gun, and placing them atop the dresser behind him. He then coolly twirled the weapon.

"These other songs are like jams," noted Horatio. "They look like they call for other instruments." He turned to the last song.

"You think there's a story there?" Johnny asked as he continued twirling his gun like a gunslinger while beaming his charming smile.

Horatio shook his head. "Don't know, cousin. But this song I'm lookin' at look like a jam and a half. I don't know all the notes, but even I can tell it feels like a storm. Lightnin' and thunder. Make Rock 'n' Roll look like a pebble standin' still."

Johnny caught his gun from its twirl and put it on the dresser as Horatio handed him the music book. "Let me see whatchu lookin' at, man," he said, book in hand. He studied the song, flipping the pages as its notation continued. "Oh, now I see. I hear whatchu mean, man." He looked up at Horatio. "I can see the jam in the notes that I do understand. This a powerful sound." Johnny flipped back to the first page of the fifteenth song and read the title aloud. "*The Long Life of Sarah the Pantomime*." He tipped his head and snapped his fingers. "Hot damn. She sound fine as the song, and like she got loooong legs." He looked at the written music and became perplexed. He said to Horatio, "This song don't look complete. I don't think it's finished. Maybe that's y'father bein' funny with the title."

"Maybe he wanted me to finish it. And I will," Horatio declared. He stood up and slapped Johnny's hand. He returned to the bed as Johnny flipped to the final song in the book. It was co-composed by his father, with lyrics by Virginia Tara-Peters. *A New Avenue In Brooklyn*. Pete Peters wrote under the title: *For Madison Goodspeed. I thank you for your advice to seek out these grand teachers, putting this story back in motion. From dream to reality.*

Johnny commented that they would learn the song once they got to New York.

Later that night, they immersed themselves in the rhythms of the song *The Long Life of Sarah the Pantomime* in Gaston's front room, played on piano and trumpet. There was no scene constructed from the music's transcendental notes. The song was a loud, thunderous jam. The boom in the swinging jazz tune didn't let up, and in some places sounded like a fight between guns, swords, and fists. The incomplete tune gave Horatio and Johnny room to improvise. The song exhausted the two of them, and even Jackson and Gaston Fable as they looked on.

The song was catastrophic rhythm at its finest, and Gaston commented that the song made the Book of Revelation cower.

Everyone slept at Gaston's house that night. Horatio stayed up past the sun's arrival. He was writing, quietly composing in magical, musical notation. He saw Mother Harmony give birth to him, and he was in awe. But it wasn't enough to keep him from slumber. Tired, Horatio finally fell asleep. He heard his own songs in his dream. They were comforting, neither taunting nor haunting.

Even in his sleep, Horatio was anxious for morning to appear, and for he to shake away sleep, rested and ready to greet the opportunity to continue composing the beautiful, otherworldly melodies serenading his slumber.

Water Bug Hollow, Louisiana
1917
"A place carved out for you and I, all of us."

The surrounding willow trees did not weep. They bowed humbly in observance to a small town outside New Orleans that evolved from slave-run plantation to a booming, bayou village. The descendants of those freed from slavery maintained the former plantation settlement. They celebrated the area's emancipation every year on August 12, the day after the plantation's owner was killed in a forty-day uprising led by a runaway slave, Curtis 'Water Bug' Hollow, whom the area was named after.

The plantation had become a mix of slippery bog, sturdy ground, and marshy bayou. The land sank and grew around it, and the earth changed. Former slaves made pilgrimage to Water Bug Hollow. They became permanent residents over time. The defeated slave-owner, Elias Jakobi, a man of French and English descent, was buried on the property. An altar was made at his burial site, and every year, on the Twelfth of August, a bonfire was lit as ritual over his grave and the Negroes of the area danced merrily around it.

The plantation's large guesthouse was now called Eve's Hallow, and its ground floor was converted into a high-class restaurant and café that turned into a barrelhouse filled with boogie-woogie dancing, gambling, and drinking come late night. The upper floors were converted to apartments rented by some of the area's permanent residents. But mostly long- and short-term guests, who often engaged in paid sexual activity, utilized the space. The main mansion was renovated into apartments where only dwelled the permanent residents of Water Bug Hollow. The slave shacks were reconditioned into various stores, including a market, outfitter, distilleries, and the offices for the town physician and dentist. Next to the market place, primary and secondary schools were built. Graduates ventured from Water Bug Hollow to pursue higher education at Southern University in New Orleans or at other Negro colleges around the country.

Joseph Pepper IV entered Water Bug Hollow through a natural archway formed from Spanish moss. Two men, armed with double-barrel shotguns, guarded the entrance, stationed on the left and right sides. More armed men were hidden in the trees. These seen and unseen men outfitted with firearms aside, Joseph Pepper IV stepped into a joyous celebration that was now entering into its late hours and still honoring the wondrous hallow day on this August 12th, 1917.

Joseph Pepper was not from Water Bug Hollow. He was from New York; born and raised in Manhattan's Five Points district. Joseph was a well-traveled man, a spiritualist and historian studying the philosophies of the Afro-American spiritualist Paschal Beverly Randolph. Joseph Pepper IV, a handsome man of forty-three years, had light, reddish-brown skin, a handlebar mustache, and a fresh haircut hidden underneath a bowler cap. He wore spectacles with brass rims, and was clothed in an elegant suit that consisted of black pants and a black double-breasted suit jacket with a gray, pinstriped vest over a white, collar shirt. Covering him was a woolen Inverness cape-coat. In his gloved, right hand was a black cane inset with seven, finely cut sapphires. Resting in the cradle of his left arm was a small and flat, wooden lockbox.

Joseph passed a sign that read: *"A place carved out for you and I, all of us."* The quote was attributed to Curtis 'Water Bug' Hollow. A crowd rejoiced in the street, and Joseph observed the men and women with a proud smile. Historical and contemporary norms and mores blended together in an interesting kaleidoscope. It felt like the border of time. An automobile sputtered across the muddy road. Horses traipsed with riders atop them, and some men still chose to strap themselves with a single-action Cattleman Revolver. People weren't holding stubbornly to old ways, and the new customs were not sprouting up in a boasting manner. It was a mutual blend. The old ways welcomed the new, and slowly stepped back for the modern era to take its rightful place like a parent guiding its child to take its first steps.

Joseph's eyes inhaled the scene. The fireflies, shimmering in various shades, gave the illusion that Water Bug Hollow was a settlement nestled among the cosmos. The pendulous foliage dipped low like galactic clouds, and the fireflies flashed among the flora. Joseph moved into the crowd, ambling closer toward Eve's Hallow. As he approached the café, he heard the residents recounting the actions of Curtis Hollow to visitors, children, and to each other.

"Curtis 'Water Bug' Hollow was either a hero or villain dependin' on who was asked about him." Joseph overheard a resident say. "White folk want to call him a 'tricky nigger' and 'a brutal murderer'. But, you ask any Negro 'round these parts and we'll proudly pro-claim his heroism. Yes, we will. And, on this day—August the twelfth, since eighteen sixty-four—and all night long, we'll show anyone how we think he a hero in dance, song, and oral account. We'll do this on any day, to tell the truth. But all of this only become louder on this day and night, August the twelfth."

Joseph continued forward, weaving through the crowd. He heard an old woman take up the account. "I knew Curtis," she bragged. "I'm four years his senior, yes I am. I remember them days of fightin'. Curtis' rebellion started, now, a year after word done trickled onto the plantation 'bout the *Proclamation*. Master Elias Jakobi referred to the Proclamation all in disgust. Went so far as to yell so we slaves could hear—because he wouldn't outright address us—that the gov'ment order was only for the low-paid Irish workers in the north. That was expected, you know. He was partly an Englishman. Them Anglos had a rivalry with them Celt-blooded boys, the Irish."

Joseph got a little closer to Eve's Hallow, the crowd becoming thicker. He heard a vibrant young man recall, "Not one among Master Jakobi's slaves believed such a thing, and word already reached and circulated through his stock of slaves before he or the other white work-hands mentioned the government's declaration." The young man slapped his hands and stomped his feet. He hollered and said, "But, there was already excitement brewin' between Master Jakobi's slaves, and it was enough to stir ol' Curtis 'Water Bug' Hollow. Now, at this time, Curtis was referred to as Curtis Jacobson, or Curtis 'Jacob's son'. He was twenty-seven, and his name had him hoppin' mad. What would you be like if you was called the son of a man that worked you to death? Curtis no longer wanted to be referred to as 'boy', or at the very least, Curtis wanted to express how he felt about it. You know?"

Arlington Johnson, the well-dressed, dark skinned and white, bushy-faced self-proclaimed mayor of Water Bug Hollow, recollected to a group of people while standing on the porch, just outside Eve's Hallow, "Curtis disappeared on a Thursday night. He wanted to find a Union unit and bring them back to the plantation to help him free the other slaves. He was ambitious, but only got as far as Alabama when an overseer who worked for a brutal plantation owner named Lachlan Mackenzie caught him. But fortune favored the bold runaway slave, because, you see, a tough Scotsman named Oscar MacRitchie was fuming over money lost to Lachlan Mackenzie. Oscar believed he could trust Lachlan because he was a fellow Scotsman. The entire deal was a con, and Oscar exacted revenge by helping Curtis escape. That Scottish boy confided in Curtis that investment and adventure was the reason for his long voyage to America. He told this to Curtis one night as Curtis awaited his fate. Mackenzie put out word on Curtis, trying to find out who Curtis belonged to. In that time, Curtis and Oscar got to talkin'. Oscar was so upset about bein' conned, he agreed to free Curtis and all thirteen of Machenzie's slaves," Mayor Johnson chuckled and patted his round belly. "Curtis—while all chained up in a barn on Lachlan's plantation—proposed a business deal with the angry Oscar MacRitchie: *'You ain't seen much of an investment. America make thieves out of businessmen. It has been an adventure, though. I'll getchu the business you need'."*

Joseph Pepper stepped inside Eve's Hallow and walked to the bar. He ordered a drink of gin and asked the bartender when the show would begin. The bartender answered as he poured a small glass for Joseph, "A couple minutes now."

Joseph paid the bartender for the drink and included a good tip. He placed his wooden box on the bar and nursed the small glass of gin. He overheard a male patron speaking next to him. "Now," the patron began talking to another, a woman he was trying to impress. "When it came to Curtis' proposal, Oscar agreed, and Curtis and the fugitive slaves returned to Jakobi's plantation. Oscar stayed behind, chained up and actin' as if Curtis and the other slaves got the drop on him. Curtis took munitions stolen from the Union and held by Lachlan to sell to the Confederate army." The man took a large swig of a drink. With his glass in hand he continued the story. "Curtis returned to Jakobi's plantation, and he brought war with him. Curtis freed his wife and two children on the first run, a quiet affair that broke out in yelling and widespread abuse of the remaining black slaves early the next morning. My grandfather and grandmother was part of it all." Joseph could see the pretty, young woman's horrified expression in his peripheral. "Curtis returned and freed his wife's mother on the second run, again a quiet affair. Gunfire was exchanged on the third excursion, and it didn't cease for more than a month. Up in Alabama, Oscar figured Curtis and his band dead." The young man had an educated flair mixed with his Southern drawl. "This small area of land was engaged in war as bloody as the one engaged in by the nation. Some days were quieter than others. Elias Jakobi and his employees and investors sought to dispatch word to local Confederate units, but Curtis' small militia made all communication impossible. They lived within the surrounding bayou and blocked the roads leading to the plantation's mansions and large fields. Curtis' life in the bayou as a fugitive slave making war with his former slave master earned him the nickname 'Water Bug'."

Joseph stepped away from the bar, taking his belongings. The floor was filled with tables and chairs prepared for the night's show, and there was space in front of the stage made for dancing. Joseph sat at an empty table, placing his drink down. He rested his lockbox next to his drink and leaned his sapphire encrusted cane against the chair. More patrons shuffled into Eve's Hallow. A woman named Janice Heath sat with four other people at an adjacent table. She finished Curtis 'Water Bug' Hollow's story, telling the people seated with her, "Then came the final days of the war, which were loud. Master Elias tried to get his family to safety, but Curtis' army attacked them, at least that's how white folk tell it—tryin' to make Curtis a bloody murderer. Oscar MacRitchie came lookin' for Jakobi Plantation and almost got himself killed walkin' up on Curtis' army, which was larger now with more freed Negroes. Curtis moved his army into the heart of the plantation and ended the war in a furious hail of bullets and blood. Master Elias Jakobi and all his associates were killed, their bodies buried. Curtis inherited the plantation and all the acres of land. He'd carved out a free place to live deep in the South. That's supposedly why he changed his last name to 'Hollow'. He'd *hollowed* out a place to live, and the trees magically domed around us to keep us safe. We are as unified as the trees. Oscar acted as the plantation's owner until it was safe for us Negroes to be on our own. We still got business with his family, even when they moved to Maryland and New York City. Curtis moved his family to Maryland thinkin' his presence endangered us here."

Joseph removed his gloves and bowler hat, resting them on the table. He looked straight toward the stage as Mayor Johnson made his way there. The mayor stopped to converse with patrons, visitors, and residents when a man came from behind the curtain and whispered something into his ear. Mayor Johnson nodded, and Joseph could read his lips when he said, "Okay. Okay. Ten minutes. I'll be ready."

Joseph sat still, patience at the surface, anxiety down deep. His eyes wandered to incoming patrons, but he mostly watched the stage. Townsfolk, dressed for celebration, joined him at his table. He made light conversation with the people. They were excited to see Joseph, as he'd visited many times before. He saw the mayor step onto the stage just as one of his conversations ended. The lights dimmed, and Joseph put his full attention forward. The mayor blessed the evening, all of the day's events, and then he reminded everyone of the reason for the celebration by summing up the life of Curtis 'Water Bug' Hollow. A set of elderly men and women gathered on the stage, called for by the mayor. These were survivors of the Jakobi Plantation War; ex-slaves freed not by a government proclamation, but by the bravery of a man long disappeared, rumored to still be alive, and even among the crowd during every August 12th celebration.

No one knew which elderly man was the true Curtis 'Water Bug' Hollow, and no one wanted to know. The secrecy was for Curtis' protection, though, in truth, Curtis 'Water Bug' Hollow had been dead for the last three years. Mayor Arlington Johnson was the only person privy to this information, he being in close contact with Curtis' family in Maryland.

The established safety measures caused Joseph Pepper to recall the armed guards stationed from earth to high in the trees at Water Bug Hollow's entrance. Outsiders harbored ill feelings toward Water Bug Hollow's history, especially the actions of Curtis Hollow. But fears were put aside for Water Bug Hollow's festival, and Joseph Pepper didn't give the jamboree's security another thought when the curtains on the stage opened to reveal a band consisting of a guitarist, bass player, piano man, drummer, and a horn section: trombone, trumpet, saxophone. They formed a horseshow around a veiled, female singer. The drummer played first, rattling his ride-hat to sound like hail falling rapidly onto glass. The trumpet played next, its sound smooth like a sunrise. Then came the piano, and the bass followed. The other instruments remained quiet as the beat took place, smoothing out from its soft rise.

The veiled woman crooned a ballad dedicated to Curtis' love for his family and enslaved people. The song was told from Curtis' wife's point-of-view. Joseph's eyes saw only the veiled woman, the subtle undulation of her hips, and the hint of her face drawn out behind the veil's lace as the light beaming on the stage illuminated the thin areas of the fabric. The woman's haunting voice surrounded Joseph and the patrons. It conjured up such imagery that the Eve Hallow's guests felt as if the spirits of those revolutionaries who passed in the Jakobi Plantation War suddenly walked among them to experience the woman's performance. Everyone was still and silent as they bathed in the melody, lost in its draw. But Joseph Pepper smiled, feeling as if the woman was singing only to him.

Maybe she was.

Her name was Theresa Amat, and she was Joseph Pepper's sweetheart. He'd been courting Theresa going on three years, visiting her as often as his travels around the country would allow. Joseph Pepper confided in Theresa more than just the lectures he gave on spiritualism. He serenaded her with stories on myths and legends concerning the ancient soul and civilizations of the Negro, the black man and black woman. Theresa regarded the stories as romantic fairy tales, but she was attracted to Joseph's enthusiasm for telling them. It was not a complete loss to him, for some of Joseph Pepper's plan was to seduce Theresa away from Water Bug Hollow and join him on his travels across the country. His travel, as of recent, called him to go abroad.

Joseph beamed an admiring stare at Theresa as her voice vibrated sweet and beautiful. He believed she might've been looking for him in the crowd when reaching the dramatic moments of the song, her eyes opening behind the veil to scan the audience. But, she probably couldn't find him. Joseph understood that. The lights flooded her eyes as their brightness washed over the stage.

The song concluded with Theresa's silvery voice praising Curtis 'Water Bug' Hollow's courage. The music trickled away, Theresa's voice holding a note with it. The drummer had the final say, ending the song in the same manner as it began, rattling his ride-hat.

The horns hit a hard note just as the audience's applause started to rise. The music continued. The horns sounded a hard, short note. The audience began to cheer and a woman cried out, *"That's right, now!"* Theresa tossed back her veil as another note hit, and the rest of the band jumped in and added to the same wild, musical moment. Theresa's round, dark face was revealed, and Joseph Pepper leaned forward to observe all the features he'd been missing from his songbird-sweetheart. She was the sum total of all the ancient treasures he'd sought, and she was half of the heart that beat within the ancient stories concerning the Negro. Her wide, dark brown eyes closed as she tilted her head back, opened her thick, ruby lips and belted out a holler. Theresa's balled fists were on her hips, and her voice jumped from her like a growl. The song was an upbeat version of what was just sung. Theresa repeated the lyrics in a fast and ferocious, melodious bark.

This was jazz! Theresa Amat's musical training in piano, hymns, spirituals, and classics were now rolled into one dazzling, fiery spell cast from her throat. The crowd jumped from their seats and began stomping and dancing as Theresa's voice, coupled with the explosive music from the band, called out both the Good Ghosts and the demons. Theresa sang only half a verse as well as the song's chorus translated into the gritty and raucous style. Then she jumped from the stage into the audience as the band continued playing. The patrons shuffled out of Eve's Hallow, dancing as the horn section followed close behind them, continuing a riotous roar. The bassist, piano man, and the guitarist danced behind the small horn section.

Joseph Pepper stood up and threw his arm around Theresa as she passed. She hugged him tight and screamed, "Joe Pepper! You made it! *Mwen kotan!*" Theresa uttered the Creole phrase expressing her happiness, and then she and Joseph kissed with spirit and energy as the people trailed from the fancy jook joint. *"Sa'w fé?"* she asked him as they ended their passionate kiss.

"My lady, I am more than fine," answered Joseph to Theresa, his voice resonating in a Northern, erudite manner that excited Theresa's more sensual nerves. She never understood why Joseph Pepper's voice sounded so appropriate coming from a black man, his tone giving the accent a more rich, deep sound.

Theresa kissed Joseph again, feeling the need to swallow the sound of his voice. He whispered, afterward, compliments on her performance and beauty. Theresa thanked him, and then she turned and tugged at Joseph's arm, hurrying him from the establishment. They followed the crowd outside where a truck waited with the band's horn section sounding off music atop its rear flatbed. A drum set, bass, and a banjo were there as well. The drummer, bassist, and guitarist jumped on the truck's bed and picked up their instruments and started playing, grooving with the horn section. The truck headed down the street, leading the people to the grave of Water Bug Hollow's former slave master, Elias Jakobi.

All the necessary tools required to build a bonfire were already lying near Elias Jakobi's marshy grave. The flatbed truck pulled up to the last of the real estate with sturdy ground, the band still serenading the townspeople. Mayor Johnson led the charge, his associates near him. Water Bug Hollow's exuberant citizens helped to put the bonfire together, and after a small speech delivered by Mayor Arlington Johnson over a more quiet piece of music from the band, the attentive citizens watched the night light up with a large, open-air fire. The citizens yelled in unison as the fire came alive, *"Bel anteman pa di paradi!"* Joseph laughed at the Creole phrase, understanding it to mean *'a beautiful funeral does not guarantee heaven'*.

The band's music exploded again. The citizens danced around the fire. Freedom rang. Even the erudite Joseph Pepper danced; and he did so as if the heat of his surname stirred his movements. Theresa Amat danced close to him with just as much jubilance. The two of them twirled for hours, their dance changing to adapt to the shifts in the band's music. Then they retired to Theresa's living quarters, even as the ceremonious gambol continued, far away in the distance where the bonfire whirled with the same fervor as Water Bug Hollow's residents and music.

Joseph Pepper sat in a comfortable chair, removed of his coat and holding a glass of cognac. He and Theresa retrieved his other belongings that remained behind in Eve's Hallow during the outdoor festivities, his jeweled cane and lockbox. He rotated the glass of cognac while swirling the taste of brandy in his mouth with his tongue. He observed Theresa with an inquisitive look, eyebrow raised as she opened the lockbox while sitting on her bed. Joseph anticipated her reaction to what lay inside. It was a silk, black veil adorned with nine ancient indigo glass beads from Mali, and it left Theresa breathless as she lifted the illustrious fabric from the box.

Joseph Pepper swallowed the cognac swirling in his mouth. He winked at Theresa Amat as she kept her look of surprise and raised her expression to him. Joseph took another sip of cognac and smiled as he gulped it down.

"Joe Pepper," Theresa gasped his name. "What strange mythology would this piece of fabric be attached to?"

Joseph stood in haste to give an explanation. He put one hand in his pocket and recounted, "This garment belonged to a legendary, African queen that resided here in America a long time ago and long before the days of slavery." He took an excited step toward Theresa. She smiled as the folklore was molded from his scholarly accent. "My grandmother blessed it, and it will provide you with protection." He expressed these sentiments completely convinced of the notion, speaking to Theresa as he walked up to her and knelt down at her side. "This veil is an object based upon a feminine principle and design, and therefore it is of no use to me." Theresa's eyes were wide, spotlighting Joseph Pepper as he took her hand. He concluded to Theresa in a soft voice, "But, in your hands, my lady, there will be nothing but great magic produced."

A breath escaped Theresa, and the sultry performer appeared to blush as she shied away from Joseph. Her eyes went from the veil to the man who still remained mysterious and full of surprises even after all these years, and she said, "An aged piece of fabric worn by an African queen here in America?" Her tone mocked the story, but it didn't bother Joseph. He smiled at Theresa as she continued. "Oh, Joe. You almost had me until that last part. You know there wasn't no Negroes here before slavery." Theresa slapped Joseph's shoulder. "You got eight years on me, Joe Pepper, but I wasn't born yesterday."

Joseph kissed the back of Theresa's hand. He stood up and declared as he turned his back, "There were, my lady, there were. Even here in Louisiana." He took another sip of his cognac, and then he placed it down on the room's vanity. He spun around to face Theresa and he imparted, "However, I speak specifically about a West Coast sect of Negroes made almost entirely of African women. There were few men among them, and those in their company where only for the purpose of pleasure and procreation." A smile peeked through his moustache, and he raised an eyebrow as he quipped, "A paradise in my masculine opinion." Theresa chuckled, and Joseph elaborated. "The men were not even put to use as guards for protection, for these women were warriors. Fierce and beautiful." Joseph watched as Theresa kept her bright smile, her head shaking in disbelief. But, behind her skepticism was a considerable fondness for Joseph's scholarship and his romanticized tales. "The nation was led by a woman named Califia, from whom the state of California received its name." Joseph walked back to Theresa, but he didn't bend down in front of her. She looked up at him, and Joseph caressed her cheek with a single finger. Theresa blushed again with Joseph's touch, but his antics of foreplay continued not through contact with his hands—which Theresa would have preferred—but through the jovial telling of the ancient legend. Joseph paced again as he continued describing the veil's origin. "Supposedly many queens wore this veil, dating back to that ancient continent we call Africa, and passed down in a line of succession until it was worn by Califia herself."

Theresa inspected the garment again and stroked its sleek texture. She asked Joseph, "Joe, who did you con this lovely shroud away from?"

Joseph swiped his drink from the vanity and turned coolly to address Theresa. "There was no con, my lady, I can assure you that. It was gifted to me as a reward by the town Copper Lyall—a town out west made up of black men and women, and a few other colored people. I aided Copper Lyall in routing hooded whites that came baring bad intentions, firearms, and crude weaponry." He looked at Theresa closely. She again was beaming a smile and shaking her head. Joseph affirmed that he hadn't accomplished this feat alone. "I had help," he told his sweetheart, and then took another sip of his cognac. He swallowed and said, "I employed the services of Thunder John and his gang the Brother Dogs. Thunder John's wife, a powerful conjure woman that ruled over Copper Lyall as Queen-Governess, authorized their assistance. He and his gang were soldiers in her private army."

Incredulity escaped Theresa in the form of a burst of laughter. Joseph inspected the songstress, an eyebrow raised, his drink held close to his lips, as he stood ready to take another sip. Theresa drawled in her flirtatious sounding Southern accent, "Now, Joseph Pepper the Fourth! I would sooner believe that ancient, royal Negresses populated this side of the world before you have me believe you went on any excursions with that ruffian of a cowboy Thunder John and his rag-tagged Brother Dogs."

Joseph shook his head as he swallowed a dram of cognac. He chuckled, "I do not lie, my lady, I do not lie. They even gave me a riding name. They called me Scholar Joe! And I, as did they, considered myself an honorary Brother Dog."

"Scholar Joe..." Theresa scoffed, though she liked the sound of the title fitting her man like the fine suit he boasted. "Well, *Scholar Joe*, come here and give me a sip of that high-quality brandy," Theresa demanded. "And fill it a little higher for me," her instructions continued. Joseph turned around and poured more cognac into his glass. He extended the glass to

Theresa, and she took a hard gulp. She wiped her lips and said after swallowing, "Thunder John. Brother Dogs. Queen Governesses. And Scholar Joe to tell me of it all." She positioned her body seductively, arm extending back on the bed, her body at an angle on the edge of the bed for the benefit of accentuating her curves. One eyebrow raised on her. She lifted the glass of brandy and took a slow sip.

The sight stimulated Joseph, and he continued to entice Theresa with his stories. "And tell you I shall, my lovely jazz bird. I was younger, obviously. Twenty-six. It was the final year of the previous century, eighteen ninety-nine. I went looking for a bracket of seven gems collectively known as The Pillar Jewels, and romantically referred to as the Sunrise Gems. I recruited Thunder John and his Brother Dogs to help me rob a train said to be transporting the ancient objects."

"Joe Pepper!" Theresa blurted. She sat up and lost her provocative posture. "You're not goin' to stand there and tell me you involved yourself in a train robbery, and expect me to believe you on top of that."

"I am, my lady. I am." Joseph beamed a proud smile. "It would have been worth it too, should I have gotten my hands on the items I desired, those gems. The story behind them is extraordinary, but it was not my day to have them." Theresa shifted back into her tantalizing lean on the bed. Joseph returned to her and again knelt down. "The set of jewels are truthfully stones, flat stones about an inch to an inch-and-a-half in diameter. Seven stones of solid colors, each representing one of the individual bright and brilliant hued belts that make up our world's rainbow." Joseph took Theresa's free hand, and the action prompted her to lean toward him. "A distinct and intricate design is carved into each stone; symbols of theurgy."

Theresa took a sip of her drink and said, "Joe." Her wide curiosity inspected Joseph Pepper, trying to look for a semblance of something she could believe in from all his words. But Theresa simply responded, "You seem to be more enamored by these stones than the veil."

Joseph propped himself onto the bed. He sat next to Theresa, her hand still in his. "The stones represent love, Theresa. Supposedly carved by a wandering, African warrior to symbolize his feelings toward an African princess." He asked for the glass of cognac, and Theresa obliged him. Joseph drank, swallowed, and carried on as he handed back the glass. "There are so many renditions of the tale. In one, the princess' father, the king, does not approve of the wandering warrior, and he sets upon him seven of his most brutish warriors for the sole purpose of running the wanderer out of the kingdom, away from his precious daughter. The wandering warrior calculates that each of the king's servicemen have a specific weakness, and thus he devises seven, unique styles of fighting, each style designated to exploit the weakness of each of the king's seven warriors. He uses these styles of fighting to defeat the king's seven merciless mercenaries. The king, nothing less than impressed, welcomes the warrior into his family." Joseph paused and thought before expressing aloud, "Another interpretation speaks of the wandering warrior conquering, single-handedly, seven kingdoms desired by the king. He does this to demonstrate his worth. The kingdoms are ruled by demon-kings, superior combatants just as fierce as their armies. Again, in this recount, the warrior invents seven styles of fighting for the purpose of exploiting the weaknesses of the demon-kings, and ultimately, he defeats them. And, upon vanquishing these fiends, he proves his worth and takes the princess for his bride. The stones, supposedly carved by the warrior, are said to imbibe not just the power of each fighting style, but the seven virtues and the seven principles. The bearer of the stones is said to become pure in spirit and intention, and thus they would be drawn to their true love. They would also posses the ability to conquer any obstacles—mental, physical, and spiritual—that stood between them and their true love, their other half."

Theresa placed the glass of brandy on the nightstand. She sat up straight and cupped Joseph's hand with her own. Theresa said low and tender, "You believe that, don't you Joe?"

"I do," Joseph answered. "And silly as it sounds, my black, beautiful songbird, I thought these stones would lead me to *my* true love. For all the legends and stories I follow, that is what I truly seek." Joseph Pepper rarely blushed for all his flamboyant and eccentric behavior. But upon divulging this particular intimate secret, his face flushed as red as his heart. "They did, in a way. I lost the gems, but I was given the veil. I was told of its legend, and I returned home to New York where my grandmother, convinced just as I am that this is truly the fabled garment worn by Queen Califia, commenced to perform rituals day and night to draw out the veil's enchantment." Joseph looked at Theresa humbly. "When my grandmother finished her work, she passed. I traveled and lectured more to relieve myself of the sorrow. I came here as one of my stops. I met you. And, after knowing you, my darling, for so long, I present to you this magical veil." He gripped her hand tighter, and Theresa looked down at Joseph Pepper's actions. Her head lifted, and her eyes took in all of Joseph's sincere expression. Joseph knew Theresa could tell he was nervous. He confessed, "I'll be leaving, Theresa." He put his hand on her shoulder. "Not long, and definitely not you, my lady. For you, I will return."

Theresa smiled. She asked in a voice just as warm as her smile, "Where you goin', Joseph Pepper?" Theresa caressed his cheek.

Joseph put on a smile, but there was still sadness in his demeanor. "I know that you don't take seriously the stories I tell you—"

Theresa interjected. "There are enough of your stories I take to heart. The ancient African kingdoms, the—"

Joseph interrupted Theresa by saying over her protest, "But there are many people that do take what I say very seriously, and a black man with my knowledge acquires many enemies." Theresa looked concerned. Joseph affirmed, "I'll be all right, Theresa. I'm returning to New York to group with a friend, Madison Goodspeed. He's a Jamaican man, but he hails from England. He's found something for me, and it is to London where he and I must travel. Our travel may take us across Europe. Do not worry, my lady. The war will neither halt nor harm us. We will be safe." He again assured Theresa, "And I will return to you."

Theresa teased, "With more legendary treasures, Joe?"

"Yes, my lady," he answered in a sincere manner. "But, more importantly, I will present to you a ring and a proposal for your hand in marriage."

Theresa's mouth dropped and her dark skin flushed red. "Joe Pepper! Stop that!"

Joseph remained serious. He reached across Theresa and removed the veil from the box. He pulled back and said to her, "Keep this on you at all times. Sleep with it over your face. It will protect you."

Theresa instantly protested, "Joe, that garment will stop my breathing if I sleep with it on my face."

Joseph disagreed, expressed as a rapid shake of his head. "No, my lady. No. It will protect you." He tightened his grip on her hand and gave a firm shake. "And you must promise me that upon my leave, and in my absence, you will act on my orders, silly as they may sound to you." His firm expression locked onto Theresa and he asked, "Is this understood?"

Theresa hesitated. She inspected Joseph Pepper's unsmiling, stern countenance and her eyes widened in reaction to it. "Yes, Joe," she said to him. "I will."

Joseph relaxed. A breath escaped him, and he finally smiled again. "Incorporate the veil into your singing performance. Substitute it for the veil you already use to perform, and give jazz a louder voice. Give permission to no one to wear or hold it, for then they can take it from you." Joseph wiped a finger under Theresa's eye as his solemn manner resurfaced. "I want no harm to come to you, my lady."

"Joe," Theresa said lowly. "Are you in some sort of trouble...danger?"

Again, Joseph sighed, and he repeated, "A black man with my knowledge acquires many enemies, but I will be all right." He kissed Theresa's hand.

Theresa chuckled. She looked away for a moment, and then she put flirtatious, inquisitive eyes on Joseph. She said as if countering an argument, "Thunder John died in a train robbery in the year eighteen ninety-nine. Everyone knows that. It's common knowledge. You tellin' me that you was there?"

"I was," Joseph beamed with a hint of reminiscent sadness. "Thunder John did not die in that failed robbery." Joseph's smile could not completely hide the somber emotion lying behind it. "He did not die."

Theresa saw the faint emotion. She didn't question it. Instead, she allowed Joseph to have whatever moment he was reflecting on in private. But she did have more inquiries, and for that she reached over and scooped up the glass of cognac. She stood up and left Joseph Pepper sitting on the bed. She walked to the window and watched through the curtains the faint flicker of the bonfire in the distance, barely seen through the intertwined and pendulous foliage. Theresa could make out the waxing, crescent moon high in the sky above the trees. Not its shape, but mostly its light as it struggled to penetrate the dense treetops. She turned and asked, "Is it true about The Brother Dogs' uncontrollable reaction to a full moon?"

"A propagated error evolved through time," Joseph answered Theresa with mocking vexation. "No. The truth is the full moon only made these Wild Zulu-Indians greater in strength, everything beyond that was controllable, my lady. I can assure you."

Theresa rolled her eyes and shook her head, a smile beaming. "Joe, I just don't know about you. Gunslingers and lycanthrope. I'll tell that one to my mother. She just loves your stories, Joe."

Joseph beamed. "Your mother does love my stories, Theresa. She knows them to be true. She's a great old one, your mother." He stood up and walked over to Theresa. "But I need *you* to be sure about me, my lady." Theresa finished the brandy and walked the glass to her vanity, setting it down. Joseph followed her, stepping up behind Theresa and massaging her neck at the shoulders. "There resides in you a power that stretches back to antiquity." He pressed his body gently against hers, enough to stimulate her. "I can only call upon my bookish insight to convince you of your power, a power so old it goes beyond time immemorial." He turned Theresa to face him. Joseph leaned his face close to hers and turned poetic as he said, "A time where the lips of the first black woman, in her cosmological form, touched the lips of the first black man, and their potent kiss birthed our world and all the heavenly bodies against their black bodies that became our universe."

Joseph did not allow Theresa to respond to his amorous Creation Myth, as it was then that he leaned close and reenacted his sentiments by kissing her with all the passion it stirred. She inhaled Joseph's kiss, breathing out to take more of him in. Joseph took a step back, and Theresa went with him, taking extra steps to force Joseph closer to the bed. Their eyes were closed and their lips held tight to each other, turning over one another like wavy, rolling hills. Joseph and Theresa disrobed as they reached the bed, and Theresa removed her lips from Joseph's just to ask, "How 'bout I try that veil for this performance?"

Joseph smiled, swiped the veil from where it rested and placed it over Theresa's face. Theresa let free a sensual giggle, and she performed an erotic striptease. She twirled and twirled as Joseph moved the veil's lockbox to the floor. Joseph crawled backwards onto the bed, removing his clothes, and keeping an eye on Theresa's playful spins as she peeled away her clothing and exposed her fruits underneath. Naked, Theresa stopped her whimsical twirl and followed Joseph, crawling over him. He pulled her closer, and she opened her legs to straddle him. Theresa reached down and guided Joseph inside her, and then she rose and fell on him like the soft notes of a jazz melody. Joseph put his hands on Theresa's waist. He supported her as she raised, lowered, and writhed atop him, and eventually

Joseph synchronized his hip movements with hers. He pulled away as she lifted, and then he pushed his hips up as she lowered. They met in the middle, and both of them felt the cool and rousing rush of penetration and enfolding. Joseph and Theresa expressed their pleasure in low breaths.

Theresa removed the veil and tossed it to the floor. She dived down and wrapped her arms around Joseph, pushing her lips forcefully against his. Joseph reacted and wrapped his arms around her. Their bodies were tight against one another. Joseph then lay flat and still. The only movement came from Theresa's hips as she increased her undulation atop her lover. The songstress' sensual chorus heightened, echoing loud and continuous throughout the room. Joseph rolled Theresa onto her back, and slipped from between her thighs. Both used the moment to catch a breath, and then Joseph put his hands on Theresa's waist. He guided her turn and lay on her stomach.

Joseph stared at Theresa's body as it waved like water, sexual energy rising up through her no different than a song. He rubbed Theresa's shoulders and lowered himself atop her. Theresa spread her legs, and Joseph reached down and guided himself into her. Theresa, immediately upon penetration, opened her mouth wide and exhaled a long, low tone. Joseph grabbed both her arms at the wrist and worked his way in and out of her aperture. He clenched his teeth tightly, and he inhaled and exhaled streams of air that sounded like a low, electric hum. He closed his eyes and held fast to Theresa's wrists. Joseph's penetrating drive quickened, and Theresa's sensual jazz melody echoed again through the room. Joseph's upper body folded over Theresa as his penetrating thrusts became faster and faster until he joined Theresa's loud cries of pleasures with his own and climaxed.

Joseph loosened his hold on Theresa, then tightened, and then loosened again as the spirit of his climax rushed from him like a billowing wind. He exhaled the rest of the spirit, and felt Theresa do the same. He slid off her, still holding her and drawing her close into the fold of his body as he lay on his side. Theresa nestled into Joseph's embrace, and both of them giggled like school children.

"Does that count, Joe, as one of your wild excursions?" Theresa asked catching her breath. Joseph puffed a sleepy chuckle. "Now, Joe Pepper, you ain't exhausted yourself completely, have you?" Theresa reached back and ran her fingers along Joseph's cheek.

Joseph continued to chuckle, the sleepiness in his tone rising. "I've done a lot of traveling this day, my lady. I've had some good brandy, the rush of a good woman, but not a proper meal."

"Goddammit, Joe Pepper!" Theresa cursed as she turned and faced her man. She slapped him softly and jokingly on the cheek. "Ain't had a proper meal. You should've said somethin' when we went back inside Eve's Hallow to get your things." She pulled away from Joseph's embrace and jumped from the bed.

Though his eyelids stuttered as they fought against fatigue, Joseph admired Theresa's dark and curvaceous nakedness. He smiled as sleep possessed even his perking up in the moment. "You off to prepare a fine meal?" he asked.

Theresa slapped Joseph on the shoulder. "I'm goin' downstairs to the community kitchen and findin' you somethin' to warm up." Theresa walked to the bathroom and washed at the sink. Afterward, she exited and went to her closet and found an indigo-colored robe to put on. She tied it tight to her person, and then she walked out the door.

Joseph watched Theresa leave. The scholar took a deep breath and then slapped his face against the pillow. He was tired, and he wanted to get in a few minutes of sleep before Theresa woke him up when she returned to the room. It was more than a few minutes given to Joseph, twenty-two, to be exact. Theresa returned with warmed catfish and gumbo for the both of them. The meal's aroma roused Joseph from his weary state. He sat up eager to take the bowl offered to him. Theresa placed her bowl down and left the room again, announcing that she was fetching a pitcher of water from the community kitchen. Joseph waited for her return, holding his bowl and inhaling the spicy redolence radiating from the gumbo and slab of catfish sticking up from the bowl. Theresa returned moments later and poured two glasses of cool water. Joseph watched her approach and crawl into the bed next to him, carefully lifting her meal off the sheets.

Theresa placed her bowl on her lap and asked Joseph, "Is there a new ancient, ritualistic prayer you picked up in your recent travels to bless the food, Joe Pepper?"

Joseph bubbled with a light chuckle. "No, my lady. I just thank you, dark goddess, for this meal I'm about to receive."

Theresa huffed, "Joe Pepper! Don't you refer to me as some heathen, dark goddess."

Joseph's chuckle turned into a full laugh. He took his spoon, and as he shook his head at what he considered to be Theresa's willful ignorance, he crushed the slab of catfish into the gumbo stew. His laughter faded as he protested with a smile, "Do not tell me there is no Goddess. The religions of the world have forgotten Her and become overrun with masculine pride, anger, and all the sins of humanity in Her absence. But if it's proof of Her existence that you need, look no further than this room. For I spy, placed strategically around this room, three pieces of proof mounted on the wall and your vanity." With his bowl carefully following his dripping spoon, Joseph pointed to the three mirrors inside Theresa's quaint apartment. "Three mirrors, my lady. All waiting for the moment to reflect back to you your divine image."

Theresa replied, "Joe, you blaspheme all in the name of romance."

"I no more blaspheme than does Water Bug Hollow, absent as it is of a church," he responded.

"Water Bug Hollow does things different, Joe Pepper. That I agree. It might not have a church, and it might extend the Good Book's words with a sprinkling of other spiritualities and hoodoo conjure, but it knows the Good Book back and forth."

Joseph grinned and spooned into his mouth a heavy sum of gumbo mixed with the catfish. The meal was warm and spicy going down into his stomach, as sultry as the jazz songstress sitting next to him. Joseph and Theresa's next conversation centered on jazz, with Theresa mostly answering questions about where she wanted to take her singing career. Joseph told her she would flourish in New York. Theresa answered, "I feel like I would get swallowed in such a large place. You really think I could make it there, Joe?" Joseph told her 'yes', and he assured her that Harlem was the place to live. Theresa was skeptical, but she was intrigued and drawn to the possibility of moving north to New York City. There would be some time for her to decide.

Until then, Joseph Pepper entertained Theresa with wild theories about world politics, one of which included the war in Europe starting over a conference held in Berlin in the year 1884. Joseph called the conference the race to divide Africa. "They know that all the secrets of the world are there. The secrets of the universe as well, decoded by the ancient Negro long ago. They wanted nothing more than to divvy up that grand knowledge among one another—not just the land, but what is buried in it."

This is what Joseph told Theresa as he finished his gumbo and catfish. "Germany felt snubbed by not getting all the pieces of Africa they desired. That is all this war is about. The politics made public for the common man and woman is all for the papers to print and us 'common folk' to read like gossip for our intellectually starved minds. All for the purpose for us to feel smart and informed."

Joseph also entertained Theresa with romantic and strange tales about the ancient world. Joseph declared that the world once had three moons, each of a different color. "Red, black, and green," he described with uncurbed enthusiasm, though sleep seduced his demeanor. "Important colors to the Negro. I have spoken about their significance to my friend Marcus in New York. He, like Madison, is a Jamaican man. He holds great ideals, and he has established a New York chapter of his Universal Negro Improvement Association. He's contemplating creating a flag based on these colors."

"You talkin' about that Garvey fellow," Theresa commented as she placed her empty bowl down next to the bed. Then she teased Joseph with his own words, "Three moons. Red, black, and green."

"Yes," said Joseph in a declarative voice. "Each moon adorned with a brilliant, glowing, gold halo. According to ancient stories, they were a wonder to see at night and the day."

Theresa chuckled. "Joe, I don't know where you find these amazing tales." She rubbed his cheek and then moved her hand down to caress his chest. "Your stories do stir the spice in my blood." She kissed his cheek. "Hold me 'til we pass into sleep, Joe Pepper."

Joseph put his arms around Theresa. She put her arms around him, and the two of them slipped under the comforter, cocooned in one another's embrace. Theresa reached over and turned off the lamplight. Then, she returned to her tight hold on Joseph Pepper. The continued carousel was heard outside, muted as it was. The faint, flicker of the bonfire shimmered at the corner of the window. Joseph and Theresa stayed awake in the dark for a few minutes. They said nothing. They only enjoyed one another's company. Theresa wondered what dangers threatened Joseph Pepper, but she never asked. Joseph thought about his future travel to London. The two fell asleep with their thoughts.

In the morning, and for the next two weeks, Joseph and Theresa's days became routine. Breakfast, a stroll through Water Bug Hollow accompanied by more of Joseph Pepper's romanticized tales, lunch, and then night activities starting with Theresa performing a set of songs with her band. Then came their love and passion, which was not without some discourse. Joseph persisted that Theresa, through the duration of their lovemaking, wear the veil he'd gifted her until she reached climax, promising she'd feel and witness sensations like never before. But, somewhere in the heat of lovemaking, she would remove the fabric. Joseph's insistence for Theresa to keep the veil covering her was always expressed in a lighthearted tone, but he was serious.

The only break in their routine came when the drummer in Theresa's band went missing for the last three nights Joseph and Theresa were together. Theresa didn't sing on those nights, but the rest of the band played in Eve's Hallow. This only made Joseph Pepper and Theresa Amat jump into lovemaking earlier in their day, retiring from Eve's Hallow after three dances: two slow and one fast romp cooked up by the band.

And so it was that Joseph Pepper IV kept company with Theresa Amat for those two weeks. Then, he left Water Bug Hollow with a promise to return after his trip to London. Theresa led Joseph out of Water Bug Hollow and to a transport that would take him to a train heading to New York City.

Joseph again made Theresa promise to cover herself with the veil, a ritual for protection. Theresa promised, and Joseph Pepper departed with a kiss. That night, Theresa wore the veil as she slept, skeptical as she was, and as silly as she felt. But she did have a vivid dream. Theresa thought of Joseph Pepper beforehand, as she lay awake with the veil over her face. She hoped to have an erotic dream about him. But all she could remember the next morning was a dream about the cosmos. Thousands upon thousands of comets streaked toward a blazing sun. One penetrated the galactic wildfire, and the cosmic, dazzling ball of flames exploded. Theresa smiled in her sleep, and her hand moved over her belly.

The second night there came another dream, but again, Joseph Pepper was nowhere to be found. Theresa sat at a table in Eve's Hallow. She laughed and dined with a young, red-haired white woman. *"Go to New York,"* the woman told her between laughs. *"Go meet your Joseph Pepper there. You have the talent and the opportunity. Go surprise him."*

The idea spoken, and the dream itself, remained faint the next morning. Theresa was upset that the veil produced no dreams of her lover.

She took comfort in the news that the band's drummer returned. Theresa would sing tonight. She would sing to Joseph Pepper, pretending he was sitting there in the audience. She already missed him. It hadn't been more than two days, and she missed him. She was too impatient to wait for Joseph Pepper's return. Odd as his erudition could be, Theresa loved him.

Hints of Theresa's dreams appeared to her as impulsive ideas to go to New York and meet her Joseph Pepper. But instead, Theresa sang to Joseph Pepper. She manifested him nightly as a ghostly image in the audience, and as her lover next to her in bed. She continued her ritual of wearing the veil over her face, but it was only the tips of her fingers that stimulated her imagination and stirred her dreams.

The Church of Water Bug Hollow, est. ca. 1917

"I died multiple times from the midnight's touch."

Sarinda Fallows stared in awe at Water Bug Hollow. Her large, green eyes panned the scene as she stepped through the tunnel that was shaped by nature from its shrubbery. She inhaled the air. Her eyes inhaled the scenery. The sun ignored the draping and tightly hugging verdure and slipped through to illuminate the bayou village. Its golden sparkle gleamed atop the green leaves and lime blades of grass that were wet with dew while also mixing its light with the browns of the watery mud and dirt roads.

Sarinda considered the large plantation house and its guesthouse were once intimidating structures to the enslaved generations that preceded the Negroes currently residing in this now majestic locale. Sarinda considered that some of the populace of Water Bug Hollow was old enough to remember life as slaves in the old days of Jakobi's plantation.

Sarinda exhaled, and her eyes saw everything except the Water Bug Hollow citizens staring back at her, pausing in their daily routines and travel to present a curious gaze at the white, female pedestrian that just strolled into their isolated sanctuary. Sarinda stopped her stride and continued to marvel at the sight of Water Bug Hollow. Its history was invisible, but Sarinda was conscious of its presence. She closed her eyes and again breathed in deep. She could feel the ghosts around her, slaves and plantation owner alike, anger and happiness issuing from them.

"Excuse me, Miss," said an elderly black man, his voice drawing Sarinda back to reality. She opened her eyes and smiled at him. "Are you lost?" he asked Sarinda.

"Oh, dear me," Sarinda said all apologetic and in a charming, Southern cadence. "I do understand how someone like you would think so. But, dear me, child, no." She chuckled in a tone as lovely as her voice. She placed a hand on the elderly man's chest while putting an open palm on her own. Her hand laid over her breast, covering the flat, gray stone that was speckled with red markings and dangling from a gold chain. The elderly man presented a humble smile, relaxed by Sarinda's charm.

Sarinda withdrew her hand from the man and explained, "Kind sir, my name is Miss Sarinda Fallows. I'm from Tennessee. My good journey started there and brought me to New York, and from there I have come here." The old man kept his smile, but Sarinda could see the perplexity that lay behind it. "I'm related to Oscar MacRitchie, a man I believe played an intricate part in the history of Water Bug Hollow."

Sarinda moved past the elderly man and again overlooked her surroundings. To the left, down the road, she could see the foliage doming Water Bug Hollow give way to a wide field. Sarinda stopped. The elderly man walked up next to her. "I can't imagine old cousin Oscar doin' nothin' of the sorts—shootin' and killin'." She turned to the elderly man and addressed him. "I've only met his family once. Our families don't get along, mostly because of these exploits. His family is worth a fortune. I hear that's where you get your goods from."

The elderly man shook his head, yes. He stepped back and said to Sarinda, "You stay right there, Miss. There's someone here you should talk to."

Sarinda beamed and assured, "I won't move."

The elderly man disappeared. Sarinda could hear him informing the paused passersby on who she was. Their movement started again. Sarinda continued inspecting the area, and after she panned the scene several more times, Water Bug Hollow's self-appointed mayor presented himself to her. Mayor Arlington Johnson tipped his hat and bowed in a gentlemanly manner. The elderly man that retrieved Mayor Johnson stood next to him. The mayor said, "I am Mayor Arlington Johnson." He took Sarinda's hand and gave her a gentle shake.

"Miss Sarinda Fallows," Sarinda introduced herself. "If your courteous assistant has not informed you as of yet. Of course, I couldn't imagine a gentle soul such as he wouldn't have done his job proper."

The elderly man bowed his head with a smile.

"He has informed me of who you are, young lady," Mayor Johnson said to Sarinda causing her peach-colored cheeks to flush red as her bright hair. "I am honored to meet you. So few of your family cares to visit since Oscar passed away. We're lucky to still receive goods."

Sarinda replied, "I am honored to be among you all. Mayor Arlington Johnson, you are the very man I need to speak with. I carry urgent news. There are politics coming to Water Bug Hollow, and I'm afraid this small camp will not be isolated for too long."

Sarinda's words caused Mayor Johnson to fidget in place. He turned to the elderly man and dismissed him from the conversation. The mayor then aimed an arm toward a small office building located behind the former plantation house. "This way, Miss Fallows," instructed the mayor. "Please, come. Thank you." Sarinda walked alongside Mayor Johnson, the two of them strolling through the light lanes of traffic made up of Water Bug Hollow residents. He escorted Sarinda into his private office, turned on the lights, and sat her down in a chair in front of his desk. Mayor Johnson took his seat behind the desk and addressed Sarinda, "If there are any worries, I don't need Water Bug Hollow's residents aroused. We're always afraid of retaliation, though we're going on a good fifty-three years after this area's rebellion. If we remember, then white folks remember. We've had people leave Water Bug Hollow and not come back. They've been found hanging with angry signs strung around them."

"I understand, Mayor," said Sarinda. "I do. I do. My side of old, cousin Oscar's family walks with shame over what happened here in Water Bug Hollow. They talk about this place's history with such disdain, especially bein' related to a man that participated in it. I grew up more curious. I found the story of Negro struggle for freedom heart warming; and I looked to it every time I needed to overcome adversity, though I never resorted to any form of violence." Sarinda beamed a coy smile. "Now that wouldn't be lady-like, now would it?" She sat up in her chair, leaning forward over the desk. She looked concerned as she spoke, "That's why I'm here, Mayor Johnson. My family is split over this area's history. A lot of people are hurt by it. We take pride in our Confederate relatives, soldiers, captains, and other ranking officials. My family believes Water Bug Hollow's past is a scar on our family." Sarinda leaned back in the chair, her emotions worked up. "We don't believe you coloreds should be slaves. It's just about our Southern pride. It's complicated, Mayor." Sarinda looked around the room and sighed. "And all I see outside is the beauty of Water Bug Hollow's present-day culture. It has me in awe. There is a primordial mystique about Water Bug Hollow's ambiance."

Mayor Johnson went stiff. Momentum returned to his body, starting first with his fingers. On each hand, he tapped in a wave against the desk. Then it was his eyes, darting from the wall on his right to the wall on his left. Then he said to Sarinda, "Miss Fallows, we take great precaution to protect ourselves, especially on the night we celebrate this town's independence."

Sarinda nodded her head. Her expression was sympathetic. She said, "I would hope so, Mister Mayor. Unfortunately, your celebration of independence is what has many non-colored folks up in arms. It's offensive to them. You celebrate the death of an honest American businessman. And I've heard it's done with a large fire. People believe there's devilry going on in Water Bug Hollow. This beautiful place is referred to as Satan's Seat. The citizens are called black devils that perform rituals against the good, American economy, and preach hate. When I heard that, it aroused me. Scared me a little, but I'm open-minded." Mayor Johnson opened his mouth to respond, but Sarinda spoke first. "Now, I understand the history from your people's point-of-view. I empathize. I do. It's why I'm here." The mayor became attentive, returning to his unmoving demeanor. Sarinda sat back, placed a hand on the flat, gray stone that was speckled with red markings and dangling from her gold chain, and said, "Even with just a quick glance, my eyes spied no church among you all." She chuckled, a charming tone that sounded like the melodic flavor of a lute. "That's all it would take to give the outward appearance that Water Bug Hollow is not populated with heathens. It would show some remorse for the killin' of Southern Americans—wicked slave owners as they were in your people's point-of-view."

Mayor Johnson kept still. His eyes stayed fixed on Sarinda, lowering and spying her hand that lay gently on her bosom and covering the pendant that dangled from her necklace. He thought about Miss Fallows' proposition, his eyes lingering on her hand and chest. The mayor shifted in his chair. He cleared his throat, feeling uncomfortable. Sarinda removed her hand from her chest. Mayor Johnson looked up and met the lovely, red-haired woman's eyes. She continued smiling. The mayor mirrored her gesture, beaming to break what he felt was tension, embarrassed as he was for staring longingly at her. He hoped she didn't notice, or take offense if she did.

The mayor slapped his desk, a move to wake himself from being entranced by Water Bug Hollow's fair guest. He cleared his throat again, and he made his smile wider. "I agree with you, Miss Fallows, but we only have a small economy that barely affords us the benefits of electricity. We do have auto-carriages—cars. A few. Trucks for transportation of goods when goods come in."

Sarinda nodded, impressed. She waved a hand and shook her head. She told the mayor, "There is no need to worry about finance. I would put forth the money."

Mayor Johnson protested, "Miss Fallows…"

Sarinda again placed her hand over her pendant. "There's too much at stake. Imagine a precious place like Water Bug Hollow lost, Mister Mayor. There are many that don't understand the pride celebrated here, or look down on what you all commemorate. This is somethin' for Negroes everywhere. Water Bug Hollow's story must be preserved."

Mayor Johnson nodded in agreement. He paused and took a deep breath before asking for assurance, "Miss Fallows, this will not hurt your purse?"

Sarinda shook her head, no. "My purse will remain as full as a pig's belly. This won't be too much. It's all I can do. Water Bug Hollow is as much my history as it is yours."

Mayor Johnson stood and reached out his hands as he came from around his desk. He helped Sarinda to her feet and proclaimed, "Then Water Bug Hollow will have its first, official church."

Sarinda turned her cheek to Mayor Johnson and instructed in a flirtatious voice, "It's okay to seal this agreement with a kiss, Mister Mayor. There won't be a scandal."

Mayor Johnson chuckled at Sarinda's playful manner. He planted a kiss on her cheek and then the two of them walked from the office and out into Water Bug Hollow's glorious environment. The mayor and Sarinda returned to the town's entrance. Arlington escorted Sarinda with the courteous gesture of his arm folded around hers. He commented as they observed Water Bug Hollow's square, "There is very little room to build here."

Sarinda stopped walking. Her eyes looked to the open field in the distance. "Out there. An open space."

The mayor shook his head in an uneasy manner. "I can't commission building out there. That's where we hold our celebration."

"The bonfire," Sarinda responded in a gasp. "Yes, of course." Sarinda shook her head and added dramatically, "Again, I tell you, it has many white Southerners believin' this here is an estate for devil worship. The hysteria is everywhere, even up in Tennessee. Many whites are looking to take arms against Water Bug Hollow in the name of the Good Lord." Sarinda stroked her pendant. "A church built over the site where Hell's flames can be seen on an annual basis would surely cease the desire to spill blood in the name of the Good Book." Mayor Johnson agreed, though reluctant. He peered over at the open field and watched the area in silence. He shook his head as he moved his gaze back to Sarinda. Before he could speak, Sarinda advised, "A revival. You can't stop the singing and the dancin'. But you can disguise your ritual with a revival." Sarinda continued rubbing her pendant.

Mayor Johnson sighed and dropped his head. He took another breath and lifted his head to tell Sarinda, "We'll ease the town into a new tradition, Miss Fallows. We are a people used to adapting."

Sarinda put her hand on Mayor Johnson's shoulder. "This is all for the safety of Water Bug Hollow, Mayor Johnson."

"Of course, Miss Fallows," the mayor responded with a whisper of melancholy in his voice. "I will have to discuss this with my small cabinet, which is made up of Water Bug Hollow's most influential citizens."

"I understand, Mister Mayor," Sarinda said to Mayor Johnson. "Change is not an easy thing for people to accept. It contradicts their traditions."

The mayor agreed, nodding. He proceeded to escort Sarinda Fallows through Water Bug Hollow's natural tunnel and beyond the bayou village's boundary. Waiting on the other side were several taxis, two horse-drawn carriages and one automobile. Two prominent women of Water Bug Hollow owned the taxi service that carried people to the train station. Sarinda neared one of the elegant horse-drawn carriages. She turned to Mayor Johnson and said in a pleasant, winsome manner, "Water Bug Hollow seems to be coming up, offering a lady a ride in such an advanced machine as an auto-carriage." She patted the mayor on his shoulder and concluded, "But a lady like me just loves the simple sophistication of the old days."

Mayor Johnson chuckled and opened the carriage for her, shooing away the cabbie from assisting Miss Fallows in anything but steering the carriage. The mayor closed the door, offering a parting smile toward the lady. Sarinda Fallows assured her return, which she indicated, "Will most likely be this evening. I hear Water Bug Hollow has a nightspot that plays the most splendid jazz music. Now, there's a tradition that's worth keepin', Mister Mayor." Sarinda leaned her head out the window and whispered, "But I just might steal them musicians from you." She explained, "When I was in New York, I met some people that want to come here and recruit an authentic, Southern Negro jazz sound."

"You'll find that here," said the mayor. He backed away from the carriage as he tipped his hat toward Sarinda Fallows. "Water Bug Hollow awaits your return, Miss Fallows. I will see you tonight." He looked over at the cabbie and ordered him to steer the horse-drawn taxi to the train station.

Sarinda and the mayor waved goodbye to one another, and then Water Bug Hollow moved away from Sarinda's view as the coach started forward. Sarinda sat back in her cushioned seat, though she remained upright, straight and proper. Water Bug Hollow was no longer in her peripheral but behind her. Accomplishment caped her, Sarinda made contact to steer the bayou village toward a change she was most comfortable with.

Sarinda exited the coach upon its arrival at the train station. She tipped the cabbie a generous sum of money and made her way to the train going to New Orleans. The trip didn't last long, no more than twenty minutes. Sarinda thought of nothing, not even her wondrous travels from New York to the bayou. She rubbed her pendant and a smile broke through as the train came to a halt at the New Orleans station. Sarinda jumped up from her seat and made an elegant walk into and through the train station and then out into the city streets to her hotel where, waiting in the lobby of her picturesque, Southern accommodation, was Cornelius "Curly" Burneside.

Curly stood up immediately upon Sarinda's entrance into the lobby. He removed his hat and tipped it as Sarinda walked up to him and nodded her head. "You look handsome, Mister Burneside," she complemented. He was dressed in an off-white suit, with a buttoned up dress shirt, the collar of which was wrapped with a black, string bowtie. "Kenten would've looked good in a suit like this."

Curly bowed at the neck. "I thank you for this fine attire, Miss Fallows."

Sarinda nodded at the comment and then pivoted with sharp precision toward the stairs. "Follow me to the room, Mister Burneside." Curly followed in tow, keeping behind Sarinda up the stairs and through the door of the hotel suite. Curly walked to the middle of the room, after closing the door, as Sarinda made a sharp pivot and stepped to the vanity to take a seat. Curly removed his hat and waited for Sarinda to speak. He watched her grab a brush from the vanity and begin gently brushing her bright, red hair. Sarinda spied Curly's attentive gaze in the mirror. She smiled, and played up, for Curly's amusement, the brush strokes she gave her hair.

"Mayor Arlington Johnson of Water Bug Hollow has agreed to the building of a church. It didn't take much convincin', you know?" She chuckled. "Not with my charm." Her smile widened as she reflected on the moment past, continuing to brush her hair. "I think you should get to work on retrieving that disgraced, Negro pastor. The one that had all them troubles with the young girls of his congregation. I'm sure he's dying to find himself another flock of churchgoers, and I think he deserves another chance." She put the brush down and addressed Curly by looking at his reflection in the mirror. "I'm returning to Water Bug Hollow tonight," she informed with slight disgust in her tone. "I know that damn Joe Pepper fellow left the veil there. There was a kind of a..." Sarinda snapped her fingers and looked up at the ceiling, searching for the appropriate wording. "...A 'dull' tug pullin' at me—I guess that's how I could best describe it. But, no matter, I'll find it tonight. Is everything arranged with Ethan, Curly? I do hope he can keep his promise to take care of Pepper over in London. I know Ethan doesn't like me—that ungrateful little soldier. I can see him lettin' Joe Pepper and that Madison fellow get away all out of spite for me. Then these nigger conjure folk would be that much closer to recalling the entirety of their magic."

"He'll do just fine, Miss Fallows," Curly answered compliant. "He has nothing else to do in this life but his job. Even if he believes he's his own man now, he still works for us at the end of the day."

Sarinda turned around in her chair. She slapped her knees with a smile and bounced up into a two-step stride toward Curly. She played with the collar of his suit jacket, and she ran the palms of her hands along Curly's arms and chest, straightening the suit as if her hands were irons. "The night I wear that veil, Curly, and you take me to bed, I want you to wear this suit." She stepped away from Curly and inspected him again. "I'd ask you to follow me back to Water Bug Hollow, but you have your own expedition."

"You be careful, Miss Fallows," Curly warned.

Sarinda patted Curly on the collar. "Ain't a need to worry your handsome self, Curly. My charm can reflect any anathema cast my way. I will be wearing that veil and laying with you soon enough." She put herself close to Curly Burneside and hugged him tight. Her cheek pressed against his lapel, and she smiled wide. "It will be wonderful." She backed away from him and touched her belly. "And then Kenten will be back with us."

Curly shook his head and said as he cleared his throat, "I imagine Master Fallows will be turned off by his surroundings when he returns." He turned toward the window and took a step in its direction.

"Especially since it will be years before he matures," Sarinda added to Curly's sentiment. "We can only wonder how much more change can happen in this environment." Sarinda headed toward the bathroom. "Call the hotel's staff, would you please, Curly? Have them prepare the tub for a hot bath. I need a wash and a li'l freshen up before I return to Water Bug Hollow tonight." By the time Curly turned toward the bathroom, Sarinda was exiting the room clothed in a silk robe. "Tell the hotel staff that I'm in a rush."

Curly bowed at the neck and disappeared through the room's door. He reappeared moments later with two black servants, a male and female. Sarinda took a seat and allowed the help to prepare her bath while she and Curly shared conversation over a glass of sparkling wine retrieved by Curly on his forage for the help. At the start of their conversation, Curly poured champagne, and the luxurious and bubbling wine sloshed into the upscale glasses just as the sound of the running water for the bath started flowing.

"Not too hot," Sarinda called to the help in the bathroom. She turned her attention back to Curly and said, "I hope they brought the proper provisions to put together an adequate bubble bath."

Curly grinned. "I made sure they brought all the necessaries, Miss Fallows," he said as he passed her a glass.

Sarinda rolled her eyes and took a sip of champagne. She swallowed and said, "Freedom has spoiled good servants, Curly." She shook the thought away. "Where was I? I don't remember. But let me tell you about Water Bug Hollow." Then Sarinda engaged Curly with her day's exploits, sounding like a giddy and infatuated schoolgirl speaking about a brief encounter with the very schoolboy that captured her desires. Her voice was a whisper so as not to be overheard by the help. She still bubbled, however, as she explained to Curly how Mayor Arlington Johnson was taken by her charm. "That, mixed with a little worry put on him, and a church in Water Bug Hollow will be built in no time." The hotel attendants appeared from the bathroom, standing straight and humble. Their presence caught Sarinda and Curly's attention. "Yes," Sarinda asked prompting a response. Sarinda held her smile, but there was a hint of indignation in her voice for being interrupted, even though the man presented Sarinda with the news that her bath was prepared. "A city of bubbles floating over the water?" Sarinda asked.

The man bowed. "Yes, Miss."

"Miss *Fallows*," Sarinda edified in a polite tone that bordered on being condescending. "Please, remember that for future reference," Sarinda chuckled charmingly at the two servants.

"Yes, Miss Fallows," the both of them spoke.

Sarinda paused and inspected the man and woman in front of her. Their heads bowed further so as not to make direct eye contact, unsure of Sarinda's inspection. Sarinda wondered and asked allowed, "Are any of you two from Water Bug Hollow?"

"No ma'am," said the woman. She corrected quickly, "No, Miss Fallows."

Sarinda continued her interrogation; smile never melting. "Have any of y'all two been? I'd like to know what the night life is like."

"They have jazz, Miss Fallows," answered the man. "And they got a singer there whose voice knows how to harmonize every range of sound in God's universe; and her band is right there with her with them sounds."

Sarinda looked at Curly and slapped her knee as she leaned forward in her chair. "Now, that sounds like a night!" Sarinda hollered her laugh and then waved the help from the room. "Now, be on your way," she told them. Curly stood from his chair and saw them out. He turned around as he closed the door and watched Sarinda continue her caress on the stone pendant she wore around her neck. A scowl scarred her face. She aimed the champagne glass at the door and said, "Those two niggers are talkin' 'bout me right now. I can tell. All polite in my face." She gulped the last of her champagne and placed the empty glass atop the small, round table in front of her. She continued rubbing her pendant, leaning back in the chair as she massaged the stone with a coarser grip. Her eyes were focused on the door, her vision seeing straight through Curly. "The Negress thinks that boy said too much to me. The boy is tryin' to tell her his talk was nothin' more than answerin' my question. She believes his wording was too fancy. She believes it showed his education too much. Now they talkin' 'bout how foolish us *'white folk'* can be. They're makin' fun of my insistence to address me by my proper surname." Her concentration broke, but the disgust remained. "I think that nigger-boy wanted to fuck me. He was bein' flirtatious in his response." Sarinda stood up. "Trust me. I know. He was showin' off, how he can arrange words and all." She then mocked, *"A voice knowin' how to harmonize every range of sound in God's universe."* But then the slightest hint of a smile flashed quickly across her face. Her eyes became slender with salacious thought. Sarinda's facial gestures were hidden from Curly's view as she walked around the chair and then toward the bathroom.

Curly suggested as he watched Sarinda make her way toward the bathroom, "For the boy's unclean thoughts, should he be taken care of, Miss Fallows?"

"Let him have his thoughts, Curly." She turned around and teased, "As I know you have yours about that nigger-maid that was standin' here. I saw your face, all lookin' her up and down." She chuckled.

"Miss Fallows…"

"Oh, Curly. Hush," Sarinda insisted in a playful tone. "In the sweet days of the plantation, there were many half-pickaninny children runnin' around that you could definitely claim as yours with the rough prowess you showed them black heifers we owned. When you weren't showin' that same prowess to the men and them young boys to get them in line."

Curly's right hand reached for the ring on his left hand. He rubbed the stone as his brow glistened with perspiration. Sarinda examined Curly's nervous visage. She reached for her pendant and chuckled, "Why Curly Burneside, are you tryin' to keep somethin' from me? I don't think so. I know what you thinkin'." She crept closer to Curly, forgoing her entrance into the bathroom. Her walk was slow, seductive, and intimidating even to a man as tall and broad as Curly Burneside. "And, it might be true, Curly," Sarinda said in a low, alluring voice as her body snaked up under his chin. "A lot of them half-nigger boys and girls might have been from my husband's seed, but we all ate from Ham's fruit." Her smile bent, topsy-turvy. "I can tell you now, that I wondered many nights how a race of men so cursed by God could be so blessed and endowed. My *petit mort* was not so *petit*, and I died, Curly. I died, I died, and I died multiple times from the midnight's touch. Hell, a long time ago, it was by rite that I see the wolf through a Man of Ham."

Sarinda pivoted, sharp and precise, but her movement forward was like a snake's slither. She glided back to the bathroom where she bathed for an hour, soaking in the warm bath that was colonized by mountains of bubbles. She emerged from the bathroom dry, naked, and without shame for Curly's leering, as he was now sitting at the oval glass table. Sarinda took a seat at her vanity and primped with perfume and cosmetics. She brushed her light-red hair while watching Curly in the mirror.

"I'll probably be spending the night in Water Bug Hollow," she informed him.

Curly turned his head toward Sarinda and asked, "How long do you expect to play chase with whomever has that veil?"

"Lord only knows how long, but I don't reckon a great deal of time." She put down her brush and stood up from her chair and walked behind an elegant, Victorian dressing panel. This was not to hide her nakedness from Curly's following eyes, but to retrieve her clothes that hung behind it. Curly witnessed Sarinda's arms lift from behind the elaborate sheet as she slipped on her fancy dress, tailored and decorated for nightlife.

Sarinda stepped from behind the panel, twirling and posing for Curly. "How do I look, Mister Burneside?"

"As good as ever, Miss Fallows."

Sarinda spun around, feminine and playful, as she said, "This dress gives me the curves of Psyche and Cupid's daughter." And then she slipped into a pair of shoes. She picked up a handbag that matched her outfit and walked toward the door, hips swaying purposely for Curly's enjoyment. She opened the door and stepped half of her body beyond the room. She turned back, half the door covering her, and said to Curly, "Don't cause too much trouble, now, Curly." She winked, and then she was gone, retracing her steps out of the hotel and to the train station where she boarded a train for a return trip to Water Bug Hollow. There, she was welcomed back as if the residents had been awaiting her arrival. In her absence, talk circled and the town was already abuzz from its visit by a MacRitchie relative. The townsfolk showered Sarinda with warm welcomes, and again the mayor greeted her when he was informed of her arrival.

"I will be spending the night, Mister Mayor," Sarinda said to him in a cordial voice.

"A room has already been prepared, Miss Fallows," informed Mayor Johnson, his hands embracing hers. He then aimed his arm toward his office and instructed Sarinda to follow. Six of Water Bug Hollow's most influential citizens were waiting patiently for Sarinda in Mayor Johnson's office. Sarinda and the mayor entered. Three men and three women, dressed to the nines and for business, stood in wait for the mayor and Water Bug Hollow's guest. Sarinda instinctively bowed to them as she walked through the door. The gesture was repeated, again by instinct, after a proper introduction by the mayor. Sarinda's knee bent, and her body dipped as her head bowed forward. She lifted from her gesture and immediately felt light headed, causing her to clutch at her pendant, rubbing it and slowly regaining a clear head. Sarinda's heart skipped a beat, and she blushed as if naked in front of strangers. She played off her unconscious mannerism when she stated, "I just feel so underdressed. You all look so elegant, and I'm already costumed for the night."

Sarinda's excuse was respectfully overlooked. The women concentrated on her gracious bow. "Your manners are most elegant," said one of the black women in the room before mirroring Sarinda's greeting gesture.

"Always a lady," Sarinda said chuckling her way out of embarrassment.

"Please," said Mayor Johnson. "Miss Fallows, have a seat."

Sarinda placed herself in the same chair she sat in earlier that day. The three black ladies and three black gentlemen stood in a line that arced behind her. She could see one black woman in her left peripheral view, and she could see a black gentleman in her right peripheral view. Mayor Johnson sat down. "We have agreed to your proposal, Miss Fallows, in the best interest of Water Bug Hollow's safety. As I commented earlier, our residents are use to adapting."

Sarinda nodded her head, smile on her face.

The mayor continued, "We will let word spread about the project, but there will be no formal announcement until a town meeting is held. But, tonight, at Eve's Hallow, we will celebrate your presence, Miss Fallows. I'm glad to hear you'll be staying the night."

Sarinda exhaled, "Well, Mister Mayor, I might not become a permanent resident, but I will be haunting Water Bug Hollow with my presence for some time."

"Good to hear," said the mayor. "We don't get many visitors from your family. We just have the occasional telegram about goods, and their delivery."

"Would it be too much to ask to see my room, Mister Mayor?" inquired Sarinda.

The mayor replied, "Not at all. That was the next course of business. Miss Inda Gale here will show you to your room. She also owns a clothing store, should you need an extra set of attire."

Sarinda stood on cue of Mayor Johnson standing from his seat. She turned around and looked to each of the women, scoping which of them was Inda Gale. Before Sarinda could reach for her pendant and contemplate the answer, Inda Gale presented herself by stepping forward. Sarinda held her composure as the youngest of the three women took a stride toward her.

Inda might have been the youngest of the gathered women, but she was in her mid-forties. What Sarinda found most peculiar about Inda Gale was her resemblance to the maid that serviced her room earlier at the hotel. There were subtle differences besides the clothing and demeanor. Inda's hair was shorter, almost natural instead of pressed. Her skin tone was a few shades darker than even the burnished brass glister of the maid.

Sarinda wondered if the maid and this woman were somehow related, which would have exposed the maid as a liar on the many topics she decided not to reveal, or claim ignorance about, when it came to Water Bug Hollow. Sarinda considered giving Curly an order that he would see as a gift to him. She would have Curly deal with the maid's trickery by showcasing his prowess against her. He would appreciate that.

Inda extended a hand, and Sarinda received the woman's action by extending her own and giving a courteous, feminine shake. "I'll show you around Water Bug Hollow," Inda spoke as she took lead toward the door.

Sarinda beamed. "Why, thank you, Miss Gale. You remind me of our house-nurse." The room became still, impacted by Sarinda's comment. The mouths of the seven black aristocrats hung open. Sarinda reached for her pendant and rubbed it. "I just loved Little Mammy. I was closer to her than my own mother. I drank her milk and everything." Sarinda spun around, observing the still movement and the frozen expressions of the seven faces. "Forgive me," she said, an apologetic smile hovering below her nose. "I know some of my dialect may come across as offensive. I still use those very innocent words that I'm sure are a reminder to you all of a very treacherous past, which I'm aware has not completely passed. I'm doing my best to shake as much of the nefarious Southern manners from my shoulders as possible while trying to retain the charm of the South." She laughed and looked at everyone while rubbing her pendant and expressing, "A few weeks in New York City did wonders." Her laughter ceased, and the faces of the small crowd surrounding her melted into more cordial expressions, some even echoing Sarinda's jovial spirit. "I can't imagine a whole year. Why, my drawl would just cease to exist." Sarinda let go of her pendant as Water Bug Hollow's aristocrats chuckle became louder. Sarinda concluded in a sincere voice, "I do hope some time among the people of my family's true origins in this country has that same effect. I thank you all for taking me in."

"We are not xenophobes," stated Inda Gale. "Do you know what that is, *chile?*"

"A fear of strangers, or people different than you," Sarinda answered in a manner both proud and eager to show her education. She tilted her head to the side and added, "And, I'm grateful for that…that you all are not such creatures."

"That's our natural way, dear woman," responded Inda Gale. Again, she took lead toward the door. "Come, *chile*, this way." Sarinda followed Inda from the office and out into Water Bug Hollow's streets. "The women on my mother's side were much like your *Little Mammy*," Inda recalled. "They were seamstresses. They made the finest garments for Master Jakobi. His wife loved their work. They called upon no one else for their clothes. Not even the latest imports, which they could afford." Inda huffed. "I always say that it was because them white folks just wanted to see a nigger work for them, by any means." Inda waved away her angry emotion and stated, "But it was a skill; a skill passed down from many generations, even before slavery. And after that great rebellion, and with the death of slavery, it has lived on. My father, a carpenter, built the store we sell the clothes out of. And we have enough hands to create for and satisfy all tastes and styles."

Sarinda's eyes panned the Water Bug Hollow universe. "This is such a magical place."

"Don't be fooled," said Inda. "Water Bug Hollow is not just Water Bug Hollow. It is all the boroughs of New York. It is San Francisco. It is Saint Louis. It is Chicago. It is New Orleans. We have expanded our life to those cities. People move out, but they send support back. We are thriving. I'm sure that has raised many-a-white eyebrow just as much as our yearly, celebratory rituals. Any excuse to keep niggers down."

"Yes, Miss Inda Gale," Sarinda yielded. "But, the building of the church will help at least calm one excuse."

"They will find another," Inda huffed. She came to her family store and stopped to point toward the open field. "I'm glad I drank and danced wild, if that was to be the last time I get to dance properly on Elias Jakobi's grave." Inda escorted Sarinda into the store where Sarinda gazed upon the various contemporary fashions stitched to perfection and reasonably priced.

Sarinda moved to the women's section and breezed through the aisles with a wide, cheerful gaze. Brand name clothing mixed with locally seamed garments and finely crafted shoes. Sarinda brushed her hand through the dresses and expressed with wonder, "You all have made liars of religion. It seems you don't have to die to get to heaven." Sarinda's sentiment made Inda chuckle. The Water Bug Hollow aristocrat backed away to allow Sarinda to sift through the numerous selections.

Sarinda picked brand names, remarking how cheaply priced they were. She also made mention that she did not want to appear to be supporting Water Bug Hollow by buying their fashions, as great and as inexpensive and flawless as the pieces were. "If I were to be seen in New Orleans with them, Inda, I'd be tarred and feathered. But, I will buy an outfit or two to keep for my stays here." Regardless of her statement, Sarinda purchased nothing that was fabricated by the local seamstresses.

With large bags filled with brand-name purchases in hand, she let Inda guide her to her room that rested above Eve's Hallow.

The room was clean, quaint, and blended the styles of many past Southern ages. Sarinda approved. She set down her bags and asked for privacy. Inda respected Sarinda's wishes and dismissed herself after reiterating that the night festivities held in Eve's Hallow would begin promptly at sundown. There, among the festivities, Sarinda Fallows would be given a formal introduction to the townsfolk. Sarinda expressed how lovely that would be, and she thanked Inda. Not too long after, Inda disappeared from Sarinda's quarters, granting the red-haired, Southern belle privacy.

Sarinda sat down at the room's vanity and concentrated on her image reflected in the mirror. She closed her eyes and rubbed her pendant. The darkness behind her closed lids rippled into an image of war surrounding Water Bug Hollow in its final days as a plantation. The violent death of the Jakobi family, and the celebration of the self-emancipated Negroes, shook Sarinda to open her eyes again, gasping. She stared at her image and spoke to it as if it was Elias Jakobi himself.

"The horror these people put you and your family through," Sarinda said in a disgusted tone. "I know all too well, Mister Jakobi. All too well." Sarinda took a breath, and then she went silent. She again concentrated on her image, closed her eyes, and rubbed her pendant.

No image appeared. There only came a dull feeling pulling at her. Sarinda stayed focused, trying to draw either herself closer to the dull sensation or have it come closer to her. The feeling never became stronger. Sarinda opened her eyes, frustrated. She spoke to her reflection, again addressing it as if it was Master Elias Jakobi. "That veil is here, Mister Jakobi. It is." She stood up and rested her hands on the vanity's counter. She bent down and leaned closer to her reflection. Sarinda spoke flirtatiously, "And on both yours and my husband's grave, I will take it from any witch that wears it."

Sarinda cleared her head, stood straight, and then proceeded to change into a newly purchased dress. She stepped into the bathroom and took a moment to freshen herself up before returning to the front room and sitting down on the bed. She looked at the clock, her eyes focused, watching time tick away until the sun disappeared. Then she stood and snatched her purse from the vanity and walked from her room and down into Eve's Hallow.

Sarinda sat alone at a table. She ordered a plate of Southern fried catfish, with a side of mixed vegetables and a bottle of Cheerwine soft drink. Sarinda asked the waiter, "Is a smoke okay?"

"Yes, ma'am." The waiter leaned closer and added with a grin, "Reefer smoke you'll have to take outside unless it's after midnight. Then, anything goes."

Sarinda chuckled and winked at the waiter. "Thank you, darlin'."

Mayor Johnson stepped inside, blending with the regular citizens. He instantly spotted Sarinda seated alone at her table. He separated himself from the wave of people shuffling inside and bounced toward his village's new guest. He leaned over to her and whispered, "We will introduce you, Miss Fallows, as a relative of Oscar MacRitchie. All you need to do is stand and wave."

Sarinda responded, "Yes, Mister Mayor."

Mayor Johnson explained, "The citizens are aware of your presence here in Water Bug Hollow. But we'd like a formal smile and wave to the crowd, if that's all right with you, Miss Fallows."

"Why of course it is, Mister Mayor," Sarinda agreed.

Mayor Johnson moved away from Sarinda and walked to the stage just as the band members seeped in from stage left, picking up their instruments and waiting. The curtain was closed behind them. Sarinda looked around. More people filed in, some clapping and singing. All of them had a smile on their face, and they were dressed in sharp and high fashion for the night's scene.

The Water Bug Hollow mayor adjusted the microphone, which was more of a cue for the people to settle and quiet down. He tapped on the device, and the noise in the room silenced. Mayor Johnson cleared his throat and then spoke, "This night is filled with a surprise. Our yearly celebration is weeks behind us, but we have been blessed with the presence of a person that puts a footnote on this year's festivities." The mayor looked beyond the lights, trying to see through the brightness beaming in his eyes and find Sarinda Fallows. He waved his hand upward and instructed, "Miss Fallows, please stand." Sarinda did so. The mayor saw her figure, washed out in silhouette by the bright lights aimed at he and the stage. "Miss Sarinda Fallows has made her journey from Tennessee to our historical hamlet, first making a stop in New York City. She's come to observe where her family's history intersects with Water Bug Hollow. She is a relative of Mister Oscar MacRitchie." There was polite applause. "I know there has been talk already filtering through the town about a visit from one of Oscar's relatives, and here she is. Miss Sarinda Fallows. Please, Miss Fallows give a wave to the crowd." Sarinda did as instructed, a smile resonating on her face as she received more applause. Sarinda returned to her seat, her meal placed in front of her. A proud smile was on the waiter's face as he presented Sarinda her food. The mayor continued, "As usual with Oscar MacRitchie's people, not everyone in Sarinda's family acknowledges Water Bug Hollow's existence with respect. Miss Fallows, you are a brave woman."

Sarinda mouthed the words, '*Thank you.*' There was more applause, which quickly quieted, and then the mayor said, "Miss Fallows will be a temporary resident in Water Bug Hollow, and she has already declared giving a charitable donation. So, in turn, let us treat her kindly. Let us dismiss her family's disdain for us—as we do with some of Oscar MacRitchie's other relatives. And, most important, let us show her the musical magic of Eve's Hallow." The mayor concluded, "So, with the children tucked away, let us adults have our play!"

The crowd shouted various statements. "*That's right, now!*" and "*Let's make a move toward the music.*" A civil impatience filled the room, prompting the mayor to introduce the band. He stepped down off the stage just as the first chords started to play. The crowd's impatience exploded into waves of applause as the band started. The first chords of music were light and then burst into a full bloom of wild jazz. There was more applause, but the people remained seated. Sarinda ate, keeping her eye on the stage. The music became soft, and the curtain pulled back. The lights dimmed down to one bright beam glowing at center stage.

A dull feeling pulled at Sarinda Fallows.

She chewed slow, distracted, but managed to swallow the last bits of food remaining in her mouth. She stopped eating her meal. Her eyes were pulled toward the stage, head lifted, attentive as the dull feeling tugging at her became stronger. Theresa Amat made her way to the microphone at center stage. The sultry jazz singer walked in the rhythm of a slow flame, or like a snake, a slow slither. Her hypnotic hips seemed to slow the musicians' music, rather than conforming to the new speed. It was as if the men in the band could no longer concentrate on the raucous jazz played before Theresa's entrance. But none of them were looking at her, their eyes closed and focused on the music being strummed, beat, pressed, and blown.

Sarinda kept her eyes on Theresa; she barely blinked.

A veil covered Theresa's face, and though Sarinda was convinced no one else in the audience could see it, the fabric of the ancient garment swirled with the backdrop of the cosmos. The dull feeling pulling at Sarinda subsided as it yielded for a stronger tug, like the arms of a strapping lover folding over Sarinda and making her lose breath.

Sarinda removed a cigarette from her purse. A waiter lit the end of it, and Sarinda thanked him.

Then Theresa sang through the veil.

Sarinda took a drag, but the usual calming effect of the tobacco did little to sidetrack the stronger draw of the veil's presence. Theresa's sweet voice chanted, *"I had a man whose skin was light as sand, but his love was spicy like Pepper—HOT like humid weather, and, sticky too. Now, I know the origins of Voodoo and hoodoo. Who knew that magic's hand, would make even the most naughty of sins seem so bland? To be touched by midnight, even when he's bright, is like being kissed by heaven on the cheek. And, when my man speaks, the thunders cease, and my knees go weak. I know that this Pepper is more than ever the most sought after treasure."*

Sarinda continued smoking, feeling like an inspired child as she watched Theresa sing. She couldn't help but express the words, "I have found my new magic to conquer." Her voice was low, undetected by surrounding ears that were too transfixed on Theresa to pay attention to Sarinda anyhow. "I'm gonna be a jazz singer," she said in a respectful whisper that resonated in the awe she held for the songbird crooning behind the ancient, cosmic-glowing veil.

Theresa's song ended. Her honey-sweet voice simmered as the music faded away. Then came a magnificent beat, each instrument blaring a hard, heavy, and loud note. Theresa tossed her veil back over her head. Her legs spread as another beat hit, and then she put her hands on her hips and started singing in a wild and jazzy upbeat style. The patrons erupted, jumping up from their seats and dancing near the stage.

Sarinda observed, what was to her, a feral environment. Sarinda's breath was anywhere but inside her, and again her eyes were drawn to Theresa. She spotted the singer's now exposed forehead. There in the center, shining like a blazing, cobalt-blue sun was a ball of brilliant light. It swirled like a mad eye panning to scout the scenery. Sarinda clenched her teeth and clutched her pendant tight. She concentrated. The light's beam panned over her, but didn't see her. Then, the light faded from Theresa's forehead. Sarinda jumped to her feet and hurried to the bar, waving her arm to flag the bartender. He approached Sarinda, and she tossed him a clump of bills. She leaned over the bar and said into his ear for him to hear over the music, "That's enough for everyone in here to have three drinks."

The bartender peered down at the cash with mouth wide open. Sarinda slid the money closer to the bartender and he accepted. "Miss Fallows…" he said back, his voice trailing away. Sarinda was only able to read his lips over the music. She didn't address his attempt at speech. The bartender stepped away from the bar and whispered to a fellow tender while showing off the cash. The other man's eyes widened, and then he looked up and met eyes with Sarinda. She winked at him and he smiled at her. He replied to his fellow bartender, mouth close to his ear. Then he made his way to the stage.

Sarinda observed everything. The second bartender waited with an anxious look in his eyes. He signaled the bass player who then signaled the piano man that an announcement needed to be made. The piano man nodded. The second bartender walked back to the bar and scrawled a note on a piece of paper before returning to the stage and handing it to the piano player. Theresa spotted the interaction, her eye opening at a particular moment as she paused in her singing. "Oh, there seems to be an announcement that needs callin' out," the jazz singer expressed through the microphone. "Band, play a little somethin' soft while I read the announcement for everyone." The music shifted. The people waved their hips in place to the more relaxed beat, and Theresa turned around to take the piece of paper from the piano player. She repositioned herself behind the microphone, and she read the announcement to herself before making it known to the audience. Theresa's eyes went just as wide as the second bartender's when he first received the news. She fanned herself with the note while saying through the microphone, "It's a party tonight, y'all. Miss Sarinda Fallows can be thanked for that. She's just thrown her money at the bar, and everyone can get their next three drinks on her."

The crowd cheered! The band's music detonated a musical applause! And Theresa Amat jumped back into singing, her voice now a loud, raucous growl. She tossed the note behind her and hollered all her vocal soul into the microphone. Sarinda leaned against the bar, proud and beaming. She bit her lip as she looked around for the man who served her. Spotting him, Sarinda pushed herself from the bar and approached to say into his ear, "You know where I could get some of them reefer smokes, darlin'?"

The waiter looked at her with a surprised expression. He answered loud for her to hear, "Yes, Miss Fallows." He offered her a price for one, and Sarinda requested four. She handed him ten dollars from her purse, telling the waiter to keep what was left over. The waiter then disappeared among the dancing crowd. He returned moments later with his profit pocketed and Sarinda's reward in hand. She accepted her reefer cigarettes and dropped them into her purse, shutting her accessory with a snap, but not before taking a plain tobacco cigarette from it. She returned to her seat after thanking the waiter. He tipped his head in a bow and offered Sarinda another light for her second cigarette. She accepted, thanked the man, sat down, smoked, and observed.

The joyous patrons respected Sarinda's space, and more so, her generosity as they indulged in the drinks paid for on her dollar. A wondrous drunkenness ensued. Sarinda watched while smoking her cigarette and sipping on her remaining Cheerwine. She listened to the band, the music thumping against her chest like a wild lover on top of her. She watched Theresa sing, and she felt the veil tugging at her.

After a time, and through the passage of both slow and fast rhythms, the revel of alcohol soon infected the band, but not their ability to play. This gave a moment of pause for Theresa Amat to step from the stage and introduce herself to Sarinda Fallows. Theresa sat down next to Sarinda, a glass of champagne in hand. She greeted, "Hello, Miss Fallows. I'm Theresa Amat, and I hope you're enjoying the night so far." Theresa took a sip of champagne.

"I certainly am, Miss Amat," Sarinda exclaimed. She looked at Theresa with a wide, admiring smile on her face. "A star shines in Water Bug Hollow. Your voice is bigger than the grand history that handed this land over to the Negro."

Theresa covered her blushing demeanor by taking another sip of her drink. "Please, Miss Fallows."

"I'm serious, Miss Amat," playfully protested Sarinda. "What is a big voice like you doing in a small place like Water Bug Hollow?"

Theresa declared with a little force in her voice, "This is my home, Miss Fallows."

Sarinda replied in kind defense, "I don't mean to offend you, Miss Amat. But the lovely Miss Inda Gale informed me that Water Bug Hollow's reach extends beyond its borders. There's no excuse for you not to walk that reach. She even told me that many of the wandering citizens give back to Water Bug Hollow, keep its economy strong." Theresa rested her glass on the table. She stared incredulously at Sarinda who continued to cajole her. "I've been to New York, and I have been to Chicago. Jazz has reached their ears, but it's not the same. One of those cities could do with a voice like yours. Show them what jazz truly is, and show them its Southern roots."

Sarinda observed Theresa as the songstress looked around Eve's Hallow's interior. The jazz singer pondered as her eyes scoped the restaurant, thinking of New York City and surprising her fiancé Joseph Pepper with her presence when he returned from overseas. Theresa asked herself if she could leave Water Bug Hollow behind.

"Jazz is flocking to the larger, northern cities," Sarinda told Theresa. "You could help its migration. Here you are a big fish in a small pond. And trust me, even in New York or Chicago you would be the same." Sarinda leaned closer to Theresa. "I came across some producers looking to bring an act to the north. It was in New York. Many Southern Negroes are making their way to Harlem, and they're bringing a great deal of musical culture with them." Sarinda put her hand on her pendant, rubbing it. A sharp scratch ran across her hand, as if a wild animal attacked her. Sarinda opened her hand, her eyes quickly focused on the veil. Through the sting in her hand, she reached out and asked, "May I see that lovely veil?"

Theresa's voice was apologetic when she answered, "No, I'm afraid." She removed the veil from the top of her head and folded it neatly. "My man told me to keep it close. A superstition. Silly as it is, but I swore by it. He's from New York City. He just left for business overseas. He'll be back in a year. It would be lovely to surprise him on his return, all established with my singing. In the big city."

Sarinda crossed her legs. "And you would make a point to him too," she said rolling her eyes and waving her hand downward. "You'd make a loud statement that you wouldn't need a man to help you establish yourself, or be waiting around for him to return. A whole year?"

"He's worth it," Theresa said softly, reminiscing about her last days with Joseph Pepper. "The first song I sang was about Joe. He's my Pepper—that's his name. Joseph Pepper."

Sarinda sat up, legs still crossed, hands now balled and jammed into her waist. *"Joseph Pepper the Fourth?"* She started to laugh. "From a place called Five Points in New York City?"

Theresa's face burst with surprise. She questioned excitedly, "You know Joe?"

Sarinda responded. "Why he inspired me to come here with all his story and talk. I bumped into him when I was visiting the more cordial relatives toward you all down here—they didn't even know our side of the family existed, but that's another story. They're just as solitarian as you all here. But I guess you'd have to be, helpin' Negroes the way they do. And speakin' of stories, ol' Joe's stories could inspire the Devil to submit to Jesus."

Theresa chuckled. "I have a theory that there are no three other Joseph Peppers before him. I believe he's named after the holiday in July with all the excitement and fireworks in his wild storytelling, and in other ways—if I might add without losing my lady-like manners."

Sarinda stiffened as she processed and imagined Theresa's last words. Her chest tightened. She took three short gasps of air, and a carnal furor snapped within her like a pair of fingers coming together and popping on her most sensual point. "Uh, uh, oh…" Sarinda bumbled trying to gain composure. She cleared her throat and shifted herself in her chair. As the waiter passed by, Sarinda kindly asked for a glass of champagne. "Hell, if you can spare the bottle, bring the whole damn thing." A bottle of champagne was delivered to her shortly along with a glass already filled. Sarinda lifted the drink and gulped back a heavy hit. "Well," she began, "A man like that, even a free-bird of a woman like me would have to keep a promise to him." She took another gulp of champagne. "But there's nothing wrong with acting a little on instinct." She aimed her drink at Theresa and instructed, *"Go to New York,"* she said between laughs. *"Go meet your Joseph Pepper there. You have the talent and the opportunity. Go surprise him."*

Theresa paused and squinted. Her eyes rolled up in thought, and she turned away from Sarinda for a brief moment. Sarinda placed her glass down and asked, "Did I say something, Theresa?"

Theresa shook herself out of thought, composing herself proper. "No…" she recovered. "I…just had a familiar thought. Somethin' already seen, I believe. *Déjà vu.*"

"Some people believe it's a spiritual instinct to know you're on the right path," Sarinda encouraged.

Theresa looked at the red-haired charmer. She lifted her drink and declared, "I will go, then." She finished her drink in a large swallow. "Miss Fallows, if you can contact those music producers you bumped into, I would be most grateful. Can I take my band?" she asked pouring more champagne for herself.

Sarinda waved excitedly. "I don't see why not. They're part of the magic." She leaned forward and patted Theresa on the knee. "But let's not tell them anything until I can get word up north—and of course back down south."

Theresa clutched the folded veil, and Sarinda watched her action. "This garment must be magic after all," Theresa proclaimed in a relieved tone. She beamed a devious smile as she locked eyes with Sarinda. "You definitely can't touch it now." Sarinda's face remained still for a moment before managing a smile. Theresa looked back at the stage. "Two more songs, then the night is over for me. The place is clearin' out anyway. All that drink you done gave these people got them sluggish and *prayin'* they hit the bed and not the floor or the muddy earth outside."

They leaned back and hollered a barrel of laughter. Theresa choked down her girlish guffaws, stood and extended a hand. Sarinda instead stood rather than take Theresa's gesture. She lifted her glass, and Theresa pulled her hand back to lift her own. The two women tapped glasses. They drank to their union and finished their champagne. Theresa placed her glass down and returned to the stage. Sarinda took her seat again, refilling her glass and drinking as she watched Theresa complete a two-song set. Her eyes focused on the veil that was now wrapped around Theresa's arm like a coiled, fabric snake. When Theresa finished, she returned to Sarinda to dismiss herself for the night, and both women shook on a promise to hold a meeting in the morning.

Sarinda lifted her glass as Theresa departed. "To meeting your Pepper," Sarinda announced. Theresa bowed at the sentiment, and then disappeared to her room. Sarinda's eyes drifted to the band's drummer, and she rubbed her pendant saying in a low voice, "I can tell that you, mister, have an addiction to see to; a dragon to chase." The drummer stood up as he gathered his things, then he shook like a soaked dog casting off water. He dismissed himself from the band. The piano player looked disgusted and disappointed as he watched the drummer depart.

Sarinda chuckled and stood with her glass still in her mouth, drinking its contents. She grabbed Theresa's glass, the champagne bottle and her purse, and then skipped from Eve's Hallow and into Water Bug Hollow's bare streets and open night.

Dance and the overabundance of drink had shuffled the people to bed, tucked in by alcohol's influence. Amid the induced sleep, Sarinda Fallows walked down the muddy road toward the open, grassy field. She removed her shoes and let her feet sink and slosh in the mud. The few pedestrians remaining on the street couldn't see Sarinda, she stroking the pendant dangling around her neck.

Sarinda continued caressing the pendant until she came to a specific spot in the field, over Elias Jakobi's place of burial. "Here we are," Sarinda remarked. She filled both glasses in her hand with champagne, placing one down along with the bottle. She opened her purse and removed two reefer cigarettes and a small matchbook. She snapped her purse shut and dropped it on the ground. Sarinda put both reefer cigarettes in her mouth and lit them. One she kept between her lips, and the other she stuck into the ground, bending down and forcing it into the soft foundation.

Sarinda stood up and took a long drag. She exhaled and said, "Mister Elias Jakobi, these niggers sure will believe anything you tell them." She drank. She swallowed. She took another puff and exhaled. "That didn't last too long for you, I guess, with what happened with them unruly niggers in your service." She walked around the planted reefer stick and stationed champagne glass. She puffed and she drank. "My husband and I know what that was like. You remind me of my husband, Mister Jakobi. He was a great businessman too. We was cursed with niggers as unruly as the ones in your possession, handed down by my father who left the family business to my husband." When Sarinda was not drinking or puffing, she was fiddling with her pendant.

The planted reefer stick burned bright at its lit end.

The champagne in the glass slowly drained, its contents seeming to evaporate.

"This was a little after them days Mister Lynch taught us how to keep them niggers in line. We were still putting together his ideals. My husband was so good at that." She puffed. The world shifted. She exhaled. She drank. "But even the best laid plans have a shelf life." Sarinda stopped pacing. She smiled and twirled. "My husband will return to me, Mister Jakobi." She spun, smiled, and rubbed her belly. "He will come through me, and I will hold him." She stopped spinning, stumbling a bit from the whirl, smoke, and drink. Sarinda caught herself and chuckled. She rubbed the stone dangling from her necklace. The world stopped spinning, and her view straightened. The euphoric effect of the reefer and drink remained.

Sarinda's eyes drifted to the champagne glass situated at an angle on the grass, its contents lower. She spotted the small stalk of reefer planted into the ground, its body curling and disintegrating into ash while a spirit of smoke twisted up into the night. "If only the spirit of Elias Jakobi were really enjoying the moment here with me," she said to no one in particular. "Ain't nothin' but tricks make the champagne dissipate and the reefer stick burn lower." Sarinda bent down and said to the earth, "But I can still talk to your bones, Elias. They might not answer, but I can talk." Her lovely smile shifted into bright laughter. She stood and resumed spinning. "I dance for you and my husband, Elias. My charm will tickle you like it did those MacRitchies up north, and like it will tickle the Negroes of Water Bug Hollow."

The champagne in the glass lowered more, and then it was gone.

The reefer stick burned away, it's aroma and smoke drifting through the field like a peppery, aromatic, thin stream of fog.

Sarinda finished her champagne and reefer cigarette, gathered her things, said goodbye to Elias Jakobi, and returned to her room above Eve's Hallow. She skipped and rubbed her pendant the whole way back.

The few Water Bug Hollow pedestrians that roamed the streets didn't see her.

Mal-Ca-Dee

"Everything starts at the bottom, even stars."

Sarinda Fallows was a traveling socialite. Theresa Amat was a soulful jazz singer, stock-still in her birthplace of Water Bug Hollow. Joseph Pepper IV was the link between them. At least, that was the case for their initial meeting. But over the next two days the ties that bound the two ladies were conversations of jazz, the lights of New York, and champagne, with a smoky reefer stick puffed on occasion.

There was nothing more euphoric to Theresa Amat than the conversations about New York, and the possibilities the city offered to further her career as a singer. Sarinda professed that she couldn't pull herself away from Water Bug Hollow's allure. However, after the second day of her stay, she was gone, back to New Orleans. Theresa was surprised at first. Sarinda disappeared from Water Bug Hollow without notice of leave. Theresa became hopeful on the thought that Sarinda mingled with her aristocratic associates that had a connection to the big-time music producers and club owners in New York City. The end result was to meet Joseph Pepper there when he completed his business overseas, and Theresa never forgot about her ultimate goal. In hopes of dreams of her Pepper, Theresa covered her face with the veil every night before sleep.

There were no dreams of Joseph Pepper. Theresa only witnessed flashes of images not to be remembered when she awoke, but the images were very calming as she rested. The slowest, most beautiful piece of jazz played for Theresa; these were songs she would never remember when she stirred from sleep the next morning. Theresa's sleep was deep and refreshing. She awoke, stretched, and met the bright sun with an equally bright smile as she lifted from her bed. She felt sure that a new life was ahead of her; new forms of jazz and song would permeate music. All of it would radiate from her.

Theresa still showed no signs of worry when an entire week passed without word from Sarinda Fallows. Inspired, she sang just as powerful, even while waiting through a strained patience. Two days after a week went by, Sarinda Fallows traipsed back into Water Bug Hollow, elegant and as charming as ever.

"I have good news," Sarinda told Theresa with excitement glowing in her wide, bright green eyes. Sarinda had just returned to Water Bug Hollow. It was morning. She walked into Eve's Hallow and joined Theresa at their usual table. Theresa was already enjoying her breakfast. Sarinda propped her suitcase beside her. "The gentlemen I bumped into from New York, a group of Jewish fellows. They're the ones that recommended the hotel I'm staying over in New Orleans. They know the family that owns the place. They do business together." A waiter politely interrupted Sarinda, asking if she would like breakfast served to her. Sarinda ordered, "I'll have grits with Red-eye gravy, a buttermilk biscuit, two eggs—scrambled—and some country ham. Thank you. Oh, and some lemon water with ice." The waiter bowed and disappeared to fulfill Sarinda's order. She turned her attention back to an eager Theresa. Sarinda wasted no time diving back into her story. "Well, I spoke to the owners of the hotel when I arrived in New Orleans. I'm staying in a wonderful room at damn near half the price."

Theresa chuckled along with Sarinda, a hint of impatience behind her demeanor. She nodded her head affirmatively only to humor Sarinda. All the patience she had waiting for Sarinda's return was all but gone.

"This hotel is looking for entertainment," Sarinda stated, finally getting to the beginning of her point and calming Theresa's unseen impatience. "I told them that I could provide entertainment: A true jazz band from Water Bug Hollow. Why, I thought their eyes would damn near explode they got so big." Sarinda leaned closer. "I waived their generosity extended to me and offered to pay in full for the room and service I've been provided if, and only if, when they see this band I have for them—a band, might I add, that I said to them possesses a meadowlark in human form—" Theresa blushed, less from the compliment and more from the excitement. "Well, when they see this band I have for them, they must immediately pass word to them Jewish boys back in New York. They're looking to produce bands up there for several nightclubs opening up." Sarinda leaned back. Her hand went to her pendant, and her fingers caressed the stone medallion. She let go immediately when her hand felt a scratch. Her eyes searched Theresa for the veil. She realized it was being worn around her neck like a cowboy's bandana.

Sarinda concealed her disdain, which quickly turned to concern that the veil's proximity hadn't presented itself with any sort of pull or tug on her psyche. Concealing her emotions was not too hard, however. Theresa was too joyous to notice, slapping her hand against her chest, smiling wide and without shame. "Can I tell the rest of the band?" Theresa asked Sarinda with an excited voice that she managed to keep low so as not to disturb the other patrons.

"Absolutely," Sarinda encouraged, slapping Theresa's hand as a playful gesture. "The performance will take time to set up, which is why my return to Water Bug Hollow has not been so prompt. There was an incident at the hotel."

Theresa's expression shifted. "Oh, no!" she blurted.

Sarinda shook her head. "Oh, yes, I'm afraid. Nothing too concerning—to you anyway. A Negro maid who worked at the hotel was found murdered in an alley not too far from the place. She was beaten." Sarinda made a fist and pointed to it. "Dollar bills were found in her grip." She opened her hand and settled. Sarinda whispered, "There was evidence of sexual conduct. Dress all torn, undergarment below her knees. Violent. Many believe she was of ill repute. Prostituting." Sarinda paused for Theresa to consider the sentiment, and then she stated, "She served me a couple times. Always prepared the bathwater for me. Did any of this make its way to Water Bug Hollow? Did Miss Inda Gale hear anything about this?"

Theresa looked perplexed. "No, on both accounts. Did the woman know Miss Gale?"

Sarinda shook her head. "No, I guess not. It's all just my own prejudices showing themselves," Sarinda confessed in a reluctant voice. "The woman so closely resembled Miss Gale, I just thought she was a relative."

Theresa sat back and folded her arms. A scowl crept onto her visage as she expressed, "I guess we all look alike to you, Miss Fallows." A single eyebrow on Theresa rose.

Sarinda became flustered and defensive. "Oh, dear me. No. That's not what I meant. And, as I said, it was my prejudices—"

Theresa chuckled. "Chil', I'm only foolin' you," she said.

Sarinda fixed herself. Her breakfast was placed in front of her and she thanked the waiter, immediately giving a mocking, stern eye at Theresa. She lifted her fork. "You did have my emotions up and about. That was a good one, Theresa, but not very good of you. Wicked." She started to eat, and she changed the subject with her first bite and swallow. "Seven days," she said while concentrating on her food. "A whole week. Every night. That's how long you'll perform for these people." She looked up at Theresa. "Water Bug Hollow will have to deal with your absence."

Theresa paused. She thought about how her absence would affect nights at Eve's Hallow. Her eyes panned the restaurant's interior. She returned her gaze to Sarinda and said, "Well, we don't perform every night. We do need our rest. Other activities go on. There are town meetings held in here, and Mayor Johnson has put out word that there will be a grand announcement. He's been looking for a set of consecutive days where the people can gather to discuss some urgent news. He so hates to interrupt the music, even with politics."

Sarinda propped up from eating. Her expression was bright. She swallowed and said, "He'll have his time then. A little political business will get done. They won't miss the music too much; and they'll be relieved when it returns, at least before the music permanently leaves for New York City."

Sarinda's words prompted Theresa to think about arriving in New York City. "Yes," the songstress said while daydreaming, and then she called for the waiter who promptly came to her side. "Reginald, could you get word to my bandmates that I have news and business with them. Tell them to meet me behind the Hallow."

"Yes, Miss Amat," the waiter responded before rushing away.

Theresa went back to the remainder of her breakfast.

"While you speak with them, I'll make myself cozy in my room," said Sarinda.

The two women mirrored one another, delighting in what breakfast food remained on their plates. They wiped their mouths at the same time as they finished, and they stood from their chairs at the same moment. The women planted light kisses on each other's cheeks, and then said their goodbyes. Sarinda lifted her bag and made her way upstairs.

Theresa exited Eve's Hallow and walked through a clean alleyway, ending up behind the eatery and waiting for the rest of her band. They appeared quickly, one-by-one. Eugene, the drummer, was the last to arrive. He walked up to the rest of the group, fidgety, which drew a scowl from the piano player, Quincy. Theresa didn't notice the matter between the two gentlemen. She addressed all the members of the band.

"We'll be performing for a week in New Orleans," she announced with a bright smile. "Miss Fallows arranged for us to perform for a group of people with connections to producers in New York City; a big city club scene." Her bandmates lit up with excitement. Quincy's scowl melted into a twinkling grin. "Now, we'll have to wait," continued Theresa. "There's a bit of a fuss hanging around the hotel. It'll be a week or so. Things are already clearing up, as I understand it."

"What happened?" asked Eugene.

Theresa's answer was channeled through a reluctant stutter. "A Negro maid was prostituting on the side," she explained. "She was killed, and her being a Negro, I believe Miss Fallows doesn't want our presence to add to the incident."

Quincy's scowl returned. "Ain't like she was the only Negro woman, or Negro at all, in New Orleans. Shit, if anything, music could lift the mood. I'm sure if them white folks been payin' her proper, that sister wouldn'ta had to be doin' no hookin' on the side."

Theresa maintained a pleasant composure even when she contended, "Now, that's not the point, Quincy…"

Quincy waved his hands. "I know what the point is, but these white folks want to have they cake and eat it too. And at the same time they want us to entertain them while they eat it."

Theresa pressed a hard glare against Quincy, and her voice was stern when she responded, "I feel it's better than having them come here."

Quincy huffed. "They already here," he said referring to Sarinda's presence.

Theresa waved Quincy's sentiment aside. "Oh, hush!" she blared. "Miss Fallows is good people. One of the few MacRitchie people to come and visit without feeling obliged by an oath to keep us supplied with trade."

Quincy swallowed his anger before the situation got away from the excitement of the scheduled, New Orleans performances. "You're right, Theresa. Let's look at the bright side." He slapped Eugene in the belly and said with a wide grin, "All them Negroes jammin' in New Orleans, and it's us in Water Bug Hollow they want to hear." He turned his attention to Eugene. "You just stay out of trouble."

Eugene tried to suppress a guilty grin. "Whatchu mean, Q?"

"Nigger, you know what I mean," Quincy expressed, his face molded between grin and scowl.

Theresa interrupted. "Let our next performances be practice," she ordered her band. "We'll arrange our greatest numbers, but nothing too saucy."

"Nothing too saucy?" Quincy repeated as a question.

Theresa rolled her eyes. "Yes. Enough boom to show we can boom. Heavy music. The song selection will be different. Too much of what goes on in these lyrics might scare white folks. We like to say what we like to say, creative and filled with innuendo as it might be. No popular songs, though, unless requested. We stay original."

"I like that," remarked Cornelius, the trombone player.

"Now, let us keep quiet about the larger picture," Theresa suggested. "We'll make the announcement once we have confirmation that we are New York bound. No need to jinx ourselves." Everyone agreed. "Now, if there's no more to discuss, let us all go about our day. I'll see you all for tomorrow night's performance."

The band dispersed. Their daily routines and independent lives filled the remainder of the day. They joined together again, on stage for music, the following night. To them, the performance was practice, and their routine continued over the next three days. Sarinda, on a morning following a performance night, assured the band that all the commotion dealing with the death of the maid had been resolved. That night, their New Orleans performances were announced, and the Eve's Hallow audience cheered. The band and Theresa celebrated as loud and as jazzy as possible! The music swelled and burst, exploding into the first humming lights of dawn. Theresa and her band rested for a few short hours before waking up moments before noon and packing articles of clothing and wash items into a suitcase, freshening up with a shower or bath, and then traveling through Water Bug Hollow's nature-made tunnel and out toward the taxis heading to the train station.

The automobile was reserved for Theresa. The other bandmates filled the horse-drawn carriages, instruments stored up top, save for Eugene's drum set and Quincy's piano. Their instruments stayed behind, too cumbersome to drag along. But the both of them were promised their specific instrument would be provided on arrival for their performance.

The band was taxied to the train station. They exited their transportation and were greeted by Sarinda Fallows who was surrounded by four black men. Her eyes focused on Theresa's veil, the item again wrapped around the jazz singer's neck. Sarinda beamed at the band's presence. The young black men jumped forward as the band arrived and stepped out of their taxis. They took the band's suitcases and instruments, handling both with care. Sarinda handed each of the band members a ticket, and a fifth young black man escorted the band to the train's area designated for colored people. Sarinda blew a proud kiss and said as the band departed, "I'll see you all in New Orleans. It's a short ride."

And it was. The shortness of the ride didn't allow for a proper moment of anxiety about their upcoming performance, or even provide time for additional rest, having been up so late from the previous night's jam. But arriving in the grand city of New Orleans would change all of that. Theresa and her band marveled at New Orleans. Old world Paris and New world Dixie collided to create an aura of architecture that accented the perfect blend of the American South and Europe's Neo-Gothic poise of the mid- to late-nineteenth century. The blend of ages and style pricked at the band's senses. There was even a taste of the American Old West. Men dressed in elegant suits, monocles clasped to an opened eye and the chains of pocket watches dangling from the lapels on their left breast. Women, topped with flower-pinned, wide-brimmed hats to block the sun, wore elaborate dresses that were ruffled by bustles. They traipsed through the streets with men on their arms, streetcars passing by. Women with smaller hats twirled fancy umbrellas to stay hidden from the sun. The past's cultures, both local and overseas, melded together with a dash of the twentieth century, and acted as a red carpet to welcome the next decade just three years off. New Orleans' atmosphere mimicked Water Bug Hollow, but it gleamed brightly as it was opened to the shining sun. New Orleans was a diamond allowed to sparkle in contrast to Water Bug Hollow as a diamond still buried within its natural, coal encasement.

Sarinda sneaked up behind them and whispered, "New York is even more grand. Keep that in mind when you all perform." She walked past them. "Come," she beckoned.

Theresa and her band shook their heads to toss themselves back into reality. They followed close behind Sarinda into the New Orleans streets. Their items and suitcases were carried by a new set of black men. Sarinda led them on a long, arduous walk that didn't seem to end. Theresa and her band appeared to onlookers as a part of Sarinda's colored entourage. The men carrying Theresa and her bandmates' possessions started to lag, the walk taking its toll as Sarinda marched them all to a quaint, black-owned hotel named Brody's Rest Place.

Sarinda sauntered inside. Theresa and her bandmates followed, including the help carrying their belongings. A well-dressed, handsome, middle-aged black man named Hunter Brody, the hotel's owner, stepped up and engaged Sarinda. He bowed his head at the neck and asked in a courteous tone, "Miss Fallows, are these the guests you spoke about?"

"Yes," Sarinda answered. "They are from Water Bug Hollow, so be sure to treat them well. They know no other way." She turned and introduced the party. "This is Miss Theresa Amat."

Hunter bowed again. "How do you do, ma'am. Pleasure to host a talent like you. I've been to Water Bug Hollow, and I have been graced by the sweet sounds of your voice and rhythms of your band. I don't need any introduction, but please, show me around the band Miss Fallows." Sarinda introduced the others, Eugene, Quincy, the horn section, the guitarist, and the bassist. It was as if they were already famous. Hunter was star struck. "We've set up our most luxurious rooms to host you all. My staff has already helped you from the train, at Miss Fallows' request." He snapped at the men carrying Theresa and the band's belongings. "Show each of these fine musicians to their room. Take their things. Come on, now. These are Miss Fallows guests."

Hunter shuffled the band off, and the band followed the young bellhops through the lobby and toward a modern elevator. Quincy only moved forward to be away from Sarinda's ear. He stopped and waved Hunter toward him. Hunter approached, and Quincy complimented the hotel's owner on the modern fashion inside the hotel. "You got entertainment here in this dive? In need of any? We tryin' to start a tour. I know this New Orleans, there're jazz bands everywhere. But you've heard us play before. You know we get down."

Hunter chuckled. "Brother, I catch you. I catch you. We can definitely talk. I'm tryin' to expand this operation. Been tryin' to get back to Water Bug Hollow and speak to your Mayor Johnson."

Sarinda approached the conversation. "Quincy," she said sweetly. "I know you all banged out a long and loud performance last night. Might you get some rest?"

Quincy fixed his face to push away the instinctive reaction of a scornful expression and absolute annoyance. A smile came to him, and he said in a relaxed manner, "Miss Fallows, I appreciate your counsel, but I'm in the middle of a conversation."

"Excuse me, young man," Sarinda expressed as she put her hands on her hips. "You hold a smile on your face, but I can hear that hint of rudeness in dismissing me. Who do you think you're addressin'?"

"I thought I was speaking with someone that considered colored folks her equal," Quincy snapped back with less force in his voice than what he would have liked. "I appreciate what you've done for us thus far. I do. But, you don't manage the band. I got business to discuss before I take my rest. Thank you."

Sarinda remained still. Her face surprised by Quincy's lip and tone. Hunter backed away from his conversation. He stated to Sarinda in a tone reflecting his quavering smile, "Miss Fallows, we can do as you say." He looked at Quincy. "You do look tired, brother. Come on. Follow the rest of your people upstairs. Enjoy your great quarters we've set for you. It's on Miss Fallows' precious dime. In fact, more than a dime, right Miss Fallows?" Brody chuckled nervously. He said to Quincy, "Come on, brother." He pushed Quincy away in an attempt to make the piano player move in the direction of the elevator. One, two, three shoves is what it took for Quincy to budge. He turned around and walked toward the rest of the band and Theresa. Hunter followed, hissing low into Quincy's ear, "Boy, this might not be eighteen-seventeen, and Miss Fallows might be good white folk, but I ain't gon' let no nigger's mouth get my place burnt to the ground. I've worked too damn hard."

Quincy shook his arm loose from Hunter's grip. He fixed his suit and fedora and sighed away his crossness. "I apologize, brother."

Hunter stared at Quincy hard. Theresa asked, "What is the matter here?"

Quincy decided to explain to Theresa. "I got a little out of place with Miss Fallows. I was talkin' with Mister Brody here about a gig. She suggested I get sleep. I was offended, and showed it. She got a little upset. Perhaps I do need some sleep." He asked Hunter in a humble voice, "I didn't mean to put your establishment in any danger."

Hunter took a breath and calmed down. "I don't think you have. But I'm gonna have to smooth talk Miss Fallows a bit. Possibly give you all a discount; at least, suggest it. I hope she don't take the offer." He looked over at Sarinda who waited by the front desk, speaking cordial and flirtatious to the young black man behind it. "If so, you *will* be performin' in this establishment, but not for the price I was gon' pay for yo' sound."

Quincy couldn't help but smirk. "So we can still talk?"

Hunter rolled his eyes as he tried to suppress a smile. "Sheee-it. Your sound would put asses in the seat. I'd make a killin'. Yeah, Negro, we gon' talk." The elevator opened. An attendant waited inside. Hunter said in an even lower voice, "I know Miss Fallows was tryin' to split us up from a talk about business. I know she got you performin' for them white folk across the way."

"That deal could carry us to New York," Quincy explained, his smirk growing into a wide grin. "Miss Fallows ain't got nuthin' to worry about. That's why I said we tryin' to tour."

"Didn't work," Hunter noted. He shook Quincy's hand. "Enjoy your stay. Enjoy your room. And Miss Amat—" Theresa leaned closer as Hunter finished, "—keep this one out of trouble, please. This Negro gon' get y'all shot, hung, and burned."

Theresa took Quincy by the arm and pulled him into the elevator. "I most certainly will. Come on, Q. Let's keep you out of trouble and get you some much-needed rest."

The band and their assigned attendants shuffled into the grand, mechanical contraption. "Is this thing safe?" Theresa asked. "I've never been in one."

"It's safe, Madam," Hunter assured as the barred doors closed and the ride lifted upwards. Theresa and the other occupants, save the attendants accustomed to the ride, felt their stomachs leave them. Just as they went to take a breath, the ride slowed. The doors opened with a clunk and Theresa, bandmates, and attendants stepped out of the elevator and onto the hotel's sixth floor.

Below, in the lobby, Hunter Brody mustered as much humility as possible into his voice when he addressed Sarinda Fallows. Sarinda pardoned the entire scene, and she didn't blame Hunter for Quincy's ill manner. Hunter still presented his proposition of a discount, and to his luck, Sarinda declined. He insisted twice, for good measure, but Sarinda never took his offer. She left with a pleasant smile on her face, and the hotel resumed its daily operations, Hunter overseeing them with his wife and eldest son and daughter.

The band settled into their individual quarters. They were too tired to enjoy the impressive scenery, but they were each given an extra-large bedroom suite that included a full kitchen and a private balcony that overlooked the New Orleans streets, a full bathroom with indoor plumbing, a queen-sized bed and a seating area that held a sofa and chairs. However, the minute their belongings were placed inside their rooms, and their attendants cleared, exhaustion set in. It was not even noon. There was a long stretch of time before their night's performance, the first of seven. New Orleans was going to be their home for a week. Right now, all each of them cared for was the bed and pillow.

Theresa slipped into her bedclothes minutes before noon. She set her hair, covering it in a silk wrap, and then she slid into the bed, laid flat on her back and closed her eyes, covering her face with Joseph Pepper's gift. The veil. Her sleep was deep until an echoing voice penetrated her slumber. *Wake up and hear me knocking on your door, ma'am*, said the voice. If there was a dream, Theresa didn't remember it, but when she awoke from sleep she felt well rested and replenished, ready to start the night. At the end of her rest she heard again, *Wake up and hear me knocking on your door, ma'am*. Theresa's eyes opened. She took a breath, inhaling and exhaling the last of sleep.

It was six in the afternoon when Theresa opened her eyes. She stared at the door before heavy taps knocked against it. Theresa lifted the veil from her face and jumped out of bed. She checked the clock situated near the lamp on the side table, wrapped the veil around her arm, and rushed over to the door. She opened it and saw an elderly maid on the other side holding out a fancy plate of mixed fruits.

"I'm here on orders of Mister Brody," the woman announced politely as she strolled into the room, walking past Theresa. "This is your wake up service and snack. Compliments of the house." The woman placed the plated fruit on the bed at Theresa's command.

"Thank you," Theresa responded with a bright smile. She searched the pockets of her nightgown for bills and handed the maid two dollars, to which the elderly maid responded that she couldn't. "But, you will," Theresa insisted, placing the bills into the woman's hands and folding the woman's fingers over the money. "Now, you keep that." And to change the subject, Theresa asked, "Is the rest of my party also receiving wake up service and snack at this time?"

"Yes, ma'am," the woman answered putting the bills into her pocket.

"Then let me get dressed. Those are my bandmates. We have a performance tonight."

The elderly maid responded, "Should I prepare your bathwater, ma'am?"

"Why, thank you, but no," Theresa told the woman. "I have to practice notes for my voice. I like to sing over the running water. Again, thank you."

"That's okay, ma'am. I understand. Everyone has their ritual." The maid bowed and made exit through the door, closing it behind her. Theresa turned around, and darted across the room to the bathroom. She started a bath, plugging the tub's drain first, and then using the hotel's provided toiletries to make bubbles. Theresa turned the knobs for the water, placing her hand under the spout to feel for the water's warmth. When the temperature was right, Theresa dried her fingers and walked back into the front room. She tossed off her nightgown and loosened her slip and under garments. Naked and free, with just the veil wrapped about her forearm, and the rushing water flapping over itself and playing behind her, Theresa tested the ranges in her voice. She manipulated the musical scales fabricated by the air in her body and shaped by her throat and tongue to raise high and dip low. Her audio was never too loud or powerful. It was practice, and she didn't want to strain her voice before the performance.

Theresa picked out her clothes for the night, dressing herself to impress a man that was not there. She would sing to Joseph Pepper tonight. Theresa was only seven performances away from meeting him in New York City when he returned from overseas. She imagined her Joe Pepper was in the room with her, watching her as she twirled around naked, the only thing dressing her a wide, girlish, flirtatious smile. She plucked cherries, strawberries, and cubed watermelon bites from the plate of fruit given to her. Theresa periodically checked her bathwater, and she stopped it when it rose high enough in the tub. She ironed her clothes and returned to her bath, running more hot water to steam the bathroom up again.

Theresa unraveled the veil from her arm and placed it over her face as she stepped into the bath and soaked in warm memories of her and Joseph Pepper. She wore the veil thinking how much Joseph would have loved to see her bathing while wearing the garment, and then she wondered how he was doing and what lost stories he was uncovering at the moment. She pondered the items he would deliver to her, declaring them some sort of magical gift from an ancient African culture, or from Negro gods and Negro goddesses lost to time and myth.

Theresa soaked for fifteen minutes before she removed the veil and reached over to drape it on the bathroom counter. She retracted into the water, underneath the cloud of bubbles and continued to soak and cleanse. She used the soaps that she brought from Water Bug Hollow along with soaps provided by the hotel. After another fifteen minutes or so, completely scrubbed and feeling clean, Theresa unplugged the drain and stood up. She grabbed a towel and patted herself down, wiping away the moisture from her skin. She stepped out of the tub and dried her legs. When finished, she wrapped herself in the towel and walked to the front room. Theresa went to her suitcase and removed lotions made in Water Bug Hollow. She returned to the bathroom, towel tossed away on the bed, and lotions in her hand. She anointed her body and cleaned her face, the final act to her cleansing ritual. She uncovered her hair; it was short, flat, smooth and straight.

Theresa dressed in a fitted gown that glittered like stars against the night and she put on her veil, wearing it back to keep her face exposed until the performance. She stepped out into the hallway and locked the door to her suite. In the hall, she joined her bandmates who looked sharp with fancy suits and fedoras. The horn players, the guitarist, and the bassist were armed with their instruments carried in cases. Eugene held tightly to a pair of drumsticks. He was eager to sit behind his provided drum set and begin playing. Quincy moved his fingers as if they glided along a set of piano keys, practicing the chords to the songs on the night's set list. The band was met by a hotel attendant and escorted down the hall. The elevator ascended to meet them as they arrived, and they walked in and descended to the lobby.

Sarinda Fallows was there to greet them, Hunter Brody at her side. He grinned from ear to ear and he complimented Theresa on her style and beauty. He also extended compliments to the band, specifically how sharp they were dressed. "If your style is any indication on how you'll play tonight, we should be able to hear you from here," Hunter joked. "It will be a show. Hot damn. Miss Fallows, your audience will not be disappointed."

Sarinda agreed and then directed Theresa and the band to follow her. She explained as they walked through the hotel lobby and toward the door, "There is a fleet of carriages outside. You will be taken to *Le Pomme Rouge*. You all will enter from the back, through the kitchen. The hotel's lower level will be your space to prepare. There you will stay, until called for."

Theresa and the band stepped out of the hotel to an awaiting fleet of horse-drawn carriages and an automobile for Sarinda Fallows to ride in, the driver of which hopped from the vehicle and escorted Sarinda to the back, opening the door for her. A hotel attendant escorted Theresa to the nearest carriage behind the car, and each bandmate was taken to his own personal carriage as well. Theresa settled into her carriage seat, impressed and ready to enjoy the ride. The anxiety to perform dispersed and was substituted by an emotion of awe that made Theresa feel like royalty.

The automobile chauffeuring Sarinda pulled into the street and the carriages followed in tow. Theresa noticed the New Orleans' pedestrians marveling at her cavalcade of musicians. She kept her eyes focused forward, spying the foot traffic as it paused and stared at her fleet. Her line of vision was able to decipher the crowd's bodily gestures indicating the curious onlookers' admiration. Her bandmates acknowledged the crowd, mostly the women folk. They tipped their hats and beamed charming smiles. The hornsmen had their encased instruments propped up next to them like a second passenger. Theresa didn't look directly at the pedestrians that watched them pass. She truly felt as if she was not ready yet. They were just curious; they didn't recognize her. Eventually they would, and she would wave to them.

Theresa took a breath and thought about the contemporary style of jazz music, its ability to be recorded with such ease and even now being spread through radio. In this year alone the Dixieland Jazz Band made the first jazz recording. Jazz was ablaze across many American cities. It was growing, evolving, but it was the white boys that were taking all the credit from the style's Negro originators. Theresa and her band would record an album and spread jazz as the gospel. They would make it larger than life. The onlookers had no idea they were watching history in the making. And Theresa thought to herself that when she received the proper recognition, then she could wave back.

Theresa wondered if Joseph could stomach the attention from the various lookers-on that would recognize her. She took comfort in the thought that Joseph Pepper would spin a tale of the two of them being the reincarnations of some great royal couple from Africa's ancient past or from some lost African mythology.

Theresa smiled. She was tempted to wave back, but she thought it would be silly now. She stayed her hand and enjoyed the ride, watching the spectators color go from dark brown, light brown to white. The spectators' facial expressions were removed of smiles when the crowd became white.

The ride ended in an alley next to the *Le Pomme Rouge* hotel. The building's garbage littered the back lane. Sarinda exited the automobile, her driver leaping from the vehicle first and coming around to open the door. She stretched one leg long to straddle a dirty puddle. The driver reached for her hand and pulled her the rest of the way across the shallow, murky pool. She walked around to the front of the building and disappeared inside through the hotel's front doors.

Theresa and her band sat in their horse-drawn taxis patiently. The hotel's side door leading into the kitchen opened. A flock of black servants poured out, all men. They attended to the carriages and helped the band out. Sarinda stood in the doorway. She made a quick pivot as the black servants rushed by her and gathered Theresa and her band to escort them to their dressing room. "To the lower level," Sarinda instructed with a subtle sharpness in her tone.

Theresa and her band were led through an empty kitchen. Then they entered into the back of the hotel, through a long corridor, down three, short flights of stairs and into a dingy, gray room that resembled an unfinished basement. An old desk and chair lay against the wall to the left. A faucet and sink was placed at the far end of the room. A light dangled from the ceiling in the middle of the room, the bulb of which was exposed without shade. There were no windows and the sole, dangling light did little to brighten the far ends of the space. The room's middle glowed with a cone of light shining down on it, keeping the worn, Victorian style loveseat in a bright spotlight. Three chairs, just as worn (but were at one time very elegant and chic) lay at the borders of the spotlight's circular, radiance.

The attendants took leave, commenting that they received a good tip from Miss Fallows and needn't receive pay again from Theresa or her bandmates. Quincy was already shuffling bills in his hands when this was told to him. But the escorts had already left. The door closed. Quincy pocketed his money. The band stayed silent as their eyes went to and fro, inspecting the dreary room. Theresa moved to the desk, a bounce in her step. In a piquant voice she said, "This is the bottom, gentlemen. Everything starts at the bottom, even stars." She bent over and looked at herself in the mirror on the desk, her reflection barely visible with little light shining on that side of the room.

Quincy snickered and moved farther into the room, stepping beyond the huddle of his fellow band members. "I guess," he commented.

Theresa observed Quincy by way of the mirror. She stood up straight, prompted by his sentiment, and she turned with her legs elegantly bestride, tightening the dress to her shape, and her hands on her hips. "There's no need to guess, Q, when you know the facts. There's nothing more impressive than an ascending star; and baby, that's what each of us be." She looked around the room. "Why, when we get to New York, and after we make a recording, they'll be new constellations in the sky. And no room will ever be too dim. The brilliance we cast as stars will brighten a room absent of light." She coolly walked over to the loveseat and wiped a single finger over the frame. "Our elegance and cool will mend the fabric of the most ragged material. Our musical magic will polish the tarnish from any worn piece of furniture. And that's if anyone so dares—even white folks—to throw us in a dungeon like this."

Quincy snarled as he suppressed a grin, "You even startin' to sound like that nigger of yours. Joe Pepper."

Theresa straightened herself and reached over the loveseat to slap Quincy on the shoulder. "Oh, hush, Q. Have a seat."

Quincy shook his head. "Oh, no. My suit is much too clean to touch somethin' of that nature."

The other band members started chuckling. The lighthearted mood was broken up by Sarinda Fallows' entrance into the room. The band members that were still huddled near the door moved closer to the middle of the room to make way for Sarinda. "It's seven-thirty. You all have thirty minutes before the performance. Take deep breaths. The piano has been tuned. The drum set is there. You'll be introduced shortly as the musical entertainment for the night." She smiled and put her hands together adding, "All the big-time players are in the building. They'll be listening and watching. You all take their breath away." Sarinda started to step backwards toward the door. "Backstage, there will be brandy and finger foods. Enjoy." Sarinda exited through the door with a smile wide on her face, eyes remaining on the band.

Theresa sat down on the chair near the desk. Eugene took a seat on the dingy loveseat, and other band members took the remaining seats. Quincy remained standing as he went over the band's arrangement, "We'll start off with two simple numbers; ease this audience into music. The second number will be a li'l louder. Then we'll get quiet again. Theresa will make her entrance."

"As planned," Theresa acknowledged.

The horn players, guitarist and bassist opened their cases. The guitarist and bassist tuned the strings on their instruments. Eugene twirled his drumsticks. Quincy exercised his fingers. Theresa fixed her veil and cleared her throat. Sarinda Fallows disturbed their various rituals when she once again entered the room. "Let's make our way to the stage. Come. Up. They're ready for you."

Those sitting stood up. Theresa was completely veiled and Sarinda's eyes became fixed on her. There again, from behind the veil, Sarinda spotted the faint glow of the sun-like, cobalt-blue blaze peering through. Sarinda cleared her throat and clutched her pendant. She blinked and the peculiar manifestation was gone. Sarinda exhaled. "Come. Follow," she instructed.

The band filed out of the dingy room and followed Sarinda through the various corridors that led to the back of the stage located in the hotel's grand ballroom. The musicians took their place on stage from behind a closed curtain. Theresa tucked herself away behind a second black curtain that blended with the stage's background. She sat on a stool, waiting for her cue. Sarinda Fallows wished them luck, and then she disappeared to watch the show from the audience.

The Master of Ceremonies introduced the band as a group of Negroes come from Water Bug Hollow to entertain them. Then the curtain opened. There was light applause. The band started playing a whimsical number. Each band member beamed wide, toothy smiles as they looked out into an audience they could barely see with the lights showering the stage.

The ballroom was fanciful. Men dressed in tailored-to-fit tuxedos and women who wore ornate and glamorous gowns sat at circular dining tables. Very few paid much attention to the band. Their conversations and dining continued. Quincy wondered how they would prove to a group of music producers that they were a party-pleasing jazz band without really getting down. But he knew that somewhere in the audience was a batch of men that presided over the decision that would lead to a bigger meal ticket. For the most part, Quincy, through the light's glare, could only see an opened and unoccupied dance floor. Beyond the dance floor, before the light's glare blurred out the audience, there sat a host of white men and women that talked and dined through the band's playing. The Water Bug Hollow jazz band was just background music, and barely that.

The first number lasted ten minutes. There was a slight pause before the second would begin. There again was mild applause from the audience at the close of the first song. The band members kept their smiles and rolled into the second number. Theresa squirmed in her seat, still waiting behind the black curtain. She concentrated on the songs she would sing, and that calmed her. This was her moment.

The second number faded. The lights dimmed. The atmosphere changed. Theresa slipped from the stool and waited. The band's music hummed a slow jazz melody. Theresa stood in a pose, hands on her hips. She felt the vibration in the bassist's strings. She felt the fluttering waves of sound purred by the horns. The curtain opened, and she walked forward until she came to the microphone.

She sang. Her sweet voice dived into the music like water, becoming one with its sound and complimenting its flow. *"Charles. Chuck. Buddy Bolden. Your music—Jazz your creation—it's holdin' my soul."* The dining stopped. Conversations ceased. The band had the full attention of the audience. Theresa continued singing, *"To your jazz I say, 'Hello'. Yes. Charles. Chuck. (My) Buddy Bolden. Your music—Jaaaazz your creation—it's holdin' my soul. And do you know, Bolden that your music's got me open to love that melts all the cold that's frozen our world to war and hate. Can you my audience relate—to the sounds of jazz?"*

Sarinda sat in the back of the audience and watched their reaction. They were stiff but attentive. Sarinda's eyes went to the stage. She watched the veiled woman croon. The glow underneath her veil resonated to life again and became brighter. No one but Sarinda could see it, not even Theresa herself could feel the warm glow resonating from her.

The music accompanied Theresa as she growled the lyrics, engulfing the audience's attention more. *"King Bolden, ain't no other royalty more deservin'. Coronate with your cornet. Catch me with the notes in your cor-net. Charles. Chuck. (My) Buddy Bolden. I turn to your music when my heart is broken. Your city's lights holds all the ghosts that possess you at this moment."*

And she crooned and crooned until a crescendo bloomed. The song reverberated with an explosive ending, complimenting Theresa's voice with a heavy, melodic crash of notes. The audience jumped to their feet and applauded. The band paused for only a moment's notice before jumping into a traditional ragtime song. Theresa tossed back her veil at the boom of the first note. She jumped into a song made of lyrics that lured the sitting and dining people to swarm the dance floor. The open space became occupied with bodies performing very conservative dances, but enjoying themselves none-the-less.

The music became heavier as the night went on. The instrumentals performed by the band in an effort to allow Theresa to rest her voice bordered on raucous, but never quite boiled over. Quincy was more satisfied playing the heavier pieces, believing it showcased the band's musical prowess than the intricate arrangements of the slower songs.

Sarinda met Theresa backstage to compliment her and tell her that everyone in the audience was enamored with her and the band. "Thank you," Theresa said as politely as possible as she took a swig of brandy to help her throat. "Right now, Sarinda, I'm in my element. I'll speak after the show. Please, let me be."

Sarinda's teeth scraped together, offended by Theresa's brush off. But she managed to hold a smile as she replied, "Absolutely, Theresa. Miss Amat, if you prefer at the moment." She backed away and returned to her seat in the audience. Theresa returned to the stage to end the show. The performance settled down promptly at midnight. There was applause as the band left the stage. In the back, the members congratulated one another. The first night was a success. "But, far from over," spoke Sarinda as she stepped into the band's circle. "There's an after party that I'd like you to attend. Mingle with the names that will help put you all's names in lights."

Quincy exhaled as he smiled. The exhilaration from the night's performance became overrun by exhaustion. "Miss Fallows, we never seem to be on the same page," he commented while giving his belly a slap. "I think I'm going to finally catch up on rest, if you don't mind."

"Not at all, Quincy," Sarinda said, happy to hear the piano man yield to his fatigue. "We just need a representative from the band, and I believe just one or two will do." She turned to Theresa. "Miss Amat?"

"I'd be too nervous," Theresa blushed. "I wouldn't know what to say."

Sarinda assured, "Say nothing at all, dear. That's all you'd have to say. Nothing. I'll introduce you to people, and you would just shake hands and smile."

"No offense," Theresa started, "but, white folks…"

Sarinda waved the comment away. "Honey, everybody mingles at The Lounge." She cupped her hand and whispered. "Don't tell that to the government." She laughed. "Of course, you'll see some senators and local representatives lettin' loose their inhibitions." Sarinda put her eyes on Eugene. "You've been, Eugene. Would you like to join in the festivities tonight?"

Quincy's mood changed. He looked at Eugene with a stern expression. The rest of the band looked at Eugene with surprise, including Theresa. She said to Eugene, "I'd feel more comfortable with your presence if you're use to this sort of atmosphere."

Quincy spoke up, "No you won't. That won't be your scene, Theresa. I recommend you get some rest too."

Sarinda scoffed, "She is a grown woman, Quincy. And a larger career is on the line." She turned from Quincy and addressed, "Eugene, the question still stands."

Eugene answered in a hesitant tone, "I'll be there."

"Theresa," Quincy protested as he stepped forward.

"I will be fine, Q," Theresa affirmed. "Eugene and I won't be long. It's just for a little wind down. Some wine, a smoke." She turned to her drummer. "Come on, Eugene. The rest of y'all get some rest."

Quincy suppressed the desire to speak again. He listened as Sarinda instructed he and the remaining band members on taking the taxi service back to Brody's Rest Place. Then, she and Theresa, who was linked arm-in-arm with Eugene, went their separate ways once the other band members left the building. Sarinda, Theresa and Eugene jumped into an automobile and were chauffeured to a converted mansion resting in a New Orleans suburb. This was The Lounge. Lights in the mansion glowed from every window, and the large house looked as if it was a multi-eyed monster peering through the low-hanging foliage. The vehicle drove closer, winding onto the driveway. Theresa could hear the recorded ragtime music blaring from the house and filling the social scene. Reefer and cigarette smoke blazed the joint and poured from the opened front door. People mingled inside and out on the lawn. A train of giggling bodies drank and smoke, an intoxicated chorus line leading from outside on the lawn and snaking into and throughout the house. Closed curtains perfectly previewed people's silhouettes, carrying on no differently than the people outside.

"Is this where you disappear to, Eugene?" Theresa asked.

Eugene kept his eyes on the scene as he answered in an uninspired voice, "Yes, ma'am." He looked anxious. The taxi stopped. Sarinda, riding in the front, stepped out first. Eugene followed, and Theresa slid after him, exiting the automobile. An anxious feeling came over her, but she hid it from the others. She stroked the veil wrapped around her arm as if it was a pet. She took a breath and looked at Sarinda who had a smile on her face. "Let's go inside, shall we," Sarinda instructed.

Eugene was several strides ahead of Theresa, and she reached long for him. Eugene stopped. Theresa looped her arm around his. Her reach for him made her trip, but she remained on her feet, using Eugene's body for support. Sarinda chuckled at the display and continued leading the way.

It was bright inside. The foyer was decorated with photos, scenic paintings and portraits, and carnival masks. The area was clogged with people that spilled from different rooms, and even lined the stairs. Theresa's heart skipped when she realized she'd lost Eugene as she waded through the mostly white crowd. A hand grabbed her by the wrist, and Theresa looked up to see Sarinda smiling and drawing her closer to a large study that was filled with reefer smoke blown from most of its occupants. The strong aroma made Theresa lightheaded on contact, and out of nowhere appeared a stocky, well-dressed white man with a mustache and receding hairline. He carried a drink in his hand and what seemed like the whole party in his greeting. The man looked at Sarinda and complimented, "Miss Fallows, that was fine entertainment you brought to us this evening. Splendid. Wonderful." He took a sip of his drink. "The colored jazz singer, a beautiful voice. Have you brought her here to be a doe for gentlemanly purposes?" The man never acknowledged Theresa and spoke about her as if she wasn't present.

Sarinda answered, "No, no, Martin. Not this one. There's enough entertainment here as it is. She's here to relax. One of her bandmates frequents The Lounge. It's just a cool down." Sarinda's grip tightened and she dragged Theresa into the study. Sarinda stopped a butler as he passed by. A fancy silver dish lined with reefer sticks rested in his hand. Sarinda grabbed two, slapped down four dollars and waved the man away. She gave one to Theresa and said, "To relax you."

"Thank you," Theresa said graciously.

The butler didn't move despite being waved away. He stood there to light the cigarettes, and when he saw the two women take a puff and long drag, assuring that their reefer was lit, he disappeared into the crowd. Theresa puffed more, seeking to relax. Sarinda handed her a drink. More people came up to them. Theresa remained calm. She was never spoken to directly, though she was the subject of much of the talk, mostly her performance. Sarinda handled all the chatter, all the while keeping her charming smile and rubbing her pendant. Theresa's anxiety increased, and as it did she puffed and drank more. Sarinda introduced her to more people. There were more compliments on the performance, and possibly one or two of them were the people that were ready to pass the word about her to their contacts in New York City. Theresa never knew for sure. Her head swirled. Her arm, wrapped with the veil, felt heavy. An hour, or maybe two or three, passed. Theresa didn't know. Minutes mingled into one another, dancing in seconds. Drunken twirls of time spun off their axis. Theresa and Sarinda moved into a conservatory that was bare of any foliage, but rather occupied by cots where rested one, sometimes two, people. Theresa, her head spinning from drink and smoke, sat down on one. Sarinda bent down and spoke to her.

"Let's relax you more, darlin'," suggested Sarinda. "You need to try this. There's a reason for its name, Theresa. It is every bit a feminine savior. If there was ever a true release for a woman, this is it. Let freedom and liberation ring. You will be free with this coursing through your body."

Theresa was handed a glass-blown Pyrex tube. Smoke whirled dreamily inside. Her eyes spied Eugene on a cot. He reached up sluggishly toward the ceiling. His body swiveled and he moaned. Theresa inhaled the smoke from the tube, and everything was sealed with a venomous, intoxicating prick from a needle's tip.

Theresa lay flat on the cot. A flame resembling the celebratory bonfire that burned on Water Bug Hollow's independence day flickered in front of her. Sarinda asked to take the veil from Theresa, and Theresa answered, "No. My Pepper would not have it so." She unraveled the veil from her arm, but she did not place it on her face. Rather, Theresa blanketed her belly.

She relaxed. There was no anxiety. There was only space between here and everywhere, and Theresa was there. She dreamed while wide awake. She could hear jazz's evolution. The dream of music evolved into the reality of the next six nights' performances. The shows were perfect, and the nights were capped with the continuing ritual of going to The Lounge and relaxing with drink, reefer smoke and golden-dragon smoke and liquid cocaine. The ritual followed Theresa back to Water Bug Hollow, which had been in disarray since her music had gone to New Orleans. Disagreements and petty grievances over a new order to build a church in the field sullied Theresa and her band's return.

Theresa didn't bother with the news, nor did any of her bandmates. That night, the air of disdain cleared with a true, jazzy and raucous performance that exercised the demons that had the townsfolk in dispute. And after the performance, liquor and smoke perfumed Theresa's apartment. Sarinda joined her. They laughed and smoked and drank.

Theresa twirled around, nightgown hanging off her frame. "This has me free, Sarinda. Freedom. This is culture," she said taking a sip of her drink.

Sarinda coaxed with a smile, "Slow it down, child. We ain't in Harlem yet." She took a drink and a drag of her reefer stick. "Word is being passed north. Save some of your upbeat spirit for when we get there. It won't be long."

Smoke and alcohol drenched Theresa's senses, and she fancied more. She rested on her bed and spoke in a slurred, dreamy speech, "This damn town. Ungrateful. There's a threat. They're mad 'cause they need to make change. Damn politics have these people inside and out. Got them forgettin' what needs to be preserved. And you done good Miss Fallows by bringing that information here. Ain't a need for people to get upset. We just need to be a li'l mo' quiet for caution's sake. Ungrateful." Theresa slumped down in the bed. She exhaled. The smoke and drunkenness dragged her closer to an unconscious state.

Sarinda stood from the chair resting in front of the room's vanity and bent down by the bed. "Theresa, you need me to take this veil from you?" she asked.

Theresa shook her head and responded as she had done for the last seven nights, "No. My Pepper would not have it so." Then Theresa removed the veil that was wrapped like a snake around her arm. She unfolded the garment and laid it over her belly with a smile on her face. Sarinda left the room.

The door closed and then the dream came. Its arrival was like a scream, but that was as furious as its scenery ever got. The environment was serene in contrast. The dream presented a gray, misty day in Water Bug Hollow's wide-open field. Strands of mist came from the ground and formed into translucent images from Water Bug Hollow's past residents. There were slaves, the slave master and his family, and other plantation hands. The dream allowed Theresa to recognize Slave Master Elias Jakobi. His ghost stood atop a wide tree stump and yelled to the ghosts of his plantation overseers. *"There is still hope,"* screamed the ghost of Elias Jakobi. *"We will not rest. We have been awakened. These rebellions will stop. They happened long ago but we have a plan. There are new ways to put them in line. I give you a new plan. A friend has spoken to my bones. She will lead us. She will help us. She has seen this before."*

Then Theresa heard another voice. It was young, soft and feminine. It was the voice of a little girl. She was pleading to her mother. *"Mamma, I'm fighting him. Mamma, don't let him in."* Theresa realized the little girl's voice was speaking to her and she turned around. A breeze ruffled the trees as if it was the breath of the little girl's cries. *"Great Grandmama's blessing is protecting me, but don't let him in, mamma."* The girl's voice, though soft, muted the loud rally held by Elias Jakobi's ghost and the apparitions of the overseers. Sarinda appeared with her smile and charm. She walked up to Theresa and cupped her wrist, holding it up.

"May I take a bite, Theresa? On the wrist?" She chuckled and waved her hand. *"Don't mind that silly rally. Ghost can't harm you, even if they haunt you. May I take a bite, Theresa? On the wrist? If not, just go to sleep."*

"I'll go to sleep." Theresa answered. Sarinda let go of her wrist, and Theresa walked back into Water Bug Hollow proper, and to her room in Eve's Hallow. She opened the door and a rat scurried out. She paid the creature no mind and noticed Sarinda was already in the room sitting in a chair stationed next to the bed. Theresa crawled into bed, her right arm extended and bare. A snake slithered over the bed and bit her on the wrist.

Theresa woke up. It was morning. Her stomach gurgled. She jumped from the bed and charged to the bathroom where she vomited in the sink. Her dream was distant. All that remained were feelings, but all that she concentrated on at the moment was emptying her stomach in a sickly fashion. Theresa ran the faucet to clean the sink. She cupped her hand under the faucet, caught water, and scooped it into her mouth. She gargled the water and then spit into the sink. She walked back into the room, breathed out and kept the back of her hand against her forehead. She prepared herself a drink with the cognac resting on her vanity. She took a large gulp. The liquor bubbled away the uneasy feeling in her stomach and Theresa drank more.

Sitting at her vanity, with her legs crossed, Theresa panned the room with her eyes. Joseph's gifted veil lay on the bed neat and undisturbed. She put her glass down, stood, and walked over to the bed. She fixed the veil around her face and twirled around. She giggled as she danced, then she stopped and wrapped the veil around her arm. Theresa walked to her closet, opened it, and inspected its contents. Her stomach gurgled again, but quickly settled. Her eyes spotted an outfit for tonight's performance. She removed the dress from the rack and laid it out across the bed. She also found an outfit to wear for the time leading up to the performance.

Theresa checked the clock. It was twelve-thirty. She prepared and slipped into a hot bath, tidied her person, dressed and then went downstairs to have a mid-day brunch in Eve's Hallow café. Theresa noticed that on the clearest day, Water Bug Hollow was in a fog; it was more about its current, sullen mood. There was still the air of disdain and bitter politics. Theresa ignored the thick atmosphere of public affairs and the gossip it stirred. She ventured out to the open field and surveyed the empty scene.

A church would fit right nice here, she thought to herself. *It wouldn't interfere with the authentic culture of Water Bug Hollow, or its celebratory rituals.* Theresa heard more political gossip and disdain coming from two townsfolk behind her. She looked up at the sun and smiled as she said with a sigh, "I appreciate your day, great star. But, I long for the moon's ambience. These people are so miserable in the daytime as of late; we can only give them solace by night with song and dance, jazz and blues. And Lord knows I have my own solace to find in a little smoke and drink. If you could run instead of walk, great star. Run to the other side of the world. We need the moon right now, the lesser stars and the dark background."

The day, despite Theresa's plea, took its time (as the day usually does). Nevertheless, the night made an appearance, and it was not too soon after that Eve's Hallow vibrated with the sounds of Theresa's band. Soon after that, Theresa fell back into her ritual of booze, reefer and heroin smoke with a shot of cocaine in her arm. Sarinda was there to share the moment in Theresa's room. And as Theresa lay back on the bed with the veil wrapped around her forearm, and her intoxication lulling her into a deep sleep, Sarinda came next to her, knelt down and asked in a polite manner, "Theresa, you need me to take this veil from you?"

Theresa shook her head and responded as she had done the previous nights: "No. My Pepper would not have it so." Then Theresa removed the veil wrapped like a snake around her arm, unfolded the garment and laid it over her belly with a smile on her face. Sarinda left the room empty-handed.

The door closed and another dream broke through sleep's initial darkness.

Theresa's dream was set aboard a train. She was heading north to New York City. A beautiful young black woman sat next to her. The young woman was in her early twenties and beaming as she looked outside the window at the passing scenery. Sitting in front of Theresa and the young woman were two black men talking about politics. One said to the other, *"They send drugs in Harlem down here to pacify us. They send alcohol down here to pacify us. They send prostitution down here to pacify us."* The other commented, *"And they will reduce me to nothing more than a dreamer, us to opposing views, and the most important of what I have to say will be hidden from view of our people."* Theresa and the young woman looked out the window. There were the ghosts from Theresa's earlier dream. Elias Jakobi shook his fist at the passing train. He turned to his audience of plantation hand specters and yelled something that Theresa could not hear. Jakobi was holding another rally.

The young woman turned to Theresa, smile still on her face. *"Grandmama!"* she expressed. *"I'm going to find papa's paintings. They're in Harlem. I will sing like you when I'm there."*

Theresa looked away from the young woman who appeared to be her granddaughter. The young woman repeated what she had said. Theresa looked forward. The two black men seated in front of her continued to speak politics. Her eyes drifted to the end of the train car, near the door. There stood Joseph Pepper. He mingled with three other men. One was a dark-skin man in a suit and tie. The other was a brown-skin man wearing an elaborate headdress, a turban with a feather. He was in a long, beige white jacket and brown slacks. The last looked like a mulatto, or Creole. His skin was light and his hair was wavy and jet-black. He had a mustache, as did all of the men who congregated. He wore a suit from the late eighteen hundreds.

Then came the voice of a little girl, the same from the night before. *"Mamma. He's coming. Mamma, help!"* She sounded frightened.

Joseph stopped his conversation and approached Theresa with hurried steps. A raggedy-haired wolf, a snake with blistered skin, and a dingy rat scurried up the aisle. Joseph kicked the animals away. *"Get away. Get back."* The animals turned and ran away. Joseph then reached for Theresa. *"Come,"* he told her. *"We're going. Get up. Hand-in-hand."*

Theresa looked at Joseph. Both she and he shared a concerned expression. *"Grandmama,"* said the woman next to her as she faded away. Theresa stood up and followed Joseph to the back of the car. Then all went dark. Theresa could hear the little girl crying. There was a soft glow that appeared from out of the darkness. In the center of the light was the little girl, her color the mix of Joseph Pepper's reddish-brown skin and Theresa's dark swirl. She was eight years old and dressed in a traditional, white Southern Belle dress with white lace-trim and a wide-brim hat to match. She immediately reached up and put her arms around Theresa and held her tight. *"Mamma, he's coming again. I'm scared. Don't let him get me."*

The wolf, snake, and rat came from out of the darkness. First, appeared their bright eyes. Then the wretched animals stepped into the light baring fangs. *"Theresa,"* came a familiar woman's voice. Theresa recognized it as her mother's voice. *"Breathe, little girl,"* her mother instructed. *"Breathe deep. Like you're trying to sing. Exhale and lift up, deep. Like a loud note. Exhale, little girl. Make it come up. From the deep. Come on now."*

Theresa woke up. Her stomach felt as if it was filled with tar, and the feeling was rising, gurgling up into her throat. She jumped up, rushed to the bathroom, and vomited in the sink. Her morning ritual started again. She washed her mouth out, washed the sink, and then made herself a glass of cognac to tame her stomach. She picked out her clothes for the day and her evening attire. She went about her daily activities and jumped into her night's performance, routine and ritual. And it all happened all over again: booze, dragon chasing and a kiss from a syringe, all with Sarinda Fallows present. Sarinda always asked to remove Theresa of the veil, but was never allowed to do so.

"No. My Pepper would not have it so." Theresa's answer remained unchanged.

Sarinda would leave her room. The door would close.

Dreams.

Theresa remained on a steady diet of smoke and booze for three months. Her consumption was handled well enough to wait after performances, but her nightly ritual with Sarinda Fallows, or alone on some occasions, was rarely missed. Theresa was never too intoxicated to forget the superstitions of Joseph Pepper, however. And so, every drugged and drunken night ended in a ritual whereby Theresa placed Joseph Pepper's grandmother-blessed veil across her belly after refusing Sarinda's kind advance to relieve her of the garment. Then Sarinda Fallows would leave the room.

Dreams.

Mamma Indigo
"I can be many things; but, what I won't be, is ignored."

Theresa awoke this morning feeling fine. She had not indulged in her after-performance ritual the previous night. She freshened up, dressed and had a delicious breakfast downstairs in Eve's Hallow café. By three o'clock in the afternoon, she would lose her delicious breakfast to nausea, and would remain in that state for several days straight. The constant regurgitation left her so exhausted that several nights' performances would have to be canceled.

The band played without her, and her after-performance rituals with Sarinda Fallows also ceased, which seemingly did no good for Theresa's body as it ached and broke into cold sweats from lack of liquor, heavy smoke, and needle pricks of cocaine to the arm. She rested most of the day, undisturbed and with Joseph's blessed gift laid across her belly. Wearing the veil calmed her anxiety and soothed her aches and pains to a degree. But, the nausea seemed to increase, and most often lead to vomiting.

Quincy visited Theresa on the afternoon of the fifth consecutive day of her absence from the band's performances. She was feeling better, and informed her piano player, "I'll be singing tonight. I feel fine. I had breakfast delivered up to me, and I've been able to keep it down." Theresa was sitting up in her bed, veil laid across her stomach. She stroked the fabric like a cat, a Cheshire grin on her face. "And I've felt inspired, Q. I got new songs. The band will learn them in time." She then asked, "Have we heard anything on Miss Fallows' end about New York?"

"No," said Quincy as he sat on the edge of the bed. "She's been around, though. She asks about your health." He hesitated before asking, "You okay to perform tonight?" Theresa didn't answer audibly. She shook her head, yes, which made Quincy believe that she wasn't too confident in the possibility. "You sure, now?" he pressured.

Theresa spoke. "Yes, Q. I'm sure. And after the performance I will speak with Miss Fallows and get some answers for us." Theresa shifted. Her body ached. Quincy again asked if she was okay and she responded, "The ghosts are leaving me, Q. I ain't had a drink or a puff of hard smoke, or anything else, for a good while now. My body is exorcising itself of those demons." Then Theresa admitted, "But, I'm scared, Q. Frightened."

"You'll be fine, Theresa," Quincy assured her. "Maybe you should give it one more night."

"I will perform tonight," Theresa insisted. "And dammit, I know I'll be fine, but…" Her hand clutched the veil. "That's not the problem. I don't need a doctor to give me a prognosis on what's going on. I know." A smile quivered into existence. Her eyes watered. "There's no ailment that I suffer from. I'm pregnant, Q. I'm carrying my Joe Pepper's baby, and I've been abusing that child." Her clutched hand opened. Theresa palmed her belly and started crying. "I've been a terrible mother, Q. Terrible. My baby girl."

Quincy reached for Theresa and put his arms around her as he wondered about Theresa's choice of words that specified the unborn child's gender. Theresa leaned forward and came into his arms, putting her own around him. Quincy rubbed Theresa back and said softly, "Easy, sister. Easy." He pulled away to look at her face. He wiped her tears from her cheek. "You don't know anything yet."

Theresa pleaded, "I know, Q. I know. I have that child sickness that a mother gets when pregnant. My sickness over the last days has been different from the sickness I get from being all hopped up on drink and smoke and party. I know, Q. Don't tell me I don't! I haven't seen a stream of blood come from me in months. I thought it was all the activity of drinking and smoke delaying my flow."

Quincy said to her, "Okay, Theresa. But, there's no possible way, now, that you could know you're carryin' a little girl. Come on, now. Let's talk some sense."

Theresa sniffed back her tears and smiled. "I know, Q," she repeated. "But that's not what scares me. That's not what scares me at all." Before Quincy could inquire, Theresa reassured, "I will sing tonight." She sniffed again and wiped her tears with the veil. *"Mwen mande w' padon m' p'ap fè sa anko,"* she expressed in Creole. "But I can only sing. I can't smoke. I can't drink. I can't kiss no needles. I need to rest."

Quincy shook his head. "You'll be okay, Theresa. I promise."

Theresa disagreed, shaking her head. "That's what's got me

spooked, Q. You see, I say that I can't drink or smoke or be kissing any needles…" her lips began to shake. The tears resurfaced in her eyes. "…But, I don't think I mean it. I…can't…but I want to. I could drink right now. I could smoke, Q, Lord I could smoke. The reefer too, not no damn tobacco." Quincy stood up, his eyes fixed on his friend. Theresa looked possessed, her eyes wide, blotched with tears and a sudden sweat. She continued speaking while shaking her head, a smile trembling into existence. "And, I swear the needle has seduced me with a kiss just as powerful as my Joe Pepper's."

Quincy cleared his throat. "I'll make sure you're fine, Theresa. And supposedly, so will the government. People got a push to make alcohol illegal. Water Bug Hollow gon' be dried up."

Theresa leaned back in the bed. "Sheeit, Q. This here is Water Bug Hollow, and you know good-and-well that Water Bug Hollow goes by its own rules, governs itself. There's a whole lot of goings-on here that the government wouldn't approve. We've always had ladies of the night, gamblin', and reefer smoke and heavy drink. Shit, now we got niggers fuckin' white women and white men, and we also got cocaine use along with the golden-dragon smoke of heroin."

Quincy shook his head, hands in his pockets. He agreed and added, "Yeah, but them last indecencies ain't domestic, they imported, ever since Sarinda Fallows done showed up here. It seem like we got a train that go straight to The Lounge."

Theresa presented Quincy with a stern look. She ordered him, "Please, write my mamma and papa in Scotlandville. Tell them to come, especially my mamma. I need her and my little sister. My mamma will know what to do."

"I'll do that," Quincy promised. "Until then, we're going to have Maggie Rhodes come up here and give you a proper inspection. And, also, we gon' postpone your return to the stage. Let's get this pregnancy confirmed, and I'll send off your letter." Theresa agreed. Quincy walked to the door and opened it. "You take care now, Theresa. I'll try and have a word with Sarinda tonight, should she show up. Maggie will be here shortly. Don't go nowhere."

Theresa responded, "I won't." Quincy left the room and shut the door behind him. The close of the door revealed the figure of a young black girl in the corner wearing a white Southern Belle dress with white lace-trim and a wide-brim hat to match. She and Theresa stared at one another. The little girl moved to the vanity and sat down, her legs dangling in the chair. She looked as disappointed as a child could look toward their mother. "I'm sorry," Theresa told her. "I'm so sorry…Philomena. I'm sorry." Theresa's voice was low. "My Philomena. That's what I'll name you." Theresa looked away from the little girl and rubbed her belly. She looked back at the little girl and asked, "You like that name?"

The little girl nodded, yes, and she managed a soft smile. Her image remained even when Quincy returned with the elder Maggie Rhodes, one of Water Bug Hollow's resident doctors and practicing midwives. She carried with her a large metal bowl filled with warm water. A face towel was draped over her shoulder and Quincy carried for her a bar of soap. Maggie entered and greeted Theresa with a pleasant smile, asking Theresa how she was doing and giving her an early 'congratulations' on her intuition of being with child. "But, we have to make sure, now."

Maggie put the bowl of water next to the bed. Quincy placed a chair adjacent to the bed for Maggie to sit on, and she sat down next to Theresa. She thanked Quincy and dismissed him. Before the piano player left the room, he gave Maggie the proper payment for her visit and placed the bar of soap on the nightstand. Then, Quincy was gone from the room. The little girl continued to observe the situation. Theresa kept her attention on Maggie as the aged midwife began conducting her tests. Maggie had Theresa lie on her back, remove her underwear and open her legs. Then the midwife and doctor washed her hands in the water with the bar of soap. She left the bar of soap floating in the bowl, and dried her hands with the towel that had been draped over her shoulder. She asked a series of questions as she inserted two fingers in between Theresa's opened legs. Theresa took a breath, looked up at the ceiling, and listened to Maggie's first question. "When was the last time you saw blood, girl?"

Theresa thought. "Well, I saw blood a week or so after the child's father left for business, but I know that doesn't mean anything."

"No, it doesn't," agreed Maggie. She continued examining with her fingers inside Theresa. "Nothing after that?" she questioned.

Theresa shook her head. "Not that I can recall, Mother Maggie. My life has been filled with consuming too much party smoke and, uh, the wrong things for my body."

Maggie groaned at Theresa's confession. The midwife didn't make a comment, but her grumble was sentiment enough of her displeasure. She removed her fingers and explained as she bent down and washed her hands again. "It's soft in there, girl. Real soft, even at the spots that supposed to feel as hard as the tip of your nose. Your body is preparin' itself." She dried her hands and ordered Theresa to sit up in the bed. She asked for Theresa to expose her breasts and then she put her hands on them, feeling around and under them. "They been feelin' tender? Swollen?" Theresa answered, yes. Maggie told her to cover up again. "No blood for how long?"

"Several months," Theresa answered.

"Swollen breasts, sickness," Maggie listed and then confirmed what Theresa had already guessed for herself. "You take care of yourself, girl. You have a child on the way."

"I've done so much harm to myself," Theresa blurted as she rubbed her belly. Tears swelled up in her eyes. "I've hurt this child. My child! I might do more. I can't have this child's father return to know that I've put her in harm's way. He'll be devastated."

Maggie, in a calm, grandmotherly tone asked, "Have you had any bleeding, especially with pain? Heavy or light?"

Theresa relaxed her tears. "No."

"Then that child should still be inside you," Maggie expressed. "We won't know anything until we know somethin'. You take it easy. Less stress the less harm. Make a good home for your child, startin' with your body." The subject was over. Mother Maggie had spoken. She asked, "Now, how's the sickness?"

Theresa rolled her eyes and groaned.

"Well," started Maggie, "limit your meals to plain crackers or dry cereal in the morning," she suggested to Theresa in a stern, matter-of-fact way. Theresa couldn't help but smile at Mother Maggie. She was more relaxed. Maggie said, "That will help ease your nausea. Drink ginger water with and after meals, but limited. The ginger will settle the stomach. Eat only the *freshwater* catfish. It'll be less toxic to your system. But don't over do it. You can still eat shrimp. No exotic seafood. Stay cool, and get plenty of rest. Tiredness plays a big role in your sickness. But don't worry. The sickness is just a signal your body is tellin' you that a great change is comin', though it can wear you out. Eat something salty before a meal; that will help you get through the meal should you start to feel nauseous. The sickness will go away soon. Let's be safe and say you about twelve or thirteen weeks in." The doctor stood. "Congratulations, Miss Amat."

Theresa shifted herself in the bed. Maggie lifted her bowl and Theresa asked her, "Can I still perform?"

Maggie answered as she stood up with her bowl, "When you feel up to it, yes. I'll keep coming back to tell you you're okay to perform until I tell you that you ain't."

Theresa expressed a light chuckle, feeling relieved. Maggie congratulated her again and left the room. Theresa looked in the direction of where the eight-year-old girl had been sitting at the vanity. She was gone. Theresa slumped back into her bed and covered her face with the veil. She burst into tears and pleaded, "I'm so sorry, my child. Please stay with me. Please be okay." She cried some more and placed the veil across her stomach. Theresa closed her eyes and cried until she was asleep. A few hours later, she was made to stir by the sound of light knocking on her door. She stood up, walked over and opened the door after asking whom it was. Quincy answered, "Your piano player. I got you a dinner." Quincy walked inside. "Mother Maggie told me what would be good for you. I got you some ginger-water and gumbo that's not too spicy. There's shrimp but no sausage. I had them put in eggplant, as I know you prefer." He placed Theresa's dinner on the vanity. He gave her a gentle hug and said, "Congratulations, my sister. The whole band knows. We play to you and your health tonight."

Theresa accepted the compliment and replied, "Thank you, my jazz brother. I'll have that later." She saw the look of concern on Quincy's face. "I'm fine. Just not too hungry right now, but I'll get there soon. Very soon. I'm eatin' for two now."

Quincy smiled and then informed Theresa, "I had a letter sent to your parents. Your family will be here soon."

Theresa expressed her gratitude, "Thank you, Q." Quincy stood still with a grin. "What?" Theresa asked.

"I'm thinking of the look on Joe's face when he sees you in New York holding his child—daughter as you say it is."

"I don't know what he'll be more surprised to see," chuckled Theresa. "Me, or me holdin' his baby girl." Theresa sat on the bed and said light-in-heart, "Joe had a plan for marriage, and I guess with marriage comes children. We're just doing this a little different. I wouldn't expect anything less from Joe Pepper. It's always an adventure with him, whether it's a story he's tellin' or an outing. There's always something fun with him." She smiled as she reminisced about her years with Joseph Pepper the Fourth. But soon her smile faded. The palm of her hand caressed her belly. "I'm more ashamed of the way I've acted. What I've poisoned my body with. The possibility that I've put our child in harm's way…I think she's disappointed in me. I can feel it."

Quincy walked closer. "You put them superstitions down, Theresa. That child will be fine."

Theresa changed the subject when she asked, "How's the politics in Water Bug Hollow? I heard a man was stabbed while debatin' with someone."

Quincy sighed, "Booker Boone was stabbed. His older brother, Bucky, did it. Heated debate. Booker'll be okay, though. Bucky repented, cried next to his brother. Booker forgave him, laughed it off. Said it was just a scratch." Quincy snickered. "Maybe this town needs a church after all." He shook his head, lifted his shoulders and sighed again. "People have simmered, but there's still some resentment. It ain't in any offense to the Good Lord, but it's just the interruption of who we are that got people's attitudes bent all crazy. But they understand the danger. Most of the craziness has been quelled. Mayor Johnson and some of the others have worked around conducting our annual celebrations within the church. Construction begins early next year."

Theresa pondered and then asked, "How's Eugene? I know he ain't got inspiration to walk away from his demons as I do."

Quincy lifted his eyebrows and exhaled while looking away from Theresa, eyes on the floor. His gaze finally came up, and he volleyed an uneasy chuckle as he said, "Well, he constantly be on that train that go straight to The Lounge." He wiped his brow and added, "But he cool, though, Theresa. He, uh, take that trip to The Lounge after performances. Ain't no up and disappearin' for days. Just every-so-often. Sarinda escorts him. People talkin' 'bout them two. I told him to be careful, but you know how he gets…and of course how I get when he gets like he gets, blowin' my advice off as if it ain't nothing." Quincy stood up straight, his expression changed to stern. "I don't care how much carefree mixin' go on up over at The Lounge. White folks will hang a nigger when good and ready, and for any reason. To hell with him for givin' them one." He took a breath and a step back. "You enjoy your food, Theresa. I'll take care of the band. Everybody's doin' fine."

Theresa bowed her head with grace and subtlety of movement. She beamed a thankful smile and flapped her beautiful eyes as she watched Quincy back away toward the door. "Thank you, jazz brother. I'll be listening."

Quincy nodded, opened the door, and departed from the room. Theresa stood and walked over to her vanity to inspect the food Quincy delivered. She opened a drawer and removed from it a pad of paper and a pencil. Then she stirred her gumbo, inhaling its aroma. She took a spoonful and then sipped some ginger-water. She paused and waited. Her stomach felt fine, and she continued eating, all the while feeling fine and keeping her food down. No feelings of nausea ever surfaced, but she didn't push her appetite too hard. With the bowl still very much full, Theresa took another sip of ginger-water to keep her stomach from unsettling, and then she picked up her pencil and began to scribble lyrics on the sheet of paper. The sun disappeared and, in an instant, Theresa felt the floor rumble with the vibration of her band's music coming from below.

Theresa tapped her feet. She closed her eyes and worked her shoulders. She continued to write. Theresa wasn't sure when she had wrapped the veil around her arm, but there it was twisted like a snake. She stood up and began to sing the lyrics she'd scribbled, rewriting them to make her singing smoother, taking out words or changing the syllabic rhythm. The music from downstairs shifted in accordance to Theresa's imagination so that she could sing her new lyrics in proper tone. She unraveled the veil from her arm and put it around her face, smiling and dancing to the new music surrounding her; she scribed more lyrics and seemed to memorize them as fast as she wrote them.

Theresa twirled and she thought of the words she would use to announce to Joseph Pepper that he had a child on the way. *You have a daughter, Joe,* she thought. *I have not treated your princess well, and I'm sorry. But our baby will grow to be fine. She will love her papa. She will love her mamma.*

Theresa's twirling stopped on cue of the music. She tossed back her veil as if she was conducting her own performance. She was smiling, happy. Then the smile faded into a curious expression. She inspected the floor of her room, which was covered with all the paper from her tablet. Lyrics to different songs had been composed on each side of each sheet.

The sight left Theresa perplexed, and she wondered how it was possible for her to have written all of the lyrics in such a short time. She remembered writing and writing and writing and not stopping, but all this was still too much. Every sheet of paper was torn from the pad, tossed and scattered about the floor. They were numbered too, so order could be kept.

Then Theresa's eyes were drawn away from the floor as a magnificent glow shined through the closed curtains, putting Theresa's thoughts on pause. Her attention focused on the awe-inspiring brilliance. The glow bubbled with the swirl of sunrise colors. Orange shifted into red that shifted into yellow, existing together and separate. Theresa moved closer to the window, taking a quick glance at the clock on her vanity. It was two-thirty. It was not the afternoon, it was the dark of night shifting hours early into morning. Here, unexpected, was the sun. Theresa moved the curtains open to get a better look at the sudden, splendid luminosity, but it disappeared, sucked back into the night sky.

Someone knocked on her door. Theresa stayed at the window, her bemused expression still present. She retracted her hands from the curtains and the sheets glided toward each other to close, waving into one another and then settling still. Someone knocked harder on her door. Theresa stepped away from the window, turned, and walked to the door. She opened it to find Sarinda Fallows on the other side with a smile on her face, a bottle of cognac and two glasses in one grip, and several reefer sticks in the other.

Sarinda noticed the puzzled look on Theresa's face. She said to the jazz singer, "Nothing hard for you tonight, Miss Amat. Just a small celebration to the news of you as a mother-to-be."

Theresa was frozen, her eyes fixed on the paraphernalia in Sarinda's hands. Fixed. Unmoving. The bottle. The reefer. All of it. She could smell the narcotics, the peppery aromas blending into one another. Eyes fixed. Sarinda shook the bottle of cognac, and Theresa blinked wildly coming out of her fastened stare. She said, "Please, Sarinda. Come in. Please." Her eyes stayed on the bottle and reefer sticks.

Sarinda entered smiling. She wiggled her shoulders in a dance and trotted to the vanity to lay the party tools down, all the while she stepped over sheets of paper, placing her feet carefully onto exposed floor. "I see you've been busy up here gettin' creative, Miss Amat," Sarinda chuckled. Her eyes scanned the floor then crawled up to spot Theresa who continued staring at the contents now resting on the vanity. Theresa fixed the veil atop her head and walked to the narcotics present, taking a seat in front of them. She stared, and Sarinda waited.

Theresa spoke soft, continuing her stare at the narcotics in front of her. "Sarinda…you have to leave," she said, voice driven by urgency. Sarinda straightened her posture. She fixed her clothes and stepped toward the vanity to grab the cognac, glasses, and reefer sticks. She reached for the items and heard Theresa order, "Leave them. Leave them be. Come back, though. Have with you a tincture of cocaine, and a small bar of golden-dragon smoke."

Sarinda backed away. "I won't be too long then."

Theresa heard the door close. She stared at the cognac bottle. Her lip quivered. She picked up a reefer stick and inspected it, ran it under her nose and smelled it with her eyes closed, and then she put it back down. Theresa took a breath and kept still until she heard knocking. "Open," she called. Sarinda walked in with the remaining ingredients. "Put them on the vanity," Theresa instructed. Sarinda placed the items down, moved behind Theresa, and then put her hands on her shoulders. "Now go, Sarinda Fallows. Leave." Theresa turned her head, and from her peripheral view, kept an eye on Sarinda. "You tell them boys in New York to hurry and make a decision, y'hear, because, I've made mine. They'll have to wait for my daughter to be born, and they will have to accept that." She turned her torso to get a better look at Sarinda. "You tell them, Miss Fallows, that I can be many things; but, what I won't be, is ignored. And should they want me, they will have to wait for my baby's arrival."

"Absolutely, Miss Amat. Absolutely."

Theresa turned back to the vanity. She heard the door close and knew she was again alone, but not entirely. The eight-year-old girl walked up and stood next to her, standing close. Her eyes, much like Theresa's, remained fixed on the narcotics sitting on the vanity.

Theresa swallowed and said, "I will fight temptation, Philomena. I will look it in the face and stand filled with pride to show that I can conquer it. That pride will not be a sin. You are my pride, Philomena. I will no longer harm you." She blinked, and inside the small space of time absent of light and sight, she saw a vision of Sarinda Fallows standing still on the other side of the door. Sarinda appeared contemplative, and then she hurried away.

Someone knocked on the door.

Theresa blinked, and in that instant she saw the image of Quincy on the other side of the door. "Come in," she permitted. Quincy opened the door and walked inside. He stopped abruptly as his eyes glimpsed, and then focused on, the various narcotics on the vanity. Theresa watched from her vanity's mirror Quincy's wide-eyed expression drizzle into anger. "Miss Fallows showed," Theresa informed in a calm voice. Theresa continued watching Quincy from the mirror. His anger halted, and then he looked down at the floor at all the papers. Perplexity widened his eyes and left his mouth agape. Quincy bent down and gathered and inspected several sheets. Theresa finally turned around in her chair to look at Quincy directly.

The piano player expressed to Theresa, "These all songs? You wrote these?"

"I've been inspired," Theresa said. She turned back to face the mirror. Her eyes scanned the narcotic contents on the vanity. "And my inspiration has nothing to do with any of the opiates here. My inspiration grows inside me." She watched Quincy in the mirror as he gathered a few more sheets off the floor. "You can set them papers down, Q. I'll gather them later."

Quincy did as told, and then he stood up straight. With his hands in his pockets he asked, "You wrote all this tonight or over the last couple days?"

Theresa projected a coy smile. Her eyes locked onto her reflection. "Oh, now, some of them tunes been on my mind for a while. Others, like jazz, I improvised." She turned her head and aimed her eyes at Quincy. "We'll put music to them in time. I have them all memorized."

"Theresa…"

She stood up and interrupted Quincy. "Do you still own a pistol?" Theresa asked him. He nodded, yes. "Your brother still provide guard with his shotgun?" Again, Quincy nodded, yes. "Q, there are diabolical forces in Water Bug Hollow, deviltry that no church will cure. Narcotics and spirits have possessed our hard-won, emancipated village. Mayor Johnson has lost control, and we will bring it back to him. I have a proposition, and I demand an audience with the mayor and all the influential bodies in Water Bug Hollow. Tomorrow night, while the band is on two-day rest. Can you arrange that for me?"

Quincy said to Theresa, "Mayor Johnson and the others will be holding a town meeting in the café tomorrow night." Quincy added, "I can't guarantee you a private audience, though."

Theresa conceded, "That's not a problem, Q." She took a step toward him. "Now, listen to me. I want you to leave this room and find your brother. I know he's holed up with that Catherine woman." Theresa chuckled. "The two of them will be finished soon. By the time you arrive at your brother's room, he'll be up to the task I assign." She returned to her seat and instructed, "Find our dear Eugene, Q. Show him that reefer smoke and drink, all in moderation, are fine. But anything else is a sin, especially since it's been so tainted and don't quite have Mamma Nature's wholesome touch as an ingredient. Persuade him to stop," she directed. "Pull from that anger you have for Eugene's behavior, but don't go too far. A little should do. He's still the best drummer in Water Bug Hollow after all. Hell, if not in all Louisiana." Then Theresa concluded, "That will be all, Q." Then she stopped him, "Oh, wait. I don't mean to be rude, Q, but could you take this back to the café?" She handed him the half-finished bowl of gumbo and the finished glass of ginger-water.

Quincy accepted the bowl and empty glass. Theresa thanked him for bringing the meal, and then Quincy tugged on the brim of his hat, turned, and left the room a little bewildered as to why he felt compelled to carry out Theresa's more violent order without question.

Theresa covered her face with the veil as the door closed. The sun-like glow rekindled and beamed through the window. There was no reflection of the light in the mirror, but it shimmered brilliantly on her right. Theresa turned to face the illumination. It's color shifted. The red, orange, and yellow dissolved away into a fresh, forest green. Theresa could feel and hear the soft sounds of her heartbeat. She stood up and walked to the window, her footsteps in synch with the beats of her heart. She stood in front of the partition, reached out with her hands, and drew back the curtains to let in the luminescence.

The electrical light in Theresa's room was inhaled by darkness and extinguished as if it was a flicker of flame blown out by a quick breath. The intense green coming from the horizon was the only light in Theresa's reality, and it rose into the sky like an emerald sun. Theresa opened her window. She looked up into the sky and peeped through a small clearing in the entangled dome of flora that shrouded Water Bug Hollow.

The celestial, green sphere blazed bright. And, though Theresa never removed her veil, she viewed the heavenly body with pristine vision. She watched as the vibrant, emerald coloration funneled into the center of the sphere and left behind a bursting, bright blue color for the strange, celestial body to glow as. Theresa smiled. Her stomach bubbled with laughter expressed through her parted lips. Then the blue too funneled away, and indigo glowed in its place. Dazzling. The saintly sphere extended an indigo tendril down toward Theresa. The slender, indigo-colored, celestial appendage touched Theresa's forehead.

Theresa closed her eyes and smiled. She pulled her body back inside the room and stood in front of the open window. The glowing sphere burned away, and the stars returned. The darkness inside Theresa's room folded and collapsed as the lights in the apartment glowed again. The window shut. Theresa opened her eyes and lifted the veil from her face. Her head, by reflex, turned toward her vanity, her eyes sweeping the floor as her head rotated. The floor was void of the papers earlier tossed upon it. They were stacked nice and neat on her vanity. The eight-year-old girl sat smiling in the chair. Her cute, beaming expression warmed Theresa, and as she walked over to the light switch she said, "Just like Water Bug Hollow, child. It just needs a little cleaning. It just needs to get its music right." Theresa turned off the lights. She got into bed, removed the veil from around her head, and gently placed it on her belly. She fell fast asleep, greeted by a violent dream.

But the violence didn't scare Theresa into believing her dream was a nightmare. This particular dream was clear, no foggy blemish. Theresa could see everything. It was night in Water Bug Hollow during a cool down period between the end of the band's music and the last drink or smoke taken by Water Bug Hollow's citizens. A crowd trickled from Eve's Hallow, dispersing into the night. Laughter and loud talk became more faint, and after a while, all there was in Water Bug Hollow was a subtle breeze.

Eugene stumbled from Eve's Hallow onto the porch leading to the entrance and exit of the establishment. He twirled a single drumstick and leaned against the railing to ease his drunkenness. His back faced the street, and his front faced the Eve's Hallow entrance. He stood up straight, careful with his balance. He slipped the drumstick into his left jacket pocket where lay its twin and then he reached into his right jacket pocket for a cigarette and matches. The orange glow of the match's flame burned the end of the cigarette and then was shaken out before Eugene flicked the extinguished match away. He took a puff from his cigarette and stepped down onto the street, making his way home. No Lounge or Sarinda tonight, only his bed and a few more drinks before going to sleep. He started down the road.

The silhouette of two male figures flickered like black flames from out of the darkness. One of the figures traipsed up behind Eugene, and as he neared, he removed a revolver. The man cocked back his arm and hit Eugene over the head with the butt of the pistol, and then he grabbed the drunken Eugene from behind. The second man shifted. He lifted his firearm, a shotgun. He panned the surroundings, aiming his gun, making sure no one saw what was happening. The first man dragged Eugene into an alley. The second man followed, walking backwards and keeping his shotgun up and at the ready.

Muffled sounds of a scuffle came from the backstreet. There was indecipherable speech, the only instance where the dream was incoherent. Then the dream faded into another just as the scuffle ended. Now Theresa was walking barefoot toward a mighty tree. She was in her nightgown, and it was the morning. There hung from a strong, thick branch two, black bodies. A man. A woman. They were dressed in rags, and the wind played with their bodies. Theresa walked around the murdered pair. She touched them and inspected their dead expressions. Their eyes were closed and their color had turned to a purplish gray.

Theresa sang, *"Ain't nothin' new here to see. Heartbeats done stopped, but not the spirit of the drum. Ain't nothing' new here to see, 'cause there ain't nothin' new under the sun. This ain't my beginning, but I've seen this so much I believe this is where I come from. I've seen this so much, seen this scene so much of a lot that I wonder if it was the Master's hands or mine that tied this knot. For average health and to gain a spot of wealth, I've got it in my brain to tell Master, 'Don't bother. I can now do this to myself.'"* Theresa continued walking around the bodies, and then she leaned against the tree, keeping the bodies in view. *"Sure as it rains, I've been well trained. It's taken some time, but I now think with someone else's brain. I see with another's eyes. I think with another's thoughts. If rhythm ain't lost, if my rhythm ain't caught, then it's at least off key. And like the only one in the room that gets the joke, Lord I sho' do kill me!"* Theresa belted, *"Oh, no! But, there ain't nothin' new here to see. Heartbeats done stopped, but not the spirit of the drum. Ain't nothing' new here to see, 'cause there ain't nothin' new under the sun. But, this ain't where I'm from, and my story ain't done. And my song ain't been sung! I've got more verses, a whole chorus line of curses, another life and story to tell. So, I beat that drum and ring, ring, ring the re-bell. I ring the re-bell. I ring the re-bell. And I rebel, rebel, rebel, rebel, rebel, rebel.* "Theresa's voice erupted into a mighty crescendo. The brawny branch holding the hanging, black bodies broke and dropped. The bodies crumpled to the earth with the fall.

A young black man, no older than nineteen and wearing slave rags, ran up the hill and inspected the bodies. He wiped his hand across the branch and looked over his shoulder to see if he was being watched. He said a prayer to the once hung black man and black woman, and then he looked up at the sky. Theresa tilted her head to see what the young man was looking at. There floated an angel whose face resembled hers. The angel smiled down on the young man and then turned to Theresa, put her hands together, and bowed her head in appreciation. Saint Theresa winked at her.

Theresa studied close every identical feature on the divine apparition. She backed away from the tree, and after a few steps, she turned around to see she was on the coastline of an island. Gone was the rural, southern field. Gone were the tree and the once-hung bodies lying on the ground. The angel and young man were gone too. A shoreline was before her, and a jungle was behind her. Out into the sea there were ships in the distance. Theresa walked closer toward the water, her bare feet sinking into the soft, warm sand. Waves of water rushed toward her and caressed her feet with a wet and chilled massage. Her eyes remained focused on the approaching armada. Then her dream rippled like the waves of the sea in front her. The rippling effect came with the blare of a magnificent horn. There were shouts.

Theresa woke up. The memory of her dreams gone, but a determined feeling remained. She sat up in bed and scanned the room. Theresa first looked at the time. It was just after eleven in the morning. Then she looked in the direction of her vanity. There rested the stacks of paper and the illegal paraphernalia. Nothing had been disturbed.

Theresa wrapped the veil around her arm and hopped from the bed. She put her hand on her stomach. She didn't feel any discomfort, which made her nervous that her child was lost. But she removed the notion from her thoughts. She'd seen her daughter as an eight-year-old child manifested from the blue. The little girl smiled at her and no longer carried a disappointed expression when they looked at one another. Last night's experience was too beautiful to symbolize loss. Theresa knew that change was coming; and she was going to bring it.

Theresa took a step toward the bathroom. She prepared a bath after tossing her nightclothes onto the bed. She rubbed her naked belly and ran her hand along her stomach's small, pregnant bump. It was the first time she'd seen the spectacular sight that hinted at new life growing inside her. Theresa grinned and thought of Joseph Pepper. Keeping her thoughts of family, and a wide grin on her face, Theresa picked out an outfit for the day. Afterward, she bathed, freshened up, and dressed in an indigo gown that rippled when she moved. It looked as if she wore a fabric stitched from both wind and water. The veil, fastened atop her head, was worn like a crown.

Theresa left her room and locked the door, placing her key in her purse. She had a small bite to eat in Eve's Hallow café and then returned to her room to pace and run through her talking points for the town meeting. She paused only to return to Eve's Hallow for lunch. The size of her appetite, and also the size of the meal she consumed to satisfy it, surprised her. Not a morsel was spared. She tapped her belly when she was finished. "I guess that's a meal for two," she said leaving money and getting up. She returned to her room and continued to polish her talking points.

Then it was night, only minutes before the town meeting.

Theresa opened the door with consummate grace, noticed by Quincy and his brother who were approaching to greet her. Theresa observed that both men were armed. Quincy with a pistol holstered at his hip, and his brother holding close a shotgun. Theresa bowed her head at the neck, acknowledging the two of them. She said, "Quincy. Avery."

"Madam," spoke Quincy as he tugged at the brim of his hat. "The meeting is about to begin."

Theresa responded as she walked by the two men, "Let us go then."

There was something regal in her step, and the two men reacted accordingly by forming up behind her like guardsmen. Theresa and her small entourage walked downstairs to the café where at the front, seated at a long wooden table, were Mayor Arlington Johnson and the six influential aristocrats of Water Bug Hollow. A little more than half of Water Bug Hollow's one hundred and twenty citizens gathered in the café. Heads turned to witness Theresa's arrival.

Mayor Johnson stood and acknowledged Theresa's entrance. "Your voice has been missed, Miss Amat. Your presence has been missed." He walked from around his table to greet Theresa, giving her a kiss on both cheeks. "Congratulations, Theresa. We've heard the news that you're with child."

Theresa smiled. "Yes. Thank you Mayor Johnson," she expressed. "That's a big reason as to why I wanted to attend this meeting. Water Bug Hollow's recent happenings have me concerned. Politics have put a stranglehold on us, and it has people concerned that it will interrupt our way of life and culture."

The mayor escorted Theresa to the front and then returned to his table holding his governing cabinet members. Theresa took a seat while Quincy and Avery broke away, posting guard near the café's entrance. Theresa shook hands and smiled at the people around her as she received congratulations on her pregnancy. Then it became quiet. Mayor Johnson stood again and addressed the audience with details on the schedule for building the church in the field. There were groans from the audience, and one man stood and shouted, "Are we still going through with this? Convert the old stable into a church, not our field. That's sacred ground that we done used too long to be coverin' over, even it is with God's house."

"An excellent idea," said the mayor. "I've said that before. Same words. But, we need this church to be observed on the outside by outsiders. White folk are already up in arms—and ready to pull arms—about the foundation of Water Bug Hollow and our annual festival celebrating it." Mayor Johnson's voice became gruff with frustration. "There are many among you that can recite the Bible back and forth. *For where two or three are gathered in my name, there I am with you,*" quoted the mayor. "Don't need a *place* to worship. We all going to Heaven 'cause we've been through and seen enough hell on Earth, but all white folk need to put you through it is an excuse, and I'll be damned if I give them one. We have a culture beyond their understanding. They're angry for that, and I will not put you or your children in the path of their anger. I will not put you in harm's way. This ain't no different from what was done when we were in chains. Fool the Master that we're doin' one thing when we're doin' another." The mayor paused to overlook the crowd with stern eyes. "Yes," he finally broke his silence. "Yes, we're goin' through with this. That's *my* word."

People groaned.

Theresa stood up. Mayor Johnson and the gathered people looked at her with odd expressions. She bowed her head at the neck to all of them, and then she turned to Mayor Johnson and asked in her regal tone, "May I speak, Mister Mayor?" Mayor Johnson granted Theresa the right to articulate her position. "Thank you, Mayor." She turned to her audience and addressed, "I know this is a town meeting, but I have a problem with the use of the word town, or village as we might be classified. You see, with our history, both founding and recent, and even with our present, it would be offensive, with all that we've been through, to call us a town or village. Just the same, if Water Bug Hollow were to expand in size and population I still would believe it to be offensive to call us a city. If we became larger than Louisiana itself, I would still find it offensive to refer to us as a capital or state. Nor would we be a kingdom should Mayor Johnson and his wife decide to wear crowns." Her last statement elicited several muffled chuckles from the audience, and Theresa too smiled at the sentiment, but her stern tone returned as she continued, "I would also consider it an affront that if after all of America looked to us to lead it in world politics, Water Bug Hollow was referred to as a country. Water Bug Hollow is none of these things." Theresa paused for effect, and then with a completely embodied grace, she communicated, "We are a family. We might have our dysfunctions, but what family doesn't, right? Well, a little dysfunction can be healthy, but I have witnessed too much of it. Muggings and stabbings and fights in the streets. I declare, no more!" She addressed Mayor Johnson, saying over her shoulder, "You may have me arrested for mutiny, because for the next while or so, I will be usurping your power." She turned to the mayor and smiled. "Only to give it back, and with greater strength, Mister Mayor."

The mayor responded, "Then you may proceed, Miss Amat."

Theresa turned and faced the audience. "Like any family, there are rules. We have rules, and we are in need of some new rules to get Water Bug Hollow back on track. You are right, Mister Mayor. We have been through hell on Earth, but we've also built heaven on Earth here in Water Bug Hollow. There's no need to not keep that going." Theresa's voice faded, and then trembled as she tried to speak the next set of words. She paused again and cleared her throat, starting over. "I have sinned. I've put my unborn child in harm's way. I've indulged in hard narcotics. Being unaware of my pregnancy is no excuse." She coughed, clearing her throat, and then sniffed back the tears forming in her eyes. "I will keep my body clean. It will be treated like a sacred temple. So too shall Water Bug Hollow be treated. I demand some cleanup. Reefer sticks and drink are fine. But in months passed, we have seen an introduction to harder opiates. Water Bug Hollow needs a cleansing from these narcotics. We've gone from fun and laughter, having a good time and waking up clean for work the next morning, to acting as if a bokor-priest done sprinkled dust on us and turned us into a nzumbi, the living dead. Water Bug Hollow is losing money to two trucks that make deliveries of these opiates. That will be dealt with." She turned to Mayor Johnson. "With your approval, of course."

He answered, "Absolutely, Miss Amat. I give my approval."

Theresa turned back to the audience. "I propose some other rules. Women earning wages by keeping the company of men will not keep the company of foreign men. Not in Water Bug Hollow. Wages earned at The Lounge will receive a forty percent tax. Tribute will be paid to Water Bug Hollow. These white men pay top dollar for colored flesh. Fine. Water Bug Hollow will profit." Theresa spoke her next words with slight disdain. "The same goes for you playboys out there getting paid a pretty penny by white women up at The Lounge who want to be tossed around all-the-night by a black buck." Theresa stressed again. "Forty percent of your earnings from The Lounge. Is that clear?" The male and female escorts sitting in the audience agreed without reluctance. "That's for you independent folk. To the brothel-keepers, your business will follow the same rules plus the taxes already paid." She paused waiting for an objection, but no one dared protest against Theresa's glare and stern voice. Her proposal was considered fair. "I also believe that Eve's Hallow needs only be a café and small club. Meeting here for politics, or rearranging the place to accommodate gambling nights, is too much." Theresa faced the mayor and his cabinet. "The old stable that Mister Heath proposed be turned into a church should be re-fashioned a gambling parlor." The audience applauded the proposal. "It could host games just the same, and bring revenue. Eve's Hallow could provide food and drink, so that there would be no competition between the two nightspots. Eve's Hallow is not big enough to support the small games already played in its backrooms."

Mayor Johnson agreed, jokingly adding, "I can't argue against the people's enthusiasm, Miss Amat."

"Yes, Mister Mayor," Theresa spoke. "I also propose that this church we build be used for political meetings. Discussions ranging in all manner of politics can then be held at whim."

"That would be fine, Miss Amat. A fine proposition," the mayor approved.

"One last request, Mister Mayor."

"Indeed, Miss Amat."

Theresa turned her body so that her profile was in view, but she turned her head to the audience. "Water Bug Hollow will only accept the goods delivered by the MacRitchie family. No more heavy narcotics. But we will have some exports." Theresa then abridged national politics, "The government of America has proposed a ban on liquor. It will most likely pass. We have several distilleries here in Water Bug Hollow. Let our well not run dry, and let us keep America's well a little wet. Also, I believe our seamstresses are the best. Let us blaze fashion. And most of all, should our population bleed to the outside, let us continue to pay tribute back to Water Bug Hollow."

Theresa again faced Mayor Johnson and his cabinet. She bowed her head, turned to the audience, and repeated the gesture. Then, she returned to her seat and waited. The mayor stood up straight. He addressed Theresa, "All your points will be taken into consideration. We will give a final approval of them after some revision," Mayor Johnson stated with authority. "Miss Amat, your father—my good friend and retired judge of Water Bug Hollow—would be proud. This meeting is adjourned should there be no further business." He looked out to the audience and waited to see if another citizen had other issues to bring up, or object or add to what Theresa proposed. No one spoke. Mayor Johnson then concluded the town meeting. He slammed a fist on the table and hollered, "Adjourned!"

The citizens stood up. Many swarmed Theresa and congratulated her on her proposals and again on her pregnancy. The crowd surrounding Theresa was not too smothering, but Quincy and his brother formed up around her as guards, and many backed away out of respect.

"Escort me to the infirmary, please," she ordered Quincy and Avery. "I'd like to talk to Eugene. I know you boys put him there last night."

"On your orders, madam," said Quincy.

"Miss Amat," spoke Avery. "The mayor's calling you."

Theresa turned around and saw Mayor Johnson pop up in her face. "I'd like your input while we're putting all this together, Miss Amat."

"Absolutely, Mister Mayor," Theresa beamed. "It would be an honor. Do you need my assistance now, Mayor?"

"No," Mayor Johnson assured her. "We're done for the night."

"That's most good. I have it on good authority that a truck is making a delivery of narcotics tonight." Quincy peered at Theresa through squinted eyes. He quickly straightened himself. Theresa concluded, "I'd like to have that situation handled with your permission."

The mayor's eyes went to Quincy and Avery. He noted that both men were armed and that their positioning around Theresa was as guardsmen. He said, looking back to Theresa, "You have full authority to deal with the truck, Miss Amat. Send a message that Water Bug Hollow will no longer be poisoned. Do you need more, uh, assistance?"

"No, thank you, Mister Mayor. Keep the regular town guards on patrol for the night."

The mayor thanked Theresa for her assistance. "I will call upon you when needed, Miss Amat. Until then, sing, great songbird. We miss your voice and jazz. We've always listened to your command and authority in song." He then allowed her leave.

Theresa exited Eve's Hallow flanked by Quincy and Avery. They walked to the infirmary and stepped inside, asking for permission to see their assaulted drummer, Eugene. Without fuss from the infirmary's night staff, they were escorted to Eugene's room. Quincy and Avery waited outside, each posted on either side of the door.

Theresa pulled up a seat next to Eugene's bed. She sat down and crossed her legs, inspecting Eugene's bruised, purple-swollen face. She dropped the veil over her face and greeted, "Hello, Eugene." She reached for his hand and held it with both of hers. "You will be fine with another day's rest. We will be practicing some new material." Eugene nodded his head, eyes closed. "There will be nothing more than reefer smoke and drink, understand? Straight to bed with you. No Lounge. Keep company with a female, even if it's Miss Fallows. But, stay in Water Bug Hollow. And I'll know if you defy me, Eugene. I'll know." She stroked his fingers, playing with them. She added, "Don't defy Mamma Indigo, Eugene, or she'll take your fingers so that you won't ever play again."

Eugene nodded his head, eyes closed.

Theresa pulled back her veil and stood. She walked out of the room and said to her guardsmen, "He'll be fine. Like new. Like magic." She then asked, "Gentlemen, may you escort me back to my room?" Quincy and Avery did so, walking Theresa all the way back to her apartment above Eve's Hallow. Quincy walked inside while his brother stayed in the hall. He noticed the floor had been cleaned of all the sheets of paper, and that they had been stacked neatly on Theresa's vanity near the untouched narcotics. Theresa sat down at her vanity and removed the veil from atop her head. She said, "My night is over, but your night begins. You have a truck to meet."

"Theresa…"

Theresa turned to Quincy. "Yes, Q, what is it?" Quincy hesitated. "Q…" Theresa prompted.

"Did I happen to tell you that we got the information on tonight's delivery from Eugene?"

Theresa smiled. "No, Q. You didn't."

Quincy looked down at the small bump of Theresa's pregnant belly. He looked up at her and said, "It's going to be a girl, isn't it?"

"Yes, Q."

Quincy stepped back.

Theresa called for him before he turned to leave. "Q, could you have sent up from the café two orders of freshwater catfish, a wide bowl of gumbo—as it was prepared for me before—cornbread on the side, greens and sweet potatoes? I'm eating for two, y'know." Quincy laughed as Theresa added, "And a bowl of ice cream for desert. I'll get to it before it melts. Also, bring two glasses of ginger-water with ice. Oh, hell, make it one glass and a pitcher of ginger-water. It's such a shame how when you don't know you pregnant you can't keep an ounce of regular food down, but the minute you find out, you can keep down the strangest and largest of meals."

Quincy tugged on the brim of his hat. "Yes, ma'am." Theresa thanked him, and then he left the room.

Theresa changed into her nightclothes. Moments after, there was a knock on her door. Theresa opened it and welcomed in the Eve's Hallow waiters. "Put it all on the bed, neatly." She noticed one of the waiters spy the narcotics on her vanity. "Don't worry," she addressed the young man. "It's just a reminder. They will not be touched."

Theresa paid the waiters, giving a generous tip, and then she indulged in every last bite of the meal brought to her. She topped off her meal with her desert and by finishing a third glass of ginger-water. She practiced songs for an hour before turning in for the night. Lying down in her bed, with the lights out, she placed the veil over her pregnant belly and then fell into the dreaming.

Theresa saw a truck on fire. A man was shot dead. There was screaming. A second man was beaten, and there was shouting coming from his attackers. *"No more! Not here. Understand? We won't have this in our home no more! Get out. And we'll kill anyone who come back."* The beaten man scattered into the night, gunshots behind him fired to instill and fortify his fear.

Theresa then dreamed of dancing with Joseph Pepper.

The Stars Look Very Different Today
"I remember you. Yes, I do. Sarah. Sarah the Pantomime."

Routine. Some call it tradition, and there was nothing wrong with tradition in Water Bug Hollow, especially every night at Eve's Hallow where the sounds of jazz and blues were always blaring. It was only Theresa Amat that held the power to either break or add to tradition, because this night, her first night back, she had new songs.

Theresa's band rolled the music to welcome her to the stage. The audience got to their feet and clapped. This was Theresa's first performance in days, and she was as equally excited as the audience. Her excitement was not inspired by belting out jazz or blues, or the roar of the awaiting audience, but rather that the audience had grown by three: her mother, her father, and her sister.

Theresa sang with a smile behind her veil. Her band played a jazzy jingle behind her. *"We could use a Psalm or two. Know that I reach my arms out unto you. Princes come from Ethiop and Egypt, and my king do pleaseth. Dreams like unto Joseph were sent down unto me. I unlocked their hidden actualities, and I found my spirituality, and I sing jazz with a voice as free as can be."*

Theresa sang through the remaining dream-like lyrics, bringing the song to a cool finish. Then, there was the familiar hard beat. Theresa flipped her veil up and dived into a fast and heavy tune. The audience jumped, and when they did, tradition appeared to be restored to Water Bug Hollow. All that was different was Theresa's time on the stage. She excited the crowd with song, and they cheered and danced, but the music simmered and she retired from the stage just a little before midnight. Her band continued playing, a slow tune humming as background music to cool the crowd down.

Theresa refreshed backstage and then joined her family at a table in the back of Eve's Hallow. "Mamma, Papa!" she said giving both her parents a kiss on the cheek. She hugged her seventeen-year-old sister and said, "Carolyn. How have all y'all been?"

'Papa' Charlie Amat, a dark-skinned and powerfully built man that carried his muscle as a symbol of his authority, smiled proudly at his eldest daughter through a thick mustache and answered, "We've been fine. I'm speaking with people over in New Orleans to help Southern University's Scotlandville campus to be its own branch, with its own president. I've been corresponding with your brother Delmon. The boy's mind is sharper than mine when it come to jumpin' through the loopholes white folk wanna put in our way."

"That sounds excitin', Papa. I knew retirin' wouldn't stop you from doin' work." Theresa asked, "How is Delmon and his family up there in South Carolina?"

"They doin' all right," Charlie answered his daughter. "Movin' farther north to Virginia. A job is callin'. He ain't gon' let that opportunity slip from him."

Theresa turned to her sister. "Cal', you look lovely," Theresa said with an excited smile. "I know them boys treatin' you with all types of attention." Carolyn Amat giggled, and the two sisters began swatting at one another playfully. They relaxed and Theresa interrogated, "You graduate next spring, right. You got any plans?"

Carolyn waved her hand and rolled her eyes. "You sound like mamma use to before I told her about where I'm goin'."

"And where are you goin'?" Theresa inquired again.

Theresa's mother answered before Carolyn. "Anywhere her boyfriend's gon' be," she said in her thick Creole accent. "Boy Cal' dealin' wit' fell down and got bruised. Cal' nursed them bruises. Now my baby want to nurse full time like her mamma."

"Why that's wonderful, Cal'. I'm proud of you!" said Theresa joyfully. "Now who is this boy?"

Carolyn blushed, giving ample time for 'Mamma' Qarla Elizabeth Amat to speak in turn for her daughter. "Boy named James. Good boy. Gone up to South Carolina to the Army. His trainin' takin' him to New York City."

"He's a year older," Carolyn said giddily to her older sister. "And he's handsome, much like your Joe Pepper, a tad darker in color, though."

Charlie Amat shifted his arm around his wife and leaned back in his chair as he asked, "Where is Joe Pepper these days?"

Theresa took a deep breath, hardly containing her smile. "Mamma, Papa, little sister, I have some news." It seemed like even the band went quiet in anticipation. A smile spread over Theresa's face. "Joe asked me to marry him."

Qarla Amat chuckled. "It's about time," she said. "My big girl goin' on thirty-six wit' no proper family. All that gon' change."

Charlie leaned over the table and cupped his eldest daughter's hand with both of his. "A fine man is receiving a fine woman. You know we like Joe, crazy as that New York nigger can be with all his wild stories. At least he got money." He pulled away from his daughter, loosening his grip, and returning to his position leaning back in his chair with his arm around his wife.

"Papa!" Theresa barked, playing at being offended.

"I suspect you two will make a home in New York," Charlie continued. "But he'll have you travelin' the globe. Is Joe here?"

Theresa answered, "No he's not. He's overseas in England." Theresa looked embarrassed, her father being right about Joseph Pepper and his travels. "But he's going to settle. He's clearing up business. He will continue to lecture, however. He wants to be a professor. I don't know when that will happen, but what I do know is that in several months time…he will be a father." She looked at her mother and father, her eyes panning back between them. "Mamma, Papa, I'm with child."

Carolyn gasped.

Qarla Amat clapped her hands together. She kissed her daughter on the cheek. "My baby!" She then sat up straight and looked at both her daughters. "My babies!" she emphasized. "One gon' to be a nurse like her mamma, the other gon' have a proper family."

"And it *will* be a girl," Theresa said with authority. She then teased, "She can challenge them two boys Delmon got." There was a sly smile on Theresa's visage. Carolyn shook her sister with heavy excitement. "I wore this particular dress so as to not be obvious when I performed. I wanted to hide my bump."

"I am happy for you, Theresa," said Charlie. "But what's this I here you runnin' Water Bug Hollow, now?" Charlie asked. "Mayor Johnson told me some things."

Theresa grinned innocently while she looked down. Looking up at her father she replied, "I just had a few suggestions for some rules that would bring order back to Water Bug Hollow. There's been an influx of heavy narcotics and violence. And politics have turned neighbor against neighbor. My child can't be born into such a place. I won't have it."

"Arlington told me about them politics," said Charlie. "I've always pleaded for Water Bug Hollow to do something like this. My daughter has finished my business. So, you going to follow your old papa and pursue a career in politics and law?"

Theresa shook her head, no. "Me and my band have been scouted to possibly perform in New York City. We've performed in New Orleans several times now. We've even played for white folks. I mean, I'm not tryin' to be a star in picture shows, but I'm gonna pursue what I like and what I can do best. Perhaps you'll hear me on the radio or play my record." Theresa quickly assured her parents, "I approach with caution, and I don't want to be blinded by some music shylock out to swindle my band and me. Music is startin' to be big business with clubs and records and all, and there are plenty of honest and dishonest sharks looking to profit. We just have to hope these sharks callin' for us don't have the sharpest teeth, and their taste is out for a dollar we can share in."

"Joe won't let harm come to you," Charlie assured. "Hell, you won't let harm come to you. My baby, you'll be alright."

"Thank you, Papa." Theresa sipped on a glass of water. She remained uncomfortably quiet until she realized everyone at the table was waiting for her to say what was on her mind. Theresa looked at her father and said, "Will you excuse Mamma and I? Carolyn too. There's just some women affairs that I'd like to—"

Charlie said to his daughter, interrupting her, "That's fine. I understand. I'm going to find Arlington and enjoy a cigar and a drink."

"Thank you, Papa." Theresa stood up. She signaled for her mother and sister to follow, and both of them walked close behind Theresa as she led them up to her apartment. Theresa sat on her bed while her sister and mother inspected her studio. Mamma Amat's eyes settled on the narcotics resting on Theresa's vanity. She became still as Carolyn noticed her older sister crying.

Carolyn joined her sister on the bed and comforted her. "What's wrong, Theresa?"

Theresa sniffed and wiped her tears. The noise of Theresa crying broke Mamma Amat's concentration on the paraphernalia, and she turned to her daughter. She walked up to Theresa and asked, "Big girl, what got you all teary?"

"I've sinned, Mamma!" cried Theresa. "I've sinned…" Carolyn moved to make room for their mother to take a seat next to Theresa. Mamma Amat put her hands on Theresa's shoulders and held her daughter close. "I was taking drink, reefer smoke, and harder narcotics before I realized I was pregnant. I've stopped, Mamma, but I still shake. I still shake with want. There's somethin' in my body that still needs them narcotics; and it has me scared, Mamma. I might hurt my child, if I haven't already."

Qarla held her daughter tighter. "Here, now, child."

"I keep them narcotics to remind me," said Theresa as she looked up at the paraphernalia, her eyes bent on them in scorn. She sniffed again. Mamma Amat asked her youngest daughter to go into her bag and get a tissue. Carolyn did as her mother ordered and Qarla handed the tissue to Theresa who wiped her eyes and nose. "I do a small ritual to keep the urges down, but they come strong and heavy. That's why I called for you Mamma. I had Quincy, you know, my drummer, I had him send you that letter."

Qarla let go of her daughter and stood up. She instructed in a voice that would brook no protest, "Get up and go wash your body, a good wash. Come out here with nothing on but your robe, nothing underneath. I got ingredients for a brew." Qarla sifted through her large bag. "Mamma always got a concoction at the ready. Go on, child. Hurry."

Theresa relaxed her tears and stood. She walked to the bathroom and started the water. There came knocking at her door, and Theresa answered. Sarinda Fallows lay on the other side with a wide smile. She reached out and hugged Theresa. "Welcome back, songbird. Welcome back." She stepped back and inspected Theresa. "I met your father downstairs, a handsome man, very charming. He looks good enough to eat. Why I could have sworn that was your brother and not a man old enough to be your daddy." Sarinda couldn't see the disdainful look in Mamma Amat's eyes. Sarinda continued, "Seein' him had me wonderin' just where the rest of the family is, and he told me you all scattered quickly. He didn't know where I might find you, so I tried your room. Am I disturbin' anything?"

"Yes," screeched Mamma Amat.

"Oh," said Sarinda catching the contemptuous tone and look given by Mamma Amat.

Theresa turned around and hissed, "Mamma! This is a friend. Miss Sarinda Fallows. She's related to the MacRitchie's. She's good folk, and she came by the strength of her goodwill to warn Water Bug Hollow of danger." Theresa quickly turned back to Sarinda. She made a gesture and the two of them moved into the hall. Theresa closed the door behind her. "I apologize, Sarinda. My mother isn't use to white folk around here. She's seen some of the MacRitchie family come and visit on a delivery, but that's all she's used to. She's mostly seen the aftermath of white folks around Water Bug Hollow, family and friends found hung miles away."

Sarinda assured, "I understand, Theresa."

"I'll speak to you in the morning, Sarinda."

"Well, wait a minute," shouted Sarinda as she grabbed Theresa by the arm. "Let me get one last hug and give another congratulations. Let me give *Mamma* Theresa a hug."

"Thank you," said Theresa as she and Sarinda embraced. "Thank you."

"Now, you may go Miss Amat. Tell your mother I apologize for my intrusion."

Theresa told Sarinda that she would deliver the message, and then she stepped back into her room, closing the door. Mamma Amat said as Theresa made her way to the bathroom, "I apologize for my demeanor in front of the MacRitchie woman. Didn't know she was a MacRitchie."

"I explained, Mamma," said Theresa as she removed her earrings and placed them on her vanity. "Her name is Sarinda Fallows," Theresa reminded. She walked into the bathroom, closed the door, stripped, and bathed. Her wash was quick. She jumped from the water, dried herself off, and snatched her robe and her veil that was dangling out of the sink. She put on her robe and tied the veil around her arm, and then covered her arm with the sleeve of her robe. Theresa stepped back into the front room and was instructed by her mother to disrobe and lay down on the bed. Theresa obeyed her mother's orders. She lay still and unraveled the veil from her arm and put it beside her on the bed.

"That's a beautiful garment," said Mamma Amat dragging the vanity's chair to her daughter's bed. She sat down.

"Joe gave it to me. That being said, you know it came with a story."

Mamma Amat chuckled, "Yes, I do."

"Some African Queen supposedly wore the veil. But this black woman didn't rule in Africa, supposedly she ruled in America a long time ago. Joe claimed California is named after her."

"Ah, Queen Califia," smiled Mamma Amat.

"I figured you'd know the story," Theresa teased. "And good too. I can't quite spin the tale like Joe. Saves me the trouble." Theresa rolled her eyes as she smiled and thought of Joseph Pepper. "Told me he had an adventure with Thunder John and them Brother Dogs when he was younger. Can you believe that?"

Mamma Amat answered, "Yes, I can child. Man like Joe been everywhere."

"One thing I do love about Joe's story concerning this veil is that his grandmother blessed the garment. I've kept it close to me ever since. I wear it at night over my belly. If it's magical, I want its power to save my child from the…" Theresa started to choke up tears. "…From the poisons I've put into my body." She relaxed. Mamma Amat rubbed dried and crushed boneset leaves all over Theresa's naked frame.

"This will take care of that, big girl," Mamma Amat pronounced. She called over her shoulder, "Cal'. Go downstairs and boil some water in the kitchen. Make some boneset tea. You know all that need to be put in there to make it right. Go on, now."

"Yes, Mamma." Carolyn spirited away from the room to fulfill her mother's command.

Mamma Amat rubbed her eldest daughter's forehead. "Close yo' eyes, big girl. Close yo' eyes."

Theresa did as her mother ordered. "If that veil is so special, maybe one day I'll be remembered for it as much as my singing, incorporating it into my act and all. That'll be the story of me: *The Jazz Singer and Her Veil.* Someone like my Joe Pepper will tell it. It'll be a story like the ones you and Miss Wright, from New Orleans, use to tell." Theresa smiled, eyes still closed. "Miss Wright was such a truculent woman. Don't know how you could stand to be around her. Is she still raising them boys, her grandchildren? The two that came from that small town outside Saint Louis?"

"Them boys are men now," Qarla stated. "Music teachers, I've heard. They moved to Mississippi. They found brides up there and settled."

She continued rubbing her daughter's forehead. She hushed her gently and said, "Just relax child. I know many medicines, but there is nothin' better than a li'l natural folk remedy. Just relax. Almost sleep."

Theresa quieted and lay still with her eyes closed. She heard the door open minutes later, and the aroma of hot boneset tea filled her nose. Her mother touched her forehead and told her to open her eyes and sit up in the bed. Carolyn passed the hot cup of boneset, herbal tea to her mother. Mamma Amat in turn passed the cup to Theresa who blew on the top of the liquid and then eagerly sipped the tea.

Mamma Amat advised, "Take it slow, child. Take it slow. That should hold back those urges and cleanse that body." She took a breath. "I'll leave some of the herbs for you."

Theresa sipped. "I'm sorry, Mamma. I just got too into that life. I swear, *mwen mande w' padon m' p'ap fè sa anko.*"

"I just hope that to be true, child. Now rest," Mamma Amat directed. Theresa continued to drink. The tea warmed her body and she felt as fresh as when she stepped from her bath. Mamma Amat took the tea from Theresa after most of it was gone. Qarla said to her daughter as she placed the cup onto the nightstand, "Now get your nightclothes on, big girl. Then get back into bed."

Theresa completed her mother's command, dressing in her sleeping clothes and then getting back into bed. She lay flat, and her mother placed the blessed garment over her humped belly. Mamma Amat covered her daughter with the bed's comforter and tucked her in. She started to hum. Carolyn harmonized with her mother.

Theresa fell fast asleep, but her body started to move as if uncomfortable. She shifted, her face making expressions. She groaned. Her movement was slight, not erratic, and all the while her mother and sister continued harmonizing until Theresa's body relaxed, and her sleep was undisturbed.

Theresa slept through the night without having to stir to relieve herself, which she had been doing often during the night since her pregnancy. Theresa relieved herself in the morning, ran a bath, freshened up, and put on a new set of clothes for the day. She met her family downstairs and shared breakfast with them.

"How long y'all gon' be home in Water Bug Hollow?" Theresa asked as she dived into the large breakfast prepared for her.

"You tryin' to get rid of us already?" her father joked.

"Papa!" Theresa protested.

"I'm funnin' you, girl. You know that," Charlie explained. "I'll be leaving ahead of your mother and sister. Tonight. I have business to attend to in the mornin'."

Theresa turned to her mother just as Mamma Amat spoke, "Next mornin' after that, we'll be headin' out. Cal' got to get back to school."

The Amat family continued their meal. Conversations about politics and school were put aside to focus on the family's well-being and the growth of new life, and Theresa's coming family. The Amats finished their breakfast and strolled through Water Bug Hollow, continuing their talk about the past and growing up within the small town's culture. And then, two hours before Theresa returned to the stage, the family escorted 'Papa' Charlie Amat to a transport. He climbed into the back of the automobile and remarked, "We should've drove here. You should see the new car, Theresa. Need one in Scotlandville."

"Next time, Papa," Theresa replied with a smile.

The family said its goodbyes. Mamma Amat told her husband she and Carolyn would be home the next night, and then the automobile pulled away. Theresa led her mother and Carolyn back to her room where she engaged a large meal coupled with ginger-water. She bathed and prepared for her performance. Shortly after, Theresa Amat found herself on Eve's Hallow's stage continuing the nightly tradition of song and entertainment. New numbers were performed, and the crowd loved every note. The band's horn section added fuel to the musical fire by sounding off in a friendly competition that the audience enjoyed and hollered at. Theresa's set ended at midnight. Her band continued playing even after she left the stage and returned to her room with her mother and sister. Upstairs in her apartment, Theresa indulged in her new after show ritual. She bathed, was then rubbed with boneset leaves by her mother, drank more boneset tea after dressing in nightclothes, and then went fast asleep, face up in the bed and veil covering her pregnant hump.

The next day followed the same pattern, with Theresa's mother and sister leaving in place of her father. Theresa then ate a private meal in her room, bathed, and returned to the stage for another night of jazz. After her performance, the routine continued. Maggie Rhodes, having been briefed by Theresa's mother, assisted in the after show ritual. Theresa fell asleep.

This night, however, her ritual did not produce a sleep that kept her from getting up and going to the bathroom, but Theresa didn't mind. When she got up she looked at the contents of narcotics on her vanity.

There was no urge.

Theresa got back into bed once her business in the bathroom was finished. When she awoke next, there was knocking so heavy on her door that it caused her to jump from sleep and from her bed. Quincy shouted her name from the other side of the door, his voice in rhythm with the incessant banging. Theresa flung her robe around her, tied it tight, and then opened the door.

"Q!" Theresa scolded. "What is your black problem, Negro?" She turned and looked at her clock as she asked, "What time is it?" Her sleepy, blurred vision came into focus just as Quincy answered her question. It was nine-thirty in the morning. Theresa allowed Quincy and his brother Avery into her room. "What is all this about?"

Quincy caught his breath. "I apologize about the disturbance, but there's a man downstairs. He's a white man. He's in the café talking to Head Lawman Kenneth."

Avery waved his hand and shook his head. "He ain't white-white. He's an I-talian boy," Avery noted specifically. "Name is Samuel Lupino. He pushed past security at Water Bug Hollow's entrance. Got five other I-talian boys with him. He demandin' to see the mayor."

Quincy and Avery both took a deep breath and looked at one another. Then their eyes, possessed by worry, drifted back toward Theresa. Quincy broke the silence. "It was his delivery truck we hit on your orders. We took out one man, but we let one survive to tell the tale. The story done come full circle."

Theresa relaxed. Sleep melted away from her. She was now up, and a smile crawled onto her countenance. "And now there's a new chapter." Theresa walked to her bed and snatched the veil laying on it. She scurried into the bathroom and told the two brothers, "Let me freshen up, boys. I'll only be a minute or two."

Theresa took forty minutes, however, and that included the bath. In that time, Avery went downstairs to check on the situation's progression. Mayor Arlington Johnson was in conference with the well-dressed, middle-aged Italian man. Avery returned to Theresa's room just as she was leaving the bathroom, freshened up and fully dressed. Atop her head she wore her veil, crowned, as she preferred to be as of late.

"Gentlemen," Theresa greeted without the slightest hint of worry in her voice.

Quincy and Avery formed up behind her, staying close until they were downstairs inside Eve's Hallow's café. Samuel Lupino, five of his goons, Mayor Johnson, and Kenneth Adams occupied the front area. There were no patrons. Theresa coolly sauntered toward the conversation. She assessed that the situation was growing more tense. Samuel Lupino scowled, pointed, and spoke harshly at Mayor Johnson.

Theresa interrupted. She beamed as if nothing was the matter and said, "Mayor Johnson, who here has come to visit Water Bug Hollow?"

Mister Lupino turned his scowl toward Theresa. Mayor Johnson took the moment to stand up. He patted Theresa on the shoulder and said with a nervous smile, "Miss Amat, I apologize. I'm busy dealing with a misunderstanding."

Theresa's smile remained. "Why there's no misunderstanding, Mayor Johnson." She surveyed Water Bug Hollow's visitors. She looked down at the Italian man. "I believe Mister Lupino is just a bit upset at how we had to handle one of his delivery trucks. And Lord, was it ever effective. We haven't seen the second truck pull up to our fine residence." She faced Samuel Lupino and reached out a hand. "Hello. Mister Samuel Lupino, is it not? I'm Theresa Amat. How do you do? There's no need to keep the mystery going, it was I who ordered your truck destroyed, which means that it was I who was responsible for the death of your soldier and the beating of another of your employees—to be so kind as to describe the man. The men surrounding me are the men who carried out those orders." Theresa's smile never faltered. Everyone around her was silent. Their mouths hung open in awe at the woman's audacity.

Theresa took the mayor's unoccupied seat. She crossed her legs and her arm remained extended, waiting for Lupino to accept her gesture. The Italian man did. Theresa then clasped her other hand over his, and she held onto Lupino with a surprisingly tight grip.

Lupino didn't try to retract his hand.

Theresa leaned forward and explained, "You must understand, Mister Lupino, that poison of such nature is no longer tolerated in Water Bug Hollow. I understand you seek retribution for our actions that you've interpreted as against you personally, which they are not. They may have hurt your business—for a while—but our intentions had nothing to do with weakening you as a businessman." Theresa opened her hands and let Lupino go. Both of them leaned back in their chairs. "Remove the idea of retribution, Mister Lupino. A war with Water Bug Hollow would not be ideal. As favorable as killing Negroes may be, it would bring unwanted attention to you and your business ventures—I'll make sure of that. Then our attacks against you would be both personal and for the sake of weakening your business." The situation became more remarkable with what happened next. Theresa spoke to Samuel Lupino in his native Italian. *"As I understand it, Mister Lupino, the business you're in—especially along the New Orleans waterfronts—garners rivals. Competition. I might be able to assist you in that."* Theresa paused, contemplating. She pressed her lips together and hummed for a short time, and then she said, *"Mister Babineaux. Otes Babineaux. You two have a feud, no?"* Theresa let out a light laugh. *"Cajuns against Italians."* Her laughter dampened, and she continued, *"Well, not only can I guarantee that this feud will come to an end, but I can also guarantee that all of Mister Babineaux's controlling interests will fall into your hands."*

Lupino cracked a genuine smile.

"Don't smile just yet, Mister Lupino," Theresa said to him. *"There's more."* She turned to Quincy and asked him in English, "A bottle of Water Bug Hollow's finest, and a glass for our guest, please." Quincy disappeared to fulfill Theresa's order. She returned her attention to Lupino, who was now beaming with delight. *"There's no need for war when we can profit instead, no?"* spoke Theresa.

Quincy returned with a bottle of Water Bug Hollow-made wine and a glass for Mister Lupino. He handed the Italian man the glass, popped the wine bottle, and then filled the glass with wine. Lupino thanked him. Theresa instructed for Lupino to have a sip.

Lupino did so, first smelling the contents, pretending to take in its aroma.

Theresa said to him, "It's not poisoned, Mister Lupino." Lupino raised an eyebrow as he drank, offended, though Theresa's accusation of his actions was correct. When his gulp was finished, his smile returned. Theresa beamed, "Isn't that just delightful?"

"Very much so," Lupino responded.

Theresa put an elbow on her knee, and then rested her chin atop a balled fist. Theresa said, "I'm sure an intelligent man like you plans for the future. Not too far in time's schedule, this government will make sure all of America is dry. Water Bug Hollow will remain wet, I assure you. There will be demand for good wine and liquor. We have distilleries here in Water Bug Hollow. And as you can taste, Mister Lupino, we offer great flavor. We have the supply. We will keep you supplied so that you may fill demand."

Lupino took a moment to contemplate.

Theresa pronounced, "I know you might have partners already lined up for this trade, but none can offer you the flavor you will get from Water Bug Hollow wine and beer. We can also supply you with the finest reefer cigarettes. We can begin that transaction immediately."

Lupino smiled. He cupped his hands and leaned back. In Italian, he said to Theresa, "*Babineaux. You have one week to deal with him. I will then consider your offer, and then we will meet again, Miss Amat.*"

"Mamma Indigo," Theresa politely corrected. "Call me Mamma Indigo. *Madre Indaco.*" She reached out and cupped both her hands around a single, extended hand offered by Samuel Lupino. She said to him, "One week is more than enough time for Otes Babineaux to be dealt with, Mister Lupino. However, should it take longer I warn you to be cautious. If you jump in your automobile with anger and ill intentions toward Water Bug Hollow, then you too will meet the same fate as Otes Babineaux. I curse you to that."

Lupino laughed away Theresa's words.

Theresa beamed a confident grin, and then both parties stood and all shook hands. Theresa invited Samuel Lupino to the night's show, and the Italian businessman accepted Theresa's offer, staying for breakfast, lunch, and dinner. Theresa and her band treated Lupino to a rousing performance, and then he and his associates departed Water Bug Hollow at three in the morning. Theresa turned in at midnight, but wished Water Bug Hollow's Italian visitors a goodnight.

Three days later, New Orleans newspapers reported the death of Port boss Otes Babineaux. It was reported that the forty-six-year-old Acadian died of a sudden heart attack, and no one was happier than Samuel Lupino. A competitor was dead, and the death could not be traced back to him. The blood was not on his hands. Blood was on no one's hands but nature's. And despite many attempts in man's history to do so, no one could arrest Her.

Samuel Lupino met with Theresa Amat and Mayor Johnson, agreeing to a partnership of 'supply-and-demand'. Samuel Lupino also wished to obtain several female escorts for his own business, and a share in Water Bug Hollow' gambling profits.

"I have no ill intentions toward Water Bug Hollow," Samuel Lupino expressed. "But I know many powerful men that might. They would make war with Water Bug Hollow, and they would take what they wanted, divvying it up among themselves. I would be hurt, Mamma Indigo, but as a businessman, I would also ask to share in the take."

Theresa replied, "Water Bug Hollow will get back to you on that, Mister Lupino."

The Italian racketeer beamed. "Most definitely, Mamma Indigo."

Samuel Lupino received an answer two days later. It was a letter reading a simple, 'No' in Theresa's handwriting and signed *Mamma Indigo*. The signatures of Mayor Johnson and his cabinet were also scrawled across the bottom of the one-word letter.

Alberto Cuore, a high-ranking man in Samuel Lupino's business, visited Water Bug Hollow not too long after Theresa's letter was received. Water Bug Hollow's matriarch watched from her window the residents scurrying about their day while she calmly sat and sipped on honey-spiced boneset tea, veil fixed atop her head.

Knocking.

"Come in, Q."

Quincy walked inside and reported, "There's an Alberto Cuore here. He's an associate of Samuel Lupino."

"Escort him upstairs, please, Q," Theresa directed.

Quincy left the room. Theresa stood and placed her cup of tea on the vanity. Quincy returned with Alberto Cuore, a handsome olive-skinned man dressed in a brown suit. Theresa extended a hand and a smile. "Mister Cuore. How is everything? I take it my letter was received."

Alberto removed his hat, rotating it at the brim as he responded in a low, uneasy voice, "Yes." He straightened his arms to his side. "A seat, please, *Madre Indaco*."

Theresa pointed to the seat near the window. "You may take that seat and pull it up to the bed," she said sitting down on the edge of the bed.

Alberto went to the window and pulled up the seat as instructed. Theresa asked, "Is it all right if my ward stays?"

Alberto took a quick look over his shoulder at the armed Quincy. He said to Theresa, "That is no problem. Not at all." He shifted in the seat and continued to rotate his hat at the brim.

Theresa reached for Alberto's hat. "Let me take that for you, Mister Cuore. Would that be okay?"

Alberto handed Theresa the hat. He rubbed his knees and sat up straight as Theresa placed the hat on the bed next to her. "Mister Lupino was far from happy with your response," said Alberto.

"Oh," said Theresa.

Samuel Lupino's loud rants came back to Alberto, having heard them in the racketeer's New Orleans office. *"That goddamned, nigger witch,"* he shouted in Italian. *"Does she think she has a deal without this part of the bargain? Who does she believe she is? I'll burn her and her whole town!"*

Theresa added, "He sent you to kill me, didn't he?"

Quincy moved his hand toward his holstered pistol.

Alberto was unaware of Quincy's actions behind him. The Italian man protested, "I argued against him. I did. He wanted to make war, but I told him not to. I don't believe it's right. Outright war does not make profit. I agree to your terms. Mister Lupino did not. He is headstrong. That's what makes him a great leader."

Alberto remembered Samuel Lupino turning to him and saying, *"You disagree with my actions, don't you Alberto? You disagree because this nigger witch reminds you of that colored woman you were fucking all those years ago. She was a witch too. Her and her hocus pocus, and you believed every superstition she had. And this one! This woman believes this country will run dry of liquor. No way. None. She is crazy. That fantasy will never become law, no matter the protests and push for it!"*

Alberto looked at the floor. He breathed deep. Looking at Theresa he said, "He didn't send me to kill you. He sent an army. His army. He screamed at me to get into his car. We were to meet his soldiers at a warehouse. Sixty armed men ready to make war with Water Bug Hollow."

"My goodness," Theresa gasped.

Alberto cleared his throat and shook his head. "I got in the car, *Madre Indaco*. Mister Lupino sped away from his office building. He was going to the warehouse." Alberto stopped, his words fading. His lower jaw trembled as it hung open. He jumped from his seat and snatched his hat from the bed. The sudden reaction startled Quincy, and he quickly pulled his pistol. Theresa signaled Quincy to holster the firearm. Alberto simply crumpled his hat. He turned his back to Theresa just as Quincy holstered his weapon.

"I, I, I don't know why I'm here, or, rather, I don't know *how* I'm here," said Alberto, his voice trembling. "It's a miracle, madam." He spun around, looking Theresa in the eye. "The trolley slammed into the car on the driver's side. Mister Lupino, my former boss, he was killed instantly. I suffered a few scrapes and bruises, nothing more."

The scene came to Theresa as she blinked. Samuel Lupino angrily speeding down a New Orleans street, and never focusing on traffic or traffic directors. Theresa saw the crash and then blinked her eyes back to her present surroundings.

"Our Lord," Theresa declared in a low voice.

"I now sit at the head of the Lupino family, *Madre Indaco*, and I agree to your terms—the terms of Water Bug Hollow."

Theresa stood. She took a step toward Alberto Cuore and reached out a hand. He accepted, and they shook cordially. But, on contact with Alberto's hand, sadness crept inside Theresa, an emotion she touched with sympathy. She surveyed Alberto, scoping his expression. "I remind you of someone, Alberto. Someone you loved."

Alberto shook his head. He said in Italian, "*He called her a witch. He called you a witch, Madre Indaco.*"

"I've never heard a finer compliment," Theresa retorted teasingly. "It's an old word, some say Arabic, that means *wise woman*. The word goes back, back before that land was known as Arabia. Before politics severed its umbilical cord from Mamma Africa. Far back. As all things go, Mister Cuore." Theresa expressed a stern look. "Speaking of which, have you ever heard of the Moors, Mister Cuore?"

"Yes, Madre Indaco. Of course I have."

Theresa took back her hand. "Then I most certainly will look forward to our trade, Mister Cuore. Thank you for your time."

Alberto put his hat on. He kissed Theresa on the back of the hand and shook Quincy's hand before leaving. Avery met Alberto in the hall and escorted him back to his four-man entourage, and then, out of town. Theresa sat down on the bed. Her eyes met Quincy's. She scoffed, "Samuel Lupino. The nerve of that man marchin' in here the way he did, believin' he could flaunt his impudent lawlessness to a community of Negroes the government's law don't protect. We depend upon ourselves." She huffed and reached for her cup of tea. "Good riddance to him. Shit."

"Yes, Theresa," Quincy said still astounded by her cool demeanor. He stared at her, humbled. There was admiration and fear in his look. Then he dismissed himself to catch up with his brother.

Theresa and her band had the night off, which Theresa was thankful for. She needed the rest. In two days, musical tradition was restored. No one made mention of Theresa's handling of what was being called the *Lupino Affair*. No one asked about her sudden understanding of the Italian language, but most ventured a guess that she picked it up from her erudite fiancé, Joseph Pepper IV, coupled with her fluency in Creole and French.

Theresa shared the story with Sarinda Fallows, and Sarinda was charmed by it.

The months faded, one after the next, and Theresa's belly grew. She became more excited, but she performed less. Her family returned to Water Bug Hollow for Christmas, staying through the New Year.

Water Bug Hollow became routine with daytime work and late-night music. In mid-February, the ground was ready for construction. The church's foundation was built, and soon after, construction was fully underway. Theresa helped to shape Water Bug Hollow's new laws, sitting in on Mayor Johnson's cabinet meetings. This routine continued throughout the months, but became challenged on the night of the twenty-fourth of May.

There was no music this night. Theresa Amat and Sarinda Fallows enjoyed conversation. They sat across from one another at a newly purchased table in Theresa's apartment. The circular table rested near the window. Theresa enjoyed boneset tea while Sarinda nursed a glass of Water Bug Hollow wine. Sudden knocking on the door interrupted the women's conversation, causing Theresa to roll her eyes. Light laughter escaped her and she said to Sarinda, "Oh, it's Q." She turned her head toward the door and called, "Come in, Q. It's not locked." Theresa said to Sarinda, "What could be the matter this late at night?"

Quincy opened the door and entered the room. Madame Lucille Harper followed Quincy into the room. She was clothed in a violet dress, and atop her head was a matching wide-brim hat. Theresa's face brightened when she noticed Madame Lucille behind Quincy.

"Madame Lucille," Theresa said excitedly. "To what do I owe this pleasure?"

Madame Lucille stepped from behind Quincy as he stayed near the door. She responded to Theresa unsmiling. "I can't say there is much pleasure, Mamma Indigo. I've decided to talk with you before things get out of hand." Her eyes quickly shifted toward Sarinda. "Privately, Mamma Indigo."

Sarinda lifted an eyebrow.

Theresa turned her attention to Sarinda and said in an apologetic tone, "Sarinda, could you wait for me in the café. I know it's late, but please don't go to your room yet. I'll send Quincy down to get you when I've dealt with this business."

"Absolutely, Theresa," said Sarinda, her civilized demeanor challenged to remain in place in Madame Lucille's presence. She got up and started to walk away when Theresa grabbed her hand. Sarinda looked down. "Theresa…"

"Don't go nowhere, you hear," Theresa instructed, her eyes looking sad. "There are some things I do need to speak with you about."

Sarinda chuckled. "I'll be downstairs, Theresa. I won't stray."

"Thank you," Theresa expressed. Sarinda left the room, and Madame Lucille sat in her chair across from Theresa. Mamma Indigo gave the elder woman her full attention. "What unpleasant matter brings you to me, Madame Lucille?"

Lucille's eyes stayed on the door, eyebrows bent, brow furrowed. Her eyes turned to spot Theresa. "You let that white woman address you by your given name? She need to address you proper. Mamma Indigo is who you are."

Theresa waved Lucille's sentiment away. "Sarinda and I have known each other too long. I'd feel queer to hear her call me that. It's quite all right." Theresa then expressed, "Your matter, Madame Lucille."

Madame Lucille fixed her demeanor. Her expression shifted from anger to concern. "My girls aren't being honest, Mamma Indigo. They are not reporting all their earnings. I caught one, and I brought her to you."

Theresa looked surprised, and she said in the same tone, "Why, I'm no gangster or pimp, Madame Lu—"

"Adina!" Madame Lucille called. "Come in here, girl."

Theresa turned her head and watched as a young, brown-skinned girl walked inside her apartment. The young woman named Adina looked shameful, like a child. She wore a simple wool skirt patterned with braid and a blouse with insets and pintucks. Madame Lucille instructed her to have a seat at the table. Adina sat down, seated at Theresa's left.

Madame Lucille, voice angry and eyes looking the same, gave another instruction. "Tell Mamma Indigo what you've done."

Adina's voice was low and stuttering when she declared, "I've held some of my earnings."

"Speak up!" hollered Madame Lucille.

Adina's body jumped at the sound of Madame Lucille's voice, and the young woman repeated with greater volume in her voice, "I've held some of my earnings."

"Tell her!" Madame Lucille shouted.

Theresa lifted her hand, palm aimed at Madame Lucille. She said in a calm voice, "Please, Madame Lucille. Please. I need you to be quiet. Either that or wait in the hall, which I would consider to be a shame, considering that I need your presence when I settle these matters." Madame Lucille relaxed in her seat; her face still composed of a scowl. Theresa asked Adina, "You and other girls have been holding back the taxes owed?"

"Yes," Adina answered in a soft voice.

"And why is this?" Theresa interrogated.

Adina took a moment and a breath before speaking. "I don't want to do this no more, Mamma Indigo. Not me, and not a lot of the other girls too. Not even the male escorts." She looked up at Theresa more confident than before. "I've given my tribute for all my earnings in Water Bug Hollow, but not at The Lounge. Them white men pay twenty dollars to us colored girls. Twenty dollars, Mamma Indigo. Twenty. The boys get paid the same when they service a white woman at The Lounge. Some of us want to go to school, but…"

"But what, dear?" Theresa asked in a motherly manner.

"Can't afford school," replied Adina. "Tuition can be as costly as a hundred and seventy-five dollars a semester. This is the only job we have, but I want to be a school teacher like Miss Lucille used to be." Surprise splashed across Madame Lucille's face. Theresa smiled at her, and then she returned her eyes to Adina. The young woman continued, "I mean no offense, Mamma Indigo, but your law has made it hard for some of us in this profession to do any saving. And we don't much like it anymore. I mean," Adina's eyes looked at the floor. She smiled as she reminisced. "In the beginning it was fun, an ongoing party. The men. The drink. The smoke. The music," she said looking up and pointing her wide eyes at Theresa in a teasingly accusing manner. "Your music, Mamma Indigo." Adina's expression then became sincere. "But, I want more."

Theresa leaned forward and put her hands on Adina's wrists. "Absolutely, child. Absolutely. Where's your mother and father?"

"Scotlandville," Adina answered. "They moved there with my brother just after I graduated the twelfth grade. I stayed. I love Water Bug Hollow."

Theresa removed the veil from atop her head. She placed it on the table and asked the young woman to put her hands over the garment. "Close your eyes, Adina. Close them." Adina did as Theresa ordered. "You no different than me, child. Now, put your head on that fabric. Just lay it down." Adina did so, and she fell fast asleep. Theresa looked at Madame Lucille. Her gaze was stern. "The brothel is closed, Madame Lucille. No more business. You and your husband will re-open the establishment as a trade school for the young men and women that graduate from Water Bug Hollow's Secondary School. I'll talk to Mayor Johnson about the funds for the school. The surplus we're seeing through trade with our Italian associates should probably cover it. Is all this understood?"

Madame Lucille replied, "Y-y-yes, Mamma Indigo."

Keeping her stern gaze on Madame Lucille, Theresa spoke, "Adina. Rise."

Adina lifted her head and took a deep breath.

"This is not the first time I've had to do this to one of your employees, Madame Lucille," Theresa confessed. "But, this is the first time I've had inspiration for us to turn around the practice of that archaic profession you and your husband indulge in. Perhaps your presence was my inspiration. Usually, the young man or young woman comes to see me about these troubles by themselves. Q," Theresa called. "Please bring Madame Lucille a copy of my mamma's cleansing ritual."

Quincy traveled around Theresa's bed and to her dresser. He opened the top drawer and removed a sheet of paper that was printed with

Qarla Elizabeth Amat's cleansing ritual. He closed the drawer and walked it over to Madame Lucille, laying the sheet of paper in front of her.

"I've been giving copies to young men and women that are now your former employees," Theresa explained. "I usually charge for this service, but this will be free."

Madame Lucille expressed to Theresa as she folded the piece of paper, "I will repay you, Mamma Indigo, by committing to your command. I will build a trade school for people to learn a skill that will get them employed outside Water Bug Hollow, and help them with a college education. Yes. My husband and I will do just that. Today is a new day, Mamma Indigo."

Madame Lucille adjusted her glasses and then stood up. She called, "Come, Adina."

Adina stood.

"You treat her right, now," said Theresa, her voice a warning.

Madame Lucille bowed her head. "I will, Mamma Indigo. I will."

The two women, Madame Lucille and Adina, left the room. Quincy stayed, closing the door as the women disappeared down the hall. "Are there any important matters, Theresa?"

Theresa chuckled. "I sure hope not," she said. "I'm tired of all this. Have my emotions up and riled. Don't these people know I'm almost due?"

"Why don't you get some rest, Theresa?"

"I can't yet. I do have matters with Miss Fallows. Please escort her back up, Q. Prepare a pot of boneset tea for me. Make it the way I like. Bring it back to my room with a clean cup, and then post up with your brother outside. The two of you may retire when I'm done with Miss Fallows."

"Yes. I'll be back, Theresa."

Quincy left the room.

Theresa exhaled. She rose from the seat, struggling with the weight of her pregnant belly. It was no longer a small bump, but a large, protruding mound. She groaned as she got to her feet. She balanced her weight on the chair, and then dragged the chair to the bed. She remained standing and waited. Quincy knocked on the door several minutes later. Theresa took a second breath, "It's open, Q." Sarinda walked in. Theresa looked over her shoulder and commented, "Oh." She could see Quincy holding the door open for Sarinda as she entered the apartment with a pot of tea and a cup. "Sarinda. Now you let Q handle that."

Sarinda walked to the table and replied teasingly, "Let Quincy hold his post, your majesty." She set the pot of tea on the table, and there her eyes spotted the veil sprawled out. Sarinda swallowed the next words she meant to speak. She was too transfixed on the veil to talk.

The door closed.

"Sarinda," Theresa called her.

Sarinda didn't move.

"Sarinda!" Theresa called again.

Then her eyes blinked. Her head shook, and she turned around. "Yes, Theresa."

"Come sit on the bed, please."

Sarinda took one last glance toward the veil, and then she slowly turned her body and walked to the bed. She sat down. Theresa sat in the chair.

"Give me your arm, sweetie," Theresa said caringly. "Come on." Sarinda held out her arm without protest. Theresa moved the sleeve of Sarinda's blouse up, exposing the puncture marks riddled up and down Sarinda's bare arm. Theresa caressed Sarinda's forearm. "Oh, baby. I've been meaning to speak with you about this. I can't see you hurt yourself any longer, Sarinda."

Sarinda took her arm back. She laughed and said, "I'm fine, Theresa. I'm okay." She jumped to her feet and changed the subject. "Them boys in New York are just waiting for you to be a mamma, Theresa. They want you to get your rest, and then when you're ready, come and play at a club. You and your band."

"Sarinda," Theresa drawled turning toward her. "Don't try and duck my focus."

Sarinda twirled and said proudly in protest, "I have slowed my ways, Theresa. You know that. I mean, the party is not completely behind me, but it is slowing its steps." Theresa groaned at Sarinda's comment as she again shifted in the chair. "Now, look at you, Theresa," Sarinda continued, "you still tryin' to regulate things while this child is in its coming days."

Theresa held her belly and breathed out hard. "Oooh," she expressed. She took a moment and relaxed. "Sarinda, you are a friend of mine. You are a friend of Water Bug Hollow. I just want to offer my help. You've offered yours. You've brought us warning. You brought me and my band an opportunity."

"I got you hooked on narcotics, girl," Sarinda reminded.

But Theresa simply waved away Sarinda's protest. "We were having fun. And, I could have said no, which I eventually did. Who's to say that I didn't have to go through that darkness and trial to get here? I'd like to return the favor."

Sarinda took a step back. She turned and stood over the veil. "Any favor, Theresa? Then, might I try on this lovely veil? Yes or no?"

Sarinda waited for an answer.

Theresa responded, "I'd like to do a cleansing ritual, Sarinda. That veil will be a part of the ritual. You'll sleep with the veil over you."

Sarinda kept her back to Theresa, eyes locked on the veil. She turned. "You're my friend, Theresa."

"Yes, I am."

"Then I will partake in your cleansing ritual." Sarinda was excited. "What do we do?"

Theresa nodded her head toward the bathroom. "Prepare yourself a bath and wash. You can use my bathrobe. Under the sink, there's a towel to dry yourself off with."

Sarinda moved her eyes toward the veil and grinned, then she made her way to the bathroom to take her bath. Theresa stood, groaning the entire time she rose to her feet. She held her pregnant stomach underneath and put her hand at the base of her back. She walked to the vanity, opened a drawer, and pulled out a bag of dried boneset leaves. She returned to her seat, placed the bag on her nightstand, and waited for Sarinda to finish her wash.

Twenty minutes passed before Sarinda emerged from the bathroom clothed with Theresa's robe. Heat and steam followed her. She walked to the table to retrieve the veil, first asking, "Should I take the veil and bring it to you?"

"Leave it on the table, Sarinda," Theresa said to her. "Take off that robe and lay on this bed."

"Theresa!" Sarinda exclaimed.

"Come on, now. You got the same lady parts I do. Take that robe off and lay flat on this bed."

Sarinda kept her smile. She untied the bathrobe's belt and then let the garment fall from her figure. Theresa looked at Sarinda unfazed by her naked frame. "You ain't totally naked yet, Miss Fallows. Take that necklace off."

Sarinda hid the surprise stirred in her by Theresa's command. She hesitated, but then obliged, removing the necklace and laying it next to the veil. Theresa asked her to pour a cup of tea, and again, Sarinda complied with Theresa's orders. She faced Theresa, and the woman now known as Mamma Indigo motioned for Sarinda to get in the bed. Sarinda obeyed after handing the cup of tea to Theresa who placed it on the nightstand next to the dried bag of boneset leaves. Sarinda lay flat and didn't speak. She closed her eyes without being told.

Theresa removed the dried boneset leaves from the bag, crushed them up in her hands, and then rubbed them over Sarinda Fallows' body. Sarinda inhaled the dried leaves' aroma. It felt like soap or oil was lathered across her skin. Sarinda did not feel the dried, crushed leaves as sharp pricks. The sensation was soothing, and it continued for several minutes before Sarinda heard Theresa command, "Sit up, now, Sarinda. Sit up." Sarinda lifted and put her back against the headboard. She felt more relaxed than any narcotic had ever made her. "Have some tea," Theresa instructed giving Sarinda the cup.

Sarinda took the cup in a gentle grip. She breathed in the aroma, blew on the tea, creating ripples, and then put the cup to her lips and sipped. Her body instantly warmed. Sarinda quivered with the heat. She tilted her head back and let out an excited cry. Theresa smiled and watched her friend drink more and more until she was finished. She took the cup from her and placed it back on the nightstand.

"Now, put that robe back on, Sarinda. You'll sleep here tonight. I'll be right next to you. Come on. Up." Sarinda lifted off the bed, feeling as if gliding. When she walked, it felt as if she was floating. Her smile never left. Theresa remarked, "Now, don't you feel better?"

Sarinda replied, "I sure do." Then something bubbled in Sarinda's stomach. It twisted and turned. Her stomach felt heavy, as if she had just eaten a large meal. Then came the foul taste of tar and ash. Her stomach jumped, and Sarinda hiccupped. She cupped her mouth as it opened. The tarry taste and heavy feeling traveled up from her stomach and into her throat. Sarinda charged the bathroom. She slammed the door shut and dropped to her knees over the toilet. A loud retching sound expelled from her and she vomited.

Theresa stood quickly, the burdening weight of her pregnancy not an issue. She walked carefully to the bathroom and called, "Sarinda! Sarinda! Honey, are you okay in there?" Sarinda replied with heavy retching and gags from the other side of the door. "Oh, dear me!" Theresa exclaimed in a low breath. "Sarinda," she called again. "Sarin—" Theresa's voice funneled back down into her throat. She gasped and backed away from the door while holding her pregnant stomach. She gasped again as she felt her child move. It wasn't a kick. It was a push.

Theresa's breath quickened. She stepped back, carefully. She turned around, being just as careful and mindful to keep her balance. She put one foot forward, and she felt a heavy push. Theresa stiffened, trying to hold back the sudden pangs. She put another foot forward, breathed in and out, and then took another step. Another. A fifth step. Theresa was upright, but she moved as if she was crawling with a mortal wound. Another sharp push caused her to again stiffen up straight. A cold sweat wiped her brow. Her mouth hung low. She continued to gasp, staring at the bed and continuing her slow trek closer to it. Theresa felt like the bed was in another state, and it might as well have been. But she continued forward, slow as it was. Each step was heavy. Each push forward came with another jarring push from her child.

Sound dampened around Theresa.

Closer.

Theresa reached out for the chair where she'd been sitting. She stopped and rested her weight there, breathing rapidly. She looked at the bed. It was close now. She took a deep breath and then moved forward, lifting herself with her arm on the back of the chair. She turned around and slowly lowered her body, the pressure of birth increasing. She was now sitting. On the bed. She rested again, slowing her breath and looking at the headboard. Theresa aimed her eyes down at her legs, and then she looked back at the headboard. She breathed deeply again, and then she swung her legs up and onto the bed. She laid flat, head elevated from the pillow. She relaxed her breath, and as she did, she saw movement come from across the room.

The bathroom door opened. Sarinda Fallows, naked, staggered from the room. Her hair was a mess, and she was panting. The warm feeling that embraced Sarinda following her first sip of tea became a burning flame whipping her body. Sarinda crawled up the wall in order to stand. Her perspective blurred foggy with haze. Her vision faded in and out as if a dying light flickered.

Theresa could see Sarinda was no use to her. She tipped her head back onto the pillow, looking up at the ceiling. Her breath quickened again. She concentrated and relaxed. Tears streamed down the side of her face. She breathed in. Out. In. Out. In. Out. In. Deep. She screamed, "QUINCY! QUINCY!"

Quincy broke through the door. His eyes swung first to Theresa as she lay on her bed, the heels of her feet rubbing her bed as if trying to escape something crawling toward her. She was disheveled and sweating. Quincy ran to her. "Theresa," he said grabbing her hand as she reached up to him. Her grip was tight, squeezing Quincy with uncomfortable might.

"The baby's coming, Q!"

Quincy actually smiled. "Right now?" he asked.

"Right now. Go. Get. Doctor Rhodes."

"You gon' have to let go of my hand, sister."

Theresa only squeezed harder until she felt confident to open her grip. Her bed sheets became her hands' next victim. Quincy stepped away from the bed. He turned and saw Sarinda Fallows naked and struggling in the bathroom doorway.

"Miss Fallows…?" He covered his eyes, but his perplexed expression remained.

"I'm fine, Quincy. Something didn't quite agree with my stomach. Fetch me that robe on the ground and—" Another gurgling sensation bubbled in her stomach, stopping her words. Sarinda jumped up and rushed back to the toilet where she vomited again.

"Avery!" Quincy called. His brother appeared in the doorway. "Help Miss Fallows. Bring her the robe on the ground. I'ma find Doctor Rhodes."

Avery placed his shotgun against the wall and stepped inside, Quincy rushing by him. Avery took a glance at Theresa who was busy keeping herself relaxed, controlling her breath. He walked over to the crumpled robe on the floor and scooped it up.

Finishing another heave into the toilet, Sarinda said in a civilized manner, "Avery. Would you be so kind as to also bring my pendant to me." She coughed and said, "Thank you, dear."

Avery picked up Sarinda's necklace and then walked toward the bathroom door with both items in hand. He entered slowly, keeping his eyes away as he handed Sarinda her necklace. He covered her with the robe, draping it over her shoulders like a cape.

"I thank you," said Sarinda out of breath. She snapped her necklace in place, her pendant swinging to and fro. On one swing toward Sarinda, it hit her chest and Sarinda bucked as if struck by lightning. When her body settled, her breath disappeared, and she began choking. Sarinda clutched her chest while on her knees.

Avery knelt down and asked, "You okay, Miss Fallows?"

Sarinda could not answer, and at that moment, Theresa screamed as another birthing pang rippled through her. Sarinda's breath then came back to her. She took in breaths as if she was eating after suffering a long starvation.

Avery patted her back. "Can you stand, Miss Fallows? Can you stand and put this robe on proper?"

Theresa cried again, and this time Avery turned around to view the condition of Water Bug Hollow's matriarch. Sarinda again lost her breath. One hand clasped her chest, the other grabbed Avery's arm for support. Her grip was tight. The hand on her chest slowly reached out until her fingers clasped her pendant and started caressing the curio.

The bathroom door closed.

Avery felt a sting shoot up his left arm. He felt a sensation as if his arm had become stone. It was numb and heavy. There was no feeling at all, and slowly the numbness began rising and spreading through his body. Sarinda gripped tighter Avery's right arm. The numbness reached his chest and then escalated up through his throat. Avery struggled to breathe. He wanted to use his free hand to knock Sarinda's grip from his arm, but his left arm wouldn't move. He opened his mouth to scream, but there was no sound. His legs started to tremble, and his knees buckled, eventually bending. Sarinda's grip tightened again, and one of Avery's knees hit the floor.

Sarinda started to stand upright, the robe slipping off her as she straightened.

Avery wheezed. His mouth opened wide with his tongue hanging out as he choked. His body stumbled and turned on its side. Sarinda stood as Avery slumped to the bathroom floor dead. She kept a tight grip on Avery's arm until she knew for certain that Avery would never stir again.

Sarinda exhaled. She picked up the robe and covered herself properly. She pulled back a sleeve and examined her arm. The marks made by needle punctures were gone, as if no sharp object had ever penetrated Sarinda's flesh. She stepped over Avery's body and listened at the door. She heard voices. Quincy had returned with Doctor Maggie Rhodes and three of her nurses. Sarinda opened the door. Quincy turned around. His eyes could see his brother on the ground.

"Avery," he said as he stepped away from Theresa's bedside. He ran up to Sarinda and asked, "What happened?" But he didn't wait for an answer. He pushed past her and fell to his knees in front of his brother's body. Quincy lifted Avery into his arms. He put his brother's mouth to his ears to hear or feel a breath. There was nothing. "Oh, no. Please, no. Avery, can you hear me? Avery you there? You there, brother? You there?" Quincy started trembling. He turned and shouted to Sarinda, "What the hell happened to my brother?" But Sarinda didn't respond, enraging Quincy. "Hell's wrong with you, woman? Go get some more help, goddamnit. Go. Maggie, we need Doctor Terrence to—"

"STOP!" Sarinda yelled.

And everything did.

Quincy didn't move. Maggie Rhodes and her nurses were motionless, hovering around Theresa's bed. Sarinda turned around. Theresa stirred. Her eyes, wide with wonder, went from Maggie and then to the nurses. They were as still as life in a photograph or painting, caught within their last movements that should have flowed seamlessly into their next. Sarinda took time to gather a cigarette from her purse. She lit the end of it, took a drag, and coolly released smoke from between her pursed lips. She sat down in the chair positioned at Theresa's bedside and she declared, "You're going to give me that veil, you black witch. Tonight."

Theresa caressed her pregnant stomach. "I don't feel a thing. My baby isn't moving." She looked over at Sarinda whose hair appeared to darken an entire shade. "Sarinda, what's the meaning of this?"

Sarinda looked at Theresa with sad eyes, shaking her head. "All that magic, and you still have no idea." Sarinda laughed as she took another hit of her cigarette. "I will readily admit this here, I have used you time and again, Miss Amat—Mamma Indigo, if you prefer. But you have always seemed to stray from my direction. You have been an unreliable instrument, surviving one trial after the next. There must be more to you than I know. There's definitely more to you than you know." Sarinda calmly rested her cigarette on the nightstand. She grabbed Theresa's arm with one hand, rubbed her pendant with the other, and then squeezed.

Theresa trembled. Her vision became blurry. She closed her eyes and tried to scream. Smoke and liquid bubbled in her throat, and Theresa remembered. There came the taste of golden-dragon smoke combined with reefer's puff and all the liquors she ever ingested. She swallowed to keep from drowning. The sensation of needle pricks stung her arms, and Theresa opened her mouth to scream, but there only escaped intoxicated laughter.

Sarinda let go.

Theresa continued her bubbly, inebriated cackling. She slumped down in the bed and covered her mouth, trying to hold the laughter in. Her laughter simmered to a drunken, hazy expression. Her eyes were dusty with sleep and she said dreamily to Sarinda, "All my sins were still inside me."

Sarinda replied with a charming smile, "You're going to die, Miss Amat."

Theresa chuckled at the realization. "Lord, this flesh sure has its disadvantages," she said in an otherworldly voice that surprised both she and Sarinda. The two of them looked at one another, recognition in their eyes. Theresa declared, "I remember you. Yes, I do. Sarah. Sarah the Pantomime." Theresa snickered, "That's what we called you."

Sarinda scowled. "Don't you call me that, nigger. Don't you use that name on me, hear?" But as she looked closer at Theresa, Sarinda's recognition became clearer. She smiled as if delighted, and she greeted Theresa anew. "I know *you*, Mamma Iyansan." She took back her cigarette, and before puffing said, "Oh, dear me. This couldn't be more perfect. Perhaps I should've stuck them drugs in you with a hexed needle." She took a drag and defiantly breathed the smoke into Theresa's face. "It's a shame that your self-realization comes at the moment your corporeal form acts out its greatest drawback." Both women laughed as if all that had just transpired had not tarnished their temporal friendship.

"Now, Sarinda, giving birth is not a drawback."

"You know that's not what I mean, you little pickaninny witch," Sarinda said with a smile. "You must have forgotten all about yourself the minute you were conceived physical and born through your mother's wretched, nigger womb."

"Sarinda," Theresa said in a weak voice, grin on her face.

"What can I help you with, Mamma Iyansan?" She mocked the name.

"I'd just like to give you a lesson, Sarinda," Theresa smiled back at her. "That word? Nigger? It comes from an old language. It means god or goddess. It has its derivatives throughout many ancient languages—all close to meaning the same thing. It gave us the words 'king', 'queen', and even the word 'energy'. Snake too, if I remember correctly. The Nubians and Egyptians called their leaders 'neggur'. Thank you for reminding me and my people, even if them British boys in the seventeenth century did twist its meaning into a slur. I wonder what them Africans must have thought when being beaten by a man who was calling them god or goddess at the same time. Oh, and Sarinda," Theresa then concluded, "I pass Joe's veil to my daughter."

"You don't believe I'll snatch it from her vile, pickaninny hands? You just cursed her life, Mamma Iyansan," Sarinda told Theresa.

"Do as you will to her, Miss Pantomime, but my daughter will never curse me."

Sarinda stood. She bent down, blew a final breath of smoke into Theresa's face, and then put the cigarette out on Theresa's shoulder. Theresa didn't cough when the smoke was blown in her face. And no matter how hard Sarinda pressed the cigarette into her shoulder, she felt no pain, and no scar blemished her flesh. She looked at Sarinda curiously, her eyes going from her shoulder to Sarinda's determined expression.

"You're still going to die," Sarinda reminded.

"I only get stronger as my breath grows weaker, Miss Pantomime."

Sarinda's face blistered with anger. Her hair darkened another shade of red as she composed herself and then said mockingly, *Hekua hey Yansa!* Sarinda left the room, slamming the door shut.

Theresa rested her head back against the pillow. She stared up at the ceiling. Her breath quickened, and she felt weak. She shut her eyes and started humming, eventually exploding into a loud, harmonious cry. Her eyes opened. The veil that once rested on her table was now lying across her pregnant belly. Theresa put her hands over it, and all manner of motion was restored, including her child's determined pushes to be birthed.

Everything was blurry to Theresa and blurry too for Quincy as he held his dead brother in his arms. Tears welled in his eyes. He rocked his brother back and forth as if Avery was a baby in his arms. The sound of shouting voices dampened and rose back to audible noise. Maggie Rhodes yelled for Theresa to breathe and push, and Theresa screamed loud, sounding as if she was blaring a musical number. Quincy heard more commands, more breathing and screaming.

Then came the birth of life. Child and mother hollered together in harmony. A piercing sound tore through the ceiling, penetrated the heavens, and left a crack in the midnight sky that stretched for miles in all four directions. The stars looked different. They appeared zigzagged rather than glowing globes. Miles away from Water Bug Hollow, in a Mississippi sky that looked down on a wide, grassy field, the crack opened up to drip forth a celestial teardrop. The moon's light followed the drip's descent as it splashed against the grass and formed into a trumpet case made of oak. The celestial dew dissolved, and it was then that the sky returned to normal.

In Water Bug Hollow, Theresa Amat held her daughter close. The baby girl was wrapped comfortably inside the veil. Theresa spoke her daughter's name as the baby girl simmered its birthing cries. Theresa became more and more weak. "Philomena. Philomena. The veil is yours, Philomena. It was blessed by your great grandmother, Philomena."

Maggie Rhodes took the child from Theresa. "Rest, Mamma Indigo. Rest."

Theresa put her head back on the pillow. *Dooley is a lilac flame, fluttering and flickering and shooting up into the sky where I see three moons reside. Red. Black. Green. There are golden halos surrounding them and they beam a kiss. Ah, procure this grand conjure and wish.* " She smiled and said in the same dreamy voice, "The gypsy was right." These were Theresa Amat's last words, said with her last breath, and then she died peacefully.

Maggie Rhodes held Philomena Amat close. The midwife's eyes fell on Theresa's body. Life faded. Maggie turned around. She and Quincy shared the same look of disbelief. She passed Philomena to one of her nurses and gave instructions. She ordered the second nurse to attend to Theresa's body, whispering her command. The third nurse was instructed to find Doctor Terrence Benjamin to attend to Quincy's brother, and then she walked to Quincy inside the bathroom and knelt down. "Amanda is going to find Doctor Ben, Quincy. He's going to see to your brother."

Quincy said through tears, "Doctor Ben can't help, Miss Rhodes. My brother's not conscious. He's dead. My brother's dead. He's gone."

Maggie touched Quincy gently on the hand. Tears came to her as she said, "Theresa passed in childbirth, Quincy. Mamma Indigo is gone."

Quincy gritted his teeth. Still rocking his brother, he asked, "Was it a girl?"

"Yes," Maggie answered. "Theresa gave birth to a healthy, baby girl. She's beautiful. Theresa named the girl Philomena."

"Where is Miss Fallows?"

"Quincy…"

"Where is she?" he hollered. Quincy didn't wait for an answer. He let his brother's limp body drop to the bathroom floor as he stood up and stormed from the apartment. He ran through the hall and came to Sarinda Fallows' room. He broke through the door and found the apartment empty. He huffed, turned, and charged out of the apartment complex. He pulled his gun and walked through Water Bug Hollow's nature-made tunnel. He thumbed back the hammer on his pistol and aimed the revolver at the taxi driver stationed next to the automobile transport. "Back away. You hear me? Back away!" The taxi driver lifted his arms and did as instructed. "Start this thing up," Quincy ordered. The driver did, and then walked away from the automobile. Quincy slipped inside. He tossed his gun onto the passenger seat and took off, New Orleans his destination. He was no more than a mile away from Water Bug Hollow when he slammed on the brakes. He wrapped his arms around the steering wheel, dropped his head on it, and burst into tears. "I'll take care of her, Theresa. I'll take care of her until Joe comes back. I'll take care of her. I will. I'll take care of her until Joe comes back. I swear." Quincy took a breath. He pounded the steering wheel with his fist and shouted numerous curses. He gripped the wheel and tugged back, screaming, crying, and cursing. Then he relaxed, took a moment, and turned the automobile back to Water Bug Hollow. He wiped his face of tears. He smiled and chuckled. "Shit. I'll take her to Scotlandville, Theresa. It's probably best that your family raise her. Yes, it is."

Water Bug Hollow was now in front of him. New Orleans was behind him, wherein that city Sarinda Fallows sulked in her apartment.

Curly Burneside stood over her as she sat down. He rubbed Sarinda's shoulders to comfort her. "There is some good news from all this, Miss Fallows," he said to Sarinda who wondered what that could possibly be. "I have word from London. Joseph Pepper is dead. It happened a month ago. Madison Goodspeed is nowhere to be found, but Joseph is dead. Ethan kept his promise. At least half."

Sarinda beamed, though still sad and fuming over the night's events. She reached back and touched Curly's hand as he rubbed her left shoulder. "Tell Mister Cassidy that I'm grateful. I know he and I don't see eye-to-eye on things, and I'm aware he's done what he's done for his own reasons, but you tell him I appreciate his accomplishment."

"Ethan was killed too, Miss Fallows," Curly further reported.

The faint hint of a smile appeared across Sarinda's face. "Oh…" she said, surprised at the news.

"That's why the news was so slow coming," Curly divulged. "Mister Brice Cadogan sent the word."

Sarinda paused. She'd heard the name before, but wasn't very familiar with the man. Then she said, "Well, then, thank Mister Brice Cadogan for me when you get the chance." Curly remained stone-faced. Sarinda didn't have the time to know why, but she could guess. Curly's jealous streak. But she had other directives for her right-hand-soldier to attend to, telling Curly, "I need some orders carried out tonight."

"Anything Miss Fallows," Curly assured her.

"There's a place called Scotlandville that I need you to visit," Sarinda told him. "Theresa Amat's family is there. This can't wait until morning, Curly. Tonight. When you come back we'll discuss more about bringing Reverend Ladon here. We'll modify his actions a bit, Curly. We'll still bring him to Water Bug Hollow when its church is complete. But we'll need his skills aimed at someone specific." Sarinda twirled her pendant as she looked down at it. "We'll suppress his urges until the time is right for him to express them."

"Yes, ma'am," said Curly in a low voice. He let go of Sarinda's shoulders and left the room, knocking on doors of apartment suites rented by men he called soldiers. White Knights. And on Sarinda's command relayed, Curly led these four men to Scotlandville, Louisiana. He rubbed his ring and gave directions while riding in the passenger's seat. In an hour and forty minutes' time, Curly's driver was turning into the Amat family driveway. All five men exited the automobile wearing potato sacks made for hoods. They walked up to the front door, looked around to verify the streets were quiet and empty, and then Curly kicked the door in.

The men walked inside, quickly scattering to different rooms of the ranch-styled house.

Qarla Amat was killed first. Two bullets struck her. One hit her in the chest, the second in the head. Charlie Amat, lying next to his wife in bed, received a bullet in the neck that paralyzed him instantly. Three more bullets struck him, piercing his lung, heart, and abdomen. Curly discovered Carolyn Amat's room. The young woman jumped up and screamed for only an instant before Curly swung the butt of his pistol into her temple and knocked her unconscious. Curly holstered his gun, dragged Carolyn Amat's body from the house and tossed her in the back of the automobile. His soldiers regrouped with him outside, and all five men got into the car and removed their masks. Curly took the passenger's seat. The driver jumped in and waited for the other three men to situate themselves. They were snug in the back with Carolyn Amat laying across them with her eyes closed and blood dripping from the side of her head.

The car backed out of the driveway and returned to New Orleans where Curly was dropped off at the hotel. His soldiers pleaded with him to stay for the fun, but Curly refused. They had been asking him to accompany them for the whole ride back to New Orleans. He never changed his mind. He did leave his soldiers with some advice. "Ain't a need to use a syringe on her. Far as I know, this one ain't got no conjure work about her. Miss Fallows got the real witch."

His soldiers acknowledged the information with a nod. The automobile sailed down the street, away from the hotel. Curly watched his soldiers drive away with Carolyn Amat in the back seat. She still lay unconscious and across the three soldiers in the back of the automobile. Now, she was being taken away. Her remains would eventually be discovered and identified in a rural area located in Pennsylvania fifty years after her disappearance—a long time after and a long way from where she was captured. Curly waited until he could no longer see the automobile in the dark distance before he entered the hotel and returned to Sarinda Fallows with a report of her orders accomplished.

News of the Amat family killing reached Water Bug Hollow the following afternoon. Upon hearing the news, Quincy retired to Theresa's apartment. Maggie Rhodes was there, rocking Philomena Amat in a new crib. The child was still wrapped in the blessed veil.

Quincy dragged a seat over to the crib and sat down.

"They haven't found Carolyn," he reported to Maggie Rhodes. "They're going to bring the bodies here for burial alongside Theresa. I sent a letter to her brother in Virginia. Hardest thing I ever had to write."

Quincy watched baby Philomena closely. He heard Maggie say, "Don't tell this child nothin' more than her mother's passin' on this day. Her mamma was sick, but she was smilin' in the last few minutes of her life. That's what this child will know. She made her mamma smile as she passed. Tell this girl nothin' more. You may not like Miss Fallows, but no foul word about her. My nurse told me Miss Fallows went and told Doctor Ben about your brother before she left. Doctor Ben said she looked frightened. This child will know no hate, hear? This child will only know the grand deeds of Mamma Indigo. Last night, Philomena was born, nothing more."

Quincy nodded in agreement. "Yes, ma'am."

"Grandparents and aunt were victims of the Klan. She can know that. But that did not happen on the night she was born. Hear?"

Quincy nodded in agreement. He chocked back tears as he again spoke, "Yes, ma'am."

"When Joe come for her, you tell him that. He should be here soon. A couple months or so."

"Yes, ma'am," Quincy said, and nothing more after. He watched baby Philomena closely. Maggie Rhodes stood next to him, a comforting hand on his shoulder. He thought that Joseph Pepper was too smart, and the erudite Northern-born Negro would see straight through him. But all that would saunter back to Water Bug Hollow resembling Joseph Pepper would be news of his death in London, two days after the Amat family funeral.

Quincy cried.

Water Bug Hollow, Louisiana
1933
"John, chapter eight, verse thirty-two."

"I decline your invitation to tonight's ceremony, Reverend Ladon. I'm not here to partake in the candlelight vigil. I won't interfere with the night's festivity. It's not my place, even if I am invited, and even if I am a MacRitchie. I'm here to see my niece," explained Sarinda Fallows to Reverend Lionel Ladon, current mayor and patriarch of Water Bug Hollow. "While you all hold vigil around the church, I will be here, watching from a distance, enjoying a nice dinner on this patio."

The Southern socialite and the reverend spoke cordially, witticisms expressed on occasion between them causing the two to laugh as they ate their brunch. They sat and enjoyed their meal within Eve's Hallow's exterior, waist-high, wooden fenced-in eating area.

Sarinda Fallows and Reverend Ladon were having a marvelous time. A cloudy day filled with haze could not stop Water Bug Hollow from shining. The sun still managed to extend brilliant shimmering rays of kisses through the tightly gathered clouds and the bonded foliage. The unusually cool, early August breeze did not disturb Miss Sarinda Fallows and Reverend Lionel Ladon from enjoying their brunch. The crisp air did prompt them to order cups of coffee with their meals. Sarinda was first offered tea, and when she inquired what kind, and the waiter answered, *"Boneset tea, Miss Fallows,"* she politely declined, expressing how that particular tea didn't sit well with her stomach. She ordered coffee instead, and Reverend Ladon joined her in a cup to accompany his brunch.

"I do enjoy your visits, Miss Fallows," relayed the broad-shouldered reverend, his gray suit matching the day. "Your visits around this time always give me the opportunity to express my gratitude to you for finding me a new congregation to pastor. So, let me say again, thank you. For the thousandth time."

Sarinda raised her cup of coffee and saluted the reverend. Before she replied, or took a sip of her drink, a young man, eighteen years of age, stepped out from Eve's Hallow. He walked onto the muddy road, saying to an older gentleman who trekked alongside him, "That's not what we learned in school, mister."

"That's 'cause your teachers don't know a damn thing," said the older man with a scowl. "And they too damn scared to tell you how Water Bug Hollow truly got its independence. We fought for this place, boy. We died."

Sarinda and the reverend made nervous glances toward the conversation as they sipped their coffee.

"My uncle says the same thing as you, mister. He talk all that militant history. My father says its nonsense."

The older man grabbed the boy by the collar with one hand and dragged him close to his face. "You listen to me, boy, your father just as stupid as your teacher. Just another forgetful nigger—like so many niggers 'round here—that don't know a damn thing about they history, believin' that mess brought in here by that Mississippi nigger!"

The young man pushed the older man and yelled, "Getcho hands off me, you ol' crazy fool." The young man's force, although powerful, did not relieve him of the older man's grip.

Sarinda curled her body away from the situation, eyes taking a peep back at the scene as it escalated. The boy's father appeared and demanded to know what the older man was doing to his son. Her eyes went to Lionel. His title as reverend fell by the wayside. He now had to resume patriarchal responsibility as the current mayor of Water Bug Hollow. Mayor Ladon angrily slapped his cup of coffee down onto the café table. He stood up and wiped his mustache with a napkin as a way to dispense some of his anger into another activity. But his crumpling and toss of the napkin only reset his anger, and he exited the fenced-in area and approached the situation with broad shoulders looking intimidating and authoritative.

The mayor ordered, "Gentlemen. Let's settle this. Now. Disperse."

The older man turned and looked Mayor Ladon up and down, the young man still in his grip, the boy's father continuing his approach and yelling for the older man to take his hands off his son.

"Mississippi nigger," growled the older man continuing to scope Mayor Ladon up and down. He opened his hand and let the young man go.

He turned his attention to the father and yelled, "Teach your boy right, you forgetful nigger."

Mayor Ladon repeated, "Gentleman. Disperse. Now."

The father cocked back a balled fist and swung hard, hitting the older man in the jaw. The older man toppled back. His body slammed against Mayor Ladon, and he used the mayor's body as leverage to balance himself straight, springing forward and tossing a clenched fist at the young man's father. Disoriented from the hit he'd taken, the older man's fist smacked against the father's shoulder. The father twisted with the impact, and the older man took the moment to strike the young man's father on the cheek.

Sarinda looked up and watched the fighting men. Her eyes focused on the men's aggression. She gasped, and her hand laid over her chest, covering the flat, gray stone that was speckled with red markings and dangling from a gold chain worn around her neck. Sarinda exhaled, and she began rubbing the pendant between two fingers.

Mayor Ladon grabbed the older man, locking the man's arms behind his back. Two of Water Bug Hollow's police officers jumped into the scene and subdued the boy's father. He was on the ground, face and clothes bathing in the muddy road. Handcuffs were clasped against him, and at the same time, Mayor Ladon had thrown the older man to the ground. An officer handcuffed the older man, and both he and the boy's father were lifted off the muddy road, clothes and face stained with the mix of earth and water.

The young man protested, "Officer, my father did nothing wrong! That drunk, old fool attacked me."

"Back away, son or you'll find yourself sittin' next to your father in jail." The officer turned to Mayor Ladon and asked, "Mayor, are you okay?"

"I'm fine," he assured, straightening his suit.

"Darren," the boy's father called. "You go on home. Tell your mamma I'll be home before church and tonight's vigil. Go on. No need for trouble. I broke the law, and this is what happens. It could be worse. It could be white officers with real authority. Now, go on."

"Listen to your father, son," Mayor Ladon encouraged. The older man mocked the boy with the same words. Mayor Ladon scolded the old man, "Keep your mouth hushed, y'hear? Officer, take these two away." The officers did as commanded, escorting the fighting men away. The young man returned home. Mayor Ladon returned to his table, sighing and flattening the front of his suit jacket with his hand as he sat down. "I apologize that you've had to see that, Miss Fallows. There always seems to be an incident or two during this time of year."

Sarinda sipped her coffee and took a bite of her eggs. "Well," she began as she swallowed her food and respectfully wiped her mouth. "You settled the matter."

"Mississippi Nigger, Miss Fallows," Lionel declared.

"Excuse me, Lionel?" Sarinda asked.

Lionel explained, "That's what they call me. The Mississippi Nigger. They've been callin' me that for eight years now, ever since I became Water Bug Hollow's mayor. Arlington got too sick to help ease the transition from his command to mine. Sick as he is, people still go to him, but he is always kind enough to remind these people who their current patriarch is."

"Lionel," Sarinda drawled with her charming, Southern accent. "The people respect you highly. You have—" A feeling tugged at Sarinda. She clutched her pendant and then turned around to see the piano player Quincy Mathews and her niece, Philomena Amat. Sarinda jumped from her chair and charged Philomena. The fifteen-year-old girl rushed up to Sarinda with a bright smile. "Now, there's my songbird of a niece!" shouted Sarinda. She and Philomena embraced one another, warm and tight. They backed away, all smiles. Sarinda inspected her niece. Philomena wore a light-blue, sleeveless dress. Her mother's veil was wrapped around her left arm. Sarinda complimented, "This is such a lovely dress, Philomena. Is that what you're wearing tonight for the vigil?"

"Just for the day's festivities," Philomena answered.

Sarinda's eyes panned up toward Quincy. "Hello, Quincy," she spoke skittishly.

Quincy nodded his head. "Sarinda," he spoke back in a low voice, beaming a strained smile.

"Come, the two of you. I'm having brunch with Reverend Ladon." Sarinda took Philomena by the arm and guided her toward the table with Reverend-Mayor Ladon. "Pull up a chair from that empty table over there—one for you and your Uncle Quincy."

Philomena did as Sarinda asked. Quincy and she sat in the chairs pulled from an empty table. Quincy said to Sarinda, "Your presence always surprises me, Sarinda. You always manage to remind Water Bug Hollow who you are."

"A MacRitchie," Sarinda expressed in a sharp tone.

Quincy smiled softly at Sarinda's reply. He asked, "How are things up in Harlem?"

"They're good, Quincy. They're good." She turned her attention to Philomena and stated, "I'll be in Water Bug Hollow more often now that I've cleared up a lot of business. I'll be able to see my niece more than once a year." She wiped a hand over Philomena's shoulder. She said to the two men at the table, "There are still troubling matters I have to deal with in Harlem. I've been helpin' these three boys run a club up there. The Mud Hare, the club is named. But them boys have gone and fallen into some legal trouble. They've been implicated in murder."

"That sounds mighty serious, Miss Fallows," Lionel commented.

Sarinda waved the reverend's comment aside. "Now, Lionel, them boys are innocent." She inquired, "Any of you ever heard of Pete Peters?"

Quincy's expression brightened. "Absolutely," he replied. "Missed him the two times the band and I went up there to New York, back in twenty-six and twenty-seven. He was away, him and his girl. Been meanin' to jump a train up to Harlem and go see him play. That young man supposed to be somethin' powerful." Quincy spoke regretfully, "Now there's no chance. Word in the jazz circle is that he was shot and killed in a quarrel."

"And that's the trouble these three boys are in," Sarinda interjected. "The piano player in his band, a close friend to Mister Peters, killed him. Fight was over a woman—and not the woman carryin' Pete Peters' child. It was a woman from an earlier romance, a romance that didn't have a proper endin'. That piano player found out his four-year-old child wasn't his child at all, but Pete's. Anyway, it's this piano player who killed Mister Peters. Tragic. They were the best of friends, I hear. But, I got a good lawyer for these boys. You best believe that piano player is going to jail."

"That's quite noble of you, Sarinda," Lionel said finishing his brunch.

Sarinda chuckled. "Noble my foot. I'm protectin' my business interest. Shoot." She then said, "But I don't want to talk all this nonsense in front of my niece. Quincy, take Philomena upstairs, please. I'm in my usual room. The door's unlocked. I have a gift for her. It's boxed and wrapped on the bed."

Philomena said bright and all smiles, "Oh my, Aunt Sarinda!" She jumped up. "I should be practicin' anyway," she concluded. Quincy stood from his chair, and then the two of them pushed in their seats.

"Not too hard now, dear, you don't want to strain your voice," Sarinda advised sweetly.

Philomena bent down and hugged Sarinda. "I won't, Aunt Sarinda. I'm so glad you're here." She kissed Sarinda on the cheek, bounced up and said, "Now, let me see this present." Philomena rushed away, enlivened. Quincy was right behind her.

Sarinda kept her eyes on Philomena and Quincy. She watched them enter Eve's Hallow to take the stairs up into the building's apartment section. She fiddled with her pendant and turned to Reverend Ladon. "Philomena looks so grown. Don't you think, Reverend? You could almost mistake her for a woman. Those curves. The way that dress hugs her ripe, young body." Sarinda gasped up laughter. "And that sky-blue dress against her golden-brown skin. Lord, I wish I had a glow like that. She will make a beautiful woman. Am I right, Reverend?"

Lionel was silent. He stared at Sarinda, his lips trying to form words but never speaking.

"I should be ashamed," Sarinda said, mocking a confession. "I've lost track on how old that child is. How old is Philomena now, Reverend, sixteen?"

"Fif—fifteen," Lionel corrected in a swallowed voice.

Sarinda continued toying with her pendant. Her voice sounded instructive when she said to the reverend, "That's still ripe enough for you, isn't it Lionel? When a young lady is just beginning to fill and feel herself out?" The reverend didn't answer. He stared at Sarinda. She teased, "You don't feel that urge anymore, do you Lionel? Power over them young girls."

"Miss. Fallows…"

Sarinda got up. "I'm going to talk to my niece, now. Thank you for brunch, Reverend-Mayor." She glided past Lionel, one hand tapping him on a broad shoulder, the other playfully rubbing her pendant.

Sarinda entered Eve's Hallow. Quincy was sitting at a table ordering a meal. He looked up at Sarinda and informed, "Philomena's upstairs."

"Thank you, Quincy," Sarinda responded, walking by and barely giving him a look. She rushed up the stairs and into her room. Philomena was already wearing Sarinda's gift to her, a long-flowing, cream-colored gown. It was a dress daring enough for nightlife, but respectable for church. "It's from a seamstress in Manhattan," Sarinda told Philomena.

"It's lovely," Philomena replied as she twisted left and right and watched herself in the mirror.

"The woman also has a shop in New Jersey," Sarinda expounded.

Philomena posed in front of the mirror, and then, whimsical and carefree, she turned around to face Sarinda. "It makes me feel like mamma. This dress makes me feel as close to her as the veil she left me." She walked over to the bed and picked up the garment. She placed the veil up against her. "And the two seem to go well together. Look, Aunt Sarinda."

"It does look nice," Sarinda commented. "But the veil is black, little girl. Black goes with everything. It even goes well against your pale Aunt Sarinda." She thought and grinned. "Trust me, child. I know." She raised an eyebrow, reminiscing harder on a thought. Then she fixed her face.

Philomena spun around, once again facing the mirror. She held the veil close against the new dress she wore so as to observe the complimentary colors. She put the veil atop her head but kept it from covering her face. Philomena placed her hands on her hips and again posed. "I will walk as my mother, Aunt Sarinda. I will walk as my father. My voice will carry and travel all over this world. I will sing in every one of its corners. This veil will amplify my voice greater than any microphone."

Sarinda sat at the bed's end. Her smile trembled. Her eyes were concerned.

Philomena could see her aunt's reflection in the mirror. She turned around and addressed the concerned expression on Sarinda's face. "Are you okay, Aunt Sarinda?"

Sarinda nodded, yes, but Philomena could see that there was more to her demeanor. Sarinda knew she could not bluff her keen-eyed niece. Her voice hesitated, but then she spoke to Philomena, "Your mamma put all her hopes into that veil, Philly. I loved your mother, but her hopes were very misguided. Your father, good intentions as he had—I'm sure— promised a return to your mother, and he didn't. He never wrote to your mother. He died overseas." Philomena's bright conduct retracted. Sarinda said to her, "You do understand, Philly?"

Philomena nodded, head dropping. Her breath slowed. Her inhale and exhale became more like sighs. Her excitement was drained, running from an emotional wound opened up at her chest and running down to her stomach. But Philomena quickly fixed her face, straightened the veil atop her head, and twirled back around to the mirror. "My mother and father were not perfect, Aunt Sarinda. But, my mother was a great singer. My father was an adventurer. I am both of them," Philomena declared. "People will know my voice, all over this world. They will build jazz clubs just for me to sing in." The fifteen-year-old girl grinned and posed in the mirror. "I'll sing in all the hot spots this world has to offer." Her eyes spotted Sarinda sitting on the bed. "Maybe I'll start in New York City at the jazz club you acquired."

Sarinda chortled. "Child, you know you too young for New York right now." She tapped the bed and instructed Philomena, "Come. Sit." Philomena followed her aunt's orders. Sarinda put a loving arm around her niece. "Your mother had that ambition to travel and sing in New York City. You tryin' to complete her crooning crusade?"

Guilt invaded Philomena's face. "I appreciate Uncle Quincy so much. But I feel like I've held him back, him having to raise me. He got to play in New York a couple times with mamma's old band."

Sarinda interrupted. "Now, Philly, you don't feel guilty about all that."

"But he didn't pursue those bigger dreams because of me," Philomena fussed. "I'd like to make things right. We're comin' up with somethin' with him on piano and me singing some of mamma's old songs. Oh, Aunt Sarinda, you should hear it. We sound beautiful. It took time to convince Uncle Quincy, but when he jumped to the piano, he was sold. He looked so alive."

Sarinda's smile faded, and she explained to young Philomena, "Your uncle had his chance, Philly. But by the time he and the band got up to New York there were just so many bands playing the sound, they didn't stand out quite as much. You don't have to blame yourself."

"I know," Philomena replied. "But mamma wasn't there to sing. And now, Uncle Quincy has me. Together, he and I have a sound. A good sound."

"I'm sure the two of you do," said Sarinda rubbing Philomena's shoulder as she held her close. "I'm sure the two of you do."

"Aunt Sarinda, you should hear us. I swear. Not tonight at the ceremony. Uncle Quincy isn't playing. You should hear us when we perform nights at Eve's Hallow. But I do a private show I'd like to open to you. I come back here after I perform at the church, just to take a small rest before the vigil begins, and I sing. Uncle Quincy doesn't disturb me. I…I…I sing to mamma and papa. I started this private show two years ago. But I invite you, Aunt Sarinda. Would you come?"

Sarinda combed her fingers through Philomena's hair. "Philly, I wouldn't want to profane that very private moment. But I will hear you sing with your uncle," Sarinda promised. "For now, young lady, let me leave you to practice." Sarinda stood. Philomena followed. Sarinda told her, "Take that dress off for now. Put back on what you had. You save that New York City garment for later."

"Yes, Aunt Sarinda," Philomena acknowledge.

Sarinda dismissed herself from the room. Philomena removed the dress her aunt purchased for her and replaced it with what she had on previously. She kept the veil atop her head, stood in front of the mirror, and started singing. She practiced the melodic hymn she would perform at the night's ceremony.

Philomena took it easy when she sang. She kept her voice low, but produced a candied sound of praise and glory as she harmonized the hymn's lyrics. She put extra emphasis on parts of the song where her voice would grow and erupt into a mighty sound. She remembered cues for herself, but never stressed her voice. Philomena was confident that her voice would not fail her in the night's ceremony, but she also longed to sing one of her mother's songs rather than the same old religious hymns. She was more anxious for her private performance.

Philomena covered her face with the veil and closed her eyes.

She could still see the mirror. In her vision, behind closed eyes, there played a scene of her singing one of her mother's tunes. Philomena watched the scene, thinking it beautiful. She saw herself giving praise to her mother by singing a song speaking about her adventuring father. It was night. It was this night. The twelfth of August. This was Philomena's private ceremony held away from the church, away from the vigil. This was what she celebrated, parents she never knew. Philomena saw the door in her vision open. Reverend Ladon walked in. He stopped after taking several steps into the room and just looked at her. Her Aunt Sarinda followed behind doing the same. Both watched her. Uncle Quincy entered next. He looked upset.

Philomena opened her eyes and flipped the veil up and away from her face. She rolled her eyes and batted a hand at her image in the mirror.

"I'm comin' back here to have my own celebration. Shoot. I'm gonna sing to mamma and papa, and nobody need to hear it but me. As has been."

Philomena removed the veil from her head and placed it on her aunt's vanity. The young woman stepped back to the center of the room as if it was a stage, and she practiced the hymn several times more. After a few more rounds of practice, Philomena joined Sarinda and Reverend Ladon outside at the table they still occupied. Reverend Ladon was making a move to stand, dismissing himself from the table, just as Philomena returned. A smile jumped onto his face when he saw the fifteen-year-old girl exit Eve's Hallow. He sat back down in his chair, his smile remaining as Philomena joined them.

"There's my little songbird," said a proud Sarinda.

Reverend Ladon placed a hand on Philomena's wrist and shook playfully. "Today is always a hard day for the people of Water Bug Hollow, but your voice, child, puts everything in order. One hymn. That's all." Reverend Ladon stopped shaking Philomena's wrists, his actions turning into a soft rub of the young woman's skin.

Sarinda observed the reverend interact with Philomena. She could tell that her young niece didn't know what to make of the reverend's slow caress of her wrist, getting familiar with her. Philomena's heart skipped, and her expression concentrated to keep a smile. Her eyes darted from the reverend's caress of her wrist to his eyes. Lionel stopped, a diffident smile beginning to quaver.

Sarinda said to Reverend Ladon, "Philomena has her own rite for tonight's occasion. A rite going on three years, as I've been told." She looked at Philomena with an expression indicating the young woman to continue the conversation with an explanation of her personal August twelfth ritual.

Reverend Ladon opened his hand and took it away from Philomena's wrist.

Philomena corrected, "I started this ritual two years ago, Aunt Sarinda." Her eyes stayed on the reverend-mayor. Philomena blinked, and then she looked up at Sarinda. "The reverend-mayor has noticed my disappearance."

"Yes, yes," Lionel chuckled. "Where *do* you disappear to, Philomena? I can't even get an answer from your uncle."

Philomena shied away.

Sarinda answered, "She slips back here to sing a song for her mother and father." Sarinda leaned close to Philomena and wrapped her arms around her. "I hope I'm not exposing you and embarrassing you too much, Philly."

"No, Aunt Sarinda," Philomena answered sheepishly, leaning into Sarinda's embrace.

"Good, child," Sarinda said as she planted a kiss atop Philomena's head. She rubbed Philomena's shoulder and suggested, "You slip away and pay your reverence to your mother and father. You come back to my room, hear? I'll be sitting right here to give you privacy." Sarinda opened her arms and released Philomena who sat up straight in her chair. "Right now, however, I think I'll be using my room for some rest. Travel has made me tired. Lord knows I could use some sleep." Sarinda rummaged through her purse to find bills to pay for her meal, even as Reverend Ladon protested the gesture. Sarinda placed down enough money for the entire meal and a good tip. "Reverend-Mayor, I am too tired to argue. So, you just let this be. Here, now. There we go."

Lionel furrowed his brow and pouted his lips in jest. He quickly broke into a light laugh. He simmered and said to Philomena, "Your voice will be well appreciated tonight, Philomena. As usual."

"Thank you, Reverend," said Philomena politely.

The reverend continued, "People say you sing with your mother's soul. I never heard her, but I am compelled to agree. There is a mature soul inside you, for such a young girl. You are a big reason people come to the vigil. People haven't been showing up out of protest, disagreeing with what has been uncovered about Water Bug Hollow's past—the glorious rebellion just a legend, the facts of history now known. But your voice unites the citizens. You make Water Bug Hollow whole again."

Philomena again beamed sheepishly because of the reverend's comment. Sarinda interjected her own remark. "How can someone so modest perform to such a large audience?" she uttered.

Reverend Ladon retorted with a belly of laughter before Philomena could answer, "The audience isn't so large, Miss Fallows." He stopped his laughter and cleared his throat. "Regardless of the turnout, I still have to prepare things. I was on my way to the church just before you showed up. Service to honor Water Bug Hollow begins at sundown. But I have to prepare my sermon, just as you have to prepare your song." He looked at Philomena and advised as he stood up from his chair, "Now, it's the same as always. After I give my sermon, I'll call the former mayor up to speak. Then, you'll sing once he's finished with his words."

"Yes, Reverend-Mayor," Philomena replied.

"Good day to you both," the reverend addressed the women at the table, giving an extra kiss on the back of Sarinda's hand. "I do hope you join the service, Miss Fallows. That is the last contention I will make against your protest to join."

Sarinda chuckled, "Reverend-Mayor…"

The reverend smiled. "I tried." He looked at Philomena, standing up straight. "I will see you tonight, young lady." The reverend walked away from the table and toward the church.

"Let me retire, too," spoke Sarinda. "Would you care to join, Philly? Get some rest before you sing tonight?"

"I will, Aunt Sarinda."

The two jumped up from their seats, pushed in their chairs like polite, civilized Southern women, and walked inside Eve's Hallow and up the stairs to Sarinda Fallows' room. When Sarinda opened the door, her eyes immediately fell upon the veil sprawled out on her vanity. She made a sudden stop that caused young Philomena to bump into her. The gentle collision didn't shake Sarinda from her opened-mouth stare at the dark, otherworldly shroud. Her eyes widened. The garment had always pulled at her with a dull feeling, but not now. There flirted a stronger, more intense draw emanating from the veil.

Or maybe it was just Philomena tugging at her arm.

"Come on, Aunt Sarinda," pleaded Philomena. "Let's get some rest."

Sarinda blinked and came to. She took a breath and looked around until her eyes fell on Philomena. Sarinda beamed a quavering smile and said, "Yes, child. Rest. Like I said, the Good Lord knows I need it." Sarinda exhaled and followed Philomena to the bed. They slipped into bed and curled up comfortably against one another. Philomena didn't fall asleep quickly. She spoke about her dreams to travel, her wish to fulfill her mother's dream to sing in New York City. Harlem. Sarinda kept an eye on the veil, barely listening to Philomena articulating her ambitions with enthusiasm. But, when Philomena's voice did bounce into Sarinda's ears, the sound ruffled Sarinda. She reached for her pendant and rubbed it. Sarinda's eyes watched Philomena. She rubbed the pendant and smiled.

Philomena's voice softened.

Sarinda rubbed the pendant.

Philomena's eyes became heavy.

Sarinda rubbed the pendant.

Philomena exhaled one last breath, and she fell asleep.

Sarinda joined her in rest after giving the veil one last admiring glance. She dreamed of Philomena giving her the ancient garment, and the dream was so real, so palpable, that Sarinda believed it to be true. Her excitement brought her from sleep where she discovered the sun was in its last breaths of light, and young Philomena had disappeared from her embrace.

Sarinda swung her legs around to sit up on the edge of the bed. She reached for the lamp and switched on the light. Her head turned toward the vanity. There was the veil, close yet out of her reach. Sarinda ignored the garment. She stood and decided to freshen up. She picked out a new outfit and she started a bath. She glanced at the clock. It was seven-thirty. Water Bug Hollow's vigil was just beginning.

Sarinda bathed for thirty-minutes before emerging from the washroom dry, wearing nothing but her open bathrobe. She sat down at her vanity and stared at the veil. She closed her eyes and rubbed her pendant while humming.

Something touched Sarinda's neck. It was gentle at first, caressing her, and then it became threatening. Sarinda continued twirling her pendant between her fingers. Her hum was chocked, but a vibrating purr resided in her throat and opposed the suffocating grip around her neck.

The vanity shook.

Sarinda rubbed her pendant and purred, forcing herself to create a louder drone until the squeeze around her neck released and she squealed loud like a morning bird's call. Sarinda opened her eyes in time to see the veil flutter as the vibration of her squawk billowed underneath it.

Sarinda grinned at the veil. "No aegis tonight. No comfort. Just watch."

Sarinda stood up, grin remaining and her eyes on the veil. She dressed and left her room, going down stairs and taking a seat outside of Eve's Hallow. A man immediately asked for her order, and Sarinda replied, "Water for now. But I do need to see a menu."

"Yes, Miss Fallows," he beamed. He wanted to ask Sarinda if she was going to join the vigil, and Sarinda could feel the question resonating behind his polite demeanor. But the man never spoke his query. He left Sarinda to fetch her menu and a glass of water.

Sarinda turned her head and spotted Water Bug Hollow's church in the distant field. She peered deeper until a vision of all the activity transpiring inside the church came to her. The church looked nice, and its pews were filled with eighty-five of Water Bug Hollow's citizens who waited eagerly for the night's ceremony and sermon. Reverend Lionel was just now stepping to the pulpit, decked in his robe.

The organ played to a haunting hum, and the church choir and some of the audience hummed in an eerily perfect harmony with the organ's consistent thrum. Then, together, in synch, the noise dropped away in a flawless fade of sound.

Reverend-Mayor Ladon spoke, "John, chapter eight, verse thirty-two." His ecclesiastical voice boomed authoritatively. *"And ye shall know the truth, and the truth will set you free.* This old phrase has been used to the point of banality, squeezed so much of its meaning, that it almost seems unfair to state it. It's too easy to assert such a trite phrase even into Earthly, mundane affairs, but there is nothing trite written in God's book; and every August twelfth, there can be no more appropriate words spoken from His Good Book that describe Water Bug Hollow." Reverend Ladon paused, allowing some of the audience members to speak in one-word approvals. Others nodded their head. The reverend's eyes panned the audience before diving back into his sermon. "I saw a fight this afternoon. An older gentleman, he was inebriated. He and a young boy were fighting over Water Bug Hollow's history and how the Negro came to be here. The boy—knowing the truth—was freed from the anger and resentment built up in the older man. He was free from the hate pumping through the old man's veins; and he stood firm against the older man's disdainful behavior.

"The old man suffered from the myth of Water Bug Hollow's eighteen-sixty-four ordeal. He believed in the bloody uprising that had been believed by so many for so long. Killing. Murder. Even under the circumstances, they leave the Negro looking like a vile savage. But we have access to the truth! Like so many have access to The Holy Bible. But we are mortal and stubborn. And, holding onto historical falsehood leaves us bitter. It leaves us hateful. It is hateful to believe in bloodshed. It is hateful to believe in an uprising. But the truth, much like the Bible, will set you free."

"Yes, it will," spoke members of the audience. *"Yes, it will,"* they repeated.

The reverend paused again, looking down at the church podium in front of him. He looked up and said, "But the truth can always be reiterated. There's no need to celebrate hate when you know the truth. The citizens, ex-slaves of Water Bug Hollow—Jakobi's Plantation—had love in their hearts. History tells us that Oliver MacRitchie, for reasons unknown, led Union troops here to Jakobi Plantation. Nestled among the plantation hands and holding the slaves and Master Jakobi's family hostage were desperate Confederate troops. Curtis Jacobson sneaked away from the plantation and helped the Union soldiers, as he knew the layout of the land. The Confederate troops were subdued with little bloodshed. Curtis Jacobson stowed all of the slaves inside the slave houses and barn while the fighting commenced. He waited, armed with other Negro slaves, but he fired no shot. Elias Jakobi, fearing arrest—though his family was as much a hostage as any Negro slave under the desperate Confederate troops—fled his plantation.

"But when Elias Jakobi passed, the ex-slaves, still living, brought his body back to what is now called Water Bug Hollow, and they buried him here on his land. The ex-slaves had so much love within them they also welcomed Master Jakobi's family back until they too passed. There's no hate within this story. There's no hate within this truth. And when we claim the truth, hate lifts, and then we are truly free. But, even with freedom, the citizens of Water Bug Hollow were still slaves. The citizens were slaves to hatred. The citizens were slaves to celebrating violence and bloodshed. Water Bug Hollow Negroes, you danced on graves under a high fire—the devil in you all. But we have the truth. We have history's truth. We have historical truth that *I* brought to you with the love in *my* heart. My *research*. We have God's truth. And tonight, this August twelfth, let us celebrate that." Reverend Ladon concluded his sermon by declaring, "Freedom, truth sets us unto thee."

Applause and verbal appreciation rang through the church. The organ hummed back to life and play. The reverend-mayor bowed his head graciously to the left and right. He waited for the audience and the organ to cease, and then he said, "Your former mayor, Mayor Johnson, would like to express a few words before we are blessed by young Sister Amat's voice."

Former Mayor Arlington Johnson walked to the pulpit with the assistance of his son-in-law and Reverend-Mayor Lionel Ladon. Once behind the pulpit, the former town patriarch assured both men that he was stable, using his cane for balance. They respectfully backed away and took their seats.

"There has been conflict over conflicting history," he said after a time of making sure his balance was indeed stable.

Sarinda Fallows lost concentration on the scene. Her attention turned to Quincy who was stepping out of Eve's Hallow with a lit cigarette in his mouth and a woman named Clora Rodgers on his arm.

"Quincy," said Sarinda in a surprised voice and expression. "You not goin' to see Philly sing?"

Quincy took a long, cool drag from his cigarette. He exhaled the smoke away from Clora and then removed his arm from her embrace. "Go on 'head, baby. I'll be there soon," he said to her. She smiled, and as she walked away he slapped her bottom. Clora swung her hand to hit Quincy's away, but she missed. She protested flirtatiously and continued on toward the church. Quincy watched Clora's figure disappear into the night shadows, and then he turned to Sarinda, took another drag and exhale of his cigarette and said, "I know the exact time my niece steps to that church stage and turns into her mother. I'll be there just in time. No need to see the bullshit that happens beforehand." He chuckled and took another drag. "You got Lionel sayin' his bullshit. Then you got Arlington trying to control his facial expressions as he hears a bullshit history of Water Bug Hollow that makes no sense. I do like seein' Arlington cleverly cut down Lionel's sermon as he tells whoever gathered to *remember as you like, the history of Water Bug Hollow*. But, I'll miss that. By the time I get there, my niece will sing. She'll be her mother."

Sarinda watched Quincy staring at the church with a smile of admiration for Philomena. His smile did nothing to hide the sadness and reminiscence in his eyes. Sarinda said, in a subtly deriding tone, "You loved Theresa, didn't you Quincy?"

There was another puff of the cigarette before Quincy turned a curious eye and sly grin in Sarinda's direction. "You mean romantically? No," he said as cigarette smoke left his lips through every word. "Joe loved her like that. Theresa loved Joe like that. Theresa was my sister. That's why Philomena is *my* niece."

Sarinda heard Quincy's emphasis, and she corrected, "*Our* niece, Quincy. I love that little girl."

"You just play 'auntie', Sarinda," Quincy retaliated in a smooth, jazzy voice. "But I raised Philomena—and no, not entirely by myself. Theresa's brother, Delmon, he sends money and visits. Philomena loves her cousins like brothers. That's family. Eugene helped before he moved to Chicago and settled to make a family of his own." He shook his head, concluding, "I don't see you here much, though. Not a dime from 'auntie' Sarinda."

Sarinda sat back in her chair. "If it's money you want, Quincy, I can give it. And when I come here, I do treat my niece. When I'm here, Philly smiles. She loves me."

Quincy sat down, pulling the chair close to Sarinda before sitting. He leaned forward and said, "I don't know why these incidents always stick out to me, but I remember a couple of them times when Theresa would drop her veil by accident, for one reason or another. She would let me retrieve it from off the floor for her. You, on the other hand, she'd always shoo away when the same thing happened. Oddly, Philomena does it too."

Sarinda shifted in her seat. "They're just takin' part in your role as a gentleman. And I think there's a superstition surroundin' that veil about its current female owner allowin' another female to hold it." Sarinda burst into laughter that sounded forced. "Or some story Joe Pepper left behind when he gave it to Theresa."

Quincy said, breaking into Sarinda's guffaws, "I like to think that deep down Theresa didn't trust you no more than I do. And she somehow passed that down to her daughter, *my* niece." Quincy stood, his eyes still on Sarinda. "Who I'm gon' watch sing tonight while you sit right here."

Quincy walked away. Sarinda called, "You not trusting me because I'm white is no different than my people not liking you because of your color, Quincy."

Quincy pivoted mid-step, facing Sarinda. "I don't know a great deal about history, Miss Fallows, but from what I've gathered, my people done never put your people through the terrible things that's been done to us— and continues to be done to us. Never. If I've distrust for you in my heart, based on any prejudice thoughts, it's been well earned by white folks. You need to go 'head on and talk to your people 'bout that." Quincy turned and walked away, not stopping even when Sarinda called to him.

"The MacRitchie's have done their part," Sarinda barked. She watched Quincy disappear into the shadows. She peered into the darkness and saw the lights of the church beaming through its windows. She concentrated hard until once again the scene of the church's interior appeared to her. She saw Quincy's entrance into the church, cigarette extinguished before entering. He sat next to Clora Rodgers. She smiled wide at Quincy when he sat down. He took her arm, and she leaned closer to him.

Philomena walked up to the podium and sang a haunting, operatic hymn that turned grand and soulful. Members of the audience swayed, others jumped up and praised the young woman's gift of song. Many in the audience started weeping. Sarinda watched while seated at Eve's Hallow. Philomena was wearing the dress she purchased for her. And when she brought the song to a powerful crescendo, she became more than just her mother's child. She was Theresa. Alive.

Philomena softened her voice. The song ended and the audience burst into standing applause. Sarinda remarked, "Who are you behind that flesh, Philomena Amat? I *am* curious, but I have no time."

Sarinda blinked. The church's interior disappeared from her eyes. She picked up the glass of water placed in front of her earlier and sipped as she patiently waited. Sarinda's waiter returned, asking if she was ready to order. Sarinda replied, "Nothing heavy. Just a glass of wine and some dream cake. Thank you." The waiter took the menu from the table, bowed at the neck with a smile, and then he disappeared to fetch Sarinda her order.

Sarinda heard rustling coming from the path leading to the church. She turned her head toward the noise, quick paced footsteps. She reached for her pendant and started rubbing it. Philomena appeared from the darkness. Sarinda watched her. The fifteen-year-old girl hurried past Sarinda, never looking at her. Sarinda continued to rub her pendant, the only movement she made besides her eyes following Philomena's every step.

Philomena stopped just before Eve's Hallow's entrance. She turned around and inspected the area. She saw nothing. Sarinda grinned and continued playing with her pendant. Philomena walked inside. Sarinda's fingers let go of the stone charm dangling from her necklace. She turned her head toward the dark path leading to the church. Reverend-Mayor Lionel Ladon appeared, no longer wearing his pastors robe. He was focused, and he was just as quick in his steps as Philomena before him.

Sarinda watched him too, a single eyebrow arched. She sipped her cool water. Reverend-Mayor Ladon paused in his approach, stopping in front of Sarinda. She again sipped her water. Lionel turned his head toward her. She looked up at him, his face drenched with apprehension. His head swung back toward Eve's Hallow's entrance like a creaking door. People exited the establishment, some asking Lionel Ladon if the candlelight vigil had started.

"They're preparing. I'm just taking a breath. Arlington will lead the ceremony. I'll be there shortly," the reverend told them.

The stream of people flowed by him, disappearing on the path toward the church.

It was just the reverend and the Southern socialite. She sat. He stood. There.

Lionel remained facing Eve's Hallow. He was stiff. Sarinda reached up toward her pendant, twiddled the stone, and nodded her head. Lionel moved forward, up the steps to the patio, and then inside.

The night brought humidity, and returned the summer to its natural, muggy state. Gone was the unnatural crisp atmosphere that ruled earlier in the morning. August's heat bubbled this night. Sarinda took another sip of cool water. She swallowed and looked up at Eve's Hallow. She watched with focused eyes until she saw the interior of her apartment materialize in view. Philomena sat at the vanity, performing an original song by her mother as she looked at a small, unframed picture of her mother and father. The photograph rested atop the veil.

Lionel entered, interrupting Philomena's second song just as she began. She witnessed the door crack open in the mirror's reflection and turned around with a smile, expecting her Aunt Sarinda's entrance. She expressed surprise when the reverend walked through the door.

"Reverend-Mayor!" Philomena exclaimed.

Lionel shut the door, taking his time, and then he took several steps to the bed and sat down. "Your voice is always so moving, Philly. It's always so inspiring. I'd like to thank you, again. You give me hope for Water Bug Hollow."

"Thank you, Reverend-Mayor," Philomena replied.

Lionel shifted awkwardly. "I'm sorry, Philomena. I didn't mean to disturb your sacrament to your late mother and father." Lionel got up. "I just…I don't always feel as if I'm keeping Water Bug Hollow together. It's been split ever since I've come to town and delivered the accuracies of its history. Some people show up for this honorable service, but more come through to hear you sing…or regret not seeing you because of their defiance."

Philomena divulged to the reverend-mayor, "I picture my father to have been a lot like you, Reverend-Mayor. He was a traveler." Philomena smiled shyly. Her eyes were aimed toward the reverend, but she imagined her father in his place. "He came bearing tales."

Lionel shook his head, eyes dropping away from Philomena. He tried to keep his expression from completely melting into sorrow. He looked up and conveyed again to Philomena, "As I say, young Philomena, you give me hope." He opened his arms out to her. Philomena walked over to Reverend Ladon, and the two embraced each other. Reverend Ladon held Philomena tightly. He sat on the bed and guided Philomena to sit with him as she remained in his arms. He loosened his affectionate hold on Philomena once she sat next to him. He leaned away to examine her countenance. "You are too beautiful to be a child, Philomena. You are a woman to me."

"Reverend," Philomena blushed.

Lionel caressed Philomena's cheek. She shied away. Lionel leaned in after her and kissed the fifteen-year-old girl's forehead.

"Reverend," Philomena said again with faint, cracking protest in her voice.

Philomena moved away from the reverend, but he grabbed her arm with a tight grip.

"Miss Fallows."

Sarinda looked away from the scene just in time for her cake and wine to arrive. The waiter said to Sarinda as he placed the plated slice of cake and fork in front of her, "I'm headin' on over to the church to partake in the vigil, Miss Fallows. Is there anythin' I can do before I leave, Miss?"

Sarinda answered, "No. This will be all."

The waiter bowed his head, smiled appreciatively toward Sarinda, and then walked away to attend the Water Bug Hollow vigil. More citizens came from their homes to attend the silent, candlelit reverence outside the church.

Sarinda picked up her fork and started eating her cake, bite by bite. Her eyes looked up at Eve's Hallow every-now-and-then, but she never peeped in on Reverend Ladon and Philomena's activities. She sipped her wine, and then she returned to eating her cake. She sat up just as Quincy approached. He was ready to ask Sarinda where Reverend Ladon had disappeared to when the answer was presented to him. The reverend emerged through Eve's Hallow's doors.

"Reverend-Mayor," Quincy acknowledged. "You got people waitin', now. Arlington's gettin' restless. He's tired. Where's Philomena?"

Lionel didn't reply. He only fixed his suit, wiping his hands down his attire to smooth away wrinkles. "I—I, uh," he stammered. He walked over to Quincy and patted the piano player's shoulder. He looked at Sarinda and said in the same stammering tone, "Miss Fallows. Uh, yes. It's, uh…yeah." He walked past Quincy and toward the church.

Quincy followed the reverend's departure with his eyes, his body twisted around to get a better look. Then he looked at Eve's Hallow and hurried inside. Sarinda sat back in her chair after one last bite of cake. She looked up at the café and apartment complex and she stared, focusing until the vision of her room appeared. Philomena occupied the bed. She lay shivering with covers piled over her, buried deep inside as if to hide.

Quincy entered the room and saw his niece in the bed. He approached her and sat down. He said in a concerned voice, "Philomena. You okay? Everybody's outside." Quincy noticed Philomena was shaking underneath the covers. He leaned closer and asked, "Philomena, you okay, little girl?" He tugged at the comforter to uncover Philomena. She tugged back, staying wrapped inside like a cocooned caterpillar. Philomena's pull surprised Quincy. He pulled at the covers again, this time harder. "Girl, what's wrong with you?" he asked with irritation heavy in his voice.

"Please, don't, Uncle Quincy," Philomena winced. "Please don't make me come out." She sniffed back tears, and then her one whimper became two, then three, and more successive.

Quincy froze. It was a while before he asked in a soft tone, "Whatchu cryin' for, girl? You can tell me. It's Uncle Quincy, now." He looked up and saw the photo of Joseph Pepper and Theresa Amat. Quincy considered Philomena overwhelmed herself with her private performance to her late parents. But then he took a deep breath and thought of something else. He closed his eyes and exhaled anger to his surface. His mind recalled Reverend-Mayor Lionel Ladon coming from Eve's Hallow looking disheveled and in shock, or more appropriate, with wide guilt splashed across his face. Quincy opened his eyes. He made one last effort, sincerity in his voice as he spoke, "Philomena…"

The fifteen-year-old girl turned in the bed and slowly removed the covers from her. Her dress was torn. Her exposed shoulders were bruised, as if a heavy force had been holding her down. Her lower lip bled, cut from a forceful bite.

Quincy took another breath, his eyes closed again. He started to ask, "Did he…" but then Philomena tossed her arms around her uncle and burst into tears. "I'm going to make everything okay, little girl."

"Please, Uncle Quincy, no. Don't."

Quincy patted Philomena on the back and held her tightly. "Shhh," he comforted, and then said in a low voice, "It's gon' be okay, little girl. It's gon' be quite fine."

Philomena pleaded, "Please, Uncle Quincy, don't do nothin'. We can leave this place. We can leave. We can play piano and sing. We can go to New York."

Quincy held Philomena even tighter. "Shhh," he said again. "Just lay down and rest. I'ma go get you a doctor. You need a doctor." He let her go and stood up.

Sarinda looked away from the scene. She grabbed her glass of wine, turned her head in the direction of the church, and exhaled. She finished her wine and placed the empty glass down. She sat back and noticed a revolver's muzzle in her face. Sarinda flinched, and her eyes widened. Quincy thumbed back the hammer. He said to her, "You got any heart for that girl, you go up there and you comfort her right now. Hear?"

Sarinda spoke fast. "Quincy, what in the world…"

"Do as I say!" Quincy interrupted. "Or Water Bug Hollow loses a MacRitchie as well as its mayor tonight." He gave the trigger a light squeeze, and at the same time, using his thumb, he guided the gun's hammer back to a safe and uncocked position. Quincy turned from Sarinda Fallows and stormed off toward the church.

Sarinda jumped from her seat and hurried into Eve's Hallow and up to her apartment. She entered and saw Philomena, bed comforter half covering her. Sarinda spotted the tears in Philomena's dress and the girl's bruises, and then she approached with a horrified look, arms outstretched.

"My little girl!" Sarinda bellowed. "Who, who did this to you?"

Philomena held out her arms and tightened them around her aunt as Sarinda came closer. "Aunt Sarinda!" she cried with heavy tears. "Aunt Sarinda!"

Philomena explained her ordeal through tears and loud, sorrowful cries. Sarinda didn't listen. She turned her attention to the vanity mirror and focused until she could see Quincy yelling as he charged toward the church where outside people gathered and lit candles for the vigil.

"Where is he?" Sarinda heard him scream as he came through the crowd with his gun raised. "Lionel! Where are you, goddamnit? Reverend!"

Citizens dropped their candles and scattered from Quincy's angry rush. The small flames from the loosed candles fizzled away as they hit the marshy earth.

Reverend Ladon ducked through the panicked crowd.

"Lionel!" Quincy called as the reverend's foot touched the first stair leading to the front door of the church. Lionel turned around. Quincy cocked back the gun's hammer.

Sarinda watched.

Water Bug Hollow police came to the scene and removed their weapons. "Put that gun down, Quincy," one ordered.

Arlington Johnson staggered to the scene, his cane barely keeping him balanced. "Quincy, what's all this about, now?"

Reverend Ladon lifted his arms.

"He forced Philomena to bed," Quincy winced. "My little girl that I swore to protect."

Arlington's expression mixed with shock and sorrowful disbelief. He fixed his face and put a stern gaze on Reverend Ladon. "Is this true, Reverend-Mayor?" His voice broke as he asked the question, sadness tearing through.

Quincy kept the gun aimed at Lionel.

Lionel kept his eyes on the gun. He hesitated, but confessed, "Yes. I did lay with that young girl. I forced myself upon her, God help me. But, I swear there is deviltry at work…"

Quincy fired all six shots from his gun at the reverend-mayor. Pops of gunfire snapped through the night. Six flashes shouted miniature threads of lightning. Lionel's suit burst with spats of blood, and his body danced. Most of the bullets tore through his chest; and two pierced his neck. The reverend-mayor's body crumpled dead in front of the church. Arlington hollered, but it was too late.

The Water Bug Hollow officers fired on Quincy just as he fired on the reverend-mayor. Their gunfire came as quick, loud bursts—louder than Quincy's gun. Their bullets riddled him, but his finger still managed to fire his shots. Quincy fell dead. His body sprawled out on the murky ground.

Citizens hollered. There was confusion. The hysteria was loud and trailed all the way to Eve's Hallow. The pops and loud bursts of gunfire were heard even over Philomena's distress as she recounted her ordeal. The fifteen-year-old girl jumped at the popping and bursting sounds, fright frozen on her face. She shut her eyes tight, and the ghastly scene appeared to her. There was her Uncle Quincy's body lying on the ground. Dead. Reverend Ladon too lay dead on the ground.

Philomena could see the images. She cried harder. She held Sarinda tighter. "Take me away, Aunt Sarinda. Take me from here."

"I will take care of you, Philomena," Sarinda promised. "But the spirit of your mother will not have you gallivantin' the streets of New York City. I will stay here. I will care for you here, Philomena. I will not leave." Sarinda rocked Philomena back and forth. Her gaze floated across the room and landed on the veil draped across the vanity. "Should I leave, it will be only for a short while to handle the business in New York City. Then, when you are ready, when you are old enough, I will take you from Water Bug Hollow." Sarinda kissed Philomena's forehead. "You are not my niece, Philomena. You are more than that to me. You are my daughter, and I love you as a mother."

Sarinda's eyes stayed fixed on the veil, and then she blinked. The hysteria from outside was coming closer. "Lay down, child," said Sarinda. She kept Philomena in her arms but guided her to lie across the bed. "Close your eyes," Sarinda told her. Philomena nodded her head in agreement, choking back tears. "Hush, child. Mamma says to relax." Sarinda loosened one arm and reached for her pendant. She rubbed the charm as she loosened her other arm. She caressed Philomena's forehead with her free hand. "Sleep, child. Sleep," she said soothingly.

Philomena drifted away.

The door opened. Sarinda turned and spotted the officers. "Get this young lady a doctor, now. My niece needs a doctor. Where is her Uncle Quincy?"

"Dead, Miss Fallows," informed an officer. And then the same uniformed man admitted with regret in his voice, "We put him down after he shot Reverend-Mayor Ladon. The reverend-mayor confessed to roughing the girl and violatin' her. Rest of the officers are tryin' to calm the people outside."

Sarinda appeared bewildered. "Well, find a doctor among them, please. Now," she reiterated.

The officers stormed out at Sarinda's command.

The Southern socialite stood and walked over to the vanity. She took a seat and peered down at the veil. She said with a victorious grin, "No aegis tonight. No comfort. Just watch." She leaned closer and whispered, "I'm mamma now." She sat up and looked over her shoulder at the sleeping Philomena Amat. Sarinda took a deep, refreshing breath. She turned back to the mirror and watched her hair turn a darker shade of red.

Portraits of Paul Benson
"I'm Paul Benson. How do you do?"

Paul Benson sat atop a broad, solid branch. He used the sturdy limb for rest and as an escape. The twenty-two-year-old sulked as the fresh sting of another argument with his parents weighed heavy. He smoked to relax, but the puff on tobacco did little to calm him, making him wish for a reefer stick.

It was Paul's eyes that put him at ease. They traced his surrounding environment as a light afternoon fog passed over the grass. His eyes outlined the trees' designs, the Water Bug Hollow field, and the church.

Paul sat back. He balanced with ease while on the tree's appendage, legs crossed and stretched out over the branch. He smoked and observed the trees bordering Water Bug Hollow proper and its wide, open field. He gathered his thoughts after a minute or two, or three, or ten when a soft, feminine voice called his name and penetrated the calm. "Paul! Paul! Paul! You okay?"

Paul looked down while exhaling a quick drag of his cigarette. There was his girlfriend, looking up at him. It was nineteen-year-old Philomena Amat. Paul smiled immediately as he saw her. His anger soothed and he said down to her, "How you doin', sweet baby? Ain'tchu supposed to be workin' at the school?"

"My shift ended early today," replied Philomena. "One o'clock," she specified. "I saw you run out your parent's house." There was concern in her voice.

Paul sat back again, knocking the rear of his head against the tree with all his frustration. His action hurt him, and Paul wasn't able to remain cool about the pain. He tilted his head forward and rubbed the area where he'd given himself a wallop. "Ow," he groaned. "Ain't that a sonnava bitch?"

Philomena hollered up at him, "Boy, you crazy? Don't go losin' what little sense you got. Paul-baby, what's wrong? Come down here and talk to me."

Paul rolled his eyes and then leaned to his right. He legs remained straight. His body dropped from the branch, and he quickly reached up with his left hand and caught the branch he had been sitting on. His arm flexed as his strength held him up. His legs remained extended, straight out. A grin ran across his face as he heard Philomena gasp. Through his concentration to hang on, he rolled his eyes as he wondered why Philomena was gasping. This had to be the umpteenth time she'd seen him perform such an act.

Paul straightened his legs, aiming them to the ground, and then he dropped and landed perfectly. Philomena crossed her arms and shook her head. She looked frustrated. "Goddamn you, boy. You a damn one-man, travelin' circus act."

Paul grinned wider, and he took another drag from his cigarette. He exhaled the smoke away from his sweetheart. He saw the veil wrapped around Philomena's arm and commented, "That will never not be sexy, Philly. You look like a woman of the night."

Philomena raised an eyebrow.

Paul staggered over his words. "No, baby. Not like that. Not a prostitute. Like, a classy woman. Y'know. Like you still carryin' the spirit of the previous decade."

Philomena huffed and reached out to Paul. "Uh-huh. Let me get a puff of that cigarette, Negro. I just might not whip yo' butt for that remark."

"My cigarette! It's been in my mouth, baby," Paul said playfully guarding his cigarette from Philomena's hands. "You might catch a disease."

Philomena retorted sassily, "Is that all it's gonna do, Paul-baby, kill me? Shit, I've been through worse than death." She swallowed what she wanted to express next, feeling the sentiment too morose. *Hell, I've been the cause of death,* she kept to herself. "Now give me that cigarette and tell me what the matter is with you," she demanded.

Paul handed her the smoke. Philomena puffed. A single eye spotted Paul, and a silent interrogation appeared on Philomena's face. Paul put his hands in his pockets and leaned against the tree. His frustrated expression returned. "My mom and dad, that's all—as usual. I love 'em, but damn. They don't want me to go to school in Chicago. I tried talkin' 'bout it again. They think it's too far." Paul huffed. "It's like I done gone and wasted the last four years of my life savin' up money to travel and go to school somewhere besides the state of Louisiana." He positioned himself with his back against the tree rather than using his shoulder. "You'd think they'd be mad I wanted to study art. They ain't mad at the profession, just the place of study. I guess they figure I can always teach." He managed half a grin. "I know my heart might be locked on the School of Art Institute of Chicago—they lettin' colored folks in—but I just believe ain't no other place like it."

Philomena returned the smoke to Paul and said as Paul took a drag, "It is a long way from home, Paul-baby. Your mamma and daddy just worried 'bout you. You're an amazing artist. Very good. Probably too damned good."

"Too damned good?" Paul questioned as he dropped the remainder of his cigarette on the ground and smothered it under his foot.

Philomena clarified, "I've seen your grade school art teachers look jealous, Paul. You takin' that same talent and puttin' it in white teachers' faces. I don't know, either, baby. I can see your parents' concern."

"Ain't nuthin'," declared Paul. He smiled and said, "The movement in Harlem might not be as loud as when it started, but it's opened minds to what the Negro can accomplish in all fields of art. Poetry. Paintin'. Writin'. Music. The door is open, Philly-baby. We got to run through it while we can 'cause they closin'." He stepped away from the tree and crept toward Philomena. He put his arms around her and kissed her on the cheek. "You could come with me and study music like you plan. I'd paint. You'd sing. We'd reignite Harlem's fire in Chicago." Then Paul suggested, "Ask your Aunt Sarinda for the money."

Philomena thought about Paul's offer. She countered, "I will, if you let my aunt see your paintings. She could get you a show—maybe even in New York." Paul started to groan. He rolled his eyes. Philomena talked over Paul's bellyaching. "I've been sayin' this for a year. What's the problem?"

Paul started to explain, "I want to—"

But Philomena had heard it before and finished the statement. "—Do this on your own," she mocked. "That's ridiculous. You met me for a reason. I'm your way in, baby. Take this opportunity. I would never hold it over you, if that's whatchu afraid of. We together, Paul-baby. Let's be a team about this." She shook him inside their embrace, rubbing her hands up and down his back. "C'mon."

"Hey, hey," Paul said in an attempt to get Philomena to relax. "Hold up, Philly. You gon' join me?"

Philomena beamed and leaned back, swinging left and right while holding Paul. "Of course. You know I got travel in my blood. My papa traveled the world, and so will I. I'll start with Chicago. Shit, I'm half-Northern girl as it is. My papa was from New. York. *Cit-ay.*" She tapped Paul on the chest whimsically and stated, "I got Uncle Eugene in Chicago. I could get in contact with him. I'm sure he'd help out."

Paul kissed Philomena on the forehead. "Thank you, Philly-baby."

Philomena rolled her eyes and jokingly waved Paul's comment aside. "Negro, please. I've been done suggested this—the part about my aunt, that is. You just finally comin' around to it."

"I'm desperate," explained Paul with a grin followed by a sigh.

"Is that what it takes, Paul-baby? Desperation?" Again, Philomena rolled her eyes. "Shit, we all desperate. There's a lot to get away from here."

Both of them reflected, Paul with a grin, and Philomena trying to hold onto the happy moment surrounding her. Paul could see Philomena's bright spirit sinking as her focus moved toward past events. He said to bring Philomena back, "You remember the time when my parents had to go away to Mobile for the weekend? You stayed over. We locked all the doors, shuttered all the windows, stayed awake until the sun came up while indulgin' in refer sticks—our pick and sip of every bottle in my parent's bar. We was naked as Adam and Eve. That was our garden, and there was no outside law."

Paul's words only drew Philomena more into contemplation. She tried to keep her smile, but her words betrayed her thoughts. "That was the first time you seemed very, very, very relaxed to take me to bed," she said. "And I don't believe it was the smoke or drink, Mister Paul Benson."

Paul tried to keep his grin afloat too, but his mannerisms as he swung his head around to avoid Philomena's gaze made him look guilty. He braved to look at her as he admitted, "Yes I was very comfortable, Miss Philomena Amat." His smile faded. "You've been through so much. Every time I took you to bed, Philly-baby, I felt like I was intrudin' on you. There was like a wall all around you 'cause of what you'd been through."

Philomena nodded her head, acknowledging Paul's words. "I was closed off, but I wasn't completely shutdown. I didn't become a hermit."

She sighed and looked up directly at Paul. "When Lionel Ladon did to me what he did, well, I have far from forgotten or overcome the incident. I take it day by day even to this day, and as we speak. My concern that night was for my Uncle Quincy. I knew what would happen next, and it did. I prayed that my uncle would only be arrested for killing Lionel Ladon—Lord knows I wanted the deed done, but I just wanted my uncle to go to jail for granting my wish."

"Do you feel guilty?" Paul asked honestly.

"No," spoke Philomena with the same sincerity. "But, I tussle with my memories every day. Sometimes in the morning I still feel that man holding me down, the weight of his anger and violence and violation. I can be having the most beautiful dream, and just by the way I'm relaxed coming from it, I'm back in that nightmare. The weight. That oppressive weight."

Paul admitted, "That's what made me so nervous taking you to bed, Philly."

Philomena kissed Paul's cheek and assured him, "My private battle is my private battle, Paul-baby—a daily struggle. But, I can tell you, I am with you, and I feel safe. I can sing and shout my troubles away in harmony. I can open myself to you. I can become naked and comfortable. And I can breathe, breathe, breathe in heavy breaths because of the love you make to me." She put her head on his chest. "Thank you, Paul-baby. I've said it before, though I don't know if you as a man are listenin', but I never thought I'd feel this way or this safe again." She lifted her head and grinned. "You've done your part to help me with my life. It's my turn to help you with yours." She resumed tapping on Paul's chest with every word of her last statement.

"Okay," Paul conceded. "Your smile has me convinced. Set me up with your aunt."

Philomena kissed Paul again. "Okay, Paul-baby!" she blurted. She instructed with the same wide-eyed fervor, "Your best works, now. Show her some of them deep ones, the abstract ones. Not just the Negro dancin' scenes or posin' scenes. I want her to know my good man has intellect as well as talent." Philomena played with Paul's shirt, straightening it as he held her close. "Aunt Sarinda might be more than the average white folk, havin' an open mind and all, but she still got her notions about colored folk."

"I'll give her what I can give her," Paul promised. "We'll make the display in your apartment. I can't be havin' strange white folks roamin' through my parent's place." Paul rolled his eyes with a grin and commented, "Look at me, Philly. I walk around here tryin' to talk all cool, but as a grown-ass man I can't even stand up to my mom and pop."

Philomena smacked Paul on the shoulder. "That makes two of us, honey. I'd love to run north like any slave, but I'm at the mercy of my aunt." Philomena burst into laughter as she concluded, "And she a white woman. Lord, I'm more a slave than you could ever know." She relaxed her laugh and said, "That aside, I believe all this that we're plannin' will help us make a grand exit. My aunt will help you impress your parents, and make them feel safe. She'll get you that show, Paul-baby, and then we're Chicago bound."

"And your uncle up there?" Paul questioned.

Philomena answered coolly, "I'll contact him when it's official. Let's take this one step at a time."

"Okay, Philly. First step."

Philomena declared, "The first step, Paul-baby, is to do as you said. We'll set up my apartment like a gallery. Go pick out your best art. And I also want you to take a moment to apologize to your mamma and papa. Settle things with them. We want them in a good mood. Tell 'em what it is you're doin' when you leavin' the house with all your art. Tell 'em my aunt is interested, knows some people in New York. Tell 'em you tryin' to catch the last wave of all the uproar Negro artists created up there."

Paul grinned and responded, "I will, Philly-baby." He took a moment to admire Philomena as he held her in his arms. "You sure know how to plan a thing or two."

"People always said I knew how to organize and put things together," Philomena responded. "They say I got that from my mamma. Said she was a great organizer for Water Bug Hollow. Makes me interested in studyin' somethin' like law or politics, beyond just music when I get to college."

Paul ordained Philomena aloud, "Philomena, the great community leader. Organizer of community law. I like that. It fits you." He added jokingly, "It's a sophisticated way of sayin' schemer and grifter."

"Paul!" Philomena scolded. She pushed Paul away from her, but he grabbed her arm and pulled her back to him.

He apologized, "I'm sorry, Philly-baby. I was just funnin' you—and you know that. Stop pitchin' a fit like you serious, or think I'm bein' serious." He kissed her. "You go run along now. I'm gonna put my pieces together." Paul then emphasized, "And apologize to my parents."

"Good. I'm gonna make a call to my aunt on the Eve's Hallow phone. She's in New Orleans. She's returning on the weekend, but I'll tell her what to expect when she comes."

Paul and Philomena turned and walked hand-in-hand back to Water Bug Hollow proper. They parted with a kiss, Philomena walking to Eve's Hallow and Paul going home. He entered cautiously, expecting to see his mother and father in the front room. His father was sitting down in his chair and enjoying a smoke. He exhaled and turned to his son. "You come back?"

"Yes, sir," Paul answered with a crack in his low, polite tone.

Papa Benson clarified, "To your senses, I mean."

Paul sighed and rolled his eyes. But then he snickered and said, "I'm just tryin' to come up with a new angle for you and mamma to see my point of view, Pop."

Paul's father stood. He puffed his cigarette and said, "How can I trust your point of view when I can't even trust you to stay away from my cigarettes. You lucky I have this spare."

Paul's mother walked into the room, scowl on her face. She stood next to her husband and extended her stance. "Well," she said.

"I got a show," Paul told both of them while wearing a smile. "For my paintings. Philomena's aunt is interested in my work," he embellished. "She wants to see a few and pick which ones she can show. She know some people."

"In Chicago?" Paul's mother said folding her arms and making a face.

"Mamma, please," Paul pleaded. "Philomena is helping me with this. And no, it ain't in Chicago, but it might take me to Harlem if all goes right." Papa and Mamma Benson took a simultaneous deep breath. "I won't be alone. Philomena will be there."

"You gon' marry that girl," Paul's mother asked, eyebrow firmly arched on her face.

"Most likely, Mamma," Paul stated in a voice showing his frustration for hearing the question for the umpteenth time. "She's done so much for me. We care about one another, but I do have to say this here. All these opportunities might lead me to Chicago. But, she'll be there, and she has an uncle up there that will help out. I'd be okay."

"So you didn't come here to apologize for your behavior?" said his mother.

Paul dropped his head and then raised it to say, "I *am* sorry for my behavior, Mamma, Pop. Ain't no way to set an example to my younger brother and sister."

"You just be glad they at school right now," Paul's mother stated.

"Yes, Mamma," Paul said humbly. "But about my offer. I have opportunities. I can't squander that away."

Anna Benson turned around as she waved her arms and shook her head. "You so damn talented in what you do, but bein' so far away got me worried." Paul kept his smile well hidden. His father looked over at his mother and took another puff. "Patrick," Anna said to her husband, "put that damned cigarette out. You smokin' up the house makin' it hard to breathe in here. It's makin' me curse. Shit."

Pat Benson crushed out his cigarette in the ashtray after savoring its last taste. Pat said to his son as he stood up, "Paul, you our first child. We just don't want to let you go…too far. That's all."

"Can I pursue these opportunities then?" Paul smirked. "I left this house with dreams and came back with potential. Let me just take this chance. Philly's aunt will be here by the weekend to see my pieces."

"Anna," called Pat.

Anna Benson turned around. She said to Paul, "I'm so mad at you. I'm so mad at the world for not givin' you the chance to show that talent of yours."

Paul walked to his mother, arms out and expressing as politely as possible, "No need to be mad, Mamma. I got that chance. I can only be mad at you for bein' so damned scared."

Anna slapped her son. "Boy," she growled.

Paul rubbed his cheek. "It's true, Mamma. It's true. And I'm grateful for that. It tells me you care. But you and Pop gotta let me do this."

"I just want my pack of cigarettes back," Pat Benson propositioned in a quip.

Anna put her hands on her hips. She told her son, "You can go if you flush them smoke sticks of his."

Paul wanted to laugh at his mother's jibe, but he sighed instead. He said, "There's still a lot that needs to happen before I go anywhere."

Anna kissed her son on the cheek and then left the room. Paul turned to his father and tossed him the pack of cigarettes pulled from his back pocket. Pat caught the pack and approached his son. The elder Benson said, "Ain't much left here in Water Bug Hollow, especially when it comes to us traditionalists. Your mother and I ain't so much scared as we are seein' so much of this community disappear. This is a free community. The Negro fought for this place. We freed ourselves and claimed this land. We fought for that white man in all his wars, ain't got nothin'. Fought for ourselves and we got this land here. What that tell you, boy? Most forgot. Most believe somethin' else. But we one of them families that don't forget—the few that we are around Water Bug Hollow. The Keepers. The outside world ain't offered us colored folk much. Ain't a need to participate in it. We fine right here. Them white folks don't come into our house, and we don't go in theirs. I'm fine with that, but I just might be old-minded."

Paul reminded, "Oh, Pop, you've seen my paintings. You've seen my scenes of rebellion. Curtis the Water Bug and his people shootin' at slave owner Jakobi. Oscar MacRitchie in the scene. There's no forgettin' here."

Pat placed the pack of cigarettes on the arm of his chair. "You might want to leave that kind of paintin' out of any showcase."

"How else can I make the sun rise on Water Bug Hollow, Pop? Get its real story told."

Pat considered the thought. "You just be careful. Your mamma and I still gotta put all this through a private talk. Until then, you hustle this opportunity your sweetheart and her MacRitchie-related aunt got for you."

"I'll do that, Pop. And most important, and to you and mamma's likin', I'll be careful."

Pat returned to his chair and sat down. "You do that, boy."

Paul kissed the top of his father's head. "Thank you, Pop. I gotta go gather some art for Philly to show her aunt." He rushed to his bedroom, the inside of which resembled a storage facility for art. His personal paintings were stacked around the room surrounding the bed, a dresser, and a small desk holding supplies on its surface and in its drawers. There was an easel holding an unfinished piece. Paul put together a collection of compositions, laying them out on his bed. He stacked them carefully, lifted them, and then walked outside. Paul said goodbye to his parents in an excited voice as he hurried through the door and toward Eve's Hallow. He walked inside, through the café area and up the stairs to the apartments. He came to Philomena's room, turned his back to the door, leaned against it, and hit his head to make a knock.

Philomena opened the door and Paul turned around. She welcomed him in and he set his artwork on the bed. "I got some good pieces," said Paul, still excited. Philomena walked up behind him. He spun around and embraced her before she could inspect the works he brought with him. He pulled her close and informed, "I reconciled with my Mom and Pop. Had a good talk. My Mamma even slapped me for tellin' her the truth." He turned his cheek to her.

"Paul," Philomena said rubbing his face.

"It's okay," he assured. "She deserved to hear it, and I probably deserved gettin' slapped for throwin' it in her face. But we all came to an understandin'. If your aunt can come through—"

"I gave her a call," Philomena interrupted. "She's upset at you for waitin' so long to ask for some help, but she is as excited as I am—maybe more so."

"How you figure?" asked Paul.

"She's never seen your art, Paul-baby." Philomena gasped and tilted her head back. "Ah! She's going to be floored."

Paul grinned and said victoriously, "Well, if she can come through, my Mom and Pop give their blessin' for whatever."

"That is wonderful. You see? I told you," Philomena teased. "Follow my word." She turned around, still in Paul's arms. She looked at the paintings. "What we got here?" Paul opened his arms and Philomena stepped forward, bending down and sorting out the artwork. "These are exactly what I wanted to see. I love these pieces," she proclaimed. She looked around the room and rearranged the apartment in her imagination into a gallery to present her sweetheart's artwork. Philomena nodded her head. "I got this all planned out, Paul-baby." She took the paintings, one-by-one, and lined them up against the wall for the time being. Paul watched her, and when she was finished, Philomena returned to his arms. "I just wanted to clear the bed," Philomena smiled.

Paul leaned in to kiss Philomena deeply. They shed their clothes and melted onto the bed to make love. They cocooned themselves in the sheets afterward, snuggled close and grinning. Philomena teasingly cursed Paul for giving his father's smokes back to him. "You ain't got nothin' around here, girl?" Paul responded.

"Don't put this on me," huffed Philomena. "All this excitement ticklin' at me and nothin' to calm my nerves."

"You ain't got a refer stick hidden somewhere 'round here?" Paul asked while catching his breath.

"Ain't had a stick of puff 'round here for three weeks or so. The last one we puffed was *the last one*. And it was your turn to get more," Philomena reminded.

Paul said in a guilt-laden voice, "Yeah…I was. I was also cursin' myself out today that I wasn't smokin' somethin' stronger up in that tree." He chuckled and pulled Philomena closer to him. "Just ride the excitement. Ain't a reason to let it fritter."

Philomena did just that. She opened her legs and wrapped them around Paul's. She rubbed herself on him until she climaxed again, digging her nails into his chest. Her excitement heightened into soft laughter. She bit Paul's shoulder until she relaxed. He took the pain, enjoying Philomena's excitement. Philomena was relieved, and then, after she caught her breath, the two of them conversed about their futures, romanticizing their time to come. Philomena, after a while, swept her hand over Paul and felt him getting aroused again.

The horizon inhaled the sun and exhaled the night sky and all the stars.

Paul and Philomena made love again and then fell asleep. Paul awoke to the aroma of a cooked meal and Philomena standing over him dressed in her mother's indigo robe. She was holding a bowl of gumbo that had a slab of catfish sticking from it. "From downstairs, Paul-baby."

Paul sat up in the bed and accepted the bowl. He thanked Philomena and she bent down and kissed his forehead. She walked away and sat at her vanity to enjoy her own bowl of gumbo and catfish. Philomena waved her arm around the room, and while chewing she said, 'I'm gonna make this all right for you, Paul-baby." She swallowed. "Your art is gonna shine. This won't be an apartment room. This will be a gallery by the weekend." She then stated, "Got some cool water over here if you need."

"Thank you, Philly. For all this."

"Not a problem, Paul-baby," she said with a sly grin. "I love you."

Paul stopped eating. He paused and took in Philomena's last words. He put his bowl on the floor and moved to the end of the bed. Philomena left her bowl and spoon on the vanity and pulled her chair closer to the end of the bed where Paul lay.

"My baby love me," Paul smiled.

"Oh, hush. You've heard me say that before."

"Not in them words, Philly."

Philomena bent down closer to Paul. "You tellin' stories."

"No I ain't." Paul rolled on his back and shouted to the ceiling. "You heard that, God? My baby love me. Hot damn!"

"Boy, what you doin' cursin' while talkin' up to God?" Philomena warned, "Do you know you can get yourself—"

"I love you, Philomena," Paul interrupted. He turned over and sat up on the end of the bed. He reached for Philomena and guided her from the chair to his lap. "I love you. Thank you. We gon' do this here together, sweet baby. Together. My parents seem to like you. They was askin' if we'd stay together."

Philomena looked at the bed and then at Paul. "We'd better, or we'll be sinners in they eyes."

"Yeah, so, let's eat up and clean up. Can't give them anymore suspicion than they already got."

They went back to their meals. Philomena described to Paul, as they ate, the details of how she would lay out his art and rearrange her apartment. He was excited, and he imagined her vision as she recounted it to him. Paul returned home after his meal, and in the morning, he returned to Philomena's room with more artwork, and they repeated the events of lovemaking and sharing a late meal. In between, Philomena redecorated her apartment, transforming it into a gallery for Paul's paintings. She sang as she worked, and Paul watched her. He volunteered to help, but Philomena playfully insisted he'd just get in the way of her vision. So Paul sat back comfortably in the bed and watched Philomena as she sang and mounted his art around the room.

This ritual was repeated day after day. Paul's display was finished by Friday night, and Philomena even allowed him to help her with the final touches. The weekend arrived, and Sarinda Fallows entered Water Bug Hollow Sunday morning.

Philomena gave her aunt little time to rest from her trip, calling her up to the apartment. Eleven of Paul's paintings greeted Sarinda Fallows as she stepped into the apartment. Her voice was drawn from her, exclaiming upon seeing the pieces, "Magnificent, Paul." Philomena and Paul walked close behind her. "You cover so many styles here. It shows you got range. Good. I'm glad."

Sarinda noted the imagery, but the context of the paintings didn't grab her completely until her second look around at them. Then she stopped. Paused. Her mouth hung open, and she could feel a dull tug pulling at her.

Paul stepped up to Sarinda's side. He pointed to the first painting and started to explain. "These first three paintings, Miss Fallows, were inspired by James Wells Champney's *Death of Crispus Attucks at the Boston Massacre*. You can see I used the same colors and drawing scheme, but they're images of Curtis the Water Bug. We got *Curtis Fires on Jakobi*. The second I call *Uprising*, and the third, *Dancing in Freedom*. There's actually two that come before these. Curtis runnin' from the plantation, and one of him meetin' your relative, Oscar MacRitchie. Of all of them, I'm, uh, most fond of *Dancing in Freedom*. I got the newly freed slaves dancin' around a bonfire. I wanted it to reflect that old tradition of celebratin' what used to go on in Water Bug Hollow."

"Oh," Sarinda said, barely audible. Her eyes were fixated on the other paintings lining the room. She moved her head slowly to examine Paul's works of the Jakobi Plantation uprising, forcing her eyes in the same direction. She made a step toward the paintings and reached out to them, keeping her hand inches away from the painted canvas. "Breathtakin', Paul. My niece's words, and all their excitement, did not prepare me for your remarkable talent." Sarinda's eyes, by reflex, moved to the next set of paintings. "And from concrete to abstract. Look at all this." She turned to the fourth painting. "What is this about?" she inquired.

"Oh, Miss Fallows, I call that one *Announcing Life*."

Philomena proclaimed proudly, "It's the day I was born, Aunt Sarinda." She pointed to the picture, arm outstretched over Sarinda's shoulder. "You see?"

Sarinda's eyes flickered. A brief moment produced an illusion to her. She believed the veil that was wrapped around Philomena's arm writhed, animated like a snake. All in the blink of an eye. But, what Sarinda could not mistake was the movement and sound emanating from the picture in front of her. Paul's abstract creation became a picture show.

To the average eye, the picture was still. Nurses surrounded Theresa Amat, brought back to life in her final moments by the gifted artist Paul Benson. Her mouth hung open. Her final cry. A nurse held baby Philomena in her arms, also crying. Above the scene was a male, African angel, blowing his horn and doing just as Paul Benson had titled the painting: *Announcing Life.*

But, to Sarinda Fallows, the picture moved and produced sound. She heard baby Philomena's birthing cry mix with the last, loud harmony shouted from Theresa Amat. New life. Lightning snaked through the sky like a twisted javelin. And from the stars above dropped a trumpet case. The case opened by itself, and inside laid a magnificent horn that started to play on its own.

The animation ceased, and the still picture painted by Paul Benson focused back into place.

"It was such a sad day," said Philomena. "Uncle Quincy's brother passed. Mamma passed."

"But you were born," Paul expressed as he came up behind Philomena and embraced her. "I want you to remember that. That makes the day happy." He kissed her neck. "You were born, sweet baby."

Sarinda looked at the two of them. "And, as so many men do that possess the talent and passion for art, you incorporated your sweet baby here into your imaginative craft of oil on canvas. And I just imagine, Philly, that you bless him with song as he paints."

"Sometimes, Aunt Sarinda," Philomena confessed blushing.

Sarinda cleared her throat. "Well, Paul, let's see these other works. Philly dear, point to them while Paul explains."

Philomena pointed to the next painting. Paul commented, "I call this one *The Lion Witness.*"

The scene was morose and looked more sketched than painted, though that was just the technique used. The colors employed were black, as if everything was a shadow. There was also red. The artwork depicted a murder scene. Three gunmen in black suits, physiques rendered elongated like shadows, mirroring the snaking stream of smoke exhaled from their firearms, stood over the body of the only figure in the painting that was not warped, but portrayed realistically. The murdered man on the ground was a black man, but there was an oddity in his image. His blood drained from three gunshot wounds, as did the color of his skin and clothing. The blood's serpentine trail pooled and spelled the word *TREACHERY* on the floor. A scorpion stood at the foot of the man on the far left, its pincer pointing to the shooting. Behind the three men was a lion, shaded black like a shadow. It's position looked cowardly and crouched as if he was the imagined lion of L. Frank Baum.

Sarinda again saw the split-second slither from Philomena's veil, and the scene in the picture moved just for her curious, anticipating eyes to see. The animation retained the art style rendered. The blood flowed back into the murdered man on the floor, and he got up. His three wounds healed, the bullets jumping from the closing injuries and traveling back to their source. The bullets were swallowed by angry mobs of billowing, flashing fire that was sucked back into the firearms as they inhaled the bullets.

The image of the pointing scorpion washed away and was replaced with another shadowy figure. The lion turned into a kneeling figure that watched the grim murder take place. Then the scene moved forward. The shadowy figure that was once a scorpion pointed toward the resurrected man. The three ruffians pulled the triggers on their guns. Three bullets broke through the standing man, hitting him respectively in the shoulder, head, and heart. The murdered man's body hit the floor. Blood seeped from under him and once again spelled the word *TREACHERY*. His color faded. The scorpion returned and crawled atop the murdered man's head. The man in the corner shifted into the cowardly lion. The scene paused and returned to the still painting by Paul Benson.

"My, my," expressed Sarinda. "Sulky and gloomy, but beautiful. What inspired this?"

"Things changed in Water Bug Hollow," said Paul after thinking for a moment or two. "When my father gets on his talkin', he say that for the past twenty years or so, Water Bug Hollow has lost more and more of itself. Things just ain't the same here. I don't know what he means, but this is how I expressed it. But things seem fine to me."

"Well," Sarinda answered, "I can say that when Mayor Johnson was alive and runnin' things, there wasn't so much tension. He knew how to calm the waters, especially with the help of your mother, Philly. But let's continue on the tour, shall we? What's this over here?" Sarinda turned her attention to the next painting, taking a step in its direction.

Philomena pointed. "This is my mother and father. It's based on a picture someone took of them before my father left for overseas."

Paul clarified, "I call it *The Promise*."

Sarinda inspected the art. Joseph Pepper IV held Theresa Amat close, smiles on their faces. She knew the photograph it was inspired by, and it captured its likeness in oil paint remarkably, fleshed out with color and shadow by Paul's artistry. The painting remained still, and Sarinda stepped to the next. Her eyes widened, and she asked as curious as before, "And what mystery do you conjure here on canvas, Paul Benson?"

Philly didn't point. She noticed her aunt's eyes moving back and forth between the next two paintings. Paul expounded, "These two here symbolize burden. My burden and Philly's burden. Something haunting us."

Paul said he named the first picture *Passing to Shadow*. There was Philomena, again captured on canvas. She was of present age, every line and curve of her true to form. She was in the very apartment they all occupied. Paul put a sorrowful expression on her face, and from an outstretched hand she presented her veil to a feminine figure painted in silhouette that stood behind her. The feminine shadow's hair burned with fiery strands, and Paul explained that the ghostly woman was symbolic of the burden Philomena suffered from.

The shadowy, fire-haired woman made a second appearance in the next painting. She pulled at her emblazoned hair and tossed the fiery strands at paintings that lay on the ground in front of her. They were Paul's paintings, flames flapping atop them. "We all have our fears and burdens," said Paul. "I can just express mine, but that don't mean I ain't scared. It helps me face 'em, but I still got my hang ups—as you know, Philly-baby. If you can see, the fire in this paintin' is above the artwork, it's not really burnin' it. That's 'cause my art is too blessed." He said of the other, "I made the paintin' of Philly so she could face her fears and burden."

Philomena drew closer to Paul and embraced him and leaned her head on his shoulder. Sarinda moved to the next, admiring its simplicity. There was an exposed, pregnant belly. Above the belly twirled an object that looked similar to Sarinda's pendant. Paul informed, "I call it *A Baby's Toy*. I was just havin' fun. I thought of it one day when you were around, Miss Fallows. I saw your pendant, that peculiar stone. I drew on that inspiration. I made it a part of this collection just to sweeten you up."

Sarinda turned around. She rubbed her pendant and smiled at Paul with her head cocked to the side. "Why thank you, Paul. I am indeed flattered to be part of such fantastic artwork." She made a whimsical pivot to face the final painting, and in the same motion, completed a step toward the final piece of art. "I don't know any buyers, but I do know people wanting to keep Harlem's artistic movement goin'. They would love your work…" Her voice trailed away, words stuck in her throat, eyes again becoming wide.

The murdered man from Paul's work, *The Lion Witness*, was the subject of this painting as well. He was alive, and he was revealed to be a trumpet player. He played at a riverbank, standing in front of a bridge. Next to him was a little boy doing the same. From the bell of their horns issued the musical notations of the song they played. The notes curved over the bridge to the other side. Across the river were scenes of an African kingdom, African enslavement, rebellion, and freedom.

Philomena pointed. "I love this one, Aunt Sarinda."

The veil snaked. The picture moved.

The notes coming from the horn fluttered and flapped like faeries. The water, already painted to look like the cosmos, rushed in a flow of galactic black and twinkling stars. But Sarinda could not hear the music the boy and the man played on their horns.

The picture focused still as Paul revealed its name, *"Play a Bridge to the Past."* He explained, "Music was the best art I thought of to show how our hearts connect to who we are. The Negro. The Black. There were societies of free Negroes in the early eighteen hundreds that called themselves Afrique-American. African-American." Paul hesitated before he expressed, "No offense, Miss Fallows, but no matter what, your people will still call us 'niggers'." He lifted his shoulders and looked at his paintings. "I hear so many older folk around here talkin' about the past. This is my way of showin' how to reclaim it. We can sing about it. We can write about it. We can play a song about it. Some say, we can even paint a picture." Philomena and Sarinda chuckled at Paul's last statement. "Either way, we can procure that grand wish to have peace."

Sarinda faced Paul again. "And you have definitely done that with your talent, Paul. I want to showcase every one of these, and more, in a gallery, somewhere. I have a contact. He's in New Orleans. A man named Curly Burneside. He's a white man. He loves Negro art. He has an affinity for the movement in Harlem. He wants to find new artists to keep the movement going. I will have you meet him immediately. You'll come to New Orleans."

Paul and Philomena beamed with excitement. "Yes, ma'am. Yes, Miss Fallows," Paul exclaimed. "Indeed. I'll have a suit and everything."

Sarinda advised, "Have your weekend free, Paul. I will contact Mister Burneside tomorrow. Rest easy for the week. Does your family have a car?"

"No," Paul answered feeling a little deflated of spirit.

"Well, then, we'll figure a way to get your art to New Orleans. Perhaps we can take three a day over the week. You can store them at my apartment there."

"Yes ma'am," said Paul.

Sarinda expressed as an order, "I want all of these paintings on display for Mister Burneside, even the ones about the uprising in Water Bug Hollow. This selection displays your wide range of artistic talent." She walked forward and passed Paul and Philomena. "Let me get to work, now. I'll make my call to Mister Burneside."

Philomena stopped Sarinda. She hugged her aunt. "Thank you, Aunt Sarinda. Thank you."

"It's all Paul's doing," Sarinda responded. She looked up at him while still embracing Philomena. "His damned stubbornness lifted. He's let me see his artwork, and now I'll reward him for it." She stepped away from Philomena. "Now, let me be on my way. I'll give you news soon. It's just a simple phone call. Let me head downstairs."

Sarinda exited. Philomena turned to Paul and the couple threw their arms around one another. Philomena kissed Paul hard. "This is wonderful!" she blared. "We'll wait for news, and then you go ask your mother and father for permission to visit New Orleans next weekend."

"You gon' be there with me, Philomena?"

"Absolutely, Paul-baby. Absolutely. I'll be by my man's side." She added, "I got to setup the display anyway. After we hear the news, and you tell your parents, come back here and we'll begin dismantling this display."

Knocking.

Philomena turned, walked away from Paul and answered the door. Sarinda jumped into the room and announced, "Next weekend. All is set. Saturday afternoon." Philomena clapped her hands. Paul stepped forward. "Mister Burneside has a building he wants you to put the display in. He'd like to see how your art would look on display in a gallery."

"An actual show," declared Philomena.

"Not truly, Philly dear," Sarinda corrected. "It would just be myself, Paul here, and Mister Burneside."

"I'll be there too, Aunt Sarinda," Philomena interjected.

"Of course," Sarinda acknowledged. "But my point is that it will be a small audience. The main person to impress will be Mister Burneside."

Paul nodded. "Yes, ma'am."

"Put your best suit on for the morning," Sarinda mandated. "Over the week, you and I will take the paintings into New Orleans. How many paintings do we have here?" Sarinda looked at each of Paul's paintings and counted. "Eleven. We'll carry six tomorrow, five the next day."

"I can help," Philomena suggested.

Sarinda assured, "And you will, Philly. While we travel to the city, and after your shift ends helping at the elementary school, you can string a protective cloth around Paul's paintings. The two of you can get the first six done tonight, or at least four."

Paul informed, "I've got some supplies at home. It should be enough."

Sarinda grinned and concluded, "Well, I'll leave the two of you to, uh, *celebrate.*"

Philomena blushed and retorted, "Aunt Sarinda, now whatever are you implyin'?"

Sarinda's grin remained. "I'm implying that the two of you are young, excited adults. That's all, Philly." She leaned her lips into Philomena's ear and said, "I'm happy to see you happy, Philly."

"Thank you, Aunt Sarinda."

Sarinda wished Paul well and then left the room. Paul once again embraced Philomena from behind and said, "We'll get to celebratin' once I get back with the supplies and tell my family. I hope they're excited."

"They will be," Philomena reassured. She patted Paul's cheek and then kissed him in the same place.

Paul let Philomena go, assured his return with a kiss, and left her apartment to inform his mother and father. Just as Philomena said, Paul's information excited them, and his family decided to celebrate at dinner, with an invitation extended to Philomena. Paul returned to Philomena's apartment and presented his parents' invitation. She freshened up and put on new clothes to accompany Paul home. Mamma and Papa Benson were cordial to her, reminding the young woman how much they loved her presence and influence on their son. Paul and Philomena kept their hands locked together under the table the whole while. Philomena loved being surrounded by Paul's family. She interacted with Paul's younger sister, who was twelve years old, a month away from being a teenager. Paul and his sixteen-year-old brother discussed baseball, the Negro Leagues. Their father chimed in every-now-and-then. Mamma Benson sat back and observed the goings on at her table.

Paul and Philomena didn't stay long, and Mamma and Papa Benson gave blessing for the young couple to take their leave. Paul went to his room and gathered supplies for he and Philomena to wrap up his paintings. He informed his mother and father that he would be home late, and then he and Philomena returned to her apartment.

The routine to assemble the display played backwards, taking the paintings down, redecorating and getting distracted with lovemaking. Paul and Philomena started wrapping the artwork late in the night, and finished six paintings by two in the morning. Philomena didn't realize how difficult the process would be, and when they were finished, Paul decided to stay the night. He told Philomena before they dozed off to sleep, "Let the people of Water Bug Hollow talk. I'm too tired to care."

Paul woke early in the morning and left for his parent's place to wash and dress himself in one of his Sunday church suits. His father gave him money and advice, telling Paul to be careful walking around New Orleans with a white woman—even if it was for business. Paul said he would mind his setting, and then he left, returning to Philomena's apartment. He knocked and heard Philomena say the door was unlocked. Paul entered and found Sarinda inside stacking three of his pieces, Philomena helping.

"Come on, Paul-baby," said Philomena. "Gather your things. We gotta move quick. I'm already a little late for work." Paul rushed over and lifted the paintings stacked by Philomena. He turned and saw her looking him up and down. "You. Are. Handsome."

"Thank you, sweet baby." He placed a kiss on Philomena's cheek.

"I agree," Sarinda concurred. "Come on, now, you two lovebirds. We need to get goin'." On Sarinda's word, they quickly shuffled to the outside. Philomena locked her space, and then they exited Eve's Hallow. Philomena followed Sarinda and Paul through Water Bug Hollow's organic entrance and walked them to their taxi. The art was placed in the cab's trunk, and just before Sarinda and Paul slipped into the car, Sarinda said, "Philly, don't you worry none, Paul will be back shortly, probably before your shift ends. And I want the two of you to finish the rest of those paintings."

"Yes, Aunt Sarinda."

The taxi moved away from Water Bug Hollow. Paul waved goodbye to Philomena, keeping her in sight until they were well on their way to the train station. There, reality set in and Paul and Sarinda sat in separate sections of the train, even though there was a minor protest made by Sarinda. She informed the conductor that Paul was with her as help, but Paul remembered his father's words and said politely, "It's okay, Miss Fallows. Let me put these paintin's up, and I'll go sit 'round the way. Ain't a need to cause a stir, now." Paul stationed the art on a shelf above Sarinda's seat, and then he made his way to the train's 'Colored Section'.

The two, however, shared a cab in New Orleans, and acting as Sarinda's help, Paul brought his paintings up to her apartment complex. Sarinda told him to lay the paintings down in the front room, and then she expressed she was ready for a bath before returning to Water Bug Hollow.

Sarinda changed, prancing around Paul in her tied bathrobe with nothing on underneath. The silky robe clung to her figure as she fluttered around her apartment. She made conversation with Paul, poured champagne for them, and indulged in a smoke while she waited for her bath to fill with bubbles and heated water. She pulled a new outfit from her closet and walked it to the bathroom. Returning to the front room, she said to Paul, "This is a lovely space, isn't it, Paul." Paul agreed. "Before Philomena was born, I was wastin' so much money payin' for a hotel room and travelin' back and forth from here to Water Bug Hollow. It was cheaper to pay for an apartment here in New Orleans *and* have one in Water Bug Hollow." She puffed her cigarette and said excitedly, "I got a call from Mister Curly Burneside, Paul. He is excited to see your work. He's putting together a show in Washington, D.C. for new, Negro artists. He wants the show to move up to Harlem. He has the space in Washington set. He's still negotiating for the Harlem space. He also plans on bringing the show to Boston."

"That sounds right with me, Miss Fallows," Paul responded as he anxiously sipped his champagne.

"I told him about your more abstract works," Sarinda continued. "That got him really goin'. He wants the thinking pieces, Paul. That's what he told me. Not the easy pieces, the thinking ones. The world is ready for the Negro's thoughts. It's the new direction for expression. The visual thought, Paul. Music can be too abstract. It gets reinterpreted with every set of ears, even if the artist is standin' right there and telling you about the musical number. Your thought, your eye, your talent, is moving in the proper direction—especially for the Negro. You're a pioneer." Before Paul could answer her, Sarinda put her glass of champagne down and moved to the bathroom. "I think that bath is ready. I'll be out shortly, Paul." Sarinda hurried to the bathroom, closing the door behind her.

Paul drank the last of his champagne and sat. Anxiety caused a tremor in his legs. He believed there were eyes watching him closely. He'd just accompanied a white woman into her apartment. He'd appeared as her help, but Paul didn't feel secure about that. He thought about the bath water running, lapping loudly. He believed that could be heard. He believed the 'pop' of the champagne bottle, and the fizzing pour of its contents into glasses could be heard, and he wondered what the other white occupants would be suspecting.

Paul took a breath to settle himself from his frantic thoughts. He looked around the posh room, observing its furnishings, curiously noting a crib at the far end. Paul began to relax as he imagined Philomena and he living as successful artists in a place no different than this. They would have an apartment in Chicago, another in New York. Philomena and he would visit Water Bug Hollow as often as they could, or invite his family up to stay.

Paul remembered Philomena remarking that she would like to study law or politics. Then Sarinda emerged from the bathroom, dried, primped, and fully dressed. "Come, Paul. Back to Water Bug Hollow." She played with her stone pendant and remarked, "Forget this place."

"Yes, Miss Fallows."

Their journey reversed. Taxi. Separate areas of the train. Taxi. Water Bug Hollow. Paul politely thanked Sarinda for her help before returning home and informing his parents about his day. He showered and changed. It was close to three o'clock when Paul made his way to Philomena's apartment. She was home and had already started wrapping the remaining paintings. Paul dived into helping his sweetheart. Their routine started up again. Wrapping Paul's work. Rearranging Philomena's living space to what it once reflected. Then they made love again, close and passionate. Paul and Philomena could feel the change in their lives, and their excitement for life became the rhythm in their lovemaking. Paul stayed the night. He didn't want to leave Philomena's side. He held her through sleep and dream, at peace.

The previous morning's activities repeated. Paul woke up, kissed Philomena as he left her apartment, rushed home, showered, primped and changed into another suit, and then returned to Philomena's place. Sarinda was again already there, two covered paintings stacked in her arms when she answered the door to let Paul in. Paul's other three works were on the bed, neatly stacked by Philomena. She emerged from the bathroom ready for her day. Paul stepped inside and approached her. A wide smile decorated his face. He gave Philomena a loving kiss.

"Okay you two," yelled Sarinda. "We're running late as it is. Come on, now."

Paul stepped away from Philomena, both of them giggling. "This is it, Philly-baby," exclaimed Paul. "My pieces for demonstration will be in New Orleans. Then come Friday night, you and I will go there and set it up for Saturday. We'll stay at your aunt's place." He turned around and asked Sarinda, "That okay, Miss Fallows? For Philly and I to come up Friday?"

"Absolutely, Paul. Not a problem at all. She's been there before plenty times. The people know I have a Negro niece. They're fine by her presence—at least they don't say nothin' to me. Now they'll know you as the man on her arm. But come on. I can't hold this mess all day. Come."

Paul grabbed his works off the bed. He led the way out the door, Philomena and Sarinda close behind him. They walked to the taxis waiting outside Water Bug Hollow's organic entrance and picked a driver to shuttle them to the train. They put the five paintings in the trunk, closed it, and then Paul turned and kissed Philomena on the cheek. "Okay, now, baby. I'll see you when I get back. Go on now to work. Help them teachers."

Paul and Sarinda slipped into the car. Paul waved to Philomena as the car drove away. The previous day's travel was repeated. Arriving outside Sarinda's apartment door, they could hear the phone ringing incessantly from inside. Sarinda set the two paintings down that she was handling. She fumbled with her keys trying to unlock the door and rush to the phone. But, the phone's ringing stopped by the time Sarinda was able to handle her keys properly and open the door. She cursed, "Dammit!" Paul walked inside ahead of Sarinda. He set down the three paintings in his hands next to the group delivered the previous day. He returned to the hall, grabbed the other two paintings left there by Sarinda, and stacked them on top of the others.

The phone rang again!

Sarinda picked it up in a hurry. "Yes," she answered forcefully. "This is she. Who…? Oh. My dear! Mister Burneside." She turned to Paul and smiled, pointing to the phone. "Yes, I know. I'm sorry," she conversed. "I said I'd be here earlier. It's been a time lugging these works into the city." She paused, listening to Mister Burneside. "Yes, he's here with me. Yes, still here. I'm lookin' at him right now. Yes. Oh. Well, I hope I didn't miss our opportunity. Really," she said excitedly. "Now? Absolutely, Mister Burneside. Absolutely. You'll send a taxi right over? That would be nice. Thank you, Mister Burneside. Uh, Mister Burneside, should we bring the works with us? Yes. Okay. We'll see you shortly. Excuse me? Yes, that's the correct address. Thank you, again, Mister Burneside." Sarinda hung up. She clapped her hands together and said with glee, "He wants you to come and see the spot for Saturday. He also wants to see your works."

"Really, Miss Fallows?" Paul jumped with excitement.

"Yes. But don't worry. He won't judge. Mister Burneside likes to observe works of art in their natural environment, on display." She exaggerated her movements, widening her arms and pretending to examine the walls of her apartment as if she was a curator setting the scene. Paul laughed. Sarinda relaxed from her playful gesture and asked, "You do have time, Paul, don't you? You're in no rush to get back to Water Bug Hollow?"

"No, ma'am," Paul spoke, grinning from ear to ear. "No Miss Fallows. I can't let this opportunity slide. I'm nervous, though."

"Don't be, Paul. You're too brilliant with your art. He's sending a taxi now." She walked to a bottle of champagne, opened it, and poured the contents into two glasses. "We will celebrate in the meantime, as you know I like to do." She finished pouring and handed a glass to Paul, lifting hers for him to toast. They took sips at the same time. Sarinda said after swallowing, "I wish we had time to get a little breakfast. I'd make you somethin'. Are you hungry, Paul?"

Paul swallowed in a hurry, almost choking. He shook his head before answering, "No ma'am. I'm too exited to eat." He took a moment to wipe from his chin the champagne that hadn't made it into his mouth. Then exclaimed, "I appreciate all this, Miss Fallows. If I knew one opportunity would make things move this quick, I'd had Philly set this up a long time ago."

"Don't you worry none, Paul. Your stubbornness to accept my help made things come together right on time." Sarinda expounded, "I mean, think about it. I didn't have these contacts months ago, or rather Mister Burneside wasn't looking for artists. It's all perfect timing, Paul. We're here now. That's all that matters."

"Yes, Miss Fallows. Yes ma'am." He continued drinking.

"That's right, Paul. You just concentrate on where this will take you all—and by 'you all' I mean yourself and my niece."

"I can't help but think of that, Miss Fallows." Paul sipped more of his bubbly beverage.

"Good. You just let your thoughts rest there." Sarinda finished her champagne. "Now, I believe you will be among several other Negro artists, Paul. It won't be an exclusive show, but it's a start. Mister Burneside will take good care of you. And I'm sure with your art, and a good word from me, you will be the center of attention. So don't you worry about being overshadowed." Sarinda impressed in a soft voice, "We're going to make this work for you. The American economy is slowly recovering. Small, self-sufficient places like Water Bug Hollow haven't quite felt the sting of this depression. It's terrible. Art and entertainment are what keep people's spirits up, and where one can gain a profit. You will be somethin' else, Paul Benson." Sarinda's eyes went to the clock. "I'll check downstairs to see if the cab is here. I'll be right back. You stay here."

"Yes, ma'am."

Sarinda excused herself and left the apartment. Paul's thoughts, as they did the day before, imagined the place was his. He imagined he was in Harlem. Philomena was living with him. They were married. The crib at the far end of the apartment was for their first child. Paul Benson, junior.

He wasn't buried too far in his imagination when Sarinda returned. A smile dressed her face, but she looked in a hurry. "The taxi's here. Come on. I'll take some paintings, and you take some paintings. We'll make two trips."

Paul stacked four paintings in his arms and asked Sarinda to place two more there. She did, and took up three paintings herself. They brought the works to the taxi. The driver jumped from his car and opened the trunk. Paul and Sarinda placed the art pieces inside. After the first set of paintings was tucked neatly inside the trunk, Sarinda handed Paul the key to her apartment and instructed him to get the remaining pieces and lock the door. Paul rushed right up to her apartment, gathered his two remaining works, exited and locked the door. He returned to the cab and placed the works in the trunk with the others, joining Sarinda inside the cab after shutting the trunk tight.

Sarinda instructed the driver where to go.

Paul was quiet for the ride. He stared outside and imagined New Orleans as New York City or Chicago. Sarinda left him to his imagination for the duration, though it was eventually interrupted when the car stopped near an old warehouse. For all of Paul's trips through his imagination, he hadn't imagined their final destination would be a dingy back alley next to an even dingier looking warehouse. Sarinda told Paul to get out and wait. He ejected from the car at the same moment the driver exited to come around back and unlock the trunk. Sarinda stepped out. She said to the driver as she twirled her pendant between her fingers, "Could you please take these pieces inside the warehouse there? Thank you, dear."

The driver tugged the brim of his hat and smiled at Sarinda as she handed him money for the extra work. He started taking Paul's works from the trunk and bringing them inside the warehouse.

Sarinda turned to Paul and straightened his suit. She told him as the driver went about delivering Paul's artwork inside the shabby warehouse, "Now, don't you worry when you meet Mister Burneside, Paul. You be polite like you know how to be. He will absolutely love you and your work. You'll be fine. This ain't an interview for a job. This is an informal meeting before Saturday. Remember that. Besides, like I said, he doesn't like to judge artwork until he sees it in its proper environment." Sarinda finished ironing out Paul's suit with her hand and fixing his tie. "There."

The driver returned to close the trunk. Sarinda walked with him to the driver's side. He slipped into the taxi and rolled down his window. Sarinda bent down to speak with him. Paul observed her say something into the man's ear. Her voice was low, and Paul couldn't tell what she was saying. Sarinda twirled her pendant, and then she patted the driver on his shoulder and rose up straight.

The taxi drove away.

"Should we have told him to wait, Miss Fallows?" asked Paul.

"No need," said Sarinda. "Mister Burneside will provide another ride home." She added, "And goodness, the kindness of Mister Burneside paid for the ride when the driver took your works inside." She waved Paul forward. "Now come on. Let's meet this man."

Paul walked ahead of Sarinda and into the building. The interior was gray and only lit from the day's light shining through massive windows situated high above. The ceilings were high and the space was open. Paul wondered how his display would look professional in this setting, even with Philomena's eye to coordinate his paintings appropriately. He walked past his works that had been stacked next to the entrance. In front of him, at the other end of the large area, was a well-dressed man that Paul guessed was Curly Burneside. His back was to Paul, but he spun around as soon as Sarinda called his name.

Mister Burneside's hands were tucked in his jacket pockets. He presented a friendly smile to Paul and stepped forward to greet him. First he looked at Sarinda and acknowledged her call, "Miss Fallows, how do you do? You look as lovely as ever." He looked at Paul just as Sarinda finished thanking him for his compliment. "Is this the Negro artist?"

"It is," answered Sarinda.

Paul's excitement lifted and dismissed his earlier anxiety about the warehouse's interior. He took a step. "Hello, Mister Burneside, sir. I'm Paul Benson. How do you do?"

Curly stopped. His smile remained. "How do I do, Paul? Well, Paul Benson, I do just fine. Just fine." Curly pulled his right hand from his pocket, and with it, a .45 caliber pistol. He aimed it at Paul Benson and shot him three times. The bullets ruined Paul Benson's handsome face. Blood spattered on Curly Burneside. Sarinda remained unblemished from the erratic, sanguinary spray. Paul's body crumpled to the floor, his life extinguished too fast for him to feel anything, not even surprise.

"Leave his body be, Curly," ordered Sarinda. "Take his wallet. Take the money. Then burn them paintings." She nodded toward Paul's artwork stacked near the entrance.

Curly sprang to his orders. He removed Paul of his wallet, and of the fifteen dollars tucked inside. He dropped the wallet and walked to Paul Benson's paintings. He laid the artworks out on the floor, right in front of Paul's lifeless body. He looked up at Sarinda for further order.

Sarinda spoke calm and collected, "Douse them and burn them, Curly. Go on."

Curly snatched a tank of gas placed near a tool shelf. He soaked the eleven works of art, and then he lit a match and backed away as he tossed it onto the paintings. The fire jumped up angrily into the air. It burned intensely for a short while and then disappeared. The paintings remained unscathed. Curly looked at Sarinda. She suggested, "Take off their protective coverings. Unwrap them. Douse them again, and then burn them."

Curly did as he was told. He poured gasoline over the unwrapped paintings, lit another match, and tossed it on Paul's artwork as he leapt back. The new action produced the same results. An angry fire hollered and reached up with flickering punches, and in the same moment, evaporated with a whoosh.

The paintings remained unscathed.

Sarinda bent down and felt the paintings. They were dry. Not a drop of gasoline drenched any area of the paintings. She stood up and asked Curly for the matches. She lit one and then tightly held her pendant before tossing the match to a single painting. There came a small whoosh of brilliant fire, and then it suddenly vanished. Sarinda grit her teeth.

Angry Sarinda tried again and again and again and again and again and again, but nothing happened. The paintings remained unscathed, and Sarinda, out of breath, handed the matches back to Curly. "Take these pieces. We'll leave the body."

"Yes, Miss Fallows. My car is out front." Curly started to stack the paintings. Sarinda helped. Curly told her, "Two Negroes were just arrested for a robbery. Grocery store. They will admit to kidnapping and killing Paul Benson. I'll handle that, Miss Fallows."

"Thank you, Curly. The taxi that brought us here, well, that man won't remember anything."

It took two trips to Curly's car to store the paintings neatly inside. Sarinda sat in the passenger's seat while Curly sat in the driver's seat. He started his engine and drove away.

Paul Benson's murdered body remained behind.

Sarinda Decorated
"He's here! He's here!"

It was night. Sarinda Fallows had been standing at Philomena Amat's apartment door for half-an-hour. Staring. Twiddling her fingers between the flat, gray stone dangling from the gold chain around her neck. The door faded from her sight, and she saw Philomena sitting at her vanity where the young woman rested her head and sobbed through heavy breaths. A bottle of liquor was next to her, its contents half drained. A glass lay next to the bottle with a few drops remaining at the bottom hinting at Philomena's alcoholic indulgence.

Sarinda continued to watch. Philomena cried, not only for the loss of Paul Benson, not just because she loved him, but because she believed he was such a brilliant young man. He was supposed to shine like the sun on the world. Sarinda discerned these thoughts from Philomena as she continued to play with the flat, gray stone between her fingers.

Philomena also felt guilty for pushing Paul, and Paul's mother made sure of that in her outcry of grief. Philomena was not invited to Paul's funeral, though Paul's father did his best to protest. Paul's mother didn't even care to have her son's works returned to her. *"That's what got him killed!"* Sarinda felt Philomena recall. *"Wasn't no white folks that took my boy from me. Them two nigger boys. Them thieves. And you, you harlot! Keep them damn paintings! You pushin' my Paul into all this with them damn dreams of his. You instigating harlot! You killed him too! This is your fault!"*

Sarinda watched Philomena burst into another round of tears. She knocked on the door. "Philly," she called. "Philly, dear, I won't leave. I've been here since you told me to go away, and I won't. Now open this door so I know you're all right. I will *not* leave."

Philomena remained still, save her sporadic movements caused by the hiccup of tears. But Philomena wasn't ignoring her Aunt Sarinda. She was trying to focus. There was half a bottle of liquor coursing through her. She stirred, her frame rumbling with a tremor of life. Philomena managed to rise up from the vanity, and then the chair. She kept her hand on the back of the chair for balance, and then she took a careful step forward. Right foot. Left foot. She moved away from the chair, keeping focus with as much balance as she could. Right foot. Left foot. She walked toward the door, almost falling into it as she reached and opened it. She sniffed and wiped her tears from her face.

"Philly," Sarinda sighed as she stepped into the apartment, arms outstretched to embrace Philomena.

Philomena backed away, stumbling. "No," she slurred. "No. Don't."

"Philly, dear…"

"No," she said again. She regained her stance and moved backward, directing herself toward the bed. Then she turned and ambled with clumsy, drunken steps back to her vanity. Philomena bent over, arms resting on the vanity, trembling and barely holding her up. Sarinda came up behind her, Philomena noticing. She swiped the veil from the vanity and turned to her aunt. She shoved the garment toward Sarinda and yelled in an inebriated voice, *"Here!"*

"Philly, no."

"Here," Philomena said louder. And then she repeated in a soft, soft whisper, "Here, Aunt Sarinda. My payment to you. Please. You always loved this. Take it. My payment." Her voice drowned in tears. She fell forward, crying. Sarinda caught Philomena in her arms.

Sarinda was holding the veil in her left hand.

"Philly," she whispered.

"Make my Paul shine like the sun, Aunt Sarinda," Philomena cried. She sniffed. "Make him shine like the sun. Please. Have Mister Burneside still showcase his art. Let it still be on display."

Sarinda stared at the veil in her hands, Philomena's words muted by awe. Sarinda's face was stone, but her eyes were concentrated on the veil. Philomena's words played in her head. Louder. Louder. More audible. She answered, "I believe I could arrange that Philly, but—"

"And then," Philomena continued to cry. "And then you put them up in your club. You have my Paul-baby's art mounted, please, Aunt Sarinda. Please!"

Sarinda moved Philomena to the bed. "Lie down, Philly. Lie down, little girl." Philomena lay on the bed. She continued to sob. "There, there, little girl. Calm." Sarinda wiped the veil over Philomena's face and the young woman closed her eyes and instantly fell asleep. Sarinda twirled her pendant and said, "Thank you, Philly. Thank you for this gift. I give a gift back to you. I give you life." She wiped the veil over Philomena's forehead. "You just let go of that devil-liquid you put in you. You just sweat that out, now." Philomena's skin saturated with liquored sweat. "You don't worry your head anymore about that Paul Benson boy. You look ahead. You forget about all of that. You go and keep your shifts helpin' them teachers at the school. You forget about travel. You forget about New York. You forget about all them dreams, Philly-baby." She leaned closer to Philomena's body and whispered with a smile, "Merciful Aunt Sarinda. Yes, I am." Sarinda straightened. She wrapped the veil around her arm, suffocating an excited grin, and then she stood up. She looked at Philomena and said cordially, "Goodbye, Philomena. Maybe I'll write."

Sarinda walked out of the apartment, locking the door as she left. She made her way downstairs, through Eve's Hallow, out onto the main road. She stopped and looked around and stared in awe at Water Bug Hollow, the town decorated by the night. Lamplights flickered. The windows on the buildings glowed, and some were vacant of light. Fireflies scampered through the air like will-o'-the-wisps. Her large, green eyes panned the environment. She inhaled the air and closed her eyes to the scenery around her. Sarinda beamed. Her eyes opened, her hair dimmed a darker shade of red, and she said, "Goodbye, Water Bug Hollow."

Sarinda walked into the nature-made tunnel, but she didn't emerge on the other side of it. Her silhouette disappeared into a shadow and was lost. But there flickered a dull shadowy flame in a New Orleans alley. Out stepped Sarinda Fallows with the veil now covering her face. She was only two blocks from her apartment building, and she walked down the street tall and confident. Men and women stared at her for different reasons. Sarinda paid them no mind, the women, that is. She presented a veiled smile and a nod of her head toward the men.

When she arrived at her apartment, and unlocked the door and stepped inside, there sat Curly Burneside listening to soft music on the radio. Curly stood up on Sarinda's entrance. His expression was one of awe, as he'd never seen Sarinda look more beautiful than as she did now while wearing the ancient veil.

She pranced inside. If there was any sleep stirred in Curly Burneside by the soft music coming from the radio, he now had been awakened. Sarinda twirled into the room, shutting the door and performing a pirouette away from it. She danced toward Curly, and then around him as she came close. He watched her every movement, his head turning to keep up with her. His body turned when his head couldn't turn any farther. Sarinda's dance made him dizzy. Curly smiled at her.

"I told you, Curly. I told you." She danced merrily and quoted an earlier statement to remind Curly, "You can take all the time in the world to trap someone that ain't aware you're after them." She stopped her dance and faced Curly. "And I can sing, Curly. I can feel that witch's breath in my lungs. Curly, I can sing." A bright, boyish smile appeared on Curly. He walked forward, hesitant with his steps. He was about to speak when Sarinda removed her veil and wiped it across Curly's face. *"Ha-ash-ash-gick!"* she pronounced.

Curly's face was gone, replaced with a face Sarinda had not seen in a long time. The face was handsome to Sarinda, and she glowed when she saw it. Curly's entire head was replaced, his body too. This gentleman was thinner than Curly Burneside, but was still muscular. His face was sharper in features, chiseled to a point and angle from nose to jaw to chin. His hair was more full, brown. And his skin was tanned by the sun rather than reddened like Curly's. He was just as tall, but Sarinda admired the man in front of her with a grin as if he was tall enough to stretch to the heavens. She looked up, curled under his chin with an admiring beam coming from her lips.

"Kenten. My Kenten," she said embracing him, placing her head on his chest. "My strong Kenten." The man smiled at her, but said no words. He hugged her tighter and a warm feeling coursed through Sarinda. She glided away from him, gliding her fingertips down Kenten's arms until she reached his hand. She grabbed hold of him with one hand and turned around, leading Kenten to the bed. "Come now, Mister Fallows. We have love to make." She looked over her shoulder and giggled. "Oh, I wanted everything to be perfect, Kenten. But it's been so long. I wanted a specific suit for you to wear, but hell, in the end, it was gonna come off anyway." Sarinda stopped at the bed and turned around. She put her arms around Kenten's neck and planted kisses there and on his face. "I might have had the longevity and power, but you had the strength, Kenten. You always had the strength. You would've been so proud of all I've done." She sat on the bed and pulled Kenten over her. "Come on, Kenten, dear. Come to me."

Sarinda put the veil over her, and then she and Kenten undressed. Sarinda immediately opened her legs to the man on top of her. But, as Kenten penetrated her, Sarinda's mind drifted to other men, men she'd conquered in Water Bug Hollow. And she thought about the women of Water Bug Hollow that mourned their loss. She closed her eyes and thought. Kenten looked at her. He barely blinked. Sarinda climaxed. Kenten climaxed inside her. He made no sound, and he slumped beside Sarinda exhausted.

Sarinda rubbed her belly with the veil before placing it back over her face and falling asleep. She awoke an hour later, stirred Kenten, and they made love again. Sarinda's mind once again drifted. This time Sarinda mounted Kenten, her hips swaying back and forth, up and down. Kenten watched her with an absent stare. Sarinda bent her head back and exhaled a passionate cry. Her body tightened. Kenten did the same as he climaxed inside her.

Sarinda's body collapsed beside Kenten. She turned on her back and rubbed her belly with the veil and twiddled her pendant. She draped the fabric over her face and fell asleep. When she woke, it was morning. She turned her head as she removed the fabric from her face. Kenten was gone. Next to her was Curly Burneside, naked and sitting up in the bed beside her. The comforter covered him from the waist down. He was bewildered, his expression aimed at Sarinda. She, shameless, turned to Curly with her top uncovered and the comforter hanging loosely below her waist. "What do you remember, Curly?" she asked.

Curly blinked. "Barely anything," he said. "It was like a dream, Miss Fallows. There's only a feeling of a moment." He blinked over and over. "Was he here? Was Master Fallows here? Was I…him?"

Sarinda lay on her back and threw the comforter off her. She closed her eyes but felt Curly's stare. "You've seen it before, Curly. Now get up. Use the veil and the ring. We have a ritual to continue."

Curly leapt from the bed. He gathered his underclothes and pants and put them on. He walked over to Sarinda, tugging at his ring until it came off. As he fumbled with this, Sarinda removed her veil and laid it out over her stomach. Curly placed the ring atop the veil lying over Sarinda's belly, positioned over her navel as commanded. She lifted her neck and reached behind her. She removed her necklace and handed it to Curly.

"Over my belly," Sarinda instructed. She was beaming. "Twirl it."

Curly dangled the necklace over Sarinda's belly, just above the ring. He flicked the stone pendant and it twirled. Sarinda harmonized her voice in a low, soulful burn. Her harmony grew into a song. The words were not English, but an old language. As she sang, and as the pendant twirled, her belly expanded up, ballooning. Pregnant. The veil draped, like the movement of a jellyfish, as Sarinda's belly turned into an expectant mound. The change tickled Sarinda, and in the middle of her song she burst into laughter and tears of joy. She covered her mouth.

Curly lifted the necklace as Sarinda's belly thickened and stretched. The necklace twirled in one direction until it wound too far, and then it twirled in the other. No other force but Sarinda's joyous laughter swayed the pendant's whirl.

Then the tickling stopped, and Sarinda screamed. A sharp pain pushed between her thighs. "Ah!" she hollered. "Curly…C-Curly!" The pendant paused. Curly's ring slipped from Sarinda's belly. "Curly! A doctor, Curly. A doctor…" she winced.

Curly left Sarinda's side and hastened to the phone. He dialed a local hospital and stated the emergency. "I don't believe there will be time to bring her in. Is there anyone close to our neighborhood?" He paused. "Yes. Thank you. We will expect him shortly." He stated the apartment building's address, thanked the woman he was speaking with, and ended the conversation. He informed Sarinda as he returned to her side that a local physician would arrive shortly. He swiped the veil from Sarinda's pregnant belly, lifted her neck, and spread the garment underneath her head, covering her pillow. He picked up his ring and slipped it onto his finger. "Here, Miss Fallows, let's make you presentable." Curly went to Sarinda's closet and retrieved one of her robes. He returned to her and helped her put it on. "There, Miss Fallows." Afterward, Curly clothed himself completely. He pulled up a chair and held Sarinda's hand.

Her grip tightened as the pain increased. Curly grimaced. He held his breath, then exhaled hard. There was knocking at the door. Curly and Sarinda looked over. Curly guessed it was the doctor he'd summoned. He convinced Sarinda to let him go, and then he stood up, walked over to the door and opened it. A doctor and a nurse were on the other side. "Come in," Curly said stepping aside. Curly closed the door after they stepped in. "This way. My friend believes her child is due. How do you do?" He shook the doctor's hand. "Curly Burneside."

The doctor moved his bag from one hand to the other in order to shake Curly's hand. "Hello, Mister Burneside. I've heard of you. You're an attorney, are you not? Or, you work with local law enforcement? I'm pleased to meet you. I'm Doctor Alfred Grayson. This is my assistant,

Cheryl Plum. Good day to you." Curly led the doctor to the bed. "And this is your friend, I take it." He beamed. "Just relax, Miss…"

"F-F-Fallows. Sa-Sarinda Fallows."

"Just relax, Miss Fallows. You will be fine. More than fine. You will be a mother soon." He turned to Curly and the nurse. "Put her at the bed's center."

The doctor placed his bag next to Sarinda as Curly and the nurse carefully positioned Sarinda where the doctor ordered. Curly removed the veil from the pillow and handed it to the nurse. The doctor opened his bag and asked Sarinda a series of questions about her pregnancy. Sarinda answered accordingly, and she was prepped for delivery. Curly paced as the nurse and doctor inspected Sarinda. The doctor stated, "You're really far along, Miss Fallows. This child is pushing through now. My goodness."

Sarinda called for Curly, and he came to her. She reached up and he grabbed her hand. On the doctor's orders, Sarinda pushed. She screamed and pushed. Screamed! Pushed! Her grip tightened on Curly's hand. He gritted his teeth. She screamed. Screamed! Pushed! The minutes that passed felt like an eternity. Push! Push! Scream! And then there came a pause from the chaos. From a moment of silence came a fraction of quietness. A baby boy's cry snapped the muted moment. Sarinda felt as if all her breath was thrust into the cry of her newborn child. Before long, she was holding her baby boy. Curly proclaimed, "He's here! He's here!"

There were happenings around Sarinda. She lay down on the doctor's orders. The nurse handled the newborn baby boy. There was more. Sarinda believed she was pushing through another child, but there was no pain. There was a soft pushing twenty minutes from the birth of her son, and Sarinda entered the third stage of labor. The doctor handled the afterbirth and then administered two pills and a glass of water to Sarinda. "Lie down," he instructed. He called for the nurse to return Sarinda's newborn baby boy.

Nurse Plum handed the wrapped and squirming baby boy to Sarinda, and when she believed the weakened mother was able to handle the child in a sturdy arm cradle, she let go and backed away.

The baby boy's fidgeting ceased, calming in Sarinda's arms. Sarinda could feel everyone smiling at her and her new baby boy. The doctor excused himself to wash up. Curly expected a name. He expected Sarinda to name the child Kenten, but he was surprised when Sarinda named the newborn, "Stanley. Hello, Stanley Fallows." She grinned at Curly. "Oh,

Kenten did always want to give his name to his firstborn son. But, he'll have his father's name as a middle name. Stanley Kenten Fallows." She looked back at her son. "S-F," she said, weary eyes flickering. "You'll have the same initials as your mother."

"You need rest, Miss Fallows," the doctor ordered. "But we need to get you and your sheets cleaned."

"Yes, doctor," said Sarinda, her voice succumbing to exhaustion.

The nurse took baby Stanley from Sarinda who protested with a fatigued smile and a chuckle. But she allowed her child to be taken from her. Baby Stanley was put to rest in his crib and he fell asleep immediately. The nurse went into the bathroom and started a bath for Sarinda. Curly retrieved a clean set of sheets for the bed. With the doctor's help, the nurse lifted Sarinda from the bed and guided her to the bathroom where the tub had been filled with lukewarm water. Curly changed the bed sheets as the nurse assisted Sarinda with her bath. He, instead of the doctor, helped the nurse return a weary Sarinda back to her bed when the bathing was through. The nurse, the doctor, and Curly tucked Sarinda comfortably into bed, and she fell fast to sleep. Doctor Grayson conversed with Curly as Nurse Plum bagged his things. Curly walked the doctor to the vanity where Doctor Grayson wrote out a prescription for pills and instructions for Sarinda. He also filled out a receipt. Curly inspected the bill. Doctor Grayson said, "I'll expect the first payment in two weeks."

"Expect the full payment now, doctor, with a little extra." Curly retrieved his checkbook from his inside suit jacket. Doctor Grayson protested, but to no avail. Curly's check exceeded the doctor's bill by two hundred and fifty dollars. "An honest day's work, doctor," Curly joked. "And the day ain't over yet."

The doctor declared in a gasp, "That's most generous, Mister Burneside, most generous."

Curly handed the check to Doctor Grayson, and they shook hands. Nurse Plum handed the doctor his bag. Doctor Grayson put the bag on the vanity, opened it and rummaged through. He removed a bottle of pills. "Here. These are for Miss Fallows. I will return in a day or two to check on her."

"No need," said Curly. "Her personal doctor is on vacation in Kansas." He added, "But, he's returning later today. His practice is in Montgomery, but he'll make his way down to see Miss Fallows. I'll give him a call later tonight on the hour I know he's due home."

"Good, then," said Doctor Grayson closing his bag and gripping it. "I'm glad I could be of assistance."

Curly shook the doctor's hand again. "Thank you. We expected this to happen. Just as Gene, her doctor, goes away. We knew. We knew." He and Doctor Grayson laughed all the way to the door. "I'd offer you a drink, but I know you have other business to attend to."

"And we should allow Miss Fallows rest," the doctor stated.

Curly saw the doctor and nurse out, again thanked them for their service, and shut the door. He sighed and turned around. He took a moment to watch Sarinda as she slept. He then made his way to the sofa and lied down to sleep. Several hours later, Sarinda stirred Curly from his slumber with nudges to the shoulder. "Get up, Curly. We've rested long enough. Let's go see Stanley." Curly lifted. He exhaled the remainder of his sleep and stood from the sofa. "Your ring, Curly." Curly pulled off his ring and dropped it inside Sarinda's open palm. He then followed her to the crib where baby Stanley slept.

Sarinda unwrapped her newborn baby, and baby Stanley did not stir. She draped the ancient veil over her child and placed Curly's ring on the baby's stomach. She removed her necklace and dangled it inches from the ring. She tapped the pendant and let it twirl. Sarinda hummed an ancient harmony. She started singing a lullaby in a foreign language.

Curly and Sarinda marveled as the child's body matured.

Sarinda stopped singing. She said to Curly, "We can skip some years. We'll play with this for a month or two. I still have urges to be mamma." She giggled.

Sarinda and Curly watched Stanley as he slept.

Baby Stanley was now two years old.

A Southern Belle Rings In Harlem
"Your daughter,"

Dear Mamma,

I apologize for my insubordination, but your desire to reach grandaunt Sarinda seemed so strong, though I know you've been scared to do so. I will be your strength mamma. I will talk to her. Please, mamma, don't be upset. I'm not just here to chase a dream. I have a purpose besides singing on a New York stage. And even when I sing, mamma, I will do so with your voice and spirit. I will sing with grandmamma's voice and spirit. And the two of you will see it all through my eyes. You will be here.

Mamma, I wish you decided to come. I wish you weren't so afraid. I came to this city with my eyes all wide and bright. I didn't have a choice. Oh, the lights, mamma, the lights. New York could easily swallow Baton Rouge and New Orleans, with room for several more Southern cities. That little hamlet you grew up in, Water Bug Hollow, could be swallowed by Harlem alone.

I'm here for you mamma. I am. I love you. And that is truly why I'm here. I will return to you papa's paintings and grandmamma's veil. As you said, they are our birthright. Yes, mamma, I agree. You made a foolish decision to give them up. But you didn't know that I was inside you at the time, papa's last gift to you before his untimely end. I will right the wrong you carry as a burden, mamma. Grandaunt Sarinda will understand.

Your daughter,
Delia-Larue Amat

Harlem, New York
1957
"I ain't played in Harlem yet. That's been my goal."

The streets were empty. Nothing existed on this afternoon. Not at the moment. Not to Horatio Peters as he stared up at the charred building with its burned and boarded up façade and cracked and broken neon sign that barely read "On The Hour Club". Horatio might as well have been panning the entire landscape as his head looked from left to right, up and down, but his eyes only inspected the ragged and burned club in front of him. The passersby coming into existence missed him, their traffic flowing around him as if he himself didn't exist. But as time passed, the stream of traffic increased, and Horatio did begin to exist to the people making their way up the sidewalk. He moved out of their way when he needed to, stepping closer to the building, or stepping away from it to allow people to pass him by.

Some of the people stopped and greeted Horatio, admiring him as much as he admired the old rundown building his father used to play in. He was decked in a fitted suit with his hands in his pocket and a fedora atop his head. His trumpet was slung over his shoulder like a medieval weapon. It hung from a strap that was looped through the instrument and draped on his shoulder. "Hey, music man," they would say, and he'd smile at their comments, his attention on the building in front of him diverted. He turned to the exuberant passersby that greeted him and shook a few of their hands. This was all because musicians were kings here in Harlem. Horatio learned this within the first few days of his arrival.

Eventually, the attention paid to him subsided, and Horatio returned his complete focus to the building in front of him. Not too long after, someone did speak to him again. It was a young white man. He was dressed in a light gray suit with a fedora to match. He was tall and well groomed with no hair on his face. His strawberry-blonde hair was shaped by a short, conservative hairstyle. There was a sparkle in his brown eyes that matched the beam of his wide smile. He put out his hand to Horatio and said, "How you doing today, young man. My name's Stanley Fallows."

Horatio made an enthusiastic turn and grabbed Stanley's outstretched hand with both of his. He shook with as much enthusiasm as the turn he made to face Stanley. He said, "Stanley Fallows! Fine to meet you, sir. Everyone know who you are 'round here. It's a pleasure, sir. A pleasure." Horatio stepped away, removed his hat, and then lied to Stanley. "The name's Davis Parker, sir. Trumpeter extraordinaire."

Stanley retorted, "No need with all that 'sir', talk, Davis. You can call me Stan or Stanley," he assured. "I'm not too much older than you. In fact, I can get away with being ten years younger than I am, thanks to a doctor mishandling my birth certificate." Stanley expounded, "It says I was born in nineteen thirty-seven, yes it does. But, I was born in nineteen *twenty-seven*. Aged to perfection, my mother always tells me." He smiled and chuckled and then said as he turned to the rundown building. "You know about the On The Hour club?"

Horatio nodded. "Yes, I do, Stanley. I do. My father played here a couple times…tourin'. The old days."

Stanley shook his head. "Yeah. The old days. My mother always talks about 'em. I was too young to remember those days. We fixed up the club just three blocks down. It used to be the Mud Hare. Now, it has a new body and a new name. The Harlem Dixie." He scoped Horatio's trumpet. "We could always use some acts. You ever play in front of a crowd?"

"Yes, sir," said Horatio. Then he corrected himself, "Uh, Stanley. But I ain't played in Harlem yet. That's been my goal. It's the reason I've come up with my friend. He's played at your spot. Name's Jonathan Gregory."

Stanley thought about the name. "Yeah. Johnny." He thought more and his memory matched the name to a face. "Johnny. Piano player, right? He's from Brooklyn. Yeah. Good guy. Great piano man." Stanley paused and then said, "So, you're not from around here?"

Horatio answered, "Naw, Stanley. I'm from New Orleans. That's where my mother and father settled down after havin' me." He pointed to the building and said through a grin, "This is where my mother and father met. If it wasn't for this place, I wouldn't be here. My mother and father shared their first dance here. They had their first kiss here. My mother watched my father from the audience as he played his horn."

Stanley's smile returned. "Well, Mister Parker, you might find yourself playin' in that club there. I come here when I can, morning or afternoon, and I admire it too. My mother and I bought the property. I imagine how it'll look once it's all fixed up. It too will have a new body and name, but it'll have the same soul." Horatio smiled at Stanley's enthusiasm. Stanley continued, "And I guarantee you this, Mister Parker. The first note played in there will be from your horn. As you jazz musicians say, 'Can you dig it?'"

"Really?" Horatio asked.

"I'll make it happen," Stanley promised. "I'm usually the one that gets the rock-and-roll acts, but it seems only fitting that jazz resurrect this club. My mother will be thrilled. She's not too keen on the rock-and-roll that's pushin' on through. She likes to keep things traditional. She loves her jazz. You can't argue with her." Stanley paused to think about his mother. "She will be ecstatic." He then waved it all away. "But, in the meantime, let's get you a performance at the Harlem Dixie. You and Johnny got a whole band?"

"I met these two cats he knows. A bass player and drummer," Horatio remarked with a smile. "We've jammed a couple times since I've come up. I've been here for several weeks now. When we ain't jammin', I find myself walkin' around and admirin' the sights of the city."

"Yes, yes, of course," Stanley replied to all of what Horatio had to say. He put his arm around Horatio and led him away. "A relative of my mother's just came up, her grandniece. A singer. Wonderful voice. Beautiful. She's been here for almost a month now. My mother is protective of her. She wants to surround her with the right band to showcase her voice." They started walking down the street. Stanley stopped after a few steps. He removed his arm from Horatio's shoulders and moved directly in front of him, facing him. "Why don't you come through tonight and meet her. Tomorrow morning we'll have a practice session. I'll talk to my mother before you come through. We'll see what we can get cookin'. How's that sound, Mister Parker?" Stanley extended his hand.

Horatio clutched Stanley's hand and again shook with wild enthusiasm. "That would be just fine, Stanley. That would be just fine."

Stanley patted Horatio's shoulder. "Good. Good. Let me get going. Here," he dug into his pocket. "Let me give you my card. It has all my information on it." He withdrew a small business card and offered it to Horatio.

Horatio pocketed the item. "Johnny will be excited about this. I'm gon' head back to Brooklyn and deliver the news. I might not've found a job this afternoon, like I said I would—hell, like I've been sayin' for the past couple of days—but I got us a gig. That's job enough."

"An audition," Stanley reminded with a firm, upright finger. He retracted his hand and finger and said, "But I'm sure it will lead to a gig. Might be steady work." He shook Horatio's hand. "Tonight. Get there by eight. It's jazz night. You'll meet my mother and her grandniece. You'll see my mother perform. I'll speak with her now and arrange a practice in the morning with you and your friend Johnny."

Horatio grinned. He expressed loud, "Absolutely, Stanley. Absolutely."

"I'll see you 'round, Davis Parker." Stanley turned and walked away. Horatio walked in the opposite direction to find the subway entrance he emerged from earlier. Then he heard Stanley's voice call him, *"Davis! Davis!"* Horatio spun around. Stanley waved him closer and Horatio approached. "Walk with me. Come on. Let's see if my mother and her grandniece are there now. My mother definitely should be. Come on." Horatio walked alongside Stanley. "I was thinking that I'd talk to my mother privately at first, but I think she'd be more excited if she saw you standing there. She remembers Johnny. She liked his piano. That's how I remember your friend, through my mother's excitement."

Horatio continued to grin. "You see, here, Stanley? This here is New York City. What would take months in other cities—even the big ones—can be accomplished in moments here. Hell, the only time you'd see something like this, even in Los Angeles, is in them pictures made out there." Stanley chuckled at Horatio's sentiment. "I'm serious, man."

"I know."

Horatio looked around at the Harlem environment. "Everywhere I've been—tourin' with Johnny—there's always this tension, a fear of strangers. I feel it here, just not as much. I got this horn on my back, and people are smilin' and lookin' at it."

"Must remind them of another time. The Roaring Twenties!"

Horatio agreed. "Yeah. Yeah," he said. "I find myself expressin' that answer too. But everywhere experienced the Roaring Twenties. What makes New York so special? Ah, I guess what everyone else was experiencin' back in them times was the feel New York was givin' off. Even 'round the parts of jazz's birthplace, colored folks was tryin' to run north to Harlem so they sound could be heard."

Stanley stopped at the corner. Horatio stopped too. He looked at Stanley and he was pointing to the building now standing in front of them. "Here it is, Davis. The Harlem Dixie."

Horatio looked up at the giant marquee that blared *The Harlem Dixie* in big, bold red letters. The phrase *Jazz Night Tonight* was spelled out below the club's name. The club's front entrance was located at the corner. Stanley explained that he and his mother purchased the building that was next to it and expanded the club from its original look.

Horatio crossed his arms. "What about the original club's owner?" he asked.

Stanley was thrilled to answer, "There were three. Good friends of my mother." Then he added in a sullen tone, "They passed away, I'm sad to say. Last one, named Irvin Witlow, passed last year. At least that was from natural causes. A car accident and a bookie collecting on a debt got the other two." He slapped Horatio on the back and stepped toward the corner entrance. "But let's concentrate on the present. Come on. This way."

An elderly black doorman stood at the entrance. He offered a polite smile as he opened the door wide open for Stanley and Horatio to walk in. "Here you go, Mister Fallows. How you been this day?"

"Turning out to be a good day, Sherman." Stanley stopped and brought Horatio forward. "Let me show you why, Sherman. This is Davis Parker. I believe he described himself as 'trumpeter extraordinaire'." He asked Horatio, "Did I get the title right, Davis?"

"One hundred and ten percent, Stanley," Horatio expressed with a lean in his stance. He reached out his hand to the elderly doorman named Sherman and greeted, "How do you do, sir?" Sherman presented a firm handshake and answered that he was doing fine. "You keep your eye on that marquee, Mister Sherman. It'll have my name up there soon. Davis Parker. Yes indeed." Sherman beamed a wide smile. Stanley stepped through the entrance, followed by Horatio. Sherman wished them both a good rest-of-the-day.

Through the corner entrance there was a path to the left and a path to the right. Doors lined the walls down the path on the right. Down the left path, located through the door at the far end on the right, was the entrance to the grand ballroom where all the acts performed and the people danced and drank their troubles away. Stanley led Horatio down the hall. He opened the door upon their arrival and extended his arm to allow Horatio entry into the room.

Horatio stepped inside and a genuine expression of awe exploded on his face. The club had a contemporary look, but there was a spirit of the old days that filtered through the room. Horatio hadn't just stepped through the door, he felt as if he'd also stepped through time. The area was as large as a theater. It was split into three seating areas with three sets of stairs leading to each section. Booths, spread horizontally, separated the sections of decorated tables. The lights were bright. Everything was on display for Horatio. He considered that all the small-time backrooms he and Johnny had played in were mounds compared to this mountain. This was a coliseum. It was an arena, and at the front of this magnificent room was the stage. It peeked out beyond its curtain, and was centered perfectly between either ends of the room. Exotic flora, potted near safety exits near the stage, twirled up columns. Eleven paintings were scattered around the walls, some hiding behind carefully laid out plants.

Sarinda Fallows occupied the stage, practicing with her band. She stood in front of the microphone, politely giving orders as to when each instrument was to come in and what they were to play. Horatio focused on Sarinda. He stepped closer, no prompt needed from Stanley. He kept his eyes on the curvy, mature redhead as she kept her profile to him, head turned to the all-black band behind her. Horatio took another step, and then he stopped as Sarinda twirled around and faced the microphone.

She looked no older than thirty-five. There was not a line of age, indent of skin, or wrinkle of flesh that blemished her fair and milky, cream-colored skin. Had anyone whispered to Horatio that Sarinda Fallows' curvaceous physical frame was the inspiration for all pinup girls, pictured or painted, he would have answered them, *"You ain't ever told a lie."* The shimmering indigo gown that hugged her shape further enunciated Sarinda Fallows' sensuous, serpentine stance and hourglass figure. It held her so tightly that it made observing men jealous of it.

There she was. Sarinda Fallows. In front of Horatio Peters. This was the woman he suspected was connected to his father's murder, and she lived up to every word of description detailed by Johnny Concheroot: dark-red hair, curves, and all. The only detail missed by Johnny Concheroot was the piece of fabric worn atop her head. It was a veil. She lowered the dark garment as she spoke into the microphone and, in a smoky voice, commanded her band to begin.

The band's sound boomed!

A hard beat rang first. Then the piano followed, trailing in like someone merrily skipping down a path. The hard beat came again. Sarinda put her legs apart on the beat. The next beat came and she put her hands on her hips. Two more beats, and then Sarinda flipped the veil off her face, let it come to rest atop her head, and sang, *"In the blink of an eye – I stole a witch's last breath, her power, and her li-ife! I took all that she claimed before she re-membered her name!"* Her voice was a magnificent, loud roar, and an argument could be made that she needed no microphone to project it. Further into the song, the tune and Sarinda's voice became campy, accompanied by cute, jazzy piano playing. The other instruments were in the background while Sarinda's voice and the piano expressed the celebratory song. *"And she be my reflection, 'cause this witch do as I do – and I, I, I, I sold her shoes for her to walk in – sold them at a bargain price. I exchanged my wrongs for all her rights."* Horatio chuckled at the tongue-and-cheek lyrics and the expressions Sarinda made while singing them. *"And over on the corner there hangs the witch's friends: Anne and Fran. And they been snorting the winter season and smoking splits. Slow suicide with slits on their wrists. They try to ride trains tunneled through their veins by way of the tracks on their arm! And these chemi-kills, they do surely kill. They've turned a witch's magic into something tragic. And her friends Anne and Fran have gotten ticks – and now they've become fran-tick with all their anne-ticks. Now that she's possessed, with all the sins of the flesh, and as I've said it will be in time – this witch's magic is now mi-i-i-i-i-i-ine!"*

The song finished.

Stanley and Horatio applauded, and so did someone else. There was another audience member. She was sitting alone at a table located close to the stage. Horatio wondered immediately why he hadn't spotted her sooner. Then he cursed himself for being too entranced by the woman he believed orchestrated his father's murder. While Sarinda accepted her applause and called for Stanley, Horatio stared at the young, lone black woman. He walked closer, focused on her. Closer. He could see her profile. He heard Sarinda calling her son's name. "Stanley! My boy. Come on in." She said to the band, "You all can take more than five to break. Stay close."

She turned back to her son and asked, "Why, who is this handsome trumpet player you bringin' in here?" Sarinda's voice was barely audible to Horatio, but he was thankful for it. Whatever she was saying caused the young woman to turn her head back over her shoulder and look at both he and Stanley.

Horatio walked behind Stanley, his steps were careful. His concentration remained on the seated woman. Sarinda, excited at her son's appearance, stepped off the stage, using the stairs to her left to descend onto the open dance floor. She stepped down, minding her high heels and balance. The seated woman jumped up just as Sarinda came down. She joined Sarinda at her side, and Horatio observed her features with a curious expression pinned to his face.

Horatio considered her the mold for femininity. She had a beautiful face that was slightly ovate, but mostly round in shape. Her large, almond-colored and shaped eyes fluttered wide like butterfly wings. Her coffee-brown skin resonated with a sunset tone that gave the appearance of a preternatural glow. Her full and red lips mixed with the sundown glow of her skin. Her hair was made up in a sleek, glam hairdo, and she was dressed in a short-sleeve shirt, a black pencil skirt and high heels. And as Horatio pondered, *Not even the most well designed car could drive those curves.*

Horatio stared, but not too long. It wasn't just her beauty that attracted him. The woman was familiar to him, and that familiarity intrigued Horatio. But before he could ponder long, he heard Stanley introduce him, "Mother, I bring you Davis Parker. I met him admiring the property we acquired three blocks up. He plays trumpet. I thought he could be the first member for Delia's band."

Sarinda beamed and reached out a hand. "Well, hello Mister Parker," Sarinda remarked. "Such a handsome boy. I see you carrying your musical weapon of choice." She pointed to the trumpet dangling behind him.

Horatio clumsily removed his hat and responded, "Yes, ma'am." He gave Sarinda's hand a gentle shake. "Yes, indeed. And I don't mean to correct Mister Stanley here, but I'd be the first of two additions. My friend Jonathan Gregory would also play for your grandniece. He plays piano. He's played here before. I think you know him."

Sarinda grinned. "Oh, I remember that boy, Jonathan Gregory—tall drink of water that he is. He is a fine piano player." She asked, "And where are you from, young boy? Clear as I can hear, I can tell you're not from 'round these parts."

"Oh, I was born here in Harlem, Miss Fallows," Horatio informed. "But, I was raised in New Orleans. My mother and father moved there right after I was born."

Sarinda reacted, enlivened to hear such a thing. "New Orleans!" she brightened up. "My, my, my." She turned to the young woman next to her and said, "You see that, Delia. This boy's not too far from Baton Rouge where you were raised." She looked at Horatio and introduced him to the young woman standing next to her. "Davis Parker, this here is my grandniece. Miss Delia-LaRue Amat."

Horatio exhaled surprise. He made a joke of his emotion. "I see the family resemblance." Both Delia and Sarinda chuckled at his remark.

Sarinda explained, "I'm a close friend of her family. Her grandmother and I were like sisters. Her mother was like my daughter."

"Miss Fallows, if you don't mind me sayin' so, Miss," Horatio began as he reached for Delia's gentle, coffee-brown hand. "You look too young to be close friends or like sisters with anyone's grandmamma." Sarinda reddened and thanked Horatio for the lovely compliment. Horatio turned to Stanley and said, "Your mamma best put her secret in a bottle and sell it." Stanley laughed. Then Horatio turned his attention to the young, coffee-brown woman whose hand he now held with tender and gentle affection. "But I see clearly that you, Miss Delia-Larue Amat, have sipped from that youthful potion. If you don't mind me sayin', pretty woman." Horatio bent and kissed the back of Delia's hand.

Delia thanked Horatio for the comment but corrected, "Flattering, Mister Parker, but I am the age that my youth presents. I am twenty years." Her voice carried an air of Southern, social civility and sophistication. "So you're from New Orleans, Mister Parker? How grand. I was raised in Baton Rouge but born in a place called Water Bug Hollow. Have you ever heard of it?"

Horatio answered with a grin, "Yes, I have, Miss Amat."

"Well, dear me, I am surprised," remarked Delia. "Most New Orleans jazz boys haven't. You boys tend to ignore Water Bug Hollow because some say the Hollow was the true jazz capital of the world."

Sarinda playfully shook her finger. "Now, now," she said. "Ain't a need for a territorial dispute like a bunch of Indians. We're in Harlem now."

Delia jokingly slapped Sarinda's arm. "Grandauntie, I'm just playin', that's all." She said to Horatio, "I really don't mean any harm or offense, Mister Parker."

"Davis," Horatio corrected. "You can call me Davis, Miss Amat."

Delia nodded her head. "Well that's mighty kind of you, Davis."

"In fact, my middle name is Horatio, Miss," he continued. "I always preferred Horatio. Sounds like 'hero'. If you wouldn't mind calling me by such."

Delia expressed flirtatiously, "Not at all, Davis Horatio Parker—Horatio." She continued after a pause, "And what brings you here to Harlem?"

"Just a chance to play," Horatio answered. He twirled around and panned the grand clubroom. "My father played up here. He met my mother over at the On The Hour club." He pivoted back to face Delia and Sarinda. "They danced, they kissed, they had me, and then they moved to New Orleans. My father always talked about playin' in Harlem, from the twenties to the thirties. I came to see if I could jump into what jazz sounds like now, and also fire that old sound back up." He said as if to prove something, "Johnny and I, we've been goin' 'round to small-time places." He looked around again at the club's interior. "They wasn't nothin' like this." He asked Delia, "And what brings you up here, Miss Amat?"

Sarinda answered, "She's come to swindle me out of my decorative items." She smiled and patted Delia on the back, adding, "That belong rightly to her." Then she teased, "I will not part with my favorite, decorative paintings so easily." She waved her arm around. Horatio followed Sarinda's gesture and caught sight of the paintings placed around the room. "I like Miss Amat's father's paintings right where they are. They add so much to the place."

Horatio panned the walls lined with paintings. He stepped away from the party, transfixed by one particular piece. "So your father paints, Miss Amat?" he asked.

Delia walked up alongside Horatio as he moved closer to the wall with the painting that interested him the most. "He painted, Horatio," Delia answered. "Past tense, I'm afraid. He was killed while in New Orleans. He was kidnapped and robbed of his money." She spoke as if she was a witness to the act, and powerless to prevent the tragedy. "Auntie Sarinda was helping him get a show. She knew a man, a white man that was interested in Negro artists. He was bringing these paintings into New Orleans to show Auntie Sarinda's friend. He went out to get some groceries and he was taken. The young boys robbed and shot him in a warehouse."

Horatio wanted to comfort Delia by telling her that his father was murdered when he too was in the prime of his artistry. But, he couldn't. He told Delia he was sorry for her loss, and then looked back at the painting. Etched in reds and shadowy blacks was a scene of murder. A man lay face down, dead on the floor. Rivers of blood trickled from three wounds and pooled into the word *TREACHERY*. Three shadowy figures held smoking guns and stood over the slain man. A scorpion aimed a pincer at the dead figure, and a lion witnessed the whole scene from behind the three shadowy gunmen. Horatio was piqued.

"I didn't know I'd come here and find his art to be as tragic as it is beautiful," Delia expressed. She assured excitedly, "There are more happier paintings spread around here, but I'm always drawn to this one, sadly enough. I feel like I'm watching my father's death." She laughed nervously. "I suppose that sounds dumb of me."

"No," Horatio answered while still looking at the painting. "I can imagine." Horatio made his way around the large room, inspecting the art. Delia followed him. He commented over his shoulder as he walked on, "These ain't the type of paintings you'd see from Negro artists. They seem biblical, even the simple ones. Prophetic, I mean. Negroes usually have a superstition against such things." He stopped and turned around. "Your father was an amazing artist. I'm guessin' he could see this world in ways no other person could." He asked Delia, "Did these paintings ever get put on display?"

Delia turned around. Sarinda and Stanley were conversing where Horatio and she had left them. She and Horatio had traveled to the far corner of the room, close to the exit. "Auntie Sarinda, did your friend ever display my father's paintings? My mother said she'd asked for your friend to still display papa's artwork."

"No, dear," answered Sarinda, her voice echoing in the large room. She walked toward Horatio and Delia. "My friend said he'd found another artist, and the display wasn't big enough for your father's paintings. The people were already givin' my friend such a hard time—a white man promotin' Negro art, and all." Sarinda then dramatically exhaled a breath. "But let me tell you somethin', child. My friend, Curly Burneside, sure did regret not showin' your father's beautiful paintings when he finally saw them. But there was nothing he could do by then, and definitely nothing he can do now. He was killed, murdered just recently. He was sheriff of a small town in Mississippi. Red Leaf it was called. An inmate killed him and escaped. His deputies went missing too. The people of Red Leaf suspect they had a hand in the murder. I doubt it. It was supposedly a Negro inmate. Oh, well, it's all simply mysterious, and I leave mysteries to the police." Sarinda paused to think and then commented, "There seemed like a new air about Red Leaf. People were different when Stanley and I went down for the funeral." She spoke softly. "Stanley was close to my friend, Mister Burneside. Stanley called him uncle. The closest thing he had to a father."

Horatio observed Sarinda' neckline, noticing the necklace she wore, and more so, the flat, stone pendant speckled with red markings that dangled from it. He hummed as a thought came to him. He remained cool. A picture was being painted in his mind. It was missing pieces like a puzzle but slowly filling in. His eyes went from Sarinda to Delia. "How old were you when your father was killed?" he asked Delia.

Delia burst into a breath of laughter only to keep from crying. She simmered her emotions and answered, "Lucky me. I had just been conceived."

Horatio bowed at the neck. "Well, ain't that somethin', Miss Amat. Standin' before me is your father's last beautiful work of art. If, of course, you don't mind me sayin' so."

Delia blushed as she replied, "What foolish woman would ever mind a man complimentin' her?" She aimed a stern finger and said with her eyes wide, "But don't think you can sweet talk me, hear. Mister Davis Horatio Parker, you will be in *my* band. You will take my orders like a musical waiter."

Stanley and Sarinda walked up from behind.

Horatio waved his arms. "Whoa, now! Ain't nothin' decided. My friend and I have to first audition."

"Tomorrow afternoon," said Stanley. "My mother gave it the okay." He stood next to Sarinda like a sentry. She nodded at Horatio, her approval signaled in her gesture.

"Thank you, Miss Fallows," Horatio voiced his gratitude.

"I'm sure the audition will all be for show," said Sarinda. "I can tell you know how to blow that horn. You wouldn't be travelin' with that John Gregory boy if you didn't."

Horatio agreed. "That's true, Miss Fallows. That's true." He smiled politely.

"And you'll still be joining us tonight?" Stanley asked. "We'll have you sitting up front. Best seat in the house."

Horatio reneged. "Not tonight, I apologize, Miss Fallows, Stanley. I might need some time to practice, and Johnny will need the same—plus the time for all this news to sink in. Johnny's played here before, but this is all new for me. I hope you all ain't o-fended."

"No, Davis, uh, Horatio," said Stanley. "Not at all."

"We understand," said Sarinda.

Horatio appreciated the kind assurance shown to him. He responded over and over, "Thank you. Thank you."

"There's nothin' to worry about at all," Sarinda continued to assure. "Why, I'm just glad that my son here brought in a musician playin' some real music rather than that rock-and-roll. Oh, my dear."

Stanley remarked, "Ah, Ma, that music puts assess in these seats."

Sarinda slapped Stanley lightly on the cheek. "My goodness. I should never have raised you in this savage, northern wilderness. What New York and that rock-and-roll have done to this man's mouth, Horatio."

"Ah, Ma." Stanley leaned over and kissed Sarinda on the cheek.

"Don't try to sweet me over, young man," played Sarinda. "You should be like this nice boy here. Horatio you have wonderful manners. Teach this young man something. Stanley, you could learn somethin' from this boy."

Horatio and Delia chuckled at the interaction between mother and son.

Stanley said to his mother, "Right now I'm gonna get a car to chauffer Horatio home." He asked Horatio, "Where in Brooklyn? You just name the street and the number, the car will get you there."

"Five-eleven Macon Street." Horatio recalled, "I believe the neighborhood is called Stuyvesant Heights."

"Okay. Come on, I'll walk you to the car."

Horatio bowed his head at Sarinda. "Thank you again, Miss Fallows. Thank you for the opportunity." He looked at Delia and a smile appeared by reflex. She smiled back at him. "Miss Amat, I can't wait to hold you up with music. I'm sure your voice is as wonderful as your father's art."

"It's as wonderful as my mother's voice," Delia corrected in a kittenish tone. "And her mother before her. My voice is more than song. It's lineage, an heirloom." The alluring and arousing heat from Delia's confident smile rivaled the sun. Her eyes closed and opened, and her neck popped with sass.

Horatio said to Sarinda, "No offense, Miss Fallows, but *hot damn! Ha-a-a-hot damn!*"

Delia exhaled a charming laugh. "I'm just playin' with you, Horatio."

Horatio's broad smile remained. "Oh, of course, Miss Amat. Of course." He added, "Johnny and I will be practicin' some songs. If you want to join in, see how we do together, we'll be studyin' *Bewitched, Bothered and Bewildered* and *I Could Write a Book*."

"Those selections will be fine," Delia approved. "I know them."

Horatio slapped on his fedora. "It'll be just a horn and piano, but you'll believe a whole band is behind you." He tugged at the brim of his hat. "Good day to you both." He turned around and joined Stanley, a kick in his step. Stanley escorted him through the club and to the back where a fleet of cars waited. By each car was a driver standing and waiting for an order. Horatio was informed that only very special guests were treated to such pleasures. "Thank you, Stanley. I'm sure glad I came up here today."

Stanley opened the door for Horatio and allowed him to slide in the back. "I hope you can play." He then corrected, "Hell, Davis-Horatio, I *know* you can play. You made my mom smile. Put her faith back in me that I'm not just about the dollar and the current trend." Stanley laughed. "Thank you." He shut the door and said to the man standing near the automobile. "Brooklyn. Five-eleven Macon street."

"Yessir, Mister Fallows, sir."

Stanley gave the man a couple of dollars for a tip. "Don't worry about your passenger giving you one, you just get him home."

"Yessir, Mister Fallows, sir."

The driver got in the car. Stanley stepped aside and waved to Horatio as the car pulled away. Horatio waved goodbye to Stanley. He looked out the window as the car pulled onto the main road. He kept his eye on the mighty fortress that was the Harlem Dixie. Horatio looked away to the road ahead. The jubilant behavior he'd demonstrated inside the club was exhaled in a sigh. The joy in his face melted away and he grit his teeth to keep from breaking into tears. Horatio remained this way all the way to Brooklyn.

As Father and Son
"Always know your mathematics, boy."

Jonathan Richard Concheroot understood good-and-well that his father was found guilty of murder by the justice of the City of New York. But he'd only killed another Negro. Had Joseph Concheroot been white he would've been found *'not guilty'*. Instead, it was just twenty-four years in an upstate, New York penitentiary. Not life. Not death. His stay would have been fifteen with good behavior, but an unfortunate fight extended the prison stay for another nine. So, it was on this day that Joseph Concheroot was getting out of jail, and Johnny could tell by the look on his father's face that he wasn't expecting anyone to greet him, maybe his brother now living in the Bronx, but not his son.

Joseph Concheroot was dark skinned with a round face and graying hair cut low on his head. A thick, graying mustache was over his upper lip. He wore denim overalls with a flannel shirt underneath, and workman boots on his feet. He had nothing else. Joe couldn't help but smile at the sight of his son leaning against the 1955 Chrysler Imperial automobile, waiting for him to exit the prison.

Johnny didn't smile back at his father. He wasn't being rude, defiant, or even trying to display how upset he had been at him. He simply didn't know how to act. He wondered how many kids picked their father up from a twenty-four year stint in prison. But he was here and nowhere else. So Johnny managed to greet his father as Joseph approached, "Hello, sir."

Joe crooned, "How you doin', son?" He stopped and inspected the car that Johnny leaned against. "This ride yours?"

Johnny answered, voice slightly cracking. "Yes, sir."

"You can take me to your uncle's place in the Bronx," Joe directed. "He's expectin' me." Joe continued inspecting the car. "I told him I'd find a ride. Told him not to bother." His eyes went to Johnny. "At first, I thought he had ignored me. Wasn't expectin' to see you. You look good, son."

Johnny moved aside and opened the passenger door. Joe walked closer. He looked Johnny up and down. "You got taller."

Johnny only nodded in reaction to his father's observation. Joe slid into the vehicle and Johnny closed the door. He walked around the car and jumped inside. He started the engine, eyed his father and said, "You look good too, sir." He finally broke a smile and teased his father, "You got gray, Pop."

Joe chuckled. "Ah, hell. I got some weight on me too. You just wait your turn to get old. You'll get all this too."

Johnny shook his head as he pulled away from the prison. "I'll still be pretty. My weight will be muscle."

Joe grinned. He asked, "You still play the piano?"

Johnny hesitated to answer. He checked the car's mirrors for traffic, and then responded after a moment, "Yes, I do. I'm good too, not to brag. I've been playin' around. Clubs here, down South, all along the East Coast. Me and this car been on the move."

Joe gave his son a curious look. "Was that so hard to answer?" asked the older Concheroot. "Sounds good. What's with the hesitation nonsense?" But again, Johnny didn't answer his father immediately. He cleared his throat as he stopped at a stop sign and then moved the car through the intersection and down the road. Joe looked at his son, frustration building. "What's on your mind, son? I'm out, and more than that, I'm a grown man. I can handle whatever ya gotta say."

Johnny kept his eyes on the road, inspecting the outside as if he was being extra careful in his driving. He finally said, "I play with Horatio Peters." He said it. "Pete Peters' boy. He plays the horn like his father."

Joe looked away, straight down the road he and his son traveled. "Oh."

Johnny continued. It was out now. He figured it all might as well pour. "You told them club owners where they could find Pete Peters, didn't you?"

Joe's head dropped. He'd never felt guiltier, even though his son's voice didn't sound accusing. He was just being inquisitive, like a child. Joe answered, "Yes, I did. I was angry, son. I was real angry with Pete Peters. All because of you."

Johnny's eyebrows lifted. "Because of me?" His head turned to his father, and then turned back to make sure he was still on the road, still in control of the car. His father's words caused him to repeat the action several times. He even repeated his words. "Because of me?"

Joe Concheroot shook his head in the affirmative and then lifted it. "Yep." He explained in a sullen and reflective voice, "I thought you were his son. I was told you were his. It was hinted. That's all I needed. Hell, I already suspected." He coughed to clear his throat. "Pete and ya mamma were together for a little minute. Their relationship, after a while, turned friendly. Pete met Virginia. I came in, swooped ya mamma off her feet. You know us Concheroots." He made a nervous laugh, and then settled back into the story. "But Pete and ya mamma remained good friends, and to my jealous eye it was too close, but to reality's all seein' eye, it was in fact, just friendly. Pete would never disrespect me. But when he decided to marry Virginia, he didn't talk to me about it, he went to ya mamma. They were like brother and sister. They talked all through the night. They spent the night with one another, but it was only on friendly terms. She was so happy for Pete. She celebrated with me after Pete and Virginia's wedding. Their happy day got your mamma thinking about the idea of marriage between her and I. You came nine months later, or so, and that was the problem."

Johnny interrupted his father with a comment. "Raised your eyebrow, huh? About that night they were together?"

Joe nodded. "Yep. It did." He grinned. "The music we were puttin' out was so profound, I got lost in it. Worked out my emotions on the piano. But, when dissention came, and the story turned up and confirmed my jealous suspicions…well, I didn't murder your friend's father, but I helped. I pointed out where he could be found. I made sure he was there. He was there to meet me." Joe shook his head, disappointed at himself. He sighed, "Never occurred to me that my math was all off. Even if they did spend the night intimately, was no way Pete Peters would've been your father. Your mother was furious when she'd heard about my involvement. Was no need to tell her what really happened. No need to try and defend myself in court. Either way, I assisted in the murder of my best friend. I might as well have pulled the trigger. That's the way I saw it. I figured I'd take my punishment." A low laugh escaped him. "I remember your mother hollerin' at me. She said, *'Oh, he's your child, Joe. And he'll be your child. In blood. Not in name.'"* Joe looked at his son. "You usin' ya mamma's family name?"

Johnny said with no expression. "In her presence, sir."

Joe nodded his head and looked forward. He leaned against the window as if he was going to fall asleep. "I read this old play when I was locked up. Shakespeare. Play was called Othello. You ever heard of it?"

Johnny said, "Yes, pop, in school, and of course, Paul Robeson's performance. But these two old men in Mississippi talked about it to us. Othello was what they called a Moor." Johnny explained about the two men, "These men were Pete Peters' music teachers."

"Oh, yeah," said Joe brightening up. "Where he got that otherworldly horn from. Yeah." Joe chuckled, and then he returned to his original point. "Othello listened to the wrong man when it came to his wife and what she was doin' behind his back. I was Othello, son. I was Othello. But I'm going to make things right again, now that I'm out." He asked his son, "That boy play like his father?"

"Yes, he does, Pop." Johnny stopped at a light. He looked at his father proudly and said to him, "And I play piano like mine." Joe beamed back at Johnny. "We found that horn. Pete Peters' horn. It's been showin' us things. The truth. Other lives."

"Yeah," said Joe as he remembered. "We used to take the audience on a trip. We used to jam. Pete Peters made sure they'd forget what they saw by the next morning, but not what they heard. He said it was too dangerous for black folk to remember. Said it wasn't the right time."

"We saw some of them sessions, Pop," Johnny stated. He drove forward, the light now green.

Joe exhaled and sat up. "I don't have any answers for that. I just know that one night, 'round twenty-three or twenty-four—I think it was nineteen twenty-four—an odd, older cat named Madison Goodspeed came to hear us play."

"That name sounds familiar, Pop," interrupted Johnny. "Horatio's father dedicated a jam to him. You and he composed that piece together."

"Yep. Yep," acknowledged Joe. "*A New Avenue in Brooklyn.*" Joe started spouting information on Madison Goodspeed. "Madison was a cook. Jamaican guy. Had an English accent. Strange guy. A spiritualist is what he called himself. Believed in a lot of hoodoo and whatchuknow, y'know? He was in Harlem, settled down with some honey that was as strange as he was. They had kids." Then he came to his point. "That old man said he saw somethin' in Pete. Said he needed to go and find these two music teachers in Mississippi. The Fable Brothers. Ain't that somethin', son? A jazzman going to the crossroads. That's a blues superstition."

Johnny interjected, "Only blues players see the Devil, Pop."

Joe laughed. "I like that." He leaned back against the window. "Well, son, I don't know who sees what, but I do know this: Always know your mathematics, boy. It's key. Keep you outta trouble." He paused and then reiterated, "Know your mathematics, Johnny. Know 'em good. Think about your math—calculate before you make a move. That horn gave us all the power in the world, but we couldn't see the fact someone was out to ruin all that. We wasn't aware of all the math involved. So know your mathematics."

"Yes, Pop. We will."

Johnny drove his father to the Bronx.

Narrative Circumference
"We all have the same superstitions."

Horatio sat on a couch inside Johnny Concheroot's Brooklyn brownstone living room. He conversed with Johnny's mother, Gwendolyn Gregory. He had been speaking with her for an hour, listening to her retell stories of his father and the old days of his band with her husband, Joseph Concheroot. Horatio sat back and watched Miss Gregory smile and speak about his mother and father and the strong bond between Joseph Concheroot and Pete Peters. She never mentioned any brewing animosity or rift. Miss Gregory only beamed, sipped her tea, and spoke of their friendship and music. She didn't even speak about Johnny's father being in prison, or his release, or Johnny having gone to pick him up. Horatio didn't feel the need to pry. The smile on Gwendolyn Gregory's face restored youth to her, but she'd seemed very tired and burdened. Horatio surmised that her mood was the result of the very topics she chose to leave out of their conversation.

Horatio was anxious for Johnny's return, wanting to tell his friend about the practice gig he scored for them and the events of the day. He also wanted to isolate himself on the brownstone's roof to play his father's horn. He'd been composing more of his father's song, *The Son Dial Tone*, extending the story from the point of his birth to the age of twelve. It was a sad experience to relive. African slavery. But Horatio continued to compose, his hand guided to script in the mystical, musical notations by the faint memory of yester-life. With the songbook opened and his father's horn at his side, he recalled the tale, scripted its musical syllabary, and composed a past life.

Horatio found an opportune moment to politely dismiss himself. Gwendolyn Gregory stood up and announced that she would begin preparing dinner. "I expect Johnny to be late, Horatio," she said rolling her eyes. She never said as to why. Horatio didn't feel that there was a need, but he noted that, despite the roll of her eyes, Miss Gregory's tone appeared to be extra sweet about Johnny's possible lateness.

Horatio said to Miss Gregory as he was leaving the room, "I'll be on the roof, Miss Gregory. I'll be practicin' my horn." He assured, "You don't need to worry, none. I won't disturb your neighbors."

Johnny's mother beamed a pleasant smile and replied, "I'm sure your sound will be a comfort."

Horatio thanked Johnny's mom and then hurried up to the top floor guestroom to retrieve his father's horn. The case holding the horn was on the dresser. Horatio opened it and removed the horn. He picked up his father's music book, left the room, and made his way to the roof where he was greeted by the setting sun and the vast rows of brownstone rooftops. He walked to the edge of the roof and watched the setting sun with a ponderous stare. Horatio dropped the songbook on the roof's surface and decided to go to work.

"Can't stare at the sun too long," he said to no one in particular. "You'll go blind."

Horatio put the horn to his lips and started playing otherworldly notes. The songbook lifted and fluttered in front of him, settling in the air with its pages flipping open and resting on a song he composed, an addition to *The Son Dial Tone*. He looked at the notations and played them through the horn. The neighbors only heard the first couple of notes, loud and sweet. Those that listened wanted to hear more, but Horatio made the song private and personal. The world disappeared around him, as he did to it. To his audience, the music faded. Some of the notes even faded from his ears, as his past voice took over, composed from the melody he played that recounted his slave narrative.

I was born twice in one life
The first started with a recital of tears
When my eyes were hit with light
Signal, push, pulled from the cosmic womb
Into a new space – my mother's trembling embrace
Dirge of fright playing on her face
An apology in her eyes
Mother Harmony, not off-key
But beauty withered into sadness

I knew her eyes
Because

I saw the world through my mother's eyes
9 months blossoming inside — wide and watching
Heaven breathing a gentle breeze
A tickle of air greeting long feathered,
>   *Fan-shaped leaves*
Where earth, coastal sand touches Iemanja's sea
Babalu Aye sickened her hydrous belly
The sea rolled sickly and the horizon regurgitated vessels
Stockpiled with human cattle
I, my mother's fruit, watered with this imagery
And eyes see
As eyes wide cry
Try to blur
So eyes become blind
But I see faces of me chained
>   *And walking limp like nzumbi*
Stench of death and waste, walking rot
A pale man commands, "Let the pregnant women watch."
As the system — the machine — is oiled with captured ichor
Pale men and women flush, drunk as if off liquor
I saw this through my mother's eyes
Trees were garnished with new leaves,
Bloodied, hanging bodies
Pregnant women beaten until birth came through stress
The strongest of men castrated and made genderless
Children shot, bodies boiled in large, ominous pots
Rivers of blood slither like snakes
Punctured corpses and severed heads adorn stakes
When my mother breathed in the scene, I could taste
Sated for gestation, this indoctrination
A meal that lasts for the rest of my days
How to make a slave
Obedient
Spirit broken, bent
Survival depends on obedience
And obedience is suicide

But my mother hummed witchcraft

Caressing me deep, a musical bath of protection
The only thing these tragedies did for me
    Was make me anticipate antipathy
My skin hardened
The light I was born into darkened
And there came my second birth,
Pulled away from my mother's embrace
Mother Harmony became a universal song
And pale men shared her chorus
But their voices could not reach her incorporeal notes
I heard her singing to me
As if she was there on that boat
That journey, taking me as sold property
These young hands
would be made to work
another

far
away
land

Horatio's music stopped. His feet touched the roof, floating as he was while invisible to the world and playing the horn. He appeared from out of thin air with a faint *whoosh* that announced his physical return, sounding like the flap of a bird's wings. The songbook hung in the air, floating with a subtle bob like a buoy on the water. Horatio's eyes remained closed. He gripped his horn tight, and he clenched his teeth even tighter. He opened his eyes and cried, a defiant face looking at the sun as it set. The celestial, burning sphere looked to hide itself from the young trumpeter's wrath. Horatio wished to toss the horn skyward and scream to the heavens. The images created from the melody still rolling through his head, biting every nerve in him, ruffling his anger. The scene composed from the music was unsettling to Horatio, no matter how many times he played these notes.

Horatio remained still. He moved the trumpet away from his lips and breathed in and breathed out. He relaxed, but he could still hear the man commanding, *"Let the pregnant women watch."* Even worse, he could see the man. Curly Burneside. He couldn't forget the face. He'd watched that face closely, as he was able to do since Jackson Fable made him aware of Curly's presence, informing him before he and Johnny left Mississippi.

Since then, something else controlled Horatio's horn playing while he observed the scenes playing in front of him. He concentrated more on the people, faces, looking for familiarity. Curly was the same man that helped throw Father Voice overboard. And his cruelty continued up to the moment he arrested Gaston Fable and kept him in a backroom in a town called Red Leaf. Jackson Fable put an end to Curly with a bullet to the head. The wicked man's long life was finally extinguished. "We put you down, Curly Burneside," Horatio said. "Even long lives come to an end, and we got you Sheriff Burneside." This man was an associate of Sarinda Fallows, and Horatio knew she too led a long life.

There were other facets to the melodic narrative that inspired Horatio to play this area of the song again, also inspiring him to continue composing *The Son Dial Tone* after he finished this session. And so Horatio tilted his head back and exhaled, then looked forward and stretched, loosening his shoulders, bending his neck back and forth, left and right. He puckered his lips and kissed the trumpet's mouthpiece. Music played. The first melodious notes left passersby wanting to hear more, but again Horatio's music faded to their ears, and he dissolved from existence as he was pulled back into his musical and poetic narrative.

N-Word
Inward
To ourselves bound
New word in New World – put us in Order
Brewed war
Yester-millenniums ago
Time remembers history
Speak it not to heed it
But to repeat it – the war of one word – for one word
N-Word Wars – inward wars
Battle with ourselves
Neggur, my king – Neggura, my queen
God and Goddess
Repeat through breath the decayed distress of history
Words as effective as chains – the static beat of repetitious beatings
R to blame

Rastus, tar baby, pickanniny, nigger (what?)

Rastus, burrhead, coon, shine, monkey, (oh…)
Sho' nuff nig-berry

I don't have a name – I have titles
Work boy, slave
Fingers rave, work land by hand
Slaves in droves as drones
Singing with moans, earth tones
Open field picked by day – till until noontime, then a house slave
And I see slave women sewing new seeds to reap
A new tradition of nursing the master's children
Mother Harmony's song a distant dissonance
Dismissed
Her song now tends to the master's wish
The commands from his wife's lips
Men work, whipped for sport
And for good measure, women whipped for pleasure
From 9 to die, sun up to life down

Loop, loop life, cycle, pattern
Continue 'round like the rings of Saturn
Retrograde action
A little black boy now
12 years a spirit Earth bound, bet placed if I become a man
An endangered species I am
They skin pieces of me to see how the sun
      Kisses tenderly my skin
So to them I must be little boy
      Beaten black and blue
My hue not considered being
My black mixed with red, bleeding
Whips lick my back. One. Two. Three.
All to keep as a memory
A reminder, emasculating menstruation, once a month
But at least I get to bleed – Our slave minds admire palien artistry
They draw our black blood to breathe

I see a black man upset. He's put to death.
Hanging after whips and lashes
Castration, more lacerations
When his stench is a well-planted memory, his body
        Is removed from the tree

A woman goes missing, returns bleeding
Blood streams, ripped seams down her legs
She begs the gods in the sky to let her die
But 9 months pass her by,
She is taken from life, and her song fades
When she gives birth to a lighter shade

And even when black conceives black
There is love and mercy. It happens,
Like virgins fed to volcanoes and dragons
The innocent are heaven sent
Instead of sacrificing them to live life
Under the actions of whore-able monsters
Up, freed from being earth bound
Smothered or drowned
Love's complexity
I see and live this reality
And I wonder if my Mother Harmony truly loved me
And in that thought I think
All the days I sing dirges
Mother Harmony and Father Voice
Conceived and birthed me for a purpose
I was put here for a reason, to change the scenery
And call out a new season

I think and gaze at the sky
Once a day as 2 years flutter and fly
On a noontime
There flickers a figure in my eye
I spy a little girl behind the slave shack
She black and bright
Hair wild,

Like lightning tussling in a tornado with night
Smile beaming back to the sun,
Her cocoa-colored eyes
Wide enough to swallow the sky
She talks up to the air as I approach and stare
Wonder tickles me
I am close
She still talks up to the air
I am there but she does not see me
The slave master and his overseer freeze me
Late, not in my place for house duty
My fate an example
Dragged and trucked to a newly bought stock
   Of young bucks – slaves my age
Whipped and beaten in front of them
And among them, a friend

Him called Li'l Chew
Spunk that sparks life
A smile that brightens the night
A dance to his struts and step
The last of life that is left

He tells me after house duty,
"I take these beats the master gives me
Turn them into music that will free me from slavery
I am the artist always known as an African Prince
So, let's go crazy
Morning is my glory
I have the power of Anansi's stories
I'm the cosmic spider, man
We be that Eshu trickster clan
I see that gleam in your eye, your purpose for this life."

I remark, "This world is off balance,
Unmoving. Iku's night freezes
And creates plight. Ojo's concentrated light
Keeps half this world burning

Shackled by shine and shadow,
How do we get the world turning?"

Li'l Chew replies, "Don't let this phase
          As slaves faze us.
We'll get both the night and the day's light
To chase us. Run. Run. Run. Step up.
Let our enemies try and catch up
We trickster gods, let our plots evolve
Our circular momentum will once again
          Get the world to revolve
We no slaves, we are salve
Salvaged parts of Osirus' whole
Wearing Isis' love as a cloak
Set hides the sun for us to plot
Keep secrets in song, tucked in blue skies
          And under rock
Anubis' sickles help us till the land
Let this slave master villain challenge me
          Cultivate me
Until I am unmade his slave
          And become Anu hue man."

"I saw a maiden," I tell him.
"A little girl — a ghost speaking to heaven.
Bright and black. Her glimmering shadow
          Haunts behind our slave shack.
I believe she asks Heaven if she can come in.
Her spirit trapped
Chained to what she knows."

Li'l Chew says to me, "Wish her well this night
And talk to her tomorrow."

Horatio moved his fingers away from the horn's valves. He took
the mouthpiece away from his lips and opened his eyes. The present world
covered the past like one movie scene fading into the next. He snatched the
songbook from the air where it floated, and he placed it on the ground,

closed. The sun settled just atop the horizon. Horatio wondered at the time as he spotted the sun's position. He played some notes on his horn and his body dissolved from the rooftop and materialized in the guestroom. A grin crept on his face, reveling in the trick. He set the trumpet in its case and went to the door, opened it, and walked downstairs to the kitchen. Gwendolyn Gregory was still working to put together a meal for him and her son.

"Miss Gregory," Horatio interrupted in a polite voice. He first asked, "You need help in here?"

"Absolutely not," she said without looking up at him, scrambling around. "You don't mind yourself with what I'm doin' here."

Then Horatio asked, "Has Johnny arrived?"

"Not yet," Miss Gregory answered. She looked up at Horatio and shooed him away playfully. "Now go. Go on. Can't have someone in my kitchen while I'm workin'."

Horatio turned around and skipped away, feigning fright from a potential punishment. He heard Johnny's mother laugh at his mannerisms. He said back to her, "You sound like my mother, Miss Gregory."

She laughed, "I know. We all have the same superstitions."

Horatio chuckled at her comment and walked back up the stairs. He saw a picture of Johnny when he was fourteen years old. Horatio grinned, hands in his pockets. He said to the picture, "How you doin', Li'l Chew?" He continued up to the guestroom and retrieved his horn from the open case. He played a note and faded back to the rooftop. He played a second note and the songbook returned to its position in front of him, open and floating. The pages flipped to where he'd left off. His feet lifted, and the world's scenery swirled back to a life long ago.

I remember Father Voice's graffiti
Etched inside Mother Harmony's belly
I close my eyes and see that script in me
Gypsy, glyph poetry
I close my eyes to sleep
And I see the script in my dream
I read a story etched inside me
　　　　And I learn a trick
　　　　Watching Tehuti pluck a little time from the day
As the story went, he split seconds

Hid them in a circle
Elongating rotation through the heavens
Then he pocketed time
And he had a day to himself, and let the gods be born here
Every leap year
I awoke and stole time, picked with my fingertips
And I saw the ghostly girl wandering, talking to the air
Head looking up, eyes in a stare
She only in my eyes
And when I captured enough time
I crept behind the slave shack to ask,
"Have you died? Go, go. Go to Heaven. I bless you."
Little black girl, with wild hair like black lightning
Turned to me and giggled as little girls do
"I have not died. I am in between time.
Blessed and protected by Mamma Iyansan
No villain can touch me, no slaver can slave me
Don't you
Have an angel too?"

She sees the scars through my shirt
Snakes tunneling through earth
Keloid tracks
Like lightning on my back
And she can see the words choked and trapped
In my throat
Little black girl knows my answer is, "No."

But she wiped away sadness
Painted a smile on her face and bragged,
"My people can fly. Mamma and Papa flew away.
Brother and sister went with them too.
Up into the blue, they kissed the sun
And hugged the moon
My heart was heavy, chambers echoing
        A melancholy melody
Nothing happy to make me lighter than gravity
My baby eyes had seen too much

Smothering my imagination,
I just see the tragedy surrounding me."

Little black girl grows up faster than most
She boasts maturity mixed with naivety
She can't fly, but she floats
Giggling happily

"Mamma Iyansan protected me
When the slave master wanted me
Beat me
Head under water
Beaten for being my father's daughter
Beat with a collective jealously come from generations before
Angry years in this slave master's might
Beaten for being the last of my family's light
They escaped, magically flown away
And here I was, a dove plucked of its feathers
A symbol of peace come to pieces
The slave master on top of me, ready to take me
Then Mamma Iyansan kissed me invisible
Kissed me from existence
But I saw many killed for my sudden disappearance.

Now, here I am. 3 years past ten. Whole again.
Mamma Iyansan told me about you. Mojuba.
I know your name. You will help me reclaim my family
Reconstruct my invisible wings, and
Fly to an invisible island and reunite with them."

My time runs out. I walk to the master's house.
Work. My hands. Work house and land
To take up time and create space
Chase minutes and pocket them
And stow away to be face-to-face
          With the little black girl
But I just wait.
Night, watching the moon

I talk to Li'l Chew
And he knows myths and legends
That extend to the world's end
He's heard of invisible islands

"I've heard of a haunted ship
Created from the heaven's firmament,
Silver, and haze
Captained by a fierce African maiden
Conjured by a runaway slave – a gravedigger
With his shovel the ground bubbles
And he raises the dead, stirred like lilac brew
Presenting to the African maiden captain
Slain, resurrected African slaves for a crew.
Rebellious! They fled to an invisible island.
The slave and the maiden married, and carried
          Themselves back to the cosmos."

I don't know if it's true
But next afternoon
Time in my pocket and hand
I speak again to little girl black behind the shack
She makes me smile,
Her voice is the gold to her black
She doesn't talk, she sings. Harmony.
Inspiration for me to become the Voice in this story

She sings her name. Mwana. She gives me a kiss,
Transfers protection through this bliss
I see Mamma Iyansan floating
Her image eclipsed by a voice
"Aren't you so precious."
I turn, fluid like water and stare
Tall, wild red hair
The master's daughter

No need for water, this shark lives on land
She beams seductive,

Interested smile aimed at the slave-hands
Intrigued black men found dead in the field
When their thoughts bleed her
And she entertains their flesh and thoughts
Her smile stands over me
Red, gleaming glow glittering from her lips
Flat stone pendant speckled with red markings
Dangling from a necklace, twirled through her fingertips

But she was not speaking to me
She grabbed Mwana with smile and hand
"And where have you been?"

Gods and Goddesses forgive me as I question
The effectiveness of Mamma Iyansan's protection
But chin up, I become brave
As Mwana is back in the hands of her enslavers
Little black girl, once again a slave

Horatio's soft tune faded. He appeared from the blue, on the roof, the last notes of his song breathed into the air. He dropped his hands and exhaled. Mystical music played in his head, continuing the song and story. Their sounds came to him like the rush of high tide. He took the open and floating songbook from out of the air and closed it. Horatio played a familiar, transcendental note through the horn and his image waned from the rooftop and emerged solid in the guestroom. He returned the trumpet to its case and spread himself across the bed. He opened the songbook to a blank page, snatched a pen from the nightstand and composed the notes that played in his head. Images flickered in his vision as he scribbled. They were too quick to make sense of, but by now, Horatio was accustomed to this process. He would see the story in its entirety later when he played the notes. Horatio memorized most of the supernatural, musical script, but just for good measure he would flip to the front of the book where the entire script was written just to verify the otherworldly sounds in his head. Translating the sound from internal audio to script is when the past life's images appeared most earnestly.

Horatio flinched when the images came. Loud and disconcerting static interrupted the music when they appeared. It faded as he continued writing and viewing small morsels of imagery. He wrote and saw he and the other enslaved men and women growing up. Li'l Chew became more recognizable as Johnny Concheroot, his piano-playing friend. Mojuba Kimoyo fleshed out and developed into him. Time was passing. Not much else of the story could be seen. There was Mwana, the little black girl invisible from the slave master's sight until plucked from her magical aegis by his daughter. Mwana was beautiful and maturing. Blooming. The images were quick flashes, but Horatio could see the little black girl as she matured. Older she became, a young woman. The image was quick but discernable. She was easily recognizable as the pretty, young lady he'd met earlier in the day. Delia-LaRue Amat. Much was recognizable, even the slave master's redheaded daughter. Horatio would've first considered the young, red-haired woman in her late-teenage years, who could see the little black girl, snatched her, and brought her back into the physical reality, was a long-ago relative of Sarinda Fallows. The odd stone pendant worn around her neck a family heirloom passed down from one generation to the next. But he concluded, as he had when he'd first composed the song, this was indeed Sarinda Fallows.

It was being made aware of Curly Burneside that convinced Horatio. He deduced that he as Mojuba Kimoyo, Johnny Concheroot as Li'l Chew, and now Delia-LaRue Amat as Mwana, were expressed through the music by their contemporary images as visual cues as to who they were in their past lives, but they most likely looked nothing of the sort in that actual time and place. If these were past lives, then he, Johnny, and Delia-LaRue had passed from it. Curly Burneside and Sarinda Fallows were deathless walkers wandering the Earth. Well, not completely deathless. Curly Burneside had a bullet in his head, and thus concluded his long, long story. Sarinda Fallows would soon have her final chapter scripted too.

"Horatio," Johnny's mother called from downstairs. "Johnny just pulled up." Horatio imagined a single eyebrow rose on Miss Gregory while she shook her head and said up to him from downstairs, "I knew that boy would be late, but not this damn late."

Horatio jumped up from the bed, opened the door, and replied, "Thank you, Miss Gregory." The son of Pete Peters kept his tone polite even as he had to raise it in order to be heard by Gwendolyn all the way on the garden floor of the brownstone building.

Horatio snatched his trumpet from its open case and walked to the window. Horn held up and propped on his shoulder, Horatio moved the curtain aside and peered through, observing his friend Johnny Concheroot parking his car parallel to the sidewalk. He stepped away from the window, returned the horn to its case, and took a seat on the bed. He heard Johnny get out of the car and then enter the house. "Mom," called the tall, dark piano man. Johnny's mother responded by playfully scolding her son for being so late.

"The sun all up in its last breaths out there," Miss Gregory said to him. Johnny asked his mother where Horatio was, and Johnny's mom responded, "Upstairs." Their conversation, to Horatio, was a muffle of indiscernible sounds as he listened in the quiet comfort of the upstairs guestroom.

Horatio sat still on the bed. He heard Johnny conversing with his mother, voices still low and words still indiscernible. He concluded Johnny was discussing seeing his father, trying to engage his mother about Joseph Concheroot's release from prison. The conversation appeared one-sided and not very long. Then Horatio heard Johnny making his way up to the guestroom. Johnny knocked on the door first, and then the door opened and Horatio looked up to see Johnny enter. "How is everything?" Horatio asked.

Johnny stepped all the way into the room and turned on the main light, which smothered the glow of the lamp resting on the nightstand next to Horatio. Johnny closed the door and walked over to the dresser to lean on it. Horatio followed his movements, turning on the bed to face his friend. "Everything's cool," said Johnny. "My pops is cool, man. He's doin' real good. I got an understandin' of his story." Johnny exhaled a chuckle. He turned away from Horatio, an uneasy smile on his face. Then he dropped his head and shook it. He rose up and told Horatio, "He thought I was your father's son. Turns out your pops and my mom had a thing for a while, but it faded. They remained good friends. Close. Like brother and sister. Your pops was with your mom; and that was real love, y'know?"

"I'm here, ain't I," Horatio joked.

Johnny laughed. "Yeah, Negro. You the proof. But I guess y'pops was nervous about askin' y'mom to marry him. He confided in my mother. They spent the night together—not intimately. But it didn't sit well with my pop. I was born soon enough after. My dad had his suspicions, but his suspicions were wrong. His math was all off. I'm his child, but he wouldn't really believe that until after someone entertained his suspicions and had him betray your father. He set your father up to be there that night."

Horatio took a breath as he took in Johnny's words. He exhaled. "Damn, man."

Johnny nodded his head. "Yeah. Ain't that a thing that definitely got that swing? Shit." His eyes floated to the songbook on the bed, pen resting in the valley of the open pages. "My Pop was tellin' me about the horn, all the wild imagery and sounds your father had the band playin'. Said that cat Madison Goodspeed told your father about Jackson and Gaston." Johnny delivered a slight pause in speaking.

Horatio jumped in. "Madison? Goodspeed! That name!"

Johnny clapped his hands and pointed at Horatio. "You got it," he said seeing Horatio's eyes widen upon reaching a proper conclusion. "Put the puzzle together, brother. Put the puzzle together. This Madison character said your pops needed to go and meet Jackson and Gaston. Goodspeed was a spiritualist. My pops said he was a Jamaican cat with an English accent. He was a weird cat, but y'pops connected with him. Went off lookin' for Jackson and Gaston."

Horatio responded, "A jazzman at the crossroads. Tell a blues brother about that."

There was a contemplative pause in the conversation.

"You been writin' and seein' things?" Johnny asked with a grin.

"Oh, I got my story, Negro," said Horatio. "I got all types of tellings for me to tell." Horatio stood and put his hands in his pockets. He beamed proudly and informed Johnny, "I went to Harlem today."

"And how's that different from any other day?" asked Johnny. "Let me guess, you went and saw your aunt or your uncle."

"No. Not yet," Horatio responded. "I don't want to put them in any danger." Horatio removed his hands from his pockets and counted the scenarios on each finger as he expressed, "But today I found and talked to a fine honey, I met Sarinda Fallows *and* her son, Stanley. And dig this, I got us a practice gig tomorrow afternoon at the Harlem Dixie."

"Ain't a way you did!" exclaimed Johnny.

"True I did, brother. True I did. Trust, believe, and understand I did." Horatio spread his arms wide, mirroring his smile. "And I seen some things. First, I was standin' at the ruins of the On The Hour club, lookin' at ancient history." His hands went back to his pockets. "Stanley Fallows appears out the blue, shakes my hands and asks my name. I tell him my name is Davis Parker. I told him as much truth as I wanted him to know. Gave him my history, but not. Y'know? Told him my father played up here. Met my mom. They moved South, had me. I knew it was him too. I knew. He was lookin' at the club too, checkin' it out. He and his mamma bought the property."

"Okay, okay," Johnny acknowledged with a nod.

"I had my horn with me." Horatio clarified, "*My* horn. Not my father's, just the regular old horn." Horatio returned to the story of the day's events. "Stanley and I get to talkin'. I mention playin' with you. I say all I want to do is play in Harlem like my father before me. Then he invites me to the Harlem Dixie. Man that is a place."

"I know," Johnny interjected.

"Miss Fallows was on the stage, practicin' with her band."

"Don't she got a voice and a figure?" asked Johnny with a wide grin. "She better not check her roots."

Horatio agreed, hating to do so considering Sarinda being the person who orchestrated his father's death. But he said, "She fine, she fine. Got a pretty, pinup girl shape. Had my attention, sure is shootin'." He pointed a stern finger at Johnny and reminded, "But we done checked her roots. Uh-huh. And we know she been workin' roots. Old magic. And that's why I didn't bring that horn. I walked into that club and saw some things. First was Miss Fallows, and second was her niece. *That's* the honey I was talkin' 'bout."

"Really," Johnny expressed surprise.

Horatio coolly laid out his hand, flat, as if taking a chop at the air. "She ain't Miss Fallows' real niece. Not by blood. Not even by marriage. Miss Fallows is close to this girl's family. Knew her grandmother. And she's a pretty, coffee-colored young thing from Baton Rouge, Louisiana. Her name is Delia-LaRue Amat."

"Sounds sophisticated," said Johnny.

"Oh, she is, brother. She is." Horatio reflected. His smile and excited demeanor faded, replaced with a deep, contemplative eye aimed first at the floor then up to Johnny. "I knew her before I met her." His head turned slowly, his eyes moving toward the open songbook on the bed. He put his eyes back on Johnny with a sly turn of his head. "She's that little girl, man. That's her." Johnny didn't say a word. He didn't know what to say. He was shocked, and he waited for Horatio to continue. "I saw more." He asked Johnny, "You ever notice the paintings hangin' inside the main ballroom of the Harlem Dixie?"

Johnny replied, sounding relieved to be saying something, "Yeah. You know how it is. The piano man is the only man in the band that can get away with keepin' his eyes open, lookin' out at the crowd. But, I never got a good look at 'em. They wasn't what was on my mind when I was there, and the lights were always too bright to see that far out from the stage."

Horatio said, "Delia's father painted them. He's dead. Killed in a robbery in New Orleans. Delia had just been conceived when it happened. He was working with Miss Fallows to get a show for his work. She had a contact, and guess what his name was. Curly Burneside." Horatio stopped. He noticed a single eyebrow rise on Johnny's brow. "Yeah. Somethin' to think about. When you see these paintings, you'll think even harder. One in particular looked like my dream, three men with smoking guns in their hands, a man's body on the floor, and a scorpion near the gunmen and a lion in the corner. That's the only paintin' that caught my attention. There were others. They might have a story frozen in them too."

Johnny paused to take in what Horatio told him.

Horatio concluded, "I want to show Delia the story. I want her to see the songs."

"You think that'll be a little much for this girl?"

Horatio didn't answer Johnny's question. He stepped around the bed, and then he said in a frustrated tone, "I keep composing. I see flashes, images as I write. I could see that little girl growin' up. It's her. She got to see that." He said turning to Johnny, "There's somethin' to Delia and Miss Fallows."

"Like what?" Johnny asked.

"Miss Fallows made a joke when I asked Delia why she'd come to Harlem. Miss Fallows joked that Delia was there to steal away her father's paintings. It seems like Miss Fallows don't want to give them up. She was bein' all funny with it, but she was serious." Horatio declared again, "That paintin' got a story, they all got a story. Just like that songbook got a story." Horatio appeared determined. "Miss Fallows is beautiful and intelligent.

Whatever we think we know, she knows more. She been usin' tricks since before them last times we was born."

"That just sounds confusin'," Johnny interjected, making a face. "Other lives and shit."

Horatio ignore him and continued, "We playin' guessin' games with this otherworldly, hoodoo magic dope—goin' off gut feelings about all this. But if we know our story—our *entire* story—we write her and all her tricks out of it." Horatio then spoke about Delia, remarking, "I think Delia and myself were together in that other life. Intimately. I feel that. I need her to see that."

Johnny quipped, "I bet you do."

Horatio loosened up, and a smile came through. "She fine, brother. She. Is. Fine." He warned playfully with his finger jabbed toward Johnny, "And I saw her first."

Johnny conceded. "Apparently. Lifetimes ago," he joked. "Like I said, confusin'—other lives and shit. But that's cool—that's cool, Horatio. You take one, I'll take the rest."

"Well, tomorrow we play behind her, just you and me. Then we'll get the rest of them cats you know when we score the gig."

"Oh, she sings?"

Horatio exclaimed, "Yeah, man. And she lookin' for the right men to sing with. I told her we'd do *Bewitched, Bothered and Bewildered* and *I Could Write a Book*."

Johnny pondered, making a face. "Not bad. That can be done, man. Easy, real easy."

Miss Gregory called from downstairs, "Dinner is ready, you boys!"

Horatio and Johnny jumped at her call. "Let's get on downstairs," said Johnny.

They turned off the lights and walked out the door, Johnny first and Horatio following close behind. "We'll be treated like stars tomorrow," Horatio said to Johnny as the two young men went downstairs. "I didn't tell you the best part that came at the end of the day."

Johnny led them into the dining room. He said over his shoulder as they walked into the room, "What's that?"

"I got chauffeured back here—all the way from Harlem. Stanley Fallows set me up with a fancy ride home. It wasn't a limousine, but it was a nice car."

"Ain't that somethin'?" Johnny exclaimed. Then he joked, "Of course, you've been chauffeured by me all up and down the East Coast, so it ain't nothin' new."

Horatio retorted, "Please, Negro. That was on account you didn't want me drivin' your precious car. And I offered, and I did help too. You had to sleep at some point."

Johnny nudged Horatio with an elbow. "I'm just playin', you know."

"Yeah, you suddenly playin' now when I'm firin' back at your accusation, Negro." Horatio and Johnny started laughing.

The dining room had already been set with food that rested on decorative placemats positioned over a tablecloth that lined the long table. Three areas were set for Horatio, Johnny, and Johnny's mother. Gwendolyn slipped inside the dining room with a pitcher of cold, iced tea. She poured the contents into three tall glasses as Horatio and Johnny took their places. They both thanked Johnny's mother for the meal she prepared and waited for her to take a seat. They said a small prayer and then commenced eating, little conversation disturbing the moment as they indulged in the healthy abundance of food.

Johnny broke the silence, informing his mother that Horatio got them a practice session at the Harlem Dixie. Gwendolyn complimented Horatio on his venture, and surprisingly she remarked with a comment about Joseph Concheroot and Pete Peters. "I'm glad to see their friendship resurrected in the two of you. I do hope things stay that way between you two."

Horatio spoke with a reserved tone in his voice, "Won't nothin' come between us, Miss Gregory." He thought about not saying what was on his mind, pausing for a brief moment. But then, Horatio expressed, "It's sad that someone was able to work Mister Concheroot against my father, if you don't mind me sayin' so, Miss Gregory." Gwendolyn said nothing, but believed she nodded her head, which she didn't. Horatio continued talking to keep an awkward silence from haunting the room and pleasant meal. "I know that Johnny saw his father today. Mister Concheroot explained what made him turn against my father. I do believe he's sorry, Miss Gregory. Yes, ma'am, I do."

Gwendolyn nodded her head, and this time it was visible but still slight. She asked Johnny, "How did your father look, Johnny?"

"He looked good, Ma. He looked good."

Gwendolyn beamed. She turned her head and glimpsed the piano in the other room. She turned her attention back to her food, pregnant with a memory. "The two of you gonna practice tonight before your practice tomorrow at the Harlem Dixie? I won't mind. I'd like to hear you two play."

Johnny said to his mom, "We could do that, Ma."

Gwendolyn looked content. She asked, "So what's this all for, this gig? You say it's practice?"

Horatio answered, "Yes, Miss Gregory, practice and kind of an audition. A young woman is looking for a band. The young woman's family is close to the woman who runs the club."

"Oh! Miss Fallows?" Gwendolyn chuckled. "Everyone just loves Miss Fallows. She never cared about colored or white. Though, she sure did love how us colored folks could get down. Miss Fallows admired the strong friendship between your father, Horatio, and my Joseph."

Horatio and Johnny looked up at Gwendolyn, the two of them looking at her with a peculiar stare, and for differing reasons. They returned to eating. Gwendolyn continued to inquire about their practice gig, asking what songs they would perform. Horatio answered her, and not too long after dinner was finished, and he and Johnny had tended to clearing the table and washing the dishes while Gwendolyn stored the remaining food, music filled the house with the songs slated for the next day's performance.

Gwendolyn sat on her couch and watched her son and Horatio play, a smile beaming underneath reminiscing eyes. The music went deep into the night, deviating from the songs planned for the audition. Horatio used his horn rather than his father's. He and Johnny's jazz became long stretches of improvisation. But, Horatio backed off playing when Johnny started in with Gaston Fable's favorite song composed by his father. Horatio made quick, unassuming glances at Miss Gregory. Her smile at the song was prominent, but that was her only reaction. Johnny's music eventually faded. Horatio, after bidding Johnny and Gwendolyn goodnight, washed up and returned to his room. He turned the lights on and shut the door. He put his horn away and sat on the bed. He scooped up the songbook from the bed, put the pen that was tucked between its pages on the nightstand, and started looking through his father's works. His eyes came across a song he learned while still in Clarksdale, Mississippi.

Some of the song's notes came from Jackson and Gaston Fable. Horatio guessed his father put these supernatural notations to use in melodies that were much more grand. Horatio used parts of the song. In particular, the parts composed by Jackson and Gaston Fable, to move objects closer to him, lift the songbook into the air and flip its pages. He even used parts of the song to speed up the dissolution of the world around him and render more quickly the scenery of the story locked inside the compositions.

Horatio wondered how far he could push the power of the song in front of him. However far that would be, Horatio believed he would unlock another purpose for his father's musical work.

Animated Stillness.

Magic Afternoon
"My name is Horatio Peters, Miss Amat."

Delia-LaRue Amat tapped her feet, counting the beats and waiting for her moment to step to the microphone and let her voice glide musically on the rhythms assembled by the piano man she knew as Johnny Gregory. Delia came in after Johnny played the introductory notes from *Bewitched, Bothered and Bewildered.* Her voice was sweet and delicate, vulnerable and sincere, singing as if she herself composed the lyrics to the popular show tune.

Horatio, going by the name Davis Horatio Parker, slipped into the song with a slow croon of his horn. Horatio's playing was subtle and complimentary, playing the melody of the second song chosen, *I Could Write a Book.* The musicians stirred the two songs together, mingling them like a gentlemen's handshake. Delia recognized Horatio's slow melody. She smiled, but didn't miss her beats as she continued singing. Her eyes closed and she folded her fingers around the microphone stand, confessing the lyrics passionately and playfully.

The song ended, but the music didn't. Horatio's horn came to the forefront. Johnny backed him up with a waggish drift played across the piano keys. Delia popped to life. Her eyes opened and her smile widened. She said into the microphone, "What you boys doin' here?" She listened and noticed *I Could Write a Book*'s exuberant melody. She let Johnny and Horatio play until she found her window to jump into the song. Delia sang through the piece, and again, it ended, but not the music. It was then that Delia started conducting Johnny and Horatio's playing, changing the tune. She sang improvised lyrics, *"Between the day and night, who's the one that tells the most lies. Day-Sun act like it's got the only shine. Night try to act like they ain't no light. I see them both fade from their glorious prime, into each other, cuz both have to humble themselves to time. To time."* Horatio and Johnny played along. *"I got a cosmic habit, so serenade me with supernatural sonnets, and play for me music marinated with magic."* She told Johnny. "Move over, piano man. A piano woman wants to get her fingers clean." Johnny gave a look at Horatio who continued playing. He slid off the piano bench just as Delia slid onto it. She motioned for Johnny to bring the piano microphone stand to her. Johnny did as Delia asked, connecting the microphone to the posable stand. Johnny positioned the stand in front of Delia and then backed away, leaving the stage and joining Sarinda Fallows and her son Stanley at a table in the audience. Stanley congratulated Johnny as he sat down with them. Sarinda continued to watch her niece, beaming the whole time and stroking the veil wrapped around her arm as if it was a living pet. Johnny sat back and watched Horatio jam with Delia. He also made inconspicuous glances toward the paintings mounted around the room.

Delia's fingers rolled over the piano keys and the music continued to function as if Johnny never left. She slowed the rhythm of the improvised jam. The melody remained upbeat. Delia trilled, *"Pillows on my piano. They remind me of you. Pillows on my piano. They remind me of what we do. Music and love. We sleep, play, and croon. My piano and you is all I want in my room."* Again, she changed the music's rhythm, Horatio keeping up. Delia sang, *"Harlem was never sweeter. Said the Virgin Mother to Peter when they heard Davis-Horatio's horn and Johnny's fingers on the pian-a. Don't forget when they heard the sweet voice of Miss Delia."*

Horatio remained on point with his playing. He managed to hint a smile as he reacted to Delia's playful, improvised lyrics. Their audience of three chuckled to themselves. "Hold up there, Mister Horn Player," ordered Delia. Horatio put his playing on pause. He watched Delia as she guided her improvised notes to a slower tune. It was jazz overrun with blues. She told Horatio, "Back me up." Horatio swooped in with sounds complimenting Delia's music. Delia belted out a soulful cry that melted into lyrics of love and heartbreak. It was her own song, silently dedicated to her mother's hardships and her father's passing. Sarinda deciphered Delia's song, but everyone listening was pulled into her ballad of heartache and redemption. Horatio's horn kept her afloat as she sang and sang and sang until the song reached a thunderous cry that melted into a sweet and fancy falsetto. Sarinda watched her niece closely. Delia's sweet voice faded under the music. And then, so too did the song. Sarinda remained focused on Delia, stroking the veil wrapped around her arm.

Johnny and Stanley stood up to applaud. Sarinda joined them, bouncing up quickly so as not to appear late in her standing ovation. Horatio lowered his horn and walked to Delia as she rose from the piano. He hugged her and kissed her cheek. Delia accepted the embrace and returned the kiss, planting a friendly peck on Horatio's cheek. She turned to the small audience and directed her words to her Aunt Sarinda. "I approve, Auntie Sarinda. I approve these two men. They can play." She said to Johnny, "I'm sorry for kickin' you out your seat, Mister Gregory."

Johnny replied to her, "Not a problem, Miss Amat. Not a problem at all." He turned to Sarinda and Stanley and jokingly expressed, "But I would like you people to take this as note: even if that happens during an actual performance, I still get paid full fee."

Everyone laughed at Johnny's quip, and Sarinda commented, "I actually would like to pay more than just two musicians to play around my niece's wonderful voice, Mister Gregory." She turned to Horatio and inquired, "There will be some other players in the band, Mister Parker?"

Horatio nodded his head at Sarinda. "Yes, ma'am. It's just Johnny and I today."

"Will they need a practice session, Mister Parker," asked Sarinda. "Or are they seasoned enough to jump in?"

"A couple practice sessions won't hurt," Johnny answered. "I know a space where we can practice. Miss Amat, would you be free Wednesday?" He turned to Sarinda and said in an apologetic tone before Delia could answer, "If that's okay with you, Miss Fallows. Your niece will be in good hands. Well protected."

Sarinda responded, "That would be fine. I trust the two of you boys. Mister Parker is, after all, a respectable, Southern boy."

"I'll let you believe that, Miss Fallows," Johnny remarked with a grin. "He was born in Harlem. He's got this city in his blood and skin."

Sarinda chuckled, and it was then that Delia excused herself.

"I just have to take a breath outside," she said. "Would you like to come with me, Horatio? I have some song selections to discuss. Some are original. Family songs passed down from my grandmother to me."

Horatio put his horn down on the piano. "I wouldn't mind at all, Miss Amat." He asked Johnny, "You good here?"

Johnny walked toward the stage as he said, "I am, cousin. Go on." He jumped onto the stage instead of taking the stairs. He slid back onto the piano bench and started playing a simple tune.

Delia told her aunt, "We'll be right back, Aunt Sarinda."

"Take your time, dear," Sarinda replied. She whispered to Stanley, "Let's talk about this arrangement in the office, Stanley. We'll see when it'll be best for my niece to make her debut."

"Okay, Ma," Stanley acknowledged. He shouted up to Johnny on the stage, "Are you good, Johnny? You need us to send someone to take an order? It'll be on the house?"

"That would be fine, Mister Fallows, sir. That would be grand. Thank you."

Stanley nodded. "I'll send someone out to take a lunch order." He turned and followed Sarinda out of the ballroom and to the club's main office. Johnny continued playing the piano. He looked around the brightly lit ballroom and took notice of the paintings lining the walls.

Delia and Horatio stepped outside, and Delia took a deep breath. "Fresh air," she exclaimed. "I like the open space of the club, but it still reeks of cigarette and God-knows-what other kind of smoke."

Horatio agreed. He pointed up the street and asked, "Would you like to go for a walk, Miss Amat?"

"Yes, indeed. That would be nice." She tapped Horatio on the shoulder. "And, you better start callin' me Delia like I've asked of you."

Horatio smiled at her. He walked on the outside of Delia, close to the curb, and keeping his hands clasped behind him. "Yes, Delia. As you wish."

Delia looked around at the buildings. Her eyes swallowed Harlem and all its activities. "I made it, Horatio," she announced. "I made it to New York City, and it is indeed grand."

Horatio joined in observing their surroundings. "We both have, Delia. I've been wanting to play here since I could hold the horn."

Delia commented, "It appears we've both been on the same journey."

Horatio grinned. He thought of Delia's words and connected them to the epic composition that his father started, that was now being finished by him. *The Son Dial Tone.* He reflected on the story it told. Horatio responded to Delia's comment. "Yes, it appears we are on the same journey."

Delia said excitedly, "And there is so much here, Horatio. So much. This is just Harlem. It's a city unto itself. There's still a great deal more to explore." Delia sighed happily. "My grandmother wanted so much to sing here, and so did my mother. My grandmother passed in childbirth, and my mother was so hurt when my father was murdered." Sadness seeped through Delia's sunny smile. "My mother focused her attention on gettin' things straight when she found out she was pregnant with me. She had support. Her uncle-by-blood helped a lot. Auntie Sarinda helped a little. An old friend of my grandmother's—a drummer in her band—he helped too. My mother went to school, graduated, and went from a teacher's aide to being a junior high school counselor. She went to school at Southern University. There was a house owned by my grandmother's family. They were supposedly killed there."

This part of Delia's story took Horatio by surprise. "Oh, no. Really?"

"Yes," Delia answered. "By the Klan, some believe. My grandmother's sister wasn't found. My great-grandparents were found shot in their bed."

"And you grew up there?"

"Well, I wasn't made aware of all this until about three or four years ago. My mother didn't tuck me into bed when I was a child with such horror stories." They walked farther up, moving closer to the block where the On The Hour club was located.

"Did your mother re-marry?"

Delia explained, "Well, she was never married to my father. They were planning to marry. But not havin' been declared unified under God's eyes didn't stop them from actin' grown with one another. My mother was nineteen. My father was in his early twenties." She paused, looking down at the pavement as they continued up the street. "She mingles with men, but my father has always been on her mind. I'd see men come and go. I'd see my mother glowing with their company, but her glow wasn't too bright. The tragedy surrounding my father's death stays with her."

Horatio remarked, "I understand."

"And what about your parents, Horatio?" Delia asked. "Tell me about the Parker clan."

"I intend to, Delia," Horatio said to her, a stern tone in his voice. He quickened his pace up the street, crossing to the next block. His eyes were focused on the charred remains of the On The Hour club. "Right up here, Delia."

"Oh," she remarked as they came upon the ruins of the club. "The On The Hour club. Auntie Sarinda and cousin Stanley are working so hard to get this property reopened. I don't know what the hold up is."

Horatio stopped and looked up. Admiration beamed on his face. He aimed his grin and a sly eye at Delia and asked her, "Would you like to go in?"

Delia asked, gasping, "Is it dangerous? Can we even get in?"

"No, it ain't," answered Horatio. He snapped his fingers. "And yes we can. Follow me." Horatio hurried around to the alley. Delia scuttled behind him. Horatio stopped at a window that wasn't boarded up. He lifted it, jumped up and crawled inside to what was once the men's bathroom. He turned around and reached out to Delia. "Come on." He waved for her to come closer.

Delia expressed incredulity. "I could rip my garments!" she blurted.

Horatio assured, "You'll be find, Delia. I won't let anything get at you or your clothes."

Delia huffed and scowled. She shook her head and took a step forward and reached for Horatio. She balanced herself in his grip and scaled the brick on the wall. "If I break a heel," she griped. She did her best to make only the flats of her shoes scrape and scale the brick.

Horatio backed up, hauling Delia's frame through the window. She ducked and then balanced herself on the sill. Horatio lifted her through, making sure no sharp splinters from the burned and worn sill scraped her attire or skin. Delia rested her feet on the floor and took a breath. She wiped herself clean and straightened her clothes. "Well, I've heard my granddaddy was a world-traveling adventurer of some sort."

"Really?" Horatio asked as he led them from the dilapidated bathroom to the hall.

"He was from New York too," Delia continued. "Only thing that got him to settle down, sort of, was my grandmother. He loved her so much. He died overseas on some adventurous excursion."

Horatio guided Delia to the concert room. Light filled the space. The entrance doors had been removed, allowing light from the front hall to spill inside. A stage barely existed. Much was cleared away, but a good deal of burned tables and pieces of chairs still littered the room. Resting on an unscathed table was a trumpet case. Horatio let go of Delia's hand and walked over to the case, unlocking and opening it. A trumpet glimmered inside.

Delia commented on the table's condition. "That table must've been able to hide from the fire."

"Oh, I did this," Horatio remarked.

"You made the table?" Delia asked perplexed.

Horatio lifted the horn and pivoted. "I re-made the table, so-to-speak."

Delia raised an eyebrow. "Well, Mister Davis Horatio Parker! Did you plan all this to seduce me?" She cocked her head to the side and grinned. "You didn't have to go all-out romantic to ask me on a date. I would give a handsome man such as yourself a 'yes' if you just asked kindly."

Horatio chuckled and dropped his head. He put his hand in his pocket and looked around the room. His eyes panned the ceiling. His smile faded as his gaze moved to the floor. Horatio looked up at Delia and told her, "My father was murdered right here. In this room."

Sorrow materialized on Delia's face. "I'm—I'm so sorry, Horatio. I didn't know. I was under the impression both your parents were alive in New Orleans."

Horatio shook his head. He bit the top of his lip and then confessed, "My mother passed five years ago." He took a step. "My father's murder happened on the night I was born. I never knew my father. I know him through stories. Just like you with your father."

"Oh…" Delia remarked quietly.

Horatio confessed to Delia, "My name is not Davis Horatio Parker. My name is Horatio Peters, Miss Amat. I have a story to tell you, to show you. I just need your undivided attention. There is so much about our lives that intertwine."

Delia nodded her head approvingly. Her eyes examined Horatio. His name was different, and so was he. But, he appeared more familiar to her. She recognized Horatio Peters more so than Davis Parker, if that made any sense.

Horatio said to her, "Your father's painting, the one with the murder. I think he knew my father."

"I don't know, Horatio," Delia stated unconvinced. "My father never left Water Bug Hollow. At least, he never left Louisiana. I don't think.

But I'm sure my mother would've said if he'd traveled as far north as New York City. Harlem, especially. They were planning to move here or Chicago. That much I know."

Horatio peeked over his shoulder and then looked back to Delia. He put his lips to the horn and played a series of musical notes with a sound unfamiliar to Delia's ears. The sound was otherworldly, and its reverberation made Delia gasp. From behind the trumpet case jumped an old, leather-bound songbook. It leapt into the air and came to rest next to Horatio. It floated, nothing holding it up from the ground that Delia could see as she peered curiously at the phenomenon.

Horatio played another set of notes and the book opened. He lowered the horn and said to Delia, "I know you, Miss Delia-LaRue Amat. We share a story. I'd like to show you that story."

Delia's curious gaze went from the floating, open songbook to Horatio. A smile popped onto her visage, then burst into a short chuckle. She put her hand on her chest as she laughed in spurts of surprised gasps. "Ah! What trickery is this? How did you do that? Did Johnny follow us? Where are the strings?"

Horatio shook his head and told Delia, "No strings, Miss Amat, except the ones attaching you and I to a common history."

Delia walked over to the book, her steps cautious. She swiped her hands around the floating object and felt nothing except a warm, watery feeling as her hand searched around the book, looking for a set of strings suspending the book in the air. There was nothing.

Delia put her head back, looking up and up and up until she saw the ceiling. She didn't know what she was looking for, clearly no strings held the book in place. She said to Horatio, "I'm impressed. You've managed to mix Harlem's flare and New Orleans' Voodoo. I'd like to see what other tricks you have, Mister Horatio Peters."

Horatio turned to the open songbook and started playing. Delia backed away as the trumpeter played the mystical notes again. New sounds. Delia couldn't help but wonder what lyrics she could write to them, and how her earthly voice would compare. Some of the notes became a thunderous variant of Horatio's voice. It spoke, *"I can make the scene dwindle and fade away, and put another in its place."*

The shimmering script swirled off the pages of the book character-by-character and fluttered in a swarm around the room and erased the scenery. Horatio played faster, and the shimmering script dissolved the scorched nightclub's interior. There stood nothing surrounding them save the outside cityscape. Delia twirled around with an expression of wonder. The Harlem passersby took no notice at the dissolved On The Hour club ruins. She and Horatio were invisible to them.

Delia looked at the people walking by. Mischief shone through her smile. She took a step in the direction of the people, and suddenly the shimmering musical notes constructed a new environment. Substituted for the On The Hour ruins was the grand ballroom of the Harlem Dixie. Delia spun back around to face Horatio as he continued to play his horn. She noticed the ballroom was empty of all its decorations, save her father's paintings lining the wall and the one table that held the trumpet case.

Horatio stopped playing and lowered the trumpet from his lips. He said to Delia, "Miss Fallows said her associate that was supposed to put your father's art on display was named Curly Burneside." He looked around the room. "I got to know a man named Curly Burneside. He knew Miss Fallows. He was a devil-of-a-man. Like Miss Fallows said yesterday, he kept the law in a small town called Red Leaf." He paused for Delia to take in what he was saying. He watched her closely, making sure she wasn't ready to crack and scream over all that was being presented to her in such a short time. There was more to show her. He needed her stable. Not only did she appear calm, but she also appeared intrigued to know more. She was brave. Anyone else would have thrown up their hands and left running and screaming the minute they noticed no strings held up the songbook, let alone, as they watched the scene around them dissolve and become something new. Horatio would then be forced to use the horn to calm her down and erase time and memory of this moment. But such measures would be unnecessary. And so, he said as he took a step toward Delia, "Curly Burneside kidnapped one of my father's music teachers. Gaston Fable. He'd beaten, violated, and killed Gaston's wife years earlier. Johnny, Gaston's older brother Jackson, and I went to Red Leaf to retrieve Gaston. We used tricks to free him. We put Curly Burneside down the old fashion way. A bullet in the head." Horatio felt the need to assure Delia that the fatal shot didn't come from him. "Jackson Fable took him down." He also felt the need to say, "Curly was a bad man all his life. He was responsible for the death of many Negroes. It was fitting that a Negro was responsible for his."

Grief and anger contorted Delia's face as she asked, "You think this man killed my father? Why?"

Horatio finished walking toward Delia. He held her arm at the wrist. He expected her to wrestle from his gentle hold, but Delia remained still. Horatio admitted, "I don't know if he did or not. I have a feeling, is all. This feeling is based on the strange motives surrounding my father's murder."

"And what's that?" Delia asked.

Horatio simplified the answer. "He could play otherworldly notes with this horn. He could do the things I've shown you plus more. He composed songs that took people into the past. With his music, taught to him by Jackson and Gaston Fable, he could show people who they are and where they come from." He let go of Delia's arm. He chuckled as he stated, "An intelligent Negro scares the hell out of white folk. Imagine one usin' the power in this horn." Horatio waved his finger. "But my father wasn't cheatin', now. He knew how to play before he got the horn." Then he pointed to the paintings in the room using the same finger. "I think your father could do the same with his art." He walked over to one of the paintings. Delia followed. "Look," said Horatio. "These paintings don't just show a captured image. They go beyond your father's ability to recreate life on canvas. These are stories. They say something." He looked over at Delia and declared, "And I think I can get them to speak."

Delia scanned the room, spotting each of her father's works. She grinned and said to Horatio, "Whatchu waitin' for? Spark up a conversation with 'em."

Horatio nodded. He returned to the center of the room. Delia walked with him. He took a breath and then put the horn back to his lips. He took a moment to hope what he was about to do would work. Delia and he were surrounded by the illusion of the Harlem Dixie's main ballroom. The paintings weren't really there. He didn't know if he could use the horn's music to animate the works. But he played.

Three paintings jumped from the wall and floated in front of Delia and Horatio. Two more paintings materialized in front of them. The image within one of the frames started to move like a motion picture. Curtis 'Water Bug' Hollow kissed his family and fled the plantation where he was made a slave. He fled not only into the night, but his image jumped into the second painting. It too started moving. He was captured and taken to a new plantation. There he met and befriended a man named Oscar MacRitchie. The images within the paintings didn't just move. They spoke.

Oscar MacRitchie was furious! His anger was directed toward Curtis' captors. Oscar ranted to himself about the deal he'd just signed as he walked up to the shed where Curtis had been chained. The dinner was good, but the deal was bad. *"That contract was a phony!"* he hissed. He walked inside the shed believing he would be alone. But he found Curtis chained and gagged inside. *"I feel like you, neggar. I've been swindled by ma own countrymen."* Delia saw Oscar grin and kneel down to Curtis. *"Nod if ya understand me, neggar."* Curtis shook his head and Oscar MacRitchie removed the cloth gagging him. *"Do ya want ya freedom?"* Curtis nodded again. *"Adventure and investment is all I came to America for. But I've been swindled. I thought I'd take advantage of this civil strife going on here."*

"You ain't seen much of an investment. America make thieves out of businessmen. It has been an adventure, though. I'll getchu the business you need. You lookin' to sell me to make a dollar?"

"I don't know. Maybe." Oscar continued to grin.

"Well, that won't do you no good, Mister. War puttin' an end to slavery. Negroes been freed by Northern law. Southern folk just bein' stubborn. Either way, ain't no money in me. Not entirely. I still can make you rich, though. How'd you like a whole plantation for yourself?" asked Curtis. *"I just have to kill a man, but don't you worry none. You ain't got to be involved, you just need to give me time. Then, come down my way, South. Look for Jakobi's plantation in Louisiana. Elias Jakobi is the man who owned me and my family. And Elias Jakobi is the man I'm gon' kill. After that, you and I will do business."*

Delia watched Oscar ponder. After a minute or so passed he spoke, *"Ya got a trickster's thinkin' about ya. I like that. What's ya name?"*

"You ain't gonna just keep callin' me nigger?" asked Curtis.

Oscar replied, *"Not seein' as I've been in this country but a simple minute, and I've been treated like I'm one as well. If it weren't by ma own people, I'd say that ma swindlers have mistaken me for Irish. So, let's exchange names and a handshake. I'm Oscar MacRitchie. And you?"* He reached out a greeting hand.

Curtis' chains were wrapped around a wooden beam. It was difficult for him to put out his hand, but he managed. Shaking Oscar MacRitchie's hand he said, *"They call me Curtis. That's all. It's supposed to be Curtis Jacobson. But Elias Jakobi ain't my father. I ain't his son. I'm Curtis."* Curtis' difficulty shaking Oscar's hand did give him the ability to address the situation. He showed off his chains, making them the next point in conversation.

To Curtis' surprise, Oscar removed a key from his pocket. His grin continued. *"I asked if ya wanted freedom, and I'm here to give it. Had this plan since I realized ma deal wasn't servin' ma best interests. I'd figure I'd take a small moment to get to know ya. See if ya could be trusted."* He unlocked Curtis, taking a look around as he did so. *"There's thirteen others that need the same freedom as you. If ya goin' to take a plantation, it's best ya have an army and guns. These conmen are storin' some in a shed. The guns are stolen from Union soldiers and meant for the Confederates. And no need for business, I just want to see the look on these boys' faces when their chattel is missin'."*

"And then what?" Curtis asked. *"You outlawed after that, and that's if they don't kill you while you laughin'."* He told Oscar in an assured whisper, *"You let me handle my business, then we gon' do business. I need that. You a good business man, right?"*

"Oh, the best," Oscar answered with a lighted smile. *"I know how to turn a profit well, legally, and with upright ethics."*

Curtis joked, *"Upright ethics? Then whatchu come to this land for?"*

The two laughed lowly, almost forgetting their predicament. Almost. Curtis came up with a plan to have Oscar chained. He told the Scotsman, *"I got the drop on you, and then I freed myself and the others. Hear? Good. If word get out that a group of runaway Negroes is armed, you tell them hunters that sho' 'nuff goin' be after us we had a plan to run north and find some Union soldiers to take us in. Ain't no one gon' suspect we headin' south when freedom in the otha direction. No, sir. I'm gon' back into the belly of the beast to kill me the beast. Yes, I is. I will enact that man Walker's Appeal. I will be like Christ in the Bible. There's gon' be a new holy book written. The Emancipation Revelation."*

Oscar agreed to the terms. The moving picture showed Curtis freeing the other enslaved blacks. The newly liberated black men and women hurried into the night, dodging even the light of the moon, stowing away into shadow and woods and into the next painting. They emerged into battle. Delia looked on in amazement as the battle unfolded, fading from Curtis and his army retreating with more freed black men and women, and fading into more attacks until Elias Jakobi and his family had been usurped and the foundations of Water Bug Hollow were made. There was celebration, dancing. But, there was no bonfire as portrayed in Delia's father's work.

Two of the five paintings faded. The other three paintings sprang back to their respective places on the wall. Another painting came forth. *The Promise.* Theresa Amat and Joseph Pepper IV held one another in tender smiles and embrace. Delia watched as the picture shifted into her grandfather, Joseph Pepper IV, arriving in Water Bug Hollow on a night celebrating the 1864 liberation. August twelfth. Joseph Pepper heard Water Bug Hollow's tale of liberation recounted from the mouths of various citizens as he made his way into Eve's Hallow. The painting shifted again, and Delia watched in awe as her grandmother, Theresa Amat, stepped out onto the stage and began to sing. Tears filled Delia's eyes as her grandmother belted out beautiful ballads and raucous anthems. There she was with her band. There was granduncle Quincy on the piano—a man her mother talked so much about. And there was granduncle Eugene on the drums looking so young. Delia beamed.

People filtered out as the music continued. Theresa and Joseph met one another and embraced. The two rendezvoused with the citizens and danced around a grand bonfire. The celebration blazed just as high! Theresa and Joseph Pepper returned to Theresa's apartment where Joseph presented a gift to Theresa. A veil. Delia recognized the veil, now possessed by her Grandaunt Sarinda.

Joseph explained, *"This garment belonged to a legendary, African queen that resided here in America a long time ago, and long before the days of slavery. My grandmother blessed it, and it will provide you with protection. This veil is an object based upon a feminine principle and design, and therefore it is of no use to me. But in your hands, my lady, there will be nothing but great magic produced."*

Delia's grandmother was skeptical of her grandfather's account, and expressed such.

But Joseph assured her the story was true. *"...I speak specifically about a West Coast sect of Negroes made almost entirely of African women...these women were warriors. Fierce and beautiful...led by a woman named Califia, from whom the state of California received its name. Supposedly many queens wore this veil, dating back to that ancient continent we call Africa, and passed down in a line of succession until it was worn by Califia herself."*

When Theresa asked how Joseph acquired the item, the sound dropped from his explanation. The scene played muted, causing Delia to remark, "Even magic paintings can get bad reception I guess."

The sound returned when Joseph said to Theresa that he was leaving, but he promised he would return and make her his wife. The scene bleached and returned to the original painted image just as the two kissed and started to disrobe. But life quickly came back to the image. Joseph and Theresa walked away from one another. Delia's Aunt Sarinda emerged from the shadows and scanned the area of Water Bug Hollow. She came with a warning. Delia observed her grandaunt speaking with an authority figure in Water Bug Hollow. *"Your celebration of independence is what has many non-colored folks up in arms. It's offensive to them. You celebrate the death of an honest American businessman. And I've heard it's done with a large fire. People believe there's deviltry going on in Water Bug Hollow. This beautiful place is referred to as Satan's Seat."* Water Bug Hollow was about to have arms raised against her. Sarinda proposed the building of a church, and said she would fund the project as well. She lied, saying she was related to Oscar MacRitchie's family. This revelation was made by the cloudy, animated appearance of the words *"she is a liar"*, floating above Sarinda's head. The cloud dissipated just as quick as it came.

There came another image, an image of Sarinda Fallows returning to her hotel room in New Orleans and conversing with a man in a dapper suit. Sarinda called him Curly, and Delia guessed that this gentleman was the Mister Curly Burneside she'd heard about from her grandaunt and Horatio. Sarinda spoke candidly about taking the veil that she knew was left in Water Bug Hollow by Joseph Pepper. She commanded Curly to retrieve a 'disgraced Negro pastor', and she mocked two black servants with slurs and disgust after they left her presence. New tears colonized Delia's eyes as she watched her grandaunt act with all the grace of a Southern slave owner. She watched Sarinda prance around and reminisce about having slaves and taking some to bed. She mentioned a husband, and addressed Curly Burneside as an overseer, pointing out how he had his way with the enslaved men and women of the plantation.

How could this be, Delia wondered through tears. She considered her grandaunt to look amazing for her age, but she was still far too young to have owned slaves. Maybe, Delia concluded, they were just servants around her house. And maybe, Delia tried to convince herself, maybe her grandaunt was conflicted until befriending the people in Water Bug Hollow. But Sarinda's mannerisms were as a devious trickster. Sarinda's intention was not only to take the veil given to Theresa Amat by Joseph Pepper, but it was also to destroy Water Bug Hollow.

The painting showcased images of Sarinda returning to Water Bug Hollow and speaking with some of its other authority figures. Later that night, Sarinda became enamored with Theresa Amat's singing voice, and the veil with which she decorated herself. She promised Theresa a singing career in New York City. She charmed the Water Bug Hollow residents by flashing money to pay for several rounds of drink, but she stowed away to hold a private conversation with long-buried slave owner Elias Jakobi. She spoke in ritual, pouring the buried man a drink, and lighting for him a reefer stick. Sarinda puffed on her own reefer stick and drank from her own glass of champagne.

Sarinda said to the earth, *"Mister Elias Jakobi, these niggers sure will believe anything you tell them. That didn't last too long for you, I guess, with what happened with them unruly niggers in your service. My husband and I know what that was like. You remind me of my husband, Mister Jakobi. He was a great businessman too. And we was cursed with niggers as unruly as the ones in your possession."*

Delia's tears streamed harder seeing her grandaunt act this way. She grit her teeth. She was so mad she wanted to spit and scream curses. But she continued watching the peeling of her grandaunt. Sarinda declared to the ground, *"My husband will return to me, Mister Jakobi. He will come through me, and I will hold him."*

The picture showed Sarinda talking to Curly Burneside again. This time she ordered him to attack the female Negro servant that serviced her bath, believing her to be related to a prominent woman in Water Bug Hollow. *"Break her in. Do what you will, Curly."*

Delia shook her head, anger continuing to rise in her. Tears streaming like waterfalls. She bit her lip, sniffed and continued to view the moving history locked inside her father's works. There came a flow of manipulation after manipulation from Sarinda Fallows. She worked Delia's grandmother, her band, and manipulated the citizens of Water Bug Hollow. Unfulfilled promises were always dangled in front of Theresa and her band. There were minor opportunities with assurances to lead to greater things. Theresa sang her heart out, the veil strengthening her voice and presence for all audiences. Delia, however, was most disappointed in her grandmother's abuse of stimulants. Her grandaunt Sarinda introduced the narcotics to her grandmother, doing her best to catch Theresa off guard to ask her for the veil. All of Sarinda's efforts failed. Theresa always answered her in an intoxicated tone, *"No. My Pepper would not have it so."* Delia was happy to see that, she wiped her tears away the first time she heard her grandmother utter those words, not giving in even while inebriated. After Sarinda's fourth attempt, and after the fourth time Theresa Amat uttered the phrase, the picture reverted back to its original, still image.

The picture sailed back to the wall, and another took its place. A fog swirled in front of the picture painted in the work titled *Announcing Life*. When the dense fog cleared, more history was presented. Theresa Amat discovered she was pregnant, and was heartbroken that she may have put her unborn child in danger with her abuse of narcotics and liquor. Delia wiped her tears aside. Watching her grandmother become determined to beat her addictions for the sake of the child inside her, inspired Delia. Her tears disappeared altogether. The veil's enchantments were shown. The veil's thaumaturgy allowed Theresa to see the child inside her, presented as a little girl. Theresa gave the apparition a name. Philomena.

Theresa's visions and creative song writing played out on canvas. More impressive was Theresa's involvement in residential politics, calming the dangerous fervor that put Water Bug Hollow in a cold, civil war. Delia was also surprised at her grandmother's ability to give violent orders to put people in line and stop deliveries of narcotics into Water Bug Hollow.

Theresa Amat required the Water Bug Hollow citizens to call her *Mamma Indigo*. They did, paying Theresa great respect. But Theresa still called upon her mother for a cleansing ritual. She continued the ritual long after her family made a visit to Water Bug Hollow. Delia saw that her grandmother was not afraid to handle the consequences of her actions, even when those consequences brought organized crime to the Hollow. Delia's grandmother also handled these tense situations. Theresa credited the veil and her kinsfolk ritual. She decided to help her friend, Sarinda Fallows, convincing Sarinda to partake in a cleansing.

Delia shook her head as she watched her grandmother attempt to help Sarinda Fallows. The ritual went terribly wrong. Sarinda became sick. Everything went to hell. Delia could see that Sarinda Fallows, her grandaunt, was dying. Forgetting that Sarinda was alive and well and up the road inside the real Harlem Dixie, Delia felt relieved that Sarinda's life was expiring.

The ritual was indeed cleansing.

Theresa's concern for her friend was pushed aside as she went into labor. She teetered and tottered back to the bed. Lying down, she called for her watchman, granduncle Quincy. Delia folded her arms and observed the scenario closely. Quincy rushed into the room with his brother. Theresa yelled to him *"The baby's coming, Q!"* Delia started fiddling nervously. Quincy hurried from the room on Theresa's command. His brother stayed and attended to Sarinda Fallows. Bad had already walked into this scenario, but now Delia saw worse crash the party.

Sarinda fought against the cleansing, usurping the guardsman's life to keep her own. Granduncle Quincy returned with Water Bug Hollow's midwife and her nurses, but the lifeless body of his brother on the floor quickly distracted him. Sarinda screamed, and everything stopped!

Delia stood still. She bit at her thumbnail, eyes focused on the painting, waiting for what the picture would reveal next. She saw Sarinda step toward her grandmother's propped up body. The women's images disappeared from the scene, and Delia's eyes became wide. Her mouth hung open. Before she could protest for their images to return, she heard the voices of her grandmother and Sarinda Fallows.

Grandmamma. Grandaunt.

"You're going to give me that veil, you black witch. Tonight."

"I remember you. Yes, I do. Sarah. Sarah the Pantomime."

"I know you, Mamma Iyansan… It's a shame that your self-realization comes at the moment your corporeal form acts out its greatest drawback…You must have forgotten all about yourself the minute you were conceived physical and born through your mother's wretched, nigger womb."

Horatio noted the name and title Mamma Iyansan as he continued playing.

"I pass Joe's veil to my daughter."

"You don't believe I'll snatch it from her vile, pickaninny hands? You just cursed her life, Mamma Iyansan…Hekua hey Yansa!"

A door slammed! Theresa's body materialized on the bed. There was motion, and then there was life birthed. Mother and daughter screamed. Lightning flickered across the sky. A spear of light cut through the sky and changed the stars' appearance. Zigzagged. The sky opened, and a watery comet dripped to the earth. Its splash onto the ground turned the drip into a trumpet case. Theresa said dreamily, *"Dooley is a lilac flame, fluttering and flickering and shooting up into the sky where I see three moons reside…Ah, procure this grand conjure and wish."*

Theresa was gone. Philomena was here.

Violence flickered and flashed. Anger. Granduncle Quincy jumped to find Sarinda Fallows, but he couldn't go through with it. Gunshots! Screaming! A family slaughtered. Word of Joseph Pepper dead overseas.

Horatio stopped the music. The picture floated back to its position on the wall. The scenery remained as the Harlem Dixie. Delia said desperately to Horatio, "There's more…"

Horatio nodded. "I know," he replied in a low, exhausted voice. "Let me catch my breath." He sat on the ground and put the horn down next to him. He exhaled.

Delia joined him. "Have you seen all this before?" she asked him.

Horatio shook his head. "No," he answered.

"You said we shared a common story," Delia commented.

"I've seen images before. Not these," Horatio admitted. "My father composed songs that show a story, a past life. It ends with him dying aboard a slave ship. My mother's captive and pregnant with me. I continued the song, the story. I haven't finished it. You're there. Johnny. Your grandmother is there. Her name is Mamma Iyansan, just as your grandaunt addressed her before your grandmother gave birth to your mother. Sarinda recognized her in that moment before she gave birth. Your grandmother is an angel, your guardian angel. We're on a plantation. It's the early seventeen hundreds, I believe. Mid-seventeen hundreds maybe." He looked up at Delia and declared, "It's real." His tone sounded as if he was asking, *'Do you believe me?'*

Delia responded, "I believe you. I do. How could I not?"

Horatio felt relieved. "I'll show it to you, Delia. You'll see it after we catch up on all this." He looked at the paintings around the room. He asked, "You wanna finish the story now, or do you think we should get back to the Harlem Dixie?"

Delia cupped her hips with her hands. Her head dropped. "I don't know if I could look at my auntie after what I've seen," she said. She then asked Horatio, "Is she there? Is she in your father's story? My aunt?"

"It's more than a story, Miss Amat," Horatio stated defensively.

Delia's voice was just as subtly sharp when she retorted, "I understand, Horatio. I told you I believe. Forgive me, with all I've seen, that

I'm not hip and fresh on the lingo. Please, answer me. Is my aunt there?" There was still a sophisticated tone in her stern voice.

Horatio nodded affirmative. "Yes, she is, Miss Amat. So is Curly Burneside." Hands still on her hips, Delia shook her head. She scanned the paintings. Horatio rose from the floor, swiping the trumpet as he got to his feet. "Should we continue, Miss Amat?"

Delia took a long breath. She stuttered, tears coming to her. "I know my mother was forced to bed when she was fifteen by an authority figure in Water Bug Hollow. He was also a pastor. My mother told me when I was sixteen. It was her way to tell me to be careful of the local boys, and even the boys beyond the neighborhood, should I wander. I have to know if, uh, that's all here."

Horatio nodded. Before beginning to play he asked, "You ready?"

"No, but play."

Horatio resumed the mystical song. *Passing to Shadow* strayed from the wall and levitated in front of Delia. The first of her mother's tragedies played out in front of her. It was August twelfth, a sacred night that was now in dispute over its historicity and its ritual celebration. The night's keeping was tamed. People argued over Water Bug Hollow's proper genesis. Disagreements over the area's history turned violent. At the epicenter of it all was the new patriarch of Water Bug Hollow, Reverend and Mayor Lionel Ladon.

Politics aside, fifteen-year-old Philomena Amat provided the greatest observance, and Delia watched her mother practice for the night's service, her voice perfect.

"Philomena looks so grown. Don't you think, reverend? You could almost mistake her for a woman. Those curves. The way that dress hugs her ripe, young body. And that sky-blue dress against her golden-brown skin. Lord, I wish I had a glow like that. She will make a beautiful woman. Am I right, Reverend?"

The picture showed Sarinda Fallows talking to the new mayor, Reverend Lionel Ladon.

"...ripe enough for you, isn't it Lionel? When a young lady is just beginning to fill and feel herself out? You don't feel that urge anymore, do you Lionel? Power over them young girls."

Anger throttled Delia. It was like fire in her throat. She allowed it to possess her, but she didn't swell with tears. She refused. She held them back. The planted thought manifested after the reverend's sermon. As bad as things became, once again, worse crashed the party. Lionel Ladon assaulted young Philomena Amat.

Granduncle Quincy relieved Delia of her anger when he fired it from a pistol. Every bullet. He killed the reverend, and the Water Bug Hollow police killed him. Sarinda comforted Delia's mother. She put her to sleep with words. Eyes on the veil, Sarinda Fallows expressed, *"No aegis tonight. No comfort. Just watch. I'm mamma now."*

The painting returned to its former state, but didn't move back to the wall. Instead, another painting danced off the wall and came by its side. A shadowy, feminine figure worked desperately to burn the paintings she straddled, throwing her hair as fiery strands. The artistry washed away, replaced with history in motion.

Philomena, older, comforted a handsome man near the edge of town. He sat on a sturdy branch high atop a tree. He smoked as Philomena called up to him, *"I saw you run out your parent's house."* They talked about the young man's frustration with his parents wanting him to stay close to home when choosing a school to attend. Even before Philomena addressed him as *'Paul-baby'*, Delia gasped. She knew who the man was. It was Paul Benson, her father.

Delia was happy. Here was her father, young and handsome. And her mother looked so joyful. Delia wished she could be there, born nine months earlier than when she was conceived. Held by her mamma and papa.

They talked about their current lives, their art—Philomena's gift of song and Paul's gift of sketch and paint. They discussed Paul's frustration with his parents, and their possible future together. Delia winced when she heard her mother suggest that her father show his paintings to Sarinda Fallows. He reluctantly agreed after she coaxed him with how it would all happen.

Sure enough, after an apology and reconciliation with his parents, Paul Benson, that weekend, was showing off his work to Sarinda Fallows. She was intrigued, taken in by Paul's work. Their magical purpose was revealed to her, and left her stunned. But neither Paul nor Philomena saw the paintings animate. Only Sarinda knew. And so she devised a plan, feigning interest in helping Paul jumpstart a career as an artist. She had a contact. Yes, she did. His name was Curly Burneside. Paul Benson and Philomena Amat were enticed. The future they wanted was now a possibility. Delia mouthed a warning to her father as she saw he and her mother put together the paintings that were on display and recounting all these stories. But the warning was of course unheard, and Paul Benson helped Sarinda Fallows take his artwork to New Orleans to show Curly Burneside.

Delia then witnessed her father's murder. It was on his second trip into New Orleans. Sarinda Fallows received a call from Curly Burneside. He wanted to meet Delia's father earlier than expected. Delia dropped her face into her hand. Her father was excited and agreed to the meeting. Curly met them at a rundown warehouse.

Delia peeked through the fingers that covered her face. Her hand slid down from her eyes to her mouth. Curly greeted her father, and then he shot him. Delia saw her father fall back dead. The anger came to her again, but there was no one there to act on it this time. No one stormed in and shot the two perpetrators of her father's murder. Delia only took comfort in the fact that her grandaunt's attempts to burn her father's artwork came to nothing. She watched Sarinda's face contort in frustration as Curly made several attempts. She moved Curly aside and attempted to burn the paintings herself. Nothing happened.

Defeated, Sarinda and Curly snatched the paintings and left the warehouse. Paul Benson remained on the floor, dead and unaware of the real magic he'd produced. His purpose, Delia concluded, was served in the grand scheme of the story wherein she now played a role.

The painting's static artwork returned. Delia put her attention once again on *Passing to Shadow* as it spiraled into motion. Delia saw her mother, mourning and hysterical. She was drunk, dangerously so. Sarinda had been invited into her living quarters. She tried to calm Delia's mother, comfort her with false empathy played so wonderfully and malevolently sincere. The second breaking, the sorrow, and the alcohol pressured Philomena to declare, *"Here! My payment to you. Please. You always loved this. Take it. My payment."* The veil was now in Sarinda Fallows' hands. *"Make him shine like the sun. Please. Have Mister Burneside still showcase his art. Let it still be on display....And then you put them up in your club. You have my Paul-baby's art mounted, please, Aunt Sarinda. Please!"*

Sarinda now had the veil and Paul Benson's magical artwork. She put Philomena to rest, relieved her of the liquor in her body, and left Water Bug Hollow victorious and never to return. The painting's image came back. The artworks hung themselves back on the wall. Another work came forward. *A Baby's Toy* resumed the story where the last painting left off. Sarinda Fallows stepped out into the streets of Water Bug Hollow, veil in her possession, and a smile across her face. Sarinda announced, *"Goodbye, Water Bug Hollow."* And then she vanished through a shadow, bent time and space with her charm, and stepped out of twilight's contour into the New Orleans streets. She was veiled and proud.

Sarinda returned to her apartment. She danced and chanted. She could sing now, the voice and spirit of a great old, wise woman now trapped inside her. She showed off to Curly Burneside, expressed an ancient phrase, and wiped the veil over his face to turn him into another's mortal form. Sarinda called him Kenten, and she made love to this expressionless figure. This must've been her husband. A ghost. A shell. Delia looked away as the painting spared no moment of this act of love between them. Sarinda was shown enjoying Kenten's company twice. She remained veiled throughout the ordeal. Then she rubbed her belly with both her pendant and the veil, and she fell asleep.

Curly Burneside had returned when she awoke. He looked dazed, confused of the whole act, remembering it as a dream and asking if he had truly become *'Master Fallows.'* Another ritual was conducted with the veil atop Sarinda's belly and Curly's ring placed on her navel. Curly twirled the pendant above the ring, and Sarinda's belly grew pregnant. Her belly stretched and ballooned until she cried for Curly to call a doctor, labor pangs striking her. Curly called a doctor on the phone, and one showed up to oversee the delivery of Sarinda's child whom she named Stanley.

Delia's mouth hung open and her eyes widened, all in total disbelief. She witnessed Stanley being placed in a crib, her grandaunt Sarinda falling into slumber for rest, and Curly seeing the doctor and his nurse to the door, paying them substantially. A small noise leapt from Delia's gawking, open-mouthed stare. She saw Sarinda stir awake after rest. She woke Curly Burneside, and performed the same ritual on her newborn son that had been done on her belly. Baby Stanley aged two years.

The motion in the painting ceased, and the artwork took its original form and place back upon the wall. Horatio's notes reached an operatic crescendo, his head tilted to the sky. He ended the song on a heavy beat and burst of music. He walked away from Delia and placed the trumpet back into its case. The songbook returned to the table and landed next to the case, remaining open. The scene surrounding Delia and Horatio disassembled into the otherworldly, musical glyphs that transformed it earlier. The interior of the Harlem Dixie broke away into the musical characters like puzzle pieces. The On The Hour Club's charred interior was left behind as the glyphs funneled back into the mystical songbook.

Delia exclaimed, "There's more. There're more paintings. Horatio!"

"I've seen my father's murder enough times in my dreams," Horatio said nonchalantly over his shoulder. "And I have all the answers as to his murderers' motivations."

Delia rushed to Horatio's side pleading, "But there's a final painting. Please, Horatio. Please! It's you and your father. The two of you are playing, connecting our past lives. Please. I have to see it. I have to because I remember it. I can see it, Horatio!" She grabbed Horatio's arm and turned him around. "I remember more than just yesterday, Horatio. I remember yester-*life.*" She saw Horatio's surprised expression. She let go of him and spoke as she stepped away, "*My people could fly. Mamma and Papa flew away. Brother and sister went with them too. Up into the blue, they kissed the sun and hugged the moon. My heart was heavy, chambers echoing a melancholy melody. Nothing happy to make me lighter than gravity. My baby eyes had seen too much, smothering my imagination. I just see the tragedy surrounding me.*"

Horatio picked up the horn, but instead of playing he listened to Delia recite.

"*Mamma Iyansan protected me when the slave master wanted me. Beat me. Head under water. Beaten for being my father's daughter. Beat with a collective jealously come from generations before. Angry years in this slave master's might. Beaten for being the last of my family's light. They escaped, magically flown away. And here I was, a dove plucked of its feathers. A symbol of peace come to pieces. The slave master on top of me, ready to take me. Then Mamma Iyansan kissed me invisible. Kissed me from existence. But I saw many killed for my sudden disappearance. Now, here I am. 3 years past ten. Whole again. Mamma Iyansan told me about you.*" She pointed to Horatio. "*Mojuba. I know your name. You will help me reclaim my family. Reconstruct my invisible wings. Fly to an invisible island and reunite with them.*"

Horatio blew into his horn. The seared stage behind him melded anew. He turned around and jumped onto it, horn blazing. The scene around them melted away. Delia turned her back to Horatio as Pete Peters' past life came to life in front of her. There he was as the flirtatious poet in an al-Andalusian night with tantalizing words that seduced Virginia Tara-

Peters as Mother Harmony. Then another life emerged after the first life faded. It was in Africa. Horatio's father and mother studied ancient theologies. The wrong prayers went up to the heavens and brought slavery to the entire continent. Africa falling. Betrayal by blood. Horatio's voice narrated his conception. Then came enslavement. Slave ship dirges. Horatio's father tossed overboard, but his voice becoming the waves in the sea. Terror instilled into an unborn child, seen through his mother's eyes. Birth and separation. Plantation.

There she was. Mwana. Hiding, invisible to the world. Ghostly. Talking up to her grandmother as an angel. Mamma Iyansan. Horatio—Mojuba—could see her. So could the slave master's daughter. "Auntie…?" Delia whimpered with new tears. She recited in a low whisper as she stared at the scene of her discovery, "*Tall, wild red hair. The master's daughter. A shark lives on land. She beams seductive. Interested smile aimed at the slave-hands. Intrigued black men found dead in the field when their thoughts bleed her. And she entertains their flesh and thoughts. Her smile stands over me. Red, gleaming glow glittering from her lips. Flat stone pendant speckled with red markings dangling from a necklace, twirled through her fingertips.*"

Visible and captured. The song and images faded on that note.

Horatio stepped off the stage, and it returned to its dilapidated form as he walked away. He put the trumpet in its case and walked up behind Delia. He put his arms around her. She had been exposed to so much.

"Take me back to Brooklyn with you," she asked of Horatio.

"I don't think your grandaunt would…"

"She's not my blood, Horatio!" Delia declared. "She stole my blood. Her closeness to my grandmother and mother was to fulfill a purpose. I can't. I can't do it, Horatio. I can't be in the same house as her. I can't stand next to Stanley. He's not real."

"All of this is real, Miss Amat," he reminded. "Respect everything you see. Respect everything in nature. If you disrespect it, it will attack." Horatio tightened his embrace. "I'll come and scoop you up in the morning. We can't let Miss Fallows, or Stanley—if he knows anything—suspect that you know anything."

Delia wiggled from Horatio's embrace. "*You damn fool!* You damn fool, Horatio Peters. Don't call me Miss Amat. I've told you that." She said over her shoulder. "You call me Mwana. You call me Delia." She spun around to face him. "Hell, call me 'baby' for all I care, but give me a name."

"I apologize, Delia."

"Thank you!" She straightened herself in a cool, relaxed manner. "Now you listen good, Mister Horatio Peters. Listen up. All that harpy needs to know is I want to practice with you. We walked, talked, and we lost time. You were excited to hear my songs. I'm excited to sing with a group of musicians: you and Johnny. Wednesday can't wait. I'll call and tell them I'm spending the night. I'll insist."

Horatio stayed silent.

Delia elucidated, "This would be an appropriate time for you to address me as ma'am or Miss Amat. *Yes, Miss Amat.*"

Horatio took a breath. "Yes, Miss Amat." He smirked as he added, *"Delia."*

She strode by Horatio, hips swaying. She said back to him as she made her way toward the exit, "You play your cards right, Horatio Peters, and you just might get a kiss. Come. Let's go."

Horatio stared at Delia, her walk waving like a snake's movement as she made an exit. He said to himself, "Woman, you don't need a trinket. You got natural magic." He locked up the trumpet case, left it on the table, and followed Delia back to the burned restroom. They crawled carefully through the window, exited the alley, and walked up the street.

"Thank you, Horatio. I needed that. My heart needed that." She took a moment and a careful step to turn and kiss Horatio on the cheek and keep walking. "I came here for my grandmother's veil and my father's art." She thought for a moment and then commented, "That harpy's pendant. It makes me nervous."

"Don't be," assured Horatio, his voice low. "The horn's music turned the stone in Curly's ring to dust. The blood-speckled stone's properties have their limits."

"She also has my grandmother's veil," Delia reminded. "Magic can be imperfect. It heightened my grandmother's awareness, but she couldn't see the devil standing right there in front of her. But, I'm sure Miss Harpy Fallows is very aware of that veil's properties." Delia grit her teeth. "She had my grandfather killed. He understood all this. So did your father."

"Delia. Relax."

Delia inhaled and exhaled.

"If you can't," continued Horatio, "then when we get to Brooklyn, I'll play a song to calm you. Put you at ease."

Delia assured, "I can gain my composure once we return to the Harlem Dixie. Even so, I would like very much to hear this calming song, Horatio. I need to be put at ease."

"Yes, Miss Amat."

Delia grinned. "You're learning, Horatio. Good."

They entered the Harlem Dixie, door held for them. Delia walked into the main ballroom, Horatio behind her as her sentry. Johnny still played the piano. He smirked as Delia and Horatio entered the room. He stopped playing and asked, "We all caught up?" Horatio looked around. He, Johnny, and Delia were alone. Sarinda and Stanley had not yet returned. "They ain't back yet, man," Johnny affirmed.

But no sooner had he said that did Sarinda Fallows and her son Stanley enter the room. "Oh," Sarinda uttered. "You've returned. That wasn't long."

"It wasn't?" Delia inquired incredulously.

"It's been about ten minutes. Maybe fifteen," Sarinda answered.

Delia looked at Horatio. He nodded his head and told her braggingly, "It use to take longer, but I've become good like that, Miss Delia."

Sarinda chuckled. She walked toward Horatio and tapped him on the back as she ambled around him. She whispered into his ear, "Don't boast too much about being quick, young boy. You just learn to take your time."

Horatio smirked. "I handle all things like jazz, Miss Fallows. I know how to draw out the climax of a song."

Sarinda stood up straight, face struck with surprise. Balled fists went to her hips. She turned her head to Johnny and remarked, "Well, ain't that a thing? I'm supposed to let my grandniece hang with you boys? I thought you were gentlemen."

Johnny played the piano lightly. He shook his head and reminded Sarinda with a grin, "He got Harlem in his blood, Miss Fallows. Harlem. In. His. Blood."

"And, Auntie Sarinda, Wednesday can't wait!" Delia exclaimed. "It just can't. I want to accompany the boys back to Brooklyn."

Sarinda's face lit up. "That's a wonderful idea."

Delia was ready to argue with Sarinda, but was caught off guard by her answer. "It is, Auntie? I was expecting you to put up a fight."

"Nothing is going on here tonight but some of them rock-and-roll acts," Sarinda explained. "It's going to be loud, and I don't want you three around. I'd rather have you all practicin'. Just call if you'll be late. We'll send a car." She waved her hands as if shooing Horatio and Delia away. "So go on to Brooklyn. Johnny, introduce my niece to them boys you know. Let the whole band meld. I want you to be the perfect act, Delia. I want you ready either by Friday or Saturday. A big day."

"Why thank you, Auntie."

"Until then, let's have a nice brunch," Stanley suggested. He called to Johnny, "That sandwich and beer hold you up, or can you do more?"

Johnny replied while still playing the piano, "Ain't arrived yet, Mister Fallows." He never looked up.

"Well, that will be your order." Stanley said to Delia and Horatio, "I'll get the waiter back in here and we'll order something. Ma, you in for eats?"

"Absolutely, Stanley. That's not a problem." She called, "Come on, Johnny. Your finger work on that piano is remarkable and soothing, but come on down here and keep us company. Close."

Johnny lifted his fingers from the piano keys. He turned to his audience and grinned. "Are you flirtin' with me, Miss Fallows?"

Sarinda responded, "Boy, get on down here with your charmin' self!"

Johnny stood and walked down off the stage. The party sat at a table near the dance floor, menus already placed at each seat. Stanley disappeared from the ballroom. He returned with a waiter in tow that held a bottle of the Harlem Dixie's best champagne. Stanley placed down crystal glasses in front of everyone. He took a seat just as the waiter opened the bottle of champagne with a flick, pop, and fizz. The waiter poured the champagne and asked the table if they were ready to order. Johnny informed that a meal was coming to him. Sarinda knew what she wanted for herself, as did Stanley. Delia and Horatio needed more time. The waiter respected that and walked away to put in Sarinda and Stanley's orders.

Delia tried not to stare at Sarinda. Even when Delia did look up at her, she tried hard to see the devil, but all she saw was the woman she called grandaunt. Sarinda's wide, pretty smile Delia tried to see as sinister, her charm as manipulation, and her bubbly laughter as a cackle. But there was no fire, no brimstone surrounding her. Delia knew not to trust the smile, the charm, or the bubbling laughter. Aunt Sarinda was a deceptive woman, and Delia understood that.

Delia's eyes wandered to Stanley as conversation and laughter popped from person to person. He looked human enough, she thought as an overwhelming urge to reach out and touch his features gripped her. Delia's eyes cast sorrow onto Stanley, which she quickly blinked away before anyone noticed. But it wasn't only the public setting that prevented Delia from reaching out and inspecting Stanley with her hands and a closer eye. It was also because she didn't want to embarrass him. On that, Delia concluded again, Stanley Fallows was human despite his unnatural conception. She didn't blame Stanley for what his mother did to him.

Concluding her judgment of Stanley, her eyes were drawn back to Sarinda. Delia considered her manipulation knew no bounds. It even touched her unnatural son.

Delia jumped into the exchange, smiling and giggling more at the talk around the table, trying to disguise her inspections of her grandaunt and cousin.

Then, Sarinda lifted her glass. "What shall we toast to?" she asked.

Horatio made it simple. "To music," he said.

Everyone agreed and clanked glasses.

Mythic Mojo Moon
"We all have our tricks, Mister Gregory."

It was getting dark. The Harlem Dixie's lights burst to life as the mid-fall season forced the sun to retreat early. The club's marquee lit up with the night's act and distracted Johnny from the road as he pulled up to the front of the building. His imagination erased the names tacked up against the white, lighted board and replaced them with his name and Horatio's. He also saw the words: *And Introducing Miss Delia Amat.* "Hot damn!" he blurted to himself as he again concentrated on pulling up to the curb.

Horatio and Delia waited patiently in front of the club, Sarinda and Stanley Fallows accompanying them. Each wore a jacket to ward off the mid-fall chill that now accompanied dusk's onset. Horatio stepped to the car as it slowed and stopped inches from the curb. He opened the rear door and waved Delia politely inside. Delia thanked Horatio and ducked into the backseat. She took the trumpet case from Horatio, and then made a final goodbye wave to Sarinda and Stanley just as Horatio closed the door. Horatio turned and shook Stanley's hand with both of his.

"Thank you, Stanley," said Horatio. He addressed Sarinda, "And you too Miss Fallows, for this opportunity." He let go of Stanley and concluded, "Miss Amat will be home safe and sound later tonight."

Stanley insisted, "Call, please. We'll send a car."

"Will do, Stanley." Horatio then said to Sarinda, "Again, thank you Miss Fallows for all of this."

"The pleasure is all mine, Mister Parker." Sarinda thought a moment. She asked as Horatio opened the passenger door, "What name would you like to appear on the marquee? Davis or Horatio?"

"Use his proper name, Miss Fallows," Johnny joked from the car. "Keep his mamma from comin' up here and whuppin' his behind." Horatio turned to Johnny as Sarinda, Stanley and Delia chuckled. Johnny said to Horatio, loud enough for everyone to hear, "Please, boy. Y'mamma gave you a proper name. Use it."

Horatio smiled as he shook his head and replied to Sarinda's question, "I guess that settles it. Davis Horatio Parker."

Sarinda slapped his arm and said through a laugh, "You gon' get your middle name in there one way or another, ain'tchu."

Stanley suggested, "How about D.H. Parker." Horatio's face lit up at the suggestion, forgetting Davis Horatio Parker wasn't his real name. But the initials with the last name sounded great to him. Stanley noticed. "Sounds professional, don't it." Then Stanley said while waving his arm, acting as if he was putting each word into the sky. "D.H. Parker on the horn." He looked back at Horatio for a reaction. "How's that sound to you?"

Horatio took Stanley's hand and responded excitedly, "That sounds wonderful, Stanley. Wonderful indeed."

"It's settled then," Sarinda spoke. "Now, go on. Go practice, Mister D.H. Parker On The Horn."

"You two have a good night, Miss Fallows," said Horatio sliding into the car.

"We will," she assured.

Horatio closed the door. He, Johnny, and Delia waved through the window. Johnny pulled onto the road and up the street. Horatio still tingled with the excitement of the professional name bestowed upon him. Delia looked through the back window and watched Sarinda and Stanley enter the club to get it ready for the night's session. She turned around and sighed. She noticed Horatio's grin and said, "That ain't your name, Horatio."

Horatio blinked. His determined mood returned, remembering Sarinda Fallows' true nature. He became focused. "Damn," he said as if waking up from being knocked unconscious. "Sorry about that," Horatio spoke aloud. It didn't appear as if his apology was to either Johnny or Delia.

"Well, it was a lot easier gettin' that harpy to agree to me leavin' than I suspected it would be," Delia remarked. "Maybe the conversation over the phone will be much more of a fight when I decide to stay the night."

"Possibly," said Horatio curled up to the window and staring at the passing buildings. His thoughts scrolled through his head no differently than the buildings on the street as they passed by. "She just might let you do that too."

"Really?" wondered Delia. "Why?"

Horatio looked back at her. He let out a breath and then looked forward as Johnny turned right. "I'd thought that'd be obvious." He cleared his throat. "She knows."

"You think so?" Delia inquired with an incredulous tone.

"I believe she suspects. She got to." He said turning back to Delia, "With all she can manipulate and see with her pendant, and your grandmother's veil at her command…" He faced forward again. "I know she got a feelin'. At least, I'm gon' stay overly suspicious. That'll keep my senses sharp."

Delia sat up, pulling herself up by grabbing onto Horatio's seat. She asked in a sincere tone, "What you plan on doin', Horatio?"

Johnny drove past several streets, and then he looped around to make the block. Now, the On The Hour ruins were just up ahead. Horatio answered Delia, "I have an idea." His voice was sorrowful. He played with his fingers and looked down at them, chin tucked to his chest.

"You know we there for you, Horatio," reminded Johnny as he slowed down in front of the dilapidated On The Hour club.

"Yep," Horatio replied as he opened the door and got out.

Delia sat back. She watched Horatio disappear into the alley, going to retrieve his otherworldly horn stashed inside the ruins. She asked Johnny, "You seen that history? He's played it for you?"

Johnny nodded, then answered audibly to ensure Delia knew. "Yeah, I've seen it. Horatio played all types of stories through that horn." He adjusted himself in the seat and began watching the traffic pass by. "I got to see all aspects of my father. Other sides of him I didn't know." He looked in the rearview and addressed Delia, "My father just came from prison. He pulled a Judas against Horatio's father. Sold him out. Informed Pete Peters' killers where he could be found. He made sure Horatio's father was there at that time."

"Oh," Delia murmured.

"Yeah. That's what my pops went in for." Johnny gripped the steering wheel hard. He relaxed and said, "I picked my pops up when he was released, just yesterday. He was very sorry. He explained the story as to why. He'd thought I was Pete Peters' child. But, that wasn't the case. I figure Miss Fallows had a hand in manipulatin' that." He turned his body and remarked, "I figure you've seen things from your side of the story, as well as our past lives."

Delia nodded. "Sure have, Johnny." She beamed teasingly, "Li'l Chew."

Johnny turned around, exhaling a laugh. "Aw, hell. Don't know what kind of nickname that is. I can't hear the narration, but Horatio tell it to me. He says the story don't say if other Negro slaves gave it to me or if slavin' white folks did." He peered into the dark alley, looking for Horatio to emerge.

Delia fixed her shirt just to do something with her hands. "Miss Fallows—that harpy—she's done a fair share of manipulatin' on my side of the story. My grandmother. My mother. She orchestrated my father's murder just like she did Horatio's." She asked Johnny, "You all put down Curly Burneside—is that his name?"

"That was his name, Miss Amat," Johnny answered looking forward. "And, yes, we did put him down. Horatio didn't show you that?"

Delia shook her head. "No. I had to argue with him to show me the story composed by his father, and now him. Our past lives. He figured we might've been takin' too much time—at least that's what he told me. He probably thought I'd be overwhelmed, especially after what I'd seen—that harpy manipulatin' my mother and grandmother. The terrible things she'd done to destroy their hometown. Eventually, Horatio showed me that long song of our past lives. I started to remember even before he played the story for me." Delia felt a cold come over her. When she inhaled she felt as if there was ice in her throat. She pulled her jacket tighter around her. "This all seems so odd. But regardless of what it seems, and whether or not I'm ready, I'm happy to be with you all when the trigger is pulled on Miss Sarinda Fallows."

"I don't know if Horatio's plan calls for the pulling of any trigger," Johnny mentioned. "We'll see." Johnny then pointed out, "You know, no one can lift that horn but him? That's some magic."

Delia remarked, "We all have our tricks, Mister Gregory. That one was meant for Horatio and his father, I suppose."

Johnny nodded with approval and said, "I guess you right." He spotted Horatio coming from the alley, trumpet case and songbook in hand. Horatio opened the passenger door and hopped in. "Oh, and Miss Amat, my last name's Concheroot. My mother's name is Gregory. She had me use it when my father was sent to jail." He watched for traffic and calculated where he could ease back into its flow. Johnny drove off. "I also don't want to use it in case your grandaunt knows the name." He asked Horatio, "You got everything, right? I ain't goin' back."

"Everything got, Negro," Horatio answered. "Keep drivin'."

"That's good to know, Jonathan *Concheroot*," Delia interjected. "I too have a correction to make. Miss Sarinda Fallows—that harpy—is *not* my family."

"Yes, ma'am," Johnny acknowledged.

They drove to Brooklyn. Delia's eyes, wide, inhaled every site Manhattan had to offer, and Brooklyn as well. It was dark, but Delia could still see. She was never going back to Louisiana, and she was going to find a way to bring her mother here. She was further impressed when they arrived in Johnny's neighborhood, looking around at all the brownstones glowing with a faint, golden-brown ambience from the streetlights.

Inside, Johnny introduced Delia to his mother, informing his mom, "Miss Amat is a singer from Baton Rouge, Louisiana. Horatio and I are gonna be her band. Morgan and Black Cue too. Miss Fallows is close friends with her family. Delia even calls Miss Fallows 'auntie'."

"Oh, that's lovely," Johnny's mother exclaimed. "Well, I can heat what was leftover from last night if you all are hungry."

Johnny kissed his mother on the cheek. "We had something before we left the club, Ma, but it was light. We could use somethin' fillin'. Thank you." He looked at Horatio and Delia. "That okay with you two? You got room?" Johnny slapped his stomach. Horatio and Delia nodded approvingly and gave thanks. Johnny waved them into the family room. "Go on inside, there. You two relax. I'll help my mom."

The parties went their separate ways. Miss Gregory commented to Johnny as they entered the kitchen, "That Delia is a lovely young woman."

Johnny smirked. "She's takin' a liking to Horatio, Ma."

"Well ask if she has any friends to settle you down, boy."

Johnny flapped his lips. "They'd all be southern girls. I had my share when I was down there with Horatio…"

Johnny's mother gasped. "Excuse me, boy!"

Johnny laughed as he braced himself against several slaps on his arm from his mother. "What, Ma? What? I'm a growin' boy."

"You see? These city gals got you hot and runnin' around and runnin' up in anything."

Johnny disagreed. "Not anything, Ma," he said opening the cupboard and pulling out several plates. "I got standards. They might be low, but I got 'em."

Johnny's mother slapped his arm again, this time harder. "Boy!" she hissed playfully.

In the other room, Horatio continued to pen *The Son Dial Tone* inside the songbook. Delia watched him, her eyes possessed with curiosity. Horatio noticed her. He grinned. "I can see it as I write," he told her. "Quick flashes, not like when the song is actually played." He lifted the pen off the page and rotated his hand. "It all just comes and comes. I can hear and see at the same time, but I guess the imagery has to give as I'm writing." He said looking at Delia, "I should have something by tonight." He went back to writing, his eyes on the page. "I think you should go home tonight. You should take that ride Stanley's offering you."

"And risk a convenient accident?" Delia questioned. "Oh, no." She put her hand on Horatio's wrist. He stopped composing and looked up at her. "I feel safe here. I'd like to play this off your hunch that this harpy knows or suspects."

Horatio saw in Delia's expression that the matter was settled, and there would be no more arguing. Horatio saw her point, and he agreed to it. "Okay. You put up your fight over the phone, and you stay here." He returned to writing. "Until then, I compose, we eat, and then we end this past life to see where we're going in this one." He smirked and shook his head.

"What?" Delia asked. "What's so funny?"

"Well," Horatio answered, "I can only imagine what Miss Fallows is going through. She pulled all sorts of strings to snatch that veil from your grandmother. She went through a lot of trouble. But your mother's birth prolonged her efforts. At the same time came this horn to Earth, and my father composing this song through it, learning all the magical notes from Jackson and Gaston Fable. My father's past life never crossed paths with Miss Fallows, but he must've seen somethin' that made her orchestrate his death. Maybe it was just because he had this horn, and had an instrument at his fingertips to take away her power. He's got a song in here called *Merkaba Jazz* about how we all connected. Maybe he saw how Miss Fallows connected to him—who she was. Whatever the answer, Miss Fallows handled that. She handled your mother, breaking her spirit little-by-little.

She got the veil. She took your father's paintings and all the answers drawn into them. She probably thought she was in the clear." Horatio's smile widened. "But, then you came to town wantin' 'em. And here I am, though she may or may not believe who I've told her I am. She might know. I'm sure all the while she's been walkin' this Earth the way she has, well, she must be overly suspicious of everything. Besides, Curly's dead. She has to know why, and if so, it's only so long before her story ends too. Even Methuselah was put to rest."

"What about Stanley?" Delia inquired. "Should he go too?" There was remorse in her voice at the thought of killing Stanley Fallows. She did like him, and she felt he was genuine despite his mother or his conception.

"I'm sure he's innocent of all this. Ain't no one that good an actor." He looked at Delia by cocking his eyes up at her. "But, we just might have to bury the whole family to make sure. I hate to say that. It makes me sound evil, even if I'm just bein' cautious. I don't like where caution is takin' me. Takin' us." His eyes went back to the paper, and Horatio continued composing. "But this is war. Sarinda put her child in danger when she brought him into this world and performed her tricks on him. I believe she has a plan for Stanley." He sighed. "Miss Fallows really thought that all this time she's been here, with every Negro she beat, saw beat, or orchestrated the death of, she really did think she was preventin' this moment—the end of her tale."

"Oh, I don't know, Horatio," said Delia. "I think she knows she was only prolongin' it. Like the last note in the strongest improvisation, we are at the end."

Horatio stopped writing. He tapped the tip of the pen onto the page. "No more."

Delia looked down at the composition in surprise. "You've finished?"

"Oh, no. Not the whole composition," Horatio explained. "The song faded, is all. No more images. Even magic needs to rest. All I can do now is play the song through the horn. That'll give enough time for the memories to come back to me, and I can compose again. That's how it's been workin'. We'll play the new section of the song after dinner. Even if we have time now, I'm just tired. I apologize."

"No need, Horatio. You've worked real hard with magic today." Delia cautiously reached for the songbook. "May I hold it? I'd like to see the song?"

Horatio handed the book to Delia. "Go ahead," he replied to her. "The symbols are far different than music nowadays, just some weird scripts. They make sense to me though. Musically."

Delia perused the composition Horatio was working on, and also flipped back through Horatio's father's works written early in the book. She remarked, "They make sense to me too, Horatio. They do. I know what each symbol's tone is expressing." She remarked, "I think I could actually sing these notes."

"Not surprising," said Horatio. "My mother could do the same when my father played the notes through the horn. Johnny can play them on the piano when I play the horn."

Johnny's head peeked in and he informed Horatio and Delia that dinner was being heated up. He left shortly after. Delia and Horatio passed the time with conversations about their families, growing up in Louisiana, and music. Little time was spent talking about the day's events or any mystical notations scribed in the songbook. That could wait for later.

Dinner was served twenty minutes from Johnny's announcement, and everyone gathered in the dining room. There was a prayer lead by Johnny's mother, and then they all started to feast, passing around dishes and bowls filled with portions.

Most of the talking centered on Delia, Johnny's mother asked all the questions. She inquired, in a motherly way, on everything ranging from Delia's upbringing to her ambitions. It was a bit interrogative. However, Delia didn't mind, even when Johnny protested. She said, "Miss Gregory, with this food here, I'll answer anything you ask. This food makes me feel right at home." The next question was if Delia had any friends as lovely as she that Johnny could be introduced to. Delia laughed, covering her mouth as she tried to chew and not choke. Getting herself together, swallowing and clearing her throat, she answered Johnny's mother, "I do indeed have a few friends I could introduce to your Johnny. The marryin' type, Miss Gregory. We'll have to get him back down South, or maybe I can bring them up here."

When dinner was finished, Johnny and his mother cleared the table. Johnny insisted that Delia and Horatio not touch a thing. He and his mother would clean. Johnny said to Horatio, "Take Delia on a house tour. You know it well by now. Show her the view from the roof."

Horatio and Delia left the dining area. Horatio first walked to the family room, swiped the songbook off the couch, and picked up the trumpet case. His earthly instrument was left behind in the room. He and Delia walked to the front hall and grabbed their jackets off the coat rack. Then, Horatio led Delia to the guestroom. "You think Miss Gregory might suspect somethin' fresh happenin' up here between you and me?"

Horatio replied with a grin, "If I was her son, yes. But she knows I'm respectable." He opened the door and turned on the lights. He stepped aside and let Delia enter. He followed her inside and tossed the songbook onto the bed. Horatio then slapped the trumpet case atop it. The case bounced from the bed's buoyancy.

"Don't put that old, dirty thing on those clean sheets," Delia hissed.

Horatio lifted the case and took it over to the dresser drawer. "Yes, ma'am," he said with subtle sarcasm that Delia didn't catch. He opened the case and removed the horn. He turned to Delia and asked, "You ready?"

Delia nodded her head. Horatio played a few notes, and Delia's eyes shut. She believed that she would be rushed away to their past life, returning to the world of colonial slavery. But, the darkness behind her eyes remained, and her body felt the night's cool air. Delia's eyes opened and she realized she and Horatio were now on the roof of the brownstone. She walked to the ledge to look out at the neighborhood that glimmered by way of the streetlights.

"Be careful," warned Horatio. "We're really here. This ain't an illusion like when we was inside On The Hour. This is real. Watch your step."

Delia heeded Horatio's warning. But her smile continued beaming as she looked out at Brooklyn. The cold tickled her, and she tightened her jacket. Delia looked up, her smile aimed at the glittering heavens. "Not a cloud anywhere, Horatio. Not one. The heavens look handsome," Delia commented. "But I'd like to see the clouds come together. If they did, I bet it could snow. It seems cold enough." She turned to Horatio. "I've never seen it snow, Horatio, except in picture shows and television."

"Me too, Delia," Horatio replied softly. He waved the trumpet and asked, "Would you like for me to grant your wish?"

Delia chuckled. She gazed at the sky again and thought about Horatio's offer. She looked at him and said, "Your offer is tempting, Horatio. But I'd rather wait and let it snow naturally. And we could watch it snow together."

Horatio bowed his head at the neck. "Yes, ma'am." He raised the trumpet and said, "I think we need a little more protection than only our jackets from the chill." He played a few notes and the outside temperature no longer had an effect on he and Delia. Thwarting the mid-fall chill made Horatio feel better being outside on the roof. He and Delia's breaths still condensed in the night, but their Southern-blooded frames and blood felt no nip from the cool weather. "Glad that worked," Horatio remarked as he rubbed his temple with the back of his thumb. "I saw my father play the same melody to start a fire. I just played it in a different key, made it lighter. Was prayin' I wouldn't set us ablaze."

Delia huffed playfully, "We're in enough danger as is, Horatio. No need to experiment with these tricks."

He agreed. But there were other matters. "And now, Miss Amat," started Horatio, "our feature presentation."

The jazz trumpeter started playing. He and Delia lifted from the building, the songbook rising with them and opening. The world melted away from them, and then it reformed to a life before. Both Delia and Horatio braced themselves for the imagery to come. The scene opened to an afternoon on the plantation. Horatio as Mojuba Kimoyo, now at the age of nineteen, was digging the graves of three dead males. Black men freed from slavery.

I talk to the dead — skitter and scat
My chit chat with them
My breath carried by seagulls
3 dots, hip-hop jive from the heart
4,4 my 6,8
I'm conversing with those
Referred to as 'the late'
"How have you been, my brothers
You now emancipated slaves?
Your afterlife is better than this life.
Tell Mamma Iyansan that I wish to see her soon
Send my prayers up into the air and whisper, 'hello'

If Mwana too is there — she disappeared so long ago
I can recall her melodic screams' echo
Dragged to the master like a convict to the gallows
He made her scream. And then he screamed curses
Again she disappeared before her violent sentence
Four black slave girls of the same age took her place
Relentless punishment upon them
You remember, don't you? Those four,
Four of many that went to the afterlife before you.
Give my prayers to them too."
Six feet deep. I tuck my brothers into an eternal sleep
Just so their souls can seep
And creep through the ground to soar heaven bound
The day bleeds black into routine
I believe, we've died to the dead

There are no days of the week
Weak and dazed, us as slaves
"Live loop, loop life, cycle, pattern"
Guessing and hoping games
On who will be freed from life today
I've lived this life since the first day
18 years have all been the same
But on the first day of 19,
I come clean as it rains
Standing outside the slave shack
Drizzles drip and outline an invisible, feminine frame
Giggling happily
Invisible eyes stare at me

Mwana, a year younger than I, but
Matured, aged womanly grace
With an ethereal, flirtatious grin on her translucent face
Mwana returned to me, unseen and ghostly
She looked both ways
Mamma Iyansan's rain washed the presence
Of the slave master and his associates away
And so, she steps from out of the mystery

Physical black, arms around me

She whispers,
"My shadow swallowed me and my scream followed me
Peeling my flesh from physical reality
Before the slave master bit into me, took my body
I drowned in waves of invisibility
And fed on the music of my own inner-G
The goddess within

Mojuba, I am alive, and I have music to teach you
Unheard harmonics that will release you when spoken
Open the four chambers of the heart to climb the throat
Focus the vision of the blurred eye that lies
        On the inside of your mind
And let bloom the flower wide atop your crown
I can teach you sounds that can pull thunder from the clouds
        And bury it into the ground
To make the earth rumble and bubble
Mamma Iyansan gave me these lessons
When I was cloaked invisible."

Her lips kiss my cheek
She exhales relief,
I no longer hold my breath either
Mwana has returned to me
I too can now breathe
I lead her into the slave shack
All the way into the back, into a corner
Eyes and whispers loud
Shining on us, flickering stares resonating
Wonder
Mwana, the whisper and shade — the missing girl
The subtle harmony, volume raised in our presence
Music underneath her footsteps
Everyone is silent
The sun's clouded song dims below the horizon
And the rain continues to play into the night

Mwana hides invisible, covered in shadow
House slaves give daily bread to us
Overseer, Curly, watching

Gone. Away. Safe. Mwana appears
Like lightning out of the blue
She asks all to gather,
I, with Li'l Chew peep outside through the doors
Save the clouds in the sky, and their rain, all is clear

Mwana's voice is like a hum
Sweet, singing
"Listen close
I bring mystical, musical notes
Spells as ballads
Tapped from the heart
Magic spoken when lips part
When you sing harmonies as spirit
Prayers in lyrics
There, manifested, rah's hymn. Rhythm.
Words made physical
Manifested to create a vision
I call forth Mamma Iyansan
To put an end to these days
Heart of truth extended like the sun's rays."

Mwana pounds her chest,
The men beat with her
We surround her as warriors
Soldiers
We give words anu tone and breath
The seventh sun of the 7th cycle
Sets
Anu day rises
Heartbeats resurrect
The women's voices harmonize
Coil and spiral, rising into the sky
In the electrical palms of our hands

Swirling with the wind and condensing into thoughts
The men hold red, the women hold blue
We come together,
I hold Mwana — her blue mixed with my red
Hand in hand
We perform a purple rain dance

Mamma Iyansan condenses in the center
Of our festivity
Plucked from our mythology
She vibrates beauty
Resonates harmony
And she speaks to us,

"I blew out the 3 sources of light
Contemplated that my physical form would be
Partly day and partly night
I gave birth to my own life
And brought back the day with an idea 1000 times bright

Equaling 3, putting back the trilogy
1-by-1: the stars, moon, and sun
I sung the sunrise chorus in an off-key sunbeam
When my voice was Horus
And I pulled from space's womb the new moon
And I threw the stars in your eyes to keep my thoughts hidden from you
And always in d'skies
Forcing the conscious and curious to study astrology
To know more about me — but it ain't that easy

Forgive me when I don't appear when you call me
I don't come at a moment's notice
I come when I notice moments drawn as time's line
And line times 'I' without the proper prayer and song
Can equal a divide
So I make time flow with a musical sequence of thoughts 'I' cry
Dripping time in a matter of seconds
Where in seconds matter explodes

And reality and time erode away
I can drown you in a lake called life-stream
And it seems like so that as life flows
It grows into memories — harmonic, musical keys
'I' swimming in 'C' playing Sirius in 'E'

Naturally, my thoughts have been nurtured by nature
I tell you to keep your windows open
Even on cold, winter nights
So that you can get a rough…draft
Of thoughts to compose on paper later

Drop verses because the burden
Of your negative thoughts
Are too heavy to hold
So mold them on paper."

I'm brave to speak to Mamma Iyansan,
"I apologize. Forgive my outburst and cry
But we draw blank stares from blank paper."

But Mamma Iyansan has an answer,
"Then declare yourselves abstract painters
Divide the time between 'me,' 'myself,' and 'I'
And give no thoughts about the remainder

Sooner has left with later
And all that is left is now
Humble yourselves. Bow at the bass of musical bars
Swirl in the 'C' of electric stars and fill space with silence

This slavery is not your life
All of you are who I am
We are an hour past 11 p.m.
I know because I timed it
And the Orisha, Lwa, and Neteru signed it
It's true you are both Heru and Eshu
Please to meet you — I am Iyansan, Mother of 9 Rhymes

Rah's hymn, sun- and shadow-shaded children."

So night after night
We danced as our magic produced
A spiritual light
Mamma Iyansan gracing our presence
With anu lesson
A supreme musical alphabet
We learn to sing this language,
Uplift with voices winged and feathered
If English could speak or write, it would compose 26 letters

A is the All. B is the key of Being. C is where music floats and swims
D is the key of Divinity. E is our key of Equality
And we sing and we sing. F is our Flow, how we move and go.
The key of inner-G, our god inside. We sing in Harmony, H our key
Key, I, the self. We sing as we say, 'No Justice, no peace," in the key of J
The constant state of prayer, Kinetic, K musical key, inner god, inner-genetic
L, l-evates to the key of M, magnetic of which we N-joy
O sung to Open—ciphered filled with bliss
A seed from a single flower resonates the key P, our Power
Hitting every note, holding until timing is perfect, signaled all on Q
Our nation, Rhythm, Rah's hymn, sun drenched—key R, a blazing star
The key S-ence, the royal, mother's Truth—key of T—anointed oil
For the next key to reflect U, become you
Sing to make all things Visible, V for Victory—reclaim our true history
Increase you, sing you twice and W, and fold you
Until the unknown X blooms, and the great mystery is revealed
As we ask in the key of Y—how can we zigzag-Z through All this?

And with these new notes we sing
Harmonized with the faint, lingering screams
Of the dying
With these anointed, mystical musical notes
The slave master cannot hurt us
We sing with purpose
Communicate in the field by way of a supernatural chorus

We knead these blessed keys
Massaged with throat and tongue
Capture the warmth of the sun
When the day is too cold
Mend the bones of those too old
Slow digestion when our belly's ache
And food is scarce or light
We sing to use the moon's beams to keep us warm
Through the night

These are nu days—no daze
We sing chance, make moments dance
Song notes become circumstance
We swim in the musical note C
And see time at a glance

We slaves no longer need to walk
In that old way
One knee bent, pimp limp
Slow stroll,
While the arms swing and sway
We've been released
From carrying the burden of yesterday
Even if the scars still remain
Handed down like family heirlooms
As the past's air looms over us
When we dream it tries to choke us
Hang us by our roots from our ancient
Family tree
But the space in the sky is for rent
And so many stars are selling out
We all know this man builds on land to take up space

Curious eyes peep our celebrations
Red hair sneaks a look,
We dance as the light of stars swirl around us
We are living constellations
Many among us believe our music

Can soothe the master's savage lacerations
Herkus Bar is one of them
Scared, but intelligent—fate has him wait
For his moment
That sadly comes through tragedy

Over the weeks
Sister Ure and her Brother Nat
They store lightning
And thunder
In their bodies, readied for attack
On a clear day destined for a bloodstain
A field woman was out of place
A whip crack cuts into her back
And tensions snap
Brother Nat and Sister Ure act
Lightning uncoiled and cracked
Thunder rumbled
But first, Brother Nat simply cursed
No enchantment spoken through syllables and breath
Just a simple word – frustration expressed
        In a statement
Overseer Burneside, had words of his own
Descriptive slurs, and a whip at his command
Surprised when cracked, that Brother Nat
Took no lash, but grabbed the leathery cord
With his hand, unscathed – no wound, cut, or brand

Sister Ure releases her words
She sings her verse to wield
The force of thunder as a shield
Brother Nat's movements
Fluid like water and lightning
Pulling overseer Burneside close
And striking,
Quick, deadly
A martial medley
Two men creep forward, pistols at the ready

I come from the shack,
Hear two gunshots aimed for Brother Nat
His retaliation striking
His movements like lightning
Sister Ure, the thunder – her power
Overseer Burneside's two men
>   *Become a memory*
A tone resonates at the center of me
Ringing – a whisper, "Ring the re-bell."
And I want to dive into the pool of violence
Mamma Iyansan, naked of flesh and form
>   *Tells me to be silent*
Let the voice just whisper
"There is no need to let the whisper scream."
I stay my hand
Herkus Bar watches next to me
He shakes anxiously – his expression uneasy
Desperate for peace
A possible reality that dies quickly
The slave master joins the fight
And he's quickly struck down by Sister Ure's might
Dead – hope in our eyes as the slave master dies

Summer becomes colder than ice

Wide, curious eyes peep
Red hair sneaks a look
Moves closer – confident glow on her lips
Flat stone pendant speckled with red markings
Dangling from a necklace, twirled through her fingertips
The slave master's daughter
Brother Nat and Sister Ure move to attack her
Her charm abrogates their power
Wounded, Overseer Burneside
Troubles our rising water and tide

Rebellion's song

Proud and strong
Improvised
With hopes to echo
Eternally
Becomes a threnody

We bear witness
As Brother Nat and Sister Ure
Are subdued
And under control
Tied and beaten
Bloodied
Awakening memories
Stirred in all of us
An old song and chorus
Mundane music makes us obedient

My re-bell whisper is mute
Drowned by overseer's shouts
Yelling
As Brother Nat and Sister Ure
Are hung on a tree
A reminder that keeps us from rebelling

A sly man
With a plan to make a slave
Behave
Fellow Fallows, he invited to restore order
He calmed the plantation's feud
He and the late master's daughter, intertwine devious smiles
Flirt, enthrall as we are in thrall,
Married, bonded to keep us in bondage
Order is in order for us
The crime of rebellion, still in judgment
Hanging over us
Brother Nat and Sister Ure in the distance
Swinging, swaying – behaving properly
Decorated tree holds the new master's property

Our verdict came at night
Chained and barely clothed
Lined in front of the slave shack
Plucked like crops
Four males and four females
         From our stock
A young woman of Mwana's age,
A thirteen-year-old girl
And two elder female slaves
The chosen men picked just the same
I want to fight
Red hair, the slave master's wife
Twirls pendant
My spirit and inner-g dampens
I again become a spectator to torture

We only hear screaming
The doors of the shack closed
Tearing and stripping of clothes
Then cracks of whips that give us a hint
But the screaming is dominant
Scratching and tearing, penetrating the night
Beyond the doors,
Overseer Burneside and his horde
Ravage the women and the men alike

Red hair stares at us, still curious
Twirling her pendant
The shack doors open
Overseer Burneside's artistry
On display
Stripped, broken, and bloodied
On their knees
Shamed
Then set aflame

The burning bodies seared my eyes

A brand on my mind
The plantation is reorganized
Fellow Fallows creates a hierarchy for us slaves
Titles as a wage
That makes us claw over one another
To reach the top
Our mystical harmonies, Mamma Iyansan's lessons
Fade to forgotten
As we struggle to keep from being at the bottom
Of Master Fallows' plantation

The women's minds broken — and she do cry
The climb and strides in the hierarchy
Of slave men is frozen
Only some of us make it up, as its purpose
A solution to the rebellious slave problem
Keep the restless at the bottom
Separate
Create an illusion of inclusion
Unbalanced, uneven
The women selling the 14 pieces of the men
No attempt to recreate them — recreate us
Osirus
The beam of Master Fallows' smile considered sacred
We dance and jive to be his favorite
Work hard for his prosperity
Argue among us who is the greatest of his property

Li'l Chew and I remember
The reality
The brutality
Brother Nat and Sister Ure
Magic preserved bodies
Still hanging from the tree
If this decoration is a reminder
Why not remember

Herkus Bar re-collects

The memories of being forced
To whip his mother to death
Crimson life dripping from his father's neck
Gasping for words, telling his son,
"Bring peace. Bring peace, so that I may rest."
With Li'l Chew near,
Herkus Bar tells me in a desperate plea,

"I can bring real peace.
Master Fallows' wife is
            Like us
She wields glorious magic
Brother Nat and Sister Ure
Frightened her. Killed her father. But I can talk to her.
There will be no more tension
            In this so-called order
A spiritual emancipation
Imagine real freedom on this plantation."

The song faded. The final notes resonating with uncertainty. Delia and Horatio gently touched down on the brownstone's roof. Horatio removed the horn from his lips and exhaled. His knees buckled, and he bent over to catch himself. Delia, just as the songbook closed and floated into her hands, asked Horatio in a concerned tone, "Are you okay, Horatio?"

"Writing that piece took something out of me," he answered taking deep breaths. "Playing it was even more of a chore." His knees touched the ground and he rolled over to take a seat on the roof. He backed up to the raised ledge. He took another deep breath. Delia came to Horatio's side. She placed the songbook on the ledge and looked down at him as he caught his breath. Horatio said to her, "Don't mistake, though. I love playin' this song. I feel like I'm the whole band. It's just that…I'm concentratin' on playin'. I'm watchin' the story. I feel everything. My empathy increases. I feel everyone. I feel their motives. I even think I understand the slave owners. I don't understand the reason for their actions other than just tryin' to maintain power." He looked up at Delia. "Do you feel that?"

Delia nodded her head. "Yes," she said lowly. "I feel connected. I'm there. I can see me. I have a different name, but it's me. I'm Mwana."

She rested her palms down on the ledge, balancing herself at an angle. "Seeing it all frustrates me. That harpy. Her stone. It's hard to watch. I see us festive, learning, finding an advantage and then we're put right back in our places, even with all the mystical lessons and the tricks we learn." She said in a louder, more frustrated tone, "We had an angel on our side! My grandmother. Mamma Iyansan. And we're still slaves, Horatio. I could hide, but I'm in chains just the same."

Horatio put his horn down and stood up. He embraced Delia and comforted her by saying, "That's the past, Delia. Simmer down. That's just the past. It's okay. We dismantled that plantation. It's gone somehow. I know it burned. That harpy—Miss Fallows—she's angry for a reason. We saw what she had to do to conceive her son. She had to bring her husband back through tricks. Now what can we figure from that, huh? Master Fallows is dead. We killed him. We raised hell somehow. I recognize Overseer Burneside. He survived. Do you recognize anybody besides Miss Fallows?" He stepped away. He rubbed Delia's cheek as if there were tears there, but it was an attempt to wipe away the dispirited look on her face. Delia shook her head, answering Horatio's question. "Then that's it. Ain't no one left. We just got one last big bad to take down. The story's come full circle, Miss Amat. We raised hell on that plantation. Trust me." He embraced Delia again. "You've seen a lot today. It's hittin' you all at once, southern belle. It might exhaust me but I can only imagine what's happening to you. Just be brave for a little while longer. Can you do that?" Delia nodded while still in Horatio's tight hold. "Trust me, Delia. I can see the story. It's in flashes, feelings. I just have to compose it on the paper so I can play it into reality."

Delia moved out of Horatio's hug. She turned around and looked out at the skyline. "I feel it too, Horatio. I feel it all. I remember, and now that it's back in my memory, there's this impatience. And with all bad memories, there's disappointment." She said over her shoulder, "We might've burned that plantation, Horatio. I'll take your word on that. But, we didn't put an end to the horrors for us or any other Negro in America, especially for that time." She raised her hand. "I know, I do know, Lord I do. We're here *now*. We got us a second chance. Most people don't have that, or take it when it's given. So I thank this blessing, wherever it leads."

Horatio rubbed Delia's shoulders. "That's the way it's supposed to be. We'll make the most of it."

Johnny entered. "I'm not interruptin' anything, am I?"

Horatio and Delia turned around. Horatio said, "No, man. Not at all."

"It's cold as hell—if hell is cold," remarked Johnny. "You Southern-blooded people okay out here?"

Horatio explained, "I played some notes. We ain't feelin' the cold." Horatio then said after Johnny acknowledged the comment with the nod of his head, "Just saw a new chapter. You'll see it tomorrow, plus more. I'll get to writing. Stay up late. Sleep late." Horatio paused and then asked, "When we meetin' up with the others?"

"Morgan and Cue are free tomorrow," Johnny answered. "Whenever you're ready."

"Okay, I'm gonna bring them in on this whole thing," said Horatio. "I'm gonna show them the story. They got to see it for what I got planned." Horatio snatched up the horn. "No need for secrets. They got to know what's gon' happen when we put this story right in front of Miss Fallows' eyes. And if they go crazy with all they see, I'll make 'em forget it with the next note I play."

Johnny and Delia both looked at Horatio with perplexed expressions. Johnny raised a hand. "Wait. Hold up. You want us to tell the story to Miss Fallows? Expose all this at the club? Not just to her but other people too? There gon' be more than Negroes there. White folks gon' be there too." He paused. Before Horatio could respond, Johnny asked, "Should we have guns on us?"

Horatio swiped the songbook from the ledge. "I'm workin' on that. I am. And I want your father to play with us."

"Okay," said Johnny nonchalantly. "You want me to get Lazarus for you too, since you askin' for miracles?"

Both Delia and Horatio chuckled at Johnny's sarcasm. Horatio assured his friend, "Man, I got this. Trust me." He asked Delia, "When do you think it'll be an appropriate time to call Stanley at the club?"

"Club winds down late," Delia answered. "I'll call at midnight."

Horatio suggested to Johnny, "She'll take my room. I'll take the couch."

Johnny put his hands in his pockets and shivered. "Well, whatever notes are keepin' you warm ain't rubbin' off." He aimed his thumb toward the door. "Let's go inside."

Horatio and Delia followed Johnny back down into the brownstone. Horatio was given privacy to compose. He secluded himself in the guestroom to write more memories of their past lives. Johnny made a phone call to Morgan Fields, the bass player. He spoke to him about meeting at his apartment in Brooklyn tomorrow morning, and after a proper time was established, Johnny moved on to Willie Santos, a wild drummer whose family hailed from Cuba. Delia, while having a cup of warm tea, conversed in the living room with Johnny's mother.

Time crept closer to midnight. Horatio scribed profusely in mystical notation to elucidate the flashing imagery that came to him like flickers of lightning during a storm. Johnny decided to turn in for the night, saying a quick goodnight to Horatio so as not to disturb him, and to Delia who continued her long-winded conversation with his mother. Johnny changed into his nightclothes and slipped into bed, thoughts of his father on his mind.

Johnny's decision to retire for the night prompted his mother to question if Horatio would drive Delia home using Johnny's car. Delia remarked, "Your son and Horatio invited me to stay. I was supposed to take Horatio's room and he'd take the couch here."

Johnny's mother huffed, and Delia believed it was her words that ruffled her. "That is just like my son! I could've been preparing this downstairs for Horatio. All that time he spent helping me with the dishes and preparing the meal. He could've told me something!"

"Oh, Miss Gregory, we all just sort of came up with that now," Delia lied to simmer Miss Gregory's hysteria.

Gwendolyn waved her hand. "No need to defend that boy, Delia. *Them* boys. Both. It's okay. The arrangements are fine. And I have some dresses from my youth you can slip into for tomorrow. They cute too. Don't worry. I know how to dress, especially in my youth. And some dresses ain't gone out of style." She thought for a moment, and then told Delia, "Always thought I'd have a daughter to give them to. You'll do fine." She winked at the young woman. "I'll give you money for some undergarments at the store 'round the way." Gwendolyn stood up. "Let me prepare some linens for Horatio down here. Make yourself comfortable while I head to the linen closet upstairs to find some blankets for him. It's getting cold."

Delia nodded. "Thank you, ma'am. May I make a phone call?"

"Yes, you may," Gwendolyn consented. She waved for Delia to stand up, and then led her to the house phone. Afterward, she disappeared upstairs.

Delia dialed Sarinda Fallows' office at the Harlem Dixie. Kathi Giovannelli, Sarinda Fallows' personal secretary, answered the phone. Delia introduced herself and asked for Sarinda. Kathi pleasantly obliged. Sarinda picked up the phone moments later, and to Delia's surprise, put up no fight for her wishing to stay in Brooklyn.

"The night is going well, dear," Sarinda informed. "It's a complete success. We've scheduled these rock-and-roll boys to play through the week. Saturday too. You practice and practice. We'll move your debut to next Friday." Then Sarinda said after a short pause to catch her breath, "There's some news, though. Stanley won't be here. He's taken a liking to these boys. He has a plan for them to get recorded. He's excited. Stanley will be leaving for Europe next Thursday. London. The boys' managers want to record outside the United States. There's more seclusion, I guess. Less distractions."

"Oh," Delia responded.

Sarinda assured, "But your cousin wishes you well. Stanley knows you and your boys will bring the house down."

The conversation ended with a cordial parting and Sarinda teasing Delia not to make a habit of staying in Brooklyn with *them two boys*. Delia hung up and ran upstairs. She knocked gently on Horatio's door. "Come in," he said, and she entered. He sat up on the bed and signaled Delia to take a seat by patting the empty space next to him on the mattress.

Delia sat down next to Horatio. "All is well," she informed, disbelief in her voice. "That harpy didn't even put up a fight. She wants us to practice and practice for next Friday. The band Stanley is showcasing tonight will be taking up the rest of the week." Delia paused, looking around. "That harpy teased me not to make a habit of this, staying in Brooklyn with you all. I assured her Johnny's mother was okay with the arrangements. There will be no funny business. But that was just simple talk, and I…" Her voice trailed away.

Horatio rubbed her shoulder. He inspected her face and concluded something was amiss by the expression she held. "What's wrong, Delia?" he asked.

Delia looked at Horatio and answered, "Stanley won't be there next

Friday. He's going overseas with the band that he's put on."

Horatio rubbed Delia's arm. "That's okay, Delia. That's just fine. When all this is finished, we just keep our eye on him."

Horatio's words soothed Delia. The fact of Stanley's absence stayed with her, but it didn't bother her. "How's the song?" she asked.

"It's flowing. The music and the imagery are strong." He clarified, "I also have feelings with the flashes that I can barely make sense of—as usual, before I play the piece. But our story, our history, it's a powerful moment in time. I'll finish the composition in the morning. I'm just too tired. I need more than rest. I need sleep."

Horatio closed the book, placed it on the nightstand and stretched out on the bed. Delia followed him, her head on his shoulder, and her arm on his chest. She whispered, "Is it okay if I stay with you, Mojuba?"

Horatio smiled. "I don't mind at all, Mwana."

Delia snuggled closer. "I'm nervous, Horatio," she confessed. "Sarinda and Curly didn't come back. They're not born again. They've been walking the Earth all this time. But we're here as us. We've been reborn. You know what that means?" Horatio didn't answer, but Delia did. "We died." She paused to allow Horatio to absorb her conclusive words. "I only hope we raised hell and grew old. I hope they didn't kill us. I hope we just didn't know Curly and that harpy got away. I don't know. I'm struggling to remember, but all I have are just these feelings. I guess it doesn't matter really. Curly's dead, and that harpy is soon to follow."

Horatio reached over Delia to turn off the light. "We'll just have to wait, Miss Amat. The story will come. Through me, and through the horn." He turned off the lamp. Still in their clothes, the two slipped under the covers and held one another close. Horatio's exhaustion quickly took over and dragged him to sleep. Delia, awake and contemplating, tried to remember her past life beyond faint feelings. It wasn't long before she too was asleep.

Gwendolyn Gregory stopped outside of the guestroom. She'd heard Horatio and Delia whispering to one another but couldn't make out their conversation. When the lights went out, she smiled, closed the door to the guestroom and took herself to bed.

The World Atop An Hourglass
"Your grandmother? Now she had oddities about her."

"Could you give us a minute, Kathi," requested Sarinda to her personal secretary who'd escorted to the office, as ordered, Stanley Fallows.

The secretary answered, "Yes, Miss Fallows."

Sarinda waved Kathi away with a smile. "Go and have yourself a drink. Enjoy the music up close while Stanley and I converse. And that handsome security boy, Michael Isaacs, is out there too." Sarinda smiled as Kathi blushed. "Don't distract him too much with your pretty smile. He is on duty. But go and talk it up with him. You just make sure he don't take a sip of what you havin', and you don't take too many sips either, hear. Get him a pop or somethin', or a cool glass of water to keep him healthy."

"Miss Fallows," said Kathi continuing to blush as she stood in the doorway.

Stanley smiled and said pleasantly to his mother's secretary, "For your assurance, he's asked about you plenty of times, Kathi. Strike up a conversation. Mom and I can guarantee you two get the same night off. Make a day of it."

Kathi's face reddened even more. "The two of you!" she exclaimed. But her face returned to its olive tone and she remarked to Stanley, "Let me stop playing so innocent. Thanks for the tip, Stanley. And I'll take you up on that night off offer."

All three bubbled with laughter. Kathi disappeared down the hall, a kick in her step as she moved to the music coming from the club's main auditorium. Stanley stepped all the way into the office. He shut the door and took a seat in the chair seated across from his mother, desk in between them.

"Congratulations, Stanley," Sarinda said to her son. "I'm proud of you. I really am."

"Thanks, Ma. Thank you. I love this business." He sat up and straightened his suit. "I hope you don't mind, but I'm trying to put my hand in things outside the club. But it'll all come back here. Acts that I find, and so on. They have to come through here."

"Of course, Stanley," said Sarinda. "Oh, and Delia extends her congratulations to you as well. I just got off the phone with her. She's excited for you."

Stanley stiffened. His eyes widened and he said to his mother, "Oh, that's great. Uh, does she need a car sent to her?" He rose in his chair, almost standing.

Sarinda waved him down. "No, just relax, Stanley. She's staying the night in Brooklyn. She'll be fine. The last thing those two boys mean her is harm."

Stanley settled into his seat. He asked, "Was she disappointed because I won't be around to see her debut performance?"

"It took her by surprise," Sarinda answered matter-of-factly. "But she was excited, and wished you well. And I told your cousin you wished her the same."

"Good," Stanley interjected.

Sarinda beamed, her eyes on her son. She stroked the veil wrapped around her arm. Stanley shifted in his seat. Sarinda shook her head, and her smile widened. "We're all so happy. You've exceeded your father, Stanley. That's what I always wanted. That's why I didn't give you your father's name. You know, he wanted his first-born son to have his name. But I wanted more for you. I didn't want you to just be your father. I didn't want to raise my husband. I wanted a son. I wanted you to be different. I wanted some separation." Sarinda chortled. "I didn't want to fall in love with my son—not in that way." She relaxed. "I gave you a different name, and I blessed you to appear different. But you are your father, Stanley Fallows. Deep down and in your heart you are Kenten Fallows." Then she said, as if an instruction, "Bring your father to the surface when I'm gone."

Stanley became worried. Perplexity colonized his face. "Gone? Mom, are you sick?"

Sarinda shook her head. "No, Stanley. Your mother is healthy. And your mother will stay healthy until someone puts an end to her." Sarinda stood. She paced over to the office's bookcase and removed a weathered, four-by-six, leather-bound book from the top shelf. She walked over to Stanley's side and put the book down on the desk in front of him. "You could use with a bit of health. Keep you strong. Give you a long life, like your mother."

Stanley chuckled faintly as his curiosity made him focus on the book in front of him. He leaned forward and reached for the book. He picked it up carefully and opened it, gently thumbing through the old, yellowing pages, the corners of which were browned by time. There were recipes on every page. Stanley's inspection revealed that the concoctions were for stews or drinks. Explanations that seemed superstitious preceded each recipe. Stanley postulated that he was looking at remedies. "What is this, Ma?" he asked.

"Knock-back curiosities of sorts. My mother's people." Sarinda looked at the wall behind her desk where a painting of her mother hung. Sarinda put her hands on Stanley's shoulders and looked longingly at her mother's portrait. "They work, Stanley. Yes, indeed. It's an old book, but not the original. It's a copy of a book written by an African woman long, long, long ago. She studied medicine in nigger-controlled Spain."

"Mom!" Stanley shouted, ducking out of Sarinda's hold on his shoulders.

Sarinda put a hand to her chest. "Excuse me, Stanley," she giggled. "I'm just so use to tellin' the story as I've heard it spoken by my mother. I do apologize." She reached for her pendant with one hand and rubbed it. With the other, she again cupped Stanley's shoulder and eased him back into his chair. Stanley relaxed. "Anyway, Stanley, this woman—who studied in *Moorish*-controlled Spain—was a brilliant woman of medicine. Folklore proclaims she looked for a treatment that could mend any wound, make the body's natural healing ability fight against the deepest, physical injuries. It's in there. A tawny Arab supposedly put his own spin on this particular formula of hers, much sought after as it was. Now it just keeps you healthy, youthful, like your mom. It all just might be legend, but I swear it works, Stanley. I mean, just look at me." Sarinda giggled again. She relaxed her laugh and looked again at her mother's portrait. "Ever notice anything strange about your grandmother's portrait, Stanley?"

Stanley put the book down and looked up to inspect the painting. The woman in the aged painting was named Rosetta. Stanley knew *Stuhac* was her maiden name before marrying his grandfather, Beringar Von Han. This picture depicted Rosetta Stuhac two months before her marriage. Her features in the painting made her recognizable as an Eastern European-born woman. Her nose was a perfect right triangle, aquiline. Long and straight reddish-brown hair draped far below her shoulders. Her head was heart shaped. She had a pretty face, with dark eyes. Stanley considered his mother must've looked more like her father, though he'd never seen a photograph or portrait of him.

In fact, Stanley hadn't seen a photograph of his grandmother. He'd only seen this painting. It was the only visual of a past relative. There were no photos of his father or grandfather. No one. It was peculiar, but because of his mother's constant descriptions and storytelling, Stanley felt he'd seen and known his father and other relatives.

Stanley scrutinized the painting of his grandmother more closely, leaning forward. He didn't see anything odd about the painting. He did always find it amusing as to the way it resembled the *Mona Lisa*, his grandmother's portrait at half-length within the painting. He looked more closely still. She was wearing the same type of stone pendant as his mother, but it was different in shape. It looked like a circle atop an hourglass. He noticed it before when he was younger, and he'd already made his query about it at the time. Nothing else seemed odd, he thought. But, then he considered, as he had done once or twice in the past, ultimately giving it no mind—his grandmother's clothes. Rosetta Stuhac, in the painting, wore a fanciful, eighteenth century Mantua dress with the signature elbow-length cuffed sleeves.

Stanley answered his mother, "She has an old sense of fashion, I notice. But I guess that was the time. A revival of that spirit, sort of Victorian, right?"

Sarinda smiled. "Yes. It was her way. She came from Europe in her mid-twenties. She met your grandfather, a great, great businessman. Grand, some would say. He stirred the pot of capitalism in America." She walked around the desk and swung the painting on its hinges to reveal a large safe behind the wall. She turned its dials properly until the locks opened. She pulled back and opened the door, revealing a wide, cardboard box inside. She removed the box and set it down on the desk behind her. She turned around, closed the safe, and returned the painting to its proper position on the wall.

"I always wondered what was in there," admitted Stanley. "I assumed it was stacks of money."

"No," Sarinda beamed. "No, child. No need for that. There are greater treasures than money. There are heirlooms. Priceless. This one is yours." She put her hand atop the wide box, keeping Stanley from opening it. She removed her hand when Stanley backed away from the box. Sarinda sat down. "Your grandfather had all types of servants working for him, especially at the beginning. The white servants were expensive to keep. The Negro servants were far more affordable. As time went on, it was easier to have an entire Negro workforce. Your grandfather was progressive in that way, but nowadays, some people wouldn't see it that way." Sarinda shook her head in disgust. "No one can call your grandfather a bad man. He had whites working for him too. Negro help was just cheaper." Sarinda took a seat. "Your Uncle Curly helped the business. He was a good friend to your grandfather. He was always able to find the best people to run your grandfather's business, and Curly had a way of keeping people in line." Sarinda looked back and up to her mother's portrait. She said as she returned her attention to her son, "Your grandmother? Now she had oddities about her. That's what the Negroes in the field would say."

"Oddities?" Stanley questioned.

"She always knew when a Negro working the field was sick," Sarinda answered quickly. "She'd point, or even get up close and tap them on the shoulder, and right there they would fall over dead. Peculiar, yes?"

"Yeah," agreed Stanley. "That is odd."

Sarinda continued, "My mother explained this oddity by saying she could see the tendrils of the sun wrapping around a field worker's neck. She'd point, and they would die. She would tap their shoulder to warn them, but it was too late. They would die. When she would do this, it would be midday. Always. So much so that the Negro workers started callin' my mother *Lady Midday*." Sarinda reminisced with a smile. "She did earn such a wonderful title from those field workers." Sarinda said disdainfully, "They called me *Sarah the Pantomime*. Not even Sarinda. *Sarah!*" she hissed, rolling her eyes. "Those Negro workers were so unappreciative, Stanley. Do you know they celebrated when my mother died? Yes, they did. She became sickly not long after blessing me in a cultural coronation ceremony. Her death changed my father. Oh, if those workers thought he was cruel before. What little patience he had for them was gone." Sarinda shook her head as she recollected. "Their attitude brought my father's wrath on them. Yes, indeed," she said, her voice sounding like sharp clicks. "They forced my father to be rough with them. They tested his patience." She thought about her father's behavior. "Stanley, my father was a cruel man when he had to be. He became a dictator to his field hands, even the ones that worked the house. He had a passion for control. But you can only push people so far. Those Negro field workers killed your grandfather. Two of them did, a Negro man and a Negro woman. I was there. Some white associates were killed too. Curly put the whole thing down, and later, your father stopped all-out hell from breaking loose. Your father already was an advisor to your grandfather's business. He talked about keeping the workers in line. Advice given a little too late. After my father's death, Kenten, your father, organized your grandfather's business with the same type of passion, just directed differently. There was order, and I was so smitten by him—even more so when I saw him runnin' my papa's business. I loved your father instantly. My mother and father were gone, but your father filled the loss I suffered." Sarinda's smile widened, mind in the past. "Your daddy was smitten with me too, and he learned so much of what I taught him. I felt as if I could tell him everything. He took to my history, the history that comes through my mother. He barely understood it, but he was very open to it. I want you to be open to your heritage too, Stanley."

"What's there to know, Ma?" Stanley asked lifting his shoulders. His eyes went back to the portrait of his grandmother. He observed the background. It looked like a plantation. Stanley returned his gaze to his mother. He didn't raise a question about the backdrop of the painting, but Sarinda appeared to notice something.

Sarinda didn't answer Stanley's question concerning his heritage, she only continued beaming at her son. She finally said, "I've kept you long enough, Stanley. You need to get back to the stage. Them boys will be ending their set soon. I just want to say that there are some loose papers tucked inside that old notebook I've given you. They have the name of places in Europe that I'd like you to visit. Your grandmother's people are there. They'll know her. Talk to them." Sarinda chortled again. "They'll have a strange look on their faces, though. I've broken tradition and given birth only to a male child. They'll be surprised." She said calmly, "But they'll know you're mine, so talk to them. Get to know your heritage through them. The irony is that as you come to know your grandmother's heritage, you will become more and more like your father. But, I want you to be different than your father, Stanley. From the brutal hand of your grandfather, to the slyer, charismatic business-sense of your father, things became more and more subtle when it came to intention and action. You improve upon your father's mannerisms, and your business will thrive. People will praise you for all you bring them even if it's heartache." She nodded her head at the box. "Go ahead, Stanley. Open it."

Stanley lifted the box's lid. An old, tattered bullwhip lay inside, curled up like a rattlesnake. It's once dark-brown body was weathered to a light tan, with faint red speckles spattered around it.

"It belonged to your Uncle Curly," Sarinda explained. "Your father gave it to him as a gift." Sarinda beamed proudly. "I do so love how your grandmother's picture keeps it safe. There's great meaning in that." Sarinda explained, "It's a European thing. The women of Europe know how to stand by their man's side, Stanley. We guard our men because he is a sacred thing. I hate to say this, but most colored women—Negro and others— don't understand that. They are very devious behind their men's backs. I want you to find a good woman, Stanley." She waved her hand. "But that's neither here nor there. What I would like is for you to take this whip to Curly's grave in Red Leaf and bury it with him. I think he should have it. He would want it; it was his prize possession. He took pride in his work." Sarinda pointed to the old journal. "There's a poem I wrote for him. I want you to say it over Curly's grave when you go there. It's my prayer to him. For now, I'll take this box home and you can attend to this when you return. I'd appreciate it."

"Yes, Ma, but…are you okay?" Stanley inquired. "I'll do this, but, are you not capable…?"

"Oh, Stanley I'm as fine as can be. I am," Sarinda assured. "Don't worry about your mother at all. I'll be with you when you return. But I just can't bring myself to go back to Curly's grave. You understand, Stanley? Would you do this for me?"

Stanley raised his shoulders again. "Of course, Ma," he commented.

"Thank you so much," Sarinda said to her son. "Now, don't mind that box. Set that aside for now. Go on back to your music band. Mingle with that crowd."

Stanley rose and said with pride, "Absolutely."

Sarinda came from around the desk, arms out. "Come here, boy." She embraced her son. "I am so proud of you, Stanley. I am. You are great, and you are just beginning."

Mother and son hugged tightly.

Stanley backed away just as Sarinda kissed his cheek with motherly tenderness. "Thank you, Ma. Let me get back. And I'll take care of Uncle Curly's things when I return."

"The box will be at the house," Sarinda told him.

"Okay," said Stanley as he turned. "Thanks…Mom. I'll do as you asked." He paused, tapping on the door in contemplation before opening it. He wanted to talk more, but decided against it. He opened the door and left the room.

Sarinda shut and locked the door. She turned and looked at the items left on the desk. She picked up the old journal and dropped it inside the box, and then she closed the lid down over it and sat down in Stanley's vacant chair. She spotted her handbag on the table and reached for it. She opened the bag and sifted through it for her cigarette case and lighter. She pulled out both items, set the bag down, and pulled a single cigarette from the silver case. She put the case down on the desk and lit the cigarette after placing it between her lips. She rested the lighter near the box, sat back in the chair and took a long drag while staring up at her mother's portrait.

Sarinda exhaled smoke and smiled. "I hope you're proud at what you see, Mamma," she said up to the portrait.

Sarinda continued smoking.

Them What Choose
"It's like I'm in two worlds…"

First, Horatio gasped! Then he jumped out of bed, bursting to life from underneath the covers. It was morning. Delia stirred only little, as Horatio's frantic and sudden leap from the bed didn't drag her completely from sleep. She was groggy, but moved to ask, "Horatio-baby, what's all the movement for?"

Horatio turned and bent down to arch over Delia. He answered in a hushed voice, "I gotta get downstairs before Johnny's mother sees I ain't been down there at all, been up here with you cuddled up all last night."

Delia smirked. Her head hit the pillow and she said, "Nothin' happened. It was like you said, Horatio-baby, we cuddled close all last night. Hell, I've gone all the way with my mamma in the next room." Her smirk widened as she remembered misadventures with boys that had taken place during her curious teenage phase.

Horatio put a finger to his lips and shushed Delia to lower her voice. He pointed to her with a stern look and hissed a whisper, "Well, remind me to take a trip down to Baton Rouge to your house. Right now, I can't have Miss Gregory thinkin' I was getting' all fresh in her home."

Delia chuckled. She said in a quieter voice, "You still all dressed. You ain't got nothin' to worry about. Hell, Horatio, you didn't even give me a kiss."

Horatio paused in his antics. He leaned closer to Delia, gently shook her shoulder to stir her eyes open again, and then leaned in to kiss her lightly on the lips. Delia accepted, if still a little drowsy. Horatio planted a second kiss on her cheek and then stood straight. He grinned at Delia, and then he silently slipped from the room. He quietly closed the door behind him and looked both ways down the hall and made his way downstairs. Johnny's room was on the parlor floor. His mother's room was on the second floor below the guestroom. He checked the door to her room as he came down the stairs. It was closed. He took a breath, and continued down into the living room where a folded comforter rested neatly atop the wide and long couch. There was also a new set of towels placed there for him.

Horatio inspected himself and groaned. He didn't have his bedclothes and was still dressed in his previous day's wears. He removed his dress shirt, leaving on the tank top underneath. He undid his belt, removed it from its loops, and dropped it on the floor. He unbuttoned and unzipped his pants to loosen them, but didn't remove them from his person. After removing his socks, Horatio approached the couch and spread out the comforter to sneak under it. He didn't know if he could go back to sleep, but all he needed to do was create a picture that he'd been here all night.

"Good morning, Horatio," he heard Johnny's mother greet him with a sly tone in her voice.

Horatio turned his body, midway between slipping onto the couch and underneath the comforter. Miss Gregory was leaning in the doorway of the dining area, sipping tea. She was up, dressed, and ready for work. Horatio's surprised expression dropped into a sheepish grin. "Good morning, Miss Gregory."

She raised a teasing eyebrow. "You up?" she asked. "I'm just about to make breakfast before I go to work. Or do you need a few more moments of sleep?"

Horatio assured, "And sleep is all myself and Mwana did last night, Miss Gregory. I didn't *completely* disrespect your house."

Miss Gregory chuckled. "Oh, I know, Horatio. I'm just having a little fun. I heard you two talking and I saw the lights go out. I suspected that nothing would happen between you two, of that nature. Not yet, anyway. I don't suspect the two of you being fast like that."

Horatio dropped the comforter and stood straight, fixing himself up. He zipped and buttoned his pants. "It's like I'm in two worlds, Miss Gregory. I have Johnny as a connection to my New York roots, and I got Mwana to remind me of Louisiana." Then Horatio said, "Three worlds. Both of them help me connect to music. We share all these worlds together."

Johnny's mother gave Horatio a curious look. "That is the second time you've referred to that girl upstairs as '*Mwana*.'" Then she contemplated aloud, "That's such a lovely sounding name. Mwana. Huh?" Her attention back on Horatio, she asked, "Delia-LaRue Mwana Amat?

How many names does that young woman have?"

Horatio said quickly, "It's a nickname. A Southern thing…?" he added, sounding unsure of the tale he was spinning. "African, actually. It's an African name. She told me it was a nickname. It does roll off the tongue so easily. *Mwana!*"

Gwendolyn chuckled, sipped her tea and asked, "So is the Woman of Many Names up and ready for breakfast?"

Horatio aimed his thumb toward the direction of the stairs. "Oh, she loves your cookin', Miss Gregory. That would stir her from the deepest sleep. I'll get her."

Gwendolyn sipped more of her tea. "I'll wake Johnny," she said. As she turned around she added, "Oh, Horatio, tell Delia that I've gone around the corner to get her some undergarments. I left them in the bathroom on your level. I also got her a toothbrush."

"I'll do that, Miss Gregory," Horatio confirmed as he put on his socks.

"That's good," said Gwendolyn before disappearing into the kitchen. "I put out some of my old outfits from my younger days. She can find them hanging in the hall closet outside my room."

Horatio rushed back to the guestroom. He opened the door and Delia lifted her head and said, "She was downstairs, wasn't she? I could hear you alls' voices." Delia started laughing. She teased, "You was caught, Mister Peters."

Horatio rolled his eyes, half a smirk on his face. "Yes, I was," he said. "But hey, I'm a grown man. I'm twenty-four. You barely jumped into bein' twenty. You still a child."

Delia cocked an eyebrow. "Uh-huh. That's why you got that look of a child caught with his hand in the cookie jar, Mister Peters, 'cause you so grown."

Horatio gestured and said, "Get on up, Miss Funny. Johnny's mom is cooking breakfast." He informed her, "She got you a spare toothbrush and some undergarments. They're both in the bathroom up here. Miss Gregory said she hung some clothes for you too in her closet near her room." He bent down and whispered "I called you Mwana by accident. I told her it was a nickname. You come up with the rest of the story should she ask."

But, Gwendolyn Gregory didn't question. She didn't have the time.

She prepared breakfast for her son and his guests, and after making and eating a small plate for herself, she left. Using separate bathrooms, Horatio and Delia washed up, Horatio retrieving the new towels placed near the couch. Gwendolyn had left for work by the time Horatio and Delia made their way downstairs. Johnny apologized on behalf of his mother for her absence. "Somebody got to pay the bills around here," Horatio joked as he and Delia made plates for breakfast. Johnny dismissed himself to wash up and get ready for the day.

Horatio and Delia started off eating quietly, but the quiet was interrupted with Delia asking in a soft voice, "Did you sleep well, Horatio?"

"Yes," he answered.

"Do you have any insight into what we've been through?" she asked. "The song? Our story," she clarified.

"It'll come through, Delia," Horatio assured her. "It's like having a memory of being really young. I can see it but can't explain it. The song speaks and tells the history. You know how that is—as you begin to remember. We'll have the whole story soon. There's still a lot to compose, but I know that'll be the end. That life will be over. Whatever leftover business is to be done, will end in this life here." Horatio changed the subject, inquiring more about Delia growing up in Baton Rouge. Delia was able to push aside her anxiety about the wondrous world she had stepped into. It wasn't long before they were finished and Johnny emerged dressed for the day. He prepared himself a plate of breakfast food and joined the conversation. Afterward, they all cleaned their places, stored the leftover breakfast food, and washed their dishes.

The three of them exited the house, stepping out into the cool, mid-autumn morning. Delia admired the fiery shades of the changing leaves that glowed brilliantly on the trees. Horatio gripped his trumpet case and songbook tightly, bracing himself for the light prick of the blowing, brisk air. Johnny locked the doors behind them, and then all three walked to his car. Johnny jumped in first and unlocked the passenger's side and the backdoors. Horatio opened the door for Delia who stepped into the back seat and said, "Thank you." Horatio handed her the songbook and trumpet case, and then he got into the passenger's side. Johnny started the car and pulled away from the curb.

Their first stop was a Brooklyn apartment complex in Fort Greene where Morgan Fields resided. Morgan was a thirty-year-old man who worked in the mailroom at a law firm in Harlem. He scored this day off with permission from his boss who knew Morgan was not only a hard worker, but also a mean bassist. Johnny left the car and Delia and Horatio waited while he retrieved Morgan. Horatio got out of the car and switched from the passenger's seat to the back seat. It wasn't long after that Johnny and Morgan were approaching.

Morgan was almost as tall as Johnny. He had light-brown skin, a mustache, and a triangular face. He sported gray slacks, brown shoes, and a buttoned collar shirt covered by a tan jacket. Atop his head was a brown fedora. Morgan was loud, and though the closed doors muffled the sounds of his conversation with Johnny, his words could be heard distinctly. "My bass is over at Cue's place right now." Johnny said something that couldn't be heard, but Morgan's response was, "His father's old garage in Queens." Johnny made a comment, looking slightly upset. Morgan replied, "Aw, man, you ain't got to worry. They fixed that piano over there." Morgan opened the door and jumped into the passenger's seat. He turned around and said excitedly to Horatio, "Hey, man! It's about to get loud now. I know you ready to blow through that horn." His eyes went to Delia. "And this lovely woman must be who the music gonna be behind. How are you, Miss Amat? Johnny told me about you over the phone." He reached out his hand. Delia accepted, gently returning the gesture. Morgan retracted and turned around as Johnny got into the car. "You mind if I smoke?" he asked Horatio and Delia.

"Please, no, if you have to turn the window down," Delia politely said. "It's just too cold. I'm sorry, Morgan."

"Understand," said Morgan. He explained as Johnny started the car and backed out of the parking spot and onto the road, "I got some southern blood in me too. My family is originally from North Carolina—my mother and father that is. I was born up here with my younger brother and sister. My oldest brother was born down there, though. But he was about five when my parents moved up here. I'm out here in Brooklyn but I grew up in Queens."

"Oh," said Delia.

"Horatio!" Morgan yelled.

Johnny said, "Man, he's in the backseat. Ain't a need to be all loud."

"I'm getting' his attention," Morgan argued.

"Man, you got all our attention," Johnny joked with laughter spilling out between his words.

Morgan rolled his eyes and said, "Anyway." He addressed Horatio with his original topic, "You hear that nonsense comin' from across the way? Over in Europe? About jazz?"

"What's goin' on?" Horatio asked.

"They hollerin' over in Europe about how jazz has moved forward, you know. How it's progressed. Not everybody is talkin', and the debate has kinda cooled. But, I just heard this shit yesterday at work." Morgan shook his head. "I tell you, white folks are crazy. You see, them white boys over there were cut off from jazz during that last war. So all they was listenin' to was the old-time stuff. They didn't hear or know about jazz's progression. Next thing that happens, war is over, jazz comes floodin' back with a bunch of new sounds, and now—to this day—some of them white boys is complainin' about all the new jazz sounds. And I mean, that just burns me ill! That is some arrogant shit! First off, how these white folks gon' comment on shit they didn't invent? This is *our* music. *Black* folks conduct this train called Jazz. *We* say what direction it goes in. *We* say how it evolves. I. Tell. You!" The others started laughing. "You all think I'm kidding!" Morgan hollered.

"No, we know you're serious," Horatio remarked. "That makes it more funny."

"But it's true!" Morgan protested not cracking a smile. "I mean, white folks think they control *everything*, or think they got the *right* to control everything! I mean…plus…them boys was gone from the party for years— havin' a fight, shootin' and killin' and raisin' hell all across Europe, and then when they came back to the party, they mad because they hear the band got a new sound. Ain't that some shit? Not a care in the world about how God is gon' judge the sins committed from London to Berlin and even into Asia. Oh, no. They mad that Negroes had a musical and creative move forward. Like, how dare we have a thought in their absence on the progression of our music." Morgan put his hands on his chest and expressed, "I didn't know we were supposed to put *our* cool on pause while they settled they differences with bombs and bullets. I mean the *def-in-ition* of arrogance!" The laughter only increased as Morgan continued to speak with sincere frustration. "I thought everyone had a smoke and a drink in they hand and came to have a good time. I guess I was wrong."

Johnny interjected, "Well, to be honest, a lot of them white boys here and in Europe talk about how classical European music influenced jazz."

"Lies!" argued Morgan. "Complete and total lies. I've said it before: When jazz first started, white folks had no idea what-in-the-hell we was doin'. People believed we were actually talking with the instruments. White folks said we 'niggers' were having a conversation with our instruments. They did not have clue-the-first on what we were doing. But, there were a lot of white boys that wanted to imitate the sound. So, they studied. And they used, as a reference point, what is called classical music from Europe as a way to understand what we were doing. Please, who do I look like, Johnny? Yesterday's fool?"

Johnny and the others laughed. Morgan continued to voice his opinions loudly even after they made their way into Queens and pulled up into Willie Santos' father's old auto repair establishment. Willie 'Black Cue' Santos was waiting outside, a stocky, dark skinned man dressed in a gray suit that whipped in the day's increasing wind. Cue defied the cold, and he looked unfazed as he smoked his cigar and waited. Johnny shut the car off, and everyone exited. Cue smiled as he saw everyone approach.

"Come. Come," he invited, his voice thick with a Cuban accent. Johnny and Morgan greeted their friend, and Horatio came behind them to do the same. All three men parted for Delia to step up. "Everything is setup for you, songbird," spoke Cue. "All the instruments are up. Johnny, the piano plays fine now."

"I've heard," Johnny remarked.

Cue turned and led them inside. "I do have some bad news, though," he said. "We're down to our final sessions here. My father found a buyer. All things final in a month. Then we got to look somewhere else to hold some jam sessions. It's good too. No longer have to pay for this place. But at least the radiators are still on. We'll have heat."

"Oh, that's good to hear," commented Delia.

Johnny, Morgan, Horatio, and Delia followed Cue into a large room with a drum set, Morgan's bass, and a piano. There was also a microphone attached to stand and amplifier. Stools were situated behind the drum set, near the bass, and the microphone and stand. Horatio set the trumpet case down, and placed the songbook atop it. He straightened and turned. "Everyone take a seat," he ordered.

Morgan and Cue looked at Johnny. Johnny nodded his approval, and Morgan and Cue did as Horatio directed, taking seats on the stools located near their instruments. Johnny sat down at the piano. Delia sat on the stool next to the microphone stand. Horatio remained standing. He joked, "I guess horn players don't get a seat. So, let me say this standing." He put his hands in his pockets, raised his shoulders and looked up at the ceiling as he took a deep breath in and out. Horatio asked Morgan and Cue, "Is it okay if I tell a story? I'd like to tell a story." Both men nodded. Horatio addressed Delia and Johnny. "You two know this story. You've seen it. Johnny, you've gotten used to all this by now, and Delia, you've accepted all this so quick. Morgan, Cue, I've been composing a story, not just songs. And it will be this musically composed story that we play at the Harlem Dixie. The music will kill. I intend it to. The story we play will be accompanied by visuals. Strong visuals. Morgan and Cue, I need you to be aware of these visuals, how this whole story will be projected."

Morgan and Cue nodded, though they weren't really sure of what Horatio had planned. But they were accepting, and very curious. Both assumed in their silence that Horatio was expressing experimental jazz, putting a mythology to it.

"My father was murdered on the night I was born," Horatio continued. "Sarinda Fallows, boss of the Harlem Dixie, orchestrated my father's death." Horatio ignored the surprised expressions splashed over Morgan and Cue's faces. He walked over to his trumpet case, moved the songbook to the floor, and unlocked and opened the case. He removed the horn and stepped back to his previous position. "Ain't no devil at the crossroads, boys. My father found that out when he went there. A devil at the crossroads is a fabrication. It's all metaphor and filled with eerie and superstitious imagery to keep the uninitiated at bay. Negroes been doing this for a long time with our stories and magic to preserve the secrets of this world and keep them safe." Horatio asked rhetorically, "So what is at the crossroads?" Then he answered, "Well, y'all, there are two old men at the crossroads named Jackson and Gaston Fable. The Fable brothers taught my father new sounds for music. He also learned from their wives who've since passed. Johnny and I went to the crossroads. I know it's strange soundin'. We're jazzmen, not bluesmen. But we went to them crossroads and we learned them sounds. This trumpet here can play them sounds. And when this trumpet plays, your instruments will play the same magic."

Horatio looked at Morgan and said, "Jazz has a new evolution, and us black folk are about to complete our revolution. We've come full circle, and our tricks and magic are back in our hands."

Morgan smiled. Both he and Cue absorbed Horatio's interesting story, but still they took it to be no more than the mythos behind the musical narrative he'd composed. Horatio considered as much without Morgan or Cue saying it aloud. But Horatio had more to say before he proved to them his story's authenticity.

"My father was murdered for the songs he composed," he said to his audience. "His songs revealed that evil still walks among us. It walks with a seductive frame. Sarinda Fallows. She has tricks. This trumpet has the power to stop her tricks."

Horatio put the horn to his lips. He blew and the instrument roared a powerful and pleasant sound that neither Morgan nor Cue had ever heard. Horatio held the note long. The room seemed to wave and ripple. Though the sound was amazing, Morgan and Cue started to believe that they were getting headaches. The sound faded smoothly. The ripple and wave of reality stopped, and everyone noticed the eleven paintings decorating the room's walls, materialized out of the ripple induced by the horn.

Delia beamed, her eyes focused on Horatio rather than her father's artwork imported by otherworldly means. Morgan's smile faded. His eyes darted between the paintings. His head followed his eyes. Cue clapped loudly. He broke into laughter and said, *"Oluku mi! Oluku mi!* If I told my father this he'd stop the deal ready to sell this place. It's now blessed. He wouldn't want the next person to get its blessing. He'd move back in, even if the other place *is* much bigger."

Morgan continued his inspection of the paintings, not for their art, but because of their sudden appearance. "Yeah, my mother and father got they southern, North Carolina stories and superstitions. Always got a talk about the spirit that goes beyond just the Christian speak. That talk is different. There's just this way their people down in Carolina talk about what moves this world. There's things we can't see." He looked at Horatio. "I guess we in the middle of it now. Shit, I'm too scared to get up and run." He asked, "All that you just said is true, ain't it?" Horatio answered with an affirmative nod of the head. Morgan took out a cigarette. "I'm gon' smoke now. Shit." He put the cigarette between his lips, and before he could reach inside his jacket for matches, Horatio played a few notes and the cigarette lit up at its tip.

Everyone jumped excitedly!

Morgan got up and stomped his feet. Cue continued to clap and holler from behind the drum set. Morgan took a drag, blew out smoke, and shouted, "I can get use to this shit right here! I could! Let me hit the numbers, goddamnit! Or give me some liquor, shit! Conjure me up a drink!" He sat back down, taking more hits from his cigarette and humming his approval. He said while exhaling smoke, "No, I respect this. Whatever this power got in store for us, I respect it. But, let me ask somethin'. Let me ask you this: We can hit them sounds when we play too? As long as you playin, right? That's what you said."

"Yes," Horatio confirmed.

"Let's hear these songs," Cue said grinning excitedly. He put his cigar down in an astray near him and snatched his drumsticks. "We got a house to bring down."

Horatio raised his hand and gestured for Cue to put his drumsticks down, and Cue set them aside. Horatio said, "I have a story to show you first." Cue relaxed. Horatio lifted the horn to his lips. He took a brief moment to wink at Delia. She beamed back at him, and he started playing.

The paintings came to life, one-by-one, just as before. Water Bug Hollow's history played like a movie, complete with soundtrack. Horatio played, the pictures moved, and the audience watched Curtis the Water Bug's escape, return, and rebellion that served as ritual to establish Water Bug Hollow. Joseph Pepper and Theresa Amat's love played next, followed by Sarinda Fallows' deceitful tale of procuring the magical veil. Delia tightened, teeth clenched in anger as she watched her grandmother, mother, and father's lives ruined at Sarinda Fallows' will. Horatio allowed the scene of his father's killing to play this time. The painting not only showed Pete Peters' murder, but his journey to the crossroads, his father meeting Jackson and Gaston Fable and their wives, and him bringing Horatio's mother down to meet them. The picture displayed Sarinda Fallows manipulating the three Mud Hare club owners against the On The Hour club. Sarinda wore desperation like makeup. A strong feeling aroused her to perform an elaborate ritual with her pendant, and a vision of the horn's fall to Earth appeared before her. She went to Harlem just to test Pete Peters. Delia and the others were in awe at Sarinda's manipulation to have the On

The Hour club burned with the owner and patrons inside, Curly Burneside and his soldiers at the ready for the infernal task. Then there was the slaying of Pete Peters' family. Pete Peters and Virginia Tara returned to see the carnage, and Pete Peters turned it all around with the power of his horn, restoring the club, resurrecting his family, the patrons, and the club's owner.

Sarinda never exposed herself, but Pete Peters' mystical compositions made him aware of her. The painting revealed that Pete Peters knew this was not his fight. It was a fight for his unborn child to resolve, and so Pete Peters invited every angle of Sarinda Fallows' manipulation. But, he never suspected his best friend Joseph Concheroot, or the other members of his band, would be made to turn against him.

Watching this revelation stung Johnny. He wanted to apologize again to his friend Horatio. He said a silent prayer and made an apology to the spirit of Pete Peters as atonement instead. Horatio, however, was now accustomed to the scene of his father's murder. He was now only providing it a mournful and suspenseful soundtrack.

As the story continued, inside the On The Hour club at midnight, the horn, after falling from the lifeless body of Pete Peters, dissolved into the musical notations that it was composed of. The notes disappeared into the trumpet case, and Pete Peters' assassins peeked inside. But, the case was empty, and no sooner had they opened it and found it so, did the case disappear in front of their eyes. And so the three assassins, owners of the rival Mud Hare nightclub, walked away from the scene. But the trumpet case reappeared upon the exit of Pete Peters' murderers. Leon Daniels, witness to the brutal slaying, when all was clear, retrieved the case and hurried away.

Horatio played *The Son Dial Tone* next. First, a few notes hummed from his instrument made the songbook jump off the ground, open, and levitate in front of him. Morgan and Cue grinned. They wanted to clap, but they also didn't want to disturb Horatio's fine, mystical playing.

The paintings disappeared, not even returning to the wall. The walls dropped away. The outside was not exposed, but instead there was a scene of glorious stars and moons. The cosmos swirled and the lives of Mother Harmony and Father Voice were put on display. Al-andalusia. Africa. Enslavement. There played Horatio's birth as Mojuba Kimoyo and his life on the plantation. All the notes composed to tell the tale were played. Morgan and Cue were now privy to the lives once lived by Horatio,

Johnny, and Delia.

Johnny could now hear the narration. He heard Father Voice and Mother Harmony. He heard Mojuba Kimoyo no longer as thunder, but as a strong voice. He wondered if it was because Horatio was mastering the instrument, playing the songs properly, or perhaps if it was Delia's presence. It was indeed because of Delia. She provided the proper harmony to the song's narrative voice.

And so the song's narrative was more apparent for its spectators. The story continued as Herkus Bar made his desperate plea to find harmony on a colonial plantation between a sly master and potentially rebellious slaves.

Herkus Bar wanted freedom in slavery
I plead that peace without struggle
Would continue the disharmony
"Herkus, I understand how you believe what you say is true
Brother, I've seen this through your view
Deciphered with both my eyes
One as Eshu the other has Heru
But those thoughts have set sail
I've whispered mystical, musical scales
Observed wails in this musical note 'C'
And like Moses I divided the 'C'
And split the vibe
And played the hidden, musical note of 'I'
And 'I' am as 'U' 'R'
And we 'B' rockin' in these notes on air guitars
These thoughts are so loud
I got them blasting from passing shooting stars
With observers shouting from afar:
'Man, turn down the Rah Dios station
I'm pickin' up vibrations of cosmic sensations
That are breaking the beat down soul low
I'm able to hear the grass grow and cultivate
And the beat be breakin' down culture soul low
I'm able to hear my knee grow shufflin' with the flow
Playin' that natural music – soul funky you can dance to it
Liquid flow playin' on water flu-ids

And jamming on the organ-ics
An earthly instrumental with wind instruments
And thunderous percussions
That are brushing through my ears and hair."

Herkus Bar smiles
An infinite beam stretching for miles
My words comfort him
But his ideals are too much a part of him
Night after night
Herkus Bar meets with the master's curious wife
But only words exchange between them
The slave master's wife listening
To all the mystical lessons Herkus Bar offers
A coffer of old-time magic
Passive Herkus Bar soothed his master's wife
Telling her, "We all cried when your mother died."
And she, teasing, replies, "Don't lie. Those were
            Tears of joy in your eyes, as cruel as she could be."

Herkus Bar
Would instruct her curious eye
To stay hidden and spy
To try and imitate our dances
Our magic wrapped up in prances
We caught up in ancestral trances
Herkus Bar stealing glances
Eye on the shadow where she observed us
We felt her presence
Our power, running rampant,
Would dampen
And her pendant was the only answer

But there were things she couldn't see
My attempts to bring Mwana out
            Of her invisible haze
I spent days composing to Mwana
I left her love letters

Then burned the paper
Flicker and flame back into vapor
Think me less of a man,
But when she did not appear, I cried
And when my tears dripped into the flames
I heard her reply:

"Black prince
Listen to this
Wade in the water
Of our streams of consciousness
Through ritual and prayer
Meditate on the time before space shattered
Into material matter
And all that mattered was spiritual
Before black cosmic Ixu and Gira's copulation ritual
Whole as one – holding conversation in the original embrace
Planning the birth of their children – suns, moons, planets, and stars
And the origins of themselves manifested multiple
In Man and Woman of the black race."

Something touched my head
And baldhead sprouted hair of wool
A black halo

She sang, "Hello. Hello. Hello.
Your hair of wool, curled galactic swirls
Intense twists, DNA helix
With all the power of gravity's force and pull.
The slave master has set us aflame
Our burning bodies angry, incensed
And myrrh
Burned and burned as the slave master
   Gathers with his family
To breathe in our sixth sense."

I speak, "But this makes no frankin-sense to me
Because even if you burn me at an excess of 1200°

My spirit will retain at least fifty percent
Of its original properties
Absorbing all forms of energy
Light – Heat – Sound – Electricity
Charge like cavalry – horse-powered battery
Because actually
This black body has been here for eons.
Let me sit back and think upon."

I can see Mwana's faint form
Her smile breathes
She pleads, "Yes, sit back with me
Recall every part of your memory
Before you were born in what is called physical history
Reflect on our mystery system. Cosmo-politicians.
We governed the heavens
Cruising through gala-x-seas
Astro-afro-nauts
Singing in perfect harmony with musical keys
That tightened our locks – only we can open them
We screamed! Screamed! And we screamed to the heavens!
We sang the entire musical range
Through black hole ankh-rah-phones
Until physically we took on the universe's color and tone
On our backs, scratches and scars are just shooting stars
For we are the black drip of the black backdrop
The world our private square
Soul locked, unable to think outside the box
Broken down, now lost of crowns
Our pyramid blocks
Have become our slave master's city blocks
And these city streets surround black family trees
While corporate branches steal their leaves
Because we now live in a spherical world
With corners on every block
Piled on block-by-block
And I see slaves hanging at the corners of these blocks
Trying to claim these blocks

Until we have enough blocks to rebuild our pyramids
Back to the top
To let our black drip up to our black backdrop."

Mwana pulls me into her ether
We kiss
And we cry sunbeams free
Draining the multiple colors in our eyes
Until the sun rose back into the sky
And the insects drank our tears
To become the stars' cousins we call fireflies
We intertwine and add rhythm and reason to our rhyme
We compose a love song as our spirits fly off into the distance
Toward our newborn sun
The sky resonates our daughter
Dawn
Mwana tattoos the Earth on her belly
So that 9 months from now, when pregnant and round
               Like a drum
She will hum a reminder of where we all come from

Horatio smiled, and both he and Delia blushed. The other three saw nothing, as Mojuba and Mwana remained in an invisible realm while making love. But, Horatio and Delia's eyes could see. Horatio saw Delia naked as Mwana. Delia saw Horatio naked as Mojuba. Their contemporary bodies were in full view. Not only were they naked, but they were also intertwined. Horatio opened his eyes for a moment. He caught a glimpse of Delia. She was sitting, blushing and shying away from Horatio's opened eyes.

But her eyes found his anyway.

Horatio winked. He closed his eyes and continued playing. Delia's shy behavior faded. She rolled her eyes at Horatio's audacity. All her lady-like confidence returned. She straightened her posture on the stool and thought to herself how men could always find a way to ruin the moment. So she simply continued to watch and listen as *The Son Dial Tone* played on.

I fold back into reality
Mwana with me

She hides in shadows
Our power swirling inside one another
I've found my harmony
Mother to my songs
My sun and dawn

I sing to my family seeds
Brother Li'l Chew and I

Speak in 360° of revolutions and loops
We are festive with rebellion
All of us
We ignite a ruckus
We make combat into an art
Kicks, jabs, stabs
Disguised as chants and dance
Make the slave master and Curly laugh
When they see us wild in whirl
Pirouette and twirl – butterfly float
African killer bee sting strike, a dance stroke

Li'l Chew drums
He hums a new name,
"Irakere! Irakere!
Call me! Call me!
I pound djembe, djembe!
My sound, my sound!
I am Irakere."

Mamma Iyansan sings,
"Ring the re-bell! Ring the re-bell!
Sound through the horn can dispel
Her spell – her spell."

Li'l Chew renewed as Irakere
He pounds sounds
From his bare hands
He screams, "Let the red hair spy
Let her curious eye watch

But her movements
Will never have rhythm with our rhyme!
We call her Sarah! Sarah!
We call her Sarah the Pantomime!"

The curious eye flees
We whisper her name in the field
We tease, and we tickle the air when we laugh
Speaking her name into the breeze
Even nature chuckles
But Herkus Bar tells her of our laughter
Our numbers fall at the hands of the master
Paying too much attention with amoral intensions
To his wife
Burnings, whippings, death — the rough taking of our flesh
Master Fallows, Herkus Bar at his side, points to the west
The strong tree with the bodies
Of Brother Nat and Sister Ure,
Rope around their necks
Bodies, magic preserved, serve as a reminder
As do the burnings whippings, death — the rough taking of our flesh
We sleep with nightmares choking our breath

It's the same all over again
Sun up to sun down
We are complacent
Herkus Bar walks adjacent to Master Fallows
Dressed in better rags

I disappear into the ether
Spend time with Mwana
Cosmic flora and fauna
Surround us
I spend my time with her
In the ether
I-spirit put on my physical as a garb
And manifest back in the slave shack

Irakere dragged away
Whipped and whipped
And whipped and whipped
For giving the pantomime
Her name
Spared from death
But beaten, broken
Open wounds draw blood
As he can barely draw breath
Mwana, wearing a shadow as a dress,
She puts a hand on Irakere's chest and mends his flesh

In the night, it's there. Just sitting.
A haunting. A tension.
At any time…ready to break

Morning opens wide
There's a pitch that breaks the sky
I hear her. Mamma Iyansan.
"Ain't nothin' new here to see.
Heartbeats done stopped,
But not the spirit of the drum.
Ain't nothin' new here to see
'Cause there ain't nothin' new under the sun.
This ain't my beginning,
But I've seen this so much
I believe this is where I come from."

A tree branch snaps me awake
I walk out and walk west
Brother Nat and Sister Ure
Crumpled on the ground
Mamma Iyansan floating above them
I run and run,
I kneel over Nat and Ure's bodies
I wipe my hands over the branch,
Look over my shoulder
No sign of the slave master or his soldiers

I sing a soft prayer
Mamma Iyansan beaming
Her eyes bright
She winks
"I will dream of this moment in the dreaming
I will dream when I am no longer aware of this moment."

I gather all the sounds
And I sing
My voice carving out of the branch
Borne a new form
A horn
I run to the slave shack,
Jump into a shadow
Swallowed by the ether
I breathe through the instrument
Inhale. Exhale. All the musical properties of the galaxy
All the universe's harmonies
The horn, reborn as cosmic mahogany
Anointed by the infinite ebony
Mamma Iyansan and Mwana bless the horn with their voices

I step out of the mystical
Rejoin the physical
And attend to my slavery
Sun and lash against my back
Hair pulled for its burst of fiery wool

It's the same all over again
Sun up to sun down
We sing the master's religion
Until our spirits are bound
And our ancestry is drowned in myth
Work. Work. Work.
Paid the bare minimum slave
We are punished for speaking to the air
Our spoken prayers
To the unseen, Mamma Iyansan or Mwana

We communicate with brother and sister slave
They allocated to the house
Our dealings cloaked
By myths that are soaked
In rumblings that we don't get along
But it's just for convenience
We keep the master unaware
Use these myths to our advantage
We communicate in slang and song
Through the anguish
We sing and sing and sing
Our voices ring and ring and ring
The re-bell, Rah's bell
The sunshine harmony and tone,
Twinkling cosmic foliage
Our locks unlock us from bondage
We sing together on this plantation
In coded language

The room folded over the atmosphere of the colonial plantation. The music was at an end, but the story was not finished, only on pause before Horatio composed more. The songbook closed and glided to the floor like a feather. Morgan removed his pack of cigarettes. "I know someone wants one."

"I take my cigar, *hermano*," said Cue, reaching down and taking up his cigar to puff on again.

Johnny waved his hands to Morgan and the bass player pitched the pack to him. Johnny caught them and pulled free a cigarette. Horatio played a few notes and lit the tip of Johnny's cigarette. He put the horn down and sat on the floor. Delia could see he was exhausted. She got up and walked over to Horatio, kneeling down and stroking his arms and shoulders. "You okay?"

Horatio nodded affirmatively.

Cue announced, "I brought brandy for the singer to clear her voice. But I brought enough glasses for all of us. I'm sure everyone could use a drink."

Horatio lifted a finger. He could do with a swig. Everyone else confirmed their fancy for a glass of brandy too. Cue got up and left the room to retrieve the brandy and glasses. He returned with two glasses filled with brandy and handed them to Horatio and Delia. He left again and returned with three empty glasses clasped in the fingers of one hand and the bottle of brandy held by the other. He gave a glass to Johnny and filled it with brandy. He did the same for Morgan, and then provided himself a pour in the remaining glass. He put the bottle down and took a sip.

Horatio sighed. He lifted his glass. "This does wonders. Thanks, Cue."

Cue responded in kind. He took another sip and asked Horatio, "You need some rest? There's a cot in one of the back rooms."

Horatio finished his drink in one gulp. He wiped his lips and said, "That'll do nicely." He got up, Delia helping him. He picked up the horn and groaned as he stood straight. Delia grabbed the songbook and Cue took the trumpet's case. Horatio staggered out of the room, he and Delia followed Cue to the small room with the cot. Horatio propped up the pillow against the wall, and then he stretched out. He put the trumpet down and asked Delia for the songbook. She passed it to Horatio. He thanked her, opened it to a blank page, and removed a pen from his pants pocket.

Cue set the trumpet case down. "The rest of that story is comin' to you?" he asked.

Horatio nodded. "Yep."

"So you…you remember another life?" Cue's eyes went to Delia. "Both of you, and Johnny?"

"Faintly," answered Horatio. "I see it, but I can't quite put it together until it's composed and played."

Cue accepted the answer. He stepped back and turned. "We'll be waiting, either to jam or see your picture show." Then he returned to the other room.

Delia sat on the bed and asked politely, "Would it be okay if I stayed?"

Horatio welcomed her. "I'd appreciate the company." But Horatio had a request. "Could you get the brandy, please?"

Delia chuckled. "I'll also bring a stool."

"Thank you."

Delia exited the room, returning when she had both the stool and the bottle of brandy. She set the stool down and poured brandy into

Horatio's empty glass that rested next to the bed. Horatio was already scribbling the notations for the next part of the story. He said to Delia without looking up, "We gon' give a hell of a show, Delia. We gon' bring the house down. We gon' throw this all in Miss Fallows' face. Get ready for this next part. I can only imagine what this will all sound and feel like with a band playin' behind it and you singin'."

Delia inquired, "What will I be singing, Horatio?"

"I gotta song for you, Delia," Horatio assured her. "Your voice will light up the room."

"There's great tension buildin' on that plantation," Delia commented. "Much like now."

"Yep. War is comin' to the plantation," notified Horatio. "And there will be hell up in Harlem for it."

The Bright Places
"I've seen your ships on my shore."

Delia didn't spend every night in Brooklyn. She stayed with Sarinda and Stanley on occasion, and her stays were far more pleasant than she imagined. Sarinda charmingly serenaded the young, Southern songbird with stories of her grandmother and the first age of jazz in Water Bug Hollow. Sarinda even spoke of Delia's grandfather, Joseph Pepper IV. Sarinda's charm was almost effective enough to eclipse the truths Delia learned about her.

Almost.

Delia spent most of her time with Stanley when she stayed nights at her grandaunt Sarinda's place in Manhattan. She was comfortable around him. Her mind never wandered during conversations with him as to whether or not he could read her thoughts, probe her mind, and see that she knew the truth, as she did with Sarinda. The only times she felt uneasy, and terribly tense with Stanley, was when the two of them walked around Manhattan together. Many eyes stared at them, white and black alike. Though, the black people that observed them were more inviting, even if their voices didn't sound as such when conversation arose with them. People believed she and Stanley were together as a couple, and the curious eyes of the white people watching them looked on in disdain. If conversation arose, Stanley was quick to call Delia his cousin. He was loud when the two of them sat at a table to enjoy a quick bite before she was off to Brooklyn or Queens to practice with Horatio and the boys. Stanley would take the opportunity, when Delia had a sly quip, to laugh loud and say, *"You got that right, cousin!"* or something close to it, anything that would clarify that the colored woman he was enjoying a meal with was somehow related to him and not on his arm. When that didn't calm suspicions, and people got involved, as the owners of the establishments often did, Stanley would get angry and declare Delia only family. But, of course, that would mean an interracial mingling happened somewhere, and so this didn't often calm hysteria.

Delia and Stanley passed the nights congratulating one another on their achievements, and Stanley recounted his plans for the band he was following to Europe to help manage. He was so excited, and Delia was excited for him. He was excited for her too, and often expressed, with great sincerity, his heartache at having to miss her debut. Talking with Stanley brought the terrible memories of Sarinda Fallows to the forefront of Delia's mind. He was so unlike his mother. But Delia also remembered that Sarinda was so unlike herself too, in terms of what she presented. Delia couldn't come out and interrogate Stanley as to whether there was something more to his personality than what he presented. But Delia rarely thought about that while in Stanley's company.

On the day Stanley departed for Europe, Delia accompanied he and Sarinda to the airport. They hugged and shared a final congratulations to one another, and Stanley also promised his mother before his departure, *"I'll write and call often. I'll keep in mind the time difference. And I'll visit nana's people. I can't wait to introduce myself."* And then Stanley was gone. Sarinda was overwhelmed with emotion, but she didn't cry. Delia comforted Sarinda the rest of the night. She listened to Sarinda's stories about Stanley growing up. *"And now he's growing out and moving on,"* said Sarinda while sipping a cup of hot tea. *"My child. I'm proud, but sad. My time has come to an end."* When Delia told Sarinda not to be so fatalistic, Sarinda responded, *"Oh, you'll understand when you have a child. You give birth to your legacy, Delia. You also give birth to your replacement. I'm sad to see Stanley going out on his own, but I'm proud of him."*

Delia was happy when her conversation with Sarinda ended. It was well into the night, a little after one o'clock in the morning. Delia was anxious to sleep. She had a show to rest up for. Delia was thankful that her day was eventful, helping Stanley pack, running around Manhattan with him for last minute items, getting him to the airport with little time to spare, and staying up late to console Sarinda. Thankfully, her anxiety didn't keep her awake. Delia slept soundly and well into the next day, waking a little after eleven. She started her day by brushing her teeth. She pampered herself as if she had already broke into stardom. She picked out a fancy outfit for the night's show, and then she handed her garments for ironing to one of the three members of Sarinda's staff inside the large and luxurious condominium apartment. She ordered a light breakfast, and it was masterfully prepared by Sarinda's cook.

Delia spent most of the day in a silk robe gifted to her by Sarinda on her second night in New York City. She hummed the tunes she would be singing at the night's show. Sarinda left around three o'clock in the afternoon to prepare the club. Not only was it Friday night, but it was also Sarinda's night, considering it was showcasing jazz. Delia jumped in the shower at five, and she finished primping herself by seven. She was scheduled to perform at eight o'clock. A car arrived for her. Delia gave her farewell to Sarinda's help, and then left the building to be chauffeured to the Harlem Dixie. Delia's face lit up as bright as the marquee when she arrived.

Neither Horatio's name nor Johnny's name ran across the marquee. It was collectively agreed upon that their names wouldn't highlight the event. The marquee instead read *Delia-LaRue Amat and the Upstart Jazz Posse*. Black Cue came up with the name after Horatio completed the composition and played the final segments of *The Son Dial Tone*. The Upstart Jazz Posse practiced the grand, musical piece night and day. Delia was not needed for every segment. It was in Delia's absence that the band discovered that it was her presence that allowed them to hear the poetic narration. Horatio decided that in their live performance, Delia should come in and croon a melody to amplify the lyrics and harmony.

The car drove around back. Delia kept her eyes on the marquee, barely giving a glance at the hordes of people cramming to get in to see the night's performance. Sarinda always made sure jazz night was a big night. The driver parked, jumped out of the car, and opened the door for Miss Amat. Delia stepped out. She was at the back of the club, in an alley, but she looked up and around as if flashbulbs brightly popped at her. She imagined the marquee was still in front of her, her name broadcast to all the passersby. The cold and light drizzle couldn't spoil the moment. Delia's wide-brim hat and long, thick coat protected her from the elements, allowing her to keep her daydream intact.

Sarinda appeared through the backdoor exit. Her steps were mindful as she moved into the alley with an excited smile, waving Delia closer. "Come on, child," she said. "Come on. This is your big night." Delia flinched in response to Sarinda's sudden appearance. "Your bandmates are here," informed Sarinda. "And I got a surprise or two in your dressing room. Come on." Sarinda turned to the driver and slipped him a few bills. "There you go," she said, and he thanked her. Sarinda grabbed Delia by the wrist and hauled her in. "Mind your heels. Come on. Come on." Delia chuckled and followed as she was towed, wrist still in Sarinda's grip.

They walked through the back hallway, winding through the corridor to the dressing room designated for Delia. The jazz singer was anxious to see Horatio and relax with her band for a moment, but all those emotions dispersed when Sarinda opened the door to her dressing room and hollered, *"Surprise!"* and Delia saw her mother, Philomena Amat, sitting at the lighted vanity.

Philomena jumped up! Delia's mouth hung open, tears welling in her eyes. She covered her face with her hands. "Mamma!" she gasped in a low whisper. Sarinda stood proud, observing mother and daughter. Delia turned to Sarinda, removed her hands from her face and asked with a smile, "How long ago did you plan this?"

"Last week," Sarinda confessed through a smile. "It was Stanley's idea, and I thought it was wonderful. You can thank your cousin when he gets back. I picked your mother up at the airport just after I left the house."

Delia, too excited to remember Sarinda Fallows' true nature, threw her arms around Sarinda. "You're here now, Auntie Sarinda. My thanks goes to you." Delia kissed Sarinda's cheek, and then she turned to her mother and ran over to embrace her. "Mamma!" Delia hollered loud. She squeezed Philomena tightly. "We made it, Mamma! We made it to New York."

"*You* made it, child," Philomena told her daughter. "I've just been invited for the ride. And you look so beautiful tonight."

Delia stepped back and looked her mother up and down. She commented, "And you're all dolled up. I just might ask you to jump up on stage and sing a number or two."

Philomena playfully smacked her daughter on the wrist. "No you won't, little girl. This is your night." She pulled her daughter into another embrace. "I'm proud of you."

"You mean it, Mamma? You ain't mad at all I've done?" Delia asked.

"No indeed, child," said Philomena. Then she confessed, "Well, I was hoppin' mad when you'd left, but your constant letters cooled me off." Philomena kissed her daughter's forehead. "I can't say enough about how proud I am of you." She stepped back as she opened from the embrace. She guided Delia to the vanity. Resting on its counter was a slightly opened cardboard box. Philomena said nothing. She only smiled as she continued to guide Delia closer. She moved ahead of her daughter, reached out, and completely removed the lid from the box. Delia stopped and watched her mother reach inside and pull free the veil given to Sarinda so long ago. It was her grandmother's veil, given to her by her grandfather. Philomena held it proudly in front of Delia. "Aunt Sarinda returned it to me. She presented it to me in the car coming from the airport."

Delia's eyes were wide with wonder. "That's grandmamma's veil?"

"Baby," said Philomena, "I want you to have this."

Delia caught her breath. She reached for the veil. "Mamma…" she took her hand away. "Mamma, I can't. This is yours. Rightfully. It belongs to you."

"Wear it tonight. For your performance," Philomena encouraged her daughter.

Sarinda stepped up behind Delia. "You've seen me perform with that veil. I got that from your grandmamma. That was her act, and it was my way to honor her. You do the same tonight, Delia."

But, Delia didn't take the veil. She bowed her head humbly instead and closed her eyes. Philomena pinned the veil atop her daughter's head, folding and fastening the veil for it to stay. Delia lifted her head and thanked her mother. She turned to face Sarinda, a sly grin on her face. Sarinda believed for a split moment that she'd seen the face of Theresa Amat beaming at her. She flinched and blinked in reaction. Her eyes focused. There was only Delia smiling at her. Sarinda fixed the surprised look on her face. She took in a small, unnoticeable breath, and she reached for her pendant.

Delia's smile faded, replaced with a curious inspection of Sarinda Fallows.

"You look stunning with that on," Sarinda complimented. The inflection of her voice was delicately peppered with nervousness. Delia could hear the subtle cracking and anxiety in Sarinda's tone, and it made Delia express a sly, but almost invisible, grin. Sarinda said, "Your mother will be sitting next to me. She'll be enjoying the show from my usual table."

Delia perceived the slight cadence of a threat. She raised an eyebrow.

Sarinda continued twirling her pendant. She called for Philomena, "Philly, let's go take a seat at the table. Let's order our meals so we won't be disturbed with ordering during Delia's performance."

Delia faced her mother again. Philomena hugged her daughter. "Make your grandmother's spirit as proud as I am."

"I will, Mamma," said Delia. Philomena walked away from the embrace, joining Sarinda's side. Delia said to both of them, "I will sing with the voice of Mamma Indigo tonight."

Philomena beamed. "Your grandmother would have loved to hear you say that. Her old nickname."

Sarinda was still. Her face trembled to shake away another flicker of surprise. She composed herself and choked up the words, "That Amat spirit has been passed down no different than you all's voices and beauty."

Delia didn't acknowledge Sarinda's words. She told her mother, "Mamma, you go and sit now. I'll introduce the band to you after the show. The horn player is my sweetheart, Mamma. You'll like him." She wanted to speak Horatio's true name, but she didn't want to give Sarinda any warning. "I'm singing with my man tonight."

Philomena made a face. "Okay, child. Lookin' and actin' all grown." She laughed and turned to leave with Sarinda. "Come on, Aunt Sarinda. Let's go watch this child bring the house down."

The two women left the dressing room. Delia waited a moment, and then she closed her eyes. An image of her mother and Sarinda taking their seats appeared behind her eyelids. She opened her eyes and rushed from the room. She blinked and concentrated. She followed a prickly instinct that guided her to Horatio and the band's dressing room. Delia knocked and said, "It's me, boys. I'm here."

Johnny opened the door. He stepped aside and allowed Delia entrance. His eyes fixed on her not so much as to ogle her beautiful frame, but because he was entranced with her regal poise and step. Morgan and Black Cue were charmed too. Horatio turned his head and watched Delia glide into the room. He sat in his chair, leg hanging over the arm. "There she is," he said with a sly, glowing smile. "The Queen of Sheba." He lifted a finger and corrected, "Ah, no! The Queen of the Cosmos."

Johnny shut the door.

Horatio popped up from his chair. Hands in his pockets, he stood in front of Delia scoping her from head to toe. "And here I am, just the Prince of the Plantation." He leaned closer to Delia and said, "You look beautiful, Delia."

Delia accepted Horatio's compliment. "Thank you," she replied.

"My mother's here," she informed in an excited voice. "Sarinda flew her in. It was Stanley's idea."

Horatio caressed Delia's shoulder. "That's wonderful," he said. But then he looked closer at her face. Delia appeared worried. "Isn't it?" Horatio questioned.

Johnny, Morgan, and Black Cue all exchanged looks.

Horatio peeped their gestures. Delia trembled. "That harpy returned my grandmother's veil to my mother. My mother put it on me. She wants me to perform with it as my grandmother did." Her eyes bubbled with tears. "This veil, Horatio. What my grandfather said was true. I can…feel it. I'm sensitive to so much around me. I know Sarinda's intentions. She threatened me. She gave me a warning to act proper. I could feel it. She might do something to my mother."

"It'll be okay, Delia. Your mother will be fine," Horatio assured.

Delia composed herself, but said, "She does know, Horatio. Sarinda—that harpy—knows. But she's afraid to die. I think she might put up a fight."

"Only thing that woman will put up is her hands or a white flag," Horatio declared. "Believe that. You believe what we got. She got nothin' but her stone, and when I take that away from her, all she gon' do is sit there and enjoy the show. Now let's do our part. We got all we need on that stage, and this horn right here. All we need is your voice. Miss Fallows ain't got nothin'. We got this harpy where we want her. I made sure Johnny's mom was too tired to come. But nothing will happen to your mother. Trust, believe, and understand." He moved his hand from Delia's shoulder to her face, and he caressed gently. "You together, beautiful woman?"

Delia straightened. Her regal poise returned. "I am," she replied.

Horatio looked at Johnny and Morgan and Cue.

Someone knocked on the door. Johnny opened. A well-dressed man told them, "Ten minutes."

Johnny thanked the man and then closed the door.

Out in the audience, Sarinda Fallows and Philomena Amat settled into their seats and ordered their meals for the night. "There is going to be a show tonight, Philomena," Sarinda declared. "A helluva show, as your daughter tells me." The women smoked and drank wine and conversed more until a man whispered into Sarinda's ear that it was time for the band to play. Sarinda got up and walked to the stage, waving a quick 'hello' at the regulars of her nightclub. Sarinda climbed the stairs to the stage and walked behind the microphone. The nightclub was filled to capacity. Her patrons clapped as she stepped to the mic. "How are you all?" Sarinda said through the microphone. "Settle down, just for a moment. Settle down." The room quieted. Muted from all the lingering, low conversations, Sarinda proceeded. "Tonight is special. Tonight, a girl I call family makes her debut. Her voice, as she calls it, is legacy." Behind Sarinda, behind the curtain's stage, Delia and the band got into position. "Her grandmother was a close friend of mine," Sarinda continued. "And she had a beautiful voice. She was from a small place called Water Bug Hollow, Louisiana. She always wanted to sing in New York, but she never made it. Her voice has, however. My friend, Theresa Amat, may have passed, but she also passed her gift of voice to her daughter, who also joins us tonight, sitting here in the audience. Philomena stand up for a moment. Everybody, give this songbird a round of applause."

Philomena stood and waved to the clapping audience, and then she sat down.

"We'll get her on this stage yet," said Sarinda. "Tonight, her daughter completes the journey. She debuts her voice here in New York City. Harlem. And she is backed by a powerful set of musicians. Ladies and gentlemen, put your hands together for Delia-LaRue Amat and the Upstart Jazz Posse."

The applause thundered!

Sarinda stepped down from the stage and took her seat. The curtains opened. A single, wide beam of light held Delia, following her every step to the microphone. She remained veiled and silent, waiting patiently for the crowd to settle. Quiet came in a hurried wave. Delia's voice hollered harmoniously before the music played: *"How could you do this to me?"* Horatio's horn came first. The other instruments followed, playing low behind Delia's voice, which simmered from a holler to a silky tone. *"I am the High Ram that sits high atop the sun. I play jazz when the wind blows. And I'd let you know when the day has begun and when it is done."*

The crowd was drawn in.

Horatio played sweet, mystical notes through his horn.

Delia's voice rose as she sang, *"When I prayed to praise midnight you flashed three lights, and I felt their fire in my head, heart, and chest. Shot down because I knew right, and I did write, so my poor sun had to set in the west."* Delia crooned her haunting melody. The crowd never heard such a voice, and Philomena watched her daughter as pride widened her gaze and smile. *"I composed notations that had gravitational rotation. My music spoke of the long life, and a past fight, all in rhyme. I sing you a jazzy little prelude. All. In. Rhyme. I sing of the long life of Miss Sarah the Pantomime!"*

The band and Delia's voice reached a heavy height and sound, and in a wave of rumbling harmony, the music ceased. Horatio's horn was the last instrument to scream. An explosion of sound vibrated from the horn's bell. The throbbing notes hollered from the horn pressed hard against Sarinda Fallows' chest. She reached up to grip her pendant, and her heart skipped as if pricked by a thin strand of lightning when she felt the dust of her trinket settle onto her fingertips, under her nails, and between her fingers, sliding down to the palm of her hand and down her wrist.

The seated patrons vanished one-by-one. Sarinda turned her head in reaction. The people in the audience disappeared from existence, popping out of reality like lights being relieved of their brilliance.

Delia addressed the audience as if it remained in front of her. "I am Delia-LaRue Amat, and this is my band: The Upstart Jazz Posse." Applause came out of nowhere. Philomena appeared unfazed at the phenomenon around her. Sarinda attempted to stand, but Horatio played a loud note, and she was unable to move her body from the waist down.

Delia announced, "We have Willie 'Black Cue' Santos on drums." Willie jumped into a beat and a small solo. "We have Morgan Fields on bass." This was Morgan's cue to pluck and play a groove, joining in as Cue's drumming fell back for the bass' sound to take front stage. "And on piano, we have Johnny Concheroot." Johnny jumped into the growing sound, his fingers up and down the keys. "Son of the legendary Joseph Concheroot who's here tonight. Come on, Joe. Sitchoself down at that second pian-a here." Joseph Concheroot walked out onto the stage. He slid into the piano seat, and dived into playing. "And on the trumpet, son of the legendary trumpeter Pete Peters and singer Virginia Tara-Peters of Harlem, we have Horatio Peters."

Horatio's horn erupted. A volcanic explosion of sound shook the nightclub.

Lights twinkled behind the paintings lining the walls. The illumination flashed to the beat. Sarinda removed another cigarette and lit the tip. She took a drag and scowled as she exhaled the smoke.

Philomena became aware of the spectacle around her. Delia said to her mother, "Mamma, you don't be afraid, now. My band and I have a story to show you." A spherical, indigo luminosity, the size of a human eye, swirled against Delia's forehead from behind the veil. Philomena looked into the light and relaxed. The three paintings recounting Water Bug Hollow's history danced in front of her and put the area's history on display.

Philomena's wide eyes swallowed every morsel of history fed to her. Her mouth hung low, her lover's etchings animated. Her Paul-baby's art revealed Water Bug Hollow's truth. "If it wasn't the truth, it wouldn't play in here," Philomena whispered, as if her voice would disturb the presentation in front of her. The revolution that conceived Water Bug Hollow played out, and Philomena's personal history played like a picture show on the other paintings.

Sarinda turned her eyes to Philomena. She smoked and watched Philomena's reaction as all her clandestine deeds were exposed. Tears slithered from Philomena's eyes, a constant stream expressing the sickened and saddened emotions wrestling inside her as she saw Sarinda Fallows, a woman she called her aunt, orchestrate the deaths of her mother, her daughter's father, and even her defilement at the hands of Reverend-Mayor Lionel Ladon.

Philomena slowly turned her head toward Sarinda.

Sarinda said with a smile that was losing its charm, "Philly-baby…"

Philomena shook her head and a defiant finger. "Oh, no. *Oh, no!*" she hollered. "You call me Ane. I am *Asase-Ane!*" It was just like peering deeper into Theresa Amat when she lay on her deathbed. Sarinda looked closer at Philomena and saw something else. "I know you Miss Sarah the Pantomime," Philomena declared with determined anger. "I've seen your ships on my shore. This ain't the first time you've done me and my daughter wrong." Philomena slapped her hand on the table. *"This ain't!"*

The band's music burst! Delia started scatting, and the nightclub's interior broke away to reveal an early morning on a colonial plantation.

We told the wind not to sing
We told the clouds not to gather
Or cry
Time was all that moved,
And that was only by very little

When the sun crept up into the sky

No one would work for the master today
Not even nature would be his slave
Neither he nor his wife
Would pluck us from stock
And savor our tastes
We would wait
And wait
And wait

The doors opened
And entered Herkus Bar

"Should everyone
Who works in this land
Stay their hand?
The master employs
People of his collective here too
Indentured like you
For the right to work
But they dance grateful with gratitude."

I tell Herkus Bar,
"They enjoy employment,
The indentured report also as soldiers
Extra pay given
Even if just pittance
It's their reward for keeping us submissive
We wallow in servitude
With no chance to move or grow
Unless we take your method
And sell out our own."

Herkus Bar takes offense
"My methods are a means to an end
I spared you and your friend
Outside, now, overseer's soldiers march closer

Let me extend that mercy again
To curb their violence."

I hiss my frustration
"You are an off-tuned spectator
Dancing unaware
You stand there and just stare
And blare witch projects
That throws your own people off topic
And you've believed you've rocked it
Because you've fooled a few to follow it
To search the floor below them
For a deep thought once you've dropped it.

We are the real gears of the machine
Abused in our rotation
Abuse our payment for keeping in order
And moving the currency of this plantation
Our spirits mop your mess up
Our spirits restore natural order
It is our original thoughts
The stone warriors that rock
Chiseled down at the writer's block
On a chronological spot far before you were born
Even with no physical form
We play the wind through a metaphysical horn
Our blessed music, the ripple that makes waves for the waves of today
Not just the new waves
But the all-present waves that bathes you in yesterday
To make you think you got flow
And I throw you a meta on your shore
And you have the nerve to ask, 'What's this meta for?'

I'll tell you
It's a key to a door
That keeps thoughts you can't afford
Consciously deep, unconsciously low."

Irakere booms from the corner,
"Man, this joker is only impressed
When you dress things up with the number three
I'm not talking about trilogies
But the trickery of unholy trinities
Herkus Bar believes he's a part of them:
The slave master, his wife, and him
The hat trick — the matrix
All that neo, new wave bullshit
I'm talkin' about substance substituted with the obvious
And on top of this
You be insultin' my intelligence
With that shallow puddle you defined
As deep thought art
The spell the master has you under
Is designed to make ignorant fools like you think they smart
But your final objective has made me cry
Until my tears rise and I finally sink
Brother, all we're askin' you to do is think."

Herkus Bar barked, "Please,
I'm thinking more than you ever did
My thoughts' tone Saturn's rings cosmic
They ring Sirius."

Mwana speaks herself into existence,
"You just don't get it
We were at the beginning of all this
I have a lock for every life I've lived
Me and the Aztecs use to hold think tanks
At each other's pyramids
While writing lyrics that reflect
Our philosophies and dance steps
Surviving in pictures, depicting scriptures
Is how we transcend death
My thoughts are a story for your vision
And I wrote the same story perfectly
But I distorted the same story purposely

Just so you would believe it was a religion
I don't mean to offend you, my brother
Just your blind service to this man
But maybe the best way for you to have a clue
Is if I wrote it in the palm of your hand
But you still wouldn't have it
No matter how many times you try and grab it
But for now, that's my only plan
So just sit back and relax
Let yo' belly shake like jelly
And you can listen to us real masters
Jam."

The plantation's soldiers flood the shack
A storm of threats
Rain hectic
One of them grabs Mwana
And I react
Beginning the dance electric
Irakere pounds the air solid, not hollow
(What's the use of war drums if a battle doesn't follow?)
Thunder's sound strikes
Our kicks and jabs cut like a knife
Mwana sings and becomes the air
Wind whirls and wobbles the plantation soldiers
Our partners in this artistic, martial dance
The tools we use to till the land
Now weapons in hand

The fury of our flurries sets the barn blurry
With blaze
Plantation soldiers lay dead
Our fire spreads to the field
The horizon births more soldiers
They fire lightning and thunder
And our numbers litter the arable land
Mamma Iyansan
Sings them back to life

Our fallen numbers spring upright
No bullet or whip
Delays our strike
We are the gods' and goddesses' might

I dance and take fight with Herkus Bar
His rhythm drenched
With the master's lashes
He scars me, scratches
His fists crash against me
I duck his fury
Clutch his next potential pound
And strike
He slips – loose
We move and shake
Every hit makes the earth quake
I attack his physical
He bombards my spiritual
Each hoping our kicks and jabs
Will break spirit or bone or the energy coiled around our spine
Winding up our backs

I'm grabbed!
A haunting chokes me
A phantom dampens my power
Pantomime twirls her pendant
Negating and subduing our advantage
The soldiers lightning and thunder kills us again
Mamma Iyansan's wings are clipped
Our Great Mother stripped
Herkus Bar seizes this moment
And hits
Scars scream on my body
And blood pours and drips

Master Fallows
His whip like a serpent
Attacks

The venom racks my body
The agony brings me to my knees
Master Fallows lashes me
Again and again and again and again
Curly's whip, more devastating
Than the soldiers' lightning and thunder,
He fells six in our number
The pantomime's trinket
Mutes Irakere's air drum vibration
The phantom borne of her pendant
Grabs Mwana
And chokes her until she turns to glass
Squeezing and squeezing
Ready to shatter her body to small shards of ash

I swallow my voice
Put all the mystic notations at my finger tips
Reach back
Call the horn into my grip
And with its mouth against my lips
I scream with the keys
Of all the cosmic harmonies

Herkus Bar
Skin of burnished brass
Turns to ash
I sing loud through the horn
Its melodies clash with cracked-brain
Slave drivers
I scream with the horn
Create pressure and wind
Mystical notation lessons
When properly played, form compression
Sounds resonating ancient
Shatter Pantomime's pendant
Dissolve her phantom's menace
And restores Mwana to her natural, spiritual state

Tornadoes mend Mamma Iyansan's wings
The horn sings rainbows
While the air makes thunder that screams
From Irakere's hands that slams against soldiers
Makes us slaves fluid like water
Fighting for future free black sons and black daughters
Led no more to the slave master's slaughter

Mamma Iyansan
Sword in one hand
Whip made of horsetail in the other
Her eye spies the Pantomime
Curly rushes red hair away
Mamma Iyansan gives chase
The master's lash wraps around her neck
And keeps the angel in place

Mamma Iyansan's arm twirls and spins
Her sword cuts the master's lash in half
Horsetail whip shifts into a snake
It eyes the master as prey
And strikes as its body ignites
Coils around the master
Keeping him stiff and frozen
Mamma Iyansan takes the moment,
Swipes her sword
And takes the master's head

The snake jumps back into her hand
Horsetail whip at her command
Mamma Iyansan turns to take
The master's bride
In 9 strides
Mamma Iyansan flies,
Her body twists, turns into a tornado

The pantomime waits for her
Holding a pound of pendant rock

Red spattered and blotched
No knowledge, wisdom
Or understanding
No philosophy reaped or sown
In this grand piece called a skeptic's stone

The master's bride
With her pound of stone
Vomits ghostly rumors and lies
That attack Mamma Iyansan

From inside the plantation house
Mamma Iyansan fights and strikes
We hear her cries
As she's overwhelmed by the ghosts
The lies
I howl the horn to push back the desperate attack
On our Great Mother

As I exhale melody and sound
Mwana inhales
Mamma Iyansan turns into feathers
And clouds
Spiraled, spun and siphoned down
Through all chambers of Mwana's body
She exhales, breathes
I play my Father's Voice
And connect with her Mother Harmony
Our bodies shift
No longer slaves, we are all free
We fly up into the breeze

Mwana sings happily,
Smile brighter than the sun's beam
"I fly, Mojuba! I fly!
The breeze we ride."
Up, we are, in the sky
Dwindled to fourteen pieces

We soar south
To the shore
We meet land
And water waves to us
Freed woman and man

The nightclub's empty atmosphere returned, growing over the plantation battle. Philomena was standing up, looking down at Sarinda Fallows. Sarinda looked up at her, eyes moving slowly like a shameful child caught in the act of a misdeed. Philomena was smiling at Sarinda. She backed up, joining her daughter on stage just as the patrons popped back into existence. They watched the band, unaware of the witchcraft that took place around them. "The long life of Sarah the Pantomime comes to an end tonight," said Philomena into the microphone. The band's music became a heightened, tribal sound. Cue's drum-work clapped like a rolling avalanche. Horatio's horn sounded like tap dancing as its rhythm skipped over the sounds of Johnny's piano work and Delia's scatting into the microphone. Morgan's bass complimented Cue's drum. It all came together in rhythm with the cosmos' heartbeat.

The club's interior faded again, the audience unaware of it all. The jazz club's interior gave way to the appearance of a shore as Philomena herself became the water, and standing before her were the runaway slaves.

Gospel ghost spells
Turn to spirituals
And we hum in harmony
As the waves' sound
Crash on the shore

We shout
Exercise the devil's ghost spells out
Call and response with nature, our mirror
We speak to us, glorious
Our knowledge, culture, and power
Drinking in four bars
(Blues)
Our pen and tonic
Two subdominant to tonic to dominant back to tonic

We cry freedom
Our tears, the ghosts of those slain
They too are now free
Fighting for one last chance to be heard or seen

We hear our tears sing collectively,
"Don't forget
Always remember me
The condensation of a memory
Feel the way we flow
As we pass through your eyes
Rushing like a river at 33°
On a square like pyramids of Masonic imagery
We are the voices tossed overboard
Into shark infested waters
We will be the emotion of recycled oceans
That wave goodbye with bloody hands
Held down, whipped and bound
Our voices will return crippled
Walking on hurri-canes
Waves that first rippled in Africa."

We amplify
We amp, and we be fly
Increase our tears' sound
And make the whole crowd 'def'

Irakere say,
"I remember this
Tapping on a tree's hip
When I heard the beat flip
I caught it on my lips
And called it music."

The women belt out a note so high
It rattles the sky
As stars pour over us fourteen
Burning black

Whole
X
And internally
This power burning in us
We become the ON of eternity
Mars combined with Venus
The heroes reborn as the phoenix

Irakere pounds the air and drums
I hum thunder through the horn
The water swirls angry
And from its depths emerges
A silver ship born from Irakere's myth
I play the horn
And we fourteen lift,
Landing on the deck of the silver ship
We sail away into a cloud of mist
Celebrate with an abundance of food and drink
While hours fold over one another
The ship provides, and we nurse one another
Back to health

Voices sing from beneath the sea
Stir the water and make it breathe
Their sound, through water, waves
Mwana's eyes see on the horizon
An invisible island coming into focus
Solid
Like the sun shining light
To open the day
The island is there, and we give praise
A council of eight awaits us
The Ogdoad
And behind them, a council of nine
Mamma Iyansan's rhymes
Her children, the Ennead

Disembarked
Mwana's heart
Hugs her mother
Mamma Asase-Ane
She leads us into a mystical
Tropical forest
Where frolicked freedom
And where we bathe in waters
That wash away our scars
But not the pain of their memories
Done purposefully
So says Mamma Asase-Ane

Then she directs,
"We must compose with haste
No minute made waste
Fifteen and Fifteen and Fifteen ships
Approach on hurried pace
The population here, this island of freedom
A target to be enslaved
Music, your mysticism at your command
Come together and band
The Ogdoad and Ennead that I lead
Will make this island visible
For this last stand.

My daughters, with me
We must pull Mamma Iyansan's spirit
With ritual through your father's Voice
And my Harmony

Irakere, the boom in your hands
Pound and pound
Until this sound shields this land
Mojuba,
Your horn must play
Call upon nature
To make all four elements wave

The rest of your fourteen
The remaining eleven
Take weapon
Join the rest of our army
Our deities
And should any slaver land upon our shore
Make war and bring balance."

Sadly,
We believe
Even if we embrace victory
This will make no difference
For a long time

But we take stance
We are the holy ghosts
We are the sun's tone
The cosmic dance
The universe's rhythm
Croons through us
Baritone, bass, soprano
Falsetto
We stand ready and mellow
In melody
We are something new
Our mutation is the separation
And differentiation
In time and space between the tones
Without us, there is chaos
We are the proper keys and harmonies

We march toward the shore
The voice of four winds
Mwana and her sister's ritual begins
Breath, balance of
Vocal chords, vibration of
Her M (magnetic) Ahket
Upper and lower sounds

Irakere drums
Hands rattle the air
Until collective prayer
Creates a sound barrier
We dance on the shore
Freestyle, our style is free
We chant collectively
Twelve tones from sixteen shades
God's 78 names interchanged
144 – thousand
Our spirits housing the open lotus flower
Our might and power
Chanting on this specific time of day
Chanting to the twelve signs in the sky
Light value emanates and synchronizes
Manifest triangulated thought
The four elements must obey
Different styles of music play

Fifteen and fifteen and fifteen ships
Approach
Hurl cannon fire at our coast
That knock against our sound barrier
And explode
Mwana's voice moves the tide
Waves climb and crash
Dash against the attacking slave ships
Mwana harmonizes tornadoes
Hurricanes and whirlpools race
The sea's mouth opens
And satiates her body with a fleet's taste

But they come back up
Irakere, distracted with victory
Ceases his percussion
The sound barrier drops
Cannon fire rocks

A concert of explosions
The island left vulnerable and open
Mwana and her mother and sister
Fly and sail
Sword in one grip,
In the other, a whip of horsetail
Mwana's father and brother lead a charge to the shore
They speak spells through ankh-rah-phones
Incant the proper tones
To nullify the effects of the Pantomime's hex
But a pound of pendant rests
Nestled aboard an attacking vessel

Horn to my lips
I breathe out all my energy
My body shifts
Funneled though the horn
The horn breathes me
Exhaled and streamed through its bell
An audible runnel, a booming beam
The universe at the center of me
I take the sounds of Irakere's hand pounds
Collect the harmony of Mwana,
Her sister, and Mamma Asase-Ane
And absorb the voice and tones
Of the ankh-rah-phones
Imbued with galactic hue
I dive
From high up into the sky
Down into the pound of pendant
And shatter it from existence
My physical beam twists and twirls
Swirls and funnels back through the horn
Kissed into physical form
I return
And amplify the harmony around me
The pounds, voices, and tones
Circle

Revolution
A tornado digs into the sea
A whirlpool opens
Iemanja feasts again
Without the ships' resurrection

The island remains free
A small area of peace
Mwana glides next to me
We embrace
As the island population celebrates
This small victory

Sarah the Pantomime
Is in the wind
And we know we would confront her again
We are prepared
With tricks of our own
Mamma Asase-Ane declares,
"We will be our own descendants
On our family tree
This will all be locked in our memory
Resting in her, hymn, and our story
All of us as 'we'
Passed on through our seeds
For a while,
This will be like repetition
But don't we find joy in that?
Rough drafts to rough tracks
Slave chains like hands clap
On the final
Cut
Wrists
And bleed sap
From the tree of knowledge of good and evil
Hold onto cross atop the cathedral
Preach and sing broken words until old and feeble
As works of encoded art

We will take care of our people, be as all forms of expression
As under the guise of cloud and sky
We will become wise and one with sunshine and fly
Talk about the days beyond when we die
Glide into heaven's eyes and see more than we ever could
  When we were alive
Now our birthdays are everyday and our age is eternal
Forever X and internal
Heave no sigh
Everyone returns to the elements in time
Reduce fraction of soul/body/mind
  Down to soul
  Soul low down
  Into earth's soil
  Down so low
  That soul begins to grow
  Again, by resurrection
Like what should be done with time
  Instead of killing it
We should be willing it, fulfilling it like destiny
And no longer riddling over the question that cannot be
Solved
Under the canopy from creation to creation
Our spirits will evolve
Frustrated that nothing will be resolved

360^0 revolve to the bullet in the next chamber

The thief in our temples
Losing our minds by gunshot
Pondering the difficult and not the simple
Life in danger
Danger in life
Releasing not through anger but in chorus
We don't have to steal our fire like Prometheus
We unwrap all talents and gifts
Shift
Return package in better condition than when we received it
  Used
No longer shall we ponder, 'How strong shall we be?"

What the ego said and how the id replied
That conversation is hazardous, words are pollutants
Hallucinogens
Dangerous secret agents
Our holy word is our bond
And tomorrow never dies
It's resurrected every day like people
Because we are everyday people
And I want to take you higher
My, my, my. Ain't that sly?"

Mamma Asase-Ane takes my horn
She sings our story's notes
Into its bell
Mystical harmonies
Turn the horn's body
Into faerie-like notations
Fluttering and flapping sprites
They anoint the end of a spear
Mamma Asase-Ane tosses it through the atmosphere
Up, beyond the sky
To reside and open
At the proper time on cue of collective cry

Mwana and I
On the shore
Hand in hand
There is freedom for us
But we pray for more
It can't be just us; there must be justice
Our spirits remain as music
Playing
From existence fades the island
The sun, ready for bed, on the horizon
Our music will evolve

The Upstart Jazz Posse's music came to a mighty crash of an end. No one in the audience applauded. The patrons were still. No movement, but they were caught in the midst of enjoying the band, their expressions jubilant. The audience's eyes, lifeless and seeing nothing, looked toward the stage. Sarinda's face was stoic. Like time holding back the movement of her patrons, Sarinda worked hard to keep the anger boiling inside her from spilling out. Horatio was the cause of both phenomena: Sarinda's anger and the still of time. He stared at Sarinda, and she stared at him in return.

Sarinda started clapping, slow and deliberate.

Horatio stepped off the stage and walked toward Sarinda Fallows.

Delia lifted her veil, and Philomena took a position close to her daughter.

Horatio pulled out a chair opposite Sarinda Fallows and sat down. Sarinda pulled out another cigarette. She lit it and smiled after taking her first drag. She took a second hit, aimed her head back, and blew smoke straight up to the ceiling. She returned her attention to Horatio. He sat in front of her. There was no expression on his face. The anger boiling in him held back his tears. The horn rested on his lap.

Sarinda hiccupped a chuckle. She took another hit of her cigarette and said, "I must have that same look of surprise. The one that was on your father's face the night them boys put him down like a mangy dog." She looked at Joseph Concheroot on the piano and told him, "Thank you for your contribution to that night's events, Joe. Couldn't have happened without you."

Joe said nothing. He sat on his bench in front of the piano and simply gazed at Sarinda. The occasional blink of his eyes was the only proof that Horatio didn't have him under the same spell as the other patrons in the nightclub.

"Well," Sarinda spoke, "I thank you none-the-less." She remarked looking again at Horatio, "I mean, your father, like me, knew his time was up. He saw it comin'. But it's so different when you're in the situation. It's nothing like you can imagine." Her light chuckle made her eyes water. Sarinda cleared her throat. She looked over Horatio's shoulder at Delia and Philomena. Her eyes back on Horatio, she spoke, "We might not have gotten them two specifically, but we had so much fun with the other ones, women just like them." She said to Philomena, "But I guess I finally had you held down when I set the good reverend on you."

Philomena said nothing. She held onto Delia and watched Sarinda.

"Hmmm," Sarinda pondered. "Well, we would just pluck and fuck. I had my share of you men. Mmmm. My husband, and my father before him, and Curly, they all had their share of your women. They also had their share of the men to keep you all from gettin' unruly. Definitely at early ages. Do you remember that? Every little boy got it. Had to. I didn't see all that in that little story you showed me. Conveniently left that one out, didn't you?" She smiled and smoked.

Horatio said nothing. His breath got heavier as the anger crept upward, gathering in his throat.

Sarinda took a deep breath. When the air she inhaled put pressure on her rising anger, keeping it stable, she continued her rant. "Hell," she started, "we did so much fuckin' and there were so many half-pickaninny children runnin' 'round spawned from my father and uncles, if you trace the line properly from those children, I mean, hey! You and I could be distant cousins by now in this lifetime of yours, Mister Horatio Peters. Shit, all of you bastard, nigger children of mine. You are products of a slave system."

Horatio said nothing.

Sarinda shouted, "What do you children think you can do to me?" Her eyes coughed tears. "I sleep with the feathers of angels stuffed into my pillow. I sleep soundly at night. I sleep comfortable with all I've done. I sleep very comfortably knowing I have left behind a legacy. It will resonate in a harmony more subtle than the noise I made, but it will be *my* legacy." She tapped a finger angrily on the table. "I sleep comfortably. On that, I rest assured."

Horatio stirred. He picked up his horn and stood. He pushed in his chair like a gentleman and calmly said to Sarinda, "Good, Miss Fallows. You sleep comfortably. Let your *eternal* rest be peaceful." He put the horn to his lips.

Sarinda reached up to him. She tried to use her legs but they were held in place. She cried and pleaded, "No! Please, no. Horatio. Please, no! I have nothing else. This life is all I have! This is it. There's nothing for me after. Please! Horatio! Please! God have mercy!" She reached out to him. She would've jumped over the table had she the use of her legs.

Horatio played the final segments of *The Long Life of Sarah the Pantomime* as a light melody. The sound was almost entirely grounded in earthly notes, but Horatio sneaked in the proper mystical notations composed in the song by his father long ago. He turned his back to Sarinda and returned to the stage. The soft sounds playing through the horn put feeling back in Sarinda's legs. She gasped in relief and jumped up from her chair with wild desperation splashed on her face. She tried to charge the stage, but each step was arduous, as if she was mired in mud. She almost fell, not anticipating the heaviness of her extremities and the strength she needed to muster in order to lift them. Sarinda reached for her pendant, forgetting the trinket was now a scattering of dust. She balanced herself on the table and slowly made her way around it. She started feeling colder, as if the outside chill now haunted her body. Sarinda shivered. She glanced at her skin to see if it had frozen and become ice. It was the same as it ever was, but she felt as if it was stiffening and cracking. She watched Horatio as he continued playing the soft music, walking up the stage's stairs.

It was tough, but Sarinda made her way around the table. One step. Two steps. To the stage. She was hunched over and reaching out her hands. She pleaded, "Philly-baby, Delia. Help me. Please."

Philomena held her daughter closer. The two of them watched Sarinda struggle. Horatio came around next to them and played the soft melody a little louder, but not rough. It was still a light and airy tune that crooned through the horn.

Lilac and indigo flames burst inside Sarinda Fallows' heart, and she fell down dead.

Time resumed and all the lights turned on.

The patrons jumped from their seats and stared at Sarinda's crumpled body now dead and near the stage. *"Ohmigod!"* yelled a woman. Kathi Giovannelli, Sarinda's personal assistant at the nightclub, ran toward her employer's body. Philomena jumped off the stage and knelt down near the body. "Get help!" she screamed to Kathi.

Kathi turned around and shouted at the crowd, "A doctor! Is there a doctor! Please, it's Miss Fallows. A doctor? Anyone?"

Three men hurried to Sarinda. One bent down and started to inspect her, turning her over carefully. "Miss Fallows, can you hear me?" He opened her eyelids and saw no signs of life. He said to Kathi, "Call an ambulance. Now!" Kathi rushed away to make the call. The man examining Sarinda put his hands on Philomena's shoulders and said, "I'm sorry, ma'am. I'm afraid she's dead. I don't understand. Your aunt stood up, screamed, and then she collapsed."

Horatio and the band watched from the stage. Delia walked down to be with her mother. She put her arms around Philomena, and Philomena put a hand on Sarinda's chest. Delia took the veil from her head and passed it to her mother. Philomena immediately felt that there was no life in Sarinda Fallows.

Sarinda Fallows was dead.

"Mamma," Delia spoke softly. "Mamma…?"

Philomena looked up at her daughter. She stood and embraced Delia. The both of them started to weep. Philomena opened a single, teary eye and spied Horatio up on the stage. He and the other band members watched closely. Philomena signaled with a nod of her head.

Their song was over.

Sirens played an encore.

The Avenue
"…I need Brooklyn to have you."

Sarinda Fallows died of a heart attack as reported by the early morning papers. *Harlem Dixie Owner Collapses At Nightclub*, read the headline of one paper. Similar outlets said the same. Some local papers featured the story as front-page news. Reports of Sarinda's death ran on local radio stations and television. Philomena and Delia handled Sarinda's arrangements, considering her son was overseas. When contacted, Stanley Fallows didn't return to America to tend to his mother. Sarinda Fallows' body was instead flown to Europe for burial. Stanley organized his mother's move from America to Europe with very little contact with Philomena or Delia. Aides to the Fallows estate informed them that Stanley would handle the rest of the arrangements.

That was fine with Philomena and Delia.

Philomena returned to Baton Rouge not long after. She'd made up her mind to quit her job in Louisiana and move to New York City to be near her daughter. She decided to use the coming summer to find a job in the Harlem school district.

Horatio visited his family a day after his performance at the Harlem Dixie. His paternal aunt still lived in Harlem. He'd met her only once when his mother passed, his aunt having attended her funeral. Horatio's aunt was happily married with three children, two girls and a boy, and with her husband, she ran the family funeral parlor.

Horatio believed it was safe to introduce himself, and with Sarinda Fallows gone, there was no threat against his aunt and her family. He told her Joseph Concheroot was released from prison, and he told her that he knew for a fact that Joseph Concheroot's incarceration was fraudulent. Horatio assured his father's sister that his father's best friend was not his murderer. *"Trust me,"* he told them on one of his visits. *"He's a good man. Did he make a lapse in judgment? Yes. He was angry."* Horatio explained why Joseph Concheroot set his father up for murder. He decided not to play a song to convince his relative. His words would do.

Two weeks passed.

Today was Sunday.

Horatio watched the sun rise from the brownstone roof. His horn was in his grip and the songbook lay on the ledge. He was still in his bedclothes: a white tank top and gray pajama bottoms. Shoes but no socks were on his feet, and he wore no hat on his head. The crisp, morning chill purred around him with no effect. Horatio was warm with the hum of otherworldly music playing inside him. He stood watching the sun break out into a bright song. Behind Horatio, the door leading to the stairs going into the house opened. Delia stepped out in her nightclothes covered by a thick robe. "Horatio," Delia called in a concerned whisper. "It's freezing out here."

"Not to me," Horatio grinned. He put the trumpet to his lips and played. Warmth immediately embraced Delia, and the morning's cold released her. It might as well have been a nice, summer afternoon. Horatio put the horn down on the ledge, resting it upright with its bell acting as a stand. He motioned for Delia to come over, and when she walked to him, he embraced her. Horatio asked her as the two of them watched the sunrise, "How'd you sleep last night?"

Delia cuddled closer, burying deeper in Horatio's arms. She smiled. "I spoke with my grandmother and grandfather again. They're happy, and full of stories. My grandfather said there's so much more to all this. He's like a giddy professor ready to tell his class about his discoveries." Delia chuckled, and then she let out an instinctive sigh. Horatio sensed her become downcast, and Delia answered him without a question being raised. "I would like to talk to my father again, but I understand. My mother says she dreams about him nightly. She seems so happy."

"Let them get to know one another again, Delia-baby," said Horatio rubbing his hand along her back and shoulder. "Jackson and Gaston said they get to dance with their wives once a year. No sleep needed. It's not a dream. But, of course, they got mystical real estate." He looked around at the various rooftops, the sun putting them in focus with its early morning light. "New York's magical, but it ain't got the crossroads." Just as the words jumped from his lips, a thought halted Horatio from talking. His eyes darted about, pondering. He unlocked his embrace from Delia and moved her aside. "Sorry, Delia-baby. Hold up. I'm so sorry, Delia-baby. Excuse me."

Delia stepped aside. "Everything okay, Horatio?" She stood close to him as he swiped the songbook and flipped through it.

"Just fine, sweet baby," Horatio assured her. "I'm just fine." He came to a particular song and placed the songbook, opened, back on the ledge. He said aloud, "*A New Avenue in Brooklyn.*" Underneath the musical notation were lyrics composed by his mother. He kept a finger on the page and asked Delia, "Could you sing this?" He moved his finger as Delia lifted the songbook and perused the verses.

"Absolutely," said Delia with a sultry confidence. "You play those hoodoo-Voodoo notes, and I'll match the pitch."

Horatio picked up his horn. He closed his eyes and saw the music to the song scrolling behind them. He started playing. The music from the horn sounded like applause from an audience, and then smoothed into a light, wondrous melody.

Delia started singing.

"Walk with me down this street. Oh, please. I cannot journey alone no more. Harlem has its streets and Mississippi has its crossroads. But I need Brooklyn to have you. I need all this Voodoo and hoodoo on the corner of this Avenue."

Time stilled, but there was movement. The earth moved without rumble or disturbing shake. Horatio played and played and played. And Delia sang the lyrics written on the page to his music. Their music sprang up a phenomenon. Halsey Street was no longer the next block north of Macon Street. Between these streets, and running from Bedford Avenue to Broadway, a new road emerged by song's end.

Time moved again, and the area's residents didn't appear to be in awe at the new street lined with pristine brownstone buildings. Delia and Horatio didn't move. They were as frozen as time had been before, completely ensnared by awe and wonder. Horatio blinked himself out of astonishment. Delia looked at him. They communicated with facial gestures. Their surprised looks expanded and contracted at one another like a form of Morse code.

Delia slapped the book shut, and with the sound of the book

closing, both she and Horatio ran into the brownstone and down the stairs. Horatio and Delia slipped into the guestroom and started removing their bedclothes to make a quick change.

They stopped.

Both of them realized they were stripping in front of one another. Horatio was ready to remove his underwear when he caught himself. He looked up, Delia, down to her underclothes, was looking at him. There was surprise on her face that melted into a coy smile.

Horatio stood up straight. "I've already seen you naked, Delia-baby."

"That was in another life," she insisted. "And we had no business peeping in on us while we…" Delia cleared her throat. Then she said, "I do believe we will be together, Horatio. We'll be married and have children." She explained, "I mean, I can't see myself with another man that would understand what you and I have been through, what connects us." Then she expounded, "But I will be properly courted before I completely remove my garments in front of you."

Horatio smirked. "I understand, Delia-baby. I get it. We'll keep our underclothes on, we'll throw on yesterday's clothes, and then we'll wash up later."

"At least brush your teeth," said Delia as she snatched up her clothes from yesterday.

"Yes, ma'am," Horatio responded putting on his slacks. "We'll let Johnny's parents sleep. We'll just wake up Johnny."

Delia smiled as she said aloud, "I do believe Miss Gregory will be Miss Concheroot again soon enough."

They dressed and brushed their teeth in separate bathrooms to save time. Delia kept the songbook with her as Horatio carried his horn. Downstairs and readied, Horatio knocked on Johnny's door calling, "Johnny! Wake up! There's something you need to see."

Johnny groaned from the other side. Horatio and Delia heard the bed creak as Johnny got up, and they heard his feet shuffle as he moved toward the door. "What's goin' on?" he asked as he opened the door.

"I played our fathers' song," Horatio answered excitedly.

"Which one?" Johnny asked.

"The New Avenue in Brooklyn song. That one. Delia sang its

lyrics." Horatio shook his head. *"And there's a new avenue in Brooklyn.* It's the next block up. Just popped up out of another world. Come on, let's go see."

"Oh, Lord," said Johnny. He shut the door to dress. Delia and Horatio stepped back. The door opened again and Johnny darted past them to wash up quickly in the bathroom. He came out freshened and asked, "How the hell did all them early mornin' church folk react to that?"

"People actin' like the street been there all this time," Delia explained. "They just goin' about they business."

Johnny walked into the hallway and put on his jacket and fedora. He rummaged through his jacket pockets for his keys. "That's Negroes for you. We see some mystical shit and we just roll our eyes, explainin' like, *'Child, that's just the Spirit. Pay that no mind. That's how the Spirit work. You want some pie?'"* He looked Horatio and Delia up and down. "You gon' put on a coat or a jacket or..." his words trailed away. "Oh, you two got the music in you. You two done gone and caught the Good Ghost." Johnny unlocked the door. "See? That's what I'm talkin' 'bout, right there. You two got the Good Ghost keepin' you warm, we got the Spirit outside makin' new streets in Brooklyn. Damn, I gotta keep my eye on you all! Show Negroes a trick and they run amok."

"Will you move," hissed Horatio.

Johnny opened the door, allowed Horatio and Delia to walk through, and then stepped out. Horatio unlocked the next door to the outside and opened it, permitting Delia to go first. Horatio followed her, and Johnny trailed behind and locked the door. The three walked down the brownstone steps and then up the street, turning right and approaching the new avenue in Brooklyn.

The early churchgoers and morning residents indeed paid no mind to the new street, and, as Delia expressed, walked along it—up and down and across—as if it had been there all the time. Horatio focused his eyes on the street sign. It read: *Fable Avenue,* and standing below it, bundled up with heavy coats to protect them from the late-November chill, were Jackson and Gaston Fable.

"Come on!" hollered Jackson to the approaching three-person party. "We got to get inside. It's cold up here in New York."

"Ain't that about somethin'," said Horatio.

"Is that the Fable brothers?" Delia asked.

"Yes indeed, Delia-baby," Horatio answered.

Horatio, Delia, and Johnny walked up to Jackson and Gaston.

"We woke up and heard all this noise," Gaston said in his raspy voice. "Went out to the front of my house, I see Jackson come out of his house. Ain't nothin'. We go to the backyards of our houses and the trees done disappeared."

"And we in New York," Jackson finished. He looked around. "Map in the house says this here is Brooklyn."

"Yes, sir," said Johnny as if welcoming the old men to his neighborhood.

"Sarinda's gone," Horatio informed.

"We know," said Jackson. "Saw everything in the mirror."

"Everything," Gaston emphasized. "The story composed by you and your father."

Jackson looked at Delia and added, "And all that happened to you and your family, Miss Amat. We saw that when your father's artwork started movin' like a picture show." Jackson smiled at her. He reached out a hand to Delia. "You know who we are?"

"Yes, sir. These boys talk a lot about you two," Delia answered accepting Jackson's gentle shake. Gaston shook her hand too.

"I believe your grandmother's mother was friends with our grandmother," said Jackson. "Ain't that somethin'?" He then asked Delia and Horatio, "You two cold?"

Horatio shook his head. He looked around and replied, "No. We got a trick warmin' us." Then he asked, "Who lives here?"

"Just us for now," guessed Gaston. "We gon' have to do some explainin'. Negroes own a whole street in Brooklyn. Jackson and I will drum up a trick to keep pryin' eyes off of us." All of them made their way down Fable Avenue.

Jackson said to Horatio as they started walking, "Miss Fallows' son ain't the only one you need to be concerned with and keep an eye on. There're plenty dangerous folk that know more about these tricks than us. We gon' be cautious, hear?"

"Yes, sir." Horatio looked around at the houses on Fable Avenue.

Gaston stated, "Map on the wall say there's a subway on that there Sumner Avenue. The Eight train. Avenue ain't the only thing new. Train go to Harlem. The Black line express."

Jackson and Gaston stopped walking. Horatio turned around and looked at them. Jackson aimed his finger down the road. "Go on. Pick a house. We'll catch up."

Johnny patted Horatio on the back. "Say, man. I'm goin' back to see to my parents. I'll catch up."

Horatio nodded. "Yeah, yeah. Go ahead."

Johnny ran back up the street and turned the corner.

Horatio and Delia, hand in hand, walked and walked and walked down the block. They came to 421 Fable Avenue. Horatio noticed a name on the mailbox near the main entrance, and he became excited. *The Goodspeeds.* He let go of Delia, rushed through the front gate, up the stairs, and was about to ring the doorbell when he noticed a note on the door. It read: *On holiday with family in Jamaica. Will return. - M.G.* Horatio exhaled a small sigh after reading the note. He would have to receive Madison Goodspeed's side of the story on another day. He stepped away and joined Delia on the sidewalk. He kept his eye on 421 Fable Avenue as Delia led him away.

Horatio leaned close to Delia and said into her ear, "Choose a house, Miss Delia-LaRue...*Peters.*" He nuzzled his nose against her cheek. Delia chuckled playfully. They continued down Fable Avenue and then Delia stopped and faced a splendid, golden-beige brownstone.

347 Fable Avenue.

Delia declared, "Here, Horatio. This is where we'll live."

The mailbox on the front door rattled as the house keys jingled into existence inside of it. At the same moment, in bronze, cursive lettering, appeared the name *Peters* on the mailbox. Delia and Horatio didn't rush to retrieve the keys or go inside. They looked up at the brownstone and savored the moment. After a time, Delia and Horatio took their house keys and walked inside to make a home. It was decorated to their tastes, and Delia was instantly in love with the house.

Later that day, there would be a private parade. With time stilled around them, the Upstart Jazz Posse would gather for a booming jam session in this bright new place called Fable Avenue. Jackson and Gaston Fable would watch from the stairs leading to their homes. Johnny's parents bared witness to the wonder of the band's music, his mother now a part of the grand story. Philomena Amat would observe the celebratory sounds and sights through her television that was tuned to a channel no one else but she could receive. Her mother's veil wrapped around her arm, and stacked next to her chair, eleven glorious pieces of art painted by her special Paul-baby.

The party lasted for an equivalent of three days. Up and down the block, inside the available brownstone buildings, and outside of time. When the music and the parade faded, the sky and all the gathered celestial onlookers applauded. They being content that this grand conjure story recommenced anew.

End Act I

<u>**References**</u>

Description of **LeMat revolver** *"a well-built and mighty-sounding weapon with a nine-round cylinder and a short twelve-gauge barrel in the center."* Found on this forum: **http://www.thehighroad.org/archive/index.php/t-140384.html**

Narrative, *"It was theater, operatic. But, the musical production inspired a pair of devious eyes to bend, believing Pete Peters' ruckus dreary and mundane. And so did watch these contemptuous, dubious eyes that scowled at Pete Peters."* – Inspired by dialogue from **ACT V SCENE II** of **William Shakespeare's RICHARD II**, spoken by the **Duke of York**.

The story of **"How Eshu Got the World Turning"** Peter Woodworth, **White Wolf Publishing**, September 17, 2001 referenced in *The Sun Dial Tone*.

"I will readily admit this here, I have used you time and again, Miss Amat—Mamma Indigo, if you prefer. But you have always seemed to stray from my direction. You have been an unreliable instrument, surviving one trial after the next. There must be more to you than I know. There's definitely more to you than you know." - Inspired by dialogue spoken by the character **Raziel** from the video game **The Legacy of Kain: Soul Reaver 2**, developed by **Crystal Dynamics** and published by **Eidos**.

"You remember the time when my parents had to go away to Mobile for the weekend? You stayed over. We locked all the doors, shuttered all the windows, stayed awake until the sun came up while indulgin' in refer sticks—our pick and sip of every bottle in my parent's bar. We was naked as Adam and Eve. That was our garden, and there was no outside law." Dialogue inspired by dialogue in **Young Guns II**, spoken by **Pat Garrett**, as played by **William Peterson**.

"I sleep with the feathers of angels stuffed into my pillow." - Inspired by lyrics from the song **The Regulator** by **Clutch**.

The painting *"TREACHERY"* inspired by artwork by Ray Cosico.

<u>MORE TITLES @</u>

www.TwinGriffinBooks.com